Dean Spencer

7-6-99
Good!

The Regulators

D1519988

The
Regulators

Being an account of the late INSURRECTIONS IN
MASSACHUSETTS *known as* THE SHAYS REBELLION
as witnessed by WARREN HASCOTT, ESQ.

⚜

Also conveying some idea of the interior
circumstances of *Massachusetts* and other
sections of the newly founded *United States
of America*

⚜

by
WILLIAM DEGENHARD

⚜

Second Chance Press
Sagaponack, New York
Jay Landesman Limited
London

Designed by Fred R. Siegle

Originally published in the United States 1943 by The Dial Press,
New York.

First republication 1981 by the Second Chance
Press, Sagaponack, New York.

First published 1981 in Great Britain by
Jay Landesman Limited, London.

Copyright © 1943, 1981 by William Degenhard.

Library of Congress Catalogue Card Number: 80-54849
International Standard Book Numbers:
       (U.S.) 0-933256-22-1 (Clothbound)
              0-933256-23-X (Paperbound)
       (U.K.) 0-905150-31-7

Printed in the United States of America

Contents

Narrator's Foreword 1
Chapter One 8
Chapter Two 30
Chapter Three 41
Chapter Four 54
Chapter Five 64
Chapter Six 83
Chapter Seven 99
Chapter Eight 115
Chapter Nine 131
Chapter Ten 149
Chapter Eleven 162
Chapter Twelve 177
Chapter Thirteen 186
Chapter Fourteen 197
Chapter Fifteen 213
Chapter Sixteen 221
Chapter Seventeen 235
Chapter Eighteen 246
Chapter Nineteen 258
Chapter Twenty 272
Chapter Twenty-one 292
Chapter Twenty-two 304

Chapter Twenty-three 315
Chapter Twenty-four 337
Chapter Twenty-five 350
Chapter Twenty-six 369
Chapter Twenty-seven 381
Chapter Twenty-eight 396
Chapter Twenty-nine 404
Chapter Thirty 415
Chapter Thirty-one 420
Chapter Thirty-two 432
Chapter Thirty-three 444
Chapter Thirty-four 453
Chapter Thirty-five 463
Chapter Thirty-six 476
Chapter Thirty-seven 491
Chapter Thirty-eight 502
Chapter Thirty-nine 515
Chapter Forty 527
Chapter Forty-one 539
Chapter Forty-two 550
Chapter Forty-three 563
Chapter Forty-four 571
Chapter Forty-five 587

The Regulators

Narrator's Foreword

MANY years have passed since the end of that insurrection in Massachusetts which has come to be known as the Shays Rebellion. Passions have cooled, recriminations have ceased, old wounds have healed. No longer am I looked upon as Warren Hascott, the Rebel, though I have never been ashamed of it. No longer do brawls break the peace of our tavern evenings when insurgent and government supporter come to reargue the issues and events of those trying days. Thus, I feel this narrative, long overdue, will arouse little controversy, or if there is disagreement, little bitterness.

The world has changed much since then. At home, a Federal Constitution has been adopted, the nation has expanded to include five new states, a second war with Britain has proven the stability of our union. Overseas, the French have revolted against their king, only to fall prey to a greater despot. The armies of the emperor have swept across Europe, accomplishing the ruin of weaker nations, the extinction of human rights, the beggaring of whole populations, capped by the fall of the tyrant, himself. No one can wonder, therefore, at the increasing number who are abandoning a bankrupt old world for a new land, a land where freedom and opportunity has become the birthright of every man.

It would be impertinent to imply that these blessings stem from the Massachusetts insurrections. Yet, it would not be too much to say that the rebellion gave to the Commonwealth—and to the bewildered young nation—an unmistakable signpost at a time when it stood at the crossroads. One path led to union and greatness, the other to disunion and impotence.

Few realized and fewer cared, at the end of the Revolution in 1783, that the Confederation, so useful during the war, was rapidly disintegrating. Only a handful of farsighted men recognized the need for a strong, permanent union to safeguard the independence won through the expenditure of so much treasure, so much blood. Most of the people were blind. They were impoverished, exhausted, intent upon rebuilding their own shattered lives.

But in the next few years everyone became aware that something was wrong. The seeds of a new prosperity were present. The forces of stability were emerging. At the same time, the forces of disintegration were gathering momentum. There was no real consciousness of impending disaster, yet there was a realization that some sort of change was necessary. What was this change to be? A strong central government? Those who believed in it were gaining recruits. But those who abhorred the idea were becoming even more numerous. The vast majority believed that the Revolution had been fought to drive out the tyranny of a strong government centered in London. They wanted no new tyrant set up in their own new world, not even if they had the right to choose and control the one man who would rule.

The provincial minded were in the ascendancy. It seemed certain that the end must be thirteen separate and sovereign states. That a certain stability would have emerged in such a case cannot be denied. But evils, too, would be multiplied. Yet, the breakup of the Confederation was viewed with such indifference by the various legislatures that, though they knew full well many urgent problems could be solved merely by keeping the union alive and granting Congress a little more power, they chose to ignore the opportunity. The Annapolis Convention, called in the Fall of 1786 for the sole purpose of strengthening the Articles of Confederation, not to set up a strong central government, was attended by the representatives of only five states.

Only the efforts of Alexander Hamilton, one of the first to cry out for a federal form of government, prevented the utter collapse of the convention. He managed to induce the representatives to pass a resolution which asked the states to choose delegates to a new convention to be held in Philadelphia in May of the following year. Almost single handed,

Hamilton kept alive the hope of those who saw the true destiny of the United States rested on an indestructible union, a union that could defy the predatory powers of Europe who already had designs of swallowing America piecemeal.

Then rebellion. Between September of 1786 and May of 1787, the flood of insurrection in Massachusetts reached a peak and ebbed away. Forebodings of civil war shook the complacency of those who had the wit to understand. The rebellion had ended. But no issues had been settled. No grievances had been adequately redressed. The Legislature continued to heap invective upon those who had rebelled against intolerable conditions. The legislators hemmed and hawed and conceded as little as possible to an aroused public opinion. The forces of reaction had been shaken, but not quite unseated from the saddle. A new storm seemed certain to come.

Truly, the causes of disorder were still present, not only in the Commonwealth, but in every other state as well. Who could tell where another and more violent rebellion might break out? Who could tell if the quarrels between states might not lead to open wars? It was possible. The danger was there. The danger was acute. Thus, when the convention met in Philadelphia in May of 1787, twelve of the thirteen states were represented.

The delegates who gathered on that historic occasion were of the most educated, most prosperous, most conservative classes. They had come solely to change and strengthen the Articles of Confederation. The state legislatures were watching with suspicion, lest too much of their powers be taken away. The people were watching with sullenness, lest the convention deprive them of the very liberties they had fought the Revolution to gain.

Washington, Madison, Pinckney, Gerry, Franklin, Hamilton, all the delegates were conscious of those many eyes watching their every move. They were aware, too, that patching the Articles would not be enough. They foresaw that the few powers the states were willing to give up in a crisis would be withdrawn as soon as the danger was past. They saw the return of the same dreary bickerings, the same renunciation of financial liability, the same refusal to cooperate that had so plagued the Continental Congresses. The moment had come

3

for prompt, vigorous action. They seized upon the moment. It might never come again.

They closed tight the doors of the convention hall. They knew if their proceedings were open to the constant scrutiny of all, how the states would howl and the public clamor whenever they proposed—much less adopted—a constructive, yet constrictive article. Yes, I remember well those long weeks, the wild rumors, the grumblings among my friends, not only among those who had property but also by those who had nothing to lose but their poverty. In retrospect it seems strange that the state legislatures so jealously guarded the very powers which were moving to destroy them, that the people protested against the very restrictions upon their liberties—or more accurately their licenses—which threatened to plunge them into anarchy.

Whosoever can suggest that union was inevitable at this time would cast a shadow on the moral courage of those men who framed the Constitution. They knew they had come for the specific purpose of changing the Articles of Confederation. They knew the task was hopeless. Once the door of the convention hall was closed, they blandly ignored their instructions, shelved the Articles and busied themselves with new and more practical concepts of government. After two months of debate and compromise, they emerged with a Constitution calling for a strong central government—exactly what the vast majority feared and abhorred.

The first skirmish was won. By January 9th, 1788, five states had ratified, not without a fight, but by safe margins. The decisive moment was yet to come.

Whether it was accident or some mysterious design in the pattern of history, it is a fact that Massachusetts was the pivotal state in the fight for the adoption of the Constitution. And here, the outlook was black indeed. When the convention opened in Boston in January of 1788, the anti-federalists had a clear majority. All eyes were on the Commonwealth. If she rejected the Constitution, New York and several other states were certain to follow suit.

But the Federalists, whose number included some of the keenest minds in the state, had a fresh and vivid object lesson before them—the Shays Rebellion. They had seen the feeble efforts of Congress, which, while not directly called upon, had

4

tried to assist in suppressing the revolt. They had seen how inadequate the Commonwealth had been in solving the problems which had driven their friends and neighbors to take up arms. They knew that a man of less integrity, a shrewder and bolder man than Daniel Shays, might again rekindle the fires of civil conflict.

The outnumbered Federalists immediately moved for delay, lest the voice of the majority prevail. Then, they went to work. By persuasion, by compromise, by outright political dealing, they swung over the votes, one by one. The difficulty of that task is apparent when you remember that the anti-federalists were mostly those who, while not directly supporting Shays, had recognized the justice of his cause and sympathized with the Insurgents. They had asked for a redress of grievances and received more repression. What could they expect from a more powerful central government? But when the Federalists finally proposed a Bill of Rights to amend the Constitution, the people saw that their liberties could be safeguarded. Opposition crumbled. John Hancock and Sam Adams swung over. The majority was obtained. Massachusetts had turned the tide toward a true United States.

It is strange that such a critical period in the history of our country has received so little attention from the historian. Scarcely a half dozen volumes dealing with the period have found a circulation. It can be admitted that the events may be recorded in a few brief pages and that there are few striking occurrences which seem to merit extensive commentary. The result was peace, not war. And it is unfortunately true that the road to construction ever receives less scrutiny than the road to destruction.

Certain historians have even gone as far as to express skepticism that this was, in fact, a "critical period." They seem to think that because the forces of Federalism were present, union was inevitable. This broad view of the stream of history must, it seems to me, be predicated on the proposition: "It happened, therefore it was inevitable." The evidence, weighed dispassionately, can leave little doubt that the nation was facing a real crisis with majority opinion driving it onward to destruction.

If I seem to linger overlong on the way to my narrative, forgive me. I am only endeavoring to indicate where in the broad canvas of our country's past it belongs, for it is not so much my intention to give you personal reminiscences as it is to provide you with a history of the Shays Rebellion as I saw it. And, too, I would give you a yardstick against which my words may be measured, for I cannot claim my account is unbiased. My labors and my sympathies were entirely with the insurgent cause, though fortunately I had considerable contact with the other side and thus was given the Tory view of the matter. I may not—nay, I do not—believe in much of that view to this very day, but I think I can understand it. I trust I have adequately presented the Tory case to you that you, too, may understand it and thus enjoy this tale the better.

It would be as easy to overstress the importance of the Shays Rebellion as to minimize it. Unfortunately, the latter has been done too often and too well by the general historian. I would not imply that the rebellion led directly to the framing of the Constitution. There were too many other elements involved. But behind that rebellion will be found almost all the causes of confusion and domestic unrest which were present, in greater or lesser degree, in each one of the other twelve states. In many respects, Massachusetts represented the extremes of Tory aversion to change and Rebel demand for liberal reform, both of which at times led to ridiculous lengths. Yet, as events have developed, it is one of the ironies of history that the Tory's apparent victory was his defeat and the Insurgent's defeat opened the way to an even greater victory for his cause.

In the preparation of this narrative, I have refreshed my memory by consulting official documents, court records, town records, the personal papers of my contemporaries, and newspapers of the time. In my perusals, I was struck by the utter lack of any adequate material from insurgent sources. With our defeat, the mass of official rebel correspondence became waste paper. Except for a few letters in the press, not one of the Insurgents placed his case, as he saw it, before the public. This is not hard to understand since the Insurgents were not scholars, being drawn mostly from the ranks of those who worked with their hands.

The only full length work dealing with the affair is Mr. George R. Minot's "History of the Insurrection in Massachusetts," first published in 1788. Excellent as it is, Mr. Minot's work tends to leave the reader with the Tory point of view, understandable enough since Mr. Minot was Clerk of the House of Representatives and a staunch government supporter. Indeed, working from Tory sources, very few historians have bothered to look behind the Tory interpretation of the facts to ascertain if it is the true one. Thus, casual readers of casual histories will tend to believe that the Regulators were scoundrels and demagogues and misguided fools, though they may have had some measure of justice in their cause. That impression will be misleading. In the main, we were honest and sincere. The proof lies in the fact that we were not wholly defeated in our most urgent aims and our cause was not repudiated by the people.

Just one more personal observation—and a caution. Do not accept the easy assumption that this is an example of "class conflict." Unfortunately, considerable confusion has attended the popular definition of "class." If by class you mean a group with specific interests, then conflicts between groups in any society are as inevitable as conflicts between husbands and wives. But if you permit yourself to consider groups as "castes," then you are helping to undermine democracy and forge the chains of your own enslavement. Our country has never been divided into "castes." Our country must never be so divided.

We are vulnerable. Because we believe in toleration, compromise and a free expression of opinion, we are caught between the harpies of autocracy and the prophets of perfection. Both offer bread and circuses, an easy solution to our worries and problems. The price is obedience to the state and an end to personal liberty. We reject both. Our faith rests in democracy, with all its imperfections and inefficiencies—yes, and injustices. We know democracy is an ideal, not a false promise. We know we can rule ourselves better than kings or cliques. We know progress toward a more perfect democracy is bought by work and struggle. With truth as our sword and liberty as our shield, we are slowly reaching our goal, a day when injustice is at a minimum, opportunity at a maximum, and none of our people knows want.

Chapter 1

HAD it been my purpose to provide you with a story of pure adventure, an exposition of my earlier life might well have served better. I had just turned eighteen when the Revolution flamed across that famous bridge at Concord. My home was in Pelham, Hampshire County, but I had left it the previous year to enter Harvard College at Cambridge. My eventual purpose had been to pursue the profession of law.

My father had been reluctant to allow me to follow such a career, for lawyers have never been popular in the country districts. But my interests had never been directed toward farming, though I had never shirked my duties at home. I had always been restless, discontented with the narrow boundaries of our farm and town. One of my earliest recollections is the delight with which I awaited our annual trip to Boston. Every fall my father would carry there our surpluses of flax and/or hogs, grain, wool or whatever had been a good crop that year. He would sell or exchange them for our winter's supply of necessaries, such as loaf sugar, tea, coffee, bar iron and so on and the few luxuries we could afford, as silk ribbons for my mother's dresses and spices for my father's flip. From our situation, we might as well have traded at Springfield or, farther on, Worcester. But my father, too, felt the need for a complete change once a year.

My father will ever hold my esteem and affection, for once he saw he could not reconcile me to farming or at least to entering the ministry, he bowed to my desires. My elder brother, Jonathan, and my younger brother, Increase, seemed content to stay home, so my presence wasn't necessary to maintain our family's existence. My father was not a rich man, though our farm provided us with an abundant living and enough cash to pay our taxes, buy our necessaries and a few luxuries. Nevertheless, he drew upon his savings and, with his blessings, sent me off to Cambridge. I was aware my father had been saving that money to buy a piece of pasture land he had admired for many years, though he rarely spoke of it at home. Accordingly, I determined to become as small a drain as possible upon his purse. During the fall term at college, I applied for a position as schoolmaster for the winter months at Hubbardston. In late November, I was notified by the selectmen that my appointment had been approved.

For teaching those months I received 39 shillings and my board. As was the custom, I was saddled upon a new family every two weeks and thus came to know almost all of the people in the surrounding area. I was a young man at the time, yet I was treated with as much respect as if I had been of the ministry. I was given the softest bed, the choicest of food, and if the canny householder asked me to provide little Zeb with extra schooling in the evening, I could hardly object. But, as obtained every winter at home, I did so wish I could vary my diet. It was pork, pork, pork, fresh and salted and in sausages, boiled and braised and roasted, until at length I could not hear a pig squeal without belching in sympathy.

War talk filled the air, much more in the east than back home. For many years, we had watched with growing concern as the British became more and more arrogant in their treatment of our commerce and industry. Yet, while we in the west became heated at the news of the Boston Massacre and damned the king when we heard of the Boston Port Bill, those events seemed rather remote to us. Indeed, even in Hubbardston, which is in Worcester County and far from the sea, we were hardly aware of the growing certainty of war. True, a company of Minutemen was formed in Hubbardston, but the drills were not taken so very seriously.

Thus, we were shocked when the storm finally broke on that fateful 19th of April. At the side of Adam Wheeler, with whom I was residing, and other of the friends I had made in Hubbardston, I marched forth to battle. We reached Middlesex too late to take part in the famous action at Concord

9

and Lexington. But my school days were over. My plans for a prosperous career in law, so carefully laid, were engulfed in the torrent. And too, I resigned myself to postponing the day I would claim Judith, the girl who had taken my affections and promised to become my wife.

With some reluctance, yet with a resolve to do my duty, I returned to Pelham, wound up my affairs and joined my militia company. The summons to battle was not long in coming. Early in June I bade farewell to my friends and family. My father was resigned, my younger brother envious, my mother tearful but brave. With drums rattling, our column set out for the town of Boston, then under siege. In my company was Jonathan, my elder brother, Daniel Shays, Tom Packard, Tom Johnson, and others whom you will meet in these pages. We paused in Amherst to join with the company there and so I had a final moment with Judith, whose father owned the tavern and store facing the common. I promised I would soon return. She promised she would wait. That day marked the last time I saw any of those most precious to me for eleven long years.

Of my wanderings, I shall deal as briefly as possible. Jonathan and I fought side by side in that terrifying engagement at Bunker's Hill. My brother was slightly wounded in the retreat and was sent home. But he returned in time to give his full share to the dreary task of keeping Boston under siege. I was quickly absorbed into the new army, which was reorganized under the leadership of our esteemed General Washington. But not even the inspiration of so great a commander could give me enthusiasm for a military career. Instead of excitement and gallant action, I found that army life meant ditch digging and monotony between infrequent skirmishes.

When the British finally evacuated in the summer of 1776, both my brother and I left the army. Jonathan returned home to help with the farm work and, as I later learned, reenlisted as soon as the harvest was in, serving gallantly throughout the remainder of the war. I was lured to Salem and the sea, where men were urgently needed for an ever expanding privateering fleet. I cannot deny I was as much motivated by the tales of fabulous rewards as my desire to serve my country. Common seamen were reported to be dividing fantastic sums of prize money. It was an irresistible temptation for one such as I who had never had more than one shilling to rub against another. Salem was indeed a maelstrom. Every shipyard was a hive, every tavern jammed with tough, blasphemous tars, every counting house working far into the night to keep track of the ever mounting profits. Though I had never before stepped foot on a deck, I had no difficulty in obtaining a berth. In September of 1776, I was signed aboard the *Resolve*, 150 tons and 20 guns, Aziel Green, master. Thus my career as a seaman —one I took to immediately—was launched.

For the next three and a half years, I was almost continuously at sea. During the first year, we rarely met a British man-o-war, though we did engage one frigate of 50 guns against our 20 and, by good luck and good sailing, emerged the victor. The profits had not been exaggerated. One voyage alone gave me three hundred pounds sterling as my share.

Unlike most seamen, I was not content to keep my station. I studied navigation and saved my money, for I could see that, as time went on, prey was getting harder to find. By the spring of 1780, the lush days were definitely done and the shares from each voyage were shrinking alarmingly. Accordingly, I determined to make one last effort to substantially increase my capital. I bought an interest in the *Falcon*, 130 tons and 25 guns, and was signed aboard her as second mate.

Alas, this was to be my least profitable voyage. For three solid months we cruised fruitlessly through the Caribbean and along the coast of the United States, as our country was now called. Very often we met enemy shipping, but the British naval escort each time proved too formidable for us to attempt an attack. Twice, we had brushes with the enemy, once defeating a frigate of 40 guns which unfortunately sank and deprived us of a prize. The second time we were forced to turn and run, the weight of the metal against us making the odds hopeless.

In desperation, we crossed the ocean and coasted off the shores of our ally, France. Late in May of 1780, we were off the Straits of Gibraltar. There, we fell in with an Algerian xebec of 32 guns and immediately engaged her. We fought bravely, but we were defeated—swamped by numbers, you might say, for the Turks swarmed over our decks in enormous waves. After more than half of our crew had been slaughtered, we were forced to strike.

For almost six and a half years I remained a prisoner of the Turks in Algiers. After being brought ashore, we were sold into slavery. I was placed in the Dey's marine, stripped of my clothes, chained to an oar, lashed without respite or mercy. The casualties among us were horrible, men dying right and left of the pest, of ruptures, of sheer exhaustion. How I managed to survive that ceaseless torture baffles me to this very day.

The price set on my body was a thousand Algerian zequins, a little over two thousand dollars in our money. The ransom was not forthcoming, either from Congress or the Commonwealth. I wrote to my family and told them of my plight, scarcely hoping they could raise such a sum, but urging them to apply to the Legislature for my relief. After almost a year, the French consul informed me my father had transmitted fourteen hundred dollars for my ransom. My hopes were short lived. The Dey became insulted at having been offered less than his demands and doubled my ransom. I knew my father had borrowed to send me this much. I knew another such sum would be absolutely beyond his borrowing power. I returned the money.

I spent two hideous seasons in the galleys, the seasons running from May to late November, when the Algerians laid up their ships for the winter months and set the slaves to other laborious works, such as road building. The second year, I went to the Dey's palace gardens, heaven after the hell I had been through.

One day I fell into conversation with a Moorish merchant, Hassi Suliman, who had been to the palace on business. He learned I was an American, that I could write and cipher, that I disliked the British. So, he effected to buy me for he needed a clerk. He had dealings with the British in tea and other East India goods and felt I would not favor them, which indeed I soon proved I did not.

My life became unspeakably easier and pleasanter. I was well treated and allowed considerable freedom, even to roaming the city at will. Escape was impossible, for no captain would risk taking me. Any captain caught aiding a slave to escape was himself enslaved and his ship and cargo confiscated.

Not until the spring of 1786 did my opportunity come.

Hassi Suliman sickened and took to his bed. By this time, a certain mutual esteem had grown up between us and he trusted me to carry on his business. He was an old man, childless, and I felt that if he died, my most probable fate would be a return to the galleys. Such a prospect called for desperate measures.

Our government, at this time, was negotiating a treaty with the Dey, but was offering to settle for half of the amount of ransom and tribute demanded. This, I was sure, the Dey would never accept. Accordingly, I appropriated the amount of my ransom, plus ten per cent import duty on the money and about two hundred and fifty pounds extra, from Suliman's strongbox and asked the French minister to effect my release. He was reluctant at first, but I finally persuaded him to undertake the task.

Suliman was still sick when word came from the palace that I had been ransomed. We parted affectionately and, as a token of friendship toward me, he gave me a beautiful ivory-handled dagger, both the handle and sheath studded with small rubies and emeralds. The value of the dagger was, I should judge, about a hundred pounds sterling.

I felt no sense of guilt in having cheated him, first because he would be repaid from the ransom money for the amount he had spent to buy me, second because he was a rich man, anyway, and third, because I felt that, if he had paid me regular wages, the account would have been virtually balanced. Many years later, a captain of my acquaintance visited Algiers and talked to Suliman. He told me the old Moor related with relish how he had been outsmarted by a Yankee.

I took passage on the first available ship, a French vessel, and reached Le Havre early in March of 1786. There I waited for nearly a month, taking only the time to visit Paris for a few days. Since no American vessel arrived, I went on to London. There, I also had to sit and wait. I was surprised, for I had believed we did considerable trading with the English. This was the first indication of the conditions I was to encounter when I returned to my native land.

At long last, in early April, the *Prosperous*, of Boston, arrived in the Port of London. I immediately waited upon Captain Bryce and asked for a berth. When I was informed he had a full crew, I bowed to necessity and paid for my passage.

We sailed on Thursday, the 20th of April, and our voyage consumed a total of 49 days, an excellent passage. You can well imagine my feelings as I turned my face homeward. I was mighty impatient to see the shores of America, but I was troubled, too. Eleven years had passed since I had last seen my home, eleven wasted years. Soon, I would have to pick up the threads of a life I hardly remembered had ever existed. I couldn't recover the ambitions of my youth, though I was aware opportunities for high government position, open to lawyers, had increased a hundredfold since independence. Schooling was no longer possible for me. What could I do? Return to farming? To commerce? To the sea? I had some experience in all three. But I did not know what I really wanted.

This was my state of mind as we drew closer to Boston. But before reaching port, one incident of the voyage deserves mention, an incident which shocked me and has some bearing on my tale. Thus, by your leave, I shall open my narrative on the 2nd of June, 1786, five days from Boston Light.

You will imagine me as I was then, 29 years of age, a tall man, angular of features, rather sharp nose, grey eyes, my skin browned from my years of residence in Algiers. My hair was my own, a natural brown, tied into a queue with a small blue silk ribbon. My clothes were ordinary, but neat, for I had bought them new in London. My coat and breeches were of a fine dark blue serge, my waistcoat of buff shalloon, my shirt an excellent white linen with a ruff in the front, my stockings of black thread and my shoes a stout black cowhide, fitted with pewter buckles.

On this second day of June, we were spanking along on a stiff breeze that bid fair to bring us to Boston in another four days at the very most. The air was crisp and clear and the sinking sun gave a pretty golden tint to the fore sides of the bellied canvas. Captain Bryce and I were standing with our backs to the taffrail, swapping stories of our experiences in the war, for Bryce, too, had been a privateer, commanding a ship of sixteen guns.

The tinging of eight bells—four in the afternoon—had not long since faded away when our conversation was interrupted by a hail from the foretop:

"A sail! A sail! Dead astern!"

The voice from aloft set off a stirring chain of memories in my mind. It was all so familiar—the alarmed cry, the sudden tenseness, the eager rush to the rails, the hush broken only by whispering as we strained to see if the ship was friend or foe, if we must clear the deck for action or run for our lives. For many moments, I didn't realize that the pattern was now being repeated. Then, I noticed that our crew was crowded at the rails, some clambering into the rigging, staring anxiously astern. I was puzzled. That the ship on the horizon was dangerous to us seemed absurd. The United States was at peace. Indeed, every sea power whose ships might be in these waters was at peace with us. Pirates were known to be operating in the Caribbean and the Mediterranean, but none had ever ventured this far north. So, I set down my fears to imagination and gave my full attention to the approaching sail.

Our lookout had been negligent in his duty. The ship had been long over the horizon before he noticed her. She was now only five miles astern and bearing down on us fast. Every rag on her was set and a white *V* raced before her bobbing bowsprit. She began beating to windward and my uneasiness returned, for I believed I recognized her type. Her jibs, her bulky waist, the bluntness of her bows and high poop, all suggested. . . . With a curious sinking sensation in my stomach, my doubts vanished. Yes, that ship was, in truth, a British frigate.

Captain Bryce swore and turned from the taffrail and stared aloft for a long time. There wasn't another stitch of canvas that could be shaken out to give us an extra knot of speed. Why we should want to escape from the Englishman was beyond me.

Before I could put the question to the captain, he growled an apology and hurried down into the waist of the ship. He circulated among the seamen, talking to them and sending some below. Mr. Boyle, the first mate, reached my side in his pacings and muttered something about wishing we mounted a few twenty-four pounders. We would need more than a few, I saw, for that frigate mounted at least forty guns. One of her broadsides could blow us to kindling.

"You'll pardon my ignorance, Mr. Boyle," I said, "but we are at peace with England, aren't we?"

Mr. Boyle's wedgelike face thrust forward. "Eh? Well, it's yes and no, Mr. Hascott. Personally, I don't think the Admiralty was informed of the peace treaty. Leastwise, they don't act that way. Why only last. . . ." He broke off sharply. "Your papers are all in order, aren't they, sir?"

"Papers? What papers?"

"Papers proving you're an American. Seems them damn Limeys assume you're an Englishman unless you have papers to prove otherwise. They impressed five men off the last ship I was in—one of them a Frenchman—right outside of Boston Harbor, too."

"That's ridiculous," I snorted. "By what right . . . . ?"

Boyle smiled dryly. "By right of forty guns, Mr. Hascott."

Captain Bryce rejoined us, his steps heavy with anger and anxiety. "By God, I'd like to see them take a man of mine. Every last son has papers." Then, his bulldog jowls set. "Papers won't mean much if they're shorthanded—as they usually are. I trust yours are in order, Mr. Hascott."

"I think so," I replied, feeling my pockets to reassure myself. "I have a letter from Mr. Adams. Will that be enough?"

"You can hope so," Bryce replied gloomily. "I'll be interested to see if they honor our minister's signature."

The frigate was creeping closer, though not as fast as before, since it was having difficulty in clawing into the wind to get us on the weather gauge. I could almost hear the drums beating to quarters as I watched those antlike creatures scurrying across the decks to battle stations. I doubted that the captain anticipated trouble from us, but was merely taking the opportunity to exercise his men.

Captain Bryce was cursing our foretopman, for he believed if we had been warned in time we might have had a chance to escape. I believed that, too. The frigate was handy enough on the wind, but she was a little balky on the starboard tack. Since darkness was less than two hours away, we might have been able to stay far enough ahead to have lost her. But it was too late for idle regrets.

White smoke belched from the frigate's port forechasers, the ball splashing under our counter indecently close and the boom bouncing close after on the greenish waves.

"Heave to, Mr. Boyle," Captain Bryce said quietly. "No use pretending we didn't see that one."

16

In grim silence the crew went to the braces. The main swung around slowly and the wind dumped from the sail. Our ship slowly lost headway and drifted. Only the soft creaking of a loosened block broke the sullen hush pressing down upon our decks. My own heart pounded through the silence as I watched the frigate heave to and a barge go quickly overside, followed at once by marines swarming down the ladder. Nervously I fingered my papers. It would be the irony of ironies if I was now pressed into the Royal Navy, so close to home after so many bitter years of exile.

The swaying blurs swinging the oars in clocklike rhythm soon dissolved into broad, sweat-stained backs. A young, smooth-cheeked, naval officer was sitting in the sternsheets, chatting easily with a bulky, black-browed sergeant of marines who stood at his side. The naval officer's manner was reassuring. At least we were being spared dealings with that unpleasant type of arrogant young gentleman who, too often, obtains his commission in His Majesty's Navy by virtue of a relative's purse.

The bosun of the naval barge barked an order and the oars snapped upright. As the boat drifted under our ladder amidships, the officer and marines stood up. Not a man of our crew stirred. But Captain Bryce knew better than to irritate the boarding party. He gave the command to heave a line, then went down to the well deck to greet the English. I followed along, for I knew I would be examined, too.

As soon as the barge was fast, the marines filed up, lined up and presented arms. Those beautiful red coats still aroused in me an almost irrepressible desire to punch one of the wearers in the nose. The young officer came up the ladder slowly, with great dignity, then vaulted over the rail, yanked down his waistcoat and looked around. He smiled and came directly toward me.

"Lieutenant Montrose, at your service, sir," he said with a bow. "Captain Witherspan sends his compliments and regrets for the inconvenience. Duty, you know. May I see the ship's papers, if you please, Captain?"

"This is Captain Bryce, Lieutenant," I explained, indicating him at my side.

The black-browed sergeant guffawed. No one else saw any humor in the lieutenant's natural mistake. Captain Bryce was not wearing a distinctive uniform, for it was not the custom to do so in the merchant service, and his brown kerseys were rather more worn than my new serges. The marine's smile dropped from his swart face and he looked as if he'd like to shrivel into his boots.

"Remind me to discuss this with you when we return to the ship, Mr. Malloy," Montrose purred. And this purr carried with it a strong hint of the cat. "You may search the ship now, if you will. And be quick about it. We wouldn't want to delay Captain Bryce any more than necessary."

The sergeant saluted stiffly, curtly picked off a squad and marched off to search the ship for any sailor who, because he lacked proper papers, might be hiding below decks.

Lt. Montrose was affable again. "Stupid of me, Captain. The papers, if you pleace. . . ."

Captain Bryce's mouth was grim as he passed them over. I felt the same way. This man was just a bit too polite. A moment ago we were feeling optimistic. Now, I suspected the suave Englishman might take some of our men, papers or no papers.

"Would you mind ordering your men to line up. Captain?" the lieutenant asked after he had glanced at the papers.

Captain Bryce grudgingly gave the order and the men, without grace and none too promptly, formed a semblance of a line. Mr. Montrose was not in a hurry, nor did he seem to notice the grumbled insults and mumbled curses—which were audible enough to make Captain Bryce chew on his lips to hold back an order for them to pipe down, lest they make the matter worse.

The lieutenant walked slowly down the line, gazing at each of the men with a calculating eye that reminded me of a slave buyer examining a new shipment of blacks. When he reached the far end he began looking over the seamen's papers. He worked back in complete silence, questioning only one of the entire eighteen. That smile, fixed on his smooth, tanned countenance was beginning to irritate me.

He was almost finished when the sergeant and his squad emerged from the after cabins. At once, I noticed a suspicious bulge at the bulky marine's flappy waist...something he had stolen, I was sure. My own valuables were with me, two hundred pounds sterling in gold sewn into my waistcoat, so

18

I didn't fear personal loss. But I was determined, nevertheless, that the sergeant wouldn't get away with his thievery.

"Satisfied?" Captain Bryce asked at length.

"Eh?" The naval officer returned the last man's papers. "Oh, yes, quite...You found everything in order, Mr. Malloy?"

"Everything in order, sir," the sergeant rumbled.

"Everything?" I echoed. "You're sure you didn't upset anything in your search for souvenirs, Sergeant?"

He wheeled upon me. "What's that?"

I reached out, hooked my finger under his middle button and yanked hard. The coat flew open and the jeweled hilt of a curved dagger popped out.

A moment passed before I realized it was mine. I had completely forgotten it since packing my portmanteau. I reached for it, but another hand was quicker and snatched it from the sergeant's belt. Lt. Montrose held the dagger up, turned it over and over and a thousand tiny red and green lights sparkled from the rubies and emeralds set into the ivory handle.

"You have excellent taste in souvenirs, Mr. Malloy," Montrose commented, amused. "Beautiful, isn't it? Or was it the monetary value that attracted you?"

"I'll take it, if you please, Lieutenant," I said. "It happens to be mine."

"Eh?" His head lowered a trifle and he scratched his chin with the point of the scabbard. "You're Mr. Hascott, aren't you—the passenger? I don't believe I saw your papers."

I struggled to keep my temper under control and, as I handed him the letter, I added pointedly, "Mr. Adams is a personal friend of mine."

Mr. Montrose tucked the dagger under his arm, opened the letter and read it. I was afraid my bluff was not convincing, for the letter merely related that I was recently released from captivity in Algiers and was a fellow citizen of John Adams from Massachusetts and any favor shown me would be appreciated.

The Lieutenant was smiling and his eyelids drooped as he finished the letter and handed it back. "Interesting. Oh, yes, quite interesting...Sergeant..."

"One moment," I broke in sharply. "I'll thank you for the return of my property—*now*."

The officer's smile broadened. "Oh, I'm afraid that's impossible now, Mr. Hascott. You see, Sergeant Malloy will have to face court martial proceedings. We can't tolerate thieving in the Royal Navy. I must use this as evidence, of course. It's all quite simple, isn't it?"

"Quite simple," I returned evenly. "You'll regret this, Lieutenant. When Congress hears of this, you can be sure our government will take drastic action—not only against *your* bald thievery—but against these whole outrageous proceedings."

Lt. Montrose laughed and addressed no one in particular. "Rather childish the way these rebels talk of their precious Congress—that impotent collection of bungling beggars who—"

He never got any further. Something inside of me exploded. I took one step forward and my clenched fist whipped into my line of vision. A pain streaked up my arm and Montrose staggered backward. He hit the rail with terrific violence, slipped and fell into the scuppers. Jaws slack, eyes bulging, the marines slowly turned upon me. A cold sweat broke out on the small of my back as I realized what I done.

Someone over on the left whooped with delight. "At 'em, boys!" he yelled—and sprang at the nearest marine, his big sledgehammer fists swinging.

With a wild roar, our seamen swung into action. A musket shot cracked harmlessly into the air and, through the pandemonium, I could hear Captain Bryce begging his men to desist. He might as well have begged a volcano to stop erupting.

"Over with 'em!" came a hoarse cry. "Heave 'em over!"

A rangy sailor picked up the limp naval officer, held him high overhead. Captain Bryce shrieked and rushed in to stay this mad act which would certainly bring down terrible punishment from His Majesty's Navy. I leaped forward, too, for the lieutenant still was clutching my dagger. Both of us were too late. Our yelling startled the sailor and the officer slipped from his hands. The body bounced on the rail and disappeared overside.

For one long, gruesome moment, the noises on deck faded

completely into the distance. I could hear the men below in the barge crying out in alarm. There was a horrible, pulpish crash. Then, wild babbling. Captain Bryce and I shuddered. We were in a pretty mess now, and no mistake. Captain Bryce glared at his seamen, biting his lips in anger. He met my eye and his mouth quivered in the semblance of a smile. His big, freckled fists closed. There was no use in indulging in regrets. The job had to be finished and finished decisively. Side by side, Captain Bryce and I waded into that milling mass of striped cotton shirts and vivid red coats.

I remember little after that, except that it was a brawl uninhibited by any delicate scruples about fair play. It was jag, gouge, kick, jump back from a butting head, punch and knee and cover desperately to keep vital parts from damage. I recall slugging one man who collapsed into the arms of one of our seamen, who thereupon swung the marine around as if he were a weight, let go and watched him sail overside and into the sea.

Then an ape almost got me. I lashed out and almost broke my hand on his jaw. He reached for me, but I sidestepped, lunged under his guard, caught him under the waist and drove him to the rail. Before he could gain his footing, I heaved him up onto the rail, trying to keep out of the way of his kicking legs.

"Don't!" he shrieked in terror. "Don't let me go!"

Something made me hesitate. As my eyes focused, I recognized the burly Sergeant Malloy. His swart face glistened with sweat as he tried to squirm back.

"Please, mister! I don' wanna go back! I wanna go to America! They'll give me the cat! Gimme a chance!"

I nodded seriously. "Indeed, yes, Mr. Malloy. Bring back my dagger and you shall come back with us."

I let him go, watched him turn over and over. He hit the water head first, came up sputtering curses, then swam desperately for the barge, which was now some distance from our ship.

The pandemonium had ebbed away and, with some surprise, I saw that the deck was entirely cleared of marines. Our sailors stood about grinning at each other, puffing and joking about their bloodied noses, blackened eyes and ripped shirts. My own nose, always getting in the way in affairs of this kind,

21

was puffed and sore. Captain Bryce was sitting on a hatch, mumbling about how old he was getting and dabbing a cut on his chin.

"Well, that takes care of the British Navy," I said.

His head jerked up. "The British Navy! Oh, my God!" He leaped up and rushed to the rail.

My knees suddenly felt weak. We had all forgotten about that frigate out there. I turned slowly and fearfully. The barge was paddling around, picking up survivors, but the frigate was nowhere in sight. She had disap. . . . No, there she was, dead astern! Our ship had drifted around to show the frigate our counter.

Captain Bryce wheeled, livid. "Damn your eyes!" he bellowed. "Man the braces! Lively! Lively! Want to get blown out of the water?"

It took a full second for the captain's words to seep in. Then, with a shout and a curse, the men tumbled all over each other in their haste to get to the halyards. The yards swung around and the mainsail shivered. Slowly, so painfully slowly, the wind took hold and bellied the canvas. The hull shuddered and the ship's forefoot gingerly pranced forward.

"We got a chance—a bare chance," Bryce murmured. "Maybe they didn't notice what happened. Give us fifteen minutes."

A fifteen minute start would be enough. The blood-red sun was hanging on the rim of the horizon. There was less than an hour of daylight left. The frigate could not accelerate as fast as our ship would, thus fifteen minutes of grace would give us a lead enabling us to stay out of range of those murderous guns until we could slip into the protection of the darkness.

Little by little, our ship picked up speed. Soon, every rag was drawing, every stay taut and singing, every timber groaning and straining, as if the ship, too, was aware of the terrible fate in store for us if the frigate's guns came within range.

Captain Bryce and I hurried aft to watch the Britisher. She was still standing motionless, no sign of excitement on her decks, no sign of getting under way again. The barge was moving back toward the ship now and I wondered idly if all the marines had been picked up. Not that I cared much.

22

But I knew better than to hope this would teach those arrogant English a lesson.

The minutes stretched into eternity. The Captain and I stood motionless, our eyes never leaving the big warship. The barge reached the frigate and I could just barely see the tiny figures going up the ladder. Almost immediately, the ponderous yards were squared and the Briton took up the chase. Captain Bryce left the taffrail, ordered a change of course, then returned to his vigil. There was a shuffling and creaking behind us and soon we were beating into the wind.

Almost imperceptibly at first, the distance between the two ships widened. Soon, it became evident that we were more than holding our own. Faintly and far off, a gun boomed. The ball landed so far astern that I didn't even see the splash.

The frigate became vague and shadowy and I blinked, believing my eyes were tiring from the strain. But no! The big warship was growing smaller and harder to see in the gathering dusk. A sudden, spontaneous cheer went up behind us. The men, hanging on the rails and from the rigging, were also keeping a sharp watch. And now they had true reason to cheer, for the frigate had given up the chase and was turning southward.

Within fifteen minutes more, night entirely obliterated the warship. I had only one regret, that in the stress I had forgotten to recover my dagger. I determined, however, to make a full report of this humiliating incident to Congress and I could hope that, in time, I could at least obtain monetary restitution for my loss. Meantime, I had the satisfaction of knowing I had set off the spark that had saved some American seamen from the horrors of service in the British Navy.

In the darkness we had escaped the British Navy. And in the darkness, three days later, we came upon Boston Light. You can well imagine my feelings when Captain Bryce called me up from the salon and gave me the joyous news. I would have preferred to have had my first view of my homeland in daylight. But it was somehow fitting that I arrive at night, for the light seemed symbolic of my present condition. Though this was my native land, I felt as one groping in the darkness, guided only by my faith that my country, under independence, would give me the opportunity to rebuild my life in peace and prosperity.

The lighthouse brought back memories, too, for I had been in the party under Major Tupper, during the siege, which had journeyed out here to destroy the light and deny its guidance to the British fleet. I remembered, too, watching the Redcoats blast the remainder to sorry rubble, their last act before abandoning the Port of Boston in June of 1776.

"They only rebuilt it two years ago," Captain Bryce commented when I mentioned my experience. "It took 'em eight years of squabbling before the town voted the money."

I smiled. "That sounds familiar. I take it the people are as reluctant as ever to tax themselves—even for necessities."

"Ha. I suppose the people haven't changed much, Mr. Hascott. But the country has changed...yes, changed a great deal."

Since it was too dangerous to attempt to navigate the channel into Boston by night, our ship was anchored close to shore to await the morning tide. Another ship, a schooner, was anchored in the roadstead and, as we passed her in search of our own berth, Captain Bryce spoke to her. She was the *Dragon*, from Boston, a Mr. Joseph Crane, master. The name seemed familiar and, when Captain Bryce indicated he would go over to visit, I was tempted to join him. But I observed he had some sort of business to transact, so I thought it best not to intrude.

I could have gone ashore at Nantasket, since it was still early in the evening, and made my way to Boston by road. But I was in no great hurry and I was sure the roads had not improved enough to make night traveling attractive. Thus, I decided to stay aboard. Besides, I preferred to get into Boston by daylight and thus render my reorientation the easier.

Captain Bryce was gone about an hour. When he returned he looked sober and thoughtful and his first act was to call for Mr. Boyle, his mate. After he had given Mr. Boyle some sort of instructions, he sought me out.

"I'm going on to New York, Mr. Hascott," he informed me. "A matter of a better market for my cargo. My owners gave me discretion in the matter. I'll put you ashore if you wish. Or you can go in with Captain Crane. He seems to have

24

heard your name before. Didn't you tell me you lived in Pelham?"

The connection struck me. "Joe Crane! Now, I remember. Joe is—was—a neighbor of mine. He was just a boy when I left. Of course, I'll go with him. I'll have my baggage on deck in a moment, Captain."

I was tingling with the kind of joy a stranger feels upon stumbling on an old friend in a foreign land. The Cranes had the farm up the road from our place and I had practically watched Joe grow up. But try as I might, I couldn't recall what he looked like. He was five years younger than I and, in my new found dignity of seventeen, I had ignored the mere child of twelve. I remembered, however, that he and my brother, Increase, had been schoolmates. It was a little disconcerting to know that he was now a grown man, and more, the master of his own vessel.

Within a few minutes, I was out on deck again with my portmanteau. The crew had been called aft and told of the change of plans and Captain Bryce offered to set anyone ashore who did not want to go to New York, since they had all signed on from Boston and return. He assured them, however, that he would return to the home port as soon as the cargo was discharged. Only two men decided they wanted to be paid off.

Captain Bryce walked with me to the ladder amidships. "I wish you all good luck, Mr. Hascott. But I'm afraid you'll not find employment easy to obtain here in America."

"I never heard of an American starving, Captain," I replied. Instinctively, I felt at my waistcoat to reassure myself my fortune was safe. "At any rate, I'll be a lot better off here than I was in Algiers. If I do find work, I can leave it if I like."

Captain Bryce laughed and clapped my shoulder and I shook hands with Mr. Boyle. I assured them both that I intended to make an issue of the incident recently concluded. Neither believed I could hope to receive compensation for my loss, or even satisfaction from the British government. Thereupon I groped down the dark side of the vessel and stepped into our small boat.

The lighthouse beam swung around, giving me enough light to make out a tall, broad-shouldered young man standing at

25

the schooner's rail. As far as I could make out in the dimness, he was blond and very bronzed. He didn't look a bit like the freckled, stub-nose Joe I had known. Our boat bumped the side and was made fast and I scrambled eagerly up the ladder. It was Joe, all right, grown into a truly handsome young man. He was solidly built, slim-waisted, and his nose was still slightly upturned, which was lucky, for it took away the perfection from his regular features and absolved him of prettiness. We smiled at each other and Joe shyly stuck out his hand.

"Welcome home, Mr. Hascott."

"It's good to see you, Joe." I gave him a hard grip. "And please, none of that mister stuff. You didn't call me that when last we saw each other."

Joe grinned. "I'd better just stick to Warren, then. Pa whaled hell out of me for what I used to call you." He laughed, embarrassed, and half turned. "Jason, take Mr. Hascott's baggage to the spare cabin...We'll go below, Warren. I guess we've got lots to talk about . . . Algiers and all."

Joe yielded to me at the companionway and, after giving orders to his mate, followed me down. I was brimming with questions, for his family and ours had always been warm neighbors. Under the salon lamp, his freckles showed up more clearly and I was relieved to find he hadn't changed so much, after all. Joe got out a bottle of sherry and glasses and poured.

"First, a toast to your safe return, Warren."

"Thank you." We drank and settled at the salon table. "Before we go into anything else, Joe, I'm dying for news of my family. How's my father—and mother—my brothers?"

Joe squirmed a little. "Well, to tell you the truth, Warren, I haven't been home in over two years. I hear from Increase once in a long while. I had a letter from him about seven months ago. He said then that everybody was all right. I wanted him to go to sea with me when I left home and I've been urging him on and off ever since, but I guess Increase will be a farmer all his life."

"He hasn't changed any, then," I commented. "And how's Jonathan?"

"All right, I guess. He's married, you know."

"My brows went up. "That's news. I'm glad to hear it. Do I know my sister-in-law?"

26

"I guess so—May Lambert. She used to live in Amherst, hard by Clapp's Tavern. A scrawny girl, as I remember her."

"The name is familiar, that's all." I eyed my wineglass casually. "By the way, how are the Burdicks?"

Joe chuckled. "Judith never married, if that's what you mean. The Burdicks don't live in Amherst any more. They've got a house in Boston—a very fine house." He frowned slightly. "Burdick's come a long way since those days. His trading house is one of the richest in Boston—West India goods, mostly —though he does send ships coastwise and sometimes to Europe." Then he added slyly, "She's still very beautiful."

"No doubt, no doubt." I coughed and changed the subject. "How about yourself? I hardly expected to find you a seaman—and master of your own ship."

"Oh, I've been at sea for almost eight years now. I started out as a powder monkey on a privateer. In '82, I went into the Navy. I served under Captain Barney. We brought the peace news back from France in '83. Well, after the Navy disbanded I went home for a while. I couldn't stand the farm, so I shipped out on deep water as second mate. There's no money in that—or much future—so I scraped together all the cash I had and could borrow and. . . ." He waved around. "Well, she's all mine—almost. I was lucky Pa left me something. Otherwise I wouldn't have been able to do it."

I caught myself as I was about to congratulate him. "Your father's dead? I'm sorry to hear it, Joe."

"Pa died at Saratoga in '77. Paul's dead, too. He went first —at Long Island in '76." His eyes clouded. "Joab came home in '79. It was pretty horrible—I mean, what the war did to him. Joab's a cripple now."

The news gave me a curious creepy feeling. Joab, a cripple! He was just a bit older than I. All of the Cranes were big men, but Joab was the biggest, the strongest. And how he had prided himself in his muscles. I could remember one time when Joab was helping us clear a field he alone lifted a boulder that four of us couldn't budge. There was something indecent about a war that could render such strength impotent.

"That almost finished Ma, when he came home like that," Joe went on in a flat voice. "After Pa died, something in her seemed to have died, too. But she tried to keep cheerful and keep the farm going for us when we got back. After I went

27

to sea and Joab came home like that...well, she just seemed to have lost interest in everything. She writes me a lot. I get a letter from her almost every time I'm in port. But it's funny, she never tells me what's going on at home. She keeps writing about what happened when we were kids...before the war. It's like she can't remember anything that happened after the war started. I guess that's the big reason why I left home. After Paul and Pa died, she treated me like a baby again." Joe smiled sadly. "And me over fourteen."

I nodded with understanding. "How's Reuben and Beulah?"

Joe shrugged. "Reuben's all right. He's a lot like your brother Increase. He'll be a farmer all his life. As for Beulah ..." He chuckled and shook his head. "Well, Beulah and I never did get along. I suppose you'll be seeing her. She's grown up now—quite a piece of woman, too. Take my advice, Warren, steer clear of her. Dangerous shoals ahead."

I laughed. "I can take care of myself."

"That's what you think. If she decides she wants you—and I've yet to meet the man she doesn't want, for a while—she'll get her hooks into you. Don't say I didn't warn you."

The warning brought forth the usual reaction. I was all the more interested. And the subject made me quite uncomfortable, for it had been a long, long time since I had even seen, much less known, a woman of my own kind. I edged gingerly away from the subject and Joe seemed glad enough to drop talk about his sister, whom he definitely disliked, and turn to the vital statistics of the town.

The town of Pelham would not be the same one I left. Friends of mine had married and were raising families. Some of the old folks had died off. The war had brought honor to some, death to others. Ed Stone died at Yorktown. Rick Wilson lost an arm at Trenton. Tom Packard had come back a Lieutenant, Dan Shays had come back a Captain, as had Tom Johnson, who was now our representative in General Court. Ed Greer had brought back a wife from Philadelphia. Yes, it would be hard for me to pick up the threads of my life in my native country.

Hour after hour, Joe and I sat and talked, only occasionally remembering to fill our glasses. I had to relate my adventures in Algiers and Joe told me about life in the navy.

"I always thought," Joe said, "that abandoning the navy

28

after the war was wrong. A lot of people are saying it now. Your ship wasn't the first to be stopped and it won't be the last. We won't be able to convince those damn Englishmen we have as much right to 'freedom of the seas' as they have until we can back up our shipping with guns."

"They haven't dared seize our ships, have they?"

"No, not on the high seas. But we don't dare stick our noses in a British port, I can tell you that. Their Navigation Acts make it impossible for us to trade with the West Indies. The law says we can bring in American produce if the ship is bona-fide American owned and at least two thirds of the crew is American. But proving it to a customs officer who doesn't want to believe it, anyway, is something else again. I used to go to the West Indies, but no more. Ships are being seized on the most trifling excuses. We used to take a chance. If we got caught, we let our ships be condemned and then bought them back at the auction for a pittance. But no more. Now, they burn condemned ships. Upwards of three hundred of our ships have been taken away since the peace. And the planters are crying for our goods. The British Ministry seems determined to sacrifice them for revenge on us. British bottoms can't supply them with what they need. To hell with them. Let them starve. Coastwise business isn't so good, but it's safe."

This news was disturbing. I couldn't help but conclude there was something very wrong with our country when the British could humiliate us almost within sight of our harbors and, more, take out our seamen and put them in virtual slavery in the Royal Navy. There was something wrong with a government that hadn't the strength to protect American ships in waters as close to our shores as the Caribbean. And I began to wonder if it would be easy to reestablish myself, even inside the country, as I had believed and hoped.

Chapter 2

THE pilot didn't come aboard the next morning until close to ten o'clock, which was shortly before the tide turned. I wasn't on deck myself much earlier than that, for Joe and I had talked far into the night. The weather was perfect for my homecoming, the sky a polished blue, the water almost as smooth as a well kept lawn. When the bosun's whistle shrilled, I moved aft to be out of the way of the bustling crew. The clackety-clack of the winch mingled with the squeals of the blocks as the mainsail was hauled up. Soon, the anchor was aweigh and our schooner eased into the channel between Lighthouse Island and Alderton Point, thence proceeding northward at a slow, cautious pace.

During my voyage from Europe, I had often feared that, in my long absence, my homeland would have changed so much I would feel as a stranger entering a new country. My fears were groundless. The village of Nantasket was the same tiny collection of weather scarred clapboard houses. The dories lined up along the shore were, I did not doubt, the very same boats we had used in our assault on the Lighthouse during the siege of Boston.

As we were passing Georges' Island, Joe came back to join me, for our pilot—a hunched, white haired old man who looked more like a clerk than a seaman—was a cantankerous sort who preferred to run the ship his way without the master standing by. Joe tapped my arm and pointed to Lovell's Island, which we were passing to larboard. A short distance off shore, the bones of an enormous ship lay white and bleached in the foaming waters of the rising tide.

"That's the *Magnificent*, what's left of her, a French seventy-four. She was flagship of Count de Grasse's fleet. De Grasse put in here for repairs after Rodney trounced him in the West Indies in '82." Joe chuckled. "Davey Darling put her ashore. After the French left, Darling was made sexton and undertaker of Old North Meeting. Everybody said he had served a sufficient apprenticeship at burying."

"That's a pretty cruel joke on Mr. Darling," I said.

"Yes, I suppose it was. Poor Davey, the kids made life pretty miserable for him for a long time afterward. One morning, he found this verse pinned on the church door:

'Don't you set this ship ashore
As you did the seventy-four.' "

I laughed, but I sympathized with Mr. Davey Darling. He must have been amply humiliated by the mere change of his occupation from pilot to undertaker.

Our course took us around Nick's Mate, a sandy, rocky spit of land where the town once hanged pirates. Thence, we veered northwest through the channel between Nick's Mate and Deer Island and our bows pointed directly toward Boston Town. The broad expanse of Boston Harbor made it difficult to ascertain details on any of the many islands to port, but nothing seemed any different than it had been ten years ago. Long Island, Spectacle Island, Thompson's Island, all were thickly wooded and meagerly farmed. There were scarcely more than two or three houses and a few barns on any of these places, though the barns were all of good size.

As we passed between Governor's Island and Castle Island, the full sweep of Boston from North Battery to the Neck became clearly visible. Joe was telling me of the new prison recently established on Castle Island, but I was only half listening. I was fully taken by the scene I had so often visualized in nostalgic moments during my long captivity. It was the same Boston.

On the summit of Beacon Hill stood a new beacon, replacing the one torn down by the British. It rose, tall and straight and stark against the fluffy white clouds, and the arm at the top, from which an iron fire basket hung, gave it the appearance of a gallows. Below, the steeples of the many churches were like enlarged spear points planted into a drab mass of irregular rooftops.

I cannot honestly say that the sight was impressive, for

31

the memory of London and Paris, vast and sprawling cities, was still fresh in my memory. Against a half a million in London alone, Boston at this time contained only fifteen thousand souls and three thousand houses. It was a village in comparison; but I was stirred as no enormous European city could stir me. This was home.

"Look!" I blurted in sudden excitement.

There was a bridge across the Charles River. It was a wooden structure, some fifteen hundred feet long, connecting a point near Hudson's point with Breed's Hill in Charleston. I could see workmen suspended from the roadway of the bridge on bosun's chairs, and so concluded it was not finished. It was indeed a marvelous piece of engineering.

"It opens this month," Joe supplied. "They're putting lamps on it for dark nights, too."

"Wonderful," was all I could say.

The *Dragon* slowly nosed toward the south side of Long Wharf, that most unusual dock which juts from the center of the bay, gouged into the rounded portion of the town's meager coastline. The string of two-storied, unpainted wooden houses built on the wharf, the warehouses and stores and shipyards and few brick residences along the waterfront, all seemed the same. Yet I got the feeling that something was different, that there was a certain strangeness in the air I could neither see nor name.

I was about to ask Joe if he felt the same, but he had returned to his duties, for our vessel was nearing its berth. The crew was bantering and laughing as they furled the sail, as happy as I to be home, though their journey had been shorter than mine.

A number of ships were riding at anchor in the harbor, some of them strung down as far as Nantasket Roads. A Dutch pink lay off Dorchester Flats, an East Indiaman rode nearby off Windmill Point, a cluster of British merchantmen stood off Noodle's Island to the north, a French brig was anchored near Governor's Island. Then I was struck by the numbers of foreign flags, British mostly, and the scarcity of our own Stars and Stripes. I searched carefully, but in all the harbor I could find only five.

As we came closer to the shore, I found the reason for my disturbed feeling. It was the tempo of the town, manifest by the aggregate of noise hanging over it. The tempo of Boston had definitely slackened. The shipyards north of Clarke's Wharf were almost completely silent and, below South Battery, only one yard showed life. Yet, the hour was only noon. Truly, this was not the busy, thriving port I had known before the Revolution.

We were almost in, so I went below and got my baggage. On returning to the deck, I saw that Joe was not engaged at the moment and went over to him to ask directions.

"Joe, I forgot to ask, is there coach service?"

Joe nodded. "I don't know when and how the coaches run, though, it's been so long since I was home. Pease runs ads in the papers. Buy one when you get ashore."

"I'll do that. Suppose I have to stay over, where would you suggest?"

Joe opened one palm. "Right here. I'll be in port a week or more. No use spending money needlessly. Money's too tight these days." He snapped his fingers. "That reminds me. Would you take letters home for me? I'll give them to you now so I won't forget."

I gladly took the letters, since they would give me an excuse, though I really needed none, to visit the Cranes. Joe had roused my curiosity about that girl Beulah. He had mentioned her in a disparaging manner several times and sometimes had become almost downright suggestive, in a very unbrotherly manner, when he spoke of her charms. And I was only human.

"Oh, and about that protest I want to make, Joe. Whom should I see, do you know? Is there a Federal office of any kind in Boston?"

"There's an impost office, but I think you'd better get advice from Captain Johnson—Tom Johnson, you know him. He's our representative in the General Court this year. Or you can see...." He scratched his stub nose. "What's that man's name? Blair! I know his son pretty well and I've met the old man several times. He's secretary to Mr. Minot, Clerk of the House."

The name sounded familiar. "I knew a Blair once. Is he a Hubbardston man?"

"I really don't know, Warren." He waved and shouted an order to one of his men. "You can go ashore as soon as we're tied up. Leave your baggage over there, under the ship's bell.

I'll take care of it. You can send for it later if anything turns up. Otherwise, meet me at Minot's T later, will you? There's an excellent tavern there."

I promised I would and he ran off to be about his duties. The schooner humped, shuddered, squealed along the piling and the hawsers were made fast. The schooner came to rest, rubbing her sides gently against the pilings like a contented cat. Joe hailed a stocky man on the wharf, who jumped down on deck and the two had a brief conversation, then headed for the salon. He was evidently the consignee of the cargo. The mate already had the hatches open, preparatory to unloading.

I put my portmanteau under the ship's bell and, as soon as the gangway had been set up, clambered to the wharf. For some minutes after stepping ashore, I just stood there, looking around. I felt as if I had been suddenly thrust into a world I knew well, yet was just a bit strange to me. Draymen, longshoremen, clerks, sailors with their tarred pigtails, merchants and mechanics flowed endlessly before me. There was the usual quota of nondescript idlers, too, who were leaning over the wharf and staring down at the schooner as if they'd never seen a ship before. The sound of the voices swirling around me was pleasant, for their accents were my very own. The faces seemed like the faces of old friends. Yes, I was home. With a happy heart I joined the stream and headed for State House.

Those of you who have never seen Long Wharf as it was in those days have missed a remarkable sight. It was some eighteen hundred feet long and a little more than two hundred feet wide. On the north side was a line of houses, most of them two storied, uncolored, the wood grey with age and weather. At the far end was a huge wooden crane, used to unload cargo from the ships. At about the middle was a T-shaped wharf tacked onto the north side of the main wharf. There were houses on Minot's T also, two of them taken by merchants, another by a tavern.

The majority of the houses along Long Wharf were taken by merchants, many of whose names were still familiar to me, though I had been absent eleven years. Eades, Shattuck, Bumstead, Isaac Parker, Henry Roley, John Shelling, and many more. There were shops along the row, too, most of them chandlers and provisioners. If you ignored the heavy planking underfoot and the open sea side, you could imagine you were walking along a busy street in town.

The people and their dress did not seem to have changed much since the war. The seamen could be recognized by their heavy canvas or cotton trousers which extended just below the knee. They uniformly wore striped cotton shirts and tarred pigtails. The workmen wore breeches of pliant leather, kersey or durant, this latter a sturdy stuff made to resemble buff leather. Invariably, the buckles on their shoes were large and made of brass. The dress of the wealthier merchants had remained practically the same, the coats square cut in the skirt, the cloth serge or broadcloth in blues, greens, reds, browns—any shade you can think of, sometimes trimmed with silk galloon or silver lace.

The younger men—and I noticed them particularly to see if I was in style—wore their waistcoats much shorter, the fashion in London, and their coats were of the new cut, double-breasted and cut away in the front with long tails in the back. Yes, I was in style. The humbler folk wore their own hair, tied in queues with a ribbon, but the merchants and many clerks still wore wigs or powdered their own hair to resemble wigs, a vanity I never approved. Everyone wore the familiar tricorn, the gentlemen's trimmed with lace. My own hat drew glances, for it was not cocked so high in the front, the latest in London.

When I came out on King Street—many were already calling it State Street—I felt on familiar ground. Mr. William Williams, Mathematical Instrument Maker, still had his shop at the head of Long Wharf, his shelves crammed with quadrants, compasses, time glasses, as well as fishing hooks and books and some stationery. Many of the residences had disappeared from King Street, their places taken by shops offering East or West India gods, crockery, a goldsmith's, a printer's shop and so on. The Bunch of Grapes, on the corner of Kilby Street, had not changed at all, except that the grapes had received a fresh coat of green coloring. And alas, the

British Coffee House was no more, in its stead there being a place of vendue for books.

The cobbled street was well filled with intent people rushing hither and yon on business, dodging carts and drays, coaches and carriages. But here was no comparison to the bustling congestion I had seen in London. As I approached State House, I noticed that the whipping post was still in its place and hackney coaches had reappeared at the head of the street, there being six in the line.

The covered walk around State House was, as usual, cluttered with idlers and, if Joe hadn't told me the General Court was in session, I could have known it from the oratory pouring from the open windows. The front of the upper story was taken by the Señate chamber, from which issued little noise. The chambers of the House were at the rear of the building, facing Cornhill, and you can be sure our legislators did not fail of their duties from lack of lung power. A bit hesitantly, I went up the front steps and peered into the offices opening on the long hallway. No one paid the least attention to me. Then, I realized I was looking for someone whose face I wasn't sure I'd know. I stopped the first passerby for information.

"Can you tell me where I can find Mr. Blair, please?"

The man peered over the tops of his spectacles. "First office to the right of the House chamber—one flight up."

I thanked him and proceeded to the broad spiral stairway in the center of the building. I always lose my sense of direction momentarily when I go up a circular staircase and this time was no exception. But I had only to follow the sound of the greatest babbling to locate the House. To the right of the closed chamber doors was an office, which I boldly entered.

There were two desks in the small, semi-circular room and space for little else, except a cupboard and a book case. At the desk to the left of the door was a gentleman, humming a tune as he scribbled and grunting each time he stabbed a period. He was an elderly man, slim and dried up in appearance, very wrinkled, his wig pushed back from his forehead, showing the baldness of his pate. He wore serviceable dark brown broadcloths, a white jabot, and his silver buttons were stamped with his initials. Yes, he was the same Mr. Blair with whom I had stayed for a time while I taught school in Hubbardston.

I coughed for attention and his quill poised. He looked up started to speak, then just stared, his mouth slightly open, showing his yellowed, uneven teeth.

"I know *you*. You're—you're—No, no, don't tell me. I never forget a name. You're.."

"Hascott," I supplied.

"Hascott! The schoolmaster!" He bounced up, revealing how very small he really was. "Of course, of course, Warren Hascott. Why, the last time I heard of you, you were enslaved in Algiers."

He came around the desk in small, hopping steps, seized my hand, and, treating my arm like a stubborn pump handle, beamed as he told me how glad he was to see me.

"I heard of your plight from one of your townsmen several years ago. I've never forgotten you, young man." He looked me up and down critically. "So you're just back from Algiers, eh? You must have a tale to tell. No, no, not a word until we've eaten." He dragged me into the hall and poked his head into the circular office opposite. "I'm going to dinner, Jeremy. If anything demands my attention, I'll be at the Two Palaverers."

He started for the stairway, remembered he hadn't taken his hat and scurried back for it. He pulled his wig down with a jerk, planted the tricorn firmly on his head and took my arm in a firm, though friendly grip. There was no opportunity to speak until we reached the street, for he nodded and passed the time of day with almost everyone we met.

"What brought you to the State House?" he asked finally. "Surely, not to see an old fossil like me."

"I had business to transact, too," I said discreetly.

And I told him briefly of our encounter with the British frigate. He grunted in satisfaction when I related our escape.

"Ah, those British," he said with a shake of his head. "They've always squealed about freedom of the seas—for themselves exclusively. I'm afraid we'll have to match them ship for ship before they'll admit us to partnership in possession of the oceans. Well, draw up your deposition, Warren. I'll see that it's delivered to the proper authority. I suppose Captain Bryce will send his deposition directly to Congress. Then Congress

37

will send a sharp note to England—for all the good that will do."

"And my dagger?" I asked. "It was rather valuable."

"Draw up a petition," Blair suggested. "Perhaps you'll be compensated—in twenty years or so. You'd still be rotting in Algiers if you waited for the Legislature to ransom you." He chuckled and looked up at me. "Now, tell me, how are you? You've grown, I can see that—filled out. It's been ten years, hasn't it?"

"Over eleven," I replied. "But it seems less. Nothing seems to have changed here in Boston, for instance."

"Except that the British are gone—bad cess to them." A scowl took hold of his wrinkled face. "Sometimes I think we were better off then. Not that I'd have them back, mind," he added hastily. "But business could be better."

"Times are really bad?"

"Bad! Young man, they're so bad I fear I'll lose two or three of my clerks when the Legislature gets around to economizing —which probably will be after the Commonwealth is bankrupt, if I know my politicians."

"And your sons, sir? They must be grown."

Mr. Blair smiled and wagged his head. "Indeed they *are* grown. The youngest, Sam, is at Harvard College. Matthew went to sea, the scamp. Ethan, you will see." He sighed. "I've had little control over them since my wife died."

I was a bit shocked and expressed my sympathy, for I remembered her with affection, though at the time I had been embarrassed by her mothering me when I so desired to maintain my budding dignity. Mr. Blair was silent a moment, but his loss had evidently been too far in the past to make him brood. Soon, he was rattling off the statistics of Hubbardston, the births, deaths, marriages, those who had gone to the war and those who had not come back. He himself had come to Boston shortly after his wife died, though he still retained his property back home.

By a tug on my sleeve Mr. Blair indicated we would turn into Merchant's Row. It was a narrow alley, almost completely blocked by a coach. Mr. Blair was not at all fazed. He released my arm, calmly seized the bridles and backed the horses from our path. The coachman rose in his seat, choking with rage, struggling to quiet the stomping, champing team. Mr. Blair

38

didn't even favor him with a glance, but took my arm again and resumed the conversation where he had left off.

At the sign of a Ladies' Shoemaker Shop, we almost ran headlong into two female patrons who were emerging. Both of us stopped to pardon ourselves. I recognized the two women at once. Mr. Blair bowed and removed his hat, nearly taking his wig along with it.

"Mrs. Burdick, Mistress Burdick. Good afternoon. You should teach your coachman better manners, Madam. I just now had to set him in his rightful place . . . Oh! May I present my friend, Mr. Hascott? He has just returned from slavery in Algiers."

"We know Mr. Hascott." I heard Mrs. Burdick say.

But I had eyes only for the younger woman. I stared, quite foolishly, struggling for adequate words.

"Judith!"

She smiled. "You're looking well, Warren."

Need I say she was lovely? She was indeed lovelier than I remembered her. Her features were smooth and well rounded and she needed no paints to enhance her clear pink coloring. Her chin was firm, her eyes a bold lustrous hazel, and her brown hair was gathered in soft curls over her flawless brow. She had closed her oil silk parasol and was swinging it nervously, smoothing her flared skirt of white flowered cambric. She seemed undecided whether to retain her smile or retire into lukewarm politeness.

Mr. Blair was saying something, but not until his thin fingers dug sharply into my arm did I remember my manners and bow to Mrs. Burdick. She was severe, unsmiling, quite thin, her appearance made more forbidding by her ever rustling black taffeta. She had aged much since I had last seen her and small wrinkles had formed about her small black eyes and thin mouth.

"We knew Warren many years ago," she was saying. Her head inclined slightly. "It's been pleasant seeing you, young man. Good day, Mr. Blair. Good day, Warren. Come along, Judith."

Judith did not seem to hear the command. She found her mind to smile without reservation and offered me her hand.

"Please come and see us soon, Warren. We live on Long Lane, just off Milk Street." She glanced at her mother, winked, and said, "Mama will be so interested in hearing about Algiers."

With a curtsey to Mr. Blair, she followed her mother, who by this time had almost reached the corner. My eyes did not leave her until she was out of sight. The coach moved off and I saw she was leaning forward. She smiled and waved and I distinctly heard her mother speak sharply to her.

Mr. Blair, I found, was eyeing me with amusement and I felt a flush creeping up my neck.

"I knew her in Amherst before the war."

Blair chuckled and took my arm again. "There's hope for you, Warren. She's the town's most beautiful ancient maid."

I started to protest, then realized he was right. An unmarried woman was indeed an ancient maid after she passed her twenty-fifth birthday. And Judith would now be twenty-seven. Quite irrelevantly—or was it so irrelevant—I remembered she had promised to wait for me.

Mr. Blair gave me a sharp poke. "Wake up, Warren. Her father's one of the richest men in Boston."

"I know. Joe told me so."

"Good. Then keep it in mind if you get ideas of courting his daughter."

Chapter 3

𝕾𝕾𝕾

As we came into Dock Square, our conversation lapsed of necessity, since the noise made talking difficult and we were often jostled and momentarily separated by the bustling throngs. Here was the town's market place. Stalls were set up all around the vast cobbled square and abundant supplies of fresh fruits and new picked vegetables brought in from the countryside were on display. There were numerous fish stalls, too, with everything from our sacred cod to delicate shrimps. Along the ground floor of Fanueil Hall was the flesh market, particularly well attended, for nowhere else in town could meat be bought. I was reminded with amusement of the market place in Algiers. Except for the color of their skins, the good women of Boston were very like their Algerian sisters. Here, too, the women pawed and pried and prodded and haggled shrilly over a few pence with the patient and long suffering venders.

Once we had passed into Ann Street, Mr. Blair resumed the subject of Mr. Burdick, telling me something of his remarkable rise to prosperity. It was simple progression. Having done well in Amherst, Mr. Burdick moved on to Springfield. There he had the good fortune to acquire a contract for provisioning the garrison. With the profits, which were considerable, he came to Boston and invested heavily, and most successfully, in privateers. Before that business collapsed, he had the shrewdness to withdraw all his funds and enter the West India trade, forbidden by the British, but winked at by the planters who desperately needed our supplies. When the peace was signed and the British found time to patrol the Caribbean, Burdick pulled in his horns a little more. He now had six ships which, though business was not very lively at the moment, he nevertheless managed to keep in constant operation.

Of the many details Mr. Blair added, I heard only a few, for I was fully taken with thoughts of Judith. All during my long enslavement in Algiers, I had cherished a picture of her in my heart. I remembered her shy smile, her warm enthusiasm, her solemn assurance that my ambitions were worthy, her trembling kiss when I bade her farewell. I hadn't seen that Judith just now. She had been a girl, barely sixteen, and I a mere boy. I realized it was impossible ever again to recapture that naive affection we once held toward each other. Yet, one ember glowed in the ashes of my outworn passion. Her very presence had once more awakened in me those same, keen desires, those vague, piquant longings.

With a start I found Ann Street had become Fish Street and I began wondering where Mr. Blair was taking me. We were in the part of town frequented mostly by seamen and shipwrights, a rather shabby section devoted to mariners' boarding houses, slop and chandlers' shops, though a few merchants had their businesses in the aging brick buildings. You could call this a slum area, though Boston had none of the stinks and horrible filth and half disintegrated houses I had noted along the London waterfront.

I did not have to be told that the state of the shipping industry was poor. True, drays rumbled along the streets and, at some wharves, longshoremen were unloading cargoes, and from one shipyard came the sounds of hammer and caulking iron. But on nearly every corner were gathered sailors, shipwrights, sparmakers and such laborers. They were engaged in lively discussions on the ills of man, in lieu of more profitable work.

"I must apologize for bringing you so far," Blair said at length. "I thought to dine with my son. I have a purpose in bringing you to see him. Or should I have had the manners to have consulted your preference of a tavern?"

"I don't mind where you take me, Mr. Blair," I assured him, "as long as the prices are reasonable."

Blair laughed. "The prices are reasonable. But you must be my guest while you remain in Boston. I insist upon it."

The inn was just off Ship Street, facing Salvation Alley,

and as we passed the open casements I saw that the taproom was well filled. The Salvation Inn was vulgarly known as the Two Palaverers from the signboard, which depicted two men dressed in small clothes and cocked hats, hands extended and bowing low to each other. Mr. Blair said he had chosen this inn as his residence mostly because it was convenient to his son's work and preferred by his other son while in port. As for himself, he cared little where he lived as long as the food was good and the beds soft.

As we entered, Mr. Blair waved cheerily to a stout, red-faced man with a denim apron across his ample middle.

"Mr. Rhodes, this is my friend Mr. Hascott. He will stay with us as my guest. Mr. Hascott has just returned from Algiers."

The landlord shook my hand heartily. "Algiers, eh? Were you a slave there, Mr. Hascott?"

I admitted the charge. The patrons nearby stirred and gazed up at me with interest. The whisper traveled fast and soon all eyes were upon me. Mr. Blair led me to a corner table by an open window where a chunky, blue-eyed young man was sitting. Had I not known I was to meet Ethan, I would never have recognized him. He was deep-chested, his face roundish, and only his long, thin nose gave him resemblance to his father. He wore green serges and his lacy neckcloth was spotless. But he seemed to be depressed, for he was toying with his dinner as if the very sight of food gave him a gaseous stomach. It was not until we were almost upon him that he noticed us coming.

He rose quickly. "It's you, father." He nodded at me glumly and without interest at first, then his eyes crinkled with uncertainty. "I know you, sir. You'll forgive me if I confess I can't for the life of me think of your name."

Mr. Blair laughed. "Shame, Ethan. Have you forgotten your old schoolmaster?"

"Schoolmaster?" Ethan grinned with embarrassment. "Dolt that I was, sir, I had many school. . . . " His eyes snapped wide open. "Hascott! Mr. Hascott!" His dolor gave way to boyish delight. "This is a surprise—a great surprise. I've been hearing much of you in these last few years. We hear from Algiers quite often. Captain Frost is—but you must know—

43

he's a prisoner there. His ship, the *Trimount*, belonged to our firm."

"Ethan is with Gorham & Blanchard," Blair told me as we settled at the table. "Doing very well there, too. They're taking him into the firm soon, eh, Ethan?"

Ethan's smile was suddenly strained and he tried hard not to show his distress. I gathered from this that he was not by nature acrid, but taken with a business worry of some kind.

"How is Captain Frost? And his men?" Ethan asked hastily to cover his glum mood. "Are they well treated?"

His father wouldn't let me answer. He insisted upon my eating before I told anything of my experience. The Blairs were well known to the patrons, skilled mechanics and seafaring men mostly, many of whom made excuses to visit our table. Some had friends who had been taken by the Turks and wished news of them. Mr. Blair chased them all away with the assurance that I would tell all later. That, it seemed, was to be the price of my dinner.

I finished my second piece of pie—dried apple pie—and how often I had dreamed of apple pie during my captivity! Then a pot of ale was placed before me and I was obliged to begin my tale. Everybody in the room crowded around our table and even Mr. Rhodes drew up a chair. I told how we were captured, about the auction of myself and my comrades, the miseries and tortures of the marine. I cannot deny I fully enjoyed the curses and gasps of amazement that accompanied my description of the barbarities of the Moorish overseers. Everyone chuckled and murmured approval when I exposed the manner of my escape.

"Didn't you take anything extra?" Ethan asked.

I shook my head. "Unfortunately, no. I managed to get only enough to pay my expenses home."

I wasn't fool enough to mention the two hundred pounds in gold sewn into my waistcoat, for I couldn't be sure there weren't thieves among my listeners. Ethan's disappointment was so marked that I couldn't help wondering if he was the kind who borrowed from every slight acquaintance. His eyes were too harassed to put him in the class of casual wastrels. Whatever his money trouble, it wasn't my concern, nor was it my place to pry into something that might have caused a quarrel between father and son.

44

Ethan must have sensed my thoughts, for he went on quickly to ask of the *Trimount* and Captain Frost. Most of Frost's men were in the galleys, so I couldn't be too sanguine about their treatment. As for Frost, himself, he was definitely better treated, though open to much misery and hardship, too. From all sides, I was bombarded with questions about friends, all of which I answered as best I could.

I was rudely interrupted by a heavy pounding on the floor. Everyone turned to see who was acting so unmannerly. A stocky man in badly cut green broadcloth had just entered and was knocking for attention with a heavy malacca cane. He was red-faced, with a flattened nose, and grey hairs bristled on his unshaven chin, giving him the appearance of a crushed strawberry.

"Anyone here want work?" he demanded harshly. "I can offer employment to whalers."

Curiously, no one showed much excitement, though I had heard during dinner that many were desperate for work. It was plain that everyone was suspicious of the offer.

"Well? Well?" the stranger called impatiently. "Is there no one who would ship aboard a whaler at excellent wages?" The suspicions did not ebb and the burly man shrugged. "Very well, if you change your mind report to Hume and Company in Salem."

Immediately, everyone rushed upon the stranger and besieged him with pleas to be taken. Mr. Blair, arms folded on the able, was eyeing the stranger with distaste. He rose suddenly, pulled down his wig, strode through the crowd.

"One moment, gentlemen!" he called shrilly. The crowd quieted and let him through and he confronted the stranger like a belligerent terrier. "Your name is Crawford, isn't it?" Suppose you tell us where you live—and where Hume & Company is located?"

Mr. Crawford glared at my friend, turned away in disdain and addressed the men. "There are positions waiting for you, gentlemen. Come to Salem."

"Salem?" Blair echoed dryly. "Gentlemen, it is my duty to inform you that Hume & Company is located in Halifax. The company has an office in Salem—a recruiting station, no more."

With a look of utmost contempt, Blair wheeled and came

back to our table. The crowd melted away from the stranger, muttering in angry disappointment. Crawford was almost purple with rage. He wheezed and grasped the arm of the nearest man.

"Come, come, my good man, would you throw away such a rare opportunity? Would you have your family starve? You know conditions here. Before you revolted against the King, one hundred and fifty whalers sailed from your ports. How many sail now? I shall tell you, gentlemen. This year, only sixteen are in service. We offer free houses for your families and excellent shares paid in hard cash. We pay in gold, gentlemen, not worthless Continental paper."

One or two wavered. The rest just glowered at the man. An ugly rumble went through the taproom.

"Throw the damned loyalist out!" came the cry.

"Aye, heave the Tory inter the harbor!"

Like a swiftly closing trap, the men surged about the burly British agent. Crawford cursed and roared and struggled to free himself. Mr. Rhodes pleaded to the mob to desist before they broke something. To no avail. Mr. Crawford was hustled to the door and sent sprawling face down onto the dirty cobbles.

Order was soon restored and the patrons settled at their own tables again, laughing and joking at Mr. Crawford's expense. This had put an end to my narration, which didn't bother me a bit.

"Only sixteen whalers?" I asked of the Blairs. "Did he mean from all of the Commonwealth's ports?"

Ethan nodded. "Times are bad, Mr. Hascott. Nova Scotia is trying to take away what remains of our oil business. They've sent a lot of agents down here to lure our whalers away."

"I'd heard of Crawford's activities," Mr. Blair said angrily, "but this is the first time I've seen him use that subterfuge. Hume & Company lures the men to Salem on the theory—a well founded one, I hear—that once the men go that far, some can be persuaded to go the rest of the way. They've been pretty successful with that means of recruiting . . . up to now."

"If Halifax can employ men, why can't we?" I asked.

"Halifax is British," Ethan replied. "Her oil enters London

46

free of duty. Ours has to pay a stiff duty, so stiff that we can't compete with Canadian oil. Some of the merchants are getting around that by registering their ships out of Halifax or transhipping their oil from here to Halifax and thence to London to avoid the duty. They pay extra freight, but they can still make a profit if they don't have to pay the duty."

"I should think the Nova Scotians wouldn't like that."

"There are merchants in Nova Scotia, as here," Ethan said dryly, "who wouldn't turn away a profit because of patriotism." He started, got up abruptly. "You must excuse me, sir. The hour is getting late. I have to get back to the office." He gave me a slight frown. "Will you be here later, Mr. Hascott? I'd like to talk to you—hear more of your experiences."

"He'll be here," his father assured him. "I shall insist on him remaining with us while he stays in Boston."

I chuckled. "Don't be too generous, sir. I may decide to settle in this town."

Ethan smiled. "But I shall see you later. Goodby."

What he wanted of me, I couldn't guess. Surely not to hear more experiences. Nor could he hope to borrow money from me, since as far as he knew, I was destitute. His father was watching him narrowly as he made his way to the door.

"That boy is in trouble again," he said softly. "That girl. . . ." He caught himself. "No, I imagine it's money again. He's always getting himself involved in some wild scheme. But I won't give him a penny, not a penny. If he intended to put the money to good use, perhaps. But getting married to that. . . ." He grinned at me. "A father has troubles, too. What do you intend to do now?"

"Return home as soon as possible."

Blair rubbed his thin nose. "Hmmm. Your home is in Pelham, isn't it? The Albany stage. . . . No, that left this morning and there won't be another for a couple of days. The New York stage passes through Springfield. You can take that tomorrow morning if you're in a hurry."

"Where do I get the stage?"

"Eli Pease's Inn on Common Street. It leaves at five tomorrow morning. You'll stay here tonight and I'll see that you get out in plenty of time."

47

"I promised to meet Captain Crane at Minot's T later and have supper with him. I can sleep aboard his schooner."

"Crane? That must be Joe Crane. Fetch him along with you and meet us here for supper. We'll put him up, too. I daresay he'll welcome a bed ashore for a change." Mr. Blair got up and straightened his wig. "I have to get back to the office myself. Just one more thing, Warren." He took out his purse with an air of embarrassment. "You must allow me—I mean, I know you're without funds—I'd like to. . . ."

I smiled. "You're very kind, sir." I lowered my voice. "I wasn't exactly truthful when I said I didn't take anything extra. I did take enough to cover my wages for three years."

Blair laughed and slapped my shoulder. "Your wages! A true Yankee." He picked up his hat. "Oh, and don't forget to draw up that petition and deposition, will you? I can't promise anything, but we'll do what we can."

He gave me directions to his room and left me. I in turn went upstairs to write out the petition before I forgot about it.

The Blairs had one large room at the corner facing Ship Street. It was well furnished with a massive fourposter bed, two cases of drawers, a spindly-legged desk and a number of cane-bottomed chairs, including a rocker set before the spotless hearth. The walls and ceilings were paneled in dark, oiled mahogany and the floor was cleaned and sanded. Of decorations, there was only a small portrait of the late Mrs. Blair and a musket and crossed swords set over the mantel. It was less than a home, yet comfortable enough for two undemanding bachelors.

That bed fascinated me. I pressed the cover tentatively, impressed by its softness, and decided that I must try it even though I wasn't very tired. I removed my coat and shoes and climbed aboard. The sensation of sinking deep into the feather mattress was an exquisite delight, one I hadn't enjoyed since leaving home. Despite myself, I felt drowsiness coming over me. After the first joy had passed, however, I found myself squirming for support. I had been so used to a solid bed that I now had the uncomfortable feeling of being suspended in midair.

Of a sudden, a sharp rapping came on the door and I raised my head. "Come in."

To my astonishment, a young woman walked in.

She was a beautiful little thing, blond, blue-eyed, her complexion creamy. There were two red spots on her cheeks that gave her the appearance of a fragile Holland doll made of porcelain.

She was as nonplused as I and glanced nervously around, even peering slowly behind the door, as if she expected someone would be hiding there.

"You're not Mr. Blair," she said accusingly.

I was about to admit the charge when I heard heavy footsteps coming down the hall. Then Ethan loomed behind her. "I saw you! I followed you here!" He pushed her roughly inside and closed the door. "Didn't I tell you not to come here? Didn't I forbid it? After this, you do as I say or I'll—I'll. . . ."

"You'll what?" she demanded, drawing herself to her full height which was not quite to Ethan's shoulder. "You can't order *me* about now or ever. You're a fool!"

"I am not!" Ethan shouted. "And hereafter. . . .!"

"Hereafter nothing!" She stamped her tiny foot. "I'm not going to let you ruin yourself just because you're too pigheaded to do something for yourself. Do you think I can stand by. . . .!"

I coughed. They both turned quickly, startled. I slipped into my shoes and reached for my coat.

"You'll pardon me," I said casually. "I was just leaving."

The girl bit her lower lip, frowned at Ethan, then at me. "Are you a friend of Mr. Blair's? You must be to. . . ."

"Amy! I forbid you to speak!"

She poofed. "Forbid all you like. You need help and you can't deny it." She raised herself on tiptoes, as if trying to look into my eyes. "He needs money, Mr. . . . Mr. . . ."

"Hascott," I supplied. She was such a delicate little thing it was hard to take her seriously. "I suppose you're the young lady Ethan intends to marry."

"We'll see about that. First, we have to get him out of . . . of trouble. He's sto—taken some of his firm's money."

"Amy!" Ethan cried miserably.

Amy stamped her foot again. "I don't care. Now someone

49

else besides me knows it. And maybe he can help. He can borrow it from your father."

Ethan scowled. "I was going to ask him to do it, myself."

"You both seem pretty sure he'd do it," I commented, amused. "Suppose you tell me what's wrong. Maybe it isn't as serious as you think."

"It's serious all right," Ethan growled. He sank into the nearest chair, stared at me for a long moment. "You could do it. Father likes you. And it's only fifty pounds."

"Only?" I whistled softly. "Be reasonable, Ethan. Assuming I had the temerity to ask such a sum, how would I explain my need? I've only been in the country three hours or so."

"Tell him," Amy urged sternly. "Everything."

Ethan looked very young at that moment, almost as if he were ready to burst into tears. The sunlight was behind him, shading his face and deepening the hollows in his cheeks. He rubbed his knees, licked his bloodless lips, cleared his throat two or three times.

"Go on," Amy prodded. "Or I'll tell him."

"No, no, I'll do it." Ethan coughed. "I—I have to have fifty pounds . . . now . . . tonight at the latest. Please ask him, Mr. Hascott. He'll lend it to you. I can pay it back in six weeks or sooner. I invested in a venture with my brother. He'll be back by then. Please, Mr. Hascott. It isn't for myself alone. Many lives are at stake."

I thought that an exaggeration. But it was clear that he faced prison, for he had stolen money from his firm and must now replace it. Amy's round, blue eyes held the terror of disaster befalling the man she loved. And it would be disaster, not only to her but to Ethan and Mr. Blair, too. I began to think that, after all, fifty pounds wasn't so much especially if it hadn't been earned, strictly speaking. I must deny I was swayed by any silly romantic notion of helping lovers in distress.

My waistcoat was open before I quite realized what I was doing. I took out my penknife and ripped open the lining on the left side and, one by one, loosened and placed on the desk my shiny gold pieces. Amy's mouth was very round, as if she couldn't quite get out the "Ooh." Ethan, too, was open-mouthed.

"Mr. Hascott," he said huskily. "I . . . I . . ."

50

Gingerly, he reached for the money. Amy's white little hand clapped down on his.

"No, not until you tell him everything. You owe him that. He hasn't even asked why you want the money. You must trust him, Ethan. Maybe there's some other way, some way without using his money."

"Amy's right," he grumbled. "I do owe you an explanation. But there's no other way out. I'll tell you everything, anyway."

"Nonsense," I scoffed, near dying with curiosity. "You don't have to explain. Just pay me back when you can."

"No, no, I insist. I must tell you everything." He sank back into the chair, rubbing his thighs, his eyes remote, as if gathering his thoughts. "About four months ago I fell in with a man named Moses Pugh. He said he was a smuggler. He needed fifty pounds to refit and offered me two hundred per cent in ten days if I would advance the money. I had no such sum and didn't dare ask my father for it. But I had access to a seldom touched money box in our office. So, I took the money."

I had already guessed it was something along that line. But he was in fact, if not intent, a thief.

Ethan drew a long breath and went on. "Mr. Pugh's schooner piled up on Cape Ann. When he told me, I lost my head and demanded my money back, telling him how I had obtained it. He demanded more money to keep my secret. I gave him such small sums as I could, but I refused to steal more to gratify his greed."

Ethan's voice grew more strained. "About a week ago, Pugh stumbled on a rumor that some of our merchants intended to ship specie to London. The news of this shipment has been kept absolutely secret from the public. Pugh either knew or guessed that my firm was sending some specie. He demanded that I inform him when and on what ship it would be sent. I hadn't the slightest notion why he wanted the information."

That struck me as particularly naive, though I could understand he might have been so frightened he hadn't stopped to think. Ethan stared morosely at the floor.

"I told him. Two days ago, I found out what use he will put the information to." Ethan jumped up. "Mr. Hascott, Pugh has set men aboard. Once out of sight of land, he intends to stage a mutiny, kill the captain and loyal crew members, scuttle the ship and divide the money."

"I see. When does the ship sail?"

"Tonight—on the morning tide." Ethan's hands clenched. "I've been a coward. It's just—Well, I waited and hoped. . . ."

"What do you intend to do now?" I interrupted.

"Why, replace the money in the strongbox and inform my employers of the plot."

"You said the shipment of the specie was kept secret. How will you explain the leakage? Or your knowledge of the plot? Especially, if Pugh is caught and implicates you?"

Ethan reddened. "I never thought of that."

I shook my head. "I don't like to sound like your old schoolmaster, Ethan, but your trouble is that you don't think enough. You ought to cultivate the habit." Then, I smiled and punched his shoulder playfully. "Cheer up. I'll handle the whole thing for you. Can you give me the names of Pugh's men?"

"No, and I doubt if the information could be pried from him. But I do know he's to meet a fellow named Ben Gore tonight at nine o'clock at the Sun Tavern. Gore is bosun on the *Mary*. I know him. He'd betray his own mother for two coppers, or if his neck was threatened." Ethan pouted and shook his head. "It won't work, Mr. Hascott. If you take Gore, Pugh will betray me. I'd better take my own medicine."

"Not until I've made a try, at least. I can't promise anything, but I have an idea. Meantime, put the money back and if anyone accuses you of giving information to Pugh, deny everything. If we're driven into a corner, you can say Pugh must have overheard you in an indiscreet moment . . . in a tavern, perhaps?"

Ethan blinked. "That's wonderful! And it's true—or could be. Mr. Gorham, himself, told me about the specie shipment over dinner at the Green Dragon." He seized my hand and mangled it. "Wonderful, Mr. Hascott, I don't know how I'm ever going to thank you."

"Wait and see if this works first. One thing more, what does this man Pugh look like?"

"Oh, I'd say, average height, dark skin, very much like an Indian. I think he is part Indian. Hawk nose, high cheekbones. His hands are discolored. You can't miss him."

"Good. Now get back to work, Ethan. I'll see you later."
"At supper, then." He kissed Amy and was so excited he
ran out without the money. He was back in a moment, grinning sheepishly and sweeping up the coins. "I'll never forget this—never." He kissed Amy again and went out whistling.
Amy was gazing at me like a solemn little blue-eyed owl.
"You're being very good to Ethan and me."
I waved airily. "It's nothing." As though I were rich.
Her eyes dropped. "I feel it's all my fault. You see, Ethan's
father doesn't like me. Ethan wants to be independent of his
father so we can get married right away. He's not earning
enough so we can marry. I can't understand what Mr. Blair
has against me, honestly I can't."
I couldn't either. She was tiny and very pretty and she
was undoubtedly endowed with better than average common
sense.
"I wouldn't worry about it," I soothed. "He probably doesn't
want to lose Ethan. He'd be alone then, you know. He'll come
around in time."
"I do hope so." Then, she went on earnestly. "You mustn't
think Ethan's a coward, Mr. Hascott. He isn't. He was going
to tell his employers about the plot. He told me so just this
morning. I—I would have waited." A shadow crossed her face,
but was dispelled by a radiant smile. "We'll make this up to
you someday, somehow."
I grinned. "I've already been rewarded."
Tears filled her eyes and she lifted herself on tiptoes. She
pecked my cheek and ran. I do believe she thought I was
rewarded enough by giving unselfish help to a friend. It was
not precisely that. I had gained the perfect excuse for visiting
the Burdicks.

Chapter 4

ﷺﷺﷺﷺﷺﷺﷺﷺﷺﷺﷺﷺﷺﷺﷺﷺﷺﷺﷺﷺﷺﷺﷺﷺﷺﷺﷺﷺﷺﷺ

As soon as I was alone again, I sat down at the desk, found quill and paper and wrote out the petition and deposition. I wrote a note to my host, too, thanking him for his courtesies and telling him I had found a reason for visiting the Burdicks. Since I expected—hoped, really—to remain late, I regretted I would be unable to be with him for dinner. Then I prepared a note for Joe, telling him some business had cropped up which would prevent me from meeting him. I asked him to send my baggage to Eli Pease's, from whence I would start home in the morning. I urged him to keep in touch with me and promised to write him as often as possible.

I regretted then that I didn't have my baggage with me, for I had a lovely deep maroon broadcloth coat, which I had bought in London, in my portmanteau. I found a brush and cleaned my serge as best I could. My neckcloth wasn't any too clean and, after a moment's hesitation, I looked through the chest of drawers belonging to Ethan and selected one of his. That was the least he could do for me. I pinned a note to mine, saying I'd return his as soon as possible. After washing myself, brushing off my hat and patting it on jauntily, I started out for the Burdicks.

Keeping my promise to Ethan wouldn't be easy, I knew. But I felt remarkably sanguine, though I daresay my blitheness of spirits was not entirely due to eagerness to complete the task I had set for myself. Passing into Cornhill, I made my way behind State House and was tempted to stop and thank Blair personally for his courtesies. I decided against seeing him, for he had impressed me as a shrewd old man and might question me too closely on the reasons I had so suddenly found for

"Yankee doodle keep it up
Yankee doodle da..an..dee
Yankee doodle keep it up
And with the girls be han...dee."

n her mother could be angry with this Judith.
and shook her head and even smiled a bit when
dith in singing lustily the subsequent verses. I was
tled when Mrs. Burdick, too, chimed in. In Am-
, she had been a singer of hymns exclusively, the
lous music being, in her view, the composition of
But this Judith, exuberant and delightfully impu-
ew well of old. We sang and laughed and sang
e until our very breath gave out.

cking on the front door put an end to our music.
servant hurried through the entry hall to answer
saw Mrs. Burdick composing herself with a look of
as to be chiding herself for her horrible lapse into
booming voice greeted the maid and, a moment later,
dick strode into the parlor.
ly remembered him, he had changed so. The years
well for him, giving him a comfortable paunch and
face which were eloquent of excellent feeding. He
ort man, pink-cheeked, and his thick, bushy, grey
ave his features the appearance of being ever torn
a benign smile and an austere frown. But his
drooped over keen brown eyes, hinting of shrewdness
ability to be hard when the occasion demanded it.
dressed in a fine, full-skirted dark blue broadcloth coat
lder fashion, the skirts being buttoned back to show
silk lining. His breeches and waistcoat were of buff
and a heavy gold chain was draped across his ample
.
ame toward me, extending his hand cordially. "I'm
see you again," he said, a bit vaguely. "Indeed, I'm
He coughed and glanced at his daughter. "Yes, yes,
I'm glad, sir. You're looking extremely fit since I last
u."

58

visiting my Amherst friends. At Milk Street, I turned down
and, without difficulty, found Long Lane and the residence
of the Burdicks.

The house was truly imposing, resembling the Hancock
mansion, though it wasn't quite as large. It was a two story,
red brick building with white wood trim. The high, pitched,
slate roof was pierced by four dormers and, at the peak, there
was a ballastered walk. The plot was large, sloping upward
and fenced in with a brick wall. In the front was a tastily
arranged garden of Dutch tulips in gorgeous reds and yellows
and blues and deep purples. Among the outbuildings were a
barn, a large tool house and a summer house, beyond which
was a vegetable garden and an orchard which screened the
property from the place beyond.

I walked by the gate twice before I could muster the courage to go in, for the very elegance of that mansion made my
serges seem shabby and worn. I could have had a better tricorn,
too, for this occasion. But then I thought that if they didn't
like me as I was dressed, why would they like me better in
elegant clothes? I straightened my neckcloth and walked
boldly up the flagstone path.

The sound of the knocker had barely died away when the
door opened. Judith herself stood before me, lovelier than ever.
She had changed to a low-cut afternoon gown of rose silk,
covered with tiny black fleur-de-lis figures.

"Why, Warren," she greeted in a surprised tone, mock surprise, you may be sure. She must have seen me coming to have
been so quick. "I hadn't expected you to call so soon."

"Who is it, Judith?" her mother called from inside.

The question was entirely unnecessary, for Mrs. Burdick
could see me very well from where she was standing on the
staircase at the back of the short, but spacious entry hall. Her
black taffeta rustled coldly as she approached us.

I bowed politely. "I don't mean to intrude, M'm. My call
isn't social. I have business with Mr. Burdick. Not knowing his
place of business I took the liberty of coming here."

Mrs. Burdick sniffed in disbelief. "Mr. Burdick is not home.
You can find him at. . . ."

"Oh, no," Judith interrupted hastily. "Father went to an
auction this afternoon, don't you remember, Mama? He should
be home any minute. Warren might miss him if he went to

55

the counting house. Do come in and wait, Warren. We're glad you came, even if only on business, aren't we Mama?"

Judith's mother refused to commit herself, but she could hardly order me to leave or wait on the steps. Judith boldly took my hand and took me into the sitting room. Mrs. Burdick sniffed again, frowned at her daughter's hand and followed us.

If I had not been told that Mr. Burdick had prospered, the parlor would have convinced me. The floor was covered with a large, soft-napped Turkish rug, deep blue in color and flowered in lush reds and greens—very expensive, as I had reason to know, for rugs were sold and used more in Algiers than here in America. The chairs and sofa had delicate, tapered legs and the seats and shield backs were upholstered in rich blue damask embroidered with wreaths of silver thread. The furniture was not only rich looking, it seemed so fragile that I scarcely dared put my full weight on the settee when I seated myself.

In the corner, between the two windows, was a handsome spinet and, over the spotless hearth, was a round, crystal clear mirror in a heavy silver frame. But most remarkable of all were the walls themselves. They were covered with imported printed paper, each side of the room showing a different aspect of the city of London, Westminster on the north wall, Temple Bar on the door side, Lincoln's Inn Fields to the hearth side and St. Paul's on the opposite wall. Had I not looked closely, I would have sworn the pictures had been painted directly on the plaster by a superb artist.

Judith was watching me with amusement and I quickly closed my mouth, trying to cover my confusion. Mrs. Burdick, seated in a big wing chair by the window, seemed quite delighted to note that I had been so manifestly impressed.

"Quite different from the tavern in Amherst, isn't it? Judith said slyly. "Papa bought the house for a pittance from a departing Loyalist. Papa was a war profiteer, you know."

"Judith!" her mother exclaimed, shocked. "You mustn't say such things about your father." She gave me a severe look. "Judith has such an awkward sense of humor."

Judith put her fingers over her eyes. "See no evil, Mama." She winked at me most brazenly. "Mama is like so many of our newly rich. She hates to acknowledge the truth."

56

"Judith!" Mrs. Burdick

Judith smiled placidly, a
badly treated in Algiers, W

I couldn't answer at on
a straight face. Mrs. Burdicl
a mother cat who has just

Judith evidently mistook
for she smiled encouragemer
Warren? We are old frie
Judith."

"No, no," I protested. "I
more delightful woman."

Mrs. Burdick cleared her th
regretted my impulsiveness. B
pink tinted her cheeks.

"Did you learn the art of
Moorish harems?" she asked a

I grinned. "The ladies of the
rated. They're fat, most of ther

Mrs. Burdick seemed distresse
sation, too. "Judith, perhaps o
you play. I'm sure he heard littl
She gave me a tight-lipped smi
accomplished on the spinet since

Judith sighed and rose. "How
"Twenty-seven," I replied, mi
Her nose crinkled. "The curse
her mother's cheek. "Mama some
girl has grown out of pantaloons.

Judith seated herself primly, har
keyboard. I detected an impishne
crashed out and a lively tune sprar
so well remembered tune we had su
on the high seas, yes and even as w
Judith, though, began with a sly tur

"Father and I went do
To sell to Captain G
The stores our soldier
Along with Hasty puc

57

Not eve
She sighed
I joined J
rather sta
herst days
more friv
the Devil.
dent, I k
some mor

A kno
The mai
it and I
such pai
levity. A
Mr. Bur

I har
had don
a round
was a s
brows
between
eyelids
and th
He wa
of the
the bu
nankee
stomac

He
glad t
glad."
indeed
saw y

"Papa never forgets a face," Judith put in sweetly. "His name is Warren, Papa . . . Warren Has . . . Has. . . ."

"—cott!" her father finished triumphantly. "Warren Hascott! Dear me, is it possible? Of course, it is. Warren, my boy, I'm delighted to see you home again and alive." He grasped my hand and gave it a vigorous shaking. "You were in Algiers, last I heard of you. Abigail, you surely invited Warren to stay for supper?"

"Oh, no please," I protested—too heartily. "I came on business, a confidential matter and urgent."

He nodded briskly. "You'll excuse us, ladies?" He took my arm. "We'll go into my study."

Mr. Burdick's den was small but comfortable, being right across the hall from the sitting room. The furniture was much sturdier and less awesome than the parlor appointments. The chairs were big, caned with closely woven rush, and the covering on the floor was of heavy, plain green cloth. Behind the massive mahogany desk were bookshelves, filled mostly with religious tracts, though I did notice a lower shelf with novels such as "Tom Jones," and another shelf with such items as Anson's "Voyages," the "Arabian Nights Entertainments," Smith's "Wealth of Nations," Watts' "Improvement of the Mind" and similar volumes. Mr. Burdick closed the door carefully, sighed, removed his wig and placed it on the knob of his chair. He was shaved, though not too recently, and his skull was remarkably flat in shape.

"Sit down, sit down, Warren." He opened the mahogany liquor safe and brought out glasses and a bottle. "Madeira," he said, patting the label. "The last consignment was exceptionally good. Did you say you had business with me?"

"I'm not sure it concerns you, sir. I stumbled across some information about the brig, *Mary*."

His hand jerked and wine spilled over the desk. He straightened, scowled at me a moment, then absently pulled out a handkerchief and mopped up the liquor. He kept rubbing in a hard circle until I thought he'd wear a hole in the wood.

"The *Mary?*" he asked softly. "Captain Bernard?" He handed me a glass. "What do you know of her?"

Briefly and simply, I told him about the plot which had been concocted by Pugh and his men to mutiny after the ship was at sea. I mentioned no names, however. Burdick sipped

59

his wine thoughtfully, his eyes never leaving me while I spoke.

"Where did you hear of this?" he asked when I was done.

I shook my head. "I can't tell you, sir."

His tongue clucked. "This is serious, very serious. Yes, indeed, young man, this is very serious." He finished his glass, set it down and, seating himself at his desk, reached for quill and paper. "You won't tell me where you got your information?"

"I'm sorry, I cannot."

Mr. Burdick hemmed and stuck out his lower lip, as if he would be stern with me if he could only think of the means. With a shrug, he dipped his pen into the inkpot and scratched out a brief note, which he folded and sealed with a wafer.

"You must stay to sup—" He looked up quickly. "By heaven, I forgot all about it! I knew there was some reason why I came home so early. We're supposed to dine with the Gilberts tonight." He scratched his ear and grinned and reached for another piece of paper. "You've no idea what a service you've done for me besides bringing this news which is important to myself and many of the merchants here in town. The Gilberts are good people, but I dislike dining out after a hard day's work." He scribbled the note. "That's why I entertain so much myself, I guess. Besides, Gilbert's a bore and his wife chatters too much."

He folded the second note, sealed it and got up. "You'll stay to supper, of course, Warren. I must inform my wife of our change in plans." His pinkish brow wrinkled. "She's not going to like this much. She keeps complaining I never take her anywhere." His shoulders lifted. "However, this time I have a legitimate excuse. I may be some time, Warren. Judith will see to your entertainment."

As I crossed the hall, I watched Mr. Burdick going up the stairs a bit hesitantly, as if reluctant to face his wife. Judith was still in the sitting room, idly fingering the keys of the spinet.

Dusk was creeping through the room and the shadows caressed Judith's softly moulded features. Her eyes were a deepening brown and a smile touched her half-parted lips as I came toward her. I seated myself in the arm chair closest to her, a curious warmth stirring in my pulses. Slowly, it came to me as a vast and wonderous discovery that she was very beautiful, more beautiful than any woman I had ever known.

"What are you thinking," Warren?" she asked idly.

I frowned slightly. "That it's horrible to be poor."

Her laughter was light and without mockery. "No, in America it's only horrible to be resigned to poverty. Are you?"

I pondered a moment. "I don't know. I mean, I'm not sure I could prosper quickly enough to make the effort worth while."

Her hands drew away from the keys and she turned toward me. "Warren, tell me, how long is it since you last spoke to a woman . . . I mean, one you knew well and might have wanted to . . . to love?"

I flushed. "Seven years, I guess."

She nodded gravely. "Think about that carefully, Warren, before you give your heart away."

I was thankful for the dusk that hid my discomfort, for I was all too aware of the keenness of her perception. I leaned back in a chair, elbows on the arm rests, blowing lightly my touching fingertips.

"Judith, why haven't you married?"

Her eyes lowered and she idly smoothed her dress. "You have been honest with me, Warren, and I shall be the same. I don't know, really." She lapsed into a pensive silence. Then: "I was sixteen when you went away. I was in love with you —at least I thought it was love. I cherished your memory a long, long time—perhaps too long." Judith smiled and her eyes traveled back into the remote past. "Remember Peter Willet? He courted me for almost a year. Peter was an awfully nice boy but I didn't love him. I promised him nothing when he went away to the war. He was killed at Stony Point. We left Amherst and went to Springfield and there were other boys, but Papa was prospering then, so I had no need to marry for the security a man could give me. Then, when we came to Boston, I met many more men. I'm not immodest when I say I've had more than a dozen proposals. Some of the men only wanted to further their ambitions through father. A few—I can think of three—loved me. But I think I had been spoiled by the years. I became too critical of their faults and virtues, comparing them with those of the boy who had promised to come back. You see, it was easy, because he wrote often enough to assure me it wasn't faithlessness that kept him away. I don't mean the you who sits there. I mean the boy who grew into an ideal—a silly, girlish ideal, perhaps. I know I should have grown out of it, but I didn't." She smiled gently and without mirth. "There, you have seen part of me no one has ever seen before." She stared at me steadily for a long moment, then added in a soft, husky voice, "And for the life of me, I don't know why you should."

Her words had brought to me a strange and nebulous glow. She was truly a remarkable woman, entirely lacking in false modesty, though not a little disconcerting in her intelligence. Almost without willing it, I rose and leaned on the spinet, my lips close to hers. She did not draw away, but her steady eyes forbade my impulse.

"Perhaps I can't be an ideal," I whispered. "But perhaps I can make you forget it. I think I shall see you often, Judith, if you will let me."

She tilted her head and laughed. "Remember my warning, Warren. Learn something of women before you give your heart to any one."

She pressed her fingers on the keys and the sweet strains of "The Banks of the Dee" filled the darkened room. During the late war, it had been despised as a Loyalist tune until a parody had been written to make the haunting music respectable to patriot ears. But Judith now sang the original words and, when she reached the last verse, I could not help but feel the sincerity in her low, vibrant voice.

> "But time and my prayers may perhaps yet restore him
> Blest peace may restore my dear lover to me
> And when he returns, with such care I'll watch o'er him
> He never shall leave the sweet banks of the Dee.
>
> The Dee will then flow, all its beauties displaying
> The lambs on its banks will again be seen playing
> Whil'st I and my Jamie are carelessly straying
> And tasting again all the sweets of the Dee."

The soothing tones faded into an enchanted silence. My feeling was one of standing at the edge of a sunlit pool, warm to look upon, cool to touch. Judith's eyes were smiling, but her warning made me shy from giving myself wholly to the thought that I had once more fallen in love with her. I would not believe she was amusing herself with my affections. I wanted to believe I was entering upon another, and this time welcome enslavement.

Chapter 5

ꚍꚍꚍꚍꚍꚍꚍꚍꚍꚍꚍꚍꚍꚍꚍꚍꚍꚍꚍꚍꚍꚍꚍꚍꚍꚍꚍꚍꚍꚍꚍꚍꚍꚍꚍꚍꚍ

I
T WAS almost half after seven before we sat down to our supper. As was customary, the evening meal was a cold one but the lavishness of the food was astonishing. There were cold chickens, pork and beef and various pickled fishes, breads and biscuits with canary, burgundy and rhinish wines to go with them. At first I was ill at ease for I had never before been served with such elegance. The tall, cool, bayberry candles gleamed on the white linen tablecloth. The plates were of expensive, fragile looking Straffordshire ware, the knives and forks of silver, the butterboats and bread baskets of chased silver lined with gilt. All through the meal Mrs. Burdick kept urging me to eat, which from politeness I could not refuse. Not until some time later did I learn that hostesses were required by custom, not sincerity, to keep urging their guests toward the bursting point.

The conversation during the meal was most lively. Even Mrs. Burdick seemed to have lost some of her hostility toward me. At the urging of Judith and Mr. Burdick, I related a few of my experiences in Algiers, of which, I must own, I was already beginning to weary. When I told of the manner of my escape, Mr. Burdick rumbled deep in his throat and gave his wife a pleased look, as if I had proved some argument he had used in my behalf.

"Now that you're here," Burdick said, when I was finished, "what do you intend to do?"

"I don't know exactly," I replied. "I'll go home first, naturally. I haven't seen my family in so long. By the by, do you have recent news of them? Joe's news was seven months old."

A quick, odd silence fell over the table. Mr. Burdick

coughed and sputtered something unintelligible. Mrs. Burdick's thin mouth tightened and she gazed with unwonted interest at the steady candle flames. Judith, too, avoided my eyes. "We haven't been home—that is, to Amherst, for a long time," she said at length. "When last we heard of them, everyone was all right—in good health, that is."

The fears that had gathered in my throat faded away. Yet, not completely. I wanted to believe they were only ashamed they had lost contact with old friends. But there was something more than that. Mrs. Burdick, for example, had already impressed me as the kind who would not be embarrassed at dropping old friends, especially poorer ones. Judith's way of putting it was strange, too, though her "in good health" seemed reassuring and made me think the trouble, if any, was not of that sort.

Mr. Burdick broke the awkward silence. "And after you've been home, Warren? Do you have any plans? Do you intend to go to sea again?"

I shrugged. "Perhaps. Though I've heard the shipping business isn't so prosperous at the moment."

"Nothing prospers," Burdick growled. "I've never seen business in a worse condition. Why, it's hardly worth while sending my ships out any more. It's only because it's cheaper to send a cargo out than to keep the ships in port that I keep my ships employed at all."

"I've heard the whaling industry is bad, too."

"Bad?" Burdick grunted. "It's so bad the State has to offer a bounty of two pounds per ton just to keep the remnants of our fleet from rotting at their docks. Cod fishery wasn't so bad last year, even though the number of ships sent out was far below normal. This year, I hear, the catch won't be as good. Unless trade improves soon, we'll all be bankrupt. Why, hardly a day goes by that I don't hear of another house in distress."

"Mostly importers of English goods," Judith put in. "Everyone says we've imported too much English merchandise for our own good."

Mr. Burdick snorted. "Those British! If it wasn't for their damn Navigation Acts, our trade would be sound enough. A friend of mine sent a ship to England not long ago, a cargo of lumber I think he carried. After paying all duties and port charges, and selling his cargo, he had enough money left to bring back a cargo of five bushels of salt . . . think of that, five bushels of salt for fifty thousand feet of lumber. And we're barred from Ireland, Canada and the West Indies. Not because there isn't a market there. Why, the West Indian planters are near starving because they can't get food from us."

"Joe was telling me about that," I commented. "It seems foolish for the British to starve their own people."

"Well, they don't starve exactly. But they pay through the nose for whatever they get. Some of our merchants take the risk. British law says our ships can enter their ports only if in distress. So, our captains swear they're sinking and put in. Most of the times they can sell their cargoes without trouble. But they have to pick their ports carefully. If the customs officer happens to be recently sent out from England, they're in a bad fix. The English seize the ship on some pretext—usually smuggling—and burn it. The rotten part of this whole business is that even the French—our allies—have turned against us."

"You mean the French have closed their ports, too?"

Burdick nodded glumly. "Her West Indian ports. At home, she's reestablished her high duties against our goods. I suppose we ought to be grateful for the help she gave us during the war, but dammit! winning the peace is just as important. We kept protesting to Whitehall about the illegality of keeping British ports closed to us. We had some sort of a chance of winning our point until the French did this to us. Now, when we argue for free trade those damn Englishmen just laugh at us."

"I've heard dealers in oil sometimes tranship their product from Nova Scotia. Could we do the same with other goods?"

"We do. I just sent a cargo of salted fish to Halifax. From there, it goes to Jamaica in a British bottom. But that's a damned nuisance, besides cutting the heart out of my profit. And my own ship lays idle while a British ship gets the business on the long haul. That man Adam Smith is right. The world won't prosper until there's real free trade."

"Couldn't America retaliate by closing our markets to British manufactured goods?"

"Absolutely!" Burdick replied vehemently. "But what's the

66

use? Massachusetts enacts a law to control the situation and what happens? New York sees the chance to get more business and lowers her tariffs. Virginia wants to sell her tobacco in London, so she admits English goods free. And so on and so on. These won't be a United States until Congress has the power to regulate commerce for all the states. Uniform tariff laws, that's what we need. Why, if all of us got together and embargoed English goods, those British bloodsuckers would come to us on their knees within six months. But no, the states won't cooperate."

"Papa's beginning to sound like a Federalist," Judith commented with a smile.

"Nonsense," Burdick waved a pudgy hand. "We don't have to set up a tyrannical central government just to regulate commerce."

"The Confederation hasn't had much luck in compelling cooperation this far," Judith commented with a smile. "Do you think giving Congress the power now would work better?"

Mr. Burdick glared at his daughter and lapsed into an angry silence, wrapping himself in his dignity. Judith had said very little, it was true, but she had definitely shown an awareness of affairs which, in the old days, were supposed to be outside the ken of young ladies. Until this moment I hadn't realized how completely out of touch I had been with the conditions within my own country.

"If shipping is in such a bad state," I mused, "there seems little use for me even to think of going to sea."

Mr. Burdick's bushy brows lowered. "Young man, a good seaman can always get a berth." He toyed with his wineglass a moment. "I think I can use you, Warren. I'm in need of a sharp young supercargo for my *Wasp*. I can offer wages and cargo space if you think you can handle the job I have in mind."

"That's good of you, sir. But I intended to go home and see my family before I did anything else."

"Of course, of course. The *Wasp* won't be back for another month, at least. Come in and see me then, anytime before the fifteenth of July."

Judith was regarding me with steady interest and I felt she knew what was going through my mind. My pride was resisting the acceptance of a position through influence. There were undoubtedly many men on the beach more competent and perhaps a lot more deserving than I. Yet common sense prevented me from rejecting the offer outright, for I was well aware that there are times when equity must give way to expediency.

Mrs. Burdick happily forestalled a further discussion of the subject. "Do tell us something of London, Warren."

I told her of the almost unbelievable vastness of the city, of my visit to Whitehall and my view of the king, of Westminster Abbey and St. Paul's. Judith questioned me about the theater—an amusement wholly lacking in Boston—and I related my visit to Drury Lane where I had seen a play by Richard Sheridan, he whom we had admired so much for his defense of our cause in Parliament. For the benefit of my host, I mentioned my visit to the Royal 'Change, to Guild Hall and Lloyd's Coffee House, where so much insurance business was transacted. Mrs. Burdick's many questions gave evidence of her admiration of things British, a common failing among our socially minded ladies, though they may be the staunchest of patriots otherwise.

The table had been cleared and we were just finishing our custard when a tapping came on the front knocker. Polly, the maid servant, went in answer and, returning, announced that a Mr. Jonathan Salderman was calling.

Mr. Burdick put his napkin by his plate and got up. "You'll excuse us, ladies. Mr. Salderman is here on business."

Since the supper was over we all got up, the two ladies preceding us to give greeting to the visitor. Mr. Salderman proved to be a tall, rawboned man of about thirty five, his features long, his jutting chin like a square cut spade. A country boy, his appearance made him, though his clothes were eloquent of his success in town. He wore a curled, powdered wig, a beautiful maroon coat trimmed with silver lace and silver buttons, and his waistcoat and breeches were of buff silk. He wore a constant smile, the smile of a cynic nursing some secret joke against mankind.

He bowed as the ladies came toward him. "Evening, Judith

and Mrs. Burdick. You look charming this evening, M'am. You're looking more like your daughter every day."

"You mean mother seems younger?" Judith asked innocently. "Or do I look older?"

"Both younger," Salderman returned promptly. He gave her cheek a playful tweak. "Indeed, my little blossom, you'll soon seem young enough to put over my knee."

"Such flattery," Judith exclaimed in mock horror. "Come, mother, we mustn't let him turn our heads."

Salderman laughed and shook hands with Mr. Burdick. " 'Evening, Moses, and I take it this is Mr. Hascott?"

I acknowledged my name and he shook my hand. He had long, tapering fingers and his grip was firm. But his skin was slightly moist and I couldn't quite like him on first sight. Mr. Burdick called for a light and we went into the library. Polly brought a light and a fresh bottle of brandy, anticipating Mr. Burdick's wish, and Salderman and I settled ourselves while our host poured. Salderman and Burdick exchanged idle remarks on the state of the India goods business until the door closed on Polly.

"So, Mr. Hascott," Salderman said as he accepted a glass, "we'll get right down to business. Suppose you tell me all about the *Mary.* Moses didn't reveal much in his note."

I gave him all the necessary details of the plot, as much and no more than I had told Mr. Burdick.

"And just how did you learn of this, Mr. Hascott?"

I shook my head. "I overheard it. That's as much as I'm willing to tell you, Mr. Salderman."

Salderman sipped his brandy, balanced the glass on his bony knee. "You're evidently unaware of the seriousness of this affair, Mr. Hascott. I must know how you obtained your information. Someone in a trusted position has betrayed us."

"I'm sorry," I replied.

Salderman gave me a quick glance, then shrugged. "No matter. I can guess. It was someone connected with Blanchard and Company, wasn't it?"

"No." I bit my tongue, regretting the answer. "Mr. Salderman, you needn't fish. I'm helping you to prevent a serious loss to yourself and others involved. Beyond that, I won't go."

69

Salderman eyed me with a slight distaste. "I appreciate your desire to protect a friend, sir. But with or without you, I shall discover his name."

"Perhaps." His manner was beginning to irritate me. "In that case, you needn't trouble me with any more questions."

"Come, come, Warren," Burdick rumbled. "Jothan usually gets what he wants, one way or the other."

I spread my hands. "Let it be the other."

Salderman sighed. "Very well, I bow. You can give me the names of those involved in the plot?"

"No, I'm sorry to say I cannot. I only know the name of the man who can tell you that, not the names of the men involved."

"And his name?" Salderman asked patiently.

I hesitated, considering my answer, then grinned. "I can only lead you to him. I expect to see him at the Sun Tavern on Battery Marsh Street later this evening—at nine. I understand he's easily frightened. The threat of the gallows will be enough, I think. If not, a bit of physical pain...."

"I understand." Salderman drained his glass. "Mr. Hascott, you're playing this game a mite too close to the edge of the precipice. No offense, of course. That's your privilege. I appreciate what you're doing for us. But I think you're a fool. Men willing to murder at sea won't hesitate to kill you, sir."

"The risk is mine," I replied.

"As you will." Salderman lifted his glass. "Believe me, I'm not ungrateful. Your health...continued health, sir."

It was with a certain grimness that we drained our glasses. Mr. Burdick made a motion to refill them, but Salderman lifted his hand.

"It's close to nine, Moses. I'll have to stop at my office before going on to the Sun Tavern."

Mr. Burdick led the way to the door and opened it. "You'll come back and let me know how everything went, Warren?"

"I fear not, sir," I stepped aside to let Salderman go first. "This business may take some time. If all goes well, I expect to be on the morning stage from Pease's."

"Very well. Jothan will let me know in the morning." Burdick took us across the hall to the living room. "Don't fail to stop here whenever you're in Boston. And remember

what I said about the berth . . . July fifteenth, at the latest.
. . . I've offered him a berth on one of my ships, Jothan.
I'll thank you not to steal him from me."

Salderman smiled. "I promise nothing. A man with his
sense of loyalty would be an asset to any firm."

Judith rose from the sofa as we entered and Mrs. Burdick
in her seat by the window, merely turned. I bowed to her
and thanked her for her hospitality. She answered simply
that she was glad to have seen me, but I believed her manner
was slightly less frosty than it had been when I arrived.

Judith placed her hand in mine. "I think we'll see you
soon again, Warren." She gave my fingers a slight squeeze.
"We'll always make you welcome here."

I thanked her and, without saying it aloud, determined
my absence from Boston would not be too long. As soon
as Mr. Salderman completed his farewells, we made our
departure.

The street lamps had not been lighted, for the moon was at
the half and the sky was cloudless. But the unpaved street was
bumpy and I nearly turned my ankle half a dozen times on the
way to Belcher's Lane. As we walked up the waterfront, coming past Griffin's Wharf, of Tea Party fame, Salderman
pointed to a ship riding at anchor out in the bay.

"The *Mary*. She'll be out on the morning tide, if all goes
well." Salderman gave me a sharp look. "One thing more, Mr.
Hascott. This affair must be kept a complete secret, even after
the ship has sailed. No one must know about the specie being
sent out. Will you give me your word of honor you will
mention this to no one, not even your own family?"

I thought the request odd, but readily gave my word. "May
I ask why?"

Salderman chuckled. "You have your secret, Mr. Hascott.
Permit me to keep mine. You're sure you won't reveal this
man's name for a suitable price?"

"I gave him my word, too," I said stiffly. "My word is not
for sale."

"Excellent." Salderman patted my shoulder. "I shall not forget that, Mr. Hascott."

I was thankful for the darkness which hid my scowl. Mr. Salderman might have meant well, but there was something about him that rubbed me the wrong way.

Salderman's warehouse and office stood at the end of White-horn's Wharf. As we entered, I saw one of the clerks was still at work on his ledgers, a big sperm candle giving him just about enough light. Salderman eyed the bent back speculatively, shot a quick look at me. I smiled and turned away deliberately, more determined than ever to protect Ethan if I could.

Four seamen were seated on the benches along the side wall and, at Salderman's bidding, they rose and came over to us. They were tough, hard looking men, dressed in rough kersey and short serge jackets, their shirts of striped cotton. Mr. Salderman had evidently expected and prepared for trouble. I wasn't displeased at the prospect of having men like those along in case I got into a fight.

"Stowe," Salderman said crisply, "you and Barnes will accompany Mr. Hascott to the Sun Tavern. Go in with him. Come to his aid if he needs your help. He's to meet a man there. Mr. Hascott, if you lure this man outside, we'll take care of the rest. If he refuses to come, signal to Stowe and Barnes and they'll persuade him. Since you won't take me into your confidence, that's the best I can do about plans."

"Those plans are adequate," I assured him.

"I hope so," Salderman offered me a small pistol. "I assume you're not armed? Then, take this, but don't use it unless it's absolutely necessary. We want no fuss, and we don't want the watch drawn into this. . . . That's for the rest of you men, too. Be as quiet and discreet as possible . . . Green, you and Tompkins will stay outside with me. . . . You wouldn't care to describe this man, would you, Hascott?"

I smiled and shook my head. "As soon as I see him, I'll point him out to the two who will be with me."

"Good enough." Salderman glanced at his clerk on the high stool. "For God's sake, Hector, that can wait until morning. Go on home . . . Let's go, gentlemen. Stowe, you and Barnes go on ahead. Mr. Hascott will come in after you."

The two named hurried off and were soon far ahead of us. Mr. Salderman and I followed the other two men. It was just about a quarter to nine. A queer lump was forming in the pit of my stomach, the same kind of a lump I remembered as invariably forming just before going into battle. I was a bit worried, too, that, in my zeal to help Ethan, I might cause the escape of those who could name the disloyal aboard the *Mary*. That would be unfortunate, though not fatal. The whole of the ship's crew could, in that case, be discharged and a new one substituted before the *Mary* sailed.

Ahead, South Battery seemed dismal and forlorn and dull grey moonlight covered the deserted battlements. Mr. Salderman, noting my interest in the place, informed me that the fort had been dismantled after the war. He was a cool customer. In calm tones, as if we were just out for a stroll, he went on to tell me about other improvements pending in the neighborhood. The town had ordered the land filled in between Windmill Point and the Neck in order to straighten the shoreline somewhat. I ventured that not until all of Dorcester Flats was filled in would there really be improvement in the neighborhood, for at low tide—which was now—a horrible, fishy odor permeated the very cobbles underfoot.

At Oliver Street, I parted company with Mr. Salderman and his two men, who would wait until I had progressed farther before resuming their approach to the Sun Tavern. Not a soul was in sight ahead of me, for Barnes and Stowe had already passed into Battery Marsh Street around the bend and would be, by this time, at the tavern. A slight, uncomfortable chill went through me and I instictively touched the reassuring bulge at my waist which was my pistol.

The Sun Tavern stood at the foot of Fort Hill, a weary, unpainted wooden house whose doors and casements had been thrown wide because of the warmness of the night. The clear, still air gave a sharpness to every emerging sound, the rattle of pots on the wooden tables, the incessant, unintelligible babble, the hard explosive laughter, the snatches of furry-throated songs. The signboard bore a painted sun with its flaming rays and the legend, "Here you may find the best liquors under the Sun."

I entered boldly, stood just inside the doorway, searching through the wispy smoke haze for Mr. Pugh. The place was well attended, though not crowded, and I saw that Stowe and his companion had found places near the unfired hearth. No one seemed to fit Ethan's description of Mr. Pugh. Indeed, it hardly seemed a place where men of Mr. Pugh's kind would gather. It was an ordinary tavern, the patrons mostly workmen from the nearby ropeyards and distill houses, some seamen, a liberal sprinkling of shopkeepers and a few well dressed merchants. Nothing in the atmosphere was sinister, nothing suggested that here was the rendezvous of murderers.

The landlord was a short, lean fellow with a fixed smile. He was wiping his hands on his apron as he approached me.

"Can I assist you, sir?"

"I'm looking for a friend of mine," I said. "A dark-skinned fellow—resembling an Indian you might say."

"Oh . . . Oh, yes. The gentleman availed himself of a private room." He motioned to the hearth. "The door to the left of the chimney, sir."

I thanked the landlord and directed myself to the room he had indicated. As I reached for the latch, I saw Barnes and Stowe rising from their places. I shook my head and they sank back into their seats. I gave myself no time for hesitation. Without knocking, I opened the door and walked in.

Two men were seated at the table, a bottle between them, each holding a pewter pot. Both heads swiveled about as I entered, but neither got up. I closed the door carefully behind me and walked slowly toward them.

I recognized Pugh instantly. He was facing me across the table, a slight man with a droop to one shoulder. His skin was swart, his cheekbones prominent, his sleek black hair drawn back and tied into a pigtail queue. He was indeed an Indian, though perhaps not pure blooded. The other was squat and broad shouldered, his leathery face seamed and unshaven, his small, piglike eyes filled with apprehension.

"Mr. Gore?" I asked vaguely, looking from one to the other.

The squat man grunted. "Aye."

I licked my lips, trying desperately to think of some excuse for this intrusion. Both were staring at me, neither moving a muscle. Pugh's clawlike right hand was resting on the table, close to a crumpled handkerchief. From the lumpiness of the cloth, I knew it concealed a pistol.

74

Boldness was my only possible course. As calmly as I could, I took out my pistol and aimed it at Pugh's head.

"Please move back from the table, Mr. Pugh." My voice was low and steady and the tenseness was leaving me. "One move and I shoot."

Pugh's black eyes shone like a cat's in the yellow candlelight. He made no motion to obey me. He did not move, yet he gave the ominous impression of a slow inner gathering, as of a snake coiling to strike. I advanced a step. His hand twitched. I pounced on his gun, a split second before he did. I wrenched it away as his fingers were closing on the butt. With a smile, I tossed it into the corner. The pistol clattered over the floor with thunderous loudness in that utter hush.

Ben Gore swore softly and started to rise, then thought better of it when he saw the muzzle of my gun swinging toward his nose. Both were too startled to be dangerous at the moment. I gave them no chance to recover their wits. Swiftly, I seized the bottle and swung it. So unsuspected was the motion that Ben Gore did not draw away. The bottle cracked over his ear and, with a deep rumbling sigh, he slid forward on his face. Liquor slopped over me and the stench of rum swirled into my nostrils, but I did not allow myself to be diverted by the wetness soaking through my sleeve.

I drew out the chair and sat down. "Now, Mr. Pugh, I think we can talk without being overheard."

Mr. Pugh's face was perfectly immobile, only his eyes showing his fierce anger. He said nothing.

"You'll be interested to learn," I went on casually, "that your scheme to rob and scuttle the *Mary* is known."

"You want a share," Pugh said flatly.

I shook my head. "I want you to clear out—now, while there's time to save your skin. I'm warning you, Mr. Pugh—"

A faint scuffling outside the window cut me off sharply. I knew instantly that Salderman was out there. Pugh's head did not turn, but he had heard the noise. I could see the muscles tighten along his prominent jawbone.

"That's Bl—" he started to say.

"Quiet" I cut in. I pushed the pistol closer to his mouth. "Mention that name and I shall kill you." My voice dropped to a whisper. "I'm giving you your chance to escape on that condition: Never mention that name again. I advise you to leave Boston at once, for if I ever hear anything about the *Mary* again, I'll know you've opened your mouth. In that case, Mr. Pugh, I'll track you down and put a ball into your head. Have I made myself clear?"

My warning was a sheer bluff, of course, since I would not be in Boston. But Pugh couldn't know that. What he was thinking, I didn't know. His sharp, angular features were perfectly blank, perfectly emotionless.

"Who's that?" he asked, giving his head the slightest jerk.

"Salderman," I replied.

"All right, I know when I'm done," Pugh's eyes turned upon the unconscious man. "And him?"

"He remains." I wanted to ask him if Gore knew about Ethan, but I didn't dare. I glanced right and left and saw there were doors leading into the private rooms on either side. I swung my pistol to the right. "Use that door. Hurry."

The moment Pugh rose, there was a rattle at the window. I jumped up and thrust myself before the window as Pugh sprang toward the door leading into the next private chamber. The window crashed and a pistol barrel lunged through.

"Don't move, Pugh! Damn you, Hascott, get out of the way!"

"It's all right," I called, keeping within the line of Salderman's gun. "I've got the one you—"

I caught a glimpse of Pugh wheeling and saw Barnes rushing in from that right hand chamber. With a cry, I threw myself into Barnes' path. We crashed and I tripped him and both of us fell in a writhing, cursing heap.

"Hascott! Look around!"

A shot roared through the room. I untangled myself from Barnes, got on my knees just in time to watch Pugh crumble. He was clutching his chest, his discolored hands reddening with his own blood. As his knees buckled, a knife slid down his bosom and twanged, point down, into the floor. Without a sound, Pugh fell on top of his knife. I heard the blade snap with a ping.

Outside, the taproom was in an uproar and the latch rattled. Salderman barked an order and Stowe threw himself at the door, shooting the bolt. Salderman boosted himself over the sill and dropped in lightly. He turned Pugh over, swore softly.

"Damnation! I've killed him."

With an indifferent shrug, he picked up the body and passed it out the window. He kicked the knife into a corner. then brushed a smear of blood from his cuff and went to the door. He opened it a trifle, reached out and dragged the landlord in.

"We've had an unimportant quarrel. This lout—" he motioned to Gore, who was groaning and coming to—"shot off a gun. No damage, as you see."

"Th—This is a respectable house. I can't allow—"

"Of course not," Salderman soothed. He pressed a coin into the landlord's hand. "Just inform your patrons that it was a drunken quarrel. It's all over. No harm done."

The landlord sputtered protests, but in vain. Salderman took him by the arm, opened the door a trifle and shoved him outside. The babbling became greater, then receded as the landlord shouted his explanations.

"Stowe . . . Barnes . . . get that man outside, quick." Salderman picked up Pugh's knife and pistol and pocketed them, then mopped up the blood with his handkerchief. "I should have let him stab you, Mr. Hascott. You're a fool."

"Thank you," I said coldly.

He glanced up, smiled. "Forgive me. I meant only that you were a fool to turn your back on that kind of an animal." He gave the room a searching glance and nodded with satisfaction. "Out you go, Mr. Hascott."

I crawled out the window, as did Salderman a moment later. Ben Gore had recovered his senses and was struggling and whining. Salderman went over to him and whispered something to him. He subsided and allowed himself to be led away into the darkness. The other two men, bearing the body of Pugh, were just rounding the far corner of the tavern and heading back into Belcher's Lane.

"You needn't return with us if you don't want to," Salderman told me. "We'll dispose of Pugh's body at sea and round up the rest of his villainous crew. I know Ben Gore. It won't be hard to make him reveal everything he knows."

"What will you do with Pugh's men?" ·

"We'll round them up and put them aboard the *Mary* in irons. I'll instruct Captain Bernard to release them in Europe with the warning that if they ever return to Boston, they'll hang." Salderman extended his hand. "Believe me, I'm not ungrateful for what you've done this evening. I do wish, though, you'd tell me who caused all this trouble. I'll be suspecting everyone, even myself."

I laughed. "Put it from your mind, Mr. Salderman. I can assure you my informant will never again prove himself unworthy of trust. If I believed otherwise, you'd surely have his name."

Salderman sighed with resignation. "Very well, Mr. Hascott and thank you again for what you've done. Remember this, too, if Burdick can't find employment for you, come to me. I could use a man of your qualities. And I don't say this from a sense of obligation, either."

I thanked him and we shook hands heartily and he hurried on to rejoin his men. I was gratified, of course, to have gained his good will, but I was doubtful that I'd ever avail myself of his offer of employment. Indeed, I hoped I'd never have the occasion to ask anything of him, for I sensed he had a sort of ruthlessness which would give me pause before fully trusting him.

Pease's Inn was on Common Street, a dusty and unpaved way, very quiet and unfrequented at this late hour. Across the road was the Mall, broad and lined on both sides with beautiful elms, a favorite place for strolling or riding. And beyond, as you would know, was the well known Boston Common, deserted in the evening but during the day the pleasure ground of the people.

The taproom was sparsely filled, the patrons being of a much better station than those of the tavern I had just visited. The moment I entered, I spied a familiar figure—Mr. Blair. He hopped up from his seat, hurried to my side, attempting to smile. But his thin, strained features showed only too well his inner pain.

"Sit down, sit down." His voice shook as he pulled me into a chair. He glanced nervously around, bent toward me. "Young man, you deserve a good hiding."

I grinned, for he didn't mean it that way, being so upset. "Why?" I asked innocently.

"Why?" He almost leaped into the air. He calmed and
looked stern. "Ethan confessed everything to me—after I
pried it out of him. I'm too old to be easily fooled, young
man. When I read your note and heard from Mr. Rhodes that
Ethan had come back—and that Amy had been there—well, it
was simple deduction. Now, tell me what hap—No, this first."
He drew out his purse and counted out fifty pounds in gold.
"He could have come to me," he grumbled. Then added
quickly. "I'm not censuring you, mind. You'll never know
how much I appreciate what you've done. Now, tell me, did
everything go all right?"

"Yes. No one will ever know of Ethan's—ah—lapse." And I
told him what had occurred. "You have nothing to fear.
Neither has Ethan. I believed he had just been foolish, that's
why I tried to help him. I'm sure he's had a lesson he'll never
forget."

"I hope so, I hope so." Blair sighed. "You can't know what
it means to me." He shook his head. "That girl. . . ."

"Oh, come now," I protested. "That's not fair. I talked to
her and I know she had nothing to do with it. She seems to
be a very sensible girl." Then, I added, aware I was treading
on eggs, "Naturally, a young man opposed in love is often
likely to do unreasonable things—especially if he thinks he's
being unreasonably opposed."

His sparse brows went up. "Are you suggesting I'm at
fault for what happened?"

I squirmed. "No, no. I mean, he's a grown man and in love—
an unreasoning state of mind. He needs . . . ah . . . understanding."

Blair smiled. "I understand well enough, Warren. I was in
love myself once . . . a long time ago. Mind, I don't dislike
Amy. It's just that—well, I don't think she's the girl for my
son. I'm only thinking of his future happiness. I believe his
wife should be . . . well, no matter. He'll get over that silly
notion of marrying her. He's been in this state before." He
straightened his wig. "In any case, I'm forever in your debt,
Warren. You know I am your friend if ever you need one."

I thanked him and felt that Mr. Blair, unlike Salderman,
would stand by me if I needed him, even though my need demanded a sacrifice with no hope of return.

Not being sleepy, I urged Mr. Blair to stay awhile, which

he agreed to do. We consumed many mugs of excellent flip over our small talk, Mr. Blair doing most of the talking. He kept me amused with tales of the foibles of the new Legislature. According to him, the towns, in great numbers, had turned out the lawyers and esquires who had previously represented them in the General Court and sent humbler citizens instead. The manners of these new men and their innocence of legislative proceedings often led them into ludicrous errors.

Blair suddenly became more serious. "You mustn't believe I'm laughing at these men, Warren. Their very presence is an indication of the temper of the people in the back country, yes, even of the unpropertied people here in Boston. The rich seem to be getting richer and the poor poorer. Pretty soon the government will have to make a serious effort to remedy conditions." He frowned into his mug. "I mean, if they're wise they will. I'm not too hopeful about that. The government is controlled pretty much by the reactionary asses who cannot, or refuse to, see that something is basically wrong. There's a spirit of restlessness abroad that won't be stopped unless our monied men snap out of their complacency. There's trouble brewing, real trouble."

"You mean another revolution?" I asked incredulously.

"No," Blair said slowly. "No, I wouldn't go that far. I believe there will be revolt by ballot. Although. . . ." He scratched his chin with his thumb. "With the Constitution as it stands, I'm not sure if ballots will be enough to overthrow the mercantile element now in power. It would be hard to blast them loose from the Senate, for example."

"Just what is wrong?" I asked. "The Constitution?"

"Among other things," Blair replied. "The number of things wrong with our government now can't be told in one evening. You'll understand what I mean when you get home— into the rural districts. The people are so disgusted . . . well, here's an indication: Amherst, the neighboring town to yours, has been so dissatisfied that it didn't send a representative this year. They felt there was no use supporting a man here in Boston who couldn't accomplish anything."

"They're liable to a fine for not sending a representative, aren't they?"

"It's cheaper to pay the fine than send the man, they figure.

And it isn't only Amherst. I can name a dozen. . . ." He broke off and looked up. "Yes?"

A servingman was standing there. "Mr. Hascott?"

I acknowledged my name. "I sent my baggage here earlier. Has it arrived?"

"Yes, sir. We set it in your room. Do you wish to be called for the morning stage?" When I said I did, he assured me a place would be reserved for me. Then he handed me a letter. "This came for you, sir."

I thanked him, wondering who could be sending me notes. Before I could open it, Mr. Blair rose.

"I must be leaving, Warren. You'll want sleep." He took my hand and smiled uncertainly. "Thank you again for all you've done for my son—and myself. I don't know how we'll ever repay you, but we will, somehow."

I was a bit embarrassed by the intensity of his gratitude, but pleased, too. He made me promise to visit him whenever I was in Boston, a promise I readily gave. When he had gone, I turned my attention to the letter.

> "Dear Mr. Hascott. . . . The affairs in which you played such a generous part has been settled to the satisfaction of all concerned. I need not repeat my thanks. I must add a most urgent request: Please do not mention this affair or reveal the nature of the *Mary's* cargo to anyone, not even your own family. Having experienced your capacity for absolute secrecy, I can have no doubt that I, and the other merchants involved, will enjoy the protection of your silence.
> Yr. humble s'v't,
> J. Salderman."

The amount of good will I had managed to engender during my very first day in America was naturally gratifying and, no doubt, would later prove valuable. But this note was a bit curious. I had already given my word of honor that I would not speak of the affair. I was certain Salderman hadn't sent the note merely to irritate me. Then, what was his purpose? Of what value was knowledge of the specie shipment after the ship had departed? Was there some reason why the news should be kept from the public? From hints Mr. Blair had given me, I was inclined to think so. I was inclined to believe that I would find my answers in the country districts. I sensed this was a matter affecting the many, rather than the few.

Chapter 6

THE following morning I was routed out before dawn, groggy with sleep and fuzzy-mouthed from the unaccustomed drinking. I thought to finish my rest on the road. Vain hope! If you ever have the occasion to travel, you would do well to hire a horse rather than trust your bones to the rigors of our stage coaches. Neither the highways nor the vehicles had changed an iota in the eleven years I had been away. Both were in a conspiracy to shake and bruise the body without respite. The coach had no springs, of course, those appurtenances being practical only on coaches used on the comparatively level town streets. The roads were badly rutted, washed away in places and strewn with boulders which ofttimes jounced me to the ceiling and nearly bashed in my head. So, it was a relief to crawl into bed at the Hancock Arms Tavern in Worcester at the end of the first day's run.

The discomfort was made somewhat bearable by the fact that I had interesting traveling companions, two of them merchants, the other a lawyer, all on their way to New York on business. Their doleful account of the troubles racking our country made my pains seem trivial. Business was bad, they said, a fact I already knew. Money was scarce, so scarce that I was warned not to try to change anything larger than a half crown in the country districts. Robbery and theft were rampant, and morals had almost completely broken down since the war. Desperate and dishonest debtors were cheating their creditors right and left. Knavish bankrupts were clamoring loudly for paper money to further their swindles. Most shocking of all, one of the gentlemen predicted that, unless drastic measures be taken quickly to unify the country, a new tyranny—probably a domestic monarchy—was sure to arise. Indeed, there was a strong suspicion that James Bowdoin, our governor, aspired to dictatorship.

After enduring such discomfort and distressing conversation for a day and a half, you can well understand my relief upon reaching the town of Western (now Warren) at half past one of the second day on the road. Here, the highway turned southwest to continue on to Springfield, the regular stage stop. The righthand fork of the road led northwest through Belchertown to Amherst. By hiring a horse for the trip, I figured I could be home by nightfall. Accordingly, I hauled down my portmanteau at Mr. Cutler's Tavern and bade an unreluctant farewell to my companions.

Mr. Cutler wasn't enthusiastic about letting me have a horse, since he didn't know me. But after I had convinced him I was truly a native of these parts, he saddled up a chestnut mare. He told me to leave the animal at Bruce's Tavern in Pelham, from whence Bruce could send it back. Here, for the first time, I had an inkling of the changes I would find when I got home. I remembered Bruce's name vaguely, but he had not kept a public house while I was home.

From the town of Western to Pelham, the distance was about fifteen miles as the overworked crow doth fly. The actual distance was close to twenty-five miles, for the road constantly twisted and turned to avoid marshes and forests and hills. The countryside was very lumpy, as if God, when He fashioned our New England, had indiscriminately thrown blobs of stone and mud over the land, forming hills from six to nine hundred feet high. It was wonderful to ride again over such familiar ground and see again with a fresh eye how beautiful our land could be in the spring.

The town of Pelham, as you may know, lies between two ridges of hills running north and south, the hollow in between being some four miles across. Coming up West Hill, the road ran through a deep winding cut known as The Valley. At the crest of West Hill, I paused and peered through the gathering dusk. Nothing had changed. A river—the west branch of the Swift—bisected the town. On this side was a cluster of houses, the largest being the Meeting House facing the Common. There were fewer houses on the other side of the bridge, and the highway which wound up East Hill and passed on

84

toward Greenwich and Hardwick and the sea, was empty. It was a beautiful town, peaceful in its walled setting, as if insulated from the cares of the world.

As I came upon Mr. Dick's house, which was the last one before the Meeting House, I overtook a boy driving a pair of plodding oxen. He looked up at me with curiosity and gave me a polite, "Howdy." But we had never seen each other before. He had been born while I was away.

The thought depressed me a little and reminded me of the curious reaction of the Burdicks when I had asked of my family. Yes, many things had changed in Pelham since I had left. Had my family changed? Were they all really well, as the Burdicks had said? A lump formed in the pit of my stomach and I burned for an assuring answer to my questions. I reined my horse at the Meeting House and sat there a moment, thinking.

At length, I dismounted, telling myself over and over that nothing was wrong, yet yearning for certainty. The Meeting House itself was the same. It was a bulky, two-storied frame building with a boxlike projection in front, forming the vestibule downstairs and a storeroom upstairs. How often we children had sneaked out of galley during those long, drab sermons and gone into that storeroom where we could talk and giggle over pointless jokes and. . . . The flow of pleasant memories broke off abruptly as I walked slowly around the church and into the burying ground.

There were many new headstones in that hushed sanctuary of our departed townspeople. But I had no eyes for them. My heart was beating wildly as I came upon the Hascott family plot. There was a new white marker over a well settled grave.

Here Lies
THANKFUL HASCOTT
Bn. Jn. 11, 1696
Dd. July 3, 1781
Rest in Peace

Poor Grandma. So, at long last, she had followed her beloved husband, whom she had waited with such impatience to rejoin. I was sorry, for I remembered her with a great deal of affection. A good woman and an excellent cookie baker for young men with bottomless stomachs. But she had been an old woman, so her death could not be wholly unexpected.

There were other stones, already grimy with weather, one for my sister Prudence, another for a brother, and a third for another sister, all of whom had died in infancy. One other stone caught my eye—a new granite slab. With a choked cry I fell to my knees before it.

Here Lies
JONATHAN HASCOTT
Died October 17, 1785
Aged 32

Jonathan . . . my brother Jonathan. It wasn't possible.

I don't remember walking out of the burying ground. I could almost feel him at my side, not quite as tall as myself, but broader, a quiet, inarticulate sort, generous and kind and never domineering over his younger brothers, though stern enough if we tried to shirk our chores. The stone had not told me how long he had served in the war. But I knew he had been a good soldier, uncomplaining through want and weariness, fierce in battle, gentle in victory. It was hard to lose a brother like that, for Jonathan had been, above all, a man.

Then, as I remounted, it occurred to me that this couldn't account for the way the Burdicks had acted. True, they might have hesitated to give me this news, but surely that could be no reason for entirely avoiding speaking of my family. What could be wrong? Baffled and frightened, I prodded my horse on faster, impatient to be assured that my fears were unfounded.

After crossing the bridge, I turned north on the road running along the inner side of East Hill. Up on the right was Dr. Hynds' Tavern. It was comforting to know that Dr. Hynds still ran his public house. He had not changed, I could safely wager, other than being a little more prosperous and owning more land. The houses on the left were familiar—first, the Killay place, then, a short distance onward, the Rankens'. And finally, a half mile farther on, I came to the limits of our property.

My hands held tight to the reins and I slowly straightened

in the saddle. Yes, something was wrong. The south field had not been planted this year. It was covered with weeds. With dread and reluctance I gave my horse a gentle kick. In slow, measured steps, she continued down the road. Nowhere had anything been planted. Nowhere had a plow touched the earth this year. Everywhere, weeds and emptiness. On the other side of the road, the pasture was vacant of livestock. The weathered split rails had fallen away from the opening in the stone fence and lay unheeded in the ditch.

The house came into view. No smoke came from the chimney. My mother's herb garden behind the kitchen was a chaos of weeds. The barnyard was littered with rubbish—a broken wheel, discarded papers, an old shoulderyoke, an old straw-stuffed chair whose upholstery had spewed over the unraked gravel.

I couldn't sit in the saddle any longer. I dismounted, tied the reins to the nearest fencepost and walked up the long, grass covered lane. A hard fist seemed to be closing under my breastbone. The glass in the window of the corner bedroom was broken. That was the room Jonathan and I had shared. The parlor shutter sagged grotesquely on its bottom hinge. Shingles had torn loose from the roof.

There was rust on the thumb-latch. The front door had not been padlocked. I pushed gently and the hinges creaked like aged, painful joints. I had long since stopped thinking, long since stopped asking myself what had happened. My hollow footsteps mocked me as I wandered from room to room. They were empty, immense without the furniture. I stood longest in the kitchen, gazing at the bare shelves, the dusty mantel, the blackened, yet immaculate hearth. I could almost see my mother standing by the dutch oven, peering in to be sure the bread was rising. I could almost see my father, sitting in his hard-backed rocker, whittling a new axe handle or pins for a new barn. Then the shadows grew darker and the visions faded into stark emptiness.

I don't know why I walked out to the barn. Surely, I couldn't have expected to find anyone there. The smell of dry hay and horses and oxen was strong and pleasant. But the silence was broken only by the faint squeakings and scamperings of the insolent mice.

Then, I looked up and was astonished to find the hayloft

still fairly well filled. The hay was in good condition. More amazing, the grain bin was over half filled. The grain was dusty, but only a little mould had formed on the kernels. It was not old wheat, certainly not older than last year's crop. From that, I knew my family had not abandoned the farm until spring. But why and where they had gone, I could not even try to guess.

As a blind man groping in the darkness, I returned to the road and remounted my horse. Not until I came to the branch in the road did I realize where I was headed. The Gilmores were our nearest neighbors, but instinctively I was turning to the Cranes. In some ways, the Cranes had been closer to us and I felt that, if there had been any unpleasantness about my family's leaving, they would be less likely to be reticent. I prayed my father had not failed and decided to take the family west, into the inaccessible wilderness, with all its hardship and terrors.

The road branched off toward the river in a long, curving downsweep. As I came down the steep hill, I could see the Cranes' house and barn, set some distance back from the crook of the road and up from the bank of the river. I noticed immediately that their south field, behind the house, was lying fallow. It was all very strange. It seemed almost as if an evil blight had fallen over our peaceful countryside.

In the distance, beyond the pastureland and along the sluggish river, the Cranes had put in some small patches of flax, corn and oats which seemed hardly enough to keep themselves, much less send to the market. But they did have a generous number of cattle. Just as I came to the bottom of the hill, I saw a goodly herd plodding down the river road toward me. A tall, gangling young man was prodding them along. Since daylight was almost gone, I couldn't see him very well. But I knew at once that this young man would be Reuben.

I was near bursting with impatience, but I composed myself while waiting. As he approached closer, I was more sure of his identity, though I cannot say I recognized him. He had been an infant when I left. He was now over six feet tall, rather narrow-chested, his face lean and freckled. A long, dark blue towcloth frock hung to his bony knees and he was wearing sturdy shoes, but no stockings. I waved to him. His reaction was startling. He stopped short, stood there, his nostrils quivering, like a frightened buck ready at an instant's warning to flee for his life.

Puzzled, I rode closer to him, expecting at any moment he would bolt. "I don't suppose you remember me, Reuben. You are Reuben, aren't you?"

He gulped. "Reckon so."

"I'm Warren Hascott." No flicker of recognition came to him. "Can you tell me what happened to the Hascotts? I see their property is abandoned."

An almost unbearable tautness gripped my chest as the boy just kept staring at me. Reuben cracked his knuckles, a sharp stabbing sound in that utter silence between us.

"Mr. Hascott . . . he . . . he's in jail. They took him away for debt. That's all I know," he finished sullenly.

"The rest of the family?" I prodded impatiently.

"Gone over to Amherst . . . by Uncle Enoch's."

He glowered at me suspiciously, then turned and raced down the lane to the barn. I felt almost weak with relief. Pa in jail? I couldn't feel too badly about that. He was alive and safe and within reach. My mother and Increase would be well cared for over at my uncle's. The comforting weight of the gold sewn into my vest assured me that my father's troubles would be over soon.

With my mind clear and cheerful again, I could once more be surprised at Reuben's actions. At first I thought he was shy and frightened of strangers, as country children sometimes are. But Reuben was seventeen now, beyond that age. The Cranes must be expecting trouble. My guess was confirmed when a woman came out of the barn and strode toward me in long, determined steps. She was carrying a cocked musket.

She stopped some distance down the path and let the lowing herd stream past her. That was Beulah, right enough, grown to womanhood. I couldn't resist a low whistle of approval. Joe certainly hadn't exaggerated his sister's charms. Her plain, full-skirted dress of blue homespun accented, rather than hid, her soft supple curves. The bodice was tight and the square, low-cut neckline revealed in alarming detail the perfection of her full round breasts. Her hair was a fluffy chestnut brown, drawn back and tied at the nape of her neck with a small red ribbon. Her features were regular, the slightly angular cheekbones and firm chin giving notice of strength and determination. Hers was no pinkish hothouse complexion. Her skin was lightly tanned, contrasting sharply with her steady grey eyes. Every inch of her denied any vapid emptiness within.

Her knuckles grew white on the barrel of the musket as I slowly approached, and her unyielding stance warned me she'd fire if necessary. The Cranes had never been inhospitable. But it was evident they no longer gave unstinted hospitality to every stranger. Yet I could not fear her, for I could sense she was not the kind to give way to womanly panics. As I reined my horse and dismounted, her frown softened to puzzlement and she struggled with a vague remembrance of my face.

"You were a stringy little brat when I went away," I said with a smile. "I don't wonder you can't remember me. Eleven years is a long time."

"Then you must be . . ." she began huskily. "Reuben said you were asking about. . . ." Her frown swept away and a smile burst over her. "Warren. Warren Hascott!"

Her hand thrust out. The act was so straightforward and unexpected from a woman that a full second passed before I recovered. Her handclasp was firmer than many a man's.

"I can hardly believe it . . . Warren Hascott." She laughed "You looked bigger in those days. Come in, come in, Warr. . . ." She broke off shyly. "Or must I call you Mr. Hascott?"

"By all means," I said with a grin, "if you want me to pull your pigtails like I did when you were six."

She laughed and took my arm. "It's all right, Reuben, It's Warren, Warren Hascott." She gave my arm a squeeze. "Mother will be pleased to see you again. And so will. . . ." She faltered. "And so will Joab. Reuben, take care of Warren's horse."

I was suddenly uneasy. "Perhaps I'd better not stay. I ought to get over to my uncle's. Reuben told me what happened."

"They're safe . . . and well. You have nothing to worry about. Please don't rush off now."

"Well, I heard my father is in . . . in jail."

"For debt," Beulah added placidly. She gave me a quick

glance, then laughed lightly. "Oh, I see what's bothering you. Well, you needn't feel bad. It's no disgrace to be in jail for debt—not with half the county living under the same threat."

That was an amazing statement, though a reassuring one. Beulah took me to the kitchen, chatting about the farm as if she had known me all her life instead of only to the age of eleven. She opened the door for me and bid me enter, as naturally as if she had never considered that politeness was due her as a right.

"Mother! Joab! It's Warren Hascott come home!"

Mrs. Crane, bending over a bubbling iron pot, turned slowly from the hearth, as if her daughter's words only gradually penetrated her consciousness. She had aged terribly. Her face was leathery and very wrinkled and, in her washed out black dress, she looked older than I ever remembered my grandmother. And Mrs. Crane couldn't be more than fifty-three. The wooden spoon slipped from her gnarled hand and clattered on the hearthstones, and she came toward me in hesitant steps, her eyes never leaving my face. She was completely expressionless, dull-eyed, weary. Her rough fingertips touched my cheek, as if she didn't believe I was real.

"Oh. I'm sorry. I thought. . . ." Her low, colorless voice faded away. She gazed at me a moment longer, then smiled. "It's Warren. It's good to see you again, Warren."

She edged away timidly and returned to her cooking. I shifted uncomfortably, remembering what Joe had told me about her. Then, a scrape of a knife on leather called my attention to someone sitting in the corner to the left of the chimney. It was Joab, his massive back to me, bent over a workbench, carefully carving out the sole for a new shoe. The whole corner was littered with pieces of leather and small nails and bits of string and, at his left, was a pile of finished shoes.

"Joab!" Beulah called, a bit sharply. "Warren Hascott is here. He's come home."

Joab turned and looked at me, but said nothing. His brown face was seamed and his nose seemed flatter than before. But he was still the same neat, clean Joab. His hair was well brushed and tied in a queue and his bleached homespun shirt was open to reveal his matted chest. Then my eye caught a single crutch standing next to the bench. A blanket covered his legs.

91

"Howdy, Warren." His voice was hard and gravelly and, for one swift instant, his eyes gleamed sardonically. "You'll find things a lot different around here, a lot different."

He returned to his work. I groped for some suitable reply, then realized he wanted none.

"Mother, set a place for Warren. He's staying for supper." She wouldn't listen to my protests. Reuben came in with my portmanteau and she took it. "Get washed, Reuben. Supper's almost ready. . . . Oh, Mrs. Lowry!"

A small, mousy woman with harassed eyes came from the pantry. She was a neat person, her apron clean, her sleek black hair tied in a bun at her neck. She was a stranger to me and Beulah did not introduce us.

"Mrs. Lowry, would you mind taking Mr. Hascott's bag upstairs? He'll sleep with Reuben tonight." Before I could say anything, she added to me, "You can wash, too, if you wish. Supper will be ready in a few minutes."

There could be no doubt who ran this household. I was impressed, rather than irritated, with her assumption of control over my actions, too. It was habit, rather than intention. And, from the little I had already seen here, it was a good thing that the family had one member able to assume the responsibility.

Reuben put fresh water in a big wooden bowl outside the door and provided me with a clean towcloth towel. I gave myself a thorough and much needed washing. Hardly a sound came from the kitchen while I was so occupied. The clatter of crockery, the bang of a pot cover, the rattle of knives and forks, no other noises broke the cheerless hush. There was no conversation.

When I came in again, Reuben, divested of his frock, was sitting at the table. I settled into the seat beside him and, to draw him out, remarked how he had grown and mentioned I had seen his brother Joe and asked if he wanted to go to sea and so forth. Reuben answered in monosyllables, impressing me as an incurious sort, whether by nature or from hunger I could not tell at the moment. Joab didn't abandon his shoemaking until Beulah called him to the table. He reached out for his crutch and struggled to get up. Then, I got a shock.

As I have mentioned, Joab was a truly tremendous man, six feet four, deep-chested, with thick arms and powerful shoulders. From the waist up, he was still the man who could deal bare handed with any truculent bull. But his sturdy legs were no more. His right leg was gone, cut off above the knee. His left leg was hideously withered, an obscene broomstick that seemed certain to snap under the weight of his massive torso. For one split second, Joab's stern eyes held mine. I'm afraid I couldn't quite conceal my feelings of revulsion, pity and horror.

Joab half dragged, half heaved himself to his place at the head of the table. Beulah took her place at the other end, at my right. Mrs. Lowry and Mrs. Crane were piling the food on the table, boiled fish, half a roasted ham, new bread, baked beans, succotash, and a big pitcher of milk. This was quite a contrast to the Burdick table. Here no cloth covered the boards, there was no delicate china, no silver butterboats and sugar baskets. Here, the knives and two-pronged forks were of steel with wooden handles. The serving plates were wooden and the eating plates of heavy, glazed earthenware. The candles were of tallow, smoky and smelly. But the food was every bit as bountiful and tasty and, I daresay, a lot more healthful.

Mrs. Crane sat down opposite Reuben and Mrs. Lowry took her place opposite me. Everyone bowed for grace—everyone except Joab. There was a bored, resigned look on his flat features.

"Dear God," Beulah began solemnly, "we thank Thee for Thy mercy in returning our friend, Warren, from the heathen Turk, and beseech Thee to watch over him and grant him good health and prosperity in his renewed life among us. We thank Thee, Oh Lord, for this food and ask Thy blessing upon us, Thy children, who eat of it. In the name of Jesus Christ . . . Amen."

A rustle went around the table and we fell to eating. After a moment's hesitation, I gathered that no one was going to serve me, so I scrambled for my own helpings. I did full justice to the supper, filling my plate twice with everything. No one here, out of politeness, kept urging me to eat. In this household, guest or no guest, a man took what he wanted and ate until full and the devil take the bashful.

There was no conversation during the meal, words being reserved for asking for something beyond reach. The silence

93

was depressing to one such as myself, who likes to relax and talk while supping. I had so many questions to ask. But not until Mrs. Crane got up and brought the teapot to the table did anyone raise eyes from the table. The intentness on every face was replaced by contentment and I then felt it safe to unleash my impatient tongue.

"I suppose Pa's in the Northampton jail?"

"Springfield," Beulah corrected. "There wasn't room in the Northampton jail."

I whistled softly. "I guess he has plenty of company. How much was his debt, do you know?"

"Over three hundred pounds, I heard."

"What!" I almost jumped out of my chair. "For Heaven's sake, how did he ever manage to get that far into debt?"

"Well, I understand it was partly your fault."

"My . . . Oh, that ransom. I sent the money back."

Beulah nodded. "Your father didn't know until later that it would cost him fifty pounds to transmit the money."

"That's outrageous." I felt myself getting angry, but was aware I must not take it out on these people. "How about the rest? Pa was always a thrifty man, dead set against borrowing."

"The war changed a lot of us, Warren. Your father had a crop failure in '78—just like a lot of us around here. He had to borrow money to pull through the next year."

"I can understand that, but three hundred pounds. . . ."

"He borrowed in Continental paper and had to pay back in hard money. The state went back to a specie standard in '80."

"I see." I chewed on my lips a moment. "So, Pa was sold out . . . everything?"

"Everything but the land. Your Uncle Enoch bought that. People around here bought most of your household goods, tools and livestock and such. You can get it back anytime. We were willing to give it back at the time and let Increase stay and work the farm, but Uncle Enoch wouldn't hear of it."

"Uncle Enoch's like father," I remarked. "He doesn't want to be in debt to anybody."

Beulah's brows went up. "He had to borrow money to cover his bid on your land. He put a mortgage on his own land. But the sale didn't cover the debt and Uncle Enoch couldn't raise the remainder . . . a hundred pounds or so, I think it was

94

. . . so your father went to jail. Well, he's got company enough."

"So I gather." I was relieved to hear the remainder was so little. "I'll have Pa out soon, I think. When did it happen?"

"Just before spring planting. Everybody bid as low as possible for the stuff, but that Boston factor kept bidding us up. He took away some of the things just out of spite. That won't happen again, you can be sure of it."

Mrs. Crane looked up suddenly. "Tell him about Jonathan, Beulah. He ought to know."

Joab growled something deep in his throat. He pulled himself up abruptly, staggered over to his corner and settled heavily into his chair. Beulah watched him, her elbows on the table, her eyes expressionless. She frowned at her mother, then played nervously with a bit of bread, reluctant to give me the news.

"I know he's dead, Beulah. I stopped by at the burying ground and saw the stone."

Beulah nodded slowly. "It was a blessing, in a way. Jonathan came back with Joab in '80. Both of them had been sent home after the Battle of King's Mountain—that's in North Carolina. Jonathan had been shot through the lung. The wound never did heal properly. He kept spitting up blood. But a year ago last January, it looked like he was cured, so he went and married Sue Lambert. You remember Sue— she lives in Amherst, about a mile this side of your uncle's place. Well, right after the wedding, he began getting those spells again. Poor Jonathan really suffered. He was in bed four months until he died last October."

A soft tapping filled the momentary hush. It was Joab, working on his shoes again. Only now could I see the price we had paid for independence. My brother dead. Joab a hopeless cripple. The elder Crane and Paul, dead. And my father in jail because he borrowed Continental money which was later repudiated.

Mrs. Lowry, all this time, had not spoken, keeping her eyes downcast. I had been wondering who she was and what she was doing in this household. Now, I noticed tears were running down her cheeks. By a quick nod, I called Beulah's attention to her.

Beulah cleared her throat. "You can go up to your room

95

now, if you like, Mrs. Lowry. Mother and I will clear the dishes. You've had a hard day."

The woman rose, curtsied quickly and almost ran from the room. She was sobbing as she mounted the stairs.

Beulah shook her head. "Being poor isn't so bad if you've got folks. Her husband's in jail, too, for debt. I bid lowest for her at the auction of the town poor."

I have always thought that was a barbarous custom, selling the poor at auction as if they were slaves. But since we had no almshouse in the country districts, we had to make some provision for the destitute. I don't know what Beulah got for Mrs. Lowry's keep, but it couldn't be much. And I was sure she was not like some who bid in a poor soul to save themselves the price of a servant.

"The jail must be pretty crowded," I commented.

Beulah nodded. "There's over fifty in the Springfield jail right now for debt, a few for non-payment of taxes, and maybe one or two for crimes."

I was amazed. "I'd been told the morals of the people had broken down, but I had no idea it was as bad as that."

It was Beulah's turn to be shocked. "What has debt to do with morals? You don't think your father was trying to cheat his creditors, do you? He just didn't have the money. You know why? Because he couldn't sell his crops last fall."

"Couldn't sell his crops?" I echoed. "Why?"

Beulah lifted her shoulders. "Money—or the lack of it. Don't ask me why cash is scarce. All I know is we haven't enough hard money out this way to pay our taxes, much less our debts. If this keeps up much longer, there's going to be trouble. We're not going to jail for non-payment of taxes when there's wheat and flax in our barns that can't be sold because there's no cash in circulation. We'll stand for so much and no more."

"You were expecting the tax collector when I came?"

"No, our town's reasonable. The selectmen know we're not trying to cheat them. Half the town would be in jail if they insisted on everybody's paying. You know what our taxes are? Four pounds—hard money. Why, we don't see two pounds hard money all year 'round." She snorted in a most unladylike manner. "No, it's a debt. Two years ago last July, we had a bad storm in these parts. It didn't hit everybody alike, but we were wiped out. The river rose and took away most of our cattle. The wind knocked down our apples and our wheat was washed away. So, we had to borrow money to carry us over the winter. All we borrowed was ten pounds. If that man Plummer comes here and thinks he can put us in jail for a miserable ten pounds, he's got another think coming. He tries to serve that writ and I'll fill his breeches with lead."

I had to laugh. "Plummer—is that old goat still in business?" "No, the old man's practically retired. I mean Toby—you know, the fat boy. You'd better come with me tomorrow morning, Warren. You'll want to see Toby. He represented the creditor in your father's case. They're selling out Mrs. Decker—or they think they are. You'll see how we handle those leeches from now on."

Joab's hammer banged on the bench. "Beulah!"

Beulah turned to her brother. "Now, don't worry, Joab, I won't spend a farthing. Honest. And even if I do, could we let Mrs. Decker go to jail?"

"I forbid—" Joab began, his chest swelling.

"Please, Joab," Beulah broke in patiently. "I told you I wouldn't spend a penny. I promise. . . . And that reminds me, Reuben. You stay around here tomorrow. Toby may send someone else here while I'm out to serve that writ. We need a man around the fa—" She bit her lip as the hammering stopped abruptly. "I'm sorry."

Joab didn't say a word. He didn't even look around. Very carefully, he put his tools on the shelves built within reach of his bench. He blew out the candle, got his one crutch and hauled himself to his feet. Joab planted the crutch on the floor, inched over his withered leg, then swung his crutch and thumped it down solidly, dragging his leg over into position again. The room was not warm, but Joab's broad flat face was glistening with sweat long before he reached the door. I could feel cold beads forming on my brow, too.

Beulah did not move for many moments after her brother had gone into the parlor, which had been fitted as a downstairs bedroom. She was staring at Joab's other crutch standing in the corner. Then, she shook her head sadly.

"Is there any wonder he lost his belief in God?"

Mrs. Crane, who had sat absolutely still until now, suddenly got up and started to clear the table. There was a curiously blank smile on her sallow face.

"Joab always was a good boy. I never had any trouble at all with him. Only that time . . . that time he fell out of the apple tree." Her eyes were vague and far away. "He was four then. . . . "

"Yes, we know, mother," Beulah broke in gently. She rose and took the platter from her mother's hands. "I'll take care of the rest. You can start washing if you like."

While Mrs. Crane washed the pots and pans, Beulah cleared the table and put away the remnants of the food. She frowned at me as she wiped the boards with a wet cloth.

"Sometimes I think time stopped for her the day Pa died." Her lips tightened and she shrugged. "You'll come with me tomorrow, won't you? You'll be able to get back to Amherst by noon. I don't know who you've been talking to, but I think you're a little mixed up about us. I'll show you what morals have to do with debts." Her nostrils flared. "I only hope the men have gumption enough to go through with it.'

Chapter 7

I FELT well rested and in a cheery mood when I came downstairs the next morning. Joab was hard at his shoemaking
and Mrs. Crane was white to the elbows with flour as she
kneaded the dough for what I was sure would be excellent
dried apple pies. But it was rather dampening to have my
hearty "Good morning" completely ignored. Mrs. Lowry,
too, hardly seemed to notice me as she served me my breakfast. But the food made up for the stony silence. I had good,
thick, pork sausages, indian pudding with warm milk, a
big slice of cherry pie and coffee. It was not real coffee but
the kind made from potatoes which had been diced, roasted
and ground. I preferred the kind made out of the coffee bean.

I had just about finished when Beulah came in. If you will
pardon the poesy, I must say she brought the sunshine in
with her. In daylight and wearing a calico dress, she was
downright pretty. Whoever had made that dress of hers was
an excellent seamstress, for it was well tailored, wide in the
skirt, the upper part molded to Beulah's enticing figure. I
had to be careful not to stare or allow myself to think along
forbidden lines.

"Ready, Warren? We'll have to hurry. We're late." She
went to the mantel and took down a porcelain cup and got
out some small change. She ignored Joab's glare. "I'll be
back for dinner, mother. I think I will. Don't wait if I'm
late. Come on, Warren."

The morning was beautiful, the sun warm, the air crisp,
the grass and the new leaves vividly green. Reuben had
saddled my horse and brought her outside and was waiting
for us by the barn. From the way he watched his sister,

I could see he almost worshipped her. I could understand that. And more than ever, I was wondering why Joe disliked her.

"Reuben will take the horse over to Bruce's," she told me. "He'll take your portmanteau, too. You can pick it up as you go by later . . . . Remember, Reuben, if that man Plummer comes or anybody else, don't let him into the house. I wouldn't like to have Joab get his hands on him. Now, hurry back."

I gave him a sixpence. "Get yourself a licorice or something, Reuben, with my compliments."

Reuben's eyes got very big. "Gee, thanks, Warren." And he was whistling as he mounted the horse and rode off.

"You shouldn't have done that, Warren," Beulah said chidingly. "I know Reuben. He'll buy tobacco instead of confections. I caught him smoking two weeks ago."

"Well, smoke is good for humors," I pointed out.

Beulah laughed. "I suppose you men must have an excuse for using the vile stuff. Not that I care much. For all of me, Reuben could sicken himself twice a day. But Joab goes into such terrible rages when he smells tobacco on Reuben's breath."

We walked up the road in silence. Beulah was a delightful companion for walking. She didn't dawdle or take mincing little steps, but swung along freely, almost too rapidly for me. A curious girl, Beulah, and a delightful one. It was hard to believe she was only twenty-two, she was so level headed and frank, so lacking in coy pretenses and simpering mannerisms. She certainly had an unfeminine boldness in viewpoint. Yet, paradoxically, she seemed all the more feminine for it.

"It's strange you're not married yet, Beulah," I said finally. "A woman of your mind and beauty—a rare combination."

She cocked her head slightly. "Did you say you were enslaved for seven years?"

I chuckled. "Enslaved, but not a hermit. I've learned ladies like flattery. But they value sincerity more. You must have quite a struggle keeping suitors off your doorstep."

"I've had my share of proposals—and maybe a little more." Then, she sighed. "Though I fear I won't have many more. No one's dared come around for the last three months—ever since David decided to be my husband. You know him, don't you? Dave Corbett—he lives in the south end of town."

"Dave Corbett." I frowned as I tried to place him. "Oh, yes, I remember—that fat—no, chunky boy."

Beulah laughed delightedly. "That was David. He's grown quite a bit since then. He's as big as Joab." Her smile slowly faded. "He's a lot like Joab, too. They get along fine. He's about the only one Joab can stand having around. When David comes, those two can stare into the fire an hour on end without saying a word. It's a little uncanny, sometimes. I keep getting the feeling those two are talking—communicating, at least—all the time they just sit."

"He doesn't sound very exciting," I commented.

"Well, he isn't exactly." Her lips twitched. "I mustn't give the impression David's an ox. He isn't. He's really a fine boy —a lot sharper than you'd think from just talking to him. Sometimes I think he sees right through me." She shuddered a bit. "Horrible thought, isn't it? But if I married him, I'd never have to worry again—about money or being cared for. David isn't very wordy, but I'd always have affection, too." She nodded slowly. "Yes, I may marry him. I'd be happy with him, I'm sure of it."

She sounded just a little too sure. Never having met David, I might have been doing him an injustice, but he sounded like a nice boy, only dull. Beulah had impressed me already as being too alive, too intelligent, to be satisfied merely with a good provider and a sober husband.

"Tell me more about London," she said suddenly. "Did you gamble with any of those dissolute nobles?"

Our walk was all too short. Almost before I knew it, we were on the precipitous road leading over East Hill and on to Greenwich. From the eminence—some nine hundred feet above sea level—the land to the east rolled away in a billowing carpet of green and brown sprinkled with dark masses of forests. A short distance from the foot of the hill was Conkey's Tavern, the rendezvous of those who were going to the auction.

Long before we reached them, the men spied Beulah and drifted over toward the tavern, as if they had been waiting for her before going to the auction. If they were, it was an odd commentary on the state of affairs to which I had returned, for never before had men waited on women in matters of business. It was a formidable crowd, every second man armed with a musket.

The small knots broke up and conversations died as we approached. A few hailed Beulah, but most were staring at me. My clothes alone set me apart from them, though many were in ill-fitting suits of black serge or grogam instead of the expected homespun. Recognition flickered on many faces and I couldn't help smiling. The crowd was very quiet now, slightly hostile, though mostly puzzled. Beulah took my arm and stepped with me into the hushed semi-circle that had formed across the road.

Beulah winked slyly. "I guess they've forgotten you, Warren," she said in a loud voice.

"Warren Hascott!" came the bellow.

Dave Cowden came barging out of the crowd and grasped my hand. Captain Dave Cowden, I should say, for he had led us from Pelham on that June day in '75 when we marched off to Boston. The whole crowd surged around me and everyone was trying to get my hand at once, slapping my back, roaring delighted cusses at me, laughing and peppering me with a million questions at once. I must own I felt very happy and my voice was husky as I greeted old friends. I was, at long last, home.

For the first few minutes, I was hard put to remember their names, for time had dimmed my memory some, too. Then, they were all familiar again—Jim Cowan, Joel Crawford, Steve Pettingil, Jake Eason, Tom Packard, Josh Conkey, Dan Shays, Sam Baker, Hank McCullock, and many more, not to neglect Will Conkey, the keeper of the tavern. Will looked a bit older and he had a stomach, but he was the same, genial, sharp-faced host.

"This calls for a drop to celebrate, boys," Will shouted. "It's on me, everybody!"

And I was swept into the tavern. Mrs. Conkey came out from the kitchen to see what was causing the fuss and when she saw me, she threw her plump arms around my neck and gave me a kiss. Everybody cheered. In an instant, rum was poured and passed about and everyone was drinking my health and welcoming me back. I was laughing and chattering, but the press was too close about me and the questions too many to focus upon anyone in particular.

Finally, someone pounded on the bar—Beulah. "Isn't it time we got along, gentlemen?"

Everyone gulped down his drink, recalling the business at hand, and trooped out. I lingered until the taproom was almost empty, then regained Beulah's side. Dan Shays and Tom Packard had waited, too, and we started down the road together. Tom hadn't changed a bit. He was still the same thin, slow moving, loose-jointed Tom I remembered so well. His pale, greenish eyes still held that faint, amused cynicism. Dan hadn't changed much, either. He was a little stockier, but there were no lines in his smooth, clear cut features, the perfection of his profile marred only by the slight hook to his long nose. He was as neat in his dress as ever, wearing a good, though not expensive, blue broadcloth coat and a white shirt with a plain neckcloth. He walked on the outside, next to Beulah, as self effacing as ever.

"I've been telling Warren something about the blight that's fallen on us," Beulah remarked.

Tom shifted his musket to his right hand. "Times are pretty depressed, all right. But I guess everything's going to be all right—as soon as the General Court gets busy."

Beulah snorted. "Which should be about Doomsday."

"You'll pardon my ignorance," I said, "but just what is it you expect the General Court can do for you?"

"Put money in circulation," Tom replied promptly. "We got to have money or we can't sell our crops. You know, Warren, I got about a hundred bushels of corn left over from last year that I couldn't get rid of. And I've got taxes to pay. Lord a mighty, I ain't hankerin' to go to jail. Though, I'd sure have plenty of company. I suppose Beulah told you your Pa's in for debt."

"Yes. I hear Toby Plummer's going to be at the auction. I'll see what I can do about settling with him."

"It's so silly," Beulah commented. "You put a man in jail because he can't pay his debts. Then he rots there. How can a man get out if he can't earn the money to pay off the debt?"

Tom Packard grinned. "Shucks, Beulah, you just don't understand. Warren's Pa ain't in jail because he can't pay his debts. He's willfully concealing his assets and trying to cheat

103

his creditors. That Boston factor told me so—right after Caleb's mattress was sold—the one with the gold hidden in it."

"You see, Warren?" Beulah said roguishly, "your father's abandoned the path of righteousness."

"Yah, and Mrs. Decker, too," Tom added.

There was a general laugh, for Mrs. Decker had always been noted for her piety. She was quite old, almost seventy, and she had been a widow ever since I could remember. As I recall it, her husband died of the pox, though I can't be sure on that point. Anyway, after her husband was buried, Mrs. Decker had taken up the burden of caring for the farm and her two boys. Until the boys became old enough to work themselves, she even did the plowing herself, though her neighbors helped some. Yes, hers had been a hard, bleak life and surely she deserved to face old age in peace and quiet. But Tom told me her sons were gone, one lost at sea during the war. The other, Elihu, who had remained home to care for her, had been killed by a bull over a year ago.

The distance to Mrs. Decker's was not over a mile and a half. Her tract was a good one, fertile and well wooded, placed in the shadow of East Hill. Now, only one of her fields had been planted in wheat. Beulah informed me her nephew, Pulfred, had come down from Maine to take over the farm and care for Mrs. Decker. His own farm had been foreclosed. While he had been away in the war, his wife had contracted a crushing debt—in Continental money again—and Fred hadn't been able to pay it off. A month ago, Fred believed he was starting a new life for Mrs. Decker was intending to deed over the farm to him in return for her keep for the rest of her life, a frequent custom among our unattended aged. You can thus understand why more than half of those attending the sale were Continental soldiers.

The big unshaded front yard was filled with milling men. The auctions I had attended when a boy usually had been gay affairs, a time for renewing old acquaintances from other towns nearby and an opportunity for the womenfolk to exchange gossip. There was little light hearted chatter here and few women in the crowd. This was not to be the liquidation of the goods of some shiftless neighbor whose neglect and extravagance had caused his ruin. This gathering was more akin to the kind occasioned by a flood or a fire or some other disaster beyond human control.

Just outside the door of the house a platform had been improvised for the auctioneer by putting planks across the box body of a ping. Matt Clark, the constable, who had that unpleasant duty, was sitting at the edge of his platform, chatting with a group of neighbors. No one showed the least hostility toward him for, as Beulah said, he disliked these proceedings as much as anyone else and could be counted on not to oppose any measures his neighbors decided to take. When he spied me, he hopped down from his perch and came over to give me a hearty welcome home.

It was indecent how the poor effects of the Decker household had been uprooted from their rightful places and exposed to the public gaze. Everything had been neatly tagged, furniture, a loom and a spinning wheel, wool cards and hetchels, a coffeemill, a cherry wood cradle filled with such things as snuffers, candlesticks, dippers, ladles and skimmers, and other kitchen utensils. But no one was pawing over the stuff and mentally marking out the items on which he would bid.

I guess I showed more interest in the household goods than anyone else. Some of the items struck me as extremely odd for a poor household. There was a bundle of old clothing, Elihu's, I gathered, which included a coat of drab colored Devonshire kersey, some shirts of imported cotton cloths, and a waistcoat of good buff shalloon. There was a brass kettle that looked almost new, an oil silk umbrella, a hand looking glass and dishware of heavy blue glazed Liverpool china. One trinket box held, among other things, a horn comb, some lacquered buckles, a bead necklace and, most disturbing, a cheap watch.

Beulah caught me examining the watch. "Elihu's." Then, a bit sullenly, "Are only the rich supposed to have watches?"

"No, no. It's just—well, there seems to be so much imported stuff here—cloth, for instance."

"It was lucky Elihu had a good year in '83," Beulah returned quickly, "Or he'd have gone without clothes. Don't forget we were in a war, Warren. For eight years, we couldn't replace our necessaries . . . iron and steel tools and such. Our menfolk weren't home to make us furniture. We gave up our wool for uniforms and our pewter for bullets. Why shouldn't we buy as soon as we could again? As for the other things, that watch and that umbrella—all right, they're luxuries. But don't you suppose we deserve some of them? We work. It isn't our fault we can't sell our crops any more."

"Sure, I understand," I assured her.

"That's more than the rich do," Beulah said snappishly. "The way some of them talk, you'd think we bought imported luxuries with the money we should have used to pay our debts. Count it all up, Warren, and you'll see the luxuries are worth about one percent of Mrs. Decker's debt. We're not cattle, you know. We don't live by hay alone."

I grinned. "I'm convinced, Beulah. Suppose we go over and pay our respects to the extravagant Mrs. Decker."

Mrs. Decker hadn't changed a bit, as far as I could see, though to my young eyes she had never seemed anything but old. She was a severe old lady, in her best dress of rusty taffeta and her white linen cap. She was more bent over than I remembered her and her hawk nose was more pronounced. She walked with a cane.

"Rheumatic humors," Beulah whispered to me.

Beulah didn't tell her who I was when we met her. She put a thin, leathery hand in mine, peered at me closely, then grunted.

"Warren Hascott. So, you finally decided to come home. About time, I'd say. I guess the Lord listens to me after all." She cackled and gave me a pleased poke. "You're thinner, but I guess your Ma will fix that up. How is your Ma—and Pa?"

"I just arrived," I replied. "I haven't seen them yet."

She chuckled. "Well, give your Pa my best. Tell him I'll be moving in with him soon. The place needs a woman, anyway. I hear they keep it like a pig pen."

"Don't you worry, Mrs. Decker," Beulah put in. "We won't let you go to jail."

"Hah! Don't you go tampering with the law, child. You'd be a tempting morsel to those devils in the Springfield jail." She winked at me. "There's Toby Plummer over there. He 'tended the autopsy of your home, too."

I looked around and spotted him. "Excuse me, please. I'd like to have a talk with him."

The young lawyer was standing over by the well, sipping from a wooden dipper, eyeing the crowd with slight distaste. Toby had been a fat boy. He was a fat man now, flabby jowls, flabby middle, and a sort of wistful half smile on his oddly thin lips. Toby had always been a gregarious sort and I could see he was hurt that he was left strictly alone. His clothes, being of elegant plum colored broadcloth, made him stand out in sharp contrast to the men in homespun and cheap kersey all about him.

His round face gave the impression of stolid stupidity. But the way his small brown eyes fixed on me as I approached made me feel sure he was still a shrewd young man.

"Why, it's Warren Hascott!" He put out his hand and, when I ignored it, he frowned like a pained puppy and put his hands in his pockets. "I guess you've heard about your father. I don't know why everybody blames me for these things. I can't help it. I'm just making a living."

"I'm not blaming you, Toby, but you can't expect people to love you when you help put them in jail. That's neither here nor there. How much does my father owe?"

"I don't know exactly. About two hundred and twenty five pounds, I think."

My jaw dropped. "That much? Good Lord, Toby, he couldn't have been that far in debt. How much was the full debt—before the auction, I mean?"

"Six hundred pounds. He'd paid off some, I heard." Toby spread his plump hands apologetically. "The auction only raised three hundred and eighty pounds, if I remember rightly. Times are hard, Warren. People around here haven't so much money to spend on auctions any more."

I scowled at him for a moment, then, "How much will your client settle for—hard money?"

"I don't think he'd settle for less than the amount due. It would set a bad precedent. You can ask him, though. Maybe he'll make an exception."

"Thanks. Who is this kind-hearted gentleman?"

"A fellow by the name of Graham—Ormund B. Graham. He's an importer—lives in Boston. I have to go to Boston next week. I'll talk to him, if you like. What will you settle for?"

"Don't bother," I said. "I'll see him myself."

I turned abruptly away and walked off, not that I was angry with Toby personally. After all, as he said, he was only making a living. If it weren't he it would be someone

107

else. But it's a ghoulish sort of living that's made by picking the bones of an honest man's household.

I rejoined Tom Packard and the group around him. And, naturally, they abandoned their own conversation to ask about my adventures. They had long since settled their strategy. It was simple enough. They had agreed among themselves that only one man would do the bidding and at no time more than a farthing for the goods. Any man covetous enough to bid more would be dealt with by the rest.

Tom suddenly lifted his fingers. "There he is—the fellow who holds Mrs. Decker's note. Madden's his name."

Hank McCullock chuckled. "Mad's his name, if he thinks his note's going to be paid."

Hank retired under a barrage of hoots and we all gave Mr. Madden a thorough eyeing. Madden was a bulky man, stiff-backed on his sleek black and white stallion, his short riding coat of blue with gleaming silver buttons and his black calf boots shone. He was ruddy and lumpy featured and his freshly shaven square jaw was blue. His attitude was arrogant, only his small shifting eyes revealing his awareness of the hostile stares.

"What do you think, Warren?" Sam Baker asked suddenly. "About this business, I mean. Think it's legal? Some of the boys said we'd be obstructing justice or something."

I smiled. "I suppose you would be, if you call it justice. The sheriff would have to put us all in jail, wouldn't he?"

Everyone considered that a moment. Then, Hank McCullock spat and shook his head.

"I dunno, Warren. The one who does the bidding could get jailed. And how about the rest of us? Toby knows just about which of us cooked this up."

"I can't see that bidding low is a crime," I answered. "As for the 'conspiracy to defraud' charge, it would be Toby's word against ours. I don't see anything to worry about."

Many of the men, however, were worried, not for themselves, but for their wives and children. The uneasy silence was broken by Beulah who joined the circle.

"Fred's taking it pretty hard," she said. "I haven't let on to him what we're going to do."

Everyone looked over to where Fred Decker was sitting on a keg near the auctioneer's platform. Fred was a thin wisp of a man with watery brown eyes, about my age, though he looked twenty years older. And he looked thoroughly beaten. A murmur of sympathy went around the circle and Beulah bit her lower lip to hold back a smile of satisfaction.

"Who's going to do the bidding? Have you decided yet?" The men shifted uncomfortably and avoided her eyes. Her brows went up sharply and she looked at me.

"Some of the boys think this may be obstructing justice or fraud or something," I explained.

Beulah nodded thoughtfully. "I suppose it would be. You boys are getting a reputation for defying the law—among our Tory friends, anyway. Suppose a woman did the bidding? Women are always looking for bargains—bidding low."

"Sure," Jim Cowan spoke up heartily. "It wouldn't be her fault if nobody else bid on the stuff. Beulah, you'd do it, wouldn't you?"

Beulah spread her hands. "Why not?"

Tom Packard scowled. "No, we ain't cowards, Beulah. We won't hide behind a woman's skirts."

"Nonsense," Beulah snapped. "I have nobody to think about but myself. Besides, Toby would think twice about filing charges against a woman. But he wouldn't have any compunction about throwing you in jail. Only I want to be sure nobody else bids."

Tom patted his musket. "You can depend on *me*, Beulah." A chorus of "Me, too's" went up and the men regained their good humor, as if they had been given a reprieve. Most of them were determined to back her, too, though they'd hesitate themselves to take the forward position in the affair. Beulah passed Hank's hat around and coppers showered in to make up her war chest.

A sharp rapping swung us around. Matt Clark was standing on his improvised platform, stamping his heel for attention and waving the people to come closer. The sale was about to begin.

The chattering and laughter soon died away and the sound of shuffling feet was heightened by the low droning of flies and pert chirping of the starlings hidden in the trees across the road. Until now, the auction had been taken as some sly game to be played on the Boston financier. These men were not playing now. No man spoke. No man smiled. A few glanced covertly to one side or the other. Most stared fixedly at Matt Clark, their mouths grim.

Matt Clark winked and eased the tension a bit. "I guess I don't have to make speeches about why we're here. I got a right good lot of merchandise to offer today, so speak up loud and clear if you want anything special put up. Now, suppose we get right along with the business. Abe, let's have the first lot."

The first lot consisted of two japanned candlesticks, with snuffers, two pair of good brass candlesticks, three wall holders and two glass-enclosed lanterns. Matt eyed the items as his assistant lined them up on the platform.

"What am I bid?" Matt called.

"One farthing," Beulah returned promptly.

"One farthing—all done?" Matt clapped his hands.

Someone giggled. "Not so fast, Matt."

"Oh, sure." He grinned. "I'm offered one farthing. Who'll make it two? Two for these beautiful illuminables. Did I hear someone say two?"

There was a rustle in the crowd and everyone craned his neck to see what was going on. Madden was arguing with Toby. Poor Toby looked miserable as he kept shaking his head.

"All done?" Matt called louder. "One farthing once . . . twice. . . ." He clapped his hands. "Three times. Sold!"

"Just a moment!" Madden shouted. "That's ridiculous, one farthing for all of that."

"I didn't hear no other bid, Mister," Matt said placidly. "This is an auction, remember. All right, Abe, lot two."

Lot two was a conglomeration of small kitchenware in a big 40 pound iron dinner pot. There were knives and forks, a tin sausage gun, a steel chopper, a ladle, a skimmer, and many other items I didn't catch because Abe was rattling the list off so fast.

"This is a nice lot," Matt said with a grin. "Handy for the womenfolk. Don't be bashful, fellows. What am I bid?"

"One farthing," Beulah said flatly.

Matt cupped his hand to his ear. "I hear one farthing. Do I hear two? Two? One and a half?"

"One shilling!" Madden roared.

Tom Packard's lank figure came pushing through the crowd

from behind Madden. He elbowed Toby aside, jabbed Madden's back with the muzzle of his musket.

"There's a bad echo around here somewhere," Tom said loudly. "I heard one farthing. Anybody hear anything else?"

"One farthing," Matt repeated. "I hear one farthing for this beautiful lot of kitchenware. Surely, ladies and gentlemen, it's worth two. Do I hear two?"

"You can stop this farce," Madden said angrily. His fists clenched and he trembled with the effort of keeping his temper. "I bid—"

Tom Packard jabbed him in the ribs and he broke off. Madden hunched and he turned slowly, his bluish jaw jutting out.

"Go ahead, shoot. I dare you."

"Me? Shoot? Tom Packard's long face sagged in a grin. "Shucks, Mister, you got me wrong. I ain't aiming to shoot nobody. 'Course—" He looked about slowly. "The gun might go off—accidentally? Yep, I reckon so. I got a hundred witnesses to prove it. . . . Matt, go ahead. Don't mind us."

"Do I hear two farthings?" Matt continued. "Two? It grieves me to accept such a low bid, but the law is the law. Sold to the little lady for one farthing."

"Plummer!" Madden burst out. "Do something. You can't let these miserable scoundrels get away with this."

Toby Plummer's fat hands fluttered. "Mat, this isn't legal. The court will hold you strictly to account!"

"Me?" Matt scratched the tip of his nose. "Well, fancy that. Toby, suppose you tell me what to do? Should I hop down there and grab somebody by the throat and say, 'Bid, damn you?' Talk sense, boy, I sell to the highest bidder. I guess that ain't against the law, is it?"

A low chuckle went through the crowd. Matt was enjoying himself, you could see that. Madden was near apoplexy.

"Get down from there!" he shouted. "The sale is over."

Matt took a paper from his back pocket. "It says here I'm supposed to sell all the effects and chattels of one Mrs. Adie Decker. I am to do my duty, no more, no less."

Madden took one step toward the platform. Tom Packard matched the step, poked the gun into Madden's side. Madden stopped, searched Tom's expressionless features a moment, then turned to Toby.

"What the hell am I paying you for? Stop this farce."

Toby shook his head helplessly. "I'm afraid I can't, Mr. Madden. As Matt said, he's within the law. As for these proceedings, you can swear out a warrant charging conspiracy and fraud. I venture the charge would be hard to prove, however."

Madden swung around, his eyes narrowing. "I'll see everyone in jail for this, mark me."

A low grumble went through the gathering and the circle closed about him like a slowly tightening noose. Madden's eyes grew bleak, but he stood his ground. Tom Packard reached over, grabbed the factor by the ruffed shirtfront.

"You show your face around here again," he said in a low, hard voice, "and you're going to have an accident—a bad accident—clear? Now, git!"

He spun Madden around and his foot arched up, neatly connecting on Madden's lovely buff breeches. Madden sprawled face down in the dust, came up sputtering. A dozen hands reached down and picked him up and set him in motion toward the road. As he was swallowed into the mob, I could see fists flying. Madden had guts, I'll say that for him. He swore and struck back and butted people aside right and left. It was an accident that a woman got into the path of his flailing fists. He was bleeding from the mouth and nose when he reached the road. He kicked out at the last of his tormentors and flung himself up on his horse. The horse whinneyed and reared and the crowd scattered. Madden raced up the road, leaving a defiant swirl of dust in his wake.

"Let's get on, Matt," Tom called quietly.

As Matt put the third lot up the whisper passed that Toby ought to be run off the grounds, too. That proved unnecessary. Toby had disappeared. Someone mentioned he had seen Toby riding off in the opposite direction during the brief flurry.

The tension relaxed completely and the sale went on. But there were sober undertones to the laughter and discussion. Hank asked me if I thought Madden would dare swear out warrants against us and I said I doubted it. But he still held Mrs. Decker's note and, since it would be unsatisfied, he probably would send her to jail, just out of spite, if for no other reason. Tom said Madden had better not try that. And there were plenty who were determined to back him up. I have never been one to encourage or approve mob action. But this was one time I could not find a reason for condemning my friends and neighbors. The auction went on to the bitter end. Everything Mrs. Decker owned went up on the block—her furniture, bedding, all her knick-knacks, even her preserves, all the farm equipment and tools, the anvil, churn, the sulky and the very sleigh Matt was standing on. Everything was knocked down to Beulah for a farthing a lot. Everything was duly recorded as having been sold to her and thus title to the goods passed into her name. Whether the title would stick or not was another matter which no one bothered about right then. For the land, including the house and barn, Beulah generously bid a shilling, the last twelve pence in her war chest.

Dan Shays had kept to the edge of the crowd all this time, watching with keen interest but taking no active part in the proceedings. After a time, I drifted over to him for the excitement of the auction was all over. As the goods were knocked down, Mrs. Decker's friends would take them inside and put them in place again. More than ample hands were engaged in the task, so I felt no need of volunteering and adding to the confusion. Dan brightened as I came up to him.

"Well, I guess you know how we feel now," he remarked.

"A friend of mine in Boston told me there was trouble brewing out this way," I said. "But I never dreamed the people were angry enough to consider violence."

Shays nodded soberly. "A man can stand so much. I'm only hoping this will help the General Court wake up. Sooner or later, they'll have to do something to redress grievances. If they don't, things will get worse—a lot worse."

"That sounds bad, Dan."

"It does, but it's true. But I don't believe the investors themselves will let things go too far. They must realize putting people like Mrs. Decker in jail won't help them any. They'll have to do something themselves to get the legislature to redress our grievances. After all, they have a stake in our prosperity, haven't they? No, I think they'll come around to accepting paper money soon—or some other plan for giving us a circulating medium."

"Haven't the towns petitioned for relief?"

"Petitioned!" Shays laughed without mirth. "Lord, Warren,

practically every town west of Boston has sent in a petition. We sent one this spring. Tom Johnson—he's our representative, you know—tells me the House reads them and refers them to committees. That's the last anybody hears of them."

Our conversation lapsed as we watched Beulah mounting the barrel. Matt Clark, below her, hammered on the planks for the attention of the crowd, which had broken up into small groups.

"Friends!" She motioned everyone closer. "Friends, Mrs. Decker wants to thank you all for coming and helping her. We've found two casks of rum in the barn. Mrs. Decker wants all of you to have a drink with her compliments."

The men cheered and began trooping toward the barn. Dan and I pushed our way against the stream and reached the platform just as Beulah was stepping down.

"You did very well," Beulah," Shays complimented.

"I was a little scared," she confessed. "Look!" She held out her hand. It was shaking a little. "Do you think he'll have me arrested?"

"I don't think he'd dare," Shays said.

"Well, I hope not." She took my hand. "There's some cider in the kitchen. Come along, boys. I need a drink, too."

Shays shied off. "I really must be going." He turned to me. "I suppose you're going to Springfield, aren't you, Warren? Will you deliver a letter for me? It's to Luke Day in West Springfield, across the river. If you're not too busy . . ."

"I'll be glad to take it, Dan."

He handed me the letter. "Luke can tell you how things are around that section. Ask him." He shook hands with me. "Well, I'll see you again soon. Goodby, Warren. 'By, Beulah."

I watched him as he hurried down the road. "Dan seems to be a pretty smart fellow."

Beulah nodded grudgingly. "I suppose he is. But he'll never amount to anything. He's all talk and no action."

Chapter 8

MRS. DECKER had an overabundance of help to get her furniture and household goods back in place, so I decided to get along myself. I walked back to the house with Beulah to pay my respects to the old lady. She was completely surrounded by men and women jabbering away at great length about the legal aspects of the affair. Just why everyone should look to me for an opinion, I don't know. I suppose it was because people still remembered that I had studied at Harvard preparatory to going into law.

Mrs. Decker shushed everyone, since I just couldn't keep up with the questions. "What we want to know, Warren, is this: Does Beulah have title to the property?"

I shrugged. "It's doubtful. I think the court will set aside the sale. At any rate, you've got a home for a while—at least, until Madden gets an order to imprison you."

Mrs. Decker chuckled. "If he does, he's more of a fool than I think he is. He'll have to pay for my keep in jail. I won't care. As long as Fred has a roof over his head, I'm content. He wants to bring his wife down from Maine. She's staying with her folks. Poor Fred's had his share of hard luck."

I could have pointed out that she had had a goodly share herself. She would have denied it. She was that kind.

"I've got to be getting along," I said. "If you need a hand for anything, just let me know, Mrs. Decker."

"Thank you, Warren. Everybody's been so good to me. God bless you all." She sniffed. "Now, scatter before I start sniveling. Give my love to your mother, Warren. And I'll pray for your father's speedy release."

I grinned. "I'll have him out in a week."

Beulah walked down to the road with me. "Did you mean that? About getting your father out soon?"

I nodded. "I have some money, you know. I'm quite sure that man Graham will settle when he sees the color of my gold."

"I'm glad—for your mother's sake as well as yours. She's had a hard time." Beulah stuck out her hand. "Let us know when you're moving back into the house. We have your oxen."

I shook hands with her. "I'll see you soon, Beulah."

I found myself looking back several times. She was a remarkable young woman, intelligent and sensible. But I must confess that was not the reason my head turned. She had a lovely carriage. Or should I say, she had exceedingly provocative curves? She had indeed. Yes, I was sure I'd be seeing much of Miss Beulah Crane.

I stopped at Landlord Bruce's and picked up .my portmanteau, and learned he had taken care of the horse. Mr. Bruce remembered me and urged me to tell him my adventures. But I was much too anxious to see my family to linger along the way.

Uncle Enoch's tract was particularly well situated, his ground being almost all level. But, as if God had determined to be absolutely fair, his land was more stony and rock infested than many another hillier site. Once cleared, however, the working was infinitely easier. Uncle Enoch had taken full advantage of every inch of cleared land. There was a wide brook running parallel to the road, making an excellent pasture for his large herd of cows. Uncle Enoch was a great believer in cheeses as a cash crop. On the other side of the road, he had three big lots laid down in wheat, corn and flax, all of which were well out of the ground and beautifully green in color.

The house was nicely situated, quite some distance in from the road, the rear to the brook. The barns—my uncle had erected a second since I had last been here—stood to the right of the house. As I came into the lane, I saw two children playing in the front yard, which had been trimmed of weeds and was nearly as smooth as a well kept English lawn. From the appearance of the place, one would surely think Uncle Enoch was very prosperous. The children, on closer scrutiny, proved to be two small girls—twins. They stopped playing to watch me, shying away as I approached and I thought sure they were about to run. But they only looked as if they wanted to run. They seemed remarkably old and solemn in their clean blue homespun dresses, which naturally were cut exactly as an adult's garment, full-skirted and long-sleeved.

I smiled at them. "Howdy, ladies. What're your names?"

The one on the left spoke for both. "I'm Matilda and this is Mildred. What's your name?"

"I might be your cousin Warren. I'd know better if I knew your father's name."

"Papa," Mildred burst out confidently.

I had to hurry on to hide my giggle.

From the banging and chattering in the kitchen, I knew the womenfolk were hard at work. And the pungent, acrid smell of indigo told me they were busy dyeing some cloth. I stopped in the doorway, blinked to adjust my eyes to the dimness inside. The women didn't notice me, they were so intent on their work. I spotted Aunt Hannah first, standing over a steaming kettle of dye, tamping the goods down with a stained stick, working it over and over to spread the blueness evenly. Then, I saw my mother. She was at the side table, pulverizing the big lumps of indigo in a wooden bowl. There was a spot of blue on her chin.

I dropped my portmanteau. "Anybody home?"

The two women started. Aunt Hannah glanced over her shoulder and spun—I swear it's the word—around. My mother dropped her mortar, her lips parting. But no sound emerged.

"Warren," she whispered finally. "Warren!"

I met her halfway, lifted her up and kissed her hard. She was crying softly when I set her down.

"My son . . . Warren . . . It's been so long."

I held her close. It was good to be home. No, I make no mistake, for where my family is, there shall always be home.

Mother wiped her eyes on the corner of her apron and felt my arms, reassuring herself that I was real. "You're well . . .

and you've grown . . . You're taller." Her face was radiant as she turned. "Don't you think he's taller, Hannah?"

I grinned. "You've grown, too, Aunt Hannah."

She came over to me and hugged me, groping for words. She was a lot plumper than I had known her and there was grey in her hair, but her face hadn't changed a bit.

"God has been good to us," was all she could say.

Then I noticed a third woman in the kitchen, a young woman whom I didn't remember at all. She was tiny, sparrow-like, her face palish and her V-shaped chin showing a dimple as she smiled shyly at me. Her bare arms were streaked with blue.

"Warren, this is Anzel's wife, Rowena," mother introduced.

"Anzel has excellent taste," I said, shaking her hand. She blushed to the roots of her hair. "Are those your daughters outside?" She just nodded.

"Good Heavens! We must call the men!" Aunt Hannah went—waddled, you might say—to the door. "Enoch!" she called in a voice that must have reached the south pasture. "Enoch! Increase, call your uncle and come in here, right away. Yes, you, too."

After a moment, "He's coming."

That deep, resonant voice couldn't come from my little brother. I moved over to the window. A tall, broad-shouldered young man was hurrying over from the barn. For a moment, I was deeply shocked. That was Increase, right enough. He had grown into the image of Jonathan, large nose, wide set eyes, and an air of solidness about him. When he was almost up to the house, I stepped into the doorway and confronted him.

He stopped short, stared at me, then stepped back as if hit. "Warren!" And he bounded toward me.

He remembered just in time that he was beyond the age of hugging menfolk. He grinned and grabbed my hand and nearly wrung my arm from its socket.

"When did you get here, Warren? Why didn't you write? Did they let you go? Did you escape? How was it in Alg. . . ."

"Whoa!" I cried laughingly. "All in due time, Increase."

Then I saw Uncle Enoch coming from the barn. He must have been up in the hayloft, for his long smock was peppered with wisps of straw. Uncle Enoch could be called the patriarch of our family, for he was the oldest and built along massive lines. His face was square and stern and deep wrinkles were graven about his unsmiling mouth. He saw me long before he reached the house, but his expression did not change. I have never known him to show surprise, or any other feeling. But I have never known anyone to say he was without emotions.

"Welcome home, Warren." He almost crushed my hand. "You're looking well."

"I'm feeling well, sir."

"Hannah! We'll have a goose for supper tonight."

Aunt Hannah looked at her blue stained hands. "But Enoch, we won't have time. . . ."

"We'll wait. Increase, go out and kill a goose—the fattest one you can find." The faintest trace of a smile touched his lips. "I remember Warren never liked veal." He was stern again. "I suppose you've heard about your father."

"Yes." I lifted my finger. "And that reminds me. Get me a knife, mother—a good sharp one."

I took off my coat, threw it on a chair and removed my waistcoat. When my mother handed me the knife, I slit the lining at the seams and drew it back. The long rows of gold coins glittered like the spangles on a King's coronation gown. My mother gasped and sank into a chair.

"Is—is it enough?"

I frowned. "Well, I'm not sure. But I think I can beat Graham down. If I can't, I think I know where I can borrow the money in Boston. I'll try to cover your note, too, Uncle Enoch. How much did you put up to buy our land?"

Uncle Enoch shook his massive head. "We'll worry about that later, my boy. Get Caleb out of jail first."

"That note's coming due soon, Enoch," my mother pointed out. "Times are real hard, Warren. They wouldn't give him a loan for more than six months."

"We'll worry about that later," my uncle said, a bit more strongly. "Come along, Warren, we'll get out from underfoot. Hannah, we'll have supper at six-thirty."

"Lands," my aunt breathed, "the way that man talks, you'd think he was lord and master around here."

Uncle Enoch took me out and showed me over his land.

He had cleared a lot of ground in the eleven years and had thinned his woods considerably. Out in the west pasture, I met Anzel, who was replacing rotted fence rails, a perennial job about any farm. Anzel was a lot like me, rather tall and sharp-faced, but he was very slow and easy in temper. I learned that my other cousins, Jesse and Saul, were both married and settled on farms of their own. Mercy, the youngest, had created a scandal in '79 by running off with an Irishman who had escaped from the Rutland Barracks. Anzel had to tell me this on the quiet, for Uncle Enoch forbid the mention of his daughter's name about the house. An Irishman wouldn't have been so bad, but an Irishman in a British redcoat—well— Uncle Enoch was an uncompromising patriot.

It was precisely six-thirty when we sat down to supper. The smell of roasted goose was almost overpowering and I could hardly wait until my uncle had said grace. Uncle Enoch waited sternly until the children stopped squirming and we bowed our heads.

I was travel weary and disliked the idea of going back to Boston to see Graham, but the trip was necessary. And there was no time to be lost. Uncle Enoch insisted Pa could still get in some crops if he was released within the next week or so. Accordingly, I didn't grumble too much when Ma dragged me out of bed before dawn the next morning. Since I was going to stop at Springfield, Mother and Aunt Hannah prepared a sack of victuals for Pa. The amount they included hardly showed confidence in the success of my mission. There were four cheeses, six loaves of fresh bread, four apple pies, two indian puddings and a gallon of hard cider. I certainly hoped Pa wouldn't have to be in jail that long.

I made the trip, via Belchertown and Ludlow, in a little under four and a half hours, rounding Arsenal Hill just about nine-thirty. The town of Springfield was the largest in the county, a picayune village by some standards but adequate for the trading needs of the surrounding area. Main Street, which ran parallel to the Connecticut River, was shaded with Elms, a mile long stretch of stores of every description. Here you could find every variety of enterprise available in Boston

—saddlers, curriers, a watchmaker, a hatter's, several tailors, many general importers of British and other foreign goods, an apothecary, and even a hairdresser who was patronized by both sexes. Besides these, there was the usual proportion of public houses.

The jail was on the west side of Main Street, a short distance from Meeting House Lane, which came to a dead end at the court house. It was a two-story frame building, standing alone, with a house tacked on at the rear for the jailer and his family. I tied my horse to the post outside and, taking my sack, went into the large anteroom and office on the ground floor.

In the corner of the tiny anteroom, a man was sitting and whittling, his feet up on a battered oak desk. He gave no sign of being aware of my approach.

"I'd like to see Mr. Hascott, please, I'm his son."

He cocked an eye at me. "Eh? Which one? Reckon I ain't seen you before, young feller."

"I'm Warren Hascott."

His feet came down with a thump. "Do tell! Caleb gave it out you was in Turkey."

"Algiers," I corrected. "Which is ruled by the Turks. I'll tell you about it some time. Right now, I'm anxious to see my father. So, if you please. . . .?"

"Shore, shore." He laid down his whittling, searched through his pockets, patted his belt, then grinned sheepishly and opened the desk drawer. He took out the keys and rose. "Come along, young feller. Your paw's upstairs."

As we passed the wrought iron, lattice work door, I glanced in. The first floor of the jail was one huge room. It wasn't very crowded, containing no more than twenty men, criminal offenders, the jailer informed me. Most of them were short term prisoners, in for drunkenness or such minor offenses. They were sitting around or arguing or playing cards or just sulking.

Upstairs, the smell of stale sweat and urine was almost overpowering. From the sound of voices, I could readily understand the place was badly overcrowded. The jailer told me debtors were treated with special consideration, being kept apart from those charged with crimes. There were three rooms up here. The first one was jammed to capacity. The second was equally filled. The third was the one in which my father was kept. The keys jangled and shoes scruffed with sudden interest as the lock clanged over.

The jailer looked down at my bag. "Maybe I oughta look into that there bag, young feller. You ain't bringin' your paw tools, be you? Some of these men ache mighty bad to get out."

I opened the bag and he pawed through, not very carefully. For a moment, I thought he was going to confiscate the cider. But when he saw my fist hardening, he decided he'd better not. He opened the iron door and poked his head in.

"Hey, Caleb! Your son's here to see you! He stepped aside. "Bang on the door when you want to get out."

I stepped inside and the iron door clanged and the key turned in the lock. The odor in that room almost knocked me down. And all the windows were wide open. The wall-space was lined with triple decker bunks and under two of the three windows were cots. More than half of the men were gathered at the one free window, pretending not to see me. The others were sitting or lying on their cots, reading newspapers or just dozing. A tall man, exactly my height but thinner, his face sharp and angular was walking toward me. His skin was sallow and his long chin was covered with a grey stubble. His cool blue eyes showed no surprise.

He put out a gnarled hand. "Howdy, Warren."

"How are you, Pa?" I had to smile as I shook hands with him. I could feel in the tremor of his fingers that his calmness was a sham. "You didn't expect to see me, did you?"

"Well, yes and no, son," he drawled. "I always knew you'd be back. . . ." His voice cracked and faded and his eyes filled. "Dammit, why pretend?" He put his arms about me. "Thank God you're home, son." He brushed his eyes with the back of his hand. "You're looking mighty fine, Warren."

"I'll feel better just as soon as you're out of here." I handed him the sack. "Some stuff Ma and Aunt Hannah sent along."

"Thanks." Pa took the sack and half turned. "Hey, Siby, share this up, will you? And don't forget my share. None for that louse Clem." He handed the sack to a chinless, baldish fellow and grinned at me. "Clem got a gallon of rum

122

last week and didn't want to give anybody else any." He took my arm. "Let's set over at my place."

We went over to Pa's bunk and sat down. The men in the corner were already squabbling over the spoils and the chinless fellow was pleading with the others not to grab. The sack I had thought so big wasn't half big enough. There wasn't a chance of getting real privacy in a place like this, but Pa poked the man who was lying in the bunk over us and told him about the victuals. He hopped down fast enough and went over to get his share.

"How did they come to let you go, son?" my father asked.

I told him how I had effected my release. "And I took something extra, too. I think it's enough to get you out of here. I've got two hundred pounds in gold."

Pa grinned. "You were always cut out for a trader or a lawyer. But it ain't enough, Warren. I owe two hundred and thirty, plus interest."

"I figure I can get Graham to settle for two hundred. If not, I can borrow the rest."

Pa frowned. "That don't seem right, son, you going into debt. Seems I put everybody in debt. Why, Enoch had to—"

"Let's worry about all that later, Pa. Right now, all I'm interested in is getting you out of here. Anyway, if cash is as scarce as I hear it is, he'll settle all right. Now, how about that debt, Pa? Mother said you had all the papers here."

My father burrowed under the straw and came up with his old leather pocketbook which Jonathan had made for him some fifteen years ago. He fished out the worn papers and handed them to me. Pa had always been an orderly man and one of the papers was a sort of balance sheet of his dealings with Graham. It was rather ragged, with additions and subtractions in pencil and vari-colored inks, but it was legible enough.

In 1778, Pa had borrowed three thousand pounds. Continental, which at thirty Continental to one sterling amounted to about a hundred pounds hard money. Pa said that crop failure was his own damn fault. Wheat had been going up and he figured he'd make a big killing by planting all of his fields in wheat. He had gone into debt to buy seed that year. Well, the bugs got everything, wiped him out clean. The odd part about it was that not everyone in the neighborhood had been so afflicted with the bugs as his fields had been. God must have tried to teach him a lesson, he said. He had to borrow more money to keep the family alive over the winter. He had learned his lesson. Net cost: three thousand pounds, Continental.

The next year, he had done well. After paying interest, taxes and other small costs, he still had twenty-five hundred pounds, Continental, left over. By this time, '79, the Continental pound had gone down to one sterling to forty, so Pa made on that deal. The following year, disaster. The state went back on the specie standard. Pa owed now five hundred pounds hard money. Graham, however, was generous. When Pa had to borrow the money to get me out of Algiers, Graham let him have it and even took care of transmitting the money to me.

"That dirty louse!" I exclaimed.

"Who, Graham? I thought he was right reasonable. At the prices land was bringing then he'd never have been able to sell the place for a thousand pounds. Seven or eight hundred was top."

"He's still a louse. Do you know what he did to you, Pa? I wondered why I only got fourteen hundred Spanish dollars. He made you sign for Massachusetts money and sent abroad Sterling. You got three tenths less than you borrowed, a loss to you of six hundred Spanish dollars."

Pa shrugged. "Anyway, you sent the money back. I only lost fifty pounds, the cost of sending the money."

"I'll bet he cheated you on that, too," I grumbled.

In '81 and '82, Pa had paid the interest on the loan, which was now five hundred and fifty dollars and in '83, he had managed to whittle it down to five hundred again. Then times slackened off. Pa could pay nothing in '84, either principal or interest. Again in '85, Pa defaulted. Graham sued. He got judgment for three hundred and fifty pounds, plus costs. And those costs were terrific—Court costs, 24 £; Jury fees, 2 £; witnesses, 1 £ 10d; counsel's fees, 20 £; totalling 47 £ and raising the debt to 397 pounds sterling. The sale brought in 167 pounds, a ridiculously low amount. Pa explained that the household goods had gone for practically nothing, since no one in the neighborhood had any cash and no outlanders were present. As for the land, a Boston speculator started bidding against Uncle Enoch, but shut up when Pa went for him.

"I almost committed a murder right then," Pa said, his eyes bleak. "Enoch told me all he had been able to borrow was a hundred pounds. I knew if the bid went over a hundred, I'd never step foot in my house again. I guess I lost my senses for a few minutes. I grabbed an axe and started after that feller. He ran and he was so scared he didn't come back. Enoch bid a hundred pounds and it was knocked down to him. I thought that feller would file charges against me, but he didn't." He rubbed his gnarled fist. "I'd rather stay in here the rest of my life than let my land go. At least, I always had hope and now . . . well. . . ." He gave my arm a hard squeeze. "Now I have hope again."

"I'll have you out in no time," I assured him. "Uncle Enoch says you can still get some crops down. Just wait 'til I see that man Graham. That's the rottenest thing I ever heard of, lending depreciated paper and demanding hard money in return!"

Pa shrugged. "'Course, it isn't fair. I argued that way in court, but the court held I contracted for a sum of money and that was the sum I had to pay. The jury knocked off a little, figuring three fifty was a more just sum."

"Justice!" I snorted. "You appealed, naturally?"

"Naw, what was the use? Almost everybody else appeals nowadays, but I'd figured I'd spent—haw, I mean gone into debt—far enough. See that feller over there? There's Ab Cheevers. He fought that point out a long time ago. If I was him I'd have something to complain about."

The man my father was referring to was sitting on his bunk, munching a piece of pie, chuckling over his cup of hard cider. Ab Cheevers was now over seventy, the shriveled remains of a once strong man. He was almost toothless, his skin like dry parchment, a faint, almost imbecilic smile fixed on his pale lips. Pa told me his story.

When the war came, Ab Cheevers sold his farm and put his wife in to live with his brother. He got something like a thousand pounds for his farm and took the newly issued Continental bills, then at par, in payment. He left the money with his wife and, with his five sons, he went off to fight for freedom.

One by one, his five sons were killed in action.

Ab served throughout the whole war and, when peace came, he returned home. His wife still had the thousand pounds. When he went out to buy a new farm, he found that his thousand pounds were worth just twenty-five pounds. Ab sued the man who had bought the farm, holding that he had been paid in worthless paper. The court held the sale was valid, even though the money had depreciated to practically nothing. Ab shrugged and tried to do the best he could. He was stone broke now, but he was known as an honest man and he was able to borrow enough to buy himself a new piece of land.

With his wife, he tried to rebuild his life. He never had a chance. His brother died and his nephews went under, packing up and heading into the Wyoming territory. Then his wife died. Ab tried to keep his place running, but when the fall of '84 came he found he couldn't sell enough of his crops to pay his taxes, much less the interest on his loan. Six months later he was sold out. He was alone and penniless, his five sons sacrificed for liberty, his wife dead, his land swept away.

"So there he is," Pa concluded. "And there I guess he'll die."

Ab's case was an extreme. Pa told me about many more of his fellow prisoners, most of whom were in for much more trivial debts. Some were in for as little as 15 shillings.

I was only too glad to get out of that dismal, smelly place. But I could now understand how my father managed to maintain his cheerfulness. Compared to many of these men, Pa was well off. He at least knew my mother and Increase were being well taken care of by my Uncle Enoch. I said as much as we walked to the door.

"Well, to tell the truth, Warren," he said slowly, "I'm not easy about Enoch. He bought in my land, you know. He had to borrow on a six month's note to do it. That note's coming due soon and maybe Enoch can get it renewed and maybe not."

"Uncle Enoch told me about it," I said. "But there's nothing to worry about. From what I've heard, it'll take a year before the case gets into court and another year before it's tried. By that time, we ought to be able to pay it."

126

"I hope so," Pa said, a bit gloomily. He smiled. "Anyway, I'm wishing you luck. I'm damn tired of sitting in here."

"You'll be out in a week," I assured him.

I banged on the door and waited a few moments. When the lock turned over, I said goodby to Pa and departed.

Outside again, I remembered that letter I had promised to deliver for Dan Shays and regretted I had made the offer, for I was anxious to get to Boston at the earliest possible moment. However, the side trip wouldn't take me over an hour, so I decided it wouldn't make much difference, either to myself or my father. I inquired of a passerby whether the ferry was still running at its accustomed place and was assured it was. Accordingly, I headed up Main Street to reach the foot of Elm.

I hated to pay ferry fare for the horse, but I dared not risk leaving her tied up outside some house or store. Thieves were too prevalent these days. So, I had to spend 10d to cross the river.

West Springfield was a very small town compared to Springfield itself. The road up from the riverbank, was steep and winding and in an abominable state of repairs, the ruts being gouged nearly to ravines by the rains. At the Common, the road branched, the left fork turning south to Connecticut, the western road leading on into upper New York State. There at the crossroads was the town, a few houses clumped about the green. But the way was well shaded by the tall elms, giving relief from the warming sun.

Strangely, the Common was alive with men at this early hour. More strangely, those men were armed with muskets. Most strangely, they were drilling. The drillmaster, a burly, barrel-chested man with a leonine head and a stentorian voice, was extraordinarily patient with them. Yet there were times when patience withered. Then, after a pause to glare at his men, he would lift his head and curse them until the very leaves threatened to fall from the trees. The troops, if they can be dignified by the name, hung their heads in shame.

After watching awhile, I proceeded on to Stabbin's Tavern, where a number of men were gathered outside watching the drill. They gave me curious stares as I approached.

"Could you direct me to Mr. Luke Day, please?"

A scrawny necked man pointed. "That's Luke out there!"

He cupped his hands to his mouth. "Luke! Hey, Luke. Here's a feller wants to see yer!"

The drillmaster saluted and snapped an order to his band. They turned and marched toward the tavern, their leader hupping to keep them in step. They were all young men, except one or two, and none, obviously, had ever done any soldiering.

"The militia?" I asked the scrawny one.

"Shucks, no." The man showed his buck teeth in a smile. "That there's Luke's pussenel army. They don't look like much now, but Luke'll get 'em in shape afore they're needed."

I gave the man a startled glance. But before I could ask for what they'd be needed, Luke Day came striding over.

"Mr. Day?" I asked.

"Major Day," he corrected.

"I beg your pardon." I gave him the letter. "Mr. Shays asked me to deliver this to you."

"Captain Shays," he said absently, turning the letter over. "You're a friend of Dan's?" When I admitted it, he took my hand and crushed it. "A friend of Captain Shays is a friend of mine. I thank you for the service, sir. May I have the pleasure of your company in a drink? He turned about. "Company dismissed!" he roared. Then he seized my arm and practically dragged me inside. "Please sit down, Mr. . . . Mr. . . . ?"

"Hascott," I supplied.

"Hascott." He straddled his chair and dropped down heavily, pounding on the table. "Stebbins! Stebbins! Drinks for myself and Mr. Hascott. . . . You'll excuse me, sir."

His resonant voice made him sound as if he was giving me an order. Whether Mr. Stebbins was frightened of Luke Day's great voice I cannot presume to say. But we were hardly settled before he came running with two mugs of rum. Luke Day tore open the letter and read slowly, his lips moving over every word.

"Did you attend the auction, Mr. Hascott?" he demanded. "Dan says here he was on the way to the sale of Mrs. Decker's property. Did they run that bastard Madden off?"

"Yes, after a while." And I gave him a sketchy account of what had transpired.

"Good! Good!" He slapped the table and laughed. "By God, sir, that's the spirit! It's about time the people got sense. We're through knuckling down to them Boston bastards. We're not going to be kicked around like dogs much longer, I can tell you that. They'd better steer clear of this town. My boys are ready to give a dose of lead to the first bastard who crosses the river. Excuse me, sir." And he resumed reading the letter.

Luke Day paused often to gulp down rum, as if reading was thirsty work, and work it surely was for him. He looked up suddenly, impaling me with his stern brown eyes.

"Hascott! You're related to Caleb Hascott?"

"I'm his son," I admitted.

He pointed accusingly. "The one in Algiers! Dan was telling me about you. Those bastards charged your father fifty pounds for transmitting money to release you. And now, he's in jail for it. By God, sir, if I were you, I'd tear down that jail, plank by plank."

I had to smile. "I think I can arrange his release with a lot less labor, Major."

"Perhaps, perhaps. Mark me, Mr. Hascott, the people are stirring. The time has almost come. Soon, we strike!"

"Strike!" I echoed. "Against whom? The government?"

"Against the defilers of our glorious Revolution, against those tyrants who seek to oppress the people, against those Devil's spawn who conspire to seize the people's liberties. We are not blind, sir. We see the rich wallowing in luxuries wrung from the bodies of the poor. We see the rich maneuvering to crush those who would cry out against their iniquitous machinations. Will we tamely submit to being stripped of our lands, thrown into jail, deprived of the very liberties we won by our own blood? Never! We cast out one king. We will never allow our own arrogant aristocrats to raise another despot in his place. Americans shall never be slaves!"

My impulse was to laugh and cheer his caricature of an oration. But his heavy features were deadly serious. A stir at the door made me look about. The men Day had been drilling were gathered there, staring rapturously at their leader. With some astonishment I realized they believed this man.

"You're suggesting there's to be armed conflict?" I asked.

Luke Day waved impatiently. "Nonsense. There will be no need to use arms. We need only demonstrate the strength of the people. Would they dare defy the will of the people?"

"Suppose they—meaning the rich, I take it—do defy the people?" I persisted.

"Nonsense," Day proclaimed. "They have the example of George the Third before them. They will not dare. Even they know the people will not stand idly by and allow them to trample upon our liberties. Our liberties are sacred."

I rose. "It's been a pleasure meeting you, Major. I suppose there are many who feel as you do."

Luke Day got up and escorted me to the door, his men scattering respectfully as he approached. "Mr. Hascott, there are some complacent fools who do not see what is happening under their very noses. Even those fools are awakening. Soon, these western counties will be fairly alive to the danger. Even now, there are more of us who are aware of the danger than those rich bastards in Boston realize. As soon as you have been among us a short time, you will see the truth of my words." He shook my hand heartily. "I'm glad to have met you, Mr. Hascott. I know you are a patriot. I know you will be in our ranks, when the time comes to rise and break the chains that bind us."

Chapter 9

LUKE DAY had made a deep impression upon me. All the way to Boston I kept thinking about him and wondering if dissatisfaction was as widespread as he would have it. That injustice existed, that many of my neighbors were in an angry mood, I had already seen. But whether the public was aroused to fighting pitch I could hardly determine on such meager evidence. I would have liked to have spent some time plumbing the sentiments of the people of these back counties, but I did not wish to linger and add expense to my trip. Nor did I want my father to languish in that foul jail any longer than absolutely necessary.

By hastening, I managed to reach Boston shortly before dark the second day after leaving home. I went directly to State House, figuring to catch Mr. Blair there before he left work. I wanted to get a line on Graham before visiting him, for if he had any weaknesses I was determined to exploit them. But I was doomed to disappointment. Mr. Blair was not at his desk. Indeed, he was not in Boston at all. A clerk in the office opposite his told me Mr. Blair had gone to Hubbardston on private business.

That put me in a quandary. I had decided to ask Mr. Burdick to intercede for me if Graham balked at an equitable settlement. But pride forbade me to follow that course except as a last resort. Then I thought of Ethan. Being connected with Blanchard and Gorham, Ethan might be an even better source of information than his father. Accordingly, I hurried down to Ethan's place of business on Long Wharf. I took care not to announce myself by name, for Ethan's employers might have heard of my participation in the *Mary* affair and

131

might connect our names, thus learning that Ethan was responsible for the leak. But, exasperatingly, I found that Ethan was not in, either.

"You a friend of the boy's?" the clerk asked, eagerly. "I think that young idiot's eloping. I hear his father went out to Hubbardston. If you have any influence with the boy, you'll stop him. Ridiculous idea, eloping. Why, Gorham's as much against his marrying Amy as old Blair. Ethan will lose his job." The clerk tapped me on the chest and lowered his voice confidentially. "I heard Blanchard say they'll take Ethan in as junior partner just as soon as business shows a little more life."

"I see. It would be foolish for him to give that up, wouldn't it? Where can I find Ethan, do you know?"

"Sure, at Amy's—Fitch's store. It's on Dock Square, right by Fanueil Hall. You can't miss it."

I thanked the clerk and hastened up to Dock Square. It would be just like that fool boy to rush off and think afterward. The awakening would be all the harder since he would have the responsibility of a wife on his shoulders. I couldn't resist a chuckle. I seemed fated to take a paternalistic interest in young Ethan Blair.

Dock Square was quieting down at this hour, the trucks and carts of the farmers wending their way out of the big market place, their day's business done. The fishmongers were closing down their stands, too, though many of the canny housewives were shopping and getting bargains in fish or fruits and vegetables which had been brought in fresh that morning.

I found Fitch's store easily enough. It was a rather small place, each pane of the checkered window gleaming bright. The sign overhead proclaimed Mr. Fitch's elegant selection of groceries from all corners of the world.

There was no one about and the door to the back apartment was closed. I rapped for attention and a muffled "Coming" seeped from inside. I waited patiently, looking about me, reveling in the exotic smells of pepper and allspice and ginger, which conjured up pictures—distorted ones, I'm sure—of the Indies. The profusion of merchandise was bewildering and it was some minutes before I saw that everything was in precise order.

On the left side of the room, as you entered, were the

liquors—casks of rum, Massachusetts and Jamaica, casks of Geneva, Claret, Madiera, shelves filled with jugs and bottles of brandy, sherry, Teneriff, Arack from the Cape of Good Hope, bottled porter and ale and all kinds of cordials. Next were the teas, bins of Sushong, Bohea, Hyson, chests piled up of Imperial and Toukey teas. On the shelves were fat jars of cinnamon, ginger, sago, pepper and other spices. Below were other small chests of spices. Next came a short counter on which was Mr. Fitch's brass balance and his weights. Behind the counter were the staples, bins of flour, coffee, oatmeal, rice, peas and so on. There were also piles of loaf sugar and the shelves were crammed with bottles and jars of items like marmalade, sweet oil, English ketsup, dried sweetmeats in boxes, preserved sugar plums, all sorts of other dried and candied fruits. Before the counter were small casks of currants and raisins, a barrel of salted fish, an open cask of olives and an astonishing variety of other items.

Along the back wall was a hearth, now boarded up, for a Franklin stove stood in the center of the floor. Along that wall were the heavy items, barrels of flour and of coarse and fine salt, barrels of vinegar and molasses set up in rows, their spouts outstretched. The corner held a vast assortment of china cups and saucers, dishes and assorted glassware and earthenware, the boxes showing they were all imports from England.

Along the left wall were dyestuffs, indigo, alum, madder, logwood, also brimstone and chalk, bar iron, boxes of hair powder, soaps, cases of fresh lemons and an assortment of drugs like Virginia snake root, stick liquorish, and shelves of patented medicines like Dr. Hill's Balsam of Honey or Duffy's Elixir. At the other corner, to the right of the entrance, was a section for tobaccos, kegs of Kites' Foot, Baltimore Numbers One, Two and Three, snuff in bottles and bladders and an assortment of pipes. Lastly, right alongside the door, was a huge pile of cheeses, on which was set this sign:

THESE CHEESES MADE IN MASSACHUSETTS
NONE FINER MADE IN AMERICA
More Reasonable than Imported

I sampled a good deal of Mr. Fitch's stock, almonds, raisins, a fig, even a few preserved cherries before realizing I had been waiting an inordinately long time. I heard voices coming from behind the door leading into the back apartment, so I took it upon myself to knock. The door opened and I was confronted by a small, thinnish man wearing thick spectacles. There were deep lines graven about his harassed mouth and his turned up chin and turned down nose gave him the look of one who had caught his face in a paper press. He might have, he was that near sighted.

"Mr. Fitch?" I asked and he bobbed his head. "I'm Warren Hascott. I was told I might find Ethan here."

"Ethan!" It was almost a groan. "You're a friend of his? Come in, come in." His stooped shoulders seemed to bear the weight of the world. "Ethan, here's a friend of yours."

Ethan was sitting in a rocker by the dead hearth, scowling at the blackened stones. His head turned slowly and, when he saw me, he jumped up and came over, extending his hand.

"Mr. Hascott! I'm pleased to see you again."

I shook hands with him, then spied Amy over at the table by the rear window, her elbows almost covered with bread dough. She looked absurdly like a yellow-headed doll playing at housewife.

I waved and she formed a silent greeting with her lips. "I hear your father's out of town, Ethan. I stopped by at State House. The gentleman in your office told me you'd be here."

"I suppose you talked to that ass Peckworth. He still thinks I'm a baby. He straightened to his full five feet ten. "Mr. Hascott, I've decided to go into the Wyoming territory."

"I've heard there's been a lot of trouble there, Ethan. You may have better opportunities in the Ohio region. Didn't I read somewhere that a new company was forming to open the territory?"

"Yes," Fitch put in. "The Ohio Company isn't fully organized yet, though. It's to be headed by General Putnam and Colonel Tupper." Fitch suddenly cocked his head, startled, and he peered up at me. "You think they should go?"

"They?" I echoed. "You mean you're taking Amy along?"

Amy turned from her dough board. "If he wants to go, I'll go with him."

Fitch shook his head glumly. "I don't like it, Mr. Hascott, I honestly don't. But if Amy wants to go. . . ."

"Absurd," I exclaimed. "Ethan wouldn't want to take her

134

out there, would you, Ethan?" I gave him no chance to answer. "Why, that's virgin wilderness. Ethan should go on ahead, break the ground, set up a stout cabin and plant his fields. By next fall, Amy can come out and help with the harvesting. You wouldn't want her around in the summer, of course. With her fair skin, she'd be burned to a crisp. Besides being eaten by the flies."

"I could stand it," Amy insisted. But her voice was a good trifle weaker than before.

"But if the Indians were in a warlike mood, you'd only be in Ethan's way. How have the Indians acted lately, Mr. Fitch?"

Fitch looked worried. "Badly, very badly. The Kentucky settlements have been bothered a lot. I hear General Clark is raising an expedition to go after Big Knife."

Ethan wasn't listening any more. Very slowly, he walked over to Amy. He took her chin in his hand and lifted her blue eyes to his.

"Would you go with me, Amy?" he asked softly.

Amy's eyes were glistening. "Of course, I would. I couldn't let you g . . get killed by Indians."

He sighed and his hand dropped. "No, you weren't made for that kind of life, Amy." He frowned and jammed his fists into his pocket, paced slowly. "I don't know what to do, Mr. Hascott. If only I had some capital. . . . But my father. . . ."

"Have you tried to raise the money elsewhere?" I asked.

Ethan nodded reluctantly. "I have a proposition that's unbeatable. But no one wants to give me a chance. I'm too young. I have no experience." He waved disgustedly. "I don't know."

"On a purely business basis, Ethan, why should your father lend you money if no one else can see the worth of your idea? Personally, I think you have an unbeatable proposition in Gorham & Blanchard. I understand you're due to be taken into the firm. You have a future there. Just be patient."

"What good would that do?" Ethan growled. "Even if I do get ahead there, father's still against Amy. He and Gorham are old friends. They think alike. Gorham would discharge me if I married Amy without father's consent. Don't you see? That's why I want to be independent."

I took his arm. "Your father isn't really cold-hearted. I

135

don't know why he doesn't like Amy. Maybe it's because she's so pretty. He may think she's frivolous on that account. He'll come around in time. You wait and see."

Ethan rocked back and forth a moment, then glanced at the girl. "What do you think, Amy?"

"I think Mr. Hascott's right, Ethan," Amy replied. "We should wait a little longer."

"Sure, father's bound to see your good qualities soon." Ethan grinned sheepishly. "Amy's very stubborn, Mr. Hascott. I didn't win her over until you came. Thanks." He pecked Amy's forehead. "I'll be back in an hour. Goodby, Mr. Fitch .. Oh, did you want to see my father for anything special, Mr. Hascott?"

"Well, I wanted a little information. Maybe you can help me better than your father. Do you know a man named Graham?"

Ethan frowned. "Not personally. I know him by reputation. He's in the Spanish and Portuguese trade—liquors, mostly. But his main interest is maritime insurance. He's a hard man, I understand, not very well liked."

I chewed my lips. "That doesn't sound so good. He holds a note of my father's. I was thinking of settling."

Ethan shook his head. "Not a chance. Graham will insist on full payment. He wouldn't take a farthing off." Then, his eyes narrowed. "Unless—. He had money on the *Mary*. In gratitude. . . ." Ethan broke off, shaking his head again. "No, that man doesn't know the meaning of the word."

"How's his financial position?" I asked.

"Like everybody else, he's crying for cash. But I don't think. . . ." His eyes widened. "Say, you're a friend of the Burdicks, aren't you? I understand Mr. Burdick just lent him a substantial sum of money to cover the insurance on the *Dragon Fly*. She went ashore at Nantucket two weeks ago—a total loss. Graham was hit hard."

"What sort of a note did he give Burdick? Short term, long term or what? And what sort of security?"

"I wouldn't know that, Mr. Hascott. But I think I can find out for you. I'll be back here in an hour. Won't you stay for supper? Amy, do you mind?"

"Mind?" Amy echoed. "I insist, Mr. Hascott."

"There, that's settled." Ethan kissed her again. "I'll be right back. Don't go away." And he rushed out.

Mr. Fitch peered up at me and, though his face still had that squeezed look, the harassed wrinkles smoothed away from his mouth. Then he looked about in alarm. Amy was sniffling. She wiped her hands on her apron, dabbed her eyes and suddenly ran upstairs, sending back a choked, "Excuse me."

My brows went up. "Was she happy or disappointed?"

Fitch scratched his thinning hair. "Danged if I know, Mr. Hascott. She was against the idea of going west all along." He tisked and went to the cupboard. "Guess I don't understand women at all. But we ought to have a drink on—" His jaw dropped and he looked around quickly, as if frightened, then gave me a sheepish look. "I forgot. My wife went over to Roxbury to help her sister have a baby."

Before we finished our drink—Boston made rum, he assured me—he was called out into the store by a customer banging on the counter. I followed him and watched him wait on a lady. She was very fastidious, insisting upon the finest imported powdered sugar. Mr. Fitch tried valiantly, but could not sell her the town made loaf sugar. Mr. Fitch obviously was a fanatic on home products and, as soon as he was free, I asked him why.

"It's imports that's ruining this country, Mr. Hascott," Fitch said vehemently, "British imports. Ever since the war, them damn British have been flooding the country with their goods. And what's the result? Our own craftsmen have been thrown out of work. Our hatters, shoemakers, blacksmiths, wheelrights, pewterers, none of them can compete against cheap British manufactured goods. So, Americans starve while English factors get rich. Not only that, them English suck out the life blood of our country—our specie. I haven't seen a gold piece in over a year. It ain't right, Mr. Hascott. And I, for one, won't have a hand in encouraging them damn bloodsuckers. Home manufacturers, that's the salvation of this country. Everything you buy that's made in America makes a job for an American. Everything you buy that's made in England is a tribute at the feet of George the Third. Damnation to the English and their King, say I."

I had to smile. "That's all very well, Mr. Fitch. But what can one man do? Are other merchants of your mind?"

Fitch sighed heavily. "Wish to God they had the sense to know what's good for them, sir. About a year ago, we held a town meeting. We resolved to buy no more goods from British merchants. We pledged we wouldn't lease our shops, warehouses and wharves to them. We said we wouldn't employ anybody who helped the British by trucks and carts and labor. We promised we'd encourage our own home manufactures. The week after, the tradesmen and the manufacturers got together and passed similar resolutions."

"Then what happened?"

Fitch snorted. "The week after that, everybody was trying to grab the business the other fellow let go. Patriots, bah! Anything to make a profit." He threw his hands up. "Nobody does nothing. And the General Court, damn its soul, acts the same way. Petitions come in from the country towns by the bushel. 'We need cash. We need relief from taxes. We need higher duties.' 'Sure,' the General Court says, 'we'll study the matter.' And that's the end of it. Nobody does nothing. Meantime, I'm getting poorer."

A curious man, Mr. Fitch, meek within his own home where his will could prevail, strong outside where his voice was a mere cry in the wilderness. Yet, just the same, I had to like his sort.

"My customers," Fitch went on, "are mostly shipyard workers and laborers. Almost all of them are out of work. Our merchant fleet shrinks while British bottoms carry the goods we buy. The hatter next door was put out of business because he couldn't compete with the British hats dumped on our shores by the thousands."

"But surely there must be a duty."

"The British pay the duty and still can undersell us." Mr. Fitch plopped a dried currant into his mouth, chewed furiously and swallowed. "The duty's too low. And you know why? It's because them damn aristocrats in the Senate won't raise them. They won't encourage our own manufactures. Why? I'll tell you why. The Senate's controlled by the big money men. They're getting rich by selling British imports— sucking the country's lifeblood, I say."

I could understand now why Salderman and his friends were so fearful of allowing the news of the *Mary's* cargo to become public. I couldn't know how much specie the ship had carried out of the country, but whatever the amount, it was just that much less hard money in circulation.

"It's a hard problem, isn't it?" I commented.

"Hard, yes. But the people will solve it, one way or the other. Things are stirring, Mr. Hascott, things are stirring." Fitch leaned closer, his voice dropping confidentially. "Groton's having a town meeting for the purpose of discussing grievances and calling a county convention. But they're not depending on words alone, Mr. Hascott. I hear tell Job Shattuck is drilling men up there. If nothing comes of the convention—well, the people can stand just so much. We fought for liberty once. Maybe we'll have to do it again."

Mr. Fitch nodded quickly and gave me a broad wink.

As soon as Ethan returned from his office, we had supper. Amy might have looked like a fragile doll, but she certainly could cook. She apologized profusely for the commonness of the meal, but she was apologizing for a dream. It was a stew, but no ordinary stew. In it were bits of tripe, lamb, diced potatoes, diced dried carrots spiced with caraway and cloves. After my third helping, I assured Ethan that he had only to have Amy cook a meal for his father and there would be no further question about the marriage.

I lingered until after eight o'clock, talking politics with Mr. Fitch and, when he could spare the time from Amy, with Ethan. I was feeling very good when I left the Fitch's, not only because I had an invitation to return for supper another time, but also because Ethan had managed to supply me with some encouraging information about Mr. Graham. My father's creditor was himself close to bankruptcy. If only one of his creditors gave him a push, over he'd go. Only Mr. Burdick's efforts had kept Graham from crashing. Burdick was doing it less from friendship than from a desire to save his own money invested in Mr. Graham's enterprises. But the best news Ethan had given me was that Graham was dining out this evening, at the Burdicks.

The Burdick's big house on Long Lane was gay with lights shining from every window. Since it was then about eight-thirty, I felt fairly sure that the supper was over. I dismounted at the front gate, tied my horse to the hitching post and stared up at the house. Yes, the jagged hum of feminine voices was drifting out of the open parlor windows. I still hesitated to intrude. I thought it might be an imposition to try to transact business at a time like this. I decided it would be better to leave my business until morning. But if I hesitated to go in, I had no thought of going away. Tomorrow I might not have the chance to come here. And I was determined not to lose the opportunity of seeing Judith.

My heart was beating a bit faster as I went up the path and knocked on the big front door. I chided myself for feeling so impatient, so like a callow, smitten youth. I almost wanted to turn around and run away and come back some other time. After all, I had no right to break in like this, even though I was a friend in good standing. My courage had not quite run out when the door opened. Polly's plain face broke into a broad smile.

"Oh, good evening, Mr. Hascott. It's nice to see you again, sir. I'll tell Miss Judith you're here."

"Wait!" I called after her.

She either didn't hear me or pretended not to. I was peeved. I didn't want to appear too forward in Judith's eyes or, more especially, in the eyes of her mother.

Judith in an evening gown was a breath taking sight. Her dress was of rich yellow tiffany, very sheer, edged with lace and peppered with red flowers sewed on. The flowers looked almost as real as natural roses. The neckline was low and off the shoulders—nice soft shoulders—and, having seen her without pads, I was aware her hips did not need the artificial aids that made for the fullness of her sweeping skirts.

"Warren! It was nice of you to come." Her head cocked slyly as she extended her hand. "Business, I suppose? Or may I hope I was the attraction?"

"Business is the excuse," I countered, laughing. "But most certainly you are the attraction." I became flustered and dropped her hand, realizing I was squeezing it too tightly. "I really must keep my mind on business."

Judith crinkled her nose. "Why?"

"I often wondered myself why the copybook advises it." Then, I shifted uneasily. "I didn't know you had company. I'll come back tomorrow sometime."

140

"Nonsense, Warren," was the expected reaction. "You're as welcome as any of our guests—more than some," she added with a laugh. "I'll call Papa. The men are still digesting their food with sage conversation. I wish I could say the same for the ladies."

Judith's frankness—almost brazenness—was a renewed source of amazement to me. I was reminded of Beulah. Not that Judith's frankness was of the same quality. Hers seemed more the product of sophistication. Beulah's was more native, naive. Mr. Burdick came waddling out of the dining room, a step behind his daughter. Judith wriggled her fingers at me and returned to the parlor. Mr. Burdick's smile and outstretched hand assured me I was genuinely welcome.

"I'm delighted to see you, Warren. Was it really business that brought you? Or was my daughter covering for you?"

"Truly business, sir. But I didn't know . . . I mean, I don't want to intrude with such matters at a time like this."

"Bosh, my boy." The smile faded from his plump face. "I suppose you came to Boston to see Graham. We know, of course. You'll forgive us for not wanting to impart such news to you on your first day back. I can make amends, though. We can dispose of the business tonight. Graham happens to be here."

"Oh, does he?" I asked with mock surprise. "Well, I'd be delighted to meet him. But I think it best if I leave the business matter until tomorrow. I . . . ah . . . I haven't enough to pay the note in full. I figured on trying to persuade him to settle."

Mr. Burdick's eyelids drooped. "You want me to help you?"

"Oh, no." I flushed. "I came to you for a letter of introduction. I thought perhaps . . . Well, if he had money on the *Mary* he might be more inclined to . . . if you told him . . . I mean. . . ."

Burdick laughed and patted my shoulder. "I understand." He lowered his voice. "You stopped elsewhere before you came here, eh? I suppose you know I hold most of his."

"Well. . . ." I grinned sheepishly.

Burdick winked. "Handle him any way you like. He's not exactly a friend of mine. He's shaky right now, but he's clever. I think he'll pull out of it all right. And if he doesn't—Well, I might be minimizing my losses by being nice to him . . . in a business way. See?"

"Perfectly, sir."

My host chuckled and took my arm. "Let's go in, then." The dining room was brilliantly lighted by fat sperm candles in the crystal chandelier overhead. The table had been cleared, except for the brandy decanters and glasses and plates of confections. A rack of clay pipes and a silver jar of tobacco had been set out for the convenience of the five men present. Two of them I recognized at once. Salderman's long, equine face lit up as I entered and he waved. The other I did not know personally, but I had seen his stern, bulldog face many times. He was General Artemus Ward, first Commander-in-Chief of the Continental Armies and now Chief Justice and President of the Senate. Burdick was beaming as he took me to the table.

"Gentlemen, may I present a young friend of mine, Mr. Warren Hascott? Jothan and I have spoken of him. General Ward, Mr. Lang, Mr. Trowbridge, Mr. Graham."

General Ward just grunted as he shook my hand. Trowbridge, a thin ancient, had a long neck and a small wrinkled head that made him look like a curious crane. He murmured politely in response to the introduction. Mr. Lang rose and stretched his hand across the table. He was sharp faced, his pointed chin and ears giving him the look of a shrewd foxhound. Later I learned he was one of Boston's most successful lawyers.

"The rest of these gentlemen have much to thank you for, Mr. Hascott," he commented as he took my hand.

Graham's head was cocked. "Haven't I heard your name somewhere before, Mr. Hascott?"

"He helped us to get the *Mary* safely to sea," Salderman said, drawing up a chair for me.

"Oh." Graham's hand was limp in mine, the dead fish type. "I trust you've been discreet."

Graham was a handsome man, his rugged masculine features broken by a deep cleft in his chin. His frown seemed perpetual and gave him an air of sullenness. Of all the men present, his coat was the finest, a rich blue velvet trimmed with silver lace. He wore a bobbed, powdered white wig.

"We're anxious to hear what you found in the western counties, Mr. Hascott," Salderman remarked as I sat down. "We've been discussing the situation. Graham, here, passed through on his way from Albany. He seems to think there's a possibility of armed revolt. What do you think?"

I cleared my throat once or twice, a bit uneasy in this ruffed-shirt company. "I'm inclined to agree."

"There!" Graham said triumphantly. "Those swine out there have lost the last vestiges of decency. It's disheartening to see how perverted the morals of the people have become since the end of the war. Indolence, selfishness, dishonesty, all are amazingly prevalent. Why, it's become a game to cheat creditors." He leaned forward, his eyes intense. "I met a friend of mine in Northampton. He told me he had been mobbed by a band of ruffians at an auction in Pelham. Why, they tore off his clothes and would have tarred and feathered him if he hadn't escaped in time. That's outrageous. We ought to call out troops and teach those rogues some respect for law."

As you can imagine, I began to burn. His friend must have been Madden. But I knew better than to get angry and say something I might regret. After all, I still had some business to attend with that man. So, I kept my mouth shut.

"What do you think, Mr. Hascott?" Trowbridge asked. "I have money invested out there. Should I liquidate?"

I considered my reply a moment. "Well, I wouldn't presume to give you advice, sir, but I don't think it good business to sell out those people indiscriminately. At auction, the property rarely brings a quarter of its true value and, at the same time, the sale deprives a man of his means of livelihood. As a rule, those men are honest. They're just unable to pay. Given time, I'm sure they'll honor their obligations in full."

"Bah!" Graham exclaimed. "I don't believe in coddling debtors. Give those knaves encouragement and we'll never collect anything. Time, huh! Time to conceal their assets, that's what they want. I'm on to their tricks."

"Well," Lang drawled, "it does seem foolish to throw them in jail—the honest with the dishonest. Don't mistake me. I believe the fradulent should be treated as criminals, the same as a thief or a man who adulterates the coin. But isn't it a bit ridiculous to imprison an honest man while he might be working?"

"There's two sides to that," Salderman put in. "Many of us don't want to sell those men out, especially for a fraction of

143

the debt. But business is bad here, too. Sometimes it becomes necessary to liquidate our holdings at any price, just to raise the money to keep afloat. Some men are panicked into grabbing farthings and losing pounds. But some of us can't help ourselves. Times are pinching us hard, too."

"That's still no reason for putting men in jail," Lang said. "God knows I've done enough of it, but it's wrong. There ought to be a more sensible way of tackling the problem."

"Wouldn't paper money help?" I asked.

Had I thrown a bomb into their midst, I couldn't have shocked them more. They gasped and turned and looked at me as if I were some sort of a mad dog.

"Now, I remember the name," Graham said softly, his eyes narrowing. "Hascott. I sent a man named Has . . ."

Burdick coughed and rose hastily. "Shall we join the ladies, gentlemen? I'm afraid they're wondering if we've decided to abandon them entirely."

Lang pushed back his chair. "An excellent suggestion. This conversation was getting depressing."

As the men drifted out, Burdick took Mr. Graham aside and spoke to him. Graham nodded grimly and stalked across the hall to Mr. Burdick's study. Burdick gave me a wink and a nod and I followed Graham, feeling a bit weak in the knees. But I decided that boldness, attack, was my only hope.

Mr. Graham was standing by the hearth, hands on his hips, as I came in and closed the door. He was scowling.

"Mr. Burdick asked me to talk over your father's debt. I'm afraid there's little to talk over. If you come to my office in the morning, I'll give you the exact amount due and you can pay it."

I smiled and sank into the nearest chair and threw my leg over the arm, trying to appear perfectly nonchalant.

"Well, I don't suppose it's absolutely necessary to have the exact amount, do you, Mr. Graham? I sort of figured you'd be willing to settle."

"I am," Graham said abruptly. "For the exact amount."

I drew forth three gold coins, tossed them idly from hand to hand. The color of gold and the clinking was not lost upon my friend. He became less rigid.

"How much is the debt? he asked gruffly.

"Two hundred and thirty odd pounds."

"How much do you want to settle for?"

I stared at the ceiling. "Say, a hundred and thirty?"

"Absurd. Wouldn't think of it. Young man, what kind of a fool do you think I am?" He snorted and started for the door. "There's no use discussing the matter further."

"That's what I told Mr. Burdick," I said. Graham was past my chair, but I heard him pause in midstride, so I added coolly, "Mr. Burdick assured me you'd be reasonable."

Graham came back and planted himself in front of my chair. "I'm a reasonable man, Mr. Hascott. Make a reasonable offer."

"One hundred and thirty pounds."

Graham waved impatiently. "Wouldn't consider it." He glowered down at me. "Young man, I lent your father money as far back as '78. He borrowed more in '80. He ceased interest payments in '84, two years ago. Naturally, I sued. I'm entitled to the full amount. But make a fair offer and I'll settle, as a favor to Burdick."

I shook my head. "You're not doing anybody any favors, Mr. Graham. The money my father borrowed in '80 was paid off in '81 in hard cash. That left only the original debt, which he borrowed in continental money. Actually, you cheated my father. You lent him depreciated paper and asked for specie in return."

Graham stiffened. "That has been thrashed out in the courts, young man. The courts sustained me."

"Law or no law, my father was cheated." I leaned back. "One hundred and thirty, in gold. Take it or leave it."

Graham chewed his lips. "Two hundred."

"One hundred and thirty pounds," I said, slowly and distinctly. "You already have received four hundred percent profit. I won't offer a farthing more. Since you reject it. . . ." I got up languidly ". . . you can pay my father's board bill just as long as you like. But I wouldn't be a bit surprised if he was out in a week and a certain usurer sitting in his place. Now, if you'll excuse me, sir. . . ."

"One moment!" Graham barked. He glared at me. "I happen to need cash. It's a deal."

I went over to the desk and got a piece of paper from the drawer. "We can settle it right now. Write out a receipt to me, Mr. Graham, stating that the debt of Caleb Hascott is paid in full. And I want this understood, sir. You are to send the papers for my father's release to Springfield tomorrow."

Graham was outraged and his face became very red. But he beat down his anger and planked himself at the desk. I took off my moneybelt and counted out a hundred and thirty pounds in gold. His pettiness showed in his eyes. I was giving him sterling money, which, at prevailing prices, meant that he was getting a few pounds more than our bargain entitled him to. I said nothing, for I wanted him to feel he was getting the better of me.

He scribbled out the receipt, carefully put the money in his purse and got up, a stiff smile fixed on his rugged face. Without a word he stalked out of the room. I had made an enemy.

Mr. Burdick was standing by the parlor door and, as Graham came across the entry hall, he came out. They exchanged a brief word and Graham went on. Burdick turned and looked after him, then winked at me.

"Everything went well?"

I grinned. "I settled for a third off."

I explained fully what had transpired between us, for I didn't want him to get the story from anyone else, assuming Graham was fool enough to let it get into the hands of the gossips. I was careful to explain my father had borrowed in debased paper, lest Burdick think I was merely sharping. When I was finished I was relieved to hear Mr. Burdick's throaty chuckle.

"Warren, you're still thinking of that offer I made, aren't you? I can use a man of your talents in my business." He gripped my arm. "Come along, I'll introduce you to the ladies."

The blue and silver motif of the delicate parlor furniture was enhanced by the rich red and blue and green velvets and silks of the ladies. Mrs. Trowbridge and Mrs. Ward proved to be elderly ladies, as might be expected, the former sharp-faced, the latter having features more round and less wrinkled. Both were gracious and asked polite questions about my confinement in Algiers and congratulated me on my escape. Mrs. Lang was a young woman, near Judith's age, very pretty in her green and gold gown which matched the green lights in her restless eyes. Passing on, Mr. Burdick took me to the sofa, where his wife and Mrs. Graham were seated in conversation with Mr. Lang and General Ward. Mrs. Graham had seen better days. She was . . . well, fat is the word, not plump. She had three chins and thick upper arms and shoulders which would better have been covered to hide the rolls of flesh. Her bewigged head was carried high and haughty and her hand was clammy.

"So, this is the farmer boy you were telling me about, Abigail." She dropped my hand as if it was dirty. "The war has wrought such changes, hasn't it?"

I reddened with embarrassment and barely managed to check my retort to her implication. I merely bowed.

Mrs. Burdick surprised me by the tightening of her thin lips. "I'm delighted to see you again, Warren. Delighted," she added pointedly. She smiled stiffly, her natural way. "Do rescue my daughter from Jothan, Warren. I'm afraid she'll succumb one of these days to his fine phrases and manners."

"Perhaps I can be the antidote, M'am."

And I couldn't resist bowing directly at Mrs. Graham. Both Lang and General Ward coughed and turned away.

Judith was sitting by the spinet, chatting away in gay animation with Salderman. The cynical smile and intent look on his long face made me dislike him a little more, though I knew I did not have the right to feel that way. Judith laughed and, as her eyes lifted, she saw me and beckoned with her fan.

"Warren! Jothan is asking for my hand again—for the fifty-sixth time—or is it the fifty-seventh? Do you think I should?"

"As a biased judge, I would say no."

Salderman chuckled and rose and slapped my back. "I accept your judgment, Mr. Hascott. Perhaps you can find a vulnerable spot in her armor." He bowed. "You'll excuse me?"

Judith invited me to take the seat vacated by Salderman. "Have you finished your business, Warren?"

"Yes—and very satisfactorily, too. My father ought to be out of jail in a few days. And I feel a lot freer myself."

"I'm glad. You'll forgive us for not mentioning it that day. I hated to spoil your homecoming." She patted my arm with her fan. "With that settled, you'll take the position Papa offered?"

"I'm not sure yet. I may turn out to be a farmer."

Her brows arched. 'Don't tell me you've found someone to compare with *me*." She penetrated my split-second hesitation and sighed heavily. "Ah, me, I begin to feel my age."

"You mistake me. I was only shocked into speechlessness by the absurd idea of comparing you to anyone."

"You lie as beautifully as ever I have heard, Warren."

"A man never lies to the woman he—" I caught myself, aghast at the impulse that had unbridled my tongue.

Judith was smiling. She waited a moment, then, "Loves," she finished. Then, she added impishly, "True, isn't it? Very true. Men have such a genius for hiding behind generalities."

To my vast discomfort, I blushed.

The evening went on, but I was hardly aware of anyone else but Judith, her blitheness, her shrewdness, her warmth, her beauty. I chatted with others and answered questions about Algiers and listened politely to a recital of the virtues of Mrs. Graham's illustrious parents and grandparents and great-grandparents, who were related to kings of Scotland, and I clashed again in a polite way with Mr. Graham. But I never felt irritation for I was within sight of Judith. My heart kept telling me how pleasant it would be to be always within her sight. My mind kept mocking me, showing me how distant she was from me, how inaccessible was her heart, how remote were my chances of reaching her. Yet logic ever bows to longing and I determined she would someday be mine.

Chapter 10

I STAYED there overnight at Mr. Burdick's invitation. I didn't see Judith before I left the next morning, for neither she nor her mother were up when Mr. Burdick and I breakfasted. Knowing I would need small money to buy back our household goods, I asked Mr. Burdick if he would change the fifty pounds in gold I had left. Had I known what a bother the task entailed, I wouldn't have asked. Mr. Burdick spent half the morning with me, going from counting house to counting house along Long Wharf trying to break the guinea pieces into smaller money. The wealthier merchants had plenty of gold, but silver and copper coins were almost unobtainable. When I had thirty pounds in small money I gave up. I apologized profusely for taking up so much of his time, but Mr. Burdick just laughed. The experience had amused him. When we parted he made me promise to get in touch with him first when I finally came to Boston for employment.

Having started out late, I reached only as far as Leicaster at dusk of the first day. Being anxious to get home, I started early the next morning, though it was the Sabbath. I was duly warned that, if caught, I faced a stiff fine and a session in the stocks, for the morale of the people had not so broken down as to make traveling on the Sabbath any less of a sin. At Brookfield I had a narrow squeak. I was unlucky enough to pass through that town just as meeting was letting out for the nooning. The tithingman gave me chase and the outraged elders shook their fists at me for my affront to the Lord. But I was sure the Lord understood and forgave me.

Shortly after five o'clock I arrived at Uncle Enoch's and found that the family had just returned from the meeting house. I was welcomed with due warmth by everyone except my uncle. He was most displeased that I had broken the Sabbath and mumbled something about the growing wickedness of the younger generation. Before I could eat or even tell my good news, I had to feed and water and bed down the horse. I was wolf hungry, having eaten nothing since leaving Leicaster that morning, but it made no difference to Uncle Enoch. He was a stern and righteous man.

I relieved my mother and the others with smiles and winks, but it was not until after my uncle had said grace over our cold meal that anyone dared ask the question burning on every tongue. Then it was my uncle who opened the subject.

"How did you find your father, Warren?"

"Cheerful enough under the circumstances, sir. I went on to Boston and settled the debt. I expect he'll be out by tomorrow night or sometime Tuesday."

A sigh of relief went around the table. The rest of us pretended we didn't notice my mother's filling eyes.

Uncle Enoch frowned at his plate. "My house is open to my brother and his family as long as he wishes, Warren. I hope you will remain, rather than go into debt. In the fall, after my crops are in, I believe I can advance Caleb enough to get him started again in the spring."

"We're grateful to you, Uncle Enoch, but we've imposed on you too long already. I made a deal with Pa's creditor. I have about fifty pounds left over." I jingled the copper in my pocket. We can buy back most of our household goods and equipment."

"Warren," my mother asked softly, huskily, "do you mean we can go home?"

"Yes, Ma."

Mother got up from her place and came around to me and kissed me gently on the forehead. Uncle Enoch and Aunt Hannah gave strict attention to their food. Increase was happy, too, and for a moment I thought he'd burst into tears. Cousin Anzel and his wife, Rowena, exchanged a relieved glance. No one could blame them for that. It must have been trying, at times, even to the most generous natures, to have two extra people around the house. If Pa and

I added ourselves to the household, it would be almost too much. My mother took her place again, her head high.

At dawn the next day, we all went over to Pelham to put our farm into livable shape and prepare for my father's homecoming. Uncle Enoch took complete charge, keeping me busier at hard labor than I had been for a long, long time.

All through the day, numbers of our neighbors dropped by to welcome us home. And very few of them came empty handed. None of them would accept pay for the household goods they brought. Gilmore, our nearest neighbor, brought over a cow, three sheep, a highboy, and our cradle—a useless, though sentimental, piece of furniture. He said he'd take my money if there was any left over after I'd paid off those who were less close to us. Beulah came over with some crockery and pots and pans and she, too, refused to take the money, except on the same terms. I didn't talk to her myself, being on the roof of the barn at the time, and had to content myself with waving and shouting my greetings. Our beds and bedding had never passed from our hands, having been bought in by Aunt Hannah at the sale. Anzel brought them over from Amherst in the afternoon and set them up for us. A lucky thing, too, for I was well nigh all in by the time dusk mercifully released me from work.

The next morning, I was awakened by a rattling and a thumping.

"Warren!" My covers whipped away. "Warren, get up!"

"Yes, Ma." I groaned and groped for the covers. "I'm up."

"That boy," my mother mumbled. "He hasn't grown a day."

I dressed and forced my eyelids open and looked down into the barnyard. Uncle Enoch was talking to someone half hidden by the darkness. Near them, a yoke of oxen was stomping restlessly. The man, I saw finally, was Gilmore, our nearest neighbor.

The kitchen looked terribly bare and cheerless, for all we had was a couple of chairs, a stool and a table made of two planks laid across two barrels. Aunt Hannah was hard at work, making pies. It wasn't dawn yet and she had ten ready for the oven. Mother found a corner of the makeshift table and gave me my breakfast, a porringer of bread and milk.

"I could use a piece of pie," I said wistfully.

Aunt Hannah laughed. "Raw? You wait a while, Warren."

Someone rapped on the door and came in. "Good morning, everybody!" It was Mrs. Gilmore, her arms filled with pie plates. Her brood of daughters filed in behind her, each bearing something, more flour, jars of preserves, fresh baked bread, salt and sugar. "Oh, there you are, Warren! Welcome home!"

"Thank you, Mrs. Gilmore." I took the pie plates from her. "You're looking younger than when I went away."

She giggled. "Henry ought to hear that." She turned to her daughters. "I guess you don't know them all. The little one is Ann, and here are Hope, Faith, Rejoice and I guess you remember Comfort. She's fifteen now."

"She's a mite bigger than she was then. Howdy, Comfort."

She smiled shyly, a rather stringy looking girl, but she had the marks of being pretty in another year or so.

The gabbling of the women moved me to gobble the rest of my breakfast and get out. I ran into two more women as I reached the door, Mrs. Ranken, our neighbor on the other side and Mrs. Dick, who lived near the center of town. Mrs. Ranken had a tub of pork sausages. The other woman had brought an enormous number of indian puddings, nicely wrapped in linen cloths. I helped them with their burdens, allowed myself to be examined to see how much I'd grown and then escaped outside.

Uncle Enoch was talking to Ranken, Mr. Dick and Gilmore. They greeted me warmly with the usual sentiments about how glad they were to see me again. Both Ranken and Dick had brought their oxen. Anzel must have risen very early for he was back from Amherst with my uncle's yoke. By this time I knew what was going on. We were holding a ploughing and planting bee.

"I owe you gentlemen some money, don't I?" I asked.

"You owe Mr. Dick two shillings," Uncle Enoch supplied. "Ed here gets . . . how much Ed? You brought those foot stoves, fire irons and a few other things."

"It's all right, Warren," Ranken said. "Forget it."

"You can use the money and I have it," I said, jingling my moneybelt. "How much, Mr. Ranken?"

I paid them off, three shillings to Mr. Ranken, two to Mr. Dick, three pounds four to Gilmore, who had bought a good deal at the sale, including some of our stock. As long as I showed I had the cash, they were willing—nay, eager—to accept the money. Ranken remarked he hadn't seen a real shilling piece in over four months.

Beulah arrived just as the sky was getting grey. She was driving our oxen. Reuben had charge of the Cranes' own yoke.

"Good morning, gentlemen," she greeted cheerily. "Good morning, Warren. We're ready for work Mr. Hascott. You give Reuben orders. I'll take the other yoke if you like."

"That's kind of you, Beulah," my uncle returned. "But I expect the women could use a good hand about the house."

Beulah sighed. "And I so love ploughing, the way the rest of you do. Well, if you have no use for my muscles I'll see you later, gentlemen."

"Hey, wait a minute!" I ran after her. "I almost forgot. I owe you money. How much?"

"Well . . ." She frowned slightly. "As I said yesterday, after you've paid off everybody else and you still have money left over, then we'll talk about it. I have spoken."

She winked at me and walked off. The men eyed Beulah thoughtfully and no one spoke until she had disappeared into the house. Then, Ed Ranken spat with precision to one side.

"She'll make somebody a good wife."

Uncle Enoch grunted. "She's a good girl, Beulah. Maybe she's a mite too quick to speak her mind sometimes, but she'll grow out of that." He smiled reflectively. "My Hannah was like her. After a while she learned it's easier to catch flies with honey."

"There's your chance, Warren," Dick put in, "if you want a good pie baker like your uncle has. Or maybe you could take a shine to my Eunice. She's to an age where I got to get rid of her soon or she'll be an old maid."

The men laughed and resumed their talk of crops and weather and debts and oxen. They drifted down to the pair the Cranes had been keeping for us and examined the beasts

153

solemnly. Oxen to me had always been rather stupid, ponderous brutes, handy to have around when heavy work was to be done, but hardly boasting of any personality. I was wrong, of course. If you knew how to look closely, you could tell a good ox from a bad one.

With daylight, more and more of our neighbors arrived—the Conkeys, Will and John; Tom Packard and his brothers, Tim and Joe; Eb Grey, Tim Rice, Will Hunter, Hank McCullock and so many more I soon lost track of the names. On hand, too, was our old family physician, Dr. Uriah Cameron, who had been a deacon in the church when I left and now was the principal religious arbiter in our community, since we had no regular minister occupying our pulpit at the moment. Here was another shortage in our back counties, a shortage of qualified ministers, for very few divinity students had been trained during the years of the Revolution.

My dislike of the good doctor couldn't have arisen from the fact that he had brought me into the world, though his attitude toward the feat had always irritated me. Babies safely delivered were his children, alive through his skill. The Lord took the blame for those unfortunates who did not survive. He was upon me before I could recognize him and escape. The years had dealt with him grotesquely. I remembered him as a short thin man, just developing a paunch. He was now a blob of quivering flesh. His flat chest and sloping shoulders and his big belly set upon spindly legs gave him the curious appearance of an egg with thin sticks set into the larger end. His face was flabby, too, pouches under his eyes, thick lips, a row of chins obliterating his neck. Indeed, his features seemed to be made of wax which had sagged in the summer heat. He extended his puffy hand.

"Warren, my boy! We rejoice at your safe return." He gripped my arm. "You're looking fit, boy, mighty fit."

"Thank you, sir." And I paused awkwardly, hoping I wasn't expected to return the compliment.

"The Lord tried us severely while you were away. The Lord has seen fit to reward us. Let us today take to ourselves the words from the Book of Luke, 'But it was to meet and make merry and be glad: for this, thy brother, was dead and is alive again; and was lost and is found'." He gave my hand an extra hard wring. "I must pay my respects to your mother, Warren."

The stream of friends and neighbors was unending. John Bruce came with his wife and brood, Joe Hamilton brought a load of new planks from his sawmill, Sam Rush arrived with his wife and a daughter who had grown mighty pretty. Then, I found myself greeting Dave Corbett, the boy who was courting Beulah. He was misnamed. He should have been called Goliath, he was that tremendous. But he was well proportioned, shoulders not too broad, slim hips, regular features, his chin not too prominent, and beautiful even white teeth. I liked him on sight. He was slow moving and ponderous, as if conscious of his great strength. He gripped my hand hard in welcoming me and immediately apologized. My hand was numb for a half hour afterward.

Dan Shays came a while later without his wife, I noticed, and I asked for her.

"She's ailing," he explained. "But she sends her best—and a few things I have here in this bag." He grinned and looked back. "Quite a crowd, eh? I had to leave my team down on the road. I bought in your father's harrow. It's in the wagon." He waved to some friends. Then, "Did you stop in at West Springfield?"

I nodded. "I delivered the letter to Luke Day himself. He was drilling some men on the common there. He's a belligerent sort, isn't he? He seemed to think we're heading for revolt."

Shays waved depreciatingly. "Luke's got a big mouth, that's all. But we need someone like him to make a noise. One of these days he'll fire off a gun and those damn seaboard aristocrats will wake up and do something for us."

"Well, I hope he only makes noise." I commented.

The sun was just over the horizon and some thirty yokes and ten teams of horses were waiting patiently to be put to work. Uncle Enoch didn't keep them waiting long. When most of the men he had expected had arrived, he gathered them about him and, with a stick, drew a map of our farm in the dust and assigned the men to their fields. One five acre patch of poor land was to be sown with a mixture of clover and rye grass. The rest of our acreage was only to be turned over and the ground dressed with the various composts the men had brought along. Each man had his favorite, varying from manure and urines to wood ashes and soap suds and the load of lime my Uncle had ordered from Northampton. The harrowing and planting they'd leave to my father. Uncle Enoch said Pa could get in quite a bit of corn and some flax and turnips, which would give us cash and some food over the winter. Personally, I was a little staggered at the amount of work he was laying out for us.

All morning long, the farm resounded with "Gee's" and the rattle of harness and yokes and the heartfelt grunting of sweating men. Uncle Enoch organized groups of carpenters who practically tore apart and rebuilt our barn and corncrib, then reshingled the roofs. Another gang cleaned out the well and the outhouse. The house itself bulged with women-folk, cleaning and cooking and setting in place all the furniture that had been returned and some new pieces brought along as presents to us. All the work was accompanied with whoops of laughter, ceaseless bantering and, among the younger men, horseplay that sometimes bordered on the violent.

Uncle Enoch had overlooked nothing. He had brought along four good, fat pigs to be roasted for our dinner. A gang of men dug a pit and set up the spits and hauled the firewood and with the approach of noon the air was filled with the smell of pork. The women, of course, brought out the usual baiting for the men in the fields at nine o'clock, a baiting being a light snack with milk and cider to wash it down. Mr. Conkey had brought along a keg of rum, as had Dr. Hynds, in addition to the two we had ordered. There was sweet cider and milk for the children, some hard cider, pies, breads, sausages, indian puddings, food and drink in such abundance as would feed and dethirst an army.

Shortly before noon, young Tommy Patterson came riding up from across the fields to the west. Excitement had taken his breath away and he had to gulp several times before he could let forth the shrill shout: "They're coming! They're coming!"

The chestnut mare came around the bend and we could see Pa, with Increase riding behind, staring up at the fields. A rustle and a wave of feminine giggling went over the barnyard. But when the horse reached the lane, the chatter and scruffing faded into a deep hush, a quietness filled with joyous anticipation.

Pa was a little dazed, you could see that. His mouth was agape and his eyes were very wide. He reined the horse, got off slowly, and walked with deliberate, almost unbelieving steps, up the lane toward us. Increase just sat where he was, smiling contentedly.

No one uttered a sound as Pa came into the open circle of his friends. His eyes were misted. I disengaged Ma's hand from my arm and stepped back, for I could know my father had eyes only for her.

Ma was crying very quietly when Pa put his arms around her. He kissed her brow and the worried lines smoothed away from his seamed, weathered old face. Then, Pa smiled.

"Neighbors." His voice was husky, but carried clearly through the deep silence. "Neighbors, by your leave, I would pray."

Our heads bent reverently and Pa, his face lifted to the heavens, closed his eyes.

"Almighty Father. From the fullness of our hearts, we give thanks unto Thee. We thank Thee for the hope that hast sustained us through every trial, for the love that ever ennobles our spirits, for the freedom Thou hast granted us. Help us, Oh Lord, to find forgiveness for those who trespass against us. Keep us ever from the paths of wickedness and the ways of idleness. We ask, Oh Lord, Thy blessings upon these, our neighbors, our friends. Keep them ever in health. Keep their fields ever fertile. Keep them ever from want. We ask it in the name of Jesus Christ . . . Amen."

The soft echo swept over the circle like a heartfelt sigh.

"Hannah!" my uncle called. The very volume of his voice subdued the crowd for a moment. "Hannah, isn't it time to eat?"

"Eat!" A loud cheer went up and the stampede was on for the pits where the succulent pigs were done to a turn.

From then on the celebration was in full swing. Rum flowed freely. The pigs disappeared down hungry gullets. The pies and puddings and cookies vanished.

Quite a crowd clustered around me, you can be sure, and questioned me closely about my experiences in Algiers. Most of the men, young and old, were very curious about

the harems and, I swear, they refused to believe the oc-
cupants were fat, greasy women whom none of them would
glance at twice here in America.

After eating, the elders drifted away, which didn't grieve
me. I mingled with the younger crowd. The center of attraction there, I had noticed, was Beulah. Dave Corbett kept
hovering at the edge of the crowd, smiling amiably, his
eyes never seeming to leave the girl's face. In fact, the
amount of adoration she was getting was truly remarkable. I
stopped by David and remarked as much and he nodded
absently.

"Everybody's crazy about Beulah," he remarked.

I was almost an equal attraction, however, for the moment I was spotted I was surrounded with eager questioners.
Almost without willing it, I was propelled into the center
of the group. Beulah egged them on, urging me to tell them
about this and tell them about that. I did the best I could.

"Did they whip you much, Warren?" young Pettingil
asked.

I nodded. "Sometimes with a leaded cat."

"Let's see the scars!" someone called.

The clamor became so insistent that I had to take off my
tow cloth shirt and expose my back. That wasn't much of a
hardship, I assure you, for that tow cloth itched like the
devil.

The younger boys felt the lash scars admiringly.

"Hey, look at them muscles," Tommy Rankin urged.

"Boy, lookit!" Young Salfrage was properly awed. "I'll
betcha Warren can wrestle. Can't you, Warren, huh? I'll
betcha yuh could even beat Dave."

I laughed. "An old man like me, beat Dave?"

Dave Corbett grinned. "I ain't been beat yet." It was a
statement of fact, not a boast.

"Make him eat those words, Warren," Beulah said slyly.

The shout went up and I eyed him speculatively. I hadn't
wrestled in years but, I still thought I could. Dave was a big
man—tremendous. But he seemed slow. If I could manage to
keep out of those arms of his. . . .

But the match didn't come off. As the circle was widening
for us, I saw Beulah straighten and stare out to the road.

"We've got company," she said.

Toby Plummer was coming up the lane, his plump face moist, his red lips fixed in a pout. He was getting a very chilly reception. As he approached, everyone turned his back and pretended to be preoccupied in conversation. I put on my shirt. Something told me that man was bringing trouble. He stopped before my Uncle Enoch.

"Howdy," he said weakly.

My uncle didn't answer and Toby glanced about fearfully, for our neighbors were gathering about, their faces set in grim lines. Toby mopped his moist brow with a linen handkerchief.

"It's just my duty," he said plaintively. "I'm just trying to make an honest living, that's all."

No one said anything. Toby squirmed under the hostile eyes, then gathered the courage to hand my uncle a paper.

"Don't take it!" Beulah said sharply.

Uncle Enoch gazed at her calmly, then turned back to Toby. "What is it?"

"It's a summons," Toby replied heavily. "Hooper won't renew. He's suing you for the money."

An ugly rumble went through the crowd. Everyone knew my uncle had gone into debt only to save my father's land from the Boston speculators.

"It's a crying shame," Beulah said angrily.

Dr. Cameron turned on her. "Be silent, girl. This is man's business."

Beulah stamped her foot. "I won't be silent. If this is the way man runs his business, then God help us women. The men go to jail and the creditors feed them. But what happens to the women? Just ask Mrs. Hascott or Mrs. Lowry or any of a score you can name. There's an ugly name for it, no matter how willingly it's given—charity."

"Beulah's right," came a meek voice from the crowd. The men turned to stare at mild little Mrs. Gilmore. "I say it's time you men get some gumption. Don't take that writ, Enoch."

Beulah's deep grey eyes fixed on the lawyer. "The writ comes up in Northampton on the 29th of August, doesn't it?"

There was a bleak, uncomfortable silence. Beulah turned to Tom Packard.

"Tom, can't anything be done?"

Tom's lean jaw hardened and he stared at the ground. "Dammit, Beulah, stop making me read your mind. Sure, there's something we could do—stop the court from sitting."

"Well?" Beulah asked belligerently.

A full minute went by while the thought sank in.

"Luke Day would support us," Dan Shays said slowly. "He writes me the whole south part of the county wants action, not more words. He's drilling—"

"Drill!" someone shouted. "Dan, you lead us in drill!"

The cry was taken up and the yapping voices were insistent. Dan Shays looked startled, then a bit pleased as more and more asked him to lead the drill.

He looked straight at Toby. "I guess they'd be no harm in drilling a little—for exercise, maybe."

Toby was scared. He tried to edge out of the crowd, but the men were pressing closer and closer around him. He tried to thrust the paper into my uncle's hands. But Uncle Enoch kept his fists on his hips. Toby looked like a cornered rabbit, his small black eyes darting from side to side, seeking an avenue of escape. Then a pickled cherry splattered on his forehead.

"Run him off, boys! Kick him offen our land!"

Disembodied hands came out of the mass of bodies and Toby was tossed from side to side. The shouts and angry snarls were frightening, for these were not the sounds of men. They were the sounds of aroused animals. Toby squealed and pleaded and tried to get out. A fist smashed him in the jaw. Another drew blood from his nose. Suddenly, the mob closed tight about him. Toby screamed and the human mass writhed. Then, as if shot from a gun, Toby hurtled free, headed down the lane. He stumbled, fell to his knees, scrambled up. A boot flew out and Toby squashed into the dust again. A roar of laughter went through the mob.

Toby lurched to his feet and started running. No one followed him. The men just stood and laughed and jeered and cursed him and all his gentry. The children took up their elder's game, following him and pelting him with stones. One hit him in the neck and he stumbled again. A cheer went up.

Then, like a snapping branch, the laughter broke and

died. The silence was complete, painful, and the scowls settling on every face wavered between defiance and guilt. No one dared meet the wrathful eyes of Dr. Cameron. "For shame!" he thundered. "Have we lost all decency and self respect? 'Vengeance is mine', sayeth the Lord." He closed his eyes, rocked back and forth. "I shall pray in the words of Christ, our Lord, 'Father, forgive them, for they know not what they do'."

Chapter 11

THERE was no rest. Ploughing and harrowing, ploughing and harrowing, from the crack of dawn until it was too dark to see, my father, Increase and I were out in the fields, turning the ground over and over. We put in ten acres of corn and prayed for rain. Early in July, we got in four acres of turnips. Then, we got in two acres of flax. Farming had changed some since I'd last been home. Our harrow now had iron teeth, instead of the wooden ones which used to break off constantly. We borrowed a drill plough from Dr. Hynds to put in the turnip seed, a great improvement over the old broadcast sowing method. But the work was the same —hard and back-breaking.

For the first weeks, there was no rest even in the evening. Being the best carpenter in the family, it fell to me to make the necessaries which hadn't been returned to us, a new table for the kitchen, some new chairs, a scrubbing board for my mother, a couple of new piggins for the milk, yokes for our sheep and geese. Pa and Increase did the other chores, the milking and the feeding of our oxen and such, and, when our forge was set up again, they took care of repairs on our tools and other ironwork. It was never ending drudgery.

I don't know what my mother would have done without Beulah. We menfolk had too much to do to be able to give her a hand with the extra work she had besides the cooking and cleaning for us. She had to make some new baskets we needed, and gather and prepare the rushes herself, scour our pots and brass kettles, overhaul our bedding and tend to the brood of chicks we were raising. When the wild straw- berries ripened, she had to take the time off to pick them and put them up. Then one afternoon, she and Beulah went on an herb hunt to restock our medicine jars. She even found time, with Beulah's help, to put down a respectable vegetable garden, including some beans, carrots, brocolli, cabbage and peas. It was Beulah who scouted around the countryside and rounded up the seed. And it was Beulah who made our butter and cheese until my mother could take over the task herself.

Yet, with all the work, by the middle of the second week, I found the time to spend an evening now and again with the boys in the tavern. There was no question of my returning to Boston to take that position Burdick had offered me. I just couldn't desert my family at a time like this. As soon as the corn was up, the hoeing started. Pa insisted that he and Increase could handle all the work, but I decided not to make any move, at least not until he had his wheat down. Come August, he intended to plant a crop of winter wheat and prepare another field for oats for the following year. So, I wrote to Burdick and regretfully informed him that I must perforce remain a farmer for some time yet.

I was glad enough to relax at Conkey's, over East Hill, which tavern I preferred to the nearer place of Dr. Hynds since my friends chose to patronize Conkey. Why, I can't say, except that Hynds was a big property owner and all of us were practically destitute. Conkey, having less, was illogically expected to be more lenient with his credit. But Conkey could count on being paid, in produce if not in cash, as soon as the harvests were in. Most of the farmers in our vicinity had restricted their planting this year, since they felt they wouldn't be able to sell full crops, but all had made provision for paying their tavern bills.

The talk over our cups was almost exclusively politics. I was astonished at the number of grievances these men had. First and foremost, of course, was the lack of a circulating medium which had paralyzed trade and prevented the farmers from selling their crops the year before. A disheartening amount of God's good fruits had gone to waste because buyers had no cash. Apples rotted on their trees. Wheat was rotting in barns. Oats and rye and even flax had found no market. And while the farmer's labor and produce went to waste, taxes were piling up, debts were unpaid, men were going to jail and families were being broken up. It was no wonder that the clamor for paper money was growing louder and angrier.

The effects of a tax on advertisements was readily seen in our vicinity. Beyond Worcester, there was now only one newspaper, the Hampshire Herald of Springfield. And that paper was reputed to be in shaky circumstances, for few could afford to pay nine shillings a year for a subscription. Travelers passed through Pelham so infrequently that we were virtually isolated. It was no wonder that many believed the tax, ostensibly levied for revenue purposes, was in reality designed to choke our free press.

On the tenth of July, Tom Johnson our representative in the General Court, came home. No one knew he had returned until he came into the taproom of Conkey's that evening. Indeed, we were so busy arguing and damning the General Court that no one noticed him at first. I happened to glance up at the tall, rail-like figure who had stopped at our table. I recognized him at once. His eyes seemed sharper and blacker and the wrinkles about his thin mouth seemed deeper, but otherwise he was the same.

I jumped up and stuck out my hand. "Tom!"

Tom Johnson grinned and pumped my arm. "Howdy, Warren. Blair told me you'd returned. How are things?"

"Tolerable. What brings you home?"

Tom Johnson couldn't answer at once, for everyone got up and rushed over to us, shouting greetings and clamoring for news. Tom laughed and fended off the scores of cups thrust at him and begged the crowd to desist. And, at length, he managed to get a semblance of quiet.

"Now gentlemen, what is it you want to know?"

"What brings you home?" Dan Shays asked quickly.

"Well, the Governor prorogued the Legislature the day before yesterday," Johnson answered.

"Come on, come on," Tom Packard urged. "You know what we want to know. What's been done?"

"Well," Johnson began slowly, "we passed several acts incorporating new towns. We put through an act repealing an act which restricted British imports. Then, there was an act allowing people of our state to pay their obligations in the currency of the state in which the creditor lives. . . ."

"What the hell good is that?" Hank McCullock asked.

"Well, if you borrow from a man in Rhode Island, for example, you can pay back in Rhode Island paper money. That's to protect creditors in this state from being paid in Rhode Island money . . . discourages the practice, so to speak."

"How about paper money for us?" Shays demanded.

Johnson smiled thinly. "Defeated, 99 to 18."

"Lowering court fees?"

"Died in committee."

"Removal of the General Court from Boston?"

"Died in committee."

"A tender act?"

"Oh, that was defeated—89 to 35."

Shays grunted. "Then what was done—toward redressing grievances, I mean?"

Johnson laughed nasally. "Not a damn thing, gentlemen, except pass the Supplementary Fund—another tax. It allows the Congress of the United States to levy a direct tax on us in case we don't pay our quota of the congressional requisition."

"That's infamous!" Shays blurted.

"I quite agree." Then, Johnson shrugged. "I did my best —as did several other of my colleagues. The Tories stopped us cold. We couldn't muster the strength to put through even one constructive measure."

A grim silence fell over the taproom. Tom Johnson got a fresh cup of hard cider from the tray Conkey was carrying and sipped his drink slowly, smiling thoughtfully.

"Oh, cheer up, boys. The Legislature reconvenes in October."

Dave Cowden snorted. "What do we do in the meantime? Common Pleas will be sitting soon. Lots of us will have judgments handed down against us."

"Tell them to stave off execution of the judgments," Johnson suggested. "Have them appeal."

Tom Packard chuckled. "And how about those who are appealing? The Supreme Court will be sitting in September. How will those men avoid being sold out? Any advice, Tom?"

Johnson lifted his shoulders. "Something ought to be done, I guess."

Tom Packard tapped Johnson's chest. "You'll have to do it, Tom. Not many of us can vote, you know."

"Yes, I'll do it. I'll draw up a warrant for a special town meeting to call a county convention." He set down his cup and gave his waiscoat a jerk. "Now, gentlemen, I know you'll excuse me. I have urgent business. I haven't seen my wife in three months."

By late in July, the farm was running smoothly again and occasionally we could finish up a day without crawling into bed half dead with exhaustion. The fresh green clover had covered the ugly brown of the lower fields, the corn was up and the ridges replowed, the turnips were coming along, the flax promised to prosper. Pa knew how much I detested the monotonous drudgery and several times told me that he and Increase could handle the work if I wanted to leave. I decided it was no more than my duty to stay until harvest. But I had another reason for wanting to delay my departure. I was growing fonder of Beulah.

That girl was certainly generous with her time and energy. There wasn't a household duty she couldn't handle, from making cheeses to remodeling some of Jonathan's old clothes to fit me. But it was not her domestic excellence that attracted me. She was pleasant to have around. With some surprise, I found I tended to avoid the company of other young women. I became tongue-tied and sometimes actually blushed in their presence. Not so when I was with Beulah. She was so open and forthright that I felt no need to cater to feminine foibles and could accept her almost as I would a male companion, an equal.

Yet, I could feel the tension building up. She was warm. She was desirable. She sometimes made restraint seem a spartan virtue. I wanted her. But I was not sure I wanted her forever. The more I saw of her, the more I resented the smallness of our town. Regardless of other considerations, that alone would make a man think twice before yielding to his impulses. Thus, I struggled to hold them in their place

166

and managed quite well until she caught me off guard that time after town meeting.

The special town meeting had been called for the 28th of July. Pa didn't want to go because he hadn't paid his taxes for two years and thus wasn't eligible to vote. I still had some money which I had held out for emergencies and told him I'd pay the taxes if I had enough. Pa didn't want to let me do that, but he finally agreed if I was allowed to vote, too. He doubted it, since I hadn't paid my poll taxes for so many years. I held it was absurd to think they'd charge me for the years I had been away.

So, around eight o'clock on the morning of the 28th, Pa and I arrived down at the meeting house. In the vestibule, we found Matt Clark, who was a selectman, sitting at a small table.

" 'Morning, Caleb. 'Morning, Warren. Fixin' to pay your taxes?" Matt Clark grinned at us. "Or did you just come to worry about 'em? We're reasonable men, Caleb. If you got the money, we'd appreciate your paying. If not—well, we ain't sent anybody to jail for taxes yet."

Pa smiled. "I know. That's why I dared come back here after they let me out of jail. How do things stand with my son, Matt? Can he vote if he pays his poll?"

Matt pursed his lips. "Why, sure, if he pays what he owes. You were away eleven years, wasn't it, Warren?"

I squinted. "Come now, Matt, you're not telling me I have to pay my poll taxes for eleven years back."

Matt Clark spread his hands. "That's the law, Warren. But maybe we can fix it." He got up and went to the door and called Dr. Cameron. "Doc, Warren here wants to straighten out his taxes so he can vote. Do you have to charge him for all his back polls? It's eleven years."

Dr. Cameron rocked on his spindly legs, his thick lips pursing. "Well, since he didn't vote during all that time, I suppose we could arrange to charge him a lower rate."

"Look here, Doctor," I objected, "I was out of the country six of those eleven years. The rest of the time I was serving my country in the war."

Dr. Cameron fingered his row of chins. "Yes, we consider that, Warren. We'll do for you what we did for the others who served in the war. We'll vote to scale down the taxes."

"Suppose we take it this way, sir: Assume I just moved into town and that you find me of good moral character and worthy of residence here. Can't I be admitted as a newcomer? After all, sir, I have no property here."

Dr. Cameron shook his head. "Warren, if you have no property, you can't vote. You should know that."

"I thought they did away with property qualifications for voting. I heard talk last time I was in Salem."

"It didn't go through," Matt Clark put in. "It's in the Constitution that you got to have property to vote."

"I suppose that could be arranged," I said. "Pa can deed over to me part of the farm. How much do I need?"

"Sixty pounds, free and clear," Dr. Cameron supplied.

"Sixty pounds!" I almost screamed. "Why, dammit, man, the rate was only forty pounds when I went away."

Dr. Cameron's flabby features froze. "There's no call to shout at me, young man. I had nothing to do with drafting the Constitution. In fact, I voted against it."

"But we have less freedom than we had under the King," I insisted. "We fought against 'taxation without representation', didn't we? And now look—I'm charged taxes and denied a vote because I have no property. What the hell kind of democracy is that? Come on, Pa. I'll be damned before I pay taxes to that kind of a government."

"Beware, young man," Dr. Cameron warned. "We are lenient with people who cannot pay through no fault of their own. But we can still put willful evaders in jail."

I wanted to say "bah!" but I didn't dare. Cameron was a power in our town. Pa and I got out of there.

"I'm going right home," Pa said. "You stick around and let me know what they do."

I started over to join Tom Packard and the boys, then paused as I saw a cart coming up the road from the bridge. Beulah was driving. She waved cheerfully in reply to the "Good mornings" of the men and turned the cart in toward the church door. The staid elders perked up and gave her nods and smiles. Then I saw Joab sitting at the tail of the cart, his withered leg dangling. He looked neither to the right nor to the left. Nor did he answer those few who politely greeted him.

Beulah stopped the cart at the entrance and sat there without turning her head, her hands in her lap. Joab eased his huge bulk down on his one thin leg, groped for his single crutch, then half lifted, half dragged himself to the door. No one spoke to him. No no dared offer him help. He threw himself up the one step, nodded curtly to Matt and disappeared inside.

I heard a grunt at my side and saw Dr. Cameron next to me. He was gazing at Joab with a curious pout on his large mouth.

"Strange, isn't it?" he said softly. "Joab never comes to church on the Sabbath. Yet he's always on hand for town meetings. I fear that man has turned his face from God."

"Oh, I'm sure he hasn't," I said quickly, not knowing exactly why I should be defending Joab. "It must be painful for him to get around." Then I added lamely, "I guess he doesn't want to neglect his civic duty."

"Man's first duty is to God," Dr. Cameron said coldly. The scowl deepened on his fleshy face as the cart rumbled by on the way to the shed. "I must remember to have a talk with that young man one of these days."

His tone was ominous. If Dr. Cameron ever found out what Joab really thought of the Lord, Joab would certainly be read out of the church. No greater calamity could befall a man and his family in a town such as ours. Man could defy governments, but woe to him who thought he could defy the Church.

Unless religious attitudes had changed radically while I was away, which I seriously doubted, Joab's life would become unbearable. He would be shunned by his neighbors. He would find it next to impossible to sell his crops and shoes. He would get no help at harvest. People would trade with him only with the greatest of reluctance. And moving to another town would do him no good. No man could settle in another town in the Comonwealth without the permission of the selectmen. No town would accept a man who could not show proof of good moral character. And Joab's punishment would not fall upon himself alone. The consequences would rebound upon his family, his mother and Reuben and Beulah.

Dr. Cameron had a disapproving glare for Beulah, too, for a town meeting was an affair of exclusive interest to men. Beulah had made a bad mistake in coming, even though she had no intent to interfere in these affairs of man. As soon as Dr. Cameron went inside, I hurried over to the cart and warned her about Cameron and Joab.

Since it was getting close to nine o'clock, some of the men who could vote were drifting into the meeting house. None of the group under the big oak made a move to go in. They gave us a noisy greeting when Beulah and I joined them. All, that is, except Dave Corbett. His eyes were fixed on Beulah. And he was frowning. His obvious jealousy wasn't lost on me.

"I thought you said you weren't coming," he said gruffly.

Beulah smiled. "Joab changed his mind."

"You shouldna come," Dave rumbled. "Dr. Cameron doesn't like women around at times like these." He waved her protests to silence. "You go right home, Beulah. After meeting, I'll take Joab home."

Beulah was getting angry at his brazen possessiveness. But Tom Packard broke in before she could say anything.

"Dave's right, Beulah. Let Dave take Joab back after the meeting. You don't want to court trouble, do you?"

Beulah frowned and hesitated, then yielded. "All right. I'll light out as soon as the meeting's over."

Tom Packard shook my hand with mock solemnity. "Welcome to the club, Warren. We're all in the same fix."

"And I found out we have a new constitution," I added. "Seems even if I did pay my taxes I couldn't vote. I'm supposed to have sixty pounds free and clear."

Tom chuckled. "You should know what a liberal constitution our rich friends cooked up for us while we were away."

"The best time to put something over on the people is while the soldiers are away," I commented. "What else did they do?"

"They made it compulsory for every town to support a Congregationalist church," Shays replied.

"No!" I looked around. "Do we have one?"

Tom laughed. "You can just see us good Presbyterians laying out money for that. No, by law, we're supposed to have one, all right, but that article doesn't work here."

"That's right," Shays confirmed. "But it certainly works in other towns where Presbyterians are in a minority. It freezes out Quakers and Baptists and all the rest, unless they want to support their own church over and above paying taxes to keep the Congregationalists' Church, too."

"That's fine. Any more clauses like that?"

"They changed the mode of representation," Shays said. "That was a raw one. You remember, every town sent one representative to the Colonial General Court. Some of the bigger towns sent two and Boston had four. Well, now, every town of a hundred and fifty polls sends one. And an additional representative is allowed for each two hundred and twenty-five polls."

"I should think that would make an unwieldy House."

"It does in a way. But the real objection we have is that the seaboard, having the bigger towns, sends enough men in to outvote us. That's why they've done so little for us in the Legislature. The farming counties have virtually lost their voice in the government."

"That's nice. And I suppose the Senate's as good?"

Dan scowled. "The Senate sets up an aristocracy of property. You have to have four hundred pounds to be a Senator."

I smiled. "It seems, 'All men were created equal' except men without property."

The boys laughed bitterly.

"You have to have a thousand pounds to be governor," Dan went on, "five hundred to be lieutenant-governor. You even have to have two hundred pounds to be a representative." Shays shook his head. "We didn't get democracy out of the war, that's certain."

"The county conventions may change that," I said. "At least, Dr. Cameron said he'd move to change the Constitution."

"Hey, that reminds me," Hank McCullock spoke up. "The meeting's started. I don't want to miss this."

None of us wanted to miss it, so we moved around to the side of the Meeting House. Matt Clark had left the windows open, with the approval of the other selectmen, to at least allow us to be spectators. That was one nice thing about our townsmen. They might exclude us from voting because we had not complied with the law, but they didn't treat us as criminals. Some towns acted as if the inability to pay taxes was an unpardonable crime.

Dr. Hynds had been selected Moderator and was up in the pulpit. Ormston, who had the store on West Hill, was on his feet, calling for a vote on the resolution: Resolved, that the town choose a delegate or delegates to meet in Convention on Monday, the 31st of this instant, at 10 o'clock in the forenoon, at Landlord Bruce's in Pelham.

"All in favor?" Dr. Hynds called. There was a chorus of "Ayes." No one answered the call for negatives. Dr. Hynds rapped the pulpit. "The ayes have it. The chair recognizes Mr. Thomas Dick."

Tom Dick was on his feet. "I move we choose Caleb Keith and John Ranken as delegates to represent us."

There was no opposition. Caleb Keith and John Ranken were chosen as our delegates.

"Mr. Moderator!" came the call from John Conkey. "I move we set up a committee of ten to instruct our delegates."

We watched with deep interest as the meeting wrangled over the names of the ten who would settle the policies the delegates would urge at the convention. Finally, the meeting chose the Selectmen, plus Tom Johnson, Jim Packard—Tom's brother—and Captain John Thompson. The point that struck me was that those were the ten wealthiest men in town.

Nothing more being on the agenda, the meeting adjourned to the 14th of August, when the delegates would report.

It was with a modicum of satisfaction that we turned away from the window. No one really expected a large representation at the convention on the 31st, for time was too short. But even if only a dozen towns sent delegates, a step would have been taken toward calling a convention countywide in scope. Thus, one ray of hope had emerged. Where this action would lead, no one would venture to guess. But we were all fervently hoping that we were embarked on the road toward a redress of grievances.

"You know," Beulah said soberly. "I don't think this is going to help the distressed much. We'll have a convention here on the 31st and maybe ten or twelve towns will send delegates. It will be a month or more before we can get a real big convention in session."

Shays frowned at her. "Just what are you getting at?"

"The Court of Comomn Pleas will sit on the 29th of August, Dan. The General Court couldn't be called into special session by then, could it? That's going to hurt a lot of people around here."

Shays nodded soberly. "Yes, I can see that."

"More people are going to lose their land and more men will be going to jail," Beulah said quietly. "Dan, isn't there something we can do? Tom?"

"I wish to Heaven, Beulah," Tom said in an exasperated tone, "you wouldn't look to me to say what's in your mind. Go ahead, say it yourself."

"Say what?" Shays asked, puzzled.

Tom Packard shrugged. "Maybe if we demonstrated in front of the courthouse while it was in session, they'd ease off on us. When the news got back to the Governor, he might wake up. I sort of think so myself, if it's done in an orderly way."

Dan Shays nodded thoughtfully. "A demonstration might help. I've heard talk like that, too. Anyway, it wouldn't do the younger fellows any harm to drill."

"Drill!" someone in the crowd shouted. "Tom lead us in drill!"

Instantly, the whole crowd was clamoring for Tom to lead the drill. Tom laughed and shook his head. He slapped Dan Shays on the back.

"Dan's your man for that, boys. He outranks me. I vote for Dan Shays to lead the drill."

The cries shifted to Dan. He grinned, abashed, and gave Beulah a sheepish look, probably remembering the last time he had offered to lead the boys in drill.

"All right, boys!" he called finally. "If you want me to, I'll lead the drill. Be at Conkey's this afternoon. And bring your muskets."

Laughing and whooping and chattering like frenzied magpies, the boys scattered toward their homes. Dan Shays was still smiling, as if overwhelmed by the honor shown him. I was unaccountably angry.

"I've got to get home," I announced abruptly.

"Yes, me too," Beulah said quickly. "Meeting will be letting out any minute now."

After we bade farewell to the others, we hurried down the road to the bridge and turned off on the river path. I was annoyed and hadn't exactly wanted to walk her home, but I didn't have much of a choice. She noticed my grumpiness and was silent.

Finally, "Are you joining the drill, Warren?"

"Certainly not," I replied indignantly. "I'll have nothing to do with anything subversive to law and government."

"Subversive?" Beulah echoed. "What's subversive about preparing to defend your rights? You're a fine one to talk about that, anyway. Your family suffered enough from those hateful money grabbers. Now, your uncle faces ruin. Are you going to stand by and do nothing?"

"You should hold your tongue," I grumbled. "You're inciting people with that talk about money grabbers."

"I'm only saying what everybody's thinking," Beulah said meekly. "Anyway, you heard what Tom said. Drilling wasn't my idea. Men all over the country are doing it." She gave me an uncertain smile. "For Heaven's sake, Warren, stop worrying. There won't be any violence. One demonstration will convince the Governor we mean business. Then it will be all over. He isn't stupid."

Perhaps not. But I was wondering whether, once the mob spirit had been unleashed, it could stop short of armed conflict.

Little by little, my irritation passed away and I saw how foolish it was to blame Beulah for what was happening. She was right, of course; she was only saying what other people were thinking. So, I determined to put my matters from my mind for the time. It was really too beautiful a day to worry about troubles which were essentially beyond my control.

The path was narrow and she walked close to my side, barely reaching my shoulder. The sweet clean scent of her hair was very disturbing. Inevitably, my arm brushed the softness of her bosom, and the touch of her hand against mine aroused an irresistible hunger in my heart. Somehow I knew she could be mine if I would only reach out and take her. But an inner instinct urged caution.

"Joe led me to expect something different," I said casually. "You're a remarkable woman, Beulah." Her step faltered and she looked up at me, half smiling. "I was once told no woman should ever reveal she has a mind." "Only a fool wants an empty shell." A comforting silence lengthened between us. Finally, I went on, in an amused, bantering tone. "If I were a Moor in Algiers, do you know what I'd be tempted to do? I'd be tempted to carry you off to my harem. There I'd set you on a huge silken pillow and gather around all the other women of the harem to be your servants. They would anoint you with sweet oils and set your hair in soft curls. They would clothe you in the richest satins and silks of the Indies. They would put emeralds at your wrists and rubies at your throat and a diadem of diamonds on your brow. And when they finished, I would walk slowly around the pillow and shake my head and say, 'No, she looks no better. There can be no improvement on the perfection of her beauty.' "

I frowned a little as my words faded into nothingness and I wondered what had possessed me to let my tongue slip its cable so foolishly. I waited for her laughter. She did not laugh. She was silent for a long time. Her grey eyes were shining.

"I'd like that," she said softly. "Just once . . . just once to feel silk against my skin. It must be wonderful." She gave me a quick shy glance. "Imagine me in a silken gown with hoops and pads to make the skirts fall in wide folds . . . and satin shoes . . . and powdered hair . . . red on my lips and maybe a patch on my cheek." She laughed, a bit breathlessly, a bit wistfully. Then she shook her head slowly. "No, it wouldn't make any difference. I could never be as lovely as those town bred girls, not ever."

"Would you like to live in Boston, Beulah?"

"I'd love it," she replied quickly. "I'm sure of it. Boston is so much more . . . more alive."

I considered that a moment. "Living in town would be a lot different than you imagine, Beulah. The people are colder and harder. Poverty is uglier in town. Everyone's door isn't open to you as here, especially if you . . . your husband isn't rich."

"I wouldn't mind, truly, I wouldn't," she blurted. Then, more soberly, "Not if I loved my husband."

A queer, uncomfortable lump pressed against my breastbone and my breathing was harder and deeper. The silence grew taut between us as we walked on, eyes averted from each other. I frowned at the river. The dark, murmuring waters were flecked with small white circles, like eyes mocking me and prodding me on. The path edged away from the stream and wound through a cool, darkened patch of woodland. But the fever did not leave me, for the wild young elms bent over the path and conspired to draw us closer.

All too soon we came out on the rolling fields touched with pink and brown and green. A thin white spume of smoke curled up from the house, hidden beyond the far hillock.

I stopped and took her arm and turned her toward me. "There are things a man musn't think about when he's poor." My voice was very husky. "Suppose . . . suppose someone asked you to wait for him awhile . . . months . . . perhaps a year . . . while he went away to make his way in life. Would you wait?"

"If I loved him," she answered softly, "I'd wait."

She swayed closer, her grey eyes searching mine. Her sultry lips were compelling. She crushed against me with all her softness, all her warmth, and her moist red lips claimed mine. For a blissful eternity she clung to me, trembling a little yet yielding completely; and the pounding of her heart was my own. Slowly, uncontrollably, I felt myself slipping toward the brink of an all-consuming rapture.

Reason jolted me back from the very edge.

"There will be a tomorrow, Beulah," I said hoarsely.

"Yes," she breathed.

"A time past thought," I added lamely. "Goodby."

I dared not linger. Blindly, I stumbled up the long hill to the road, angry and resenting my own timidity. Why had I let her slip from my grasp? I sensed the answer. But, for the moment, the exasperating truth was hidden in a nebula of outraged urges and jeering passions.

Not until I reached the top of the hill could I force myself to look back. My cheeks were burning. Beulah was still standing there, slim and lovely and desirable. I scowled and rubbed my moist hands against my thighs. I knew I would have a tomorrow. I wondered if I would have the courage to take it. I waved and she lifted her arm. In her upstretched hand she held my will to escape.

Chapter 12

THE convention our town had called was duly held at Bruce's Tavern on Monday the 31st of July. As I have mentioned, we held no high hopes for a large turnout, for the time between our town meeting and the convention was too short to circularize any but the nearest towns. We were, therefore, gratified that eight towns sent delegates. Their deliberations were short. They drew up another circular letter, calling for a convention to be held at Hatfield on the 22nd of August. By then we felt sure that more than half of the towns could send delegates.

In the meantime, however, we were much more interested in what the Leicester Convention in Worcester County would do on the 15th of August, for we all knew that meeting would greatly influence our own convention. Dan Shays had written to Captain Adam Wheeler of Hubbardston and asked him to send a report of the convention as soon as it was over. Dan knew Adam Wheeler very well, having served in the war with him.

On the 17th of August I made sure to be down at Conkey's early, for the post rider was due to stop there around two o'clock. As soon as I came over East Hill I knew the letter had come, for the boys were not drilling. They were grouped about the tavern door, their muskets trailing. Dan was in the middle of the crowd, reading the report. On one side of him was Tom Packard, on the other, surprisingly, was Beulah. From the stolid looks on the faces, Wheeler's report was nothing to cheer about.

Shays waved as he caught sight of me and some of the

177

boys moved aside to let me through. "I just finished reading Captain Wheeler's letter. Want to look it over?"

"I sure would," I answered.

No one spoke or commented on the subject while I was reading. I had noticed before that my friends gave me more than ordinary respect in matters of this kind. My year at Harvard College had made me, in their eyes, an educated man.

Thirty eight towns had sent representatives to the Leicester Convention, a very respectable turnout, but the work done was rather disappointing. Wheeler had appended the list of the grievances set forth to be remedied by the General Court. There were only eight of them, the sitting of the Legislature at Boston, the lack of a circulating medium, the abuses of lawyers, unreasonable grants to government officers, the excess number of government employees, the paying out of money to Congress while state accounts were unsettled, the existence of the Court of Common Pleas, and the appropriation of the excise to pay the interest on the state's securities. All of these were surely grievances, but many of the most patent injustices had been omitted.

I folded the letter and handed it back to Shays.

"Well, what do you think, Warren?" Packard asked.

"This won't scare the Governor, that's certain," I replied. "It's not even strong enough to make him think of calling a special session."

"They didn't even ask him to," McCullock added.

"You know what I think?" Beulah put in. "I think most of the delegates were Tories. That sounds like the way Dr. Hynds would talk. Sure, he's for us and all that. But he's got a lot of property. He'd be scared to holler too loud."

Dave Cowden snorted. "Hell, if our convention is as wishy-washy as that, the delegates might as well stay home."

"Colonel Bonney will be there," Shays remarked.

"No? Honest?" Hank punched air. "By Jeeps, then we'll see some action. I'm going over to Hatfield that day. The Colonel will see our petition ain't no milk sop."

"If he ain't outvoted," Packard said dryly. "How about you, Dan? Going to the convention?"

Shays shrugged. "If I can. I'm not sure right now."

Dan Shays asked me if I was going. I said I was eager to be on hand, for I suspected the Hatfield Convention would be a real lively affair. Everyone must realize that we would have to take a stronger stand than the Leicaster crowd to get results. I was sure there would be quite a tussle between Tory and Radical.

After the chattering died down a bit, I turned to Beulah. "What brings you over this way?"

"I just happened by," she answered. "I was visiting with Mrs. Decker."

I grinned with disbelief. "How's she getting along?"

"Fair enough. She's been served with papers to appear in court at Northampton on the 29th. And listen to this, Toby's father is taking the case. He's not charging her anything."

Tom Packard grunted. "If he thinks that'll make us like Toby any better, he's mistaken. Toby's got too much Boston tar on him. Or maybe he'll throw the case so Toby wins."

"That wouldn't help Toby," Beulah pointed out. "No, I think he'll win for Mrs. Decker if he can."

"I suppose you'll be on hand at Hatfield," Tom said.

"Well, I don't know. An unescorted woman. . . ."

"Shucks, Beulah," Tom drawled, grinning, "you know we'll take you. I'll borrow my brother's chaise. There's room for four. I'll pick Warren up and . . . how about you, Dan?"

Shays shook his head. "I don't know yet. Maybe."

I didn't exactly cheer at the idea of Beulah coming along. For a time after that day I walked her home I had more or less avoided her, unnecessarily, I found. I soon realized I had overinflated the importance of my vague promises and she made it quite clear she took no stock in them. She never referred to the incident again and acted as if nothing had ever occurred between us. Suspecting she knew more of feminine strategy than I gave her credit for, I made sure not to be too much alone with her. She was much too desirable. And I wasn't yet able to overcome the inconvenient habit of looking beyond the moment of pleasure. So, I wasn't unhappy that, if she must come along, we would be in Tom's company.

On the morning of the 22nd of August Tom Packard was on deck promptly at six thirty, all dressed up in his best black suit, which fit him as well as it would the rough hewn fence rail he resembled. Beulah was with him and was wearing a fresh white calico dress splashed with big red flowers. She had a straw bonnet, but she was wise enough not to wear it, for the yellow straw would have made her skin look sallow. As it was, her tawny skin and lustrous brown hair contrasted prettily with the white and red of her dress. Even Pa, who had come in from the fields a moment to bid them good morning, couldn't help but comment on how pretty she looked.

"Is Dan coming?" I asked.

"No. He says he's too busy." Packard moved over in his seat. "Hop in front here if you want to. Plenty of room."

My mother and father wished us Godspeed and Tom whipped up the horse. The front seat of that chaise was broad enough, but my left arm seemed to be in the way. It was much more comfortable behind Beulah's back. Tom's brows went up and he clucked.

"Better not let Doc Cameron see that, Warren," he warned, "or you'll be publishing the banns come Sunday."

Beulah laughed. "When banns are to be published, I'll have the say about it, you can wager on that."

"Yep, I suppose you're right," Tom drawled, "long as you stay nice and proper. Remember the Nugent girl?"

"Oh, Thebe was a fool. I'd like to see that old goat make me marry a man I didn't want to." Beulah smiled and patted Tom's brown hand. "I'm glad you're along to protect my good name. A comfortably married man and uncle-in-law of sorts, you make the perfect chaperone."

Tom shuddered. "Stop it. I ain't that old."

At Bruce's tavern we picked up Hank McCullock and, when we reached Clapp's Tavern in Amherst, we took aboard Joel Billings. Joel and I greeted each other warmly, for he had been a rival of sorts for Judith's hand in those dear, dead days. Joel was a slim man, average height, but well muscled. He had crooked teeth and what I hadn't remembered, a crooked nose. I mentioned this and he grinned and rubbed his twisted nose. "I got it at Saratoga. It was too damn straight, anyway."

The time passed swiftly in reminiscences and stories of our respective adventures. When we reached Hadley we arranged for the rig to be stabled and walked up the north road to take the ferry across to Hatfield.

The town of Hatfield looked as if a flight of locusts had descended upon it. Crowds were gathered in groups before the stores and meeting house and on the common and around the taverns. The biggest crowd, naturally, was clustered about Colonel Seth Murray's Inn, where the convention was to be held. The numbers were propitious. Tom reckoned there must be delegates from almost every town in the county.

We found Caleb Keith and John Ranken standing under the big oak near the door to Murray's and we joined them. Tom recognized the man whom they were talking to and introduced me. He was Captain Hunt, the delegate from Northfield.

"I hope you gentlemen do better than the Leicester Convention, Captain," I commented.

"Damn ri . . . ." He caught himself, blushed furiously and bowed to Beulah. "Excuse me, M'am. Da— danged right, we will, Mr. Hascott. We ain't no—Cal! Damn my eyes, Cal! 'Scuse me, gentlemen." And he bounded off.

Caleb Keith and John Ranken were gone, too. That's the way it was, just like a grand reunion of Revolutionary soldiers. On all hands, men were shouting and yelling and pounding each other on the back with delight.

Colonel Murray was profiting handsomely by having the meeting at his public house. His taproom was jammed with delegates and their friends, all insisting on buying drinks for each other. Luke Day was there, too, his booming voice revealing his presence long before I caught a glimpse of him.

The delegates soon began going upstairs and the noise died down somewhat. Most of the townspeople drifted away and some of the visitors went over to Jurges' Inn, a half mile up the road. We pushed ourselves into the taproom and, since we had Beulah along with us, turned into the other public room on the side where the delegates had left their wives. That place was jammed, too, only one corner table having empty seats. A captain in a dark green broadcloth coat and ruffed linen shirt was in one of the chairs. But we could see he wouldn't mind if we sat at his table. In fact, he wouldn't even know it. He was resting his head on the table, snoring lustily, drunker than the House of Lords. No one paid any attention to him, not even the ladies present, for such conduct was neither unusual nor especially reprehensible.

"The convention is starting, Captain," Beulah said, shaking him. "Don't you think you'd better get upstairs? Your duty, you know, Captain."

The Captain hiccuped. "Foolishness . . . damn nushance . . . Mush perfer talkin 'to you, m'dear."

"I'll wait right here for you, Captain. Now, hurry along."

The captain grumbled and got up and gave Beulah a lopsided grin. Wriggling his fingers at her, he weaved his way through the crowded room, bumping into people right and left and stopping to bow and apologize profusely.

I suggested we leave Colonel Murray's because the place was becoming foul with the stink of tobacco and rum odors. We went to Mace's Tavern which was smaller, but almost as crowded. Poor Landlord Mace and his wife were almost beside themselves with work, for evidently they had never been confronted with such a sudden press of business—nor would ever again, Tom opined.

All afternoon, men drifted in and out of the Tavern, bringing news of the convention. The intelligence was highly unreliable as a whole; the more confidential and direct the source, the less it could be believed.

As the afternoon waned, the tension grew. I was beginning to worry about being able to get home before dark, but I knew I couldn't drag my comrades away until we got the news. Indeed. I doubt that I myself could have been dragged away.

At five o'clock, Luke Day barged in. Instantly, a hush dropped over the taproom and even the rattling of the cups and shuffling of feet ceased. Luke stood in the doorway a long moment, aware that all eyes were on him, his grim heavy features upholding his dignity.

"Gentlemen," he boomed, "the convention is nearly over." He smiled slowly. "As soon as I have refreshed myself, I can give you news of the proceedings."

He strode into the room, heading for the bar. Everyone clamored to buy him a drink. He laughed and refused all offers. Then, as he came to our table, he caught sight of Beulah and stopped short. He stared at her a moment and, as his gaze moved on to me, his face brightened.

"Why, Mr. Hascott! Delighted to see you again." He shook my hand and greeted others at the table he knew, then coughed and gave a slight jerk of head toward Beulah.

"This is Major Luke Day, Miss Crane," I said.

"Delighted, Mistress Crane, delighted." He took her hand and bowed. "Do you have a personal interest in the convention, Mistress Crane? Or is your interest academic?"

"A little bit of both, Major." Beulah gave him a bright smile. "If there were a chair I'd invite you to sit."

"I need no chair, M'am." Luke Day swept the cups and dishes from the corner of the table and hoisted his thigh over it. "You live in Pelham, M'am?"

"Oh, for Pete's sake, Luke," Eli called. "Ain't you never seen a purty girl before? Here, pass this over to him."

Day laughed sheepishly and accepted the mug of rum which had been passed from hand to hand through the vast crowd. We waited impatiently while he drank the whole mug at one draught.

"Now, gentlemen," he said, wiping his mouth with the back of his hand, "let's to business. The following grievances and unnecessary burdens are held to be the cause of discontent."

In a pompous, resounding voice, he read the whole list. There were seventeen grievances, contrasted to eight in the Leicaster Convention's bill of grievances. Ours included those eight, plus such obvious wrongs as the Supplementary Aid, the embarrassments on our free press, and the neglect of settlement of money matters pending between the state and Congress. Two strong articles showed clearly the trend of thought in these rural areas. One demanded the absolute abolition of the Senate. The other complained about the present mode of taxation as it operated unequally between polls and estates and between landed and mercantile interests.

The convention further offered four recommendations. The first urged the issuance of paper money, legal tender for all obligations, to provide a circulating medium. The second urged a revision of the constitution, since many of the grievances arose from defects in that document. The third asked the towns to petition the Governor for an immediate special session of the General Court. The fourth asked the people to refrain from mobs and unlawful assemblies until a constitutional method of redress could be obtained. Obviously, this qualification was an implied threat.

"Well, what do you think, Warren?" Tom asked me when Luke Day had finished.

"It's the vigorous document we hoped for," was my comment. "It's clearly better than the one produced by Worcester."

"Yes," Beulah agreed slowly, "but it doesn't solve our immediate problems, does it?"

Luke Day grunted. "Indeed, it does not, young woman. There's no guarantee that our illustrious Governor will pay any more attention to this petition than he has to the others." His brows came together. "God help him if he doesn't, is all I can say."

"Do you think he'll act before the 29th?" Beulah asked. "I have a case coming up in Common Pleas and one in General Sessions of the Peace."

"You, involved in a criminal . . . ?" His jaws clamped shut. "Yes, I remember now. You helped a widow woman save her property." Day snorted indignantly. "Preposterous, I say, persecuting a fine young woman for helping her neighbors." He glared around indignantly. "I daresay there are many of you who stand to lose everything if the court opens at Northampton next week."

"If, did you say, Luke?" someone called from the crowd.

Luke Day jammed his fists on his hips and glared around him. A hush rippled outward until every last voice in the taproom was stilled. Luke Day's greenish eyes narrowed.

"If," he repeated softly. "Yes, that's exactly what I said and exactly what I meant."

The nervous shuffle of feet filled the tense sober hush and neighbor avoided the eye of neighbor. This had been discussed before, not only in my town, but all over the county. Yet, no man now seemed to have the courage to say outright what was in everyone's mind. Someone gulped loudly.

"Maybe the Governor'll call a special session afore then."

"What?" Day exploded. "You expect miracles? This, gentlemen, is but another petition. You know what has happened to our petitions before. We must act! We must put teeth into our demands, show that bas— rotter we mean business."

184

Beulah eyed Luke Day a moment, smiled faintly, then gazed at Tom Packard. "Tom, what do you think?"

Tom grinned. "I just ain't thinking right now, Beulah."

Beulah frowned slightly, turned to Joel Billings. "Joel, some of you have cases coming up at Northampton."

Billings glanced at Luke Day, considered a moment, running his finger over his broken nose. "Well, I guess I got the guts to say it. If I thought I'd have support, I'd raise a body of men and stop that court from sitting."

Luke Day instantly slid from the table, stretched out his hand. "Lt. Billings, you have my support, the support of the men of West Springfield, one hundred of us." He whirled on the crowd. "Who else will join us? Speak up, men!"

His voice resounded through the room. The men shifted from one foot to the other, sent timid frowns to each other, licked their lips. Some were white with fright. Many faces were hardening with resolution.

"Speak up!" Luke Day roared. "Who will strike a blow for Liberty? Now is the time to act against those aristocratic bas—rotters who would enslave us. Who has the courage to strike? Speak up! You, Trubel, will you join us?"

"Shore, Luke." A tattered, unshaven fellow replied, "I'll be there with a dozen men—relatives. Hee!"

"I'm coming!" another cried.

Enthusiasm swept the room. "I'll be there!" "So will I!" "Count on me, Luke!" Then everyone was jabbering at once.

"Men after my own heart!" Luke Day boomed. "Men of courage." He clinked a gold piece on the table. "Landlord, a drink for my friends. A drink, gentlemen, to the twenty-ninth of August—at Northampton!"

A cheer resounded through the taproom, shaking the chandeliers and rattling the cups on the shelves behind the bar. Pewter mugs clacked at the grim promise in Luke Day's toast:

"To Northampton, gentlemen. To the beginning of the end of the tyrannical ambitions of the rich!"

Chapter 13

I couldn't laugh at Luke Day's bombast this time. As soon as I got home that evening, I sat down and wrote a letter to Mr. Blair, relating what had happened and enclosing the copy of the convention's proceedings which I had appropriated from Luke Day. I advised him of the intention of the more disgruntled to march on Northampton on the 29th of August and urged him to place the information before the proper authority at once—before the Governor himself, if possible. But I warned him that empty promises and saccharine words would not help. Only quick, positive, constructive action could head off the growing movement toward violence.

On Monday the 30th, I was still hesitating, not because I wasn't sympathetic, but because I couldn't brush aside one unassailable fact—stopping the court meant breaking the law.

At five o'clock, I was still in the fields, hoeing, a task I detested. And I could hear the rattle of the drums as Tom led the boys over East Hill and across the river toward Amherst.

As soon as mother sounded the dinner horn, I dropped my work and came in from the fields and washed up. Then, I went upstairs and changed to a clean shirt and my best serge clothes. When I came downstairs, I found Ma helping Increase to comb and club his hair.

"You going to Amherst, Increase?" I asked, surprised.

"No," Increase replied gruffly.

He blushed furiously and mumbled something to mother and hurried upstairs. My brows went up and Ma smiled.

"Increase has more important business," she said, her voice lowering. "It's Hope—you know, Hope Pendleton."

"For goodness sake." I chuckled dryly. "I guess I haven't been noticing what's going on right under my own nose. I must congratulate him. She's pretty and I hear she won the spinning match Dr. Cameron held at his house last year."

"Yes, she did. She's very handy around the house, too. Hope will make him a good wife." She gave me a sharp look. "Now, I've only got you to worry about."

Pa came in just at that moment, drying his hands on a towcloth towel. "Guess you don't have to worry about him, Ma. He'll be taking himself a woman pretty soon."

"I have to find one who suits first, Pa."

"So?" Pa picked the horn comb off the mantel. "Well, if that's the case, son, you better not be seeing so much of Beulah. There's talk already." He turned and held up the comb. "Say, that reminds me, Pendleton got me aside yesterday after meeting. He says Increase asked him about marrying Hope. We both figured it's all right if they wait 'til spring to publish the banns."

I grinned. "That's fine. And if Dr. Cameron gets after me, maybe we'll have a double wedding."

Neither Ma nor Pa thought that was very funny.

It was after eight o'clock when I came down the road toward Clapp's. Long before I reached there, the drone of voices and explosive laughter told me the taproom was very full. Outside, a straggling line of men was at ease and Joel Billings, his back bathed in the yellow light falling from the open door, was talking to a thickset man in a cocked hat and an old war uniform coat.

". . . and he'll take care of our boys," Joel was saying. "My barn's full. You'll like Joe. He's a good fellow."

"All right," the other replied. "I'll get a keg of rum and take the boys over there."

To say that the tavern was crowded would be an understatement. The place was jam-packed, every table taken, extra benches and chairs were being brought in. And still, some of the men had to stand by the bar to drink.

I pushed through the crowd to the bar. "Well, I didn't expect to see you here, Beulah."

"I'm helping out. Can I serve you, sir? No fancy drinks served tonight, mind." She whisked up a mug of rum for me. "I have to go to Northampton tomorrow anyway, don't I? Besides, I didn't want to miss the excitement." Someone caller her. "Coming, sir." She huffed. "I never knew this was such hard work. See you later, Warren."

There really wasn't room on the bench where Tom Packard was sitting but somehow the fellows managed to squeeze over and give me an inch. Tom introduced me around, informing the gentlemen I had been, until recently, a prisoner in Algiers. Immediately I was deluged with questions. Before I had answered half of them, the talk had veered back to the ever so much more important subject, the Hatfield Convention and what was to be done at Northampton on the morrow.

The unrestrained temper of the talk might have scared the wits out of anyone who didn't know these men. They spoke of tarring and feathering the Tories, hanging the judges, shooting creditors, none of which they meant—at the moment, anyway. They were used to talking in exaggerations. Not that they were lukewarm in their determination to stop the court. No, indeed. But I was quite sure they would go to almost any length to prevent violence.

Business finally slacked off to a point where Beulah was able to relinquish her duties as bar maid. I couldn't deny I had been waiting for this moment. She was hot and flushed and a bit piqued as she removed her cap and apron and came out from behind the bar. On all sides, she received invitations to sit, but she declined them all and came over to our table. Joel got up politely and pulled over a chair for her.

"No, thanks, Joel," she said tiredly. "I think I want a little air. It's awfully stuffy in here."

Mrs. Clapp gave her a frown. "Now, don't you go traipsing around in the dark outside, Beulah. The woods is full of wolves."

Everyone laughed self-consciously. Beulah patted the woman's plump cheek. "Don't you worry about me, Mrs. Clapp. I'll take Warren along for protection."

Joel winked. "Them's sheep's clothes he's got on, Beulah."

I wasn't amused. Until this moment, I hadn't realized how resigned everyone was to allowing me a monopoly on her attentions. Pa had been right. I had better watch my step. And I rather resented the need, though I was aware that the attitude among the men had grown through my own fault.

I was glad enough to be out of that warm, smoke-filled taproom. The night was clear and cool and a thin silvery sliver of moon seemed to be pasted on the star-sprinkled canopy of blue velvet overhead. In the distance, a cheery red campfire cast a soft glow over a circle of lounging men. They were singing the old ballads that had eased a thousand and one heartaches around a thousand and one campfires during the horrible months of the late war. Their voices were soothingly melodious in the soft summer darkness.

"That's Captain Grover's detachment," Beulah told me in a subdued voice. "His boys didn't want to hole up in a barn tonight." She sighed. "I'd like to sleep outside on a night like this."

"Ha, you'd be sorry," I declared. "You'd wake up stiff in every joint and dripping with dew."

She poked me playfully. "Must you always be practical, Warren?" She took my hand. "Come on, let's sit down there by the brook."

The grassy bank was dry, but the tufts were uneven and it seemed darker down here, so we had to move very cautiously. We found a level spot near the edge of the water and settled to rest. Beulah pulled off one shoe, then the other, and set them on a rock within easy reach.

"I never knew being a barmaid was such hard work," she said with a slight groan. "My poor feet."

Without the slightest formality, she drew her skirts well up over her knees and stripped off her stockings. Her legs and well formed thighs were startlingly white. She dipped her toes into the purling waters, drew a sharp breath, then plunged her feet in and gave forth a long, satisfied sigh. More alarmingly, she loosened the string holding her dress together and her bosom relaxed to its full roundness. She was saved from immodesty by the inside flap of the bodice.

"There, I feel better now," she said delightedly. She gave me a sharp look. "Goodness, Warren, don't look so shocked."

"Don't be silly," I growled.

For some time, we just sat in silence and listened to the lilting tinkling and bubbling of the tumbling waters and watched the pert winkings of the restless fireflies. I was propped on one elbow a short distance back from the water, for once completely amenable to forgetting the petty turbulences of the world. But I was too conscious of her arm brushing against my knees, of the soft curve of her neck, of the disturbing firmness of her thighs. It didn't help to watch her wriggling toes.

At length, she drew away from the water, murmuring, "It's getting cold." And she sank back on the grass, settling herself with sinuous contentment. I scarcely dared look into her eyes, for my heart was throbbing with mounting insistence. I dared not reach over and draw down her skirt.

She was breathing so languorously I thought she had fallen asleep. But no. She was gazing into the heavens, as if there she sought the promise of silence from the astute stars. Her smooth heaving breast had escaped the confines of her dress and the rosy pinkness of the crest was an irresistible temptation. My lips brushed it and she drew a quick, gasping breath, pressing herself the firmer to my mouth. Her arm crept over my shoulder and she squirmed with soundless delight as my kisses raced with burning steps to her throat and her chin and her waiting lips. Her fierce ardor drew me ever down to her.

A coarse, nearby laugh swirled the mist away. Beulah stiffened, too, and for an eternity, we both stopped breathing. The gruff voices came closer. Two men emerged from the darkness. There was just enough shadow to give me hope that they wouldn't notice us. They didn't. Both were weaving slightly, absorbed in their ribald jokes and arguments upon who was the drunker. As the footsteps and the laughter receded, Beulah relaxed with a sigh.

"Men can be worse gossips than women," she said with some irritation. She smiled and rubbed the nape of my neck. "But I wouldn't care."

I kissed her again, but the fervor of the moment was gone. We both knew it. And strangely, despite my annoyance, I was not regretful. She trembled a little, as if she sensed it.

"Warren, I—I have a room to myself tonight." Her voice

dropped to a whisper. "Warren, a woman does have the right to . . . to live as she pleases."

I held her close. "You may believe it, Beulah. I want to believe it. But we won't test its truth . . . not now." I kissed the tip of her nose. "No, not now. I—I like you too much."

"Poor Warren," she murmured, a bit peevishly, "he still bears the cross of callowness."

Her full lips touched mine and her arms tightened about me. Had that kiss lasted another moment, my resolution would have melted in the fires of her passion.

"We'd better keep Dr. Cameron in mind," I said shakily.

I got up, waited until she had put on her shoes and stockings, then pulled her up. The mockery was gone from her eyes and her resentment told me I had scored.

The rattling of a drum under my window awakened me with a start. For some time, my sleep befogged mind groped for an explanation of that hideous noise. Then I remembered I was in Clapp's Tavern. The depression in the mattress beside me told me that my companion, an old fellow with the most horrible snore, had already left his couch.

I fumbled about in the half light, found my shoes, slipped into them and went over to the window. A great horde of men was gathered below. Some were standing in rude lines, but most were moving from group to group, shouting delighted greetings to old acquaintances and noisily being introduced to new ones. It was not a prosperous looking crowd. A few wore cocked hats and shabby old uniform coats left over from the late war. Most wore clean, patched homespun suits or towcloth smocks. All were armed with muskets or swords or new-cut bludgeons. This was the last Tuesday in August, the day for the sitting of the Courts of Law.

I dressed hastily, ran my horn comb through my hair and hurried downstairs. The taproom was well nigh empty, only a half a dozen or so eating breakfast. Mr. Clapp gave me a cheery "Good Morning," took my order and I went over to the table by the front window. From the look of the milling throng, it was evident that this section of the county would be well represented. I judged there were at least two hundred on hand already, and I could see two more columns coming in from eastward.

I ate hastily, paid my bill and thrust myself out the crowded doorway. I soon spied Tom Packard, head and shoulders above those surrounding him. There was much joking and laughing going on over there and, moving over, I saw Beulah was the center of attraction. She was wearing a cocked hat at a jaunty angle and, to protect her from the chill of the morning, someone had thrown a uniform coat over her shoulders.

I was still hesitating about joining the Pelham detachment when the decision was whisked out of my hands. Beulah and Tom spied me at the same moment, came over and took my arms and marched me to the head of our contingent. The boys gave me a rousing welcome. I couldn't protest without setting off an unpleasant scene. So, I kept my mouth shut and only grinned.

Our march consumed less than three hours, for the drums kept our pace brisk and lighthearted chatter shortened the long miles. Not until we crossed Goodman's Ferry at Hadley and reformed to march into Northampton did the men become subdued. They need not have worried about how the populace would receive us. Crowds lined both sides of the elm shaded road and gave us rousing cheers.

The drums were growling in stirring rhythm as the column crossed the square in the center of town toward the hill on which stood our Hall of Justice. At the door of the Court House, Joel Billings and the drummers detached themselves from the column and stood to one side while the rest passed in review. We wound around to the rear of the drummers and formed a barrier before the entrance. The maneuver was done briskly, if not smartly. As soon as everyone was in place, the order to stand at ease was given and the leaders of the various town contingents, including Tom, gathered around Joel. It was then just a little before nine. There was no sign of the other contingents which were supposed to be marching from the south and western parts of the county.

Beulah said, "Well, I have to see Plummer. Looks like the case won't come up this session. But I'll be prepared, anyway."

"I'll go along with you, Beulah," I said. "I have to have a

lawyer for Uncle Enoch's case. Might as well be Plummer."
Tom smiled. "Y'know, I have a feeling he ain't going to
be working today. Don't pay him a retainer, Warren."
Beulah returned the cocked hat and coat to Jim Cowan
and we went across the Common to Mr. Plummer's office,
which was located over Tappen & Fowle's store. I thought
Beulah might be slightly peeved over what happened last
evening, but her gay manner made it seem as if she had forgotten all about it. That suited me. I felt uncomfortable every
time I thought how foolish I had been to pass by such a
golden opportunity.

We knocked on the upstairs door and a thin, squeaky voice
bade us "Come in." The elder Tobias Plummer was behind his
flat-topped desk placed before the window. He was almost
hidden behind the books and piled up papers strewn untidily
about the desk. He was as plump as his son. Except for the
wrinkles about his eyes and the grey in his hair, he was almost
an exact duplicate of Toby. I explained my needs briefly and
after a minute's hesitation he waived the matter of retainer.

Tying my papers with a red ribbon, he threw them into a
drawer. I hoped he'd be able to find them again, though
I doubted it, the drawer was in such a mess. He immediately
confounded my fears. He opened another drawer, equally
chaotic, fumbled about a moment and came up with the
papers to Beulah's case.

"Now, let me see." He frowned at the papers. "We'll use
the same strategy as Warren, in his uncle's case. We'll call
for a postponement at this session."

A roar and a swelling volume of cheers brought us up from
our chairs and to the window. The men in front of the courthouse were yelling and cheering and waving their hats. Here
and there, a musket went off with a loud bang. Then we saw
the reason for their jubilance. Another column was coming
in from the south.

A chunky, barrel-chested man with a stiff, military bearing
was leading the column. Behind him stretched a long line,
four abreast. There were at least five hundred men in that
detachment, a truly stirring sight, for they were formed in
a much more regular line than we had attained. The drums
pounded in brisk militant rhythm as the column tramped

across the Common. The commander of that contingent was, of course, our friend Luke Day.

"Come on," Beulah said excitedly. "Let's get down to Pomeroy's. They'll be holding their consultation soon."

Two guards were standing before Pomeroy's Tavern and, as we tried to enter, their muskets crossed. But one of them knew Beulah by sight and, with a grin, let us pass. Inside, Captain Hinds was directing two of his men in taking out a keg of rum he had bought. Tom had also bought a keg for our boys, which he was helping Hank McCullock hoist to Jim Cowan's shoulder. Joel, Captain Grover, Simeon Vaughn and some other gentlemen were already at work on the petition.

Joel grabbed my arm. "Warren, sit here. We need someone who writes a good hand."

Captain Grover pushed over the ink and paper. "You're elected clerk, Mr. Hascott. I'm staying out of this. These asses want to put all sorts of seditious rot into the petition."

Before the argument could resume, Luke Day and his party barged in, boisterously greeting those already on hand. He shook hands all around, allowing only a stern half-smile to break his dignity. Cups rattled like mad in the kitchen and the serving men came running with the drinks. Then, after a toast to the success of our expedition, we settled to work.

There was little wrangling, and that on the scope of the petition. One group wanted a short statement, the other wanted to detail grievances. The latter attained a compromise when it was pointed out that the petition would, in the end, reach the Governor.

Even so, the paper was quite windy. At the very beginning, the men set forth that they had the constitutional right to protest against unconstitutional acts of the Legislature. The scarcity of cash was the only important grievance mentioned. There was no open threat in the petition, but the judges were told that, if they wanted to avoid the resentment of the people, they would forbear doing any business at this session of the court.

Six men signed the document. And they were aware of the great risk they were taking. They were grim and serious as they stepped up to the table and affixed their signatures. But there was no sign of trembling, no sign of weakness or hesitation. The six men were: John Thompson, Asa Miller, Thomas Anfolin, Luke Day, Joel Billings and Simeon Vaughn.

When the last had signed, Luke Day heaved a loud sigh. His voice was comparatively subdued. "I think we could all stand another drink. Pomeroy, rum!"

A loud voice at the door said, "The judges are coming!" I caught Beulah's hand as the men stampeded for the door. "I don't want you trampled. Wait a moment."

Beulah squeezed my hand. "Can it be love? Come on, let's hurry. I don't want to miss this."

We ran down the street, joining the streams of people rushing to the big square. The leaders scattered and took their places with their own men. The men themselves hastened back into their formations, holding their muskets ready for use. Luke Day, Joel Billings, Thompson, Miller, Anfolin and Vaughn grouped themselves directly in front of the ranks guarding the door.

A hush rippled over the gathered crowds as three men, walking with slow, solemn steps, came out of the street from the east. Behind them were a number of court retainers and lawyers. The judges maintained impassive dignity as they came up Meeting House Hill headed straight for the Court House entrance. I noticed Joel jab the tip of his sword into the turf, for his arm was trembling a little. In the other hand he held the petition.

The three judges stopped before the leaders and, for a tense moment no one spoke, no one moved.

"Stand aside!" Judge Porter finally cried.

"Eleazer," Joel said quietly, "you know why we're here. We don't want any trouble. There won't be if you—and Judge Bliss and Judge Mather—act like reasonable men."

He took one brisk step forward, handed Judge Porter the petition, then stepped back. Eleazer Porter looked at the paper, glanced at his colleagues. Without a word, the three men swung about and returned whence they had come.

Two thousand suspicious eyes held fast to the judges as they returned to Clark's Tavern. Still no one moved. Not one word was spoken until the judges had entered the inn.

"What do you suppose they'll do?" Asa Miller asked, his voice almost a whisper.

"I don't know," Luke Day returned darkly. "But if they try any tricks. . . ."

A freckle-faced boy came running up the street and came across the Common to us. "They're opening the court!" he yelled.

A roar of rage swept through our ranks. The men made a motion as if to sweep down the hill toward the tavern. Luke Day swung around and faced the men.

"Stand fast!" he bellowed. The men obeyed instantly. Luke Day counted out ten men. "Come on. You, too, gentlemen," he added, indicating the other leaders.

At double time, the men trotted down to the tavern. Beulah and I, since we had stood aside, followed along with them. A huge crowd was gathering about the tavern, but they quickly made way as Luke Day and the others came puffing up.

At that very moment, the door opened and a thin, sour-looking man stepped out. He held up his hand before Luke Day.

"The court has decided," he said nasally, "to continue all business until the next session of the court, to be holden at Springfield on the second Tuesday of November next. Accordingly the court has adjourned."

No one heard him read the official pronouncement. A wild wave of cheering swept from Clark's Tavern in ever increasing volume across the Common to the Court House where our men waited. Muskets went off, hats were thrown into the air, men hugged each other, laughing and swearing and yelling in delight. The court had been stopped.

It had been an easy victory.

Chapter 14

EVERYONE hoped that our excursion to Northampton would be the end of agitation for a redress of grievances. To our dismay, we soon learned it was only the beginning. When we got back to Conkey's late that afternoon, we found Dan Shays was there. He told us he had to go to Worcester, but I suspected he had merely found that excuse to avoid being in Northampton. At any rate, he had passed through Hubbardston on the way back and visited with Adam Wheeler. Wheeler had told him that the Worcester men were planning to stop the court at Worcester on the 5th of September.

"Artemus Ward will be the judge there, won't he?" Tom Packard asked. "The General's a tough man, brethren. He won't knuckle down as easily as Eleazer Porter did."

Shays nodded soberly. "I told Wheeler that. He says everything will be all right. Unless the militia turns out. In that case, Wheeler says he won't force the issue. But he doesn't think the militia would obey the order to turn out, even if it's given. The people are on our side."

Tom shook his head. "The Tories are yelling now that we're only trying to swindle them out of their money. It's going to be pretty bad if some damn fool starts shooting—and there's at least one damn fool in every crowd." He turned to me. "You got important friends in Boston, Warren. Maybe they can get the Governor to call a special session before that court opens."

"Yes, why don't you go to Boston, Warren," Shays agreed eagerly. "We don't want any . . . any trouble."

"Well, I'll think about it," I said. "I wrote once to a friend of mine who may be able to help. I'll write again."

"Make the letter strong," Shays advised.

And I did. As soon as I got home, I wrote an account of the Northampton affair to Mr. Blair. I took particular pains to be accurate, for I was aware he would be getting distorted accounts from Tory sources.

On Thursday, I received a reply from Mr. Blair to the first letter I had sent him. It was dated the previous Friday. His news was ominous. He said he had taken my information to several of the Governor's advisors and urged, as so many had urged, that they get the Governor to call a special session to head off a revolt. The worthy councilmen had pooh-poohed the idea that revolt was brewing and had flatly refused to advise the Governor to do anything whatsoever. I hoped they were merely stupid. Already there were whispers that certain factions were hoping and working for an outbreak of violence in order to have the excuse to clamp down martial law and then set up a dictatorship.

The 5th of September came and still the Governor had done nothing. The court at Worcester was stopped. The turnout there was not as great as at Northampton, only about five hundred being present. And the Worcester County men, as we anticipated, did not have as easy a time as we had had. General Artemus Ward lived up to his reputation as a fire-eater. He balked at the idea of being prevented from doing his duty.

As we heard the story, Captain Wheeler, Captain Smith of Barre, Captain Hazelton of Hardwick, Ben Converse and others led their men to the courthouse and threw a cordon around it. At the time appointed for the opening of the court, General Ward tried to get through. The men at the entrance fixed bayonets and leveled them. General Ward would not stop, not until he pressed himself against the points of the bayonets and found the men would not yield. He then harangued the crowd for two solid hours, threatening and cajoling. He was finally hooted into silence when he said that the Government never would yield to force that which would readily be afforded respectful representations.

For the moment Ward admitted defeat. He returned to the U. S. Arms Tavern, opened the court there and immediately adjourned it to the following day. Then, he called in the commanders of the town militia and ordered them to mobilize their men. The colonels declined politely, pointing out that the people were on the side of the Insurgents and would not turn out. Ward thereupon sent out a call to General Warner for the militia from the surrounding area. The next morning, two hundred men from Ware and Holden came in. The Insurgents paraded up and down Main Street, drums thumping, inviting all who would resist oppression to join them. Everyone was in a gay mood, for the militia gave no sign of appearing and victory was in sight. When the men returned to the courthouse, some exuberant youngsters went out into the woods and cut down a pine tree and set it up by the courthouse door. They also distributed sprigs of hemlock and one of them got up and announced somewhat in this fashion:

"There—" he pointed to the pine tree "—is the standard of our revolt. Here—" he held up the sprig of hemlock "—is the badge of our rebellion. Henceforth, we shall be known as THE REGULATORS!"

The name and badge swept across the state with the swiftness of a hurricane. Less conservative men than myself were alarmed. Such trappings, giving men a sense of comradeship and a common mode of recognition, made it simple to weld them into a stable organization. And once that organization had jelled, the Regulators would certainly gravitate inexorably toward open insurrection.

It was now well established that our excursion to Northampton had set off a whole series of these court stoppage incidents. Three more were probable on the 12th of September when the courts were due to sit in Berkshire, Middlesex and Bristol Counties. With dread and impatience we awaited the coming of that fateful 12th of September. As yet the Government had shown no sign of acting, either to call out the militia or call a special session for the purpose of redressing grievances. If the militia was called out, there was certain to be bloodshed, for the belief was hardening among the more radical of the Regulators that the Governor had sold out to the Tories and Monarchists who were plotting to steal our liberties. If Bowdoin should give proof of the truth of this accusation, the result could only be war.

Dan Shays had an astonishing number of friends scattered throughout the state, friends from army days, some as far east as Groton—he knew Job Shattuck quite well—and some as far west as Great Barrington. Dan was an indefatigable correspondent, eager for news of the movement, prompt in replying to the many letters. Thus, we at Conkey's received a fairly comprehensive picture of public opinion in the other rural districts. Shays and some of the others took the reports at face value. But Tom Packard and I were more cautious in accepting the glowing accounts of how enthusiastic the people were about stopping the courts.

Beulah, I must remark, was visiting Mrs. Decker more and more frequently. She would return just before dark and, quite naturally, stopped by at Conkey's to chat with the boys. On the rare occasions I happened to be there, I walked home with her. We confined our conversations exclusively to topics of current interest. Only once, I mentioned a personal matter, telling her of Burdick's offer and my refusal and my half-formed business scheme which I intended to arrange with Joe. I was afraid I might become so entangled with her that I wouldn't be able to leave after harvest. So I saw her as little as possible.

Just before the Worcester affair, Mr. Blair had written to me and informed me that the Governor was drawing up a proclamation. No one knew yet what would be in the proclamation, but Blair promised to send me a copy as soon as one was available. Our hopes soared. Now, surely, after most of the counties had held conventions, after two courts had been stopped, Governor Bowdoin would know that the people were aroused and he would be in the mood to do something constructive. Thus, we awaited the proclamation with eagerness.

When it finally came on the 8th of September, we read it with outraged amazement. It was dated the 2nd of September and dealt solely with the Northampton affair. The Governor stated that we had acted in contempt and defiance of government, that the high handed offense was subversive to government and tended to dissolve our "excellent" Constitution. Such incidents could only terminate in anarchy and despotism. Thus, the Governor called on all judges, justices, sheriffs and other officers to prevent and suppress such riotous proceedings and directed the attorney-general to bring the ringleaders of any future violations to condign punishment. Not a word about redressing grievances.

Most infuriating of all in the proclamation was the implication that we were ". . . misguided by the machinations of internal enemies. . . ." In other words, Bowdoin was accusing us of being incited by British agents whose purposes were to pave the way for our reabsorption into the British Empire. This directed at the soldiers of the Revolution! The unconscious or deliberate lack of understanding of the farmer's position succeeded only in aggravating an already aggravated situation.

Thus, it was in a grim and angry mood that we awaited the sitting of the courts on Tuesday, the 12th of September. We thought sure we'd get letters on Wednesday, but no news came even on Thursday. By that time we were almost beside ourselves with impatience. On Friday morning I went up to Dr. Hynds, thinking there might be a letter for me from Mr. Blair, but there was none. I was sure, however, that news had come to the boys at Conkey's, so, as soon as I was finished with my morning's work, I cleaned up and hurried over to East Hill.

Beulah was there, standing by Tom Packard who was surrounded by boys clumped about the table next to the fireless hearth.

"Just in time, Warren!" Tom called as he saw me. "News just came in. Still room on the mourner's bench."

The boys drew aside for me and I saw that Joel Billings was at the table with Dan Shays. After I shook hands with Joel, I found that Joe Hinds had come, too. He told me he had come over from Hardwich with dispatches which had been routed through Hubbardston. Dan had quite a pile of letters before him and there was a mild frown on his smooth, even features. He waved briefly to me and pushed the letters across the table.

"Look 'em over, Warren. Nothing personal in them."

There were seven letters in all, one from Adam Wheeler, one from Joe Shattuck, a third from Abe Gale, a fourth from an Obediah Collins of Taunton. The remaining three were from friends of Dan's in Berkshire, the best account being from Lt. Perez Hamlin. Since the letters generally covered the same ground, I shall give you only a summary of the events.

Taunton: Early Tuesday morning, the militia, under General Cobb, occupied the courthouse. Sentiment for the Regulators was much less in this county, a sea coast county, so the Insurgents were not able to muster enough strength to challenge the militia. A band of Insurgents did gather outside the town, but they knew it would be folly to march in. Their petition, asking the court to adjourn, was ignored. The Taunton Court opened and did business.

Great Barrington: Here, in the farthest west county of the Commonwealth, the Insurgents were the most radical and hot headed. Their actions showed it. Early Tuesday morning, Eli Parsons marched in with eight hundred men. They occupied the courthouse and a mob broke open the jail and liberated all the prisoners—criminals as well as debtors. After that, the mob marched to the tavern where the judges were gathered and, pushing their way in, demanded under threat of arms that the judges sign a paper, obligating them not to act under their commissions until all grievances were redressed. Three of the judges bowed to the threat and signed. A fourth, Judge Woodbridge, flatly refused, saying he'd rather resign his commission than submit.

However, the court of Great Barrington did not open.

Concord: On the same day that the court was due to open, a county convention sat here. Fearing bloodshed, Judge Philips, Col. William Prescott, Joseph Hosmer and other prominent gentlemen had persuaded Governor Bowdoin to revoke the marching orders given to General Brooks. Hence, the militia was not on hand when the court was due to open. Job Shattuck, with a force of two hundred men, occupied the courthouse early Tuesday morning. Around two o'clock in the afternoon, Adam Wheeler with ninety men from Worcester, came in. Job Shattuck sent a demand to Jones' Tavern, where the judges were gathered, that the court adjourn. A committee tried to persuade Job to abandon the courthouse. Job refused. The judges finally bowed and adjourned the court. Except for the outrageous conduct of one Nathan Smith, who threatened bodily harm to any who did not join the Insurgents, there were no untoward incidents. Job Shattuck and Adam Wheeler shut Smith up and drove him out of town. On Tuesday night, having won their point, the Insurgents dispersed.

When I had finished reading the dispatches, I folded them carefully and laid them on the table by Dan's hand. The room gradually became quiet as the boys broke off their conversations and looked at me. Dan had a strange, perplexed look on his face.

"Well, what do you think, Warren?" he asked. "Do you think the Governor will be convinced now we mean business?"

I shrugged. "It would have looked a lot better if the court at Taunton hadn't opened and the jail at Great Barrington hadn't been broken open."

"That's what I was thinking," Tom Packard put in. "Seems to me, we're in a bad hole."

Our discussion was broken off by a loud, booming voice which could only emerge from the barrel-chest of Luke Day. "Is Captain Shays here?" he bellowed at Conkey. "I was informed I'd find Captain Shays. . . ."

"Here, Luke!" Shays called, getting up. "Luke, I'm glad to see you."

Luke Day barged through the crowd, seized Dan's hand and almost wrung it off. "Dan, you old bast—Oh, Mistress Crane, how delighted to see you again, and Lt. Billings and Mr. Hascott."

Luke Day was so noisy in greeting those he knew that we didn't see the other four men who had entered with him until Day himself brought them to our attention.

"You know these gentlemen, I assume? Captain Grover of Montague . . . Captain Brown of Whately . . . Captain Powers of Shutesbury. I met them on the road. And this, gentlemen, is Eli Parsons of Adams, who came to give me a first hand report of events in Berkshire."

Eli Parsons was a short, stocky man with sharp, thin features and small darting black eyes. Unlike the rest of us, who all had our hair queued, Parsons' shock of black hair hung loose and was bobbed short. His smile was perpetual as if covering his self-consciousness. He showed great economy in speech, merely grunting in response to our welcome.

"I guess you know what brought us," Day said finally. "That news—damnably disturbing. We'd better discuss it

203

fully—in private." He smiled about him. "You'll excuse us, gentlemen? No offense intended."

"We'll use the front parlor," Shays suggested. "Tom, you come along."

It was virtually a staff meeting of the leaders of the movement in Hampshire. As far as I could learn, no one had called this meeting. It resulted naturally from the gravity of the news. Since Shays had been in contact with all of them, they had come here to consult on the meaning of the news and what, if anything, was to be done about it.

The meeting did not last long and the men studiously avoided talking about the movement as they drifted out.

Beulah and I corralled Dan Shays who confided that it had been decided that we had gone too far to quit now and that we must, to avoid the arrest of all leaders, stop the Supreme Judicial Court at Springfield on the 29th.

"Dan," Beulah said softly. "Will you be leading the Pelham contingent?"

Shays, who was still working on his list, did not look up. "Why, I suppose so—if the men want me." He frowned at his papers. "We wouldn't have to march if the Governor called his special session, would we?" He looked up at me, almost pleadingly. "Maybe if you went to Boston. . . . There may be bloodshed, Warren. The militia's certain to be out. And you know how General Shepard feels about us. He might call out the militia on his own."

I shifted uneasily. "I couldn't do any good."

"You could try," Shays said. "It's your duty."

When I arrived in Boston at dusk of the 18th of September, my impulse was to go directly to Mr. Burdick and see Judith. But I decided it would be better to call first upon Mr. Blair. Thus as soon as I had my supper at Pease's, I repaired to State House. Mr. Blair had finished work and gone for the day, so I went to his residence.

The Two Palaverers was filled with supper patrons, many of whom remembered me and invited me to sit with them. I begged to be excused until I could ascertain if Mr. Blair was in, for neither he nor Ethan were in the taproom. Yes, Mr.

Rhodes told me, Mr. Blair was at home. He had just finished his supper and gone to his room. Accordingly, I went upstairs. A quavering "Come in!" answered my knock and I opened the door. Mr. Blair, seated at the desk by the draped window, was just clapping on his wig.

"Warren, my dear boy!" He hopped up and took my hand in both of his. "I'm delighted to see you. Here, sit here, the rocker is most comfortable."

"I'm not interrupting your work?" I asked.

"Indeed not." He snatched off his wig and threw it on the bed, grinning at me. "What brings you to Boston?"

I related the events leading up to the meeting at Conkey's and gave him the status of public opinion as I saw it. Blair listened carefully, his arms folded, a slight frown fixed on his small, wrinkled face. When I was finished, he smiled and shook his head.

"Warren, you've come on a fool's errand. For months, I've been warning the politicians this would happen. You'll remember I told you this was brewing the first day you arrived here." He shrugged. "However, you can try, if you like. You've come at an opportune moment. There's a meeting of the Ohio Company at the Bunch of Grapes this evening. Hancock will be there—and General Putnam and several other prominent gentlemen, including your friend, Mr. Burdick."

"Burdick there? That's fine." I stood up. "If you'll excuse me, perhaps I'd better get over there as soon as possible."

Blair nodded. "But don't expect too much, Warren."

"It isn't true. . . ." I paused awkwardly. "I mean, that blather about the aristocrats wanting a dictatorship?"

Blair smiled thinly. "Some do, of course. Some would rather see a monarchy than chaos. The bulk of the wealthy do not. But they're frightened. They feel if they open the door an inch the radicals will overwhelm them and seize their power."

"You make my task sound hopeless."

Blair chuckled and patted my shoulder. "Try, anyway. Mr. Minot is there. You'll see what I have to put up with."

The Bunch of Grapes, on the corner of Kilby and State Streets, was one of the oldest and most famous of Boston's taverns. It was the haunt of the wealthier merchants and bankers and legislators. The place was expensive and crowded with well dressed men. Brocades and velvets were the rule, and I felt ill at ease in my well worn serges. I stood in the doorway, peering through the smoky atmosphere, searching for a friendly face and finding none. At length, a serving man approached and asked my business.

"Mr. Burdick is attending a meeting of the Ohio Company. Will you inform him Mr. Hascott wants to speak to him? It's urgent."

The servingman picked his way among the tables, heading for a private dining room at the rear of the taproom. I wasn't sure it was good form to follow him, but I did anyway. I waited outside and, a moment later, Mr. Burdick emerged.

"I'm sorry to bother you, Mr. Burdick," I apologized.

Burdick beamed and shook my hand. "Nonsense, my boy. They're only trying to sell me more stock. I was about ready to go home. Was there some business you wanted to discuss with me?"

"Well, not exactly, sir. I thought perhaps. . . ." I was suddenly conscious of how foolishly self important I would sound. "What I mean, sir, is that I thought you and your friends. . . ." I felt myself blushing. "You should be warned. Rebellion is brewing."

Mr. Burdick's plump face became sober. "We've heard disquieting reports. He took my arm in a firm grip. "Come in, Warren. You can give these gentlemen a first hand account of the situation. They'll want to hear you."

He almost had to drag me in, I was so scared. I had often imagined myself in the company of distinguished people and acting in a cool, suave manner. After all, people are people. The prospect of facing them now awed me. And these men were truly important. I was slightly reassured when I saw Salderman, Trowbridge and my friend Graham at the table. Besides them, there were General Putnam, Colonel Benjamin Tupper, Mr. Minot who was Mr. Blair's boss as Secretary of the House of Representatives, Mr. Lang, Mr. Samuel Breck, a merchant, and a thin-faced, aristocratic gentlemen in a rich red velvet coat, the Hon. John Hancock.

Mr. Burdick stopped me at the foot of the table and the drone of conversation died away. Mr. Salderman's long, horselike face brightened as he waved. Mr. Towbridge, too, recognized me. Mr. Lang gave me a pleasant salute. Mr. Graham just scowled.

"Gentlemen," Burdick said, "may I present my young friend, Mr. Warren Hascott. He lives in Pelham, Hampshire County. He is personally acquainted with many of the Rebels out there."

Absolute silence fell over the table. If I was ill at ease before, I was positively tortured now. With few exceptions these gentlemen stared at me as if Mr. Burdick had introduced me as the Devil. My mind became a complete blank.

General Putnam finally coughed. "We'd appreciate an account of the disturbances, Mr. Hascott. We're deeply interested and, I daresay, alarmed."

I gulped three or four times and, with horror, I found I had lost my voice. I felt like a perfect ass. Mr. Hancock chuckled and passed over a cup of punch.

"I fear we're impolite, Mr. Hascott. Your throat must be dusty. Try this . . . an excellent throat oil."

"Thank you, sir." I sipped a little and felt much better as the liquor burned the fur from my gullet. "The fact is, gentlemen, I believe the Commonwealth faces a real rebellion."

An excited murmuring went around the table and everyone urged me to go on. When I began my tale, my voice was shaking a little, but I gained confidence as I went along. I sketched the events at the Hatfield Convention and at Northampton, trying to show them the way the people in the country districts really felt about all this. I wanted them to understand that the people were behind the movement, not a group of isolated scoundrels. The assemblage listened in deep, troubled silence. When I was finished, no one spoke for a long moment.

Mr. Trowbridge, a scowl on his wrinkled face, leaned forward. "Mr. Hascott, who's leading this movement?"

"As I tried to show you, no one is leading the movement. It has grown spontaneously, the direct result of economic and political injustices which are prevalent. As you gentlemen must know, this hasn't come on suddenly. It's been brewing a long time. I can see it, and I've been back in the country only two months."

"You came from England, didn't you, Mr. Hascott?" Mr. Graham asked in an accusing tone.

"I passed through England on the way home," I replied. "That's your story," he returned nastily. "Hascott, I have information that this is being instigated by British agents. The British are trying to divide us and stir up civil war, after which they'll drag us back into the British Empire."

"Gentlemen," I pleaded, "don't be confused by any poppycock about British agents. Those men are old soldiers. They've been shabbily treated since the war. They never had a chance to reestablish themselves. They're getting desperate."

"No one starves," Putnam said bruskly.

"Good God, General, did you fight for bread? You had bread under King George. Did you fight to become a beggar, dependent on the kindness of your neighbors? That's what's happened to those men. Certainly, they don't starve. That's because their neighbors have food and won't let them go hungry. But is that just? Is that what they sacrificed eight years of their lives for? Is that the liberty they were promised? But that isn't the point, whether they starve or not. The point is that those men are being denied their right to earn a living. You know that hundreds of them are in jail. If conditions get worse, the number will be thou—no—the day won't come when conditions will be that bad. There will be a bloody civil war first."

I knew my words were intemperate, but I was struggling mightily against the indifference mirrored in every face. That I was defending something I did not wholly approve, that I was identifying myself with their cause, did not bother me. I could only consider the imminent danger, the danger heightened by the very immobility of these men.

"Northampton was the beginning," I went on. "Worcester was next, then Concord, Taunton and Great Barringon. The end is not yet in sight. Gentlemen, not one court will sit west of Boston until and unless something is done."

"What, for example? Trowbridge put in sharply. "I read the Hatfield Declaration. And let me tell you, young man, I've never seen a more absurd set of grievances."

Graham snorted. "Must we humble ourselves to a pack of malicious knaves who want to cheat their creditors?"

I ignored him, turned to General Putnam. "Those men out there were your men. They were once willing to lay down their lives at your command. Why? Because you were leading them in a fight for something you and they believed in. The war is over. What have they got? Poverty, degradation, jail. General, where is the freedom they were promised? Where is the better land you told them they would get? Are you going to let them down?"

General Putnam grunted into his neckcloth. "You're excited, young man. We don't doubt your good intentions, but we believe you exaggerate the situation. This will pass over. We'll wait and see. If the situation is as bad as you say, you can be sure we'll prevail upon the Governor to call a special session. However, I doubt if that will be necessary. The General Court meets again in November, anyway."

I shook my head, suddenly weary, suddenly realizing I had been wasting my breath. "Must you wait until civil war breaks out before acting? Isn't the justice of the people's wants enough to move you?" There was no answer. "You all agree with the General?"

No one replied. No reply was necessary.

"Well, thank you for listening, gentlemen. It was an enlightening experience. Now, I'll leave you to your business."

Of all the people in that room, only Jothan Salderman showed the slightest sign of having listened carefully to what I had said. The rest were back to their small talk about business and dreams of a Western Empire before I reached the door. But Salderman's long face seemed truly thoughtful.

Burdick waddled out of the chamber after me. He took my arm, giving me a friendly pat. Then, I saw that he, too, had been attentive. Troubled wrinkles marred the smoothness of his brow.

"Warren, don't take it too hard. I think they've been moved enough to make serious investigations. If there's evidence to back you up, they'll act, never fear." Then—"Come along, Warren. You'll stay at my house tonight."

I was not allowed to argue that point. Not that I wanted to, but I did have to object feebly, just to be polite. I was glad to walk with Burdick along the dark and deserted cobbled streets. The air was cool and refreshing. We talked about personal matters and I put aside all fears and anger and thoughts of the growing revolt. The court at Springfield would be stopped on the 29th of September, of that I was certain. And I was equally certain that I would be marching with the Regulators.

When we reached Mr. Burdick's house, we found that the ladies were not at home. Then Mr. Burdick remembered that his wife and Judith had gone to a card party for the evening. Shades of the Puritan Fathers! Card playing in Boston! Mr. Burdick wasn't sure whether the ladies played for stakes, but he was not particularly worried whether they did or not. Old Cotton Mather, though, would be wringing his hands up there in Heaven.

We spent a very pleasant two hours or so, talking about this and that and sipping excellent madeira. In the course of the conversation I mentioned that I had a business proposition in mind, but I would need some capital. Burdick assured me he would be willing to put up some money if he thought my idea was good. Having that assurance, I considered my trip to Boston well worth the while, even though I had failed miserably in my prime purpose.

It was after half past ten when the ladies finally got in. By then I was getting very sleepy for this was long past my regular bedtime. When the big front door opened, Mr. Burdick excused himself and went out to greet the ladies, asking me to stay in the den.

After a long wait, Judith slipped in. Before I could open my mouth, she put her fingers to her lips. She pointed up to the ceiling and giggled a little. I could hear voices—angry voices, the shrill voice of Mrs. Burdick, the gruffer tones of Mr. Burdick. The quarrel was growing in intensity.

Judith closed the door softly. "Even the best of families have them." Then, she added blandly, "They're arguing about you."

"Me?"

"Mama would like you better if you had money—or a noble family." She was completely artless. "Mama's something of a snob."

I was very uncomfortable. "In that case I'd better. . . ."

"Don't worry, Warren, Papa and I know your family is as noble as ours. And Papa's sure you'll be a rich man some day. I think so, too. I heard how you dealt with Graham."

My brows went up. "Your father didn't tell, did he? And Graham would hardly let it out."

"Oh, but he did. Graham complained to a friend and the friend forgot to keep the secret. Graham isn't too well liked around here, you know." She smiled and lifted her glass.

"To your success, Warren."

"A remote prospect at the moment," I remarked. "I don't even know what I'm going to do."

Judith's lips pursed. "I suppose you do have reason to be confused."

Her tone surprised me and my head cocked. "What makes you say that? Intuition? Or information?"

Judith laughed, swished her skirts around and seated herself in the chair across from me. "After all, you didn't come in July, you know."

Then I knew that she had been corresponding with some friend in Amherst, some friend who had told her about Beulah. The knowledge gave me considerable comfort. After all, it was flattering to know she was that much interested in my behavior.

"Stop grinning, Warren, it doesn't become you." She set her wineglass on the tray and stood up. "I'll leave you to your thoughts until Papa comes down." She smiled and patted my cheek. "Sweet dreams, dear Warren. But don't dream too long or you'll wake up and find emptiness." She curtsied impishly. "Good night."

"Wait!" I swung out of my chair and my arm circled her slim waist. "Judith, there's something I want to say. I'm leaving the farm after harvest. You can be sure of that. I want something to look forward to, to plan toward, to work for. Judith, I want. . . ."

Her cool fingers pressed against my lips. "No, not now. Plans are such flexible things. Men are such uncertain animals."

"I'm sure," I said huskily.

She shook her head. "Patience is a greater virtue than rashness, Warren." Her lips brushed mine and her eyes mocked me. "And the next time you want something, remember to learn if the other can give it."

She slipped from my grasp, paused at the door and crinkled her nose. "Life was simpler in Algiers, wasn't it, Warren?"

Her heels clicked on the stairway and faded into nothingness. But I still held her fragrance in my arms.

I had blundered, and blundered badly. I thought back over my words and wondered how she had taken that balderdash about looking forward and planning. Considering my position, she could have thought that I was proposing something not quite moral. And it occurred to me that this somehow had a familiar ring. I wondered why I had shied away from direct and incisive action.

I sank back into my chair, scowling. Had she meant she was in love with someone else? A tinge of jealousy made me wince. Ruefully I looked back upon my moment of smug confidence.

Chapter 15

W HEN I got home I found that Dan had sent out all the letters calling the Regulators to appear at Springfield on the 26th. From all over Hampshire, enthusiastic replies were pouring in. We knew we could count upon a thousand men being on hand when the Supreme Judicial Court tried to open on the 26th.

Only one ominous note marred our satisfaction. The rumors, too numerous to ignore, insisted that the militia would be on hand. Everyone knew that Major-General William Shepard, who commanded the 4th Division, was urging this action on the Governor.

On Monday morning, the 25th of September, the roads about Pelham were astir very early. Dan Shays had sent out the call to our men to gather on the Common in front of the Meeting House by eight o'clock, from whence we would start out for Springfield at about nine. Letters had been dispatched to the leaders in the northern towns inviting them to be on hand by that time and march with us.

I didn't have to ask my father if he was going along. The night before he had taken down Jonathan's musket and cleaned it. I armed myself with a brace of Jonathan's pistols which he had brought home from the war. Ma was less than enthusiastic about our going, but she put up a good lunch for us. Pa carried that in an old leather pouch Jonathan had carried. Increase was the conservative of the family. He had taken absolutely no interest in the affair, especially since the talk grew about putting the Insurgents in jail. Not that he was afraid, mind. But he was determined to remain free—at least until spring.

Pa and I got down to the Common at about eight-thirty. Already contingents had arrived from Montague, Shutesbury, Athol and Petersham. Most of our boys were on hand—Hank McCullock, Johnny Cobb, Steve Pettingil, Jim Cowan—and even Fred Decker, who was looking a lot more cheerful than last I had seen him. Dan Shays was conspicuous in his army uniform of a blue coat, the lapels faced with red, and white breeches. His uniform fit him perfectly and looked new, though a closer view revealed blended patches on the skirts of his coat and the knees of his breeches. However, his military bearing and precise manners gave him the air of an officer and a gentleman, which he truly was.

I was about to join Dan Shays when I spied Tom Packard coming up the road in the company of Captain Tom Johnson, our representative, and our egglike Dr. Cameron. Tom Johnson was wearing his sword and uniform coat, which was very wrinkled, showing it had been exhumed that very morning from an old storage trunk.

"Good morning, gentlemen," I greeted. "Are you coming with us, Captain Johnson?"

Captain Johnson grinned. "Might as well, Warren. I wasn't much help in my seat at the General Court. Maybe I can do better at Springfield."

Dan Shays came over and briskly shook hands with Captain Johnson and Dr. Cameron. "I'm glad you're coming, Tom. I'll be happy to stand aside and give you command of the Pelham forces. As our representative. . . ."

"No, no, Dan," Johnson broke in nasally. "You did all the work. The honor is yours. I'll stay in the ranks, I insist."

"Very well, Tom," Shays returned.

I thought I detected a slight note of disappointment in his voice. It was evident he had not made the offer merely out of politeness. He gave Dr. Cameron an anxious glance.

"Do we have your support, Doctor?"

The doctor rocked on his spindly legs, pursing his thick lips. "Frankly, Dan'l, my mind isn't made up yet. I prayed for guidance from the Lord, but the problem isn't simple. I believe wholeheartedly in the need for a redress of grievances. The way you go about forcing the Governor's hand, however, is illegal. On the other hand, our petitions have received no attention from those Boston aristocrats. Your cause is just. But your methods may be immoral."

"In that case," Tom Johnson put in dryly, "our method of throwing off the yoke of King George was immoral. My conscience is clear, Doctor."

The two fell into an inconclusive argument, as such arguments usually are, over whether the end justifies the means. After a while Tom Packard tugged on my sleeve.

"Here comes Beulah," he whispered.

Unfortunately, his voice carried and Dr. Cameron's brows arched. A scowl was settling over his fleshy features as he turned. I scarcely dared look. But when I finally did, my apprehensions receded. She hadn't come alone, so she was safe. Or was she? She was driving the rickety old cart with Joab Crane sitting on the open tail, his withered leg dangling.

Beulah was in a gay mood, laughing and waving to the younger men who drew about the cart to exchange a quip and a greeting. She was wearing her brown homespun dress, a brown shawl covering her shoulders.

Beulah drew on the reins and her lips parted to give us greeting. When she saw Dr. Cameron, she stiffened, almost imperceptibly, then glanced at Joab, fright leaping to her wide grey eyes. But Dr. Cameron was not interested in Joab at the moment. His thoughtful gaze was on Beulah, herself. In slow, waddling steps, he went over to the cart.

"Beulah," he said, his voice low and gentle, yet carrying cold reproach, "I have been told you were seen inside Conkey's Tavern several times last week."

For a moment I thought she was going to defy him. Her chin lifted slightly and her lips parted. But Beulah had too much sense to court disaster. Her eyes lowered meekly.

"I was only helping Captain Shays write letters. I thought there was no harm. I—I didn't go in the taproom."

"Whosoever exposes himself to the Devil," Cameron said, wagging his fat finger, "seeks the wrath of the Lord. Remember that."

With a small smile, he turned away and walked in heavy righteous steps around to the back of the cart. There were two bright red spots on Beulah's cheeks. She shuddered slightly, gave me her hand and jumped down from her perch.

"God help us now," she said huskily. "He never did come around to talking to Joab."

An ominous hush had fallen over those within range of the cart and everyone watched with growing uneasiness as the doctor planted himself before Joab. Joab's stolid expression did not change, though his eyelids did droop a trifle.

Dr. Cameron's smile was bland. "Good morning, Joab."

" 'Morning, Doc," Joab grunted.

"I haven't seen you at meeting lately, have I?"

Joab swung his withered leg. "Reckon I don't get around as often as I used to."

Dr. Cameron nodded gravely. "Going to Springfield?"

"Reckon so, Doc."

"If you feel able to go as far as Springfield, Joab, don't you think you'd be able to come to church on Sundays?"

Joab was silent for a painful moment. His head turned slightly and he gave Beulah a hard stare. Beulah was very pale.

"Doc, I reckon God understands why I don't get to meeting more'n Thanksgiving and Easter."

Dr. Cameron played with his lower lip, searching Joab's flat, composed features. Then, very softly. "Joab, I've heard it said you have turned from the path of God."

"The Lord is my shepherd, Doc," Joab replied simply.

Dr. Cameron gazed long at the huge cripple. Then his eye fell on the bundle under Joab's hand. One corner was open and a small bible was plainly visible under Joab's thumb. A smile broke over the doctor's flabby face. He patted Joab's thick thigh, then walked off with infinite dignity.

The crowd drifted away, but Joab did not move. Soon, only Beulah, Tom Packard, Tom Johnson, Dan Shays and myself remained. Joab's lips twisted in the semblance of a smile and he contemptuously tossed the bundle farther into the cart.

"Satisfied?" he asked of his sister. He drew his musket from behind him and placed it across his knees. "In case the shepherd ain't around when I need him most," he drawled.

He patted his musket.

Unlike our march to Northampton, the journey to Springfield was not lighthearted and carefree. Every mile of the way, the rumor grew stronger that General Shepard had called out the militia. By the time we reached Chicopee and stopped for the night, we knew the worst. Shepard had occupied the courthouse. We feared him now, for our numbers were growing. We felt sure the people would support us. But many wondered if we could conclude *this* affair without bloodshed. Originally, we had intended to make our headquarters at Parson's Tavern. But with Shepard on the field, we decided not to risk an explosion. So, without fanfare, we marched into Springfield early on the 26th and encamped in a large field on the north side of town. Stevens Tavern became our headquarters.

Luke Day was already in, as were a number of other leaders of contingents from the surrounding area. As soon as I had greeted them, I excused myself and hurried off to rescue Joab and Beulah from Parsons where they'd be waiting. As I walked down Main Street, I could feel the tenseness in the air. Armed men were constantly passing back and forth, some of them wearing hemlock sprigs and on their way to join our ranks, others wearing white strips of paper in their hats. That white paper was the identifying mark of government supporters.

The hostility in the air was evidenced the moment I entered Parsons' Tavern, which was located right next to the courthouse. The taproom was crowded with men, all wearing white strips of paper in their hats. By their dress, they were men of means, many boasting of fine broadcloth coats and ruffled linen shirts. Their conversation died abruptly as I came in and I was favored with many a cold glare.

I spied Beulah and Joab immediately, sitting at a table in the back corner of the taproom. They looked very out of place and uncomfortable. And no wonder. The air was livid with harsh condemnation of the Regulators. We were devil's spawn, shameless thieves, abandoned debtors, and so on ad infinitum. Many an epithet was gulped down as I hove into view, showing that if we were despised we were also feared.

Both Beulah and Joab were vastly relieved when they saw me, though Joab's expressionless features hardly gave sign of it. Beulah snatched my hand warmly.

"Thank Heaven. I thought you'd never get here."

217

"We only got in this morning," I explained. "We're encamped up the street. Headquarters are at Stevens' Tavern."

Joab grunted. "Beulah, go up there and reserve a room for us. Come back later and fetch the cart and me."

"All right, Joab." She got up quickly, whispering, "Don't argue, Warren."

I understood, so I made no comment.

Beulah was wearing a homespun dress, as I have noted before, but homespun or no, she attracted considerable attention. Several gentlemen grinned at me, despite my badge, as if to say that they, too, would join the Regulators if such was in our ranks.

When we got outside we discovered it was just ten o'clock and the court was about to open. A big crowd had collected, men, women and screaming children. Armed guards were posted at the doors and a file of soldiers was drawn completely around the courthouse. The troops were tense and expectant, their eyes constantly roving about to see if the Regulators were coming. Then, a stir went through the crowd and quiet descended. The judges were approaching.

There was no fuss, no outcries, no one tried to hinder them. The judicial party, headed by Judge Nathaniel Sergeant, and including the usual entourage of clerks, lawyers and clients, wound through the opening path toward the courthouse door. General Shepard of the militia was on the steps, a grim, blue-jowled man with thin lips and hard grey eyes. The militiamen were undistinguishable from our men, except for the white papers in their hats, for these men, too, were mostly farmers and mechanics. They stirred restlessly and many had doubtful looks on their faces as the judges passed through the door into the courthouse. It was evident, too, that not all in the crowd were wholeheartedly in favor of this event.

Shortly, the hoarse bellowing of the court crier came from the open window. Then came the rapping of a gavel. The court was open. A sigh, mingled relief and disappointment, came from the assembled people. No Insurgents had appeared to stay the judges. But the Insurgents were present in spirit. The rumor was strong that the court would not do business, for the court, too, was fearful that such an action would precipitate violence.

Beulah and I walked on up Main Street, neither of us saying much. We had been impressed by the explosive atmosphere. We had sensed the hardening of a large block of public sentiment against our presence in Springfield.

"Warren!"

The cry brought me up short, looking about for the source. I could see no one I knew among the passersby. We were abreast of a private residence, a modest red brick building set close to the street. I heard the cry again and looked up to the second story.

"Judith!"

She called to me to wait and disappeared inside. A short moment later, the front door opened and she came out. I could feel Beulah drawing shyly behind me. Judith was in a dark green traveling dress, beautifully tailored in long, flowing lines, with a white lace collar about her neck. Her soft brown hair was done in small curls and her fresh, pink complexion made her seem radiant.

"Warren! I was watching for you. I knew you'd be here." She turned slightly and extended her hand. "Beulah it's nice to see you again. Did you march with the men?"

"I came with my brother," Beulah answered defensively. "My—my brother couldn't come alone."

"Oh." Judith's smile faded a little. "I heard about Joab." Then she turned back to me. "You must come in. Father will want to see you. We're about to have our mid-morning tea. And you, too, Beulah, please come in."

Beulah was frowning, unconsciously fingering her skirt as her eyes traveled over Judith's fine dress. She gave me a glance that held an almost agonized plea. As a gentleman I could do no more than acknowledge it.

"It's nice of you to ask, Judith, but we must decline. I have business up at Stevens' Tavern." I pointed to my hat. "I'm a Regulator, you know."

Judith's brows arched. "Wait till Papa hears that. Papa came here on business—or so he said." Then she added impishly. "I came for the excitement, too. Will there be any?"

I shrugged. "It's too early to tell."

"There really shouldn't be any trouble," Judith said. "Not since the Governor's called the Special Session."

"What?" Beulah and I cried simultaneously.

"Didn't you know?" Judith asked. "I heard about it the

219

day I left Boston—day before yesterday, the 23rd. It's set for some time in October—the first week, I think."

"That's news." Beulah fidgeted. "The boys will want to hear about it right away."

"Of course," Judith agreed quickly. "I won't keep you any longer. But please come back, won't you? Both of you. Papa will want to talk to you, Warren. And I've so much to ask Beulah. It isn't often I get a chance to talk to someone from . . . from home. Do come, Beulah—say, about seven?"

She waved a farewell and I bowed and she went into the house. Beulah was silent as we walked on and I could see a flush burning beneath her smooth tan.

"You shouldn't feel that way, Beulah," I chided.

"What way?" Beulah's tone wasn't convincing. Her eyes lifted slowly and she shrugged. "I suppose you're right. I'm as good as she is, any day."

Chapter 16

THE whole camp was in an uproar when Beulah and I arrived. The news had sped before us. The Regulators had learned of the Governor's action and, since the victory was considered as won, everyone was talking of going home. Luke Day had taken swift action to scotch that idea. He was mounted on a barrel, delivering a vigorous oration, denouncing the news as false rumor spread by Shepard to decimate our strength. By the time he finished, the men were roused to fighting pitch and, had the word been given, I am sure they would have stormed the courthouse and hanged Shepard.

There was another, stronger argument for keeping the men on the ground. Everyone hoped that the mere presence of the Regulators would keep the court from doing business. Indeed, that hope seemed well founded, for by eleven o'clock, the court still had done nothing because no Grand Jury had appeared. If we left now, the Grand Jury might feel it could sit with impunity and hand down indictments not only against the leaders but against every man who had taken part in this affair or the one at Northampton.

The majority was convinced and someone suggested that the time was ripe to send a petition to the court, demanding that it adjourn. The idea was enthusiastically received and immediately everyone shouted for Shays to head the committee. Shays laughed and reddened with embarrassment, which covered his reluctance to serve, and tried to get silence.

"Gentlemen," he called over the clamor. "I vote for Captain John Powers for Chairman of the Committee."

"And I second the motion!" Luke Day roared.

The motion was carried unanimously. It looked to me as

if Luke Day wanted anyone except Shays as chairman, for Shays was definitely not vigorous enough to suit him.

As soon as the committee had departed for the court, Luke Day came striding over. "Now, Mistress Crane, you cannot refuse to take dinner with me. I waited long that evening, you know." He gave me a slight frown. "You must join us, too, Mr. Hascott," he added in a can't-you-refuse tone.

"You're very kind, Major," Beulah said, smiling and getting up. "I'm afraid you'll have to invite one more, my brother. I'd better fetch him now before he gets angry. You'll excuse me? I'll be right back."

Luke Day's eyes followed her out. "I can't figure that girl," he grumbled. "Do you think she likes me?"

"I'm sure she does," I replied, and immediately wondered why I had given him this encouragement.

Luke Day dined with us. But it did him little good. Beulah returned a short time later with Joab, bringing him in through the kitchen. She preempted the table in the remotest corner of the taproom and Joab painfully hauled himself to his seat. Until he was settled everyone pretended not to notice him. Then a whole flock of his friends—friends he hadn't seen for years—came around to give him an uproarious welcome. I had suspected all along that coming to Springfield hadn't been his idea, but now that he was here he didn't regret it. Joab thawed gradually. No one mentioned or seemed to notice his legs, and after a time, something like a smile broke the seamed leathery mask over his flat features.

At half-past one Shays and the committee returned. A shouting crowd had followed them up Main Street and the guards at the doors had a struggle to keep the excited idlers out. Shays and his committee ran headlong into another noisy crowd—us.

"Please! Please!" Shays begged. The shouting eased a bit. "I'll read you what the judges answered."

The tumult died to a jubilant buzzing, for the fact that the court had condescended to give a written reply—the first in any of these affairs—was considered a partial victory. But the words of the judges took away even this small consolation. They refused to adjourn the court, holding it inconsistent with honor and duty to accede to such a demand. They said they had no authority to redress grievances. That was the business of the General Court.

When Shays was done, a storm of curses went up. All thoughts of going home were set aside. Instead, anger was growing and tension was mounting close to the breaking point. The talk turned more and more to positive action, to enforcing their demands, if necessary, by arms and cold steel. Dan Shays looked very worried. He hurried through the milling men toward our table, noting the ugliness of the words being bandied about. He gave us all a brief nod, pulled over a chair and sat down by Luke Day. His voice was low and strained.

"Luke we've got to do something." He jerked his head nervously. "Listen to them. They'll be out of hand soon. If we don't stop them, somebody's going to get hurt."

Luke Day was dour. "Dan, you can't fight for Liberty without expecting casualties."

"My God, Luke, this isn't the Revolution. We've already won what we wanted. I've learned positively that the Governor called the special session for the first week in October. If we have bloodshed now, how can we hope to get the relief we want?"

"You only want to frighten the court, don't you?" Joab asked suddenly. "Well, show 'em your strength."

Dan looked up, started. "Oh, howdy, Joab." He nodded briskly. "Yes, that's it—show them our strength. We haven't done that yet. There's a thousand of us out there. That ought to impress those judges. The militia isn't over six hundred." He pointed to the girl. "Beulah, you're going to make a speech."

Beulah's brows went up. "Golly, Dan, I've never made a speech in my life. But if I can help . . . . What should I say?"

"Appeal to them not to break loose. Make them think of their wives and sweethearts—oh, yes, and their children. Think of what it will mean to the womenfolk if a bloody riot starts. Somebody might get killed—on either side. Remember, the militia is composed of men like ourselves—our neighbors. You know the stuff."

"Yes, I think I do. Now, Dan?"

223

Dan Shays got up. "This very minute." He shook Day's shoulder. "Come on. You, too, Luke."

Day just sat. "I don't believe in cowardly . . . ."

"Cowardly? To prevent men from killing their neighbors?" Dan Shays was a determined man when he was aroused. He was aroused now. "Luke, you're going to make a speech appealing for peace. I'm not going to have my neighbors' blood on my conscience. And I warn you, Luke, start something and, by God, I'll have you run out of the county. Now, let's get along."

Luke Day hesitated, glowering at Shays. He glanced at Beulah and saw that she, too, was against him. He shrugged and, with an air of disgust, allowed himself to be led outside.

Shays mounted to the barrel and faced the crowd whose raucous noise waxed to thunderous proportions. Dan's smooth, boyish face was set in placid lines, only the thinning of his lips showed his inner tautness. He stood there quietly and patiently, waiting for the hoarse voices to calm. Gradually the turbulence ebbed away and a grim hush fell over the restless multitude.

"Gentlemen," Shays began in a deliberate tone, "after due consultation, your officers have agreed to ignore the stupid and ridiculous reply the court returned to our petition. It shows conclusively that our judges are blind to the will of the people—yes, and to the will of Governor Bowdoin himself."

A scattering of catcalls went up. Many of the men showed puzzlement at his reference to the Governor.

"Let us be charitable, men," Shays called to the hecklers. "We have won our victory. We have learned that it is true—I repeat, it is absolutely true—that the Governor has called the General Court into special session for the first week in October. Thus, we are certain to obtain a redress of grievances. Thus, we can scorn the judges who, even now, do not understand the will of the people—yes, and the will of the government. They are fools, not monsters. They are ignorant, not tyrannical. We shall treat them, therefore, as they deserve—with contempt."

The crowd growled and shuffled about angrily. This was not what they had expected or wanted.

"But because we decry violence," Shays went on quickly,

"we do not mean we must accept arrogance from the court. It is evident the judges have not been fully apprised of our strength. We will awaken them. We will march in regular companies and in good order through the town to show ourselves. It is your duty to see that no one, because of misguided zeal, provokes violence or destroys property. Remember, the Regulators stand for Justice, Temperance, Liberty!"

Shays whispered something to Beulah and helped her up to the barrel. She struggled with her skirts, slipped and teetered and clutched air wildly. Half a dozen men closed about the barrel to catch her but she regained her balance and smiled sheepishly. Someone laughed. In a moment, a ripple of laughter went skidding out across the crowd. Hoots and cries and whistles went up as Beulah prepared to speak. She opened her mouth, gulped, trying valiantly to get the words out. She looked scared to death.

"Go ahead, Beulah!" came an encouraging voice—Tom Packard's from deep in the crowd. "We'll keep the rowdies quiet."

Beulah opened her mouth. "Howdy, boys!"

The men acted as if she had dropped an exquisite pearl of wisdom. They cheered and whistled and applauded her. She smiled, abashed, her confidence surging forth.

"Well, it looks like we've got what we want, doesn't it?" she began conversationally. "I don't suppose you think about it much—not aloud, anyway—but we women have won, too. You know, you didn't come here for yourselves alone, or for your friends. You've done this to help your wives and sisters and sweethearts. We've suffered as much as you have under injustices and oppressions. And, boys, remember this, we will suffer if you get hurt." Her eyes were round and solemn. "You boys know how much we can sacrifice when sacrifice is necessary to win justice and liberty. The widows of our Revolution testify to that. Now that we've won our point, now that Bowdoin has agreed to call a special session, now that fighting is not necessary to win a redress of grievances, spare us more tears. Remember that rashness on your part or on the part of one of your comrades may make some woman a widow uselessly. I know you boys will not bring sorrow upon the women of Hampshire." She smiled and lifted her fist. "Now, let's have that parade. Let's show them how strong we are—peacefully. Those stupid judges will get so tired of waiting for the Grand Jury, they'll have to adjourn."

The thump of the drums was lost in the roar that went up as Beulah finished. She waved and laughed and fended off those men who would lift her to their shoulders and carry her to the head of the column. When she got loose, her hair was disheveled and there was a small rip in her dress.

The leaders were too wise to let the men cool off. They scattered back to their companies, called the men to attention and quickly herded them into rough formation. Shays gave the order to the Pelham contingent and our men swung out into Main Street, drums crackling enthusiastically. One by one, the other detachments followed, not without confusion, but smartly enough. Shays had lost his harassed look, for it was now evident that discipline had been reestablished.

There were no incidents of any account. A few times, some of our soldiers tried to break ranks and avenge insults hurled at us by the wearers of white strips among the spectators. They were restrained by their comrades, proving the wisdom of having placed the responsibility for maintaining order upon the men themselves. The drums kept up a brisk, blatant rhythm and the fifes brought songs from the throats of our men. By the time the Regulators returned to the camping ground they were slightly breathless, but well pleased with themselves.

No sooner had the men broken ranks and gathered about the rum and cider barrels for refreshment when they were brought up sharply by the rattle of approaching drums. Instantly the officers brought them back in line. Then, before the men could really become excited, Captain Clarke of Colrain leaped onto the barrel.

"At ease, men!" he shouted. "It's the militia all right—or part of it—coming to join us!"

And so it proved, to our great satisfaction. Some hundred of the militiamen came in and exchanged the white strips of paper in their hats for sprigs of hemlock. The Regulators grew in strength to about twelve hundred.

Then, shortly after four o'clock, word came to us that the court had recessed. The Grand Jury had made no appearance. The court had done no business. Thus, the first day had ended in complete triumph for the Regulators.

Supper was a gay affair. Joab held court somewhat like a benevolent king in his corner of Stevens' taproom. I wouldn't say Beulah was of herself the attraction, for Joab had many friends of his own, but she did account for the extraordinary mob that constantly ebbed and flowed from the corner. She took the attention with good spirit, but if it hadn't been for Joab, I'm sure she would have tried to escape long before the time came for us to depart for our visit to Judith.

The chill autumn night was a relief after the noisy and smoky atmosphere in the taproom. Beulah relieved my mind by showing no nervousness. I deliberately walked past the Herrick house to see what she would do. She caught my arm and, wordlessly, indicated that this was our destination.

I removed my hat as the maid opened the door. "Will you inform Mr. Burdick—or Miss Burdick—that Mr. Hascott and Miss Crane have arrived?"

"Oh, come in, sir. You're expected." She led us to the parlor. "Mr. Hascott and Miss Crane, Mum."

There was a rustle of silks and Judith came out of the deep chair by the fireplace. "Beulah—and Warren. I'm so glad you could come." She took Beulah's hand. "Warren, the gentlemen are still at the dinner table. Tell them they're not being very polite." Her fingertips flew to her lips. "Nor am I." She took my hand, too, and led us over to the plush covered sofa where a horsefaced woman was sitting. "This is Mr. Hascott, Mrs. Herrick—the young man I was telling you about. And Miss Crane—an old friend of mine from home."

I bowed and Mrs. Herrick inclined her bewigged head in response. Beulah was frowning as she put out her hand in that same forthright manner that had upset me the first time I met her. Mrs. Herrick was unruffled and promptly accepted the outstretched hand.

"Sit down, my dear," she said in a throaty voice. She smiled faintly as she examined Beulah. "I do believe our girls are getting prettier every day. Don't you agree, Mr. Hascott?"

227

"M'am, our corner of Hampshire produces the finest." This with a bow to Judith, then to Beulah.

"Go along with you, young man," Mrs. Herrick said dryly.

The Herrick house was neither as big nor as richly furnished as the Burdicks'. The parlor wall was covered with plain buff colored paper and the clean, sanded floor was bare except for some small oval rugs scattered about, mostly near the chairs. The furniture itself was solid mahogany stuff, covered with heavy plush, obviously imported before the war. The fat candles in the crystal chandelier were of sperm and smelled a little.

Conversation about the big oval table died as I entered the dining room and Mr. Burdick, his face lighting, got up.

"Come in, Warren, come in. I guess you know everyone, except, perhaps, Mr. Herrick."

One of the guests was Salderman, who half rose and took my hand. The other merely nodded to me and I merely nodded back. He was my old friend, Mr. Graham. Mr. Herrick was a short man with dark pouches under his eyes which gave him a saddened look even when he smiled.

Graham was scowling at me, the cleft in his chin marked. "I understand you're one of the Regulators, Mr. Hascott."

"I'm afraid you swung me to that side, Mr. Graham," I returned coldly.

Salderman laughed. "Touché!"

Burdick coughed. "Should we join the ladies?"

"Ah, Henry!" Mrs. Herrick said as her husband came in. "I want you to meet a charming young friend of Judith's. Miss Crane, this is my husband. Mr. Burdick, you know . . . Mr. Graham . . . And beware of that other one. He's a bachelor, Mr. Salderman."

Mr. Burdick beamed at Beulah. "She's grown into quite a beautiful young lady, hasn't she? I've known her since she was in the cradle, Jothan."

Salderman bowed. "She's learned much about taming men since then, haven't you, Miss Crane? I believe you're the young woman who delivered a speech to the rebels, aren't you?"

Beulah nodded curtly, not that she intended impoliteness, but she was a little shy. She relaxed more and more as the talk drifted into less personal aspects of the day's events.

Mr. Burdick and I, standing a bit to one side, fell into a

228

discussion of the state of business. He asked me how much capital I'd need for the venture I'd hinted at in Boston. When I told him a thousand pounds would swing it, he said:

"Too much, Warren. If I were you I'd think of a smaller profit and less risk." He eyed me a moment, then smiled. "Tell you what I'll do. I'll put up five hundred or any part you feel you need. The less the better, young man. I want ten percent."

I grinned. "But you don't know my proposition."

He waved his pudgy hand. "If I lose, it will be worth it to find out how good a businessman you are. I have a claim on your services for spring, you know. You think the deal is fair? Remember, it's not a loan, but ten percent of the profits. However, if I get my money back I'll count myself lucky. I'll deposit that amount for you with Gerson in Northampton." He looked up sharply. "I think we'd better abandon business for the moment. Graham's off again."

Graham was indeed at it again, delivering a tirade against "those lazy scoundrels, scheming rebels and thieving debtors." Beulah's head was high and two red spots stood out vividly on her tanned cheeks. Her anger was slowly heading toward the explosion point.

"Don't let him rile you, Beulah," I soothed. "He's the fellow who thinks I'm a British agent."

Graham turned coldly toward me. "I'm not sure yet that I'm not right. Do you deny that the British have stirred up this trouble? Why, Sparhawk told me they've gathered together the scum of the state to threaten our courts, subvert law and overthrow the fruits of our government. Yes, and their camp followers are the worst trollops—" He checked himself, flushed and bowed to Beulah. "My apologies, M'am."

Judith snatched Beulah's hand just in time to stop her from slapping his face. "Don't pay him any attention, Beulah. He was very rude. I'm sure he didn't mean. . . ."

"I'm sure he did mean it," Beulah cut in sharply. "He can apologize all night and still he'd believe we're all rascals. You can go back to Boston, Mr. Graham, and deliver this message to your fine, aristocratic friends: Just as long as you insist on treating us like cattle, just so long will we remain in arms. British Agents!" She snorted in a most unladylike manner. "Thieves, scoundrels, unprincipled scum, can you think of more names for the honest farmers who feed you? Can you think of more abuse to heap upon the heads of the men you throw in jail? I suppose you think it's right to pauperize their wives and children. I suppose you think the soldiers who fought and bled for your liberties should now be your serfs."

"Now, my dear young lady . . . ." Graham protested.

Beulah was thoroughly aroused and she wasn't to be stopped. "Did you serve in the army? Did you sacrifice your civil life and go on short rations?" When he did not answer, she went on scornfully, "And I suppose you think you're better than I am. Well, look at me, look at my dress. My mother made it. I spun the thread. I loomed the cloth. Yes, I even sheared the sheep. And you! Shoes with gold buckles made in England. That lace neckcloth—made in England. Broadcloth coat—made in England. Money you sent out of the country while we cry out for cash to sell our crops. And you squeal about your liberties, your government. Yes, and you call yourself a patriot."

She paused, a bit breathless, and glanced defiantly around. Mr. Burdick was distressed. Salderman was amused. Judith was placid, showing nothing of what she was thinking. Personally, I was enjoying this and hoping she'd go on and tell him all I thought of him, too.

"You'll excuse the speechmaking," she said, suddenly subdued. "And goodnight. I won't stay under the same roof with that—that Tory."

With a toss of her head, she sailed from the room. I started after her, but Salderman caught my shoulder.

"Please, Mr. Hascott. I'd like a word with her. A remarkable girl. Indeed, yes, a remarkable girl."

Judith caught my eye. "Stay a moment, Warren."

Salderman hurried after her and I struggled with the impulse to follow. Then, uncomfortable in the knowledge that Salderman would be chatting with her outside, I lingered for another moment. I wasn't going to stay. I'd sure have a run-in with Graham. Also, I could see that the host, Mr. Herrick, was not in sympathy with our cause.

"I'm afraid I must go," I said, bowing to Mrs. Herrick.

"Oh, there's no need of your going," Herrick said gruffly.

"I think Warren wants to," Judith said, rising. "I'll see him to the door."

I ignored Graham and shook Mr. Herrick's none too friendly hand, then said goodnight to Mr. Burdick.

"If you see Joe Crane, will you tell him to get in touch with me? I'll need him in on the deal. And the funds . . . ."

"I'll deposit that money with Gerson right away for you, Warren," he assured me. He glared at Graham. "I'm inclined to agree with Jothan. That man's an ass."

Judith winked at me, took my hand and escorted me into the entry hall. I could hear Mr. Herrick make some remark about "these young people, nowadays."

"Jothan had the word for her—remarkable," Judith commented. "And she's beautiful, too."

I smiled into her eyes. "I only know one beautiful woman. I'd say Beulah was handsome." I took her extended hand. "I'm sorry I must go. But after all, I brought her. . . ."

"I understand. I hope she doesn't think we're all like him. Tell her to come back tomorrow afternoon, will you? He won't be here. I didn't get a chance to talk to her at all, you know."

"I'll tell her," I promised. I opened the door, paused, and I believe I could have kissed her had I just bent my head. I backed away, warm under the collar, a bit confused. "Goodnight."

I almost ran into Salderman as I hastened down the steps. I was irritated to find a smile on his long face.

Beulah was a short distance up the street, lingering expectantly. As she saw me, she lifted her hand and waved. No, she was showing me a small leather bag.

"Look, Warren! Isn't it wonderful? Mr. Salderman wants to help us. He's given me money for the cause. He told me to turn it over to Shays."

I eyed the bag distastefully. "Are you sure you're not the cause he's interested in?"

Beulah's brows lifted and she laughed. "Why, I never thought of that. Of course, that may be." She slipped her hand under my arm. "If he's fool enough to think he can buy me, should we be fools enough to refuse the money?"

I thought I'd let Joab answer that. As soon as we got back to the taproom, Joab cleared away the people who were hanging about his table, for we had returned early and he wanted to speak to us alone. He had been worried about Beulah. In his own curious sullen way, Joab had a lot of pride in his sister.

"What's wrong?" Joab asked gruffly.

I chuckled. "Beulah tangled with a Tory and walked out. I thought she acted a bit hastily, but it doesn't matter. They're not all like Graham, you know, Beulah."

"Maybe not," Beulah admitted grudgingly. "I suppose Salderman isn't a Tory—not an obnoxious one, anyway." She tossed the bag of money before Joab. "Look, he gave us a contribution for the cause. Should we keep it, Joab?"

Joab's scowl softened. "Why not? We need money if we expect to keep the men on the ground. Some have to be fed." He looked up and lifted his hand. "Dan!"

Dan Shays excused himself from the group of officers to whom he was talking and came over. Joab gave him the bag.

"Here's a contribution from a sympathizer, Dan. I guess we can use it, eh?"

Shays hefted the bag with delight. "I should say so! We've been worried about feeding some of the men. We got a few pounds here and there from other sympathizers, but not nearly enough. This helps tremendously. We have enough to carry us over tonight. Mind if I hold this for an emergency?"

Joab shrugged. "Do what you like with it, Dan. After all, you're the commander of the Regulators."

Dan's smile faded. "Yes, I guess I am," he said slowly. "I suppose it can't be helped."

Wednesday was very quiet in Springfield. The day was spent mostly in drilling and speechmaking. The court sat as usual. But it did no business. The Grand Jury did not appear. In this, the Regulators saw the reluctance of the people to sit and condemn them, and so we were assured we retained popular support.

The money we had turned over to Dan proved very useful. Most of it went into feeding the men who had no more funds. Except for a few odd men coming in now and then, our number was pretty well stabilized at fifteen hundred. The government hadn't been able to push its strength beyond eight hundred. But almost half of our men were armed only with bludgeons.

About noon, I had a note from Judith. Her father and Salderman, having finished their business, had decided to go on home. They felt there wasn't going to be any serious trouble, especially since the General Court was soon to sit. So, she regretted she could not entertain Beulah and me as she had promised.

Thursday, the court opened at the usual time and again no business was done for the lack of a Grand Jury. Our men were getting very restless. Small detachments were permitted to march up and down Main Street for the exercise and, invariably, as they passed the courthouse, they would set up the cry: "Adjourn!" They were getting tired of the siege and wanted to get home. This was harvest time, their busiest time of the year.

The end came abruptly about one thirty. A townsman burst into Stevens' Tavern as we were dawdling over dinner, shouting the electrifying news:

"The court's adjourned! The court's adjourned!"

Luke Day waded through the babbling mob that had almost engulfed the young man. "Has Shepard dismissed the militia?"

"N—no, sir." The young man gulped. "The soldiers are still there, all right. But he's gonna retire soon."

"It may be a trick," Day said darkly. "We'll march down there and take over the courthouse right now!"

Shays stood up on a chair. "One moment, gentlemen! We'll march in orderly fashion. Let's have no rowdyism. If the court's adjourned, we have full victory. Remember, upon our conduct in that victory depends how much the General Court will do for us in redressing grievances. Back to your companies, gentlemen. We march in five minutes!"

When the news reached our camp the men were thrown into a frenzy of cheering and shouting and hugging one another. As soon as Dan Shays appeared they gave him a tumultuous ovation. His name was shouted again and again until the men were hoarse.

Dan was almost exasperated. "I don't know why they insist on giving me all the credit."

The militia was drawn up at attention in front of the courthouse when we marched up. General Shepard, his dark, angular features set in stern lines, was standing on the courthouse steps, watching in silence as the Regulators approached. Shays gave the order and the Regulators shuffled to a halt. Several men tried to break from line, but they were quickly hauled back, either by their officers or their own comrades. No one wanted any untoward incident to spoil our moment of triumph.

General Shepard came down from the courthouse, moving with studied deliberateness. Shays, with Luke Day, Captain Foote, Captain Colton and Captain Fisk at his back, went out to meet the unbending General.

Shepard smiled without mirth. "Well, General Shays. . . ."

"Sir!" Shays cut in sharply. "My rank is Captain. I pretend to none higher." His hand fell to the hilt of his sword. "Should anyone address me by a higher title, I would consider it an insult and demand satisfaction."

General Shepard's brows went up and he put his hands behind his back. "Very well, Captain Shays, how can I serve you?"

"We demand custody of the courthouse and the immediate dismissal of the militia."

Shepard waved, an amused smile touching his lips. "I don't entertain demands, sir. But assuming that I withdraw from the courthouse, what assurance do I have that your rabble will not destroy it? And other property?"

"I don't lead a rabble," Shays answered coldly. "You have my word there will be no destruction of property. You have seen how our officers and men have conducted themselves."

Shepard nodded gravely. "I shall accept your word, sir. And I'll tell you what I'll do. I'll withdraw to a distance. You dismiss your men and I'll dismiss mine. I won't argue that point. That's my final word."

Shays hesitated, then, "Done, General."

General Shepard nodded to his aide, Colonel Burt of Longmeadow. The Colonel gave the signal and the militia's drummers went into action. One by one, the militia companies swung into line, passed down Main Street parallel to our waiting column. Our men couldn't resist jeering the departing militiamen. For a few moments, it looked as if fist fights might break out. Happily, there were none. And an hour later we were marching homeward.

Thus the Springfield affair was ended. Thus the triumph of the Regulators was complete.

Chapter 17

For me, the fight had ended just in time. The activity would have lapsed, anyway, for no courts were scheduled to sit during the busiest of the harvest season. Almost all of our neighbors already had harvested their corn but ours was just coming in. Late as we had planted it, we got an excellent crop, assuring us of indian pudding and corn bread over the winter, if nothing else. Some of our turnips were ready, too. Pulling up the turnips was a detestable, back-breaking job. But we got a fine crop, except for one field of about two acres into which the rot had settled. We cut one crop of hay, too, and thus were assured of ample feed for our cattle. I might add here that Pa had managed to gather a herd of twelve cows, trading with considerable shrewdness on the strength of his expected turnip and corn crops.

All during the time I was occupied with my farm tasks, I kept perfecting my business plans and keeping a sharp eye on the state of the commodity markets. Prices held up fairly well over last year's prices, corn selling for four shillings a bushel, wheat at eight shillings, six pence the bushel, rye at from four to six shillings, and so on. But there still were no buyers, no money in circulation. Whole apple orchards had been left to rot rather than have the time wasted in picking the apples. Some farmers were so disgusted with the failure of the General Court to provide a circulating medium that they left their wheat standing in the fields. They were without hope that this session would make the leopard change his spots. Yet, despite curtailed production, the harvests were the best in many years and the amount of produce on the market was almost normal. Thus, not even an artificial scarcity came to the rescue of the few. Trading was virtually on a barter basis, barter prices being one third higher than cash.

Originally, my schemes had been quite grandiose and founded on the theory that I could speculate heavily on borrowed cash. I soon cut the idea down to a practical level. I would need the aid of my father and Uncle Enoch and so talked it over with them. Both agreed my scheme seemed promising enough to merit backing me.

Briefly, my plan was this: I realized my father and uncle would have a hard time getting cash from their crops. My father needed cash for taxes and debts, as did my uncle. I planned to trade their crops—turnips, flax, corn and, in the case of my uncle, some wheat and rye—for shoes. Watching Joab made me realize there would be many farmers making shoes rather than raising crops, with the idea of swapping them for commodities and cash in the fall. I'd save them the trouble of going on the road. I'd take all of their shoes at once.

I had been reading the papers closely during these last months and concluded that exporting our produce would not prove profitable. Connecticut, it was true, suffered heavily from a windstorm in August, cutting down their crops and opening something of a market there. But everyone would think of that. And Pennsylvania and New York reported bumper crops of cereal grains, so those states would be exporters, not importers.

Shoes, I believed, would be a more marketable item outside our state and would sell for cash. I planned to send the shoes to New York or Philadelphia or even as far south as Charleston, depending on the market. This was where Joe came in. He would know the state of the market and could tell me the best place to send the shoes. More, I believed I could trust him, so if he was willing he could take the whole shipment and save me the expense of making the trip myself. When Beulah told me that Reuben was about ready to go on the road with Joab's shoes I told her my plan and took over the whole lot.

About the end of the first week in October, I set up headquarters in Northampton, since that place was more centrally located, and placed an advertisement in the newly established *Hampshire Gazette*. I may add in passing that the opening of this newspaper still left only one in the field, for the *Hampshire Herald* was forced to suspend operations late in September.

The response was tremendous. Within four days I had swapped all of my father's and most of my uncle's crops. I felt I could take on a little more without overextending myself, thus I drew some of our neighbors into the scheme, Dan Shays, Tom Packard, Mr. Gilmore our next-door neighbor and a few more. For the cash I needed I drew upon Mr. Gerson, who informed me that Mr. Burdick had deposited five hundred pounds to my account. I drew only a hundred pounds and set up headquarters in an old, unused barn at the outskirts of Northampton.

I shall spare you the details of the trading, for they were long and complicated. I gave notes to my father, my Uncle and the others whose crops I had handled, promising them cash at the rate of eight shillings a bushel for wheat, four for oats and rye, four for corn, the prevailing prices. For the shoes, I began by giving a bushel of wheat per pair, two bushels of oats, rye or corn. Naturally, the amount I gave out varied with the quality of the shoes, but the average would be about eight shillings. Most of the farmers complained my prices were too low, holding they could get at least a shilling more per pair if they sold the shoes themselves. My argument was that, if they took to the road, they'd have all the expenses of the trip, food and lodgings and time, which would bring their net down to the price I was offering. That argument usually prevailed.

The deals were not always simply turning over produce for shoes. Some wanted cash, too, which I doled out in small amounts to clinch a deal. Some wanted products I did not have on hand, such as pigs, chickens, geese and so on. So I swapped around with people in the surrounding area who were in need of one commodity or the other. In the end, I did pretty well in my attempts to satisfy everyone. Very few sold me their entire supply of shoes, for they swapped some for staples, such as sugar, tea and coffee, at the Northampton stores. My biggest competitors were Tappen and Fowle and I found that they had raised the amount they'd give in goods. After a while I had to raise my offer, too. The result was that I had bought the shoes at an average of nine shillings a pair.

When I closed up shop at the end of two weeks, I found I had some fourteen hundred pairs of shoes valued at about four hundred and ninety pounds. I had given out promissory notes to the amount of five hundred and ten pounds. Expenses would bring the total I had laid out to five hundred and sixty pounds. I expected to sell the shoes wholesale at 10 shillings— the retail value averaging 12—thus giving me a profit of about a hundred and fifty pounds. Not bad—if I could sell at my price.

Joe Crane came home on the 18th of October. I was at home that morning, working on the ping I was making for my father. The old sled, which Pa had used for hauling so many winters, had been sold at the auction and never returned. No one seemed to remember who had bought it.

It was a little before noon when my mother called to me from the kitchen door. I put aside my tools and went outside to see what she wanted.

"Joe!" I called.

He grinned and waved and, a moment later, we were pumping each other's arms and going through the usual inquiries about our obvious good health.

"You're staying for dinner, of course, Joseph," my mother said.

Joe came in. "I can't stay, really, Mrs. Hascott. I haven't been home yet."

"Well, set a while and have a bite, anyway."

Joe protested he couldn't eat a thing, since he expected to have a big dinner soon. Ma put a jug of cider and some new bread and cherry jam on the table just the same. After Joe had finished his second slice of bead and jam, I refilled his cider cup.

"I'm all ready, Joe. Unless you've got other plans. I can leave the shoes until later in the fall if you want me to. My storage costs are practically nothing."

"No, no, everything's fixed, Warren. I've got another cargo lined up at Machias, Maine. Fact is, things are dull right now, dullest fall I've ever had. But I have promise of some business later in the season. So, now's the time, Warren."

"Suits me. How is the market?"

"Well, I figure the market ought to be pretty good in Philadelphia. I spoke to a friend of mine last time I touched there and he said he could take about two thousand pairs at ten and a half shillings. I can push him up to eleven and a half easy."

"Try to get twelve, Joe, though eleven and a half would be all right. I can get by on eleven, if necessary."

"Sure, I'll try Baltimore, too." He picked up another piece of bread, smeared it with jelly, grinning. "I ain't had home-made bread in years, Mrs. Hascott. This is good." He stuffed his mouth full and gulped. "Fact is, Warren, I wish you'd come with me. I need a mate. Mine walked out on me when we docked. He's shipping out on deep water."

That was a tempting prospect. I would certainly love to get out to sea again and away from the smell of hay and dirt. Besides, being paid wages, the trip wouldn't cost me anything. And, although I had full confidence in Joe, I'd feel a lot safer if I did the trading myself. Another reason occurred to me. I was itching for an excuse to get to Boston.

"You've got a mate, Joe. What's the cargo—lumber?"

"No, rum and sugar."

"In Machias? I never heard Machias was exporting that sort of stuff before."

Joe laughed and refilled his cider cup. "It's simple enough. Spencer—he's the owner of the cargo—was shipping it from Jamaica to Halifax. The ship got caught in a bad blow and put in there. She sank in the harbor. Luckily, Captain Russell managed to get the cargo off before his ship went down."

"Why doesn't he sell it at Portland, rather than ship it all the way back to New York?"

Joe shrugged. "Everything considered, the freight isn't much more. If he sold the cargo in Portland he'd have to take whatever price he could get. In New York he can hold it in his own warehouse until he gets his price." Joe wiped his mouth and got up. "Can you leave with me on the stage tomorrow morning? I expect to go out on the Saturday after-noon tide."

I considered. "Listen, Joe, could you make a stop at Fenwick?"

"I suppose so. Why?"

"Well, I figure I might send the shoes there by barge

instead of paying wagons to take them to Boston. I'd save money."

"Yes, I can see that." He lifted his palms. "All right. Arrange it that way, if you like. Now, I'd better get home and let my family see me. Come over later, will you, Warren?"

I went back to my work until the dinner horn blew. I figured on going to Northampton in the afternoon and making arrangements to ship the shoes down the river. The prospect of taking that trip myself didn't appeal to me at all. But I just couldn't let those shoes go down unattended. I was aching to get to Boston for a day or two. For one thing, I wanted to talk to Mr. Blair and find out what the General Court was doing toward redressing grievances. For another, I was anxious to see Judith again.

Both Pa and Increase were already in and washed up when I reached the kitchen. I cleaned up and sat down at the table. Mother had told them about Joe's visit.

"I'd like to send someone downriver with the shoes, Increase. I'd like to spend a few days in Boston. How about it? I'll pay you five pounds—cash money."

Increase's head shaking stopped abruptly. "Cash?"

"Cash," I repeated. "And I'll tell you what I'll do. I'll buy you a new suit to get married in next spring. That's over and above what I'd give you for a wedding present, anyway."

Increase grinned. "You must want to get to Boston pretty bad." He passed his plate for another helping of pork. "How about cash instead of the suit. I got a good suit. Ma's tailoring is good enough for me."

My father hawed. "Looks like I raised two traders."

"Well, that's just good sense," Ma said testily. "He's going to have a lot of expenses next spring. Don't you go throwing your money away on imported cloth, Warren. I'll make Increase another suit this winter, just as soon as Pa gets me the wool."

"All right. I'll price the suit in Boston and give you the cash. Is that satisfactory, Increase?"

"Fine." His face saddened. "Do I have to go right away?"

"Next week will be time enough. Don't worry, Increase, you won't be away from her more than two weeks in all. I'm going over to Northampton this afternoon and make the arrangements. I'll tell you tonight how we'll work it."

Right after dinner, I went next door—which was three quarters of a mile down the road—and borrowed Mr. Gilmore's horse, for I wanted to get over to Northampton and back by dark, if possible. Mother said she'd pack my portmanteau while I was gone. I was feeling queerly buoyant and happy and free. This place would always be home to me but I was certainly ripe for a trip and the end, for a time, to farms and farming.

In Northampton I went to Mr. Gerson and made all the arrangements. I don't know what Burdick had written to him about me, but he certainly went out of his way to be nice and obliging. I felt I could trust him, too. He agreed to place the shoes on a barge sometime next week and instruct Increase where to store them in Fenwick while waiting for me. He told me he had a friend there who would not overcharge me and would see that the merchandise was given proper care. I thanked him and offered to pay for his services, which was no more than his due, but he would not take my money.

When I got home, shortly after supper time, I told my brother about the arrangements and gave him instructions and a little pocket cash. Increase wasn't a sharp sort, but I knew I could trust him to carry out my orders to the letter. He was most happy to learn that he wouldn't have to be away from his beloved Hope any more than three weeks at the most.

Joe had dropped in a few minutes before I arrived, Pa told me, and had gone over to Conkey's to see some of the boys. Accordingly, as soon as I was finished with my supper, I decided to go over there, too. I promised Ma I'd be back early.

The wind was sharp and chill as I came over East Hill. Everyone was inside Conkey's now and there was a roaring fire going in the hearth. The taproom was noisy, for everyone was crowded about Joe and telling him about the excitement we had had during the summer. The boys broke their circle long enough to welcome me and draw me inside. I was surprised to find Beulah sitting by Joe's side.

"So, you're going with him," Beulah said.

"I've got to think about making a living sometime," I explained. "Anyway, the troubles are over. I won't miss anything."

"That's what you think," Tom Packard drawled. "That the troubles are over, I mean. The General Court's been sitting for three weeks now and they haven't done a damn thing but talk."

"Well, as long as the Legislature is in session," I remarked, "we can hope they'll do something. Give them time. A lot of those grievances present complicated problems. They have to be studied carefully. After all, it wouldn't help the country any if we got what we wanted and the merchants were ruined."

Shays nodded. "Warren's right. We'll wait and see, anyway. How are things down south, Joe? I hear they've had a bit of trouble in Rhode Island."

Joe smiled. "A bit? Brother, I avoided Providence like it was a plague city. That paper money they issued last spring has the whole state in a dither. There's a law saying that it's a crime to refuse to accept the paper, but the Tories won't take it, anyway. I heard that the Supreme Court held that the law forcing Tories to take the paper money was unconstitutional. That only made matters worse. They almost hanged the judges. Now, Rhode Island paper is down to about ten to one."

"How about paper in other states?" I asked.

"Pennsylvania paper money is down about fifteen percent already. New Jersey, North Carolina, Georgia, all of them are having trouble with the rapid rate of depreciation. South Carolina paper's holding up pretty well. It's selling around par. But it's not legal tender for debts. New York paper's off ten percent."

"How about other grievances?" Shays asked.

Joe shrugged. "I don't pay much attention to that stuff, Dan. I heard a mob broke up a court in South Carolina not so long ago. The militia had to be called out. In Portsmouth, I heard there's talk about stopping the courts there. From what I've heard, most people are watching to see what happens here. If the General Court redresses grievances on account of what you boys did I guess there'll be a lot of others trying it all over America. You mark me."

There was a queer stirring in the crowd, but being absorbed

in the conversation I hadn't paid any attention. A mug slid off the table and clattered to the floor. Suddenly, I realized the room was very quiet. The crowd had melted away from our table. Beulah was very pale. Both Joe and Dan Shays were staring at someone directly behind me. I turned and my heart sank. Our visitor was Dr. Cameron.

" 'Evening, Doc," Joe said casually.

Doctor Cameron rocked like an ill-balanced egg. "Good evening, Joseph. God has kept you in good health, I see."

"Tolerable," Joe conceded.

Dr. Cameron's eyelids dropped and he gazed at Beulah a moment, then stared at me. "Good evening, Warren."

"Evening, Doctor," I answered uncomfortably, not knowing exactly why the hackles on my neck were rising.

"I hear you're going away," he said softly.

"News travels fast, doesn't it doctor?" I replied, unaccountably irritated by his red, pouting lips.

"Yes, very fast." A trace of a smile touched his thick lips. "And I suppose you're taking Beulah with you."

The taproom seemed to hold its breath and the crackling of the fire was suddenly very loud. My knuckles whitened against the pewter cup I was holding. I had more or less expected this. I tried desperately to hold my voice level and steady.

"What gave you that idea, Doctor?"

"Oh . . . things." His flabby features set into an ugly, expressionless mask. "I've been expecting you any Sabbath to be publishing the banns. And seeing her with you here, drinking and carousing. . . ."

Joe picked up the cup in front of Beulah and sniffed. "It's sweet cider, Doc," he said in an easy, almost insolent tone. "Besides, she came with me."

Dr. Cameron's small, piglike eyes shifted. "Joseph, in this town, a proper young woman does not frequent the parlors of Sodom."

Joe leaned back slightly, gave Beulah a quick, amused glance. Beulah was frightened yet angry, too, and there were two red spots fixed on her cheeks. Joe seemed to enjoy her discomfort. But she was, after all, his sister.

He cocked one brow. "I'm sure Conkey is pleased to learn

he runs a resort for Sodomites. Do you tipple here with a special dispensation from God?"

The whole room gasped. This was defiance of the boldest, the worst sort. Joe winced as Beulah gave him a kick, but his bland smile didn't waver. Underneath that smile, I knew Joe was boiling mad. I was, too, possibly with greater reason, yet I had sense enough not to court disaster. And there was ominous rage in the doctor's small, black eyes as he gazed, his lower lips protruding slightly, at the younger man.

Tom Packard's chair scraped with nervewracking loudness over the bare floor. "I've got to be getting along," he said gruffly. "Come on, Beulah. I'll see you home."

I opened my mouth to say something, but Tom gave me a quick scowl and a shake of the head. Beulah rose slowly, her expression torn between defiance and fear. She went along with Tom promptly enough, but her eyes were not cast down.

Dr. Cameron turned away abruptly, seated himself at the next table. "A rum flip, if you please, Mr. Conkey," he said heavily. "Light on the sugar."

A few made feeble, labored attempts to resume their talk. But the air was charged with thunder. Joe was elaborately nonchalant, though he too felt it. Finally I got up.

"I'm leaving. Coming, Joe?"

Joe shrugged. "Might as well. . . . Goodnight, boys." He bowed ostentatiously to the doctor. "Goodnight, Dr. Cameron."

Dr. Cameron did not look up or answer. He scowled at his cup, swirled the flip and buried his nose in the foam.

As soon as the door was closed behind us I exploded with a pent up curse. "Of all the damn fool. . . ."

I broke off sharply as I saw Tom Packard's lean figure move out of the bushes at the edge of the clearing. Beulah was with him. They had been waiting for us.

Beulah's grey eyes were cold with rage. "You did that on purpose. You tried to ruin my reputation. You. . . ."

"Aw, cut it," Joe said wearily. "I just got sore at that pompous old ass."

"Joe, you should have better sense," Tom chided. "You're going away. Beulah has to live here."

"Oh, no I don't," Beulah snapped. "I'm not going to wait to be hounded out of here. Joe, you're taking me along."

"I am not," Joe answered indignantly.

"You are," Beulah insisted sharply.

"I'm not arguing the point," Joe said icily. "You're not going with me. That's final."

Beulah's head lowered and, from the shaking of her shoulders, I could tell she was crying. Tom put his arm around her and led her toward the road.

"Come on," he said sharply to us. "We've got to get out of here." He patted Beulah awkwardly. "Shucks, Beulah, there's no need for tears. Soon as Joe's been gone awhile Cameron will forget all about this. I'll talk to him. So will Dan and Hank and Mrs. Decker and—oh, lots of us. You've done too much good around here to let what Cameron says make any difference."

"I'll be going away, too," I added eagerly. "That will stop the gossips, Beulah."

She looked up quickly, stared at me for a long moment. Then, "Joe, you've got to take me."

"Beulah," Joe said flatly, "if you try to come with me I swear to God I'll drown you soon as we're past Boston Light."

Beulah didn't answer. With the collar of her cloak she wiped away the glistening streaks on her cheeks. Her mouth thinned to an ugly, bloodless line. She shook Tom's arm away, turned and walked quickly up the road, her head high.

We followed at a distance, grim and silent. I was squirming inside, pained by the knowledge that this was partly my fault. Then, as we came over East Hill, we could dimly see Beulah up ahead. She hadn't turned up the road which led past Dr. Hynds and home. She was going into town.

"I'll bet she's going to Dave's," Tom said softly.

"Dave?" Joe echoed. "Is he still after her? Then he chuckled softly. "I hope she marries him. She'll find out that Dave's got a lot more backbone than she thinks."

Chapter 18

I TOLD my father and mother what had happened rather than let them hear it from somebody else. Ma's only comment was that Beulah had been foolish to have gone to Conkey's at night in the first place. A tavern was no place for a young woman, even one as independently minded as Beulah. Pa said nothing at all. I think he sensed what I felt. To some extent this was my fault, for Dr. Cameron wouldn't have made such an issue of her presence in the tavern if she'd been with Joe alone. People had drawn the natural conclusion from my being with her so much. Either I had been after her for marriage or carnal purposes. Since I wasn't quite sure myself, I resented the alternative.

Neither my father nor mother mentioned Beulah when Joe came to call for me. I was ready to leave, anyway, and we had no time for discussions of any kind. Joe and I planned to hire horses at Clapp's Inn in Amherst and ride to Western where we would catch the stage that passed through there in the afternoon. Thus, we could be in Boston by Friday night.

"When do you figure on being home?" Pa asked.

"Late next month," I replied. "If I think I won't be back in time, I'll try to transmit enough money to cover Uncle Enoch's loan. If it doesn't come, put in an appeal."

Pa nodded. "We'll take care of it." He stuck out his hand to Joe. "Goodby, Joe. Take care of Warren, will you?"

Joe grinned. "I'm taking him along to take care of me, Mr. Hascott. Goodby, Mrs. Hascott." His face became sober. "Look in on my mother once in a while, will you? I'm a little worried about her."

246

"We'll look out for her," Ma said. She kissed his cheek. "Godspeed, Joseph. Don't be away so long this time."

Joe promised he wouldn't. I gave Increase some last minute instructions, kissed Ma and said goodby to my father. Not until Joe and I were far down the road did I ask the question that had been bothering me.

"How's Beulah, Joe?"

Joe's shoulders lifted. "All right, I guess. She came home late after I went to bed." Then he added, "Dave brought her home. She seemed cheerful enough this morning, though." His brow wrinkled. "She even kissed me goodby and she told me to tell you not to worry about her."

"I feel pretty mean about this," I said.

"Why should you? I can't blame you for wanting her." He chuckled. "She's quite a package, isn't she?"

I thought it wasn't quite decent for him to talk about his sister that way.

"I had a talk with Joab," he went on. "Joab suspended his grouch long enough to give me all the gossip. Fact is, Warren, as I see it, she's only getting what she deserves for chasing you so shamelessly."

"Aw, now, Joe, let's be fair."

Joe shrugged. "Have it your own way."

We dropped the subject.

The stage arrived at Boston shortly before dusk on Friday evening and, since the coach had come in over Charleston Bridge, Joe and I got off at Prince and Middle Streets. Joe's ship was moored at Scarlett's Wharf, a short distance north of Dock Square, so we went directly there to stow our belongings. I had told Joe about the way Burdick was partially financing me and asked him if it would be all right for me to call upon them. Joe grinned knowingly. He said it would be all right with him if I spent the evening—or even the night— with them, as long as I was back to the ship before the tide turned at three the next afternoon.

Before going to the Burdick's, however, I decided to have supper. Being so close to Salvation Alley, I thought to have it with the Blairs if they were there. I asked Joe if he wanted to come along but he said he had some business friends to see this evening. The small amount of cargo which he was bringing to Machias had already been taken aboard under the supervision of the bosun but there was a little more cargo coming in during the morning so Joe couldn't sail until the afternoon tide. He assured me, however, that he didn't need my services in the morning. I stowed my baggage in my cabin and appeared in the salon to sign the articles.

Joe seemed a bit embarrassed as he put the papers on the table. "It's going to be queer commanding you, Warren."

"It's a queer feeling being employed again," I returned. "But you can be sure I'll obey orders, Joe. I believe friendships should be suspended—at least officially—while at sea."

It was just about supper hour when I arrived at the Salvation Inn, and the taproom was almost completely filled. Mr. Rhodes recognized me at once and after shaking my hand, led me over to the roaring hearth where the Blairs, father and son, were having their meal. Both Ethan and his father saw me at the same time and, rising, gave me a hearty welcome.

"Sit down, sit down, Warren," Blair urged. "You're just in time. Rhodes, supper for my guest."

"What brings you to Boston, Mr. Hascott?" Ethan asked.

I seated myself with my back to the fire, then, as the heat struck me, moved over to the other chair. "I've signed on as mate on a schooner—Joe Crane's ship. You know him, don't you?"

"Indeed, yes," Blair answered. "He's a good friend of Stephen's. Why didn't you bring him along?"

"He had another engagement." I smiled at Ethan. "And how are you getting along?"

Ethan lifted his palms. "About the same. Pa met Mr. Fitch, which didn't turn out to be such a good idea."

Blair humphed. "Fitch is a jackass. Don't know which side his bread is buttered on. He blathers now that all good citizens should uphold our 'happy' Constitution."

Ethan winked. "You wouldn't think my father was secretary to Mr. Minot, would you, Mr. Hascott?"

"Well," Blair said in a crotchety tone, "right is right, Minot knows my sentiments. He can discharge me if he doesn't like them. I don't know why he hasn't, to be truthful."

"How is the General Court doing?" I asked. "I haven't paid much attention since Springfield."

"They're stalling, just the way I said they would," Blair said. "Did you read the Governor's speech opening the session? That just about tells what's going to happen—nothing—except possibly the passing of some repressive measures. They're talking now about suspending the Habeas Corpus and there's a Riot Act coming up for action, too."

I whistled softly. "That's likely to lead to trouble, Mr. Blair. The Governor can bank on it."

Blair shrugged. "He's been warned often enough."

The conversation spun out for several hours and I forgot until it was too late that I wanted to call upon the Burdick's. But the call could wait until morning. So, we sat and talked and drank and talked some more and had another cup and another. . . .

My head ached a little when I got up the next morning, but Mr. Blair fixed that in a hurry with his favorite remedy for fur lined heads—gin and bitters. After a hearty breakfast I decided to make an early call on Mr. Burdick, for I knew he did not leave for his counting house until late in the morning. Both Mr. Blair and Ethan had to hurry on about their business but insisted that I refrain from bolting my breakfast to accompany them.

"Oh, and I almost forgot," Blair said, coming back. "I sent your deposition and petition to New York to be laid before the Continental Congress. I doubt if you'll ever get compensation for that dagger you lost but if you visit New York, stop in and inquire about it."

He clapped on his hat and hurried off to his work.

It was still very early when I reached Dock Square, but the place was quite crowded with farmers and fishermen preparing their stalls for the influx of housewives later in the morning. It was shocking to see how many shabby men were pawing over the refuse piles to salvage the makings of a cabbage soup or a chowder of fish entrails. Others were gathered around Fanueil Hall, searching for a bone or scraps of aged flesh no longer salable. Boston had an almhouse but a man had to be hopelessly pauperized before he'd go there, for the place was run more like a prison than an institution of charity for the unfortunate.

Since I had a little time I thought I'd stop in to see Mr. Fitch, so I laid my course past Fanueil Hall and toward Merchant's Row. As luck would have it, Mr. Fitch was outside washing the store windows. Mr. Fitch, being a very short man, was having a hard time reaching the uppermost of the many square panes that composed the window, even though he was standing on a box. I could understand, then, why store windows were so seldom cleaned.

"Can I help you, Mr. Fitch?" I inquired.

"Eh?" Fitch turned and adjusted his spectacles. "Why, bless me, it's Mr. Hascott." He jumped down from his box, extending his hand—the one with the wet rag in it. He looked down in surprise, laughed, and put it on the box. "I've thought of you quite often, Mr. Hascott, especially when I read those awful reports of riots and mobs out in the west."

"They weren't so awful, Mr. Fitch," I said, "In fact, those mobs, as you called them, were very orderly."

"No! Is that a fact?" The lines about his mouth seemed to deepen in disappointment. "I heard tell there was all sorts of violence out there. Worcester was the worst, wasn't it? I heard those rogues bayoneted General Ward, wounded two or three of his clerks and ducked all the lawyers in the town pond."

I was amused. "I suppose that made you change your mind about the need for reform?"

"Well, no," Fitch said reluctantly. "There're plenty of grievances to be redressed. But as Sam Adams said, a government bought with so much blood mustn't be torn down by mob action."

"Sam Adams said that? I thought he was for the common man. Oh, I remember now. Sam Adams is a senator now, isn't he?"

"Well, what's that got to do with it?"

"Nothing, I was just wondering." I decided to abandon that mean line of attack.

"How's business, Mr. Fitch?"

"Terrible." He gave his full attention to a stubborn spot. "I'm in the middle, don't you see? Half my customers are out of work. I owe money to the bigger merchants. I can't collect what's owed to me and I can't pay my bills. I can't last much longer."

"Wouldn't it help if the General Court did something about those grievances? If they provided a circulating medium, for instance, wouldn't a lot of your customers go back to work?"

Fitch peered into the distance a moment, then shook his head. "I don't know, Mr. Hascott, I honestly don't. All I know is I'd be even worse off if we had paper money. Suppose the General Court did set up a bank of paper money? The money would depreciate. After a while, people would be paying off their debts at a discount of maybe half the real value of the debt. 'Course, I could pay off my debts at the same rate, but then my credit would be ruined. I'd have to close up shop."

It was about eight when I knocked on the Burdick's massive front door. A cordial smile lit up Polly's plain face as she opened it for me. Yes, the master was up. He was still at breakfast.

Mr. Burdick, in a plum silk banyan and tasseled skullcap, was just helping himself to another serving of kidneys. "Well, Warren, my boy! Good morning. Sit down. Have you had your breakfast?"

"Yes, thank you." I sank into the chair next to him. "I thought I'd drop by and report on the state of your investment. I'm leaving with Joe on the afternoon tide."

"Hmm." He frowned slightly. "Gerson told me you only drew a hundred pounds. Why didn't you take the rest?"

I started to explain but he had already heard of the bartering I had done, so I went on from there. "I didn't want to make the deal too big for me to handle. After all, I'm risking a lot—not only your money, but the crops of my family and neighbors."

"Yes, that's the wisest thing to do in your position." He pulled a bundle of papers over from across the table and fingered through them, selecting one. "Here's a report from a friend of mine in Baltimore. They've just had a very bad storm down there, floods, houses blown down and so forth. He says seven mill dams were washed out in his neighborhood alone. Frightful amount of damage to the stores. I'm rerouting a ship of mine to touch Baltimore at the end of the month."

"There wouldn't be a market for shoes there," I said. "Whatever loose money is around will go for necessaries."

Burdick nodded, a bland smile on his pinkish face. "You're touching New York, aren't you? New York's had a good wheat crop. If you turn up nothing else after you've disposed of your shoes, perhaps you can take advantage of the opportunity. If you need more money, call on White & Coleman in Pearl Street. They'll take care of you. I'll give you a letter to them."

I scratched the edge of my jaw. "That's good of you, sir. I should have seen the opportunity at once."

"Poof, Warren. I'm in touch with this sort of stuff all the time and you're not. You'll take hold quickly enough."

"Oh, and New York reminds me, Mr. Burdick. Do you know a Spencer there?"

"Which Spencer? Spencer & Green, English goods, D. W. Spencer, West India goods, or A. L. Spencer, Factor?"

"It must be D. W. Spencer."

"Stay away from him. He's a sharper. He was driven out of Charleston for shady dealings in damaged tobacco." Burdick felt his second chin. "He has money, though. But you'd have to get up very early to outsmart that man."

I told him about the cargo Joe was picking up for Spencer in Machias and Mr. Burdick thought it over.

"Well, I can understand him wanting the cargo in New York. He'd get precious little for it at a forced sale in Portland." He stared upward for a moment, frowning into space. "Machias . . . Seems I heard . . . Why, yes! It was about three months ago. A friend of mine told me about that ship. . . . No, it's longer than three months. It's a good six months. Now, why hasn't Spencer sent a ship up there for that cargo before?" He wagged a plump finger at me. "You tell Joe to be careful. That man Spencer's up to something."

"I thought it sounded a bit queer," I commented.

Burdick waved impatiently. "Enough of business. How are things in Hampshire these days? Quieter?"

I said they were and we fell into a discussion of the recent tumults. We were not at it long, however, when we heard clatter of feminine heels on the stairway. A moment later, I rose as Judith swept into the room. She was dressed in an exquisite frock of light blue persian—a thin, shimmery silk—under which was a petticoat of the same color splashed with huge, yellow sunflowers. The neckline was square-cut and the dress itself was fitted snugly about the front and gathered into pleats in the back, giving it a bustle effect. It was indeed a startling creation.

"What a delightful surprise, Warren," she cried, extending her hand.

Her father burped a laugh. "Surprise, indeed. This is the first time I ever saw you with your hair dressed at breakfast."

She crinkled her nose. "Don't spoil my little artifices, Papa." She kissed his plump cheek and seated herself. "You came just in time to save me from riding alone this morning, Warren."

"Another artifice?" Burdick winked at me. "Tuesday is her day to have the chaise."

"This week it's Saturday," Judith returned blandly. "Besides, Warren won't be here Tuesday, will you, Warren?"

"How did you know he was going away?" Burdick asked.

"Spies!" Judith hissed. She winked at the partly opened kitchen door. "It's all right, Polly. No one knows you're my spy."

I couldn't help laughing as I saw how red Polly got.

Judith chattered away blithely over breakfast, I was busy admiring her beauty, her soft brown curls, her lustrous, impish brown eyes—and that dress. The bodice seemed molded to her and I was convinced she needed no stays to accent her slim, well-rounded figure.

As soon as coffee was over, Polly came in and announced that the carriage was waiting. I felt awkward, rushing out this way, but Mr. Burdick didn't seem to mind.

"I'll send that letter to the ship for you, Warren." He shook a finger at his daughter. "Have him back by two."

"Yes, Papa." She pecked his smooth forehead. "Tell Mama the walk to the dressmaker's will do her good. Bye!"

The sun was not very strong and the crisp October air nibbled at Judith's cheeks and made them glow. The fields were a harsh, mutilated brown and the forlorn, withered debris of the crops gave the earth a weary look, as if exhausted

253

and well deserving of a rest after a season's feverish work. But the trees were gay in their thinning coats of purple and red and rusty, mottled green. It was pleasant riding without destination, chatting without purpose, becoming excited almost like children at the sight of a nervous deer or scurrying rabbit or a placid porcupine waddling along in the yellowing grasses.

Our coachman, Harry, I must mention, was the soul of discretion. Never once did he needlessly turn his woolly head. Harry was a free negro hired at wages, for there was no slavery in Massachusetts since the adoption of the State Constitution in 1780. The issue had been fought out in court but the Supreme Court held that the dictum "all men are created free and equal" actually meant all.

After a time, Judith became quite restless and, coming to an inn at the foot of a rather steep incline in the road, she directed Harry to stop. He pulled up the horse some distance beyond the tavern and we got out.

She took my hand and started up the hill. From the distance it looked something like the back of a camel, two humps through which the road ran. Judith insisted on cutting off the road and climbing to the peak of the tallest hump. The brittle weeds were deceptively tall and I thought sure she would tear that lovely dress or damage her shoes. But she didn't, for we found enough bald spots to give her safe passage.

The view was really magnificent. The place wasn't very high above sea level, yet we could see a long distance in every direction, the endless undulating pastures and fields, the toy-like barns and farmhouses, the grazing cows that seemed no bigger than small dogs. Over to the west was a forest, lying like a brownish ball against a semi-circle of protecting hills. At the nearest farm we could see carts loaded with apples moving into the yard, disappearing into the open mouth of the big house and coming out empty. I could almost hear the clank of the machinery and the gurgling of the cider as the white-tipped wheel turned over and over in the sluggish stream alongside the old mill.

I spread out the cloak on a level spot and we seated ourselves, giving ourselves in silence to the beauty and the peace of the unchanging landscape. Soon, there were no more trees, no more fields, no more people, for I was content to center my view on the picture of a very lovely woman.

"You mustn't stare so," Judith teased. "What will the birds think? Such gossipy creatures, they are."

"Haven't they told you what I have in my heart?"

"Oh, of course." She smiled and patted my cheek. "They say you think you're in love."

"Marvelous. Did they say with whom?"

"Dear Warren, how could they? You're in love with . . . with visions." Her eyes dropped and she plucked at the grass. "Just as I was, once," she added softly.

"Yes, a vision . . . and a reality in one. With you, Judith."

She shook her head and was silent for a long time. Then, she turned her grey eyes away. "Warren, I'm going to marry next spring."

I sat upright. "What? No, I mean, to whom?"

"Salderman—Mr. Jothan Salderman."

"Now look here, Judith, you can't marry him. He's . . ." I fumbled for words. "Well, I don't trust that man. He's . . . Oh, I don't know. All I do know is he isn't the man for you."

Her smile faded and her hard eyes gazed to the horizon. "He's cold and ruthless in business. He'll trample over any man who stands in his way. He'll be a very wealthy man, some day—perhaps even a powerful man. His morals—" She shrugged. "He hasn't lived in a monastery. But that's in the past. He loves me as much as a man of his sort can love any woman. He'll be constant and kind and give me everything I'll ever want."

"Except love," I said bitterly. I took her shoulders and turned her to me. "You know you don't love him. You'd hate him a week after you married him. Judith, you're going to marry me."

Her eyes held steady to mine for a long moment. Then, in a soft, husky voice. "No, Warren. You say that because . . . because you've been driven into a corner."

"That's not so and you know it." I drew her toward me, but she placed her fingertips on my chest. "No, please, Warren."

"Judith, I can't find one sensible reason why you can't marry me. If there is one, tell me."

A faint smile brushed her lips. "I'm not sure . . . and this is the truth, Warren . . . I'm not sure I love you. I hardly know you, really. And even if I were sure now, I'd hesitate. This much I do know about you, you'd never be happy as the son-in-law of Moses Burdick. You'd irritate yourself to the end of your days with the knowledge that you didn't get on by your own—your very own—efforts."

"Who said I wasn't going to get on by my own?" I asked, surprised. "I asked you to wait a little while."

"You see? The merest suggestion irritates you. To be honest and practical, you may be in a position to marry me soon, perhaps within a year. Perhaps not. You might decide to go into father's firm and work for him to hasten the time. You say you love me now. Perhaps. But you'd change afterward. I've seen it. . . ."

I cut her short with a furious kiss. She didn't struggle, she didn't resist. For an eternal moment we were one. I felt her lips yielding to mine and her arms crept around my neck and tightened. . . .

Our lips parted reluctantly and Judith smiled and kissed me again, lightly and gaily. Then she slipped out of my arms, patting her curls back into place.

"Do you know your mind now?" I asked.

"Yes. . . . No." She was still a bit breathless. "I think I do. I'm afraid I'm going to marry Jothan."

She stood up and swished the wrinkles from her dress. I was confused. I was more than a little exasperated.

It was almost half past two when the carriage slowly clattered up Ship Street. The smells of hemp and tar, the bowsprits forming an arch over our heads, the far off cry of a scavenging gull, all made me glad to be going where I could forget the scent of hay and burning leaves. I wanted to be out where I could think. Somehow, I felt that she had tried to get a message across to me, something she wanted me to do to win her. And I ruefully remembered how I had admired in Judith the quality of almost male frankness and lack of feminine pretenses.

We lapsed into silence and didn't speak until the carriage

had rounded the schooner's bowsprit and rumbled out onto the wharf. I was sorry the ride was over, sorry I must leave Boston, sorry I would miss the opportunities of seeing more of Judith. . . .

She sighed and frowned a little. "At least, you won't be lonely, Warren. There . . . on the poop."

I looked and my astonishment grew. By the rail stood a girl in brown homespun. It was Beulah.

Chapter 19

꤫꤫꤫

To SAY I was stunned would be indulging in the vastest of understatement. I was numb. I stared increduously for a long time after the chaise had come to a halt. I told myself that it was a horrible mistake when that girl up there waved at me. As she came down the poop later, my last doubts vanished. Her tawny skin and contrasting grey eyes finally convinced me she was really Beulah.

"I—I had no idea," I stammered.

Judith's brown eyes were cool and a half smile was fixed on her lips. "I guess you didn't," she conceded softly.

Joe was standing by the rail amidships, grinning down at me as if he thought this was funny. I remembered myself and got out, handing Judith from the carriage. Beulah came tripping down the gangplank and I thought she was going to throw her arms around my neck. I almost died. But she stopped at a reasonable distance and put out her hand to Judith in her forthright fashion.

"Judith, how nice!" she gushed. "I was hoping you'd come before we left."

Judith was unruffled. "This is a pleasant surprise, Beulah. Warren didn't tell me. Your first trip to sea?"

I got red and mumbled something and fled up on deck to where Joe was standing. "How did she get here?"

"Reuben brought her. They arrived around noon." Joe wasn't as amused about this as I had first thought. "I'd like to wring that girl's neck, by God, I would!"

"Why don't you?" I urged darkly. "Maybe you'd let me. . . ." I bit my tongue. "I'm sorry."

"What for? Only you'd have to fight me for the pleasure."

Then he shrugged. "There's nothing we can do about it."

"Why not?"

Joe spread his hands. "She owns a share in this ship. The family made a pool for me. I've been paying interest and a little extra ever since I bought it. Now, Beulah says she'll slap a libel on me if I try to leave without her. She says she'd sue to recover her share. I'd have to sell the ship."

Suddenly—and quite unreasonably—I began to laugh. Joe grumbled that he couldn't see anything funny. I could hardly tell him I was laughing at myself. The last illusion I had ever held that I knew how women's minds worked, lay shattered on the deck. Just a while ago I had wondered how I had ever thought Judith endowed with male frankness and a lack of feminine pretenses. I had thought the same of Beulah. That foolish notion had crumbled, too.

Joe and I stood at the rail, watching the two women chat with unrestrained friendliness. Quite unconsciously I began comparing them, point by point. Physically, Beulah had all the better of it. She was a trifle taller, her curves fuller, her breasts rounder, her whole manner relaxed, like a soft, seductive animal. Judith was slimmer, her figure more boyish, though undeniably very attractive. She was unquestionably the more poised, the more patrician. The difference in their dresses was of quality of cloth, rather than cut. Yet I realized Beulah would be luscious even in a burlap bag.

From the standpoint of picking a life partner, Judith undoubtedly had the edge. Having lived so long in town, among commercially minded people, she would be more likely to understand my ambitions and the reasons for my undertakings. Having the greater social poise, she would make the better hostess. Her present position wasn't exactly a disadvantage, either. Yet, on practical grounds, why should she descend again to the bottom and climb at my side? The very lack of my material possessions and the possible slowness of my progress might cause a good deal of dissension and unhappiness.

Beulah, on the other hand, had nothing of that sort to sacrifice. I could never doubt her ability to take poverty and hardship. Whatever she lacked in social sheen, I was sure she could get in time. Her mind certainly would make her a bearable companion for all my days. She had only one drawback. Her manifest aggressiveness might, in the home, prove to be shrewishness.

With a slight shock I suddenly realized that I had omitted the highly important item of love. Then, in all honesty, I had to admit to myself that I was not emotionally ready to marry anyone. In fact, I was resenting the very thought. Six and a half years in Algiers had been imprisonment enough for a time. I wanted to stay free for a while. So, it could be that I wanted Judith so much because she was aloof, remote. I saw now that I had tried to pin her down and put her in a glass case until I was ready. With Beulah, on the other hand, I was trying to avoid being pinned down, though I certainly did want to play. Beulah had been right about one thing. Algiers had stunted my growth. But what could I do about it? I had to play the game the best way I knew how. With a chuckle I admitted that the prospect of being burnt and dragged to the altar by either one of them would not be a fate worse than death.

Judith caught my eye and smiled and waved for me to come down to the dock. I suddenly realized I liked those two women very much—separately. I tried to pretend it was Joe she was waving to, but that didn't work. Joe grinned and walked off. There was no way of sidestepping the moment so I joined the ladies.

". . . rather dangerous to be alone among so many men," Beulah was saying. She slipped her arm into mine. "But I'll have Warren to protect me, won't I, Warren?"

I coughed. "Well, there's Joe. . . ."

"Nonsense," Judith interrupted sweetly. "Beulah doesn't need protection. She can protect herself, can't you Beulah?"

Beulah nodded slowly. "Oh, yes. But it's nicer to pretend some man is taking care of you. Don't you find it so?"

"Always," Judith returned placidly.

The ship's bell saved me. The tingling of six bells—three o'clock—echoed and reechoed all along the waterfront. I disentangled myself from Beulah's possessive grip.

"We'll be casting off in a few minutes," I announced. "I have to be about my duties."

"Goodby, Judith." Beulah extended her hand. "I do hope I'll see you again when I get back."

She gave Judith's hand a hard wring and scurried up the gangplank, leaving us alone, much to my surprise.

Judith looked amused. "Transparent sort, isn't she?"

"Take care," I warned mockingly, "you speak of the woman I may marry if you keep tramping on my heart."

Judith's brows arched. "He's coming out of the fog. That's a dangerous sign." She gave me her hand. "Goodby, Warren. Good luck in your venture. And you won't forget to stop in when you get back? I'll still be free, you know."

"Of course. I'll have business to transact with your father, won't I?" I bowed slightly. "I may have other business, too. I'm not so easily discouraged."

Judith laughed. "I hope not. A woman of my age needs the flattery of male attention."

With that, I retired to my cave to lick my wounds.

The schooner was bumping the piles as if eager to be away from the land and all its bewildering problems. Although the presence of Beulah, I thought gloomily, would present other and perhaps more disturbing problems. But I had other things to think of at the moment, so I sought out the bosun and introduced myself and set about getting the ship from her berth.

As soon as the pilot was aboard, the mainsail was raised and hauled about and the lines cast loose. Slowly, sluggishly, the schooner eased astern, rubbing her sturdy sides against the piles as if reluctant to leave now that the moment had come.

She drifted out cautiously her bows swinging in search of open water. At the signal from Joe, I barked the order and the crew leaped to the halyards again and swung the boom around again. Then, as the ship straightened out, I set the men to coiling the ropes and battening down loose gear. But my mind wasn't on my work. I kept watching the dock and the carriage. Judith was standing up and, little by little, her face faded into a white blur. She waved to me once and I waved back, then the carriage turned about on the dock and disappeared into the stream of traffic on Ship Street.

Then I found Beulah at my side. "You're not angry with me, Warren, are you?" she asked in a small voice.

"Oh, for God's sake, get aft!" I exploded. "I've got duties to attend. Go on. I'll have time later to talk to you."

She went hesitantly, looking back and pouting and I was

afraid I'd hurt her feelings. But I didn't chase after her. She'd have to learn sooner or later that this was no pleasure trip. Joe was standing at the break of the poop, looking to the pilot for his orders. He ignored his sister as she stalked past him and went below.

The seaman nearby snickered and I caught a ribald remark from one of them. I reached out, grabbed his ear and whirled him around. He was a thick-shouldered, black-jowled fellow and his yellow, rotted teeth looked like fangs as he snarled a curse and swung at me, wrenching loose. I caught his arm, twisted it behind him and he howled.

"Now, my good man," I said easily, "we'll have no more remarks like that about the captain's sister."

"Leggo 'a me, yuh lousey bilge rat. Leggo!" He kicked back and I had to jump away to keep from being kicked in the shins. "How dare you lay hand on me?" he roared. "I'll—"

I hit him and he sprawled at my feet. "No more of your insolence. Now, get to your work."

He got to his hands and knees. "Why, you . . . you . . . I'll clap you in ir—" he caught himself, rubbed his unshaven jaw, then hauled himself up and, with a perfunctory salute, shambled off.

His attitude had startled me a bit, for he had neither the manner nor the reactions of a common seaman. I looked to the poop, then decided against going aft at the moment. Joe was looking off the starboard bow, pretending not to have noticed the fuss. The other seamen were slinking off to their various tasks.

Joe turned as the pilot signaled him. "Set the foresails, Mr. Hascott," he called.

"Aye, aye, sir! I returned. "Lively, there, boys! Hoist away!"

The men leaped to the halyards and put their backs to the tasks. Swiftly, the sail shook itself loose from the trailing gaskets and billowed in the freshening breeze. The deck shivered a little as the schooner felt her awakening power. All too quickly the lengthening white line of our boiling wake snapped and freed us from the receding shoreline of Boston.

By five o'clock, we had reached Lighthouse Island and there dropped the pilot. Joe ordered the topsails set and, as soon as the halyards were peaked, I was free to go aft for supper. Since we carried no second mate, the bosun, a fleshy, moon faced man with a pushed in nose, was left in charge.

Joe was grinning when he met me at the companionway. "I see you had a little trouble. What was it about?"

I told him. "Who is that fellow, anyway? I thought there was something queer about him."

Joe's smile faded. "Oh, him. His name's Buckner. I signed him on at New York. He's going up to visit his folks in Machias." He turned away, avoiding my eyes. "He's all right. I think he had ships of his own once."

The lamp over the salon table was swinging in a wide arc as I settled into my seat and gave Beulah a quick glance. She wasn't showing the slightest sign of distress, so I concluded she was lucky enough to be a natural sailor. I don't know why I should have been so disappointed. Joe ignored her completely. There was no conversation until after the weazened old black cook had put a big bowl of steaming fish chowder on the table and retired to his pantry.

Beulah fidgeted in the lengthening silence. "Well, have I done something so very terrible?"

Joe cocked one brow. "You're not worrying me."

I shifted uncomfortably as she turned her gray eyes on me. "I think you're crazy, Beulah. Things were bad enough before. What will people say when you get back?"

"No one knows I'm here," she answered in a petulant tone. "I met Dr. Cameron by Bruce's Inn and I told him I was going to visit Grandpa Crane in Attleboro. He thought the visit would do me good—the fat old pig," she added savagely.

Joe grunted. "And you think the truth won't get back?"

"Not unless you tell," Beulah replied. "Or Judith. She writes to friends in Amherst sometimes, I know. I had to tell her about Dr. Cameron. I asked her not to mention to a soul that she had seen me." She chewed her lower lip a moment. "Warren, do you think she'll tell?"

"Not if she said she wouldn't."

"I hope not." She put her hand on Joe's. "Don't be mad, Joe. I know how you feel. But think of me. I've never been outside of Hampshire County in all my life. Just once, I wanted to take a little trip. I won't bother you again. Honest."

"All right." Joe sighed and relaxed to a rueful grin. "I suppose you'll always get what you want, anyway."

After an uneventful voyage of five days and favored by fine breezes, we reached Machias in the Province of Maine. The town was wholly dependent on the sea for its sustenance, for the land was not suitable for extensive farming and there wasn't even a road connection between here and the towns farther south. There was enough grain grown to secure the people's bread supply, but almost all else had to be imported by the sea. The lumbering business, however, provided the people with an ample living.

The town itself was a mere handful of houses thrown up haphazardly behind a broad waterfront street. The Meeting House, a one story wooden building, stood in an open space in the middle of the town. It was very quiet and peaceful here. The dark green waters swished along the side of the ship, like the soft hissing of a contented tea kettle. The stillness was catching and the men's voices unconsciously grew softer as they furled the topsails and brought in the jibs. In the distance, we could hear the whine of a sawmill.

"I should think there'd be a market here for that rum," I remarked, "with all the logging camps around here."

Joe who was watching the shore, nodded. "I was thinking that myself. I wonder. . . . Look, over there, Warren."

Up river, just beyond the town, I could see the tops of two masts sticking above the water. The ship had sunk inshore, but the river was deep and there was plenty of room for other vessels to get by, so the sunken ship was not an obstruction to navigation.

"That ruined Russell, I understand," Joe commented. "He didn't have a shilling's insurance on her."

"Too bad. I'll bet the cargo was covered, though."

Joe chuckled. "Personally, I think Spencer would have been better off if the cargo had gone down, too."

By the time we were abreast of the town, the schooner wore barely enough sail to give her steerageway. Joe returned to the poop and called down to break out the anchor. No sooner had the anchor let go when we saw a small boat pull out from the town dock. The man in the sternsheets was not a townsman, I suspected, for he was wearing the kind of red and white striped shirt usually affected by seamen. From the distance he looked like all chest and nothing else. His arms seemed rather thin and his head was almost ludicrously small for his enormous torso.

As we let down the ladder for him, Joe came amidships to greet our visitor. The man scrambled up like a monkey and came over the rail. Indeed, he was the closest to a monkey I had ever seen in human form. He had short, bowed legs and a weazened face and a receding forehead and a bristling manner. He tilted his head and looked up at Joe.

"You Captain Crane? I'm Russell. Damn glad to see you, Captain. I've been sitting on my arse here almost six months."

"You're coming to New York with us?" I asked.

"Certainly not!" Russell returned indignantly. "I'm through with the sea. Sick and tired of it." He waved angrily at his ship. "Every cent I had. Dropped right out from under me. Barely had time to get the cargo out. And that bastard Spencer's kept me here six months waiting for my freight money."

"Other masters have lost ships before, Captain," I pointed out. "You could get another one."

"Work for someone else, you mean? In times like these? Who'd give me a ship, answer me that!" He hitched his breeches. "I'm going West. I'm through with—" He broke off sharply and his eyes bugged for a moment. Then he turned quickly away. "Well, get busy. I'll be at the warehouse when you want me."

He hastily slung his legs overside and disappeared. I half turned and noticed Buckner staring at the spot where Russell had been standing. His jaw was now covered with a black beard and his lips were drawn back, showing his yellow teeth in an animal-like snarl. . . .

Within a short time, we were tied up at the town dock and the hatches were broken open to receive the cargo. Labor being scarce in Machias, we could only get a few 'longshoremen so we had to use the crew, much to their displeasure. But the loading proceeded with dispatch, for the hogsheads of rum and sugar were not awkward to handle.

When Joe went ashore to settle matters with Captain Russell and visit the custom's house, he took Beulah along. And, when he returned, he let her stay ashore. In a place as small as Machias, it was perfectly safe for an unescorted woman to wander about alone, but the points of interest were extremely limited. Every so often she came back to the dock and watched the work, undismayed by the cussing and bumping and eternal squealing of block and tackle. She was restless with boredom. I'm afraid she was somewhat disillusioned, for she was learning that going to sea meant hard, unpleasant work without romantic adventuring.

Beulah didn't come back aboard until almost time for supper. Vaguely, I noticed she seemed bursting with some suppressed excitement. She mentioned she had learned something about Russell, but I was too busy at the moment to pay much attention. Later, when dusk had put an end to our day's labor, I remembered I hadn't seen Buckner around. I told Toby, our bosun, to fetch the man. Toby searched the forecastle and came back to report the man was not aboard. No one had seen him leave.

"How about his gear?" I asked.

Toby fingered his flat nose. "Now, there, sor, is a queer one. Buckner never did bring aboard no gear."

The supper was delicious, a chowder made of oysters and fresh milk, which Cookie had bought ashore this afternoon. He had bought us fresh bread, too. But none of us gave Cookie's masterful work due attention, especially after I had mentioned that Buckner was missing. Joe and I speculated at length on the possibility that Russell and Buckner knew each other.

Not until Beulah slapped the table did we notice she was squirming with impatience. "Can I get a word in? I found out something. That man Russell isn't Russell at all. His name is Kimble. Know what I think? I think Buckner's Russell."

"Whoa!" Joe cried. "Let's not get too confused. First, what makes you think that the bandy-legged ape who calls himself Russell is really named Kimble?"

"Well, I got talking to the wife of the landlord at the inn and she told me that Russell—or Kimble—got drunk one night and blubbered about his wife and children in Charleston."

"Charleston?" I echoed. "Why Burdick told me that Spencer had been kicked out of Charleston for shady dealings in tobacco. Suppose there's a connection?"

"God knows," Joe answered. He frowned and filled his plate from the chowder bowl. "Know what I've been thinking? I heard Russell's ship hit a rock and limped in here with

266

all his pumps going. I've been thinking Russell was pretty far inshore to have hit a rock around here if he was going to Halifax."

For a long time we were silent thinking over that point. We reached no conclusions.

Joe sighed. "It's nothing to us, anyway, as long as Spencer pays the freight bill. Just the same. . . ."

Our curiosity was thoroughly aroused and that very evening Joe and I went into the hold with a lantern to examine the cargo. The total number of hogsheads would amount to fifty-seven of sugar and thirty-three of rum. So, naturally, we couldn't examine them all. But those we did sample contained rum and sugar and nothing else.

When work resumed the next morning, I kept a close watch on the hogsheads as they were rolled aboard and hoisted into the hold. I don't know what I expected to find. But about ten o'clock, one of them did catch my attention. As it swung around on the tackle, I noticed there was a streak of something that looked like tar. I called Joe to relieve me for a moment and went down into the hold.

The black streak wasn't tar, but charred wood, as if a hot poker had been drawn along the side of the barrel. And, oddly, it stank stronger of rum than any of the other hogsheads, as if rum had been spilled all over the sides. I had the men turn the barrel over and examine the heads. One of them looked as if it had been off, though I couldn't be sure how recently. Then, on impulse, I called out ship's carpenter and had him take out the bung. The liquid was rum, all right. One of the men, with an awkward grin, produced some hollow straws and I let him take a drink. I took one myself. The result was nil. I was thoroughly baffled when I came up on deck again. But then, while these things might add up to something sinister, they were really none of our business, I hoped.

We were finished before dark. Joe was jubilant, for that meant we could get out on the eleven o'clock tide and thus avoid paying another day's port charges. I drove the men unmercifully, holding up their supper until they had cleaned up and battened down all our gear. By six-thirty we were finished. The men were all in bed by eight to get a few hours rest. I tumbled in myself, as did Joe, leaving Toby on anchor watch.

A low thump over my head awakened me with a start. At sea, strangely enough, my senses always cleared the instant my eyes opened. I was wide awake now. For some time, I lay still, feeling the tiredness drawing at my every muscle. Faintly and far away, I heard the tinging of a ship's bell, not our own but the bell of a lumber schooner up the river. I turned over into a more restful position, trying to sleep, wondering what that thump could have been. Sleep would not return, for my mind was filled with a vague uneasiness. I sat upright suddenly, wide awake again. That bell! Why hadn't our bell been rung? Toby was on deck—was supposed to be on deck!

I slung my legs overside, fumbled for my shoes and slipped into them. I walked softly into the salon, stopped and listened hard. No sound came from the cabin Beulah occupied. Joe, in his cabin, was snoring very softly. Then I glanced up, my ears tingling. Silence, deep, brooding silence, broken only by the gentle lap of the waters along the sides, the low groaning of the timbers, the faint squealing of the listless tackle. With a growing chill I realized what was wrong. I heard no footsteps. And Toby was the conscientious type, the kind who would not seek a nap or rest for long in any one spot on deck.

Heart pounding, I crept up the companionway stairs. Quickly I looked about the poop. Toby was not there. Nor was he in the waist of the ship. With quick, light steps I circled the deck. Then I found him—under the dory lashed to the top of the deckhouse. He was unconscious and bleeding from a gash at the base of his skull.

Fearfully, I examined him more closely. He was breathing slowly and regularly and the bleeding had almost stopped. If his skull had been cracked, neither I nor any doctor could help him. If not he would revive in due time. I left him there and prowled slowly around the deck, searching for the man who had struck down our bosun.

I stiffened sharply as I heard the clink of metal on metal. The chill night wind bit through my thin cotton shirt and coarse goosepimples crawled over my gathering muscles. Then, as my gaze swept across the fore part of the ship, I caught a sliver of light shining on the forepeak. The fore lazaret was open!

In light, soundless steps, I was across the deck and up the forecastle ladder. Below, the men were snoring peacefully, completely unaware that someone was in the small storeroom just forward of their bunks. On hands and knees I crawled across the deck to the small open hatchway and looked down. A lantern was almost directly below me, the fat candle sputtering and spitting in the warm, close air. Then I saw a man, a stocky man with a small, weazened face. It was Russell.

For some moments I was frozen into position, wondering what he was doing. As my eyes became accustomed to the dim light, I could see he was lashing down the lamp with fishline to a loose board in the decking. He got up chuckling and walked over to a small keg, pulling out the bung and spilling part of the contents. It was a keg of gunpowder.

I almost slipped and fell into the forepeak. I caught myself in time and remained absolutely motionless, watching. He lashed down the keg as close as possible to the curving stem, then ran a long waxed fuse from the powder keg to the lamp. He had stiffened the end of the waxed fuse with a needle and inserted it into a lower hole in the lamp so that when the flame reached the fuse, it would take fire and race to the powder keg and—wham! The whole forefoot of the ship would be blown out. We wouldn't have the slightest chance of getting to the leak before the ship would go under, bows first. From the look of the candle, I judged it would take from six to eight hours before the flame reached the stiffened fuse. By then, we would be well at sea. It was an ingenious scheme— and a diabolical one.

Russell passed directly under me and I considered dropping down on top of him. But I was unarmed. I saw that Russell had a wicked looking sheath knife stuck into his belt. The harsh yellow light glistened on his swart, gnomelike face and he was clucking like a contented hen. I decided against tackling him within the confines of that small locker. He would be effectively trapped if I could just get the hatch cover on.

The cover was heavy and my palms were sweaty and I was anxious. I could feel it slipping from my grasp and clawed at it frantically. The heavy cover thumped on the deck. Russell's feet scruffed in alarm, then became still. Long, tight minutes passed and neither of us moved. I didn't want to make him move suddenly, lest he knock the lamp over and set fire to the loose powder lying around. I could hear his slow, harsh breathing below.

"Don't put that hatch cover on," he called in a hoarse, subdued voice. "I'll fire the powder if you do—so help me!"

I edged over and looked down. The frightened whites of his eyes shone in the dim light. He bent down without taking his eyes from the opening, unsnapped the lantern's front and carefully took out the candle. Wax dripped on the loose powder and a lump throbbed in my throat.

"Stand back there, Mister!" he whispered. "Lay a hand on me and I fire the powder."

"And kill yourself, too?" I heard myself ask.

"Blow up or hang, I ain't particular, Mister." His knees bent and the flame of the candle dropped closer to the powder. "Last chance, Mister. You go up if I do."

I hesitated a split second before yielding. Even if he did get away, the ship at least, would be saved. Uselessly committing suicide didn't appeal to me much. I didn't doubt that he'd blow up the ship rather than surrender. As he said, it was blow up or hang, which would leave him equally dead.

"You win, Captain," I called—not too loudly, but loud enough I hope to rouse someone in the forecastle. Vain hope. The crew snored on unheedingly.

The glow over the open hatchway became brighter and brighter as Captain Russell slowly came up the ladder. I retreated, step by step, edging around toward the bow to be in back of him when he came out on deck. He wasn't going to get ashore, not if I could help it. Once loose he'd be gone forever. Once in the woods, he would easily avoid capture and, if he had any kind of resourcefulness, could easily reach the Ohio Country or Canada.

His head appeared and I tensed to spring. But Captain Russell was wary. He stopped, holding the flickering candle below the coaming and out of the wind. He looked about carefully, spotted me and chuckled hoarsely.

"Get aft, mister, and no tricks!" He listened a moment and nodded, satisfied. "Move! I ain't got all night."

He still had the advantage of desperation. I had to obey. I came around the open hatch, keeping to port of him, to the dock side of the ship. His small beady eyes never left me. Then I went down the forecastle ladder. The moment I hit bottom, I scurried to the rail, waited, ready to spring over onto the dock.

Flat, oppressive silence fell over the ship. In the distance, an owl was hooting. A cramped eternity passed before I heard the cautious shuffle of Russell's feet. Then, I heard him land with a soft thud on the dock. I was over the rail in an instant, landing with a spine jarring jolt. Russell swore as I started after him. He knew his short legs could not match my ground consuming strides.

He whirled and I caught the flash of steel. My momentum made me crash into him, twisting as the blade slashed viciously. He went down in a struggling heap and I felt the knife rake my side. Frantically, I squirmed over, slammed my fist into his face and knocked him back. I crabbed away, leaped up and kicked out. His wrist bones cracked as the knife spun away.

After that, the advantage was all mine. He surged up, his massive fists swinging. He never landed a blow. I drove in, hit him twice with every ounce of my strength. His jaw was like rock. But his belly was soft. He collapsed, moaning with pain.

Even now, no one had been awakened. I hauled Russell up, slung him over my shoulder and took him aboard. He was conscious, but harmless, for the fight was all out of him. I dumped him on the salon couch and woke Joe up. Joe grumbled and came out of his cabin groggily. The sleep swept away from his eyes as he saw the man on the couch.

"That's Russell," he said in an unbelieving tone.

"I nodded and told him what had happened.

"My God!" Joe swore softly. "What do we do with him?"

"Fetch his baggage. We're taking him to New York. I imagine Mr. Spencer is due for a mighty unpleasant surprise."

Chapter 20

ᵗᵗᵗᵗᵗᵗᵗᵗᵗᵗᵗᵗᵗᵗᵗᵗᵗᵗᵗᵗᵗᵗᵗᵗᵗᵗᵗᵗᵗᵗᵗᵗᵗᵗᵗᵗᵗᵗᵗ

THE journey from Machias to New York consumed ten days, including a half a day's stopover at Fenwick for my shoes. Those weren't entirely pleasant days, for a slight strain had developed between Joe and myself over the disposition of our unwilling passenger. Off and on, I questioned Captain Russell, trying to learn his motive for setting that infernal machine aboard. He would not talk. Joe's attitude was that, since Russell had been caught and no damage done, we ought to forget the whole matter. I even believe he would have let Russell go if I hadn't been so determined to get to the bottom of the affair.

Increase gave us a few anxious moments when he came aboard at Fenwick. He told us about Beulah's sudden departure from Pelham and said the gossip was that she had intended to join us. But Reuben had squashed those rumors. After leaving Beulah at Boston, he had actually gone to Attleboro and he brought back letters from Grandpa Crane to some of his friends in Pelham. Beulah had told us she had planned this, but Joe hadn't thought his grandfather would fall in with the scheme. Grandpa fooled him. Increase never suspected Beulah was aboard, nor was he much interested in finding out. All he wanted was to get home as soon as possible. He started up river before the shoes were in the hold.

It was on the sixth of November that we reached the southern end of Long Island Sound and approached the famous Hell Gate. The Sound seemed deserted and forlorn, for there were no boats or ships on the broad, smooth waters and the bleak, leafless woodlands were broken only by brown squares of bare fields. A wisp of smoke rising here and there from the scattered farmhouses gave the lone sign that the shores on both sides of us were inhabited. There was evidence, too, that time had not yet erased the ugly blight of war from the scarred earth. Twice on the mainland side and once on the Island side, I saw black smudges in the middle of overgrown farms, marking the place where once had stood a house and a barn and other necessary outbuildings.

Beulah was on deck by sunrise—a cold, hazy dawn that drove her quickly below for her cloak. She was eager for her first view of New York, for that city had a reputation for being gayer and more wicked than our almost equally large but more sedate Boston. Joe and I told her it would be a couple of hours before we reached the city, but that didn't matter to Beulah. She would rather endure a cold nose and wind-reddened cheeks than miss a moment of this. The only point of interest Joe could show her was Frog's Neck, where the British had landed in an effort to outflank the American armies. Even that was only trees and wind-scruffed hillocks.

From the distance, it seemed that we were running straight into a dead end bay. The land ahead was practically a wilderness. Not until we passed Hulith's Island, lying slightly south of Flushing Bay, could we see the East River and Hell's Gate. The town of Flushing itself was only a collection of rooftops in the distance, surmounted by one defiant steeple. On the mainland side, we could see Morrisannia, which must have been pretty in the summertime, for it nestled among a number of low, tree covered hillocks. It was a remote place, scarcely touched by the bustle of trade and the gay social life of the city of New York.

It was about eight o'clock when we rounded Colear's Point, where the river turns southwest and empties into the harbor. There was a small group of wooden buildings on that flat open space of land. The houses were sadly outnumbered by the pens of cows and sheep and pigs. Here, Joe informed us, was the only place in the city where animals were permitted to be slaughtered for the food supply. From there southward, the houses stood in larger and larger clumps that soon merged into a solid mass of low brick and wooden warehouses, shops, residences and counting houses. Joe said that some of the churches had not been rebuilt since the war, though he admitted this place was not as attentive to religion as Boston.

By this time, the schooner barely wore enough sail to give her steerageway. Gently and surely, Joe brought her in closer to her wharf. Spencer's Wharf—under lease, Joe had told me —was a short distance down from Catherine's Slip and near the foot of Dover Street, virtually at the farthest end of the city. I was rather disappointed, for I should have liked to have viewed the whole waterfront from offshore. I have always been, as you have probably already guessed, the incorrigible tourist.

From the little I could see of the endless wharves down along Water Street, it was obvious that there were few ships in port. Of the first ten wharves down from Spencer's, only six held ships, two of them dismantled. There could be no mistaking that New York, like Boston, was languishing in the grip of depressed times.

Depression or no, we had business to attend. Joe and I had discussed what to do about Russell and Joe reluctantly agreed that, as soon as the ship was fast, we'd send Toby ashore to fetch Mr. Spencer from his counting house across the street. Accordingly, as soon as the last of the mainsail was down and the lines were fast, Toby hopped ashore and I gathered four men armed with belaying pins and went to bring Russell up from his hole.

As the cover came off the hatch, a shaft of feeble sunlight fell full on Russell's pale, weazened face. I almost felt sorry for him, he looked so wan and thin and dirty.

"You can come up now, Captain." I showed him my belaying pin. "But remember this: One false move and your head's broken."

He came up the ladder slowly, as if his confinement had weakened him. Which probably was the case, to some degree, for we hadn't allowed him much exercise, especially since we had entered Long Island Sound. We had feared he might take the risk of jumping overboard and trying to make shore. I was alert for any attempt he might now make at escaping.

Captain Russell stuck his head above the coaming and looked about. The grim faces of the four seamen evidently convinced him that escape was hopeless. He knew the men would delight in the chance to work over him, for Toby was popular with them and had not been allowed to pay back that foul blow Russell had delivered on his skull. With a slight shrug the

Captain crawled out on deck, straightened his clothes and, with as much dignity as he could muster, marched aft to the salon.

Toby came down a few moments later and told me that Mr. Spencer was on his way. I gave Toby my belaying pin and ordered him to keep watch on our prisoner, for I wanted to be on deck when Mr. Spencer arrived. Beulah had retired discreetly to the taffrail. None of our crew showed impatience to get ashore, but were standing about in small groups, excitedly discussing the baffling case of Messrs. Spencer and Russell.

Joe was visibly nervous. He nodded briefly as a tallish, slim man came up the gangplank in long, spry steps. Mr. Spencer was a smooth looking article. His features were very regular, his nose long and thin, his chin dimpled and his eyes very blue against his pinkish skin. His dress marked him as something of a dandy, for his coat was of the latest cut, short and double breasted in the front and the tails long. His breeches were of yellow kersymere and his stockings were of white silk—this in the daytime! His black calf shoes had gilt buckles and, completing his attire, he carried a gold-headed cane.

He smiled cordially and lifted his cane. "Friend Joseph!" He hopped up the poop ladder. "Delighted to see you. And much sooner than I expected. You had a remarkably fast passage."

Joe grinned tightly. "No thanks to you, Mr. Spencer."

Spencer's delicate brows arched. "Eh?"

"He means," I put in dryly, "that we successfully weathered the hazards you set before us."

"Suh?" He rested both hands on the head of the cane. "I don't believe we've been introduced."

"This is Mr. Hascott," Joe said. "He's my mate and my friend."

"I see. Your servant, suh." He bowed slightly. "Though I cannot say I like your tone, Mr. Hascott."

"Forgive me, suh," I said with mock politeness. "Perhaps you'll understand my tone better when you see the present we brought you from Machias. After you, Mr. Spencer."

Spencer frowned quizzically, first at me, then at Joe. He shrugged and followed Joe to the companionway. He paused as he caught sight of Beulah, whistled softly and winked at her. She stared right through him and he laughed.

"Charming," he commented as he went down the ladder. "Joseph's wife? No, his sister. The resemblance is plain."

If we expected Mr. Spencer to be taken aback when he confronted Russell, we were sadly mistaken. With a cry of pleasure, he put out both hands and strode over to the captain.

"Russell! You old bilge rat! How delightful." He grasped Russell's hand and pumped away. "Imagine seeing you here. So you changed your mind about going west, eh?" He stepped back and viewed him critically. "On my word, Russell, you look as if you've been sleeping in a barn."

"He's been our prisoner," Joe growled.

"Prisoner?" Spencer's voice was shocked. "Good heavens, Joseph, why should Captain Russell be your prisoner?"

"Because he tried to blow up my ship," Joe said with mounting irritation.

"Blow up your ship! What utter rot."

I leaned over the salon table. "Let's drop the pretenses, Mr. Spencer. We caught Russell in the act of rigging up an infernal machine in our fore lazaret. That's why he's here. We intend to turn him over to the authorities."

"Well," Spencer drawled. "I fail to see any reason why that should interest me."

"Have it your way, Mr. Spencer." I smiled at Russell. "You see, he intends to let you hang alone. Suppose you tell us all about it—why you did it and everything else. That's the only way you can save your neck."

Russell's weazened face screwed up in thought and he gave Spencer a quick glance. Then, he shrugged. "I got nothing to say. You can't prove nothing. I'll get a lawyer."

"If that's the way you want it," I said grimly. "Toby, fetch a constable. Not an ounce of the cargo moves until we get to the bottom of this thing."

"Now, see here," Spencer burst out. "That cargo belongs to me. I've already made the arrangements for the unloading. It will be out of the hold by nightfall."

"Go ahead, Toby," I said quietly. "We'll see about that."

As Toby started for the door, Russell lashed out, hit him squarely in the mouth. I swore and made for Russell. Joe caught Toby as he was falling and eased him down, jumped over him and yelled something at me. Spencer coolly stuck out his cane, caught me between the legs and I felt myself flying forward. I hit the deck with bone-shaking violence. Joe sprawled out on top of me. In a moment, we were both up and I could hear Spencer laughing. As I streaked up the companionway I heard the laugh choke off as a fist cracked against his jaw. But Joe did not come pounding up the ladder after me.

Russell was over the rail by the time I reached the poop. Beulah was sitting down, nursing a bruise in her temple. I caught a glimpse of Russell scurrying down the dock toward the street.

"Stop that man!" I yelled. "Stop thief!"

The cry of "Thief!" brought prompt action. A knot of idlers broke up fast and started in pursuit of the bandy-legged little man. Some of our crew had seen him go overside and were in the chase. He was swirling in and out among the carts and trucks on Water Street, running easily and widening the gap betwen himself and the baying pack at his heels. Again and again he bowled over rash pedestrians who tried to stop him.

He had one big advantage. He knew where he was going. He ducked down one alley and I lost sight of him for a moment. By this time, I was out in front of the mob. Just as I caught a glimpse of him again, some fool came rushing at me. I shouted at him and tried to sidestep, but he crashed into me. Down we both went and I sat up and cursed him roundly as the crowd streamed by. I jumped up and went on, refusing to listen to the man's apologies.

The chase gradually petered out. When we got to Cherry Street, the crowd began breaking up into confused groups, some running up, some down, some heading along Rosevelt Street. My lungs were now tearing at my chest and I had to stop, lest my racing heart leap from its moorings. I finally had to admit the obvious. Captain Russell had made good his escape.

Reluctantly, I returned to the ship, furious with myself for having allowed Russell the opportunity. I could have expected such a move. But I never dreamed Spencer would be so brazen about helping him. I never dreamed that Joe would help, too.

He was waiting at the head of the companionway when I returned to the ship. He smiled tentatively.

"You didn't catch him."

"No, thanks to you," I returned angrily. "Joe, you know something about this. Are you mixed up in . . . in whatever Russell and Spencer have cooked up?"

"No, honest I'm not, Warren. Honest." He was so earnest I had to believe him. "Warren, let's forget it."

"Forget it?" I echoed. "Dammit, man, Russell tried to blow up this ship. He tried to murder me and you. Forget it? Like hell. . . ." I caught myself as I saw how worried Joe looked. "All right, Joe, I'll forget it—on one condition. You tell me what this is all about."

"I can't," Joe answered miserably. He clutched at my arm. "Just forget it, Warren. We've lost nothing. Russell failed in his attempt to kill us, didn't he? We won't gain anything by interfering in Spencer's business.'

"I'll gain plenty in satisfaction," I growled. "Joe, you have something to gain. That man has some sort of a hold over you. He tried to murder you once. He'll try again."

"No, he won't. I assure you he won't. He prom—" Joe checked himself. "He swears he had nothing to do with Russell's attempt to blow up the ship."

I laid my hand on his arm. The muscles were taut. "Joe, you're on a spot. Maybe I can help you, maybe not. But tell me about it. You know you can trust me."

Joe hesitated, then shook his head. "Please, Warren." He essayed a grin. "Let's not be enemies on that account. And believe me, my trouble has nothing to do with this."

"All right." But I was determined to investigate further.

I was still sore as we went down into the salon. Spencer was sitting on the couch, calmly smoking a black cigar and paring his nails with a penknife. His brows went up as he glanced at Joe.

"Well? You'll release my cargo and forget this?"

I shrugged. "As Joe says, we've really lost nothing. You can start unloading as soon as you like."

Spencer rose languidly and stretched his legs. "You're a sensible man, Mr. Hascott." He flicked the ashes from his cigar and smiled. "Just between us, Mr. Hascott, that man Russell's very stupid. I assure you again that idiotic infernal machine wasn't my idea at all."

I was inclined to believe him. If, as Burdick had told me, this man was a sharper, he wouldn't think along violent lines, except out of desperation. And his attitude when he saw Russell convinced me he hadn't known then about Russell's attempted action. I was still mad but Joe shook his head at me. With a resigned shrug, I followed the merchant up the ladder.

"I'll stay aboard, Warren," Joe said, as we stepped out on deck. "I'll send you to some people I know. Maybe you can get rid of your cargo here, instead of going to Philadelphia."

"Eh, what's that, Joseph?" Spencer turned back. "You're carrying cargo on your own account?"

"On Mr. Hascott's account. Shoes."

"Hmm." Spencer examined the tip of his cigar. "I may be in the market, Mr. Hascott. That is, if you're not prejudiced against dealing with me after what happened."

"I never allow sentiment to interfere with business, Mr. Spencer." I half turned. "Toby break open Number Two hatch."

Spencer chuckled and lifted his cigar. "Remember that, Joseph. A very sage precept to follow." His gaze fell on Beulah and his lips pursed. "Your sister is a very striking woman, Joseph. Perhaps you wouldn't mind if I took her to the theatre this evening."

"I always allow sentiment to interfere with pleasure," Beulah came back quickly.

Spencer laughed. "Delightful!" And, tucking his cane under his arm, he made his way amidships.

Joe was sullen. "If that fellow says 'delightful' once more, I swear, I'll murder him."

Spencer dressed like a dandy, but he didn't allow his clothes to interfere with business. As soon as the hatch was off, he descended into the hold to examine the shoes. Toby brought him a light and he pawed over the pile, picking out a pair here and there for close scrutiny. After some time he came up on deck again, brushing off his clothes and his hands.

"How much?" he asked abruptly.

"There are fourteen hundred pairs down there," I said. "I want twelve shillings a pair."

Spencer smiled. "That's right, start at a high figure. But twelve's ridiculous. I'll give eight. Do you know what shoes are bringing retail, suh? Eight and nine for strong, twelve for the best. Check in any store if you don't believe me."

I shrugged. "Half the lot is superfine. Some ought to bring as high as sixteen. That's Boston prices."

"Less than a hundred pairs will bring that high," Spencer said crisply. "I'll offer nine . . . . No, nine and a half. That's a fair offer and my best. My margin of profit will be very small, a quarter shilling at the most, but I think I can turn them over quick. That's my final offer, Mr. Hascott."

I figured it out quickly. Even at nine and a half I'd still be making a very comfortable profit of ninety-five pounds. I weighed Spencer's words carefully and decided he was telling the truth about the retail value. He hadn't been quite so truthful about the estimate he gave me of the superfine shoes, but I felt it would work out fairly evenly. If he separated them, he'd break even or perhaps lose a little on the ordinary shoes, and make about thirty to forty pounds on the superfine batch. I couldn't gainsay him a legitimate profit.

"It's a deal," I said finally. "Nine and a half."

Spencer clamped the cigar between his teeth and stuck out his hand. "It's a pleasure to do business with you, Mr. Hascott. Come over to my office later—or tomorrow morning, if you prefer. I'll get my cargo out first. Yours, I'll take later."

Spencer touched the brim of his hat with the gold head of his cane and scurried down the gangplank. Joe mumbled something about my being foolish to have dealings with such a man and went back to the poop. Whatever his trouble was, I felt quite sure now that Joe was not working with Spencer.

A respectful cough made me turn and I found Toby at my side. He was bruised on his jaw, but otherwise unhurt.

"What's his game, Mr. Hascott?" he asked.

"Damned if I know, Toby. But I'd sure like to find out." I considered a moment. "Toby, could you find three men we could trust? No, don't go for them now. You instruct them. We don't want the Captain to know about it."

"Leave it to me," Toby growled. "I just want to get my hands on that man Russell for a few minutes."

"All right. Here's what we'll do. Have one man hang around Spencer's establishment and follow Spencer wherever he goes. Put a second man with him to send back here in case Russell and Spencer meet. Set a third man on watch at Fraunce's Tavern. Russell is a New Englander, I think. He may try to go to Boston. If any of the men see Russell, tell them to grab him and bring him here. Tell them to try to stay out of the hands of the law. We don't want the law in on this until we know what the game is."

Toby scratched his chin with his thumb. "If we see him, we don't guarantee to deliver him in such good condition."

I smiled. "As long as you don't kill him."

When I came back to the poop, Joe was just emerging from the companionway with the manifests and other necessary documents. As we fell to a discussion of the work to be done, Joe tried hard to appear cheerful and pretend that nothing was wrong. I was a bit uneasy about setting Toby to catching Russell, for Joe might be hurt if the full story came out. But I was burning with curiosity and a determination to get to the bottom of this affair. I would try my best, if I succeeded, to protect Joe.

Beulah plucked at Joe's sleeve. "Joe, wouldn't you like to take me to the theatre?"

Joe feigned horror. "Take my pure little sister to such a den of iniquity. Haven't you heard playgoing is sinful?"

"Yes," Beulah admitted solemnly. Then defiantly. "But I don't believe it. Please, Joe. I won't have the chance again."

"I'll take you Beulah," I said impulsively.

Joe looked disgusted. "That's just what she wanted, Warren. Do you suppose she thought I'd take her?"

"Don't be mean, Joe." Beulah was flushed with eagerness. "Where is the theatre? What time do we have to be there? Do I have to wear a gown?"

"You'll sit in the pit," Joe said chuckling. "You can go in homespun. As for the other questions, where and when, go ashore and buy a newspaper. There's a bookshop up on Rosevelt Street. And come right back. I don't want you wandering around New York unescorted, not even in the daytime."

Beulah squealed with delight and scurried ashore. She scurried back to beg some change, then was off again. Joe and I exchanged a startled glance.

"Well, after all," Joe drawled, "she's never been out of Pelham before. I was excited, too, the first time I went to the theatre."

Joe was right, of course. Only it was a bit hard to realize this wasn't the same Beulah I had considered so worldly back in Pelham. The idea of taking her to the theatre tickled me a little. I was anxious to watch her reactions. Naturally, going to a play meant nothing to me. I had been to the theatre before—in London—once.

Within a few minutes, the press of work brushed all thoughts of pleasure from my mind. Spencer's longshoremen came aboard and the hatches were broken open and the cargo began streaming from the holds and across the street to the warehouse. It had taken us a day and a half, working like horses, to load that rum and sugar up in Machias. The number of men Spencer put on the job was proof that he had been in earnest when he said all the cargo would be out by nightfall. All morning and all afternoon I was kept hopping like a flea on a hot hearthstone.

Joe was gone all morning, making his call on the custom's office and settling business details with Spencer. Part of the time he spent searching for another cargo to take home, for he was reluctant to have any more dealings with Spencer. He reported no success when he came in around one o'clock. Then, he was off again. He was as glum as ever when he returned, shortly after four thirty.

"Business in New York smells to high heaven," Joe reported. "I could have had a cargo of brick, but I turned it down. Fact is, those fellows are trying to beat the rates down too far." He started. "Say, if you're going to the theatre, you'd better get ready. It starts at six."

I nodded. "The cargo's almost all out. Toby can take care of the rest."

I hurried aft and went below to clean up and dress.

As I came into the salon, I heard a rustle and half turned. Beulah was dressed and waiting, seated on the salon couch, her hands folded in her lap. The color heightened on her cheeks as I kept staring.

"W—Well? D—don't you l—like me . . . my dress?"

I just whistled. That dress couldn't exactly be called up to the prevailing mode, yet it certainly couldn't be called old fashioned. The gown was of dark blue linen timothy, cut something like a coat, hanging loose about the shoulders and fastened down the front with light blue ribbons. The petticoat underneath, which was visible only from the bodice down, was of white with tiny red flowers. A waistcoat was laced tightly to give a provocative uplift to the bosom—eminently fashionable, as well as attractive to the male eye. The skirts were full, though not excessively so, for she wore no pads on her hips, only—well, I won't guess how many petticoats.

"D—don't you like it?" she persisted timidly. "My mother made it from . . . from a dress her mother wore. W—we thought we made it like the Boston ladies wear now."

"It's a marvel," I said with conviction. "You'll be the envy of every woman in the theatre. Believe me, you will!"

Beulah slumped back a little, relieved. Then I found one criticism to make. Those petticoats underneath evidently only went up as far as her waist. The gown had parted a trifle under her bosom, showing a small patch of bare flesh of her stomach between the lacings of the waistcoat. She giggled when I pointed out this immodesty and went to her cabin to make the adjustments.

I washed and shaved and put on my best clothes which I hadn't had the opportunity to wear since coming from London. When I had had the occasion before, I didn't have them with me. I put on a clean linen shirt, my best lace cravat, waistcoat and breeches of buff colored swansdown, a coat of plum colored broadcloth. My stockings were of brown thread and I had gilded buckles on my black shoes. After combing and clubbing my hair with a red silk ribbon, I put on my tricorn, gave it a firm pat and I was ready.

I knew from Beulah's smile when she saw me that I was worthily decked out to escort m'lady to the theatre. She had thrown her hooded cloak over her shoulders for warmth and I considered taking my surtout, but I didn't believe it would be that chilly. Beulah bowed with mock solemnity as

I handed her up the companion ladder. We were indeed a handsome couple. Even Joe admitted it.

"How do we get to this place?" I asked. "The paper doesn't give the address."

"It's on John Street, between Broadway and Nassau Street. Just walk down to Goldenhull. You can't miss it. Goldenhull changes its name to John Street a bit beyond William Street." He winked at his sister. "If I didn't know you, Beulah, I'd be tempted to whistle after you. Have a good time."

"We will!" Beulah promised gaily.

If Joe wouldn't whistle, the longshoremen and idlers on the dock made up for him. Beulah ignored the uncouth sounds, but her eyes sparkled and her shoulders squared just a bit more. I wouldn't say she was pretty, for that gives an impression of fragility. But she certainly was strikingly handsome. And she was just beginning to be conscious of it.

I should have liked to explore through the streets of New York before full darkness overtook us, but the time was too short. We hurried down Water Street, a solid line of grog shops, mercantile establishments, chandlery and mathematical instrument shops. The smells were delightful—to me, at least —hemp and tea and spices from the far off Indies. But the street was in a horrible shape. The cobbles were uneven and here and there we had to skirt patches of mud.

At Burling Slip, which was at the foot of Goldenhull Street, we turned away from the waterfront. Here we encountered more residences and neater stores, farriers, a tailor shop, hatters, upholsterers, charmakers, neat little taverns, shoemakers' shops—which tempted me to go in and price shoes. After we passed William Street, I remembered that neither of us had eaten since noon and I offered to take Beulah into a tavern for a bite of supper. She was so afraid she'd miss a minute of the play that she declined. Accordingly, we stepped into a confectioner's and bought a paper of sweets—cinnamon comfits, lemon drops, corianders and some peppermints.

As Joe had said, we couldn't miss the John Street Theatre. People were hurrying from all directions toward that place, like bees winging to a hive. The theatre was about sixty feet back from the street, the pathway leading to the entrance being covered with a wooden roof. In the broad lobby, we stopped uncertainly while I searched about for the place to buy tickets.

Being bumped and jostled by the people swirling by, I regretted I hadn't attended to this matter before. Then I spotted what I wanted. On a board by the Office of the Theatre were listed the prices, four shillings for the gallery, six for the pit, eight for box seats. I considered for only a second, then went in and got our tickets. This was one night in a lifetime. I engaged a box.

An attendant at the foot of the stairs handed us playbills and led the way to our places. He parted the curtains for us, touched his paper to the candles on either side of the partition and waited, shuffling his feet. A moment passed before I realized he expected a gratuity. When we settled in our seats, which were set out beyond the partition, I squinted at the playbill, grumbling at the lack of light in that big, barnlike place. After a time, I could read that the play would be "She Stoops to Conquer," a silly farce, as I had heard in London, though very popular.

Our box was on the left side of the house in the lower tier. There were two rows of boxes, a gallery above and a pit below. Hawkers were wandering up and down the aisles, selling oranges, confections and printed copies of the play.

Our neighbors in the boxes on either side of us made both Beulah and myself very uncomfortable. They were ladies and gentlemen of means, obviously, the gentleman on my left wearing a rich scarlet coat with mother of pearl buttons and black satin breeches with paste buckles at the knees. They all wore white, powdered wigs. The hairdress on the woman on Beulah's right was very large and curled in the old fashioned aristocratic manner. Her face was nearly white with pomantum and the red spots on her cheeks made her look ridiculous. Her dress was of heavy plum colored damask brocaded with gold thread. She was staring at Beulah with almost indecent amusement.

"Remarkable child, isn't she, Henry?" she remarked to her escort. "These country rustics have such a quaint way of aping their betters—and not quite succeeding, of course."

The gentleman turned and stared boldly at Beulah. He had a fat, piggish face and protruding red lips. "She's a beauty, Stel, even without powder and patches." He leered at her. "I'll wager she's a vigorous wench."

I had determined to ignore such loutish conduct, but this was too much. Beulah caught my arm as I rose.

"Pay no heed to the boors," she said sweetly. "They have such quaint notions about being our betters."

"They have the manners of my father's swine," I said loudly. "They even smell like swine."

The "lady" gasped and whispered something about demanding satisfaction of me. It was really too bad that the violins had to start screeching at that moment. I should have enjoyed refusing to meet him on the "field of honor" in favor of beating his head off on the spot.

The house settled down as the attendants put out the candles in the hurricane lamps fixed to the walls around the auditorium. And I was relieved when that abominable orchestra of three fiddles and a horn stopped its infernal racket. The ushers lighted the lamps in the channel at the edge of the stage, the curtain parted and an actor stepped forth.

Just what the actor was saying, I wasn't able to get, for the last minute arrivals, chattering and laughing, took most of his words away. The prologue wasn't very important anyway, merely indicating what the play was to be about. The curtains parted to reveal a sitting room at the country seat of Mr. Hardcastle, who thereupon begins complaining about his stepson, Tony Lumpkin, a general no-good. Mrs. Hardcastle is defending her son.

I shall not detail the story, for you have either seen this play or will see it sometime in the future. It has remained astonishingly popular through the years. I enjoyed it immensely. One speech by Hardcastle early in the play particularly tickled my fancy, though few others in the audience laughed.

". . . There's my darling Kate; the fashions of the times have almost infected her, too. By living a year or two in town, she is as fond of gauze and French frippery as the best of them."

So, it seemed the English were as fond of fripperies as our own American townspeople, and just as prone to blame someone else for their introduction. We blame the English. The English blame the French. I wondered whom the French could blame.

There was another passage which almost gave Beulah

hysterics, though I, for one, couldn't quite see why she should be so overly amused. It occurred later in that same scene, after Mr. Hardcastle told Kate that young Marlow was coming and had given her an idea what the prospective husband was reported to be like. Kate Hardcastle, alone onstage, soliloquized thusly:

"Lud, this news of Papa's puts me all in a flutter. Young, handsome, these he put last, but I put them foremost. Sensible, goodnatured, I like that. But then, reserved and sheepish, that's much against him. Yet, can't he be cured of his timidity? . . . ."

I didn't catch the rest of the line. I was afraid Beulah was going to choke. And I was tempted to help her along.

All too soon the final happy conclusion brought the curtains together. We stood and applauded the actors and actresses and, I daresay, Beulah would have liked to have had the hours back to enjoy again. Regretfully she allowed me to drape the cloak over her shoulders and lead her from the box. I did not tell her at once, but I had determined the evening was not yet at an end. I wanted to make the occasion one she would remember for a long, long time. When we emerged from the coverway onto John Street, I turned her to the left, toward Broadway.

"Warren, you're going in the wrong direction."

"No, we're not going back to the ship yet. Have you forgotten? We didn't have supper. I'm taking you to a place where you'll get something I don't think you've ever tasted before."

She squealed with delight and took my arm. Beulah was much too sturdy a type to seem natural when she giggled or squealed in a feminine manner; but she was all woman and I could hardly be disconcerted if she acted as one.

When we reached Broadway, I wasn't prepared for the scene of devastation I found. From Thomas Street to the Battery, the whole west side of Broadway right to the Hudson River was a blackened ruin, the result of a horrible fire during the war while the British occupied the city. Trinity Church, at the head of Wall Street, was a hollow, half-crumbled shell. The moonlight was just bright enough to show up clusters of mean shacks which had been set up on the rubble. I didn't know it at the time, but gangs of footpads and thieves and beggars lived in there, and their crimes, after dark, had become a city scandal.

The City Tavern, where we were headed, was practically the first building north of the ruins. It stood close to Little Queen Street and was not much to see outside, but it was reputed to be one of the best taverns in town. Before the late war it had been a patriot headquarters. Now it was famed as the gathering place of the elite social elements of the city.

The taproom was crowded with elegantly dressed merchants and bankers and such people. But the taproom was not for us. A servingman met us at the door and conducted us to the Ladies' Dining Parlor, a smallish room facing the street, and furnished with round tables on which there were damask tablecloths. There was a carpet on the floor and the wall paper depicted a fox hunt. Beulah's eyes had to follow the pictures from the "Tallyho!" to the holing of the fox. There was a roaring fire in the hearth, which shed a comfortable glow over the room.

The servingman held out the chair for Beulah and helped her off with her cloak, then waited expectantly for my orders.

"You may bring us a supper of sea foods, please," I said. "We'll rely on your judgment as long as the amount is ample. We're hungry. And the appropriate wines, of course."

Not being a connoisseur I figured that was the best way to cover my ignorance. The meal that order brought us was astonishing and delightful. We started with a delicious turtle soup, then went on to blue fish, curried oysters, grilled terrapin—a marvel!—and finished off with a huge platter of steaming red lobsters. The wines were canary and madeira and, the *piece de resistance*, sparkling white wine, known as champagne. We both enjoyed it thoroughly, delighting in the bubbling and hissing and the tart, piquant taste. In fact, I liked the first taste so much that I ordered two more quarts.

We tore the lobsters limb from limb amid much laughter and joking, for there were no other patrons in the parlor to make us mind our manners. I thought it rather a shame she couldn't tell about this when she got home, but I didn't say it aloud for fear of spoiling her lusty enjoyment of her meal. And it was a scandal the way that girl drank. She matched me glass for glass. But then, it was I who insisted on toasting everyone I had ever known or expected to know.

There was something wonderful about that champagne, about the way the bubbles went up my nose, about the glow and feeling of well being it set pulsing through me. Whatever we talked about, I'll never know, but it must have been very funny, for the more wine we drank, the more hilarious the feeblest joke became. And the wreckage of the lobsters strewn around our table was fearful. Both Beulah and I became owlishly solemn as the waiter came and asked if we would have tarts and sweet pastries. Neither of us could bear the thought.

As soon as the waiter was safely out of the parlor again, Beulah belched daintily, squirmed and pulled on the laces of her bodice. "It's laced too tight now."

"Loosen it. See if I care."

I stood up and was knocked down. I shook my head to clear it, amazed at the potency of that shy sparkling white beverage. The candle branch on the hearth didn't stop swaying for a full minute. Yes, I was drunk, all right, but my head was perfectly clear. That had always been an idiosyncrasy—or should I say vanity?—of mine. No matter how much I had consumed I never lost my senses or my awareness of what was right and wrong. I just didn't give a damn.

I swayed a little as I came around to help Beulah on with her cloak. It occurred to me that if I felt this way, how must she feel? I was relieved. She was fully as sober as I. Yes, deep down in her sparkling grey eyes I could see it. And her moist red lips were an invitation too urgent to resist. Her stomach was very full, too, I could feel it, despite the petticoats.

Her eyelids drooped a little when I released her. "Umm. Kate should have used champagne instead of stooping."

I pecked her nose and gave her a playful slap on the backside.

We were very precise and dignified when the servingman tendered his bill. And it was a lucky thing I had imbibed so deeply. Even now, I can't bear to think of the size of that bill.

We needed that walk back to the ship. The cold, crisp air seemed to steady my legs, but strangely it did not take away my sense of exhilaration. We whispered and giggled over meaningless jokes and were convulsed by the oddest things —the grotesque shadows falling from the tall masts over

Water Street, the flecks of white on a puddle of water, the screaming of a love-sick cat. When we reached our wharf, I suggested this would be an excellent evening for a moonlight swim. Beulah had quite a task talking me out of that idea.

One of our men was keeping anchor watch and he saluted us as we came aboard. With utmost casualness, we returned the greeting. With utmost effort, we managed to follow a straight line across the deck. We were sure he had been fooled as we ducked down the companionway. In the salon, the lamp was turned very low and we could hear that Joe was sound asleep. Beulah had to bury her giggles in my lapels, for Joe snored in a very peculiar manner, with a rattle and a whistle and a snort.

"I'm not a bit sleepy," she whispered.

"Neither am I. Let's go up on deck and howl at the moon."

"All right. But I want to get comfortable." She rubbed the lacing of her waistcoat. "This thing is killing me."

She drew away, but it didn't seem right, somehow. I pulled her back and kissed her again. The warmth of her quickened my already racing pulses and some of her fervor flowed into me as her thighs rubbed gently against mine. She was very soft, but vaguely I was aware she was wearing too many clothes.

She slipped from my arms and swung around and loosened the cloak strings. Mechanically, I took it from her shoulders, kissing her lightly on the nape of the neck. She turned her head, smiled and went into her cabin, leaving the door wide open.

I blinked and felt a bit foolish holding the cloak, for I knew happily that she might as well have taken it with her. It surely didn't belong out here in the salon. I was going to throw it on her bunk in her cabin, but I just stood in the doorway. She was unlacing her waistcoat and, inch by inch, as the tension eased, the edges of her gown were parting and the curves of her smooth white flesh became more pronounced. She certainly had an attractive body. And she was not in the least perturbed by my frank and open admiration.

She threw the waiscoat over to the chair and held the loose gown together tightly.

"I really need a pin," she said, half to herself. Then she glanced over to me. "Do hang that thing up, Warren. . . . And get me my other shoes, please . . . over there, by my trunk. They're so much more comfortable."

Her voice was so casual that obeying her seemed perfectly natural. I hung up the cloak and set out the shoes before her. I wondered uneasily if her skin would be as feverish to the touch as mine, if her heart was pounding with the same vague insistence.

She lifted her skirts high and scuffed off her shoes, one by one. The gown parted carelessly to reveal the full roundness of her pink tipped busts. The temptation was too much for me. I raised one and kissed it hard. Then I drew her into my arms. Her head bent back slightly, her eyes closed and her lips half parted.

For an eternity, I felt as if I was being drawn deeper and deeper into the smothering waters of a shimmering whirlpool, toward an end to all earthly cares, toward the threshhold of all earthly delights. Her arms hung loosely at her sides, but the passion of her probing tongue, the closeness of her body to mine, gave bliss to the never-ending moment. Not by accident, her gown slipped from one shoulder, then the other. My fingers crept imperatively beneath the tightened strings of her petticoats. Slowly, her head drew back.

"Warren," she whispered breathlessly. "Your buttons. . . are hurting me."

I laughed huskily and kissed the spot she was rubbing. She slipped away a trifle, pulled on the bows at her waist. One by one, all four of her linens swirled to her feet. She stepped forth with conscious pride in her glorious nakedness.

With slight surprise, I found my waistcoat and shirt were open. I tossed the offending buttons into the pool of her petticoats.

Chapter 21

﷽﷽﷽﷽﷽﷽﷽﷽﷽﷽﷽﷽﷽﷽﷽﷽﷽﷽﷽﷽﷽﷽﷽﷽﷽﷽

A CHILL draught struck my bare shoulder blades and pulled me irresistibly from my warm, comfortable drowsiness. Some instinct kept insisting that I get up. Somewhere in the vague distance, men were shouting, pans were rattling, wood was splintering. The noises added up to the certainty that a fight was in progress amidships. But it seemed remote and unreal and outside of my personal concern. I couldn't summon the energy to be curious.

Then a scream brought me upright. Beulah, too, was suddenly wide awake. As I tried to get up, she seized my arm, so hard that I knew she wasn't just being capricious.

"Listen!" she whispered.

Someone was stirring in the next cabin—Joe's cabin. Bare feet thumped on the floor and, a moment later, Joe ran across the salon, pattered up the ladder and was gone. Beulah pressed herself against me, gave me a hard, quick kiss, then pushed me out. I jumped into my breeches and shoes and rushed up on deck.

The cold air hit me like a stinging blow, knocking the last of the sleep from me. The moon was almost gone and, through the dimness I could barely see a crowd of gabbling men gathered around the deckhouse. I pushed my way through the mob of half-dressed, barefooted seamen. A man was lying on his back by the cook's cabin, his puffed eye closed, blood drooling from his broken lips and lacerated gums.

"Who is he?" I asked quickly.

"You got me," Joe answered. He turned to Toby, our bosun, who was leaning against the bulkhead. Toby was a pretty battered looking specimen, too. "You all right now, Toby?"

The bosun wiped the blood off his chin and spat. "Guess so, sor, 'cept for skinned knuckles." He grinned and showed a broken tooth. "We had us a tussle, seems like."

"Seems like," Joe agreed, smiling. "What happened?"

Toby shrugged. "He comes prowling aboard and I see him and holler, 'Stop!' He don't stop, so I chases him around the deck and he ducks into the galley. I guess we near wrecked the place. I 'pologize, Cookie."

The little negro chuckled. "Yo' sho' welcomb, sar."

Joe motioned to one of the men nearby. "Dump a little water on this thing. Maybe we can bring him to."

It helped, but Toby had done such a good job that two buckets had to be dumped over him before he moaned and turned over on his stomach. He tried to pull himself to his knees. His arms relaxed and he slid forward on his face again. Two of our men grabbed him and stood him upright.

"Suppose you tell us what you were after," Joe suggested.

"Go 'way," the prowler groaned.

Joe slapped his cheeks and the man's eyes opened a bit. "Who sent you? We'll let you go if you tell the truth." Still no reply. "Maybe you'd like Toby to continue on that face of yours. Come on, speak up."

"I ain't sayin' nothin'," the man growled sullenly.

Joe chewed his lower lip, then looked over to me. "What'll we do with him?"

"Call the watch and have him locked up. Charge him with assault and attempted robbery. You take care of it, Toby." I grabbed the prisoner's shirtfront. "A lawyer can't get you out of this, mister. You're going to spend a lot of time in Bridewell unless you talk. Who sent you?"

The puffed eyes opened a trifle. "No spik English."

"As you will. . . . Just one thing more, Toby. Did you notice where he was headed—for the hold or aft or where?"

"Aft," Toby replied. "I cotch sight of him going up the poop ladder, sor. He led me a merry chase 'round the deck before I run him inter the galley."

Joe looked startled. "Say, do you think. . . .?"

293

"Maybe," I cut in quickly. "Take him away, Toby. Come on, Joe, let's see."

Both Joe and I were glad to duck back into the comparative warmth of the salon, for we were without shirts. Both of us were a bit excited, certain we knew what the prowler had been after. Beulah was at the door of her cabin now, dressed in a nightgown covered with a calico wrapper. I felt a twinge of embarrassment and looked quickly to Joe to see if he knew. Either he didn't or wasn't interested at the moment, for he made straight for the locker under the salon couch where we had put Captain Russell's sea chest.

"What was it?" Beulah asked.

"A prowler, that's all," Joe said as he dragged the box out. "Go back to your bunk. It's all over."

"It wasn't Russell, was it?" she asked. Neither of us answered. "Russell sent someone to fetch his box, is that it?"

"Either Russell or Spencer," Joe replied.

He threw up the cover and stared into the jumble of old clothes. Then, he pulled them out, one by one. There was an old salt-stained blue coat with brass buttons—the pockets empty; three pairs of dirty stockings, two dirty shirts, three pairs of heavy grogham breeches, an astrolobe—broken—a woollen belly band, a pair of shoes with brass buckles, a watch and a snuff box. The snuff box was marked with the initial "K." On the watch was the initial "R."

"K for Kimble," Beulah half shouted.

"Maybe," Joe conceded. He held up the watch, frowned. "Maybe that K is an R without the loop finished."

"I don't believe it," Beulah said firmly.

There wasn't a scrap of paper of any kind in that box. No notebook, no letters, no log, no nothing.

Beulah yawned. "Well, you can worry about it if you like. I'm going back to sleep. Goodnight boys."

She winked at me and went back into her cabin. Joe was putting the stuff back into the box. He looked up at me, flushed, averted his eyes.

"I thought you weren't interested in Russell any more, Joe," I said casually. "Nor in knowing what Russell was after."

"No . . . not exactly, that is." Joe let the lid drop and

294

got up. "Look, Warren, I trust you. Honest, I do. But it wouldn't help if you knew what was bothering me. Believe me, you can't do anything." His eyes grew thoughtful. "But if I had what Russell was after . . . . If I had that I'd be safe. Yes, I think I would."

"You don't know what it is?"

"I have an idea, but I'm not sure."

"Joe, we never made a search for Buckner. Was he murdered?"

Joe look startled. His voice was husky when he answered. "Maybe he was, Warren, maybe he was." He was silent a moment. "Honest, Warren, I really don't know what Spencer's game is. All I do know is that we could be rid of him once and for all if I had what Russell was after."

"I'll do my best to help you, Joe."

"Thanks, Warren, but you can't do anything. Good-night."

He took Russell's box into his cabin with him.

I flopped on my bunk, dog tired. I was up at once, a bit frightened. Then I caught a glimpse of something white in the dimness and relaxed. My clothes were neatly draped over the chair. I sank back, weary in every nerve and muscle, and soon drifted into a shallow, troubled sleep. My dreams were filled with fizzing bottles, big cuban cigars and—most terrifying of all—misshapen, bandy-legged little hobgoblins.

At breakfast, I was still tired. Beulah, too, was a little heavy-eyed. I felt uncomfortable when Joe asked us what kind of a time we had had last night. But Beulah wasn't fazed. She chattered gaily, relating the play in detail and telling all about the supper at City Tavern, giving a course by course description, not forgetting the champagne.

Joe laughed. "So, drunk again. I thought I heard you bumping around in there. Doc Cameron should hear about this."

My face flamed. If Joe hadn't kidded me about how red I looked, I would have thought he knew. I wondered idly what he would do if he did find out. Joe hadn't exactly taken the stern brotherly attitude toward his sister, but one could never tell. Yet, when I thought back, I wasn't so sure

295

I cared. That lout at the theatre had been righter than he could know.

We were almost through with our meal when a rapping came on the bulkhead at the top of the companionway. It was our friend, Spencer, dapper and smoking his perennial cuban cigar.

"Good morning, gentlemen." He bowed to Beulah. "And the bright-eyed Mistress Crane, good morning. I understand you had a little trouble last night, Joseph. Naturally, you don't expect to press charges against the man, do you?"

I answered first. "Suppose I do?"

Spencer's eyes narrowed slightly and he smiled. "Mr. Hascott, I'm afraid you misunderstood that little unpleasantness yesterday. I assure you again, I had nothing to do with Russell's despicable attempt to blow up the ship. I aided him only because court proceedings would have inconvenienced me. I have enemies, Mr. Hascott, enemies who would go to great lengths to ruin me."

The last might be true, but the rest I didn't believe. "Then, perhaps you wouldn't mind satisfying my curiosity."

Spencer nodded. "I have nothing to fear."

I didn't expect him to give me the truth, but I wanted to see how well he could lie. "How did you happen to be shipping a cargo from Jamaica to Canada? Your business is here."

"Well, I happened to be in Jamaica on business about eight months ago. Someone mentioned that no ship had put in at the new colony of Loyalists at New Brunswick for some time. I decided a cargo of rum and sugar might command premium prices there. So I employed Russell to make the trip. He was to have brought me a cargo of lumber here to New York on his return trip. That's all there was to the deal, I assure you, Mr. Hascott. If you have any commercial connections, you can easily check the facts."

"How do you account for Russell's actions?"

Spencer wagged his head. "Honestly, suh, I cannot. I do know, however, that the man has a bad reputation. I wasn't aware at the time I hired him that his usual trade was smuggling. I was worried when I found out. I was rather relieved when I heard he had put into Machias. I kept thinking he might sell the cargo for himself in some port."

"Your cargo was insured, wasn't it?"

"Naturally." Spencer flicked the long ash from his cigar and smiled. "If you think, Mr. Hascott, I would have been tempted to sink Joe's ship to get the insurance, you just don't know me. Why, I would be a fool to risk whatever commercial reputation I have left in a barratry conspiracy —especially for that picayune amount of money."

That sounded reasonable, but I had the feeling that Spencer was being just a bit too glib. Yet, everything did hang together neatly. There was the possibility that, whatever was between himself and Joe, he had not been involved with Russell in any plot against us. It was possible that Russell had tried to blow up the ship in revenge for some wrong Spencer had put on him.

"Now, gentlemen, shall we forget it?" Spencer put his cigar in his mouth and drew out a wallet. "I'll settle with you later, Joseph. As for you, Mr. Hascott. . . ." He opened his wallet and counted out a sheaf of bills. "This will cover the shoes. Six hundred and sixty five pounds, right, Mr. Hascott?"

I didn't answer at once, staring at the money. My belief of a moment ago that I might be wronging Spencer's honesty was quickly dispelled. That was New York paper money. I didn't know what it was worth exactly, but I knew it was selling at a depreciated price. I smiled, but refused to reach for it.

"If you don't mind, Mr. Spencer," I said casually, "I wish you'd hold the money for me. I don't like to carry such an amount on my person. It's not safe, you know. From your papers, I understand there's been a lot of robberies lately."

"Of course. I'll arrange a letter of credit for you, if you like, Mr. Hascott."

"Thank you, but I don't think that will be necessary. I intend to take another cargo to Boston."

"Oh, you do?" Spencer's head cocked. "Perhaps we can do more business, Mr. Hascott. What do you have in mind?"

"Anything I think I can make a profit on, Mr. Spencer. What have you to offer?"

Spencer puffed on his cigar a moment. "Well, I have that batch of paper—newsprint. I bought it at a bankruptcy a while ago. You can have it at forty pounds a ton if you take the lot, forty two if you take half or less. The whole lot amounts to a hundred tons."

I considered the offer. I had heard that there was a shortage of newsprint in Massachusetts—yes, and in New Hampshire. I remembered reading an item that *Freeman's Oracle*, published in Exeter, New Hampshire, had been forced to cut down the size of its pages because of a shortage of paper. On that basis alone, the proposition looked like a good gamble. If the General Court repealed the tax on advertisements at this session, newspapers would be opening all over the state and there was sure to be a scramble for paper. In that case, the price would skyrocket.

Joe was trying to catch my eye and shaking his head to tell me to turn down the offer. But I just winked at him.

"I may be able to swing it, Mr. Spencer. As you can see, all I have is six hundred and thirty pounds cash. However, I can easily arrange to raise the rest in Boston if you'll allow me to arrange payment there."

Spencer stared at the tip of his cigar. "Tell you what I'll do, Mr. Hascott. Since you've been so decent about this whole thing, I'll pay the freight and turn over title to you in Boston. I have a bit of business there, anyway. I'll travel with you. Do you have room, Joseph?"

"We have a spare cabin," Joe assured him.

Spencer got up and shook hands with me. "It's a pleasure to do business with a sensible man, Mr. Hascott. I'll arrange to start loading this afternoon. Good morning, gentlemen, and Mistress Crane." And he hurried up the ladder.

Joe eyed me sadly. "And I thought you were a good businessman, Warren. He offered that paper at thirty nine and no takers. I tried to tell you, but you were too cocksure of yourself."

I winked broadly. "Maybe I still am, Joe. You wait and see. I think I'll be paying less than thirty nine."

Joe stared at me a moment, then grinned. "All right. I'll bet on you."

I pushed myself away from the table. "I have to make a call. Do you need me this morning, Joe?"

"No, we only have some cleaning to do—and getting out those shoes. I can handle it alone."

"Can I go with you, Warren?" Beulah asked.

"Sure, take her along," Joe urged. "Get her out from under-foot . . . unless you'd prefer to be alone."

"No, I'll take her off your hands." I winked. "Get your cloak, Beulah. We'll visit Congress, too, while we're at it. We ought to get back by noon." I neglected to add that I intended to learn more about that man Russell, too.

Beulah and I didn't talk very much on the way down to Pearl Street. Both of us avoided mentioning what had happened last evening. I was a bit uneasy, wondering how far she thought I had committed myself. I wondered if there was any meaning in the way she held my arm, a little tighter, a little more possessively. Otherwise, she seemed to have accepted the affair casually, almost too casually. Maybe she was that kind.

White & Coleman was located in an old, red brick building on Pearl Street, just off Broad. The neighborhood smelled strongly of tea and cinnammon and roasting coffee and other spices, not forgetting the odors of garbage from the residences interspaced among the mercantile establishments. I disentangled Beulah's arm, stepped up the worn stone steps and entered the counting room. A plumpish clerk swung about on his high stool.

"I'd like to see Mr. White or Mr. Coleman, if you please. I have a letter of introduction from Mr. Burdick of Boston."

The clerk jerked to the hallway. "Mr. Coleman is in. Last door down. Knock first."

I turned to Beulah. "Will you wait here, Beulah?"

The clerk jumped down and brought over a chair, dusting it off with a flourish. "If you please . . . ah . . . M'um."

The door of Mr. Coleman's private sanctum was partly open and he growled "Come in" when I knocked. Mr. Coleman proved to be a gruff, square-faced man of about fifty, wearing a bobbed white wig and worn serge coat with steel buttons. His gnarled red hands were calloused.

"Well? Sit down, Mr. . . . ."

"Hascott," I supplied.

I handed him my letter and seated myself, drawing my chair away from the glowing grate in the hearth. Mr. Coleman was a brisk man. He tore open the letter, scanned it quickly and dropped it onto the neat pile of papers at the corner of his desk.

"Burdick says you're to have any reasonable credit. How much do you want?"

"Three thousand five hundred pounds."

His black brows went up. "Is that reasonable? Let's hear the proposition. Burdick instructed me to pass judgment on whatever transaction you contemplated taking on."

"I'm taking a shipment of paper back to Boston—a hundred tons at forty pounds a ton."

Coleman waved a big hand. "Too much. I can get you a load at thirty-nine—maybe thirty-eight. Who's trying to rook you?"

I grinned. "I'm afraid it's the other way around, Mr. Coleman. I'm buying the paper from A. V. Spencer."

"So you figure on outsmarting him, eh?" Coleman snorted. "That man's the nearest thing we have to a legal thief here in New York. All right, let's have it. How do you figure you can do it?"

I told Mr. Coleman about the sale of my shoes to Spencer, then how I intended to swing the paper deal. Mr. Coleman grunted, tittered, then broke into a rafter-shaking roar of laughter. He got red in the face, caught his breath and I thought he was going to choke. He didn't. He poured himself a stiff drink of brandy from the bottle on the small table behind him and poured it down.

Then he was solemn again. "Sounds pretty good. How do you know it will work?"

I shrugged. "He already swallowed the bait. He said he'd keep title to the paper until we reached Boston. Of course, if this leaks out the gossip might reach him."

"Don't worry about me, Mr. Hascott. All I ask is that you write after the deal's completed and let me know that it's safe to pass the tale along. A lot of us around here have waited a long time to have a laugh on him." His blunt fingers drummed on the desk. "Give me a little time to raise the money. Come back late this afternoon or early tomorrow morning."

"Fine. Thank you, sir." I felt a lot more confident now that Coleman had approved my scheme. "There's one thing more you may be able to help me with, Mr. Coleman."

"I'm at your service, young man."

I told him the full story of the Machias affair and what had happened here in New York. When I finished, Coleman lifted his wig and scratched his head. He heaved himself out of his chair and went to the door.

"Jeremy!" Then, as the clerk came running, "Fetch Captain Waldron. Try the Boar's Head first. He ought to be having breakfast by now." He poured brandies for us both, then sat down again. "Seems I remember something about this man Russell, Mr. Hascott. I can't remember offhand what it was. Captain Waldron will know. He's in the West India trade."

While we waited, Coleman asked about business conditions in Boston and about the tumults, of which he had heard. I told merely the events, not wishing to get into a political discussion. Then I asked about conditions in New York. Coleman gave me the same dreary story I had given him—trading virtually at a standstill, exports and imports off fifty percent from the year before, mercantile failures by the score, debtors crowding the jails. The arrival of Captain Waldron mercifully put an end to the doleful tale.

"This is Mr. Hascott, Captain Waldron," Coleman said briskly. "Mr. Hascott is looking for information about a Captain Russell."

Waldron's horny hand gave mine a quick mangling and he planked himself down with a creak and a grunt. "Russell, eh? Let me see . . . Ben Russell, that would be. Last I heard he was in Kingston . . . No, Machias. Wrecked his ship up there."

"That's the man," I said eagerly.

"Did he cheat you or just steal something, Mr. Hascott?" Waldron rubbed his bulbous nose as I hesitated. "Don't have to tell me if you don't want to. You had trouble with him, I suppose. That's enough for me." He shifted his bulk. "Let me see . . . Russell. Smuggling, that was his business mostly. Worked between the West Indies and Charleston, as I remember."

"Charleston?" I echoed. "Then he must have known Spencer there."

"Spencer?" Waldron's eyes narrowed. "Seems I heard . . . Oh, yes, he's the fellow who had to pull out of Charleston about a year ago. Sold some damaged tobacco as prime and refused to make good. The buyer swore Spencer showed him samples from a good batch and delivered a rotten load. Spencer refused to make good. People boycotted him and he had to leave. He's here in New York, I understand. Let me see. . . . Yes, I remember hearing rumors that Spencer and Russell were in on some smuggling deals together. Nobody could ever prove anything, though."

I was completely baffled. That Spencer was closely linked to Russell was now obvious. But just what their game could be wasn't so easy to see. I tried another attack.

"Russell was supposed to have come into Machias after hitting a rock. Could he have had any reason for wanting to scuttle his ship? I understand he had no insurance."

"Bah, that old tub wasn't worth the powder to blow it to hell. He didn't have to hit a rock to spring a leak. He had to keep at least one pump going all the time." Waldron wagged a finger at me. "That's one reason why we figured he and Spencer were in together. While Spencer was in Charleston, Russell was able to keep his ship in good shape. After the two parted, Russell started to go downhill fast."

"I suppose that would have made him want to head west and take his chances out there."

"I suppose. He didn't dare stick his nose into Charleston and Savannah. Savannah had the goods on him for smuggling. Maybe this will help, Mr. Hascott. About a year and a half ago Russell was mixed up in a murder in Charleston."

I sat upright. "A murder?"

Waldron squirmed for comfort. "Well, everybody said it was murder. It was a fellow named Bissol or Bristol, as I remember it, a dealer in West India goods. His warehouse burned up one night and he was found burned to death in his office. Among the ruins, they found two dead slaves said to have been smuggled in. They still had chains on their legs. Somebody said those chains belonged to Russell. He denied it and nobody ever proved anything. Somebody else . . . Mulhull, was his name . . . said he had seen those slaves up for sale in Kingston. He identified them positively. One of them had a big V scar on his stomach. But nobody could prove Russell had brought them in."

"That seems like fairly certain evidence," I said, and

Captain Waldron shrugged. "Do you know a man called Kimble?"

"Kimble? . . . Kimble. No, sorry, never heard of him."

"What did this Russell look like?"

"Pretty big fellow, nothing else much distinctive about him. Except he had tender skin. He hated shaving. Used to let his beard grow while at sea."

A weird crawling sensation went over my scalp. At last! Here was real progress. This much was now sure. The man we knew as Russell was Kimble. The sailor we had known as Buckner was, in truth, Captain Russell!

Chapter 22

IN JANUARY 1785, New York became the capital of the United States of America. When President Richard Henry Lee and the members of Congress arrived, they were greeted with cheers and the discharge of cannon and ceremoniously escorted by Governor Clinton to his residence on Queen Street. Congress had been offered, and accepted, quarters in the City Hall and in that place the members settled to business. Thereupon, the people of the city, never very impressed by the honor of being host to the National Government, proceeded to ignore the body that was supposedly sovereign over the thirteen Confederate States.

The City Hall was a shabby three-storied grey stone building on Wall Street at the head of Broad Street. It was built along the usual plain lines, squarish and surmounted by a cupola. It was badly in need of repairs, for the paint had weathered from the wooden sashes and doors and some of the window panes were broken and patched with paper. The grey stone itself had a dirty, smudged appearance. Throngs of intent people scurried up and down Wall and Broad Streets, but few gave the place any notice. Even fewer went in and out, and most of those, chances were, had business with the city. Congress had not even been afforded the dignity of exclusive occupancy of the building.

The weary flooring squealed underfoot as Beulah and I entered the broad, low-ceilinged lobby. A few men were standing by the winding staircase at the rear and a few more were grouped by the office doors on the right. They talked in hushed tones, as if apologetic for breaking the hush of this tomb. To our left, a sign on the open door read: "Office of the Clerk of the Continental Congress." We entered and waited to be noticed by the lone occupant, a thin-faced blond man seated behind a fine mahogany desk and scribbling away industriously. After a moment he set down his quill, rising and bowing politely.

"My pahdon, suh," he said in a soft drawl. "I didn't mean to be rude. How may I serve you, suh—and Madam?"

I couldn't help smiling. "It's rather quiet in here, isn't it, Mr. . . .?"

"Proctor," he supplied, then he shrugged helplessly. "It's no lively place when the City Council is in session. Is your business with Congress, suh?"

"Yes. But if you'll direct me to the Representative from Massachusetts, I believe he could take care of me."

Mr. Proctor shook his head. "Mr. Dane returned to Boston some time ago to report to his government. Mr. King didn't answer this morning's roll call, but I expect he'll be here later. I can direct you to his lodgings. Or perhaps I can serve you?"

"Well, perhaps you can. My name is Hascott, Warren Hascott. Some time ago, I petitioned Congress to reimburse me for a loss I sustained at the hands of a British warship. We were stopped and searched outside of Boston."

"I think I remember the incident, suh. Last June, wasn't it? The ship *Prosperous*, Captain Bryce? I remember Captain Bryce came here, demanding satisfaction from the British Government."

"That was it. I lost a jeweled dagger, valued at about eighty pounds. It was stolen from me by a British Naval Officer."

The clerk smiled slowly. "I'm afraid, suh, you'll have to write off the sum as a dead loss. However, if you'll excuse me a moment, I'll see if we've had a reply from Mr. Adams on the protest we directed him to lodge with the British Government. Won't you be seated, suh—and Madam?

Beulah and I seated ourselves and waited. In a few moments, Mr. Proctor returned with a sheaf of papers.

"On the eighth of July we sent a note to Whitehall. Mr. Adams informs us that our protest has been rejected. His Majesty's government holds that it has the right to stop and search the ship of any nation suspected of harboring British subjects who have deserted from the Royal Navy."

"That's monstrous," I said. "This is peace time."

The clerk lifted his shoulders. "Peace or war, Mr. Hascott, the United States does not recognize the right of any government to search our ships. But what can we do? Either we must accept these insults or match the British Navy ship for ship and fight them for the freedom of the seas. Humiliation is the price we pay for allowing the Confederation to be so weak."

I smiled. "I won't be drawn into a quarrel on the merits or demerits of Federalism, Mr. Proctor. I would like, however, to see our Congress in action. Are visitors permitted?"

"I must remember to ask sometime," Proctor returned with a sad smile, "in case someone else has that much interest in our Government's deliberations. Would you care to step this way? The chamber is upstairs."

Mr. Proctor took us upstairs and to the left and into a big chamber where the Continental Congress was sitting. There wasn't much to see. The room was high-ceilinged, furnished with rows of leather bottomed chairs, with a podium up front on which stood the President's desk. There were other desks for the clerks on either side of the podium. Behind the president's chair was a drooping American flag. Some twenty men were in attendance, that small number looking lost in the big room. They were lounging about in various relaxed attitudes, listening to an elegantly dressed gentleman delivering a speech in an ordinary tone of voice. Mr. Nathaniel Gorham, this year's President of the Congress, was not present in the chambers at the moment. Mr. Proctor whispered to me that eight states were in attendance on the floor, which was considered good, for often Congress had a hard time mustering a quorum.

We didn't stay long. The experience was too depressing. Personally, I was against Federalism, though I had not delved deeply into the subject, being instinctively against a strong central government which could degenerate into an aristocratic tyranny. Yet, I was not against strengthening the Confederation. There were so many pressing problems which a revitalized Congress could be dealing with vigorously. I told Mr. Proctor that it was shameful that men of such ability must be wasted in such useless work as they were now doing.

"You happened in at a quiet time, Mr. Hascott," Proctor

said. "We do have debates—interesting debates, at times. But they are just words. The delegates cannot force any state to act in accordance with the will of the majority of the delegates. Rhode Island, for example, won't be bound by anything Congress does. She even refuses to send delegates. Most of the rest consider themselves, and act, as ambassadors of sovereign nations."

"Congress can make treaties, can't it? I understand a treaty is being negotiated with Algiers. I have friends in slavery in that country. Can't Congress do anything to obtain their release?"

"Congress can negotiate the treaty, Mr. Hascott, and probably will. But only the states can pay any ransom agreed upon. The national treasury is bare. Why, not so long ago, Mr. Adams had to borrow money in Amsterdam from the money lenders to pay the interest on our debt to Holland. That's disgraceful."

Both of us were glad to get outside again into the sunshine and the bustle of crowds.

"What part of the country did he come from, Warren? He talked so funny."

"Funny? I hadn't noticed. I suppose—Oh, now that you mention it, I guess he's from the south. His accent wasn't as pronounced as some southerners I've met."

"He was nice—polite." Beulah was silent a moment. "You know, there might be something in Federalism, after all."

I laughed. "You're easily persuaded, Beulah. A nice blond man with a soft accent does it, eh?"

"No, it's not that. I was just thinking, during the war he wasn't a Virginian or a Georgian or whatnot. He was an American. You and I were Americans. It would be a shame, sort of, to break a bond like that. You fought together and died together. Why can't you live together?"

She had a point there.

My holiday was over. By the time we got back to the ship, the first of the cargo was going into the hold. I put on my old clothes, ate a hasty dinner, then got to work. The paper came in flat bales weighing around two hundred pounds each and, after our experience with Spencer, I was naturally suspicious. Accordingly, I opened several of the bales to examine my purchase. The paper was in prime condition.

Having assured myself of that, I went below and wrote a letter to Mr. Burdick, telling him about the sale of the shoes, the deal I had made with Spencer and about the loan of the money from Mr. Coleman. I explained how I expected to realize an extra profit. I told Mr. Burdick to sell the paper, if possible, before I reached Boston. I asked him to try to get forty-two pounds or better, but not lower than forty pounds, otherwise there would be no profit. I sent the letter in duplicate, one going by the Boston stage from Fraunce's Tavern, the other by boat to Providence, thence overland to Boston.

It took us two full days to get the cargo into the holds. At that the task was accomplished in such a short time because we worked into the night by the light of pitch torches. Busy as we were, however, I managed to keep those men on watch at Fraunce's Tavern and Spencer's establishment. They saw nothing of Russell—or, to call him by his right name, Kimble. Spencer, as far as we could learn had not seen or contacted him. But Toby and I felt sure that, sooner or later, the two would meet. Our only fear was that they would somehow elude our watch.

The morning of our last day in port, I returned to Coleman & White and saw Mr. Coleman. He gave me the money I needed and informed me he had made inquiries about Spencer. He had learned that Spencer was in bad financial straits. He was liquidating a number of his assets to meet his current bills. Coleman mourned that I had paid forty pounds a ton for the paper, opining that I could have gotten it for thirty-eight or less. I regretted I didn't have a wider margin to work with in case paper wasn't in demand in Massachusetts, but I could hardly want for more profit on the deal than I expected I would be getting.

Mr. Spencer came aboard with his baggage late in the afternoon. No, he was not going to stay aboard for the evening, since we wouldn't be going out until the 4 A. M. tide. Joe took him below to settle him in the spare cabin. As soon as he was out of sight, Jeffrey, who was keeping the daylight vigil on him, ambled casually up the gangplank.

"Anything to report, Jeff?" I asked.

"Nothing much," Jeff answered. "He's closed up his house and sent his valet on to Boston by stage."

"No sign of Russell?"

"No, sir." Jeff spat overside. "Did you know Spencer sold that rum and sugar we brung down from Machias? Truckmen have been carting it away all afternoon."

"Well, there's nothing unusual about that."

"Maybe not. But he put one hogshead aside. It has a big black streak on it. I'm pretty sure that one isn't going out with the rest."

"I see." I didn't want to show how much the news had excited me. Not that I had the vaguest idea what it meant. "You'd better get off the ship, Jeff. Spencer will be up in a few minutes. Follow him and see where he goes. As soon as he's at dinner, come back here and tell me where and with whom, will you?"

Jeffrey touched his hat and assured me he would. He cleared out none too soon, for Spencer came on deck not long after. He had left his gold-headed cane behind, but he was smoking one of those big black cigars. Joe left him at the break of the poop and he came down alone.

"Everything satisfactory, Mr. Hascott?" he asked.

"As far as I know, yes," I replied. "I won't worry about it until I reach Boston, anyway."

Spencer grinned. "Well, at least you know you're not being cheated, having examined the paper." He held up his hand. "Tsk, Tsk, Mr. Hascott. I would have done the same under the circumstances. Well, I'll be back later. As I told Joseph, if you change your plans and wish to sail earlier, I'll be at the Crown Tavern. You wouldn't like to join me, would you, Mr. Hascott? There's to be cock fighting upstairs later in the evening."

"Isn't cock fighting illegal?"

Spencer laughed. "Oh, yes. But the city watch has trouble enough coping with robberies and greater crimes without taking on the impossible task of stamping out such harmless amusement. Well, I'll be glad to have you as my guest, Mr. Hascott, if you decide to come. Remember, the Crown Tavern on King Street."

Never having witnessed a cock fight I was tempted to accept the invitation. But if I could count on him staying at the Crown Tavern all evening, I could think of a better—and perhaps a more educational—way of breaking the law.

By eight o'clock the last of the paper went into the hold. The waterfront was very dark and very quiet, only an odd pedestrian here and there passing along the deserted waterfront. The hatches were battened down the gear cleared up and set to rights, and, one by one, our pitch torches winked out. Stygian blackness fell over the schooner. The crew, allowed to go ashore for the last hours in New York, trampled down the gangplank and scattered. A deep silence settled over the ship.

As soon as I was alone on deck, I made my way to the forepeak and stared across the street to Spencer's warehouse. His building was completely dark. Indeed, except for the taverns spaced irregularly up and down Water Street, scarcely a light showed anywhere. All evening long, I had been thinking about Spencer and that hogshead with the black streak on its side. I had half jokingly played with the idea of breaking into the warehouse. But now, I was considering it seriously.

Jeffrey had reported that Spencer had really gone to the Crown Tavern for his supper. After supper, in the company of some friends, he had gone upstairs. I sent him back there with orders to stand watch. If Spencer should happen to come out and head for the waterfront, he was to try to hurry on ahead and warn Toby or me. Since he had not yet returned, I could assume Spencer was either still at the Crown Tavern or had gone to some other place of amusement. And my curiosity gnawed incessantly, demanding that I go and find out what was in that hogshead. Rum, I knew, for I had tasted it. Yet, there might be a false bottom, a recess where some vital clue to the mystery was hidden.

I carefully looked over the situation. There was an alley alongside the warehouse. Four doors down there was a tavern, packed with patrons who were maintaining the usual riotous noise, singing and babbling and coarse laughter. I was sure the tumult was enough to cover any noise I might make breaking into Mr. Spencer's warehouse. Toby, who was on anchor watch, came up and joined me. I talked it over with him and decided to take the chance.

"Get me a shuttered lantern and a crowbar, Toby." I said.

"You stand watch up here and warn me as if anyone comes. Get an old bottle or something that breaks and smash it against the door."

"Aye, sor. Two bottles, so you won't mistake the noise."

I went below to get my coat, for I didn't want to let Joe or Beulah know what I was doing. As I anticipated, Beulah asked me where I was going.

"I have a little business to attend. I'll be back in a half hour or an hour at the most."

Joe scowled at me. "Personal business?" He sighed and went on before I could answer. "Warren, why don't you quit? Spencer told me you have men watching him."

"Oh, he did? Guilty conscience, I imagine."

"Your business has something to do with Spencer," Joe said accusingly.

I got annoyed. "All right, what if it has? Spencer is a criminal, I'm sure of it. He may have you too scared to do anything about it, but not me—not unless you're willing to tell me what you know. How about it?"

Joe glowered at the floor for some time. Then he clapped his knees and got up. "All right, Warren. Good luck."

Joe made no attempt to follow me. Before I was off the dock, I had annoying evidence that burglary would never be my profession. There was a curious tightness in my chest. The wind seemed colder and sharper than it actually was. My footsteps sounded like the clacking of wooden clogs on the hard cobblestones. Not a soul was in sight. Not a light showed in any of the windows of the shops and mercantile establishments. Yet, unreasonably, I felt that grim eyes were watching me from behind those dark panes.

After one nervous glance back to assure myself that Toby was on the forepeak, I plunged down the gloomy alley. The raucous song and explosive laughter from the nearby taverns seemed to reverberate between those hard brick walls. The lantern leaked light, a yellow sliver wavering back and forth over my leg. The beam was just bright enough to make me feel naked and conspicuous in that utter blackness. I could see nothing ahead. Like a blind man, I groped for the wall and felt my way along.

My fingers slid off the edge of the wall and I stopped. Soon, my eyes adjusted to the gloom and I was able to make out dim, shadowy shapes—a pile of rubbish on my left, a broken barrel, pieces of broken glass that glinted like jewels. Slowly, cautiously, I edged along the back of Spencer's brick warehouse. I soon came to a huge window, closed tight with a thick wooden shutter. Then, further on, I could make out the faint outlines of a door. The door seemed a less formidable obstacle.

I set down my lantern, looked up and down carefully. There were no fences along these back yards and the wheel-tracks and small mounds of manure in the dirt told me that many of the merchants loaded or unloaded at the rear of their buildings to escape the congestion on Water Street. No one was in sight. Nothing was stirring. The sounds from the taverns were muffled, too muffled.

With a shrug, I pried into the hasp. The task wasn't going to be as easy as I thought. The hasp was bolted through the thick door. I pulled gently, little by little increasing the pressure. A screeching, like the pain-wracked yowls of a thousand cats, shattered the quiet. Instinctively, I flattened myself against the door. For long, horrible minutes, I pressed myself against the wood, every nerve taut, listening hard. Silence mocked my fears.

Slowly, my heart eased its mad pounding and my muscles thawed. I went back to my job, working more cautiously. Suddenly and without warning, the hasp snapped and the lock clacked against the wood with sharp, staccato raps. I grabbed it, then quickly pushed the door open. Quickly, I picked up my lantern and slipped inside. The door closed with a soft thud.

I stood very still, my nostrils quivering as a host of strong odors swirled about me . . . cinnamon, tea, rum, tobacco . . . the blend was almost overpowering. Then, just as I was about to lift the shutter of my lantern, I heard a scraping, then a frenzied scurrying. I lifted my crowbar, relaxed and chuckled shakily. The place was filled with rats.

I was fairly certain that the shutters over the warehouse windows were tight enough to make it safe to show a light. I had to take the chance, anyway. I pulled up the cover and a thick finger of yellow light stabbed through the blackness. The place was completely empty, except for the litter on the floor—some straw, old barrel staves, spilled sugar. The beam steadied on a huge hogshead standing by the back wall. It was the object of my visit, the barrel with the black streak.

Now I was calm, my hands were steady. I set my light down carefully, then tapped the barrel lightly, on the head, by the bung, at the bottom. There was no hollow sound. I frowned at it, considering my next step. There was no use taking out the bung. I had done that once before. I tapped the head again, though that hollowness might signify a greater airspace than normal in a barrel of this size. There was nothing else to do. I had to get the head off.

I jabbed the sharp end of the crowbar into a crack and pried. Spencer was sure to see that someone had been at this barrel. But I didn't care anymore. The wood splintered and crackled. One section snapped loose, then another, then a third. The smell of rum swirled up and made my eyes water. Rubbing them with the back of my hand, I lifted the light and peered into the dark, rippling liquid.

My hands grew cold and a hard lump formed in the pit of my stomach. The paralysis of a monstrous horror turned me to stone. There, floating on the surface of the reddish liquor, were wisps of black hair.

My whole body was numb. I could feel neither heat nor cold, dryness nor wet. As if my fingers were no longer a part of me I watched them dip into the rum. The fingers closed about the tarred cue. Slowly, a hideous, grinning face grew clear before me. It was a squarish face, wrinkled and misshapen. There were black hairs on the chin. The ugly lips were drawn back to show evil yellow teeth. The lamp slipped from my fingers and crashed to the floor. The man was Buckner.

Then I remembered I had drunk of that liquor. I got sick.

Dimly, I heard footsteps behind me, the cautious scrape of shoe leather, the slow, heavy breathing of a man. Frantically I tried to throw off my nausea, moving back, step by step. I cried out as I realized I was moving toward the man. I whirled, lashed out blindly, caught a blur rushing at my head. A searing white light exploded before my eyes. Desperately I strove to hold my slipping senses. A new wave of pain and nausea went through me as I hit the floor on hands and knees. Try as I might, I couldn't get up. I slid forward on my face.

"Don't!" came a faint, far off voice. "Don't kill him, you

fool." I felt myself turned over and an arm shoveled under my shoulders. "Here—drink this."

I obeyed, not because I wanted to. I couldn't help myself. The liquor burned down my gullet, but it eased the throbbing agony in my throat. I thought that the man holding me was Spencer. But I wasn't sure. I couldn't swear to it. A warm glow flowed through my muscles and my aches vanished. Soon I drifted into merciful oblivion.

Chapter 23

I STRUGGLED for consciousness. A black bearded man with yellow teeth was sitting on my chest, laughing and pounding on my breastbone. I knew I was dreaming. But the horror of that wrinkled face was doubled by the memory of where I had seen it before. Slowly, as if rising from a deep dive, I emerged from the terrifying darkness. I was immediately aware that I was no longer in the warehouse. The soft squeal of tackle, the hum of the wind through the stays, the low groaning of the timbers, all told me I was at sea.

I opened my eyes, vaguely frightened. When I turned my head, the tautness ebbed from my chest. I had not been shipped aboard a strange vessel. I was in my own cabin. Beulah was sitting in the chair by my bunk, her eyes closed, drowsing.

"Good morning," I called softly.

She started, stiffened. "Warren, are you all right?"

"Yes . . . No. I'm hungry . . . famished."

She rose, a bit flustered. "I'll get Joe." And she hurried out, leaving me alone.

I had been too optimistic about my bodily condition. I tried to get up, fell back, tried again and made it. But my head! It felt like a cannonball. No ache, exactly, but at any moment I expected my skull to roll off my shoulders. The heaviness gradually passed away and soon I felt almost like a human being again.

"Someone stomped into the cabin and I cocked an attentive eye. It was Joe. "Good morning, Joe. How are you?"

"Fair to middling," Joe replied seriously. "How are you?"

"I'll live, I think." Then I realized daylight was pouring through the porthole. "What time is it?"

"Two o'clock. You've slept almost sixteen hours. What happened? . . . Beulah, close the door. . . . Toby told me all about what you were doing, Warren."

I rubbed my head and eyes. "How did I get here? I can't remember a thing."

"Well, about an hour after you left, Spencer brought you aboard. He said someone had come for him at the Crown Tavern and told him a burglar was in his warehouse. Toby later told me he was just about to go in for you when Spencer arrived. Anyway, we tried to revive you, but we couldn't." Joe frowned at his shoes. "What did you find, Warren?"

I hesitated, eyeing Beulah. "You'd better go outside, Beulah. This isn't fit for a lady's ears."

Beulah stamped her foot. "No. All along I knew something was going on between you two and I kept quiet. I know Joe's in trouble. I have a right to know about it."

"Didn't you ask him?"

"He won't tell me anything."

"He won't tell me, either, will you, Joe?"

Joe waved impatiently. "What did you find?"

"Get ready for a shock," I warned. "Remember that hogshead we noticed while loading in Machias? The one with the black streak on it? Well, I opened it. There was a body inside."

Joe gasped and sank into a chair. "He killed. . . ."

"Russell," I finished. "That bandy-legged little ape was Kimble, wasn't he?"

"There, I told you so," Beulah said triumphantly. Then she frowned. "So that's why Kimble wanted to sink the ship."

"He had three reasons," I said. "First, he wanted to get rid of the body. If he buried the body or disposed of it in the bay, it might have popped up sometime to embarrass him—or Spencer. If the ship went down no one would ever know what had happened to Russell. Second, Spencer did want the insurance on the cargo. I found out he's in financial difficulties. Third, he wanted to kill a man named Joseph Crane."

Beulah straightened. "Joe? Why?"

I shrugged. "Joe can tell us that."

Joe chewed on his lips a moment, staring out the porthole. He turned abruptly and walked out, slamming the door.

"Well!" Beulah said breathlessly. "W—Warren, he's in danger. Y—you said. . . ."

"No, I don't thing he's in danger now. I don't know why. But I don't think so."

I got up a bit shakily and put on my coat.

"You ought to stay in your bunk awhile, Warren."

"I'm starving," I grumbled. "I feel fine, otherwise."

"Then put on your surtout. It's cold out."

I said it wouldn't be necessary. I insisted it wouldn't be necessary. I put on my surtout.

She was right. The air was bitingly cold and the sky was overcast, hinting of snow. Spencer was leaning on the taffrail, a cigar clamped between his blue lips, staring down into the bubbling wake. He was wearing an elegantly cut dark blue greatcoat and his stockings were of green wool. He glanced over his shoulder as I approached.

"Ah, there, Mr. Hascott! Feeling better?"

"Much better, thank you."

He gave me a level look. "Suppose you tell me what you were doing in my warehouse last night."

"Snooping," I said frankly. "I suppose you don't know what I found." I smiled as he kept silent. "I ran into an old friend of yours. Captain Russell, remember? Not that bandy legged imposter. The Russell with the beard."

"Indeed," Spencer's voice was like ice, but his assurance was not shaken. "I heard he was dead. I'm afraid we'll never see him again. Never."

I chuckled. "Don't be too sure about that, Mr. Spencer. Don't be too sure."

That got him, all right. He shoved his hands deep into his greatcoat pockets, stared at me for a long moment. Then he drew out a wicked looking clasp knife and opened the blade. Calmly he began paring his nails.

"Mr. Hascott," he said in an even tone, "you have the most annoying habit of prying into other people's business—mine and Joseph's. Really, Mr. Hascott, it's not nice—or healthy."

I wasn't one bit scared. I knew his kind. He'd kill in desperation or perhaps in cold blood. But I doubted if he had the courage to meet anyone man to man. I took out my own clasp knife and opened it. The two blades were exactly the same size.

"I've learned a trick or two about knife fighting in Algiers, Mr. Spencer. Anytime you want a lesson, just let me know. Or would you rather I turned my back?"

Spencer's eyes yielded and he turned away from me. I was smiling as I hurried fo'rd to get my dinner.

Bit by bit the tension began building up. Joe walked around tight-lipped, with a stubborn hardness in his eyes. Beulah seemed to become more and more worried. Spencer kept his veneer of geniality, but he was more often prone to lapse into long, thoughtful silences. His eyes hardly ever left me when I was within his sight. The mood transmitted itself to the crew. Our men were fairly well informed about the link between Kimble and Spencer and they hadn't forgotten that they might have been innocent victims of Kimble's diabolical scheming. Tempers became snappish and the whole ship seemed to be waiting impatiently for an explosion.

I was irritable myself, but I believed there would be no relief until we reached Boston. Then I would take a hand. Remembering what Coleman had told me about Spencer's financial condition, I was fairly certain Spencer would be meeting Kimble there. With the cash he got from me, he'd pay off Kimble for his part in this affair. If Kimble had left New York on the morning of our departure, the stage would bring him to Boston in four days—barring snow and bad weather. I was fairly certain that Spencer would lead me to him. I itched to get my fingers on that weazened, bandy-legged ape. I'd make him talk all right.

Then it occurred to me that the answers to my questions might be on this very ship. Spencer had traveled with us, I knew, to be sure the paper deal went off without a hitch. He could conceivably have another motive. He could want to get at Captain Russell's sea chest. I was sure Spencer or Kimble had sent that prowler aboard. And I noticed Joe never let Spencer get time alone in the salon. He always found some excuse to go below whenever Spencer did. Whether or not Joe knew what was in the box, I couldn't say. Perhaps he was holding whatever it was over Spencer's head. I determined to have a look at that box as soon as I could.

The opportunity didn't come until the third morning at sea. I had the four to eight watch, sleeping from eight to twelve. I didn't sleep. I waited for the salon to empty and give me the chance to get into Joe's cabin alone. The second morning at sea, Beulah and Mr. Spencer stayed below because of rain. But the weather cleared at night and the sun shone the next morning. At nine o'clock Beulah and Spencer decided to get some air. I lost no time. As soon as their footsteps had faded from the ladder, I was out of my cabin and into Joe's. The door was not locked.

I dropped to my knees and pulled the box out from under Joe's bunk. I opened the lid and stared at the clothes. Joe evidently hadn't opened the box since that night the prowler came aboard, for the watch and the snuff box were still on top. That being the case, I decided there wouldn't be any use in going through the clothes again. But what was I to look for? Obviously, a paper of some kind. And papers could easily be hidden somewhere in the wood of the box itself.

Carefully, I pushed the point of my knife into the wood here and there. The wood was solid. There was no false bottom. There was no veneer on the inside of the cover. The rope handles were frayed from age, but of no value in my search. I sat on my haunches, every nerve of me straining for the answer. I must be close to it. I refused to acknowledge my bafflement.

I emptied out the box, examined the clothes again, opened the watchcase, went through the snuffbox. I found nothing. I turned the box upside down, on its sides, examined every corner for a sign of glue. I found nothing. The box was sturdily built, the wood of oak, the sides pegged—Pegs! One by one, I examined the round pegs, which were flush to the outer sides of the chest. One seemed a bit peculiar and I scraped the dirt and grime away. It was a false peg! My heart gave a jubilant leap and, eagerly, I dug out the putty plug.

The putty went quite deep and I had to use my penknife, to get it all out. Finally, I uncovered something dully metallic. It was a slim lead pipe. I cussed and squirmed and probed with my knife and my pinky and got ready to dig that thing out with my dirk. In desperation, I upended the box. The damn pipe slid out with exasperating ease.

My hands were trembling with excitement as I opened the

319

tube and pulled out the tightly rolled paper. I unrolled it, stared at the precise writing. Then, the fog in my mind cleared away—not completely, but enough to have a fair picture of the situation. One thing was certain. If Spencer ever went back to Charleston, this would be his ticket to the gallows.

It was a receipt, made out to one Avery Bissol for two slaves, one aged nineteen and five foot three. The second slave was the important one. He was aged thirty, five foot seven, marked with a V scar on his stomach. The receipt was signed: "A. V. Spencer".

This was not exactly proof that Spencer had fired the warehouse and murdered Bissol. It was only proof that Spencer had sold smuggled goods. That was a hanging matter, too, but it was doubtful if he could be extradited from New York or Massachusetts for that offense. No, I had to have more evidence to pin the murder on him. And one of two people, perhaps even both, could give me the evidence—Kimble and Joe. I closed the lid and was about to push the box back under the bunk when I paused. Perhaps Spencer would come looking for this paper. Perhaps Joe himself would do it. There was no sense in letting them know I had been here first. I picked up all the bigger pieces of putty and scattered the rest. Then I plugged the hole with wax which I got from the base of the candle on Joe's desk. I darkened it as best I could with dust and dirt. My handiwork was not bad. Perhaps whoever else searched wouldn't find the hole. If he did, then perhaps he'd suspect someone else—Spencer would suspect Joe, of course, or Kimble.

I got up off my hands and knees and brushed myself off, feeling well satisfied with myself. Yet, something made me hesitate. Where did Joe come into this picture? I stood there a while, wondering, the faint glimmering of an idea swirling around in my head. Then, I snapped my fingers and went for the log. Eagerly, yet hoping against hope I was wrong, I flipped back the pages. The receipt was dated April 14th, 1785. A lump formed in the pit of my stomach as I sought that date in the log.

Joe had arrived in Charleston on April 11th of that year.

A scruff of shoeleather made me turn quickly, reaching for my claspknife. I relaxed with a sigh of relief. It was Joe.

"Looking over the log?" he asked. His voice was small and

strained and his fists were clenched. He was scared. I decided to do no fencing but give it to him straight.

"Close that door, Joe. . . . Now, sit down." When he was seated on his bunk, I put one foot on the chair. "Joe, I'm going to tell you what I know. Then, you're going to tell me the rest." I held up my hand. "No more of this stubbornness, Joe. I'm a little sick of it. Maybe I am a paul pry. It's too bad I have a curious nature. But I do want to help you."

"What do you know?" Joe asked coldly.

"Just this: On April fifteenth, or thereabouts, of last year, Avery Bissol was murdered in Charleston, South Carolina."

Joe gasped. "How did you know?"

"Shut up and listen. Bissol's warehouse was burned down. Two slaves were found dead in the ruins. One of them was marked with a V scar on his stomach. Those slaves had been smuggled into Charleston. I have evidence to prove they were sold to Bissol by our friend Spencer."

Joe leaped up. "You have?"

"I have. Now, you tell me the rest. Where do you come into this? No talk, no evidence, that's final."

Joe sank back on the bunk, his head lowering. For a long time he stared at the floor, rubbing his sweaty hands together. Joe's face was very pale.

"All right," he said huskily. "You know everything else. You might as well know the rest. I smuggled those slaves in." He looked up quickly. "But I didn't know it. I swear. . . ."

"Let's have it from the beginning."

"Well, a year ago March I was in Jamaica . . . Kingston. Russell came aboard and told me he had been in Jamaica on business. His own ship was in Charleston being refitted. He asked me to take him back to Charleston. He paid me passage money. I didn't know his reputation at the time. I hadn't been in the game long. I wondered at the time why so many of my men didn't show up when sailing time arrived. I know now he kept them away. He put his own men aboard. Well, we arrived outside Charleston harbor at night time— I think Russell arranged that. I went below for some sleep and, after a while, I heard a boat pull away from the side. I got dressed and went on deck and, a short time later, Russell came back."

"You never knew he had slaves aboard your own ship?"

"I swear I didn't. He'd put them in the hold the night before we sailed. The hatches had already been battened down. Those poor devils had practically nothing to eat for ten days."

"Then what happened?"

Joe shrugged. "I passed through customs and everything was all right. Russell warned me not to say that he had come in with me. So, I said nothing. The minute I paid off the crew most of them disappeared. The rest hardly knew that Russell was aboard because he stayed out of sight during the day. The mate's watch was all Russell's men and he only came on deck then."

"How were you tied to the murder?"

"I found Russell had stolen my hand shackles."

"Oh, I see. And those shackles were on the bodies of the slaves found in the ruins of the warehouse?"

Joe nodded miserably. "I had no idea. The newspapers said Russell had been questioned and he denied they were his and nobody could prove they were."

"Then how could they be proven yours?"

"The ironmonger had stamped his initials on them. Ramsey was his name. That's why Russell came under suspicion. I met Spencer in a tavern one night and he treated me to drinks and we got talking about shackles. He asked me where I had bought mine and I told him Philadelphia, not knowing what he was after. Later, he told me. He said he'd pin the murder on me if I didn't do as he said."

"What did you do—what crimes did you commit—for him?"

"None. He wanted me to do some smuggling and I told him to go to hell. I said sooner or later I'd get caught and hanged. I might as well be hanged for a murder I didn't commit. I said I might have a chance to get away with it. But this thing— well, everything looked all right. Naturally, he had to tell me his game. I suppose that's why he wanted to murder me."

"What was—or is—his game?"

"I don't know everything. All I know is that I was to bring Russell up to Machias. Russell came aboard at New York and told me Spencer had stolen his ship. He wanted to get up to Machias. . . . I suppose to get that sea chest of his."

"That's a very good guess. Go on."

"Spencer hired me and told me I'd find Kimble posing as

Russell. All I was supposed to do was to bring Russell up to Machias and bring back the cargo. Whatever happened between Kimble and Russell was none of my business."

"He sure picked an elaborate way to lure Russell up there. Why?"

"That I don't know." Joe sighed and got up. "I feel better now. But what am I going to do?"

"There's one thing you've forgotten, Joe. Russell's dead. He's the only one who could testify against you and prove you helped smuggle in those slaves."

"But his crew," Joe objected.

"Neither Russell, if he were alive, or any of his crew would dare testify against you without risking their own necks."

"Spencer would turn one of them in. He knows them."

"No, he won't. He's not going to get the chance. We're going to put a noose around his neck first."

"How?"

"You leave that to me." I smiled wryly. "And pray."

You can imagine our impatience and eagerness to get to Boston once this part of the mystery was cleared up. But our luck ran out. Our trip down from Machias had been accomplished in extraordinarily good time. Off Nantucket, we ran into a storm, the granddaddy of all Nantucket storms.

When the storm finally blew over, we had to beat into unfavorable winds. The weather seemed to be conspiring to keep us away from Boston. Our food held up fairly well, for Joe never put to sea without a month's provisions. He had met situations like this before. But the storm had staved in two of our water casks. Another week and we would have been in a serious plight.

Thus, it was on the 27th of November, seventeen days from New York, that we dropped our hook off Lighthouse Island. My homecoming this time was a lot different, but I was no less glad to see familiar shores again. I was wondering if I'd be so happy to be home after I had heard what transpired while I was away. In New York I had seen newspapers now and again, which had told me all was not going well for our cause. I hadn't delved deeply into the matter then, however, for I had been, in a manner of speaking, on vacation from the Regulators.

But before I could worry about affairs of State, I had personal matters to attend. I had planned to stay on in Boston for a few days and send Beulah home ahead of me, lest both of us arrive home at the same time. Beulah and I had a mild argument on this point and I suspected she was thinking I'd be seeing a good deal of Judith. But I might have been wronging her. To my relief, and some puzzlement, she had never mentioned that night, nor did she seem to assume a claim on me because of the intimacy. Naturally, I was prepared to marry her in case of accident; but I wasn't quite sure my feeling toward her was love. So, it was just as well that further opportunities had not presented themselves, for habit can be the shortest route to the recorder's office.

Winding up the Spencer-Russell affair promised to be slightly more difficult. Naturally, I laid plans and took precautions. Shortly after we dropped anchor, I sent one of the men ashore at Alderton Point with a letter to be delivered to Mr. Burdick. I outlined the situation to Burdick and told him how to act when we met at the dock. Our messenger would get to Burdick in plenty of time, for we didn't expect to dock much before noon. We made no attempt to conceal his departure, even inviting Spencer to go ashore if he was in a hurry to be in Boston. I told him I was informing Mr. Burdick of our arrival to enable him to have the money ready to pay for the paper. As I expected, the explanation satisfied Spencer and he declined with thanks our offer to set him ashore.

On schedule, the tide turned at ten o'clock and, with the pilot in charge, the schooner gingerly treaded her way along the channel into Boston Harbor. Both Beulah and Mr. Spencer were on deck, ready to go ashore, Beulah in her brown homespun traveling dress, Spencer in his blue greatcoat and perennial cigar. They stood aft by the taffrail and Spencer, who was evidently familiar with the harbor, pointed out the places of interest to her—the bones of the French Seventy-four laying off Lovell's Island, Nick's Mate where the pirates had been hung, and later, after we had turned northwest and headed in toward town, the many islands dotting the smooth waters. Spencer was making the most of his opportunity. Beulah had given him precious little attention during the voyage. And I rather doubted this short interlude would do him any good. The schooner slowly and cautiously nosed in toward her berth on Long Wharf. Having given orders to strike the mainsail, I hurried fo'rd through the scurrying crew and took my place on the forepeak with the seaman who held the line ready to cast. Our arrival caused no stir among. the throngs flowing back and forth over that busy dock. Only a few moved to the stringpiece to look us over. It wasn't hard to spot Mr. Burdick, for his roundish, well-fed figure covered with an elegant greatcoat of plum colored broadcloth, the collar of black velvet, made him stand out among the drab corduroys and kerseys and serges.

The lines flew over and, as if glad to be home, the schooner rubbed her sturdy sides against the quivering timbers. All of us, Joe and Spencer and I, converged amidships where the crew was setting up the gangplank. As soon as it was fast, Mr. Burdick came aboard, surprisingly nimble for a man of his age and bulk.

"Warren, my boy!" He seized my hand and gave it a hard wring. "You had a prosperous voyage, I trust?"

"Not yet, Mr. Burdick," I replied with a smile. "This is Mr. Spencer, the gentleman from whom I'm buying the paper."

"Mr. Spencer, sir!" Burdick extended his hand. "I believe we met before."

"Indeed, suh." Spencer's lips twitched. "Under circumstances not quite as pleasant as now."

"Tush!" Burdick waved a plump hand. "We must keep our wits about us in business, sir. The devil takes the hindmost. I happened to be the hindmost at the time. No hard feelings."

"I'm sure there will be none this time, suh." He bowed slightly. "Suppose we close the deal, Mr. Burdick."

Burdick cleared his throat. "I'm afraid there must be a slight delay, Mr. Spencer."

Spencer frowned. "I don't understand."

"No hitch, I assure you. I just haven't been able to gather the cash as yet. I expect to have it in an hour or so. You know it's astonishing how little cash there is, even in Boston. I never realized it until I tried to raise it this morning. We do most of our business in bills of credit and such paper, you know."

"Yes, of course. You'll have the cash shortly?"

"On my word, sir. In an hour, a little more or less." Burdick

325

pulled out his big globular watch. "It's eleven o'clock now. By one o'clock, without fail, I'll have the money for you."

"That's satisfactory to me." Spencer took out his watch and frowned at it. "I have a little business to clean up in the meantime." He snapped his watchcase shut. "I'll be back around one o'clock—right after dinner."

I thought Joe would spoil it by shouting with glee. But he managed to restrain himself. Spencer had done exactly what we wanted him to do. As Spencer hurried up the gangplank, Burdick turned slightly and nodded to a small, nondescript man in shabby black grograms. The man returned the nod and casually fell into Spencer's wake.

"I told Jason to return here the moment Spencer contacts your man Kimble. Jason is an excellent man." He smiled and turned to Joe. "Now, Joseph, my boy, will you order the hatches opened? I'd like to see that batch of paper."

"Did you get a buyer for it?" I asked quickly.

Burdick nodded. "It wasn't easy. I could have sold it here in Boston at 40 or 41 pounds the ton. But I thought you'd want more profit than that. I sold fifty tons to a man in Portsmouth who happened to be in town, for 43 a ton, twenty five to a Salem man at 42 and the other twenty five to a Plymouth concern at forty two and a half. Joseph, you can make Salem first, then Portsmouth, then Plymouth. I have a cargo of flour for you in Plymouth for Nantucket. Is that satisfactory with you, young man?"

Joe grinned. "Yes, sir. It's a pleasure to be kept busy. I'll go out on the afternoon tide so's I won't lose another day."

"Excellent." Burdick eyed me. "I suppose I must wait until one o'clock for an explanation of all this rigamarole? I confess I don't understand why, if you've already drawn the cash from Coleman and White. . . ."

"One o'clock, please, Mr. Burdick," I broke in.

He sighed. "Ah, well. . . . Oh, and that reminds me. I saw Mr. Lang this morning. He's holding a small party—supper and cards—at the Cromwell's Head Tavern up on School Street this evening. When I told him you were arriving, he urged me to bring you along. Mrs. Burdick and Judith will be out this evening, so if you'd care to join me. . . ."

"I'd be delighted," I returned promptly.

I'd never been very keen on cards and gambling, but I

felt in the mood for some relaxation. And I wasn't overlooking the fact that I would be extending my business acquaintances.

"Six-thirty, Warren. And you may bring a guest if you like —male," he added quickly, as he caught sight of Beulah. "How are you, my dear? Warren didn't tell me Joseph was taking you along. Did you enjoy the trip?"

"Very much," Beulah replied shyly. Then, a bit fearfully, "Didn't Judith tell you she saw me?"

"Why no, she never even mentioned it." He started as Joe called to him. "Excuse me. Business, you know."

I winked at her. "Now you know how well she kept your secret. I'll tell her to take care of her father."

"I should have stayed below," Beulah said soberly.

We went over to watch Mr. Burdick. For all his excess weight, he was still very spry. He was in the forehold, examining the paper. He was suspicious, as I had been. But he found, as I had found, that the paper was as represented.

A hail from the dock made me turn. A young man with a roundish face and a curiosly thin nose was waving at me.

"Ethan!" I called. "Come aboard!" I grasped his hand as he came down on deck. "How did you know I was here?"

"News of arrivals travels fast on Long Wharf, Mr. Hascott. It might have been one of our ships, you know." His brows went up as he saw Beulah. "She's pretty. Introduce me."

I laughed. "That reminds me. How's Amy?"

"Fine, just fine. Papa's still balky and Amy still loves me. But I haven't lost my eyesight on that account."

I called Beulah over. "I want you to meet a friend of mine, Beulah, Mr. Ethan Blair. I was his schoolmaster once."

Ethan bowed. "You must be Joe's sister. The resemblance is marked. Though I must say you're far prettier."

"Thank you, Mr. Blair." She smiled. "I see Warren was a very good schoolmaster."

"That part of my talent is native, M'am. I was going to ask you to dine with us this evening, Mr. Hascott. Father will want to see you, I know. Why not bring Joe and Mistress Crane along?"

"I don't know if we can make it, Ethan. Joe's going out on the afternoon tide. Beulah's going home tomorrow and I have an urgent supper appointment myself."

327

"You live in Pelham, Mistress Crane?" Ethan asked. "But this is Monday. There won't be a stage until Wednesday."

I snapped my fingers. "Glory, I forgot all about that. I'll have to find a place for you tonight, Beulah."

"If you'll permit me," Ethan offered quickly. "Amy has a room to herself. I'm sure she'd be delighted to have you, M'am."

"Well, thank you, Mr. Blair," Beulah returned slowly. "But perhaps a convenient inn. . . ."

I got the point immediately. I was sorely tempted. But the situation wasn't without its drawbacks. Perhaps I was of too cautious a turn of mind, but I figured there'd be safer times.

"Beulah wouldn't like to impose on Amy," I said.

Ethan gave the expected answer. "Nonsense. Amy will be only too glad of the company. Besides, she's to be my wife one day, so she does as I say. And I must insist."

"Then, Beulah can't refuse," I returned quickly.

"Fine." Ethan beamed. "Then I'll call for you at . . . Joe will be leaving at four . . . say, two thirty?"

"I'll be ready then and thank you, Mr. Blair."

"Right! I know you're going to like Amy." He bowed. "I'll be back at two thirty. 'Til then!"

Ethan hopped up the gangplank and was soon lost in the crowd. Beulah was mad. Without a word, she turned and started aft. I wasn't willing to let that pass without explanations.

"Beulah, don't be foolish. I was thinking of you, not myself. I'm expected to call at the Burdick's tonight or tomorrow. How long do you suppose Judith would keep your secret if she knew you were staying with me overnight?"

"How would she know . . . unless you told?"

I smiled sadly. Her father will mention he saw you, won't he? Judith will know there's no stage until Wednesday. If you're with Amy, she won't be able to suspect anything. Be sensible, Beulah."

"All right. I understand." She touched my cheek. "That's your biggest trouble, Warren—you always want to be sensible."

She went below to pack her things. I squirmed a bit under her rebuke, but I had to admit it was deserved.

Mr. Burdick emerged from the hold and I went over to rejoin him and Joe. Burdick brushed off his clothes and straightened his wig and gave me a pleased smile.

"Better than I expected from the sample, Warren. I could have sold some of it as book paper. I hope the profit is better than I expect, too. I'll have to leave you now. I'll be back at one. You know where my establishment is if you need me before."

Mr. Burdick hadn't gone five minutes before Jason returned from his mission. Both Joe and I rushed to meet him as he came down the springy gangplank.

"Well?" I demanded.

Jason grinned. At close range I saw he had heavy features and loose lips. He talked from the side of his mouth.

"He went to a sailor's boarding house up in Gallop's Alley, right off Middle Street. After he went in, I waited awhile and went in myself. He's on the second floor, last room down at the back. I heard them talking." Then, he added apologetically, "I couldn't see if he was with a bandy-legged man."

"You've done nobly," Joe assured him. "Come on, Warren, what are we waiting for?"

"You're staying here," I informed him. "You have to be here when Spencer gets back. Tell him Burdick sent me off someplace."

"That's not fair," Joe grumbled. "After all, I'm the one that's most interested. You can't go alone."

"I'm taking Toby with me. I can count on him to handle our friend Kimble if he gets troublesome."

Toby was more than eager to go. He still had that old grudge against Kimble, though his head wound was long since healed. I only hoped he could be held within bounds. Jason, of course, had to go along to show us the place. Joe became sulky and refused to say goodby to me. But he changed his mind as we reached the gangplank. He caught my arm, grinned sheepishly, then furtively passed over his pistol.

I was strangely calm as I strode down Long Wharf and into the less congested State Street. The prospect of facing a callous, vicious murderer didn't bother me. Rather, I was relieved that the strain would soon be over. I had a greater fear of meeting Spencer on his way back to the ship. But I couldn't take a roundabout route, lest Kimble leave the house before I got there. I regretted now that I hadn't asked for two men, one to keep watch while the other returned to report.

My calmness ebbed away a bit as we approached Gallop's Alley. At the corner, Jason stopped me and pointed.

"That's the house, sir."

It was the second one from the corner, a shabby, grimy red brick building, the windows opaque with dirt and dust. There was a small sign proclaiming that rooms were available. The sagging, weathered old door was wide open, though the day was quite sharp. How anyone could choose to live in such a hovel was beyond me.

"You stay right here, Jason. Spencer may still be up there. If you hear any shooting or commotion, fetch a constable. Now, where's that room again?"

"Up those stairs and straight ahead. It's the last room at the back. You can't miss it."

With Toby at my back, I went in. The dark hallway stank of sour sweat and urine and bad liquor. The door to the front parlor was open and I peered in. The landlord was lying on the mussed bed, snoring, a bottle cradled in his arms. The floor squealed under Toby's feet and the landlord snorted. He didn't raise his unshaven face from the pillow and was snoring lustily again before we reached the stairs.

We went up the steps one by one. The house was old and dilapidated, deserving of being torn down, but the workmanship of the long dead builders had been honest. Not a creak came from any of those stairs. I glanced back once, saw that Toby was right behind me, his face intent. He was carrying an open claspknife, a wicked looking blade fully seven inches long.

"Careful how you use that," I whispered. "We don't want to kill anyone—or have doctors in on this."

Toby promised with a curt nod and we continued on up. At the top, we paused, listening intently. The darkness closed about us in unpleasant, acrid waves. Only feeble grey light managed to push through the grimy window at the front of the long hall. There was no window at the back. I caught a host of small, disturbing noises—the scratching of a mouse, the heavy breathing of a sleeping man, the echo of footfalls from the street. . . .

As soon as my eyes had become accustomed to the dimness, I counted the doors—two toward the front, three toward the back. I put my mouth to Toby's ear and, in a whisper, told him to go halfway up the stairs to the next floor and wait there while I made sure Spencer wasn't with Kimble. If he was, I'd duck up there, too. Toby nodded and quietly left me. I listened a moment. I heard nothing remotely resembling a human voice.

I took one step, then another, then a third. I stopped abruptly. I struggled to relax a little, wondering why I had halted. Then, I heard a faint murmuring. My heart skipped a beat and my ears strained. Yes, someone in that back room was talking. The voice was very low and faint, but I was sure it was Spencer's. I turned and started back to join Toby.

A latch clanged and I froze. I turned swiftly, barely managed to see that the rear door was slightly ajar. A painful crawling sensation went over my scalp.

". . . and that will be the last," Spencer was saying. "I'll be back after one o'clock. Don't leave. . . ."

Sudden panic swept over me and I heard no more. But I didn't lose my senses. Quickly and silently, I lifted the latch of the nearest door and stepped inside, closing the door noiselessly. My pulses were throbbing so wildly that I wasn't aware of the room's occupant until he spoke.

"Wha' shish?" came a low mumble. "G'wan. . ."

He said no more. In two steps, I was at his side and my hand clapped over his drooling mouth. I rammed my pistol at his throat. His eyes bulged and he relaxed, probably expecting that his last moment had come.

Footsteps went by the door at a brisk pace and pattered down the stairs, they faded into the distance and were gone. I took my hand off the poor slob's mouth and he remembered to breathe again. So did I.

I waited a few moments more to make sure Spencer wouldn't return, then went out into the hall. The man on the bed was much too scared to cry out or make a fuss. He was in the process of sleeping off a drunk, anyway, and would probably think he had dreamed the incident. I called softly and Toby joined me. Together, we went to the end room, the need for silence and caution gone.

I picked up the latch, threw back the door and barged boldly in, my pistol leveled. Kimble made a dive for the knife lying on a chair next to his bed. I kicked his wrist and he grabbed it and the knife spanged against the wall.

"Be nice, Kimble," I said softly. I waited until Toby closed the door. "I'm sure you're going to be reasonable, Mr. Kimble. You're going to answer a lot of questions for us, aren't you?" He maintained an indifferent silence and I chuckled. "You already have a noose around your neck, you know. Remember that night you found me in the warehouse? Well, you didn't get away with that hogshead unobserved. We know where you disposed of it."

"You're crazy," Kimble snarled impulsively. "Nobody could follow us across that marsh. I—" His jaws clamped together and he went pale, realizing he had said too much.

I was quick to seize my advantage. "He didn't have to follow you all the way. Did you, Toby?"

Toby had his wits along. "Nope. It was purty hard work crawlin' on hands and knees. Got me all muddy."

"You see, Mr. Kimble? We have your neck in a noose. But I'm not interested in you."

Kimble's eyes narrowed quickly. "What's the proposition? If I talk will you let me go?"

"Talk!" I said crisply.

He talked. His tale was simpler than I had thought it would be. Kimble had been Russell's first mate and for years they had worked at smuggling with Spencer. When Spencer was driven out of Charleston, Russell had to leave, too. Russell thereupon fell upon hard times, for he had no reliable shore contacts for his smuggling activities. About eight months ago, Spencer turned up at Jamaica. He and Russell had a violent quarrel—over what, Kimble did not know. At any rate, Spencer came to Kimble later and arranged to dispose of Russell.

The plan was this: Spencer had given Russell a cargo of rum and sugar to take to New Brunswick. The ship was not to go there. As soon as they were at sea, Kimble was to murder Russell. Kimble would then put in at Machias in a sinking condition and pose as Russell. He was to give out the story that he was going west. Thus, the news would go out that Russell had been ruined and, having fallen on evil times at his trade, had abandoned it in disgust. No suspicion of murder would ever fall on any of them.

But Kimble bungled. Russell evidently suspected something was up, for the ship had no sooner left than Russell decided Jamaica was healthier. He took the dory and skipped back to shore. Kimble searched for him and finally found the dory on the beach, proving that Russell had made good his escape. Kimble didn't know what to do, for Spencer had already left Jamaica to return to New York. He did the only possible thing for him. He proceeded to Machias and got the cargo off and scuttled the ship. Then he wrote to Spencer. Kimble, you can see, was not overly bright.

Spencer was furious, naturally. He wrote back and told Kimble to sit there and wait. Russell was sure to appear up there sooner or later. Then Kimble was to murder Russell, which he did. The original plan had been for Kimble to send Russell's sea chest back to New York with one of the other men, who wouldn't be paid his share until the sea chest was delivered. Kimble figured there was something valuable in it, though he didn't know what, so he hung on to it to assure himself he wouldn't be double crossed. He intended to deliver it himself—at a price.

The rest I knew. To get rid of the body of Russell and to get cash for the cargo and, finally, to get rid of Joe, Kimble was ordered to make sure Joe never arrived in New York. On questioning, I learned that Kimble hadn't the faintest idea why Joe had to be disposed of. That made me think over the situation.

I finally decided not to rake up the Charleston affair at all. I would pin the murder of Russell on Spencer as an accessory and send him to New York to trial, for I was sure I could crack Kimble and get him to reveal where Russell's body was hidden. At the trial, Spencer in a mood of vengeance might accuse Joe of being in on the affair. Joe could deny everything and, if we had a good lawyer, we could discredit Spencer thoroughly. That oughtn't be hard.

"This has been interesting, Kimble," I said finally. "Now, if you'll write out the tale as I dictate it and then sign it, we'll put Mr. Spencer on the scaffold."

333

"And let me go," Kimble added with an evil grin.

I didn't answer, turning to Toby. "Go down and tell Jason to fetch us a hackney."

"They're scarce in this part of town, Mr. Hascott."

"There's a stand at State House. He'll find one, all right. Tell him to come up and inform us when he arrives."

Thereupon I set Kimble to writing out his confession. It was slow work, for I had to be sure I had all the salient points in the manuscript. I even got him to set down the exact location of Russell's body. It was perfect. Spencer was doomed.

Before we were quite finished, Jason was back with the coach. Kimble signed the document with a satisfied flourish. I looked it over and put it in my pocket.

"All right, Kimble, come along."

Kimble went grey. "You promised. . . ."

"I promised nothing," I said coldly. "However, I shall testify that you aided us in catching Spencer. Perhaps the jury will mitigate your punishment, perhaps not. I guarantee nothing. You'll have to take your chances. And remember, I can shoot you at any time with impunity."

Kimble stared at me a moment, then at Toby's grim face. His small, weazened face became resigned. He came along quietly.

The coach bucked against the heavy traffic on State Street and plowed through the crowds on Long Wharf. A short distance from the schooner, I directed the coach to stop. I gave the pistol to Toby, telling him to use it if necessary. I went down to Burdick's counting house and got him myself. Before I brought Kimble on the scene, I was going to make damn sure that I had that paper deal settled.

Burdick bubbled with questions as we hurried back to the schooner. But I could only urge him to be patient. With some satisfaction I saw that Spencer was seated on the hatch, chatting with Beulah.

He rose as Burdick and I came down on deck. "Ah, I assume we're ready to finish our business?"

I nodded. "If you'll go below, Mr. Spencer."

As Beulah and Spencer started aft, I sought out Jeff, one of the crew members who had helped me before, and told him to stay at the head of the companionway. I'd be sending him on an errand soon. Joe came down from the poop and brushed

334

past Spencer, his flushed face mirroring his excitement. Spencer's brows went up and he turned back to watch Joe. My heart gave a bound, fearing Spencer might catch on. But he didn't.

"How did it go?" Joe asked breathlessly.

"Fine. Stop jittering. You'll give the game away."

We went down into the salon and proceeded about our business. Burdick took charge, keeping up a rapid chatter about the condition of business in Boston. I hoped he wouldn't overdo the moaning. Spencer was aware that something was wrong, but he didn't know exactly what. Joe provided the quill and ink and Mr. Burdick set out the contracts for him. Spencer hesitated before signing, puzzled.

"You have the money?"

"As soon as you've signed," Burdick purred. He was magnificent, really.

Spencer affixed his signature, turning title to the paper over to me. I thanked him and went into my cabin. I put the documents into my sea chest and brought out a box of money. Spencer was frowning as I placed it on the table.

"Just what is this, Mr. Hascott?"

"Your money—according to the contract . . . four thousand pounds. That's the correct sum, isn't it? Count it."

Spencer lifted the lid and swore violently.

"Paper money!" he half shouted. "I won't accept it! This is a cheat!"

"It's New York paper," I said icily. "May I remind you that you paid me six hundred and sixty-five pounds in paper?"

"See here," Spencer burst out angrily, "you can't get away with this. I'll sue you. This is Massachusetts. Massachusetts is on a hard money standard. I demand to be paid in hard money."

"This is Massachusetts, Mr. Spencer," I returned, "but you are a New Yorker. Sue all you like. The deal is legal. Being a New Yorker I don't suppose you know Massachusetts law. Let me inform you: The debt of any Massachusetts man contracted with anyone outside the state may be paid in the legal tender of that state. This currency is legal tender in New York. The law was passed at the Spring session of the Legislature."

335

Spencer sat very still for some time. "I see. I guess you've beaten me, Mr. Hascott."

"More than you realize," I said curtly. "No, please don't leave. I have another surprise for you."

I called up the hatchway and told Jeff to fetch Toby. Spencer was very nervous while we waited, fingering his lapels, the paper money, his lips. Had I not been sure his career was at an end, I might have feared his vengeance.

Mr. Spencer looked to the companionway as the heavy footsteps clomped down. The blood drained from his face. He trembled with rage when his bandy-legged friend stopped before him.

"You stupid bungler!" he said hoarsely. "What have you done now?"

"He's confessed everything," I supplied. "Even to where Russell's body can be found. You'll be returned to New York, Mr. Spencer. I imagine you'll hang there, too."

Spencer was livid as he turned on Russell. "Why, you . . . You'll never live to testify aga . . . ."

He never finished. His hand started into his coat. Before any of us realized what was happening, Kimble pounced like a nimble cat, grabbed Spencer's hand. There was a short scuffle and Kimble whirled back. In his hand was Spencer's pistol.

The threat stopped us in our tracks and Kimble grinned.

"I can kill one of you." He motioned to Toby. "Lay that pistol on the table. No funny business."

Toby looked to me and I nodded. No sense jeopardizing his life. Toby put the pistol down and Kimble took it. The weazened little man fingered the banknotes, then stuffed them into his pocket.

"Seems like it's getting to be a habit—me escaping."

He backed around to the companionway. All of us moved mechanically, well aware that he would shoot without the slightest compunction. He fixed his gaze on Spencer.

"You all stay here, folks, and nobody gets hurt. Follow me and I shoot to kill. Remember that."

He leveled one pistol and fired. Before the sound had died away, he was up the companionway. Not one of us had moved. Spencer was clutching his chest, his features twisting in agony. He pitched forward on his face and lay still. The case against A. V. Spencer was closed forever.

Chapter 24

※※※

JOE was the first to recover. He bounded up the ladder, swore lividly as he found the hatch closed and locked. He pounded and shouted until finally one of the crew came to let us out. By then, it was too late. Kimble was gone. Joe immediately informed the constabulary, who proceeded to send men to Boston Neck and the Charleston Bridge. No one really expected them to catch Kimble. Personally, I didn't care much. Sooner or later, Kimble was sure to come to a violent end. As for Spencer, he was better dead than alive to make trouble for Joe.

The event caused considerable excitement, naturally, but by three o'clock, it was all over. The huge crowd that had been drawn to Long Wharf melted away, leaving only the stubborn curious who insisted upon standing around, staring at nothing and chewing over crumbs of misinformation. We on board quickly recovered from the shock and horror. It was with profound relief that, at last, we watched the body being removed from the schooner.

We had been extremely lucky that we had a man of Mr. Burdick's standing as witness to the tragedy, for his presence eased considerably the ordeal of interrogation by the constables. After all explanations had been made, Mr. Burdick and I were ordered to appear at the inquest to be held the following morning. For a time we feared Joe would not be allowed to sail. But, irregular as the precedure was, the constables yielded to Mr. Burdick's insistence that justice would not be served by holding the ship. Truly, manifold are the advantages of prestige and wealth—especially wealth.

"I must get back to the office," Burdick said, as soon as we were alone. "Let me have that contract and bill of sale. I'll see the deal through for you. You'll have to wait for your money awhile, though. By the way, what was the discount you got on the money in New York?"

"Ten percent. New York paper depreciated less than I thought. But it just about doubles my profit."

Burdick chuckled. "And mine, too. I made no mistake about asking a percentage instead of interest." He frowned slightly. "Under ordinary circumstances, it would have been unethical."

"He actually cheated me on the shoes, sir."

"I know. And he cheated me on a deal once, too, so I'm only getting a little of mine back." He picked up his hat. "I'll see you at six-thirty, Warren. You'll stay at my house, of course. I'll send Jason down to take your baggage over."

The finality of his tone precluded argument, which was fine with me, for I had wondered how I could accept the almost inevitable invitation without arousing Beulah. Despite Judith's announced intention of marrying Salderman, I was eager to see her, eager to explore the sincerity of that intention. Yet, in my male egotism, I didn't want to relinquish what I already had. I wondered uneasily how long that could go on.

As soon as Burdick was gone, I packed my portmanteau and turned it over to Jason. Beulah had retired to her cabin to gather her things together and I had a moment alone with Joe. I took out the paper I had found in Russell's box and gave it to him.

"Better hang on to that awhile. If there's ever any trouble about those shackles, this proves Spencer had a hand in the murder. In case you're ever arrested on that charge, tell the whole truth. Personally, I think the case is closed."

"I hope so," Joe said fervently.

Beulah finally came out of her cabin with her old traveling trunk—one that Joe had discarded on a visit home some years ago. She tried, without much success, to appear cheerful.

"It's been nice, Joe," she said softly. "You've been good to me. I'll never bother you again. Honest."

Joe grunted. "I hope you remember that." He relented and kissed his sister. "If you weren't such a bitch at heart, I wouldn't mind having you around. I'll say this for you, though, you're a lot smarter than you were when I was home."

Joe laughed and picked up her traveling trunk and we went

up on deck. There I heard someone shouting my name from the wharf. It was Ethan, who had been barred from the ship with everyone else who had tried to get aboard and bother us with silly questions. The three of us went down to the waist and I called to Toby to let Ethan come aboard.

Ethan was bursting with curiosity, but too polite to broach the subject directly. "I managed to get off early. Everyone was so excited about . . . about . . . You know, we did business with Spencer. Naturally, we're all interested. . . ."

"Beulah saw everything. She'll tell you."

"Oh, fine. I didn't mean . . . Say, I saw Amy before. She'll be delighted to have you, Mistress Crane. And you, Mr. Hascott. Mr. Fitch sends a particular invitation to you to dine with us . . . and me, too. I'm going to be there. Pa may be angry, but. . . ."

"I'll take care of your father, Ethan," I said. "Express my regrets to Mr. Fitch. I won't be able to dine with him. I have another engagement. I'll take your father with me, if he can come. Will he be free, do you know?"

"Oh, yes, as far as I know." He gave my hand an impulsive wring. "That will fix things fine, Mr. Hascott. I'm sorry you can't be with us, Joe. Don't fail to drop in on us next time you're in port."

I shook hands with Joe and Toby and bade them goodbye. Toby was happy to see me go, for Joe wasn't going to be able to get another mate in time, so Toby had the job. Joe had also promised to teach him navigation.

State House was very quiet. No oratory was rattling the closed windows, either from the Senate or House chamber. Few people were going in and out of the front door, but the clerks in the offices along the hushed corridor were as busy as ever. Truly, without the Legislature in session the place was like a tomb.

Upstairs, the silence was profound. As I stepped from the circular stairway, I looked around to orientate myself, then spied Mr. Blair in the office to my left. His wig was askew, as usual, and his quill was wriggling like the frantic tailfeather of a diving goose. Mr. Blair looked up as I entered, scowled at me, then threw down his quill and pulled up a chair for me.

"Sit down, Warren. I heard you were in. I've been expecting you. Here's a letter for you."

I was surprised when I saw it came from Pelham. "That's queer. As far as I know, nobody in Pelham knows you've been in correspondence with me."

"Tom Johnson guessed. He remembered you had taught school in Hubbardston and put two and two together." He wriggled his fingers. "Open it. It's important."

I tore open the letter and noticed at once it was signed by Dan Shays. It was dated October 31st.

"Dear Warren:

The most alarming reports have reached us from Tom Johnson concerning the activities of the Legislature. The Habeas Corpus has been suspended. The Riot Act has been passed. The people are alarmed, needless to say. I beg of you, seek out those friends of yours who have influence and persuade them to protest this tyranny. The evil consequences can bring only sorrow to us all. If you can do nothing else, try to speak with Sam Adams or John Hancock and win either or both over to our cause. If the struggle continues—as God grant it will not—we shall need the aid of some men of their fame and standing on our side.

DANIEL SHAYS."

I swore softly as I handed the letter over to Mr. Blair. "So, there's to be more trouble."

"To be?" Blair echoed. "There's already been. Abe Gale— You remember Abe. He lives in Princeton. He's Adam Wheeler's son-in-law. Well, Abe, with a hundred and fifty men, closed down the inferior courts at Worcester on the 21st of this month."

"No militia?"

"No militia. But that's beside the point." Blair's eyes narrowed. "Warren, what's Daniel Shays like?"

"Like? What do you mean?"

"There are all sorts of stories going around about him. The mildest say he's in the pay of the British and aspires to dictatorship."

"That's Tory rot," I replied. "If it weren't for Shays, there might have been serious riots in Springfield. He's a peaceable man, thoroughly anti-British and as honest as they come."

"Strange, isn't it?" Blair folded his gnarled hands and stared into space. "Remember how the situation was when you left? The General Court had been in session three weeks then. Not a thing had been done. One group wanted stern repressive measures. The men from the country districts wanted a redress of grievances. A third faction—holding the balance of power—wanted to keep the insurgent cause alive until they could push personal measures through. Well, sir, the debates went on and on. You never heard such an outpouring of blather in all your life. Meantime, the Supreme Court sat at Taunton. As was the case in September, the militia was on hand. This time a group of Regulators came in. They delivered a petition to the court, demanding that it close. The petition was rejected. The Regulators dispersed and the court went on to do its regular business. From that, the Tories concluded that the courts could be upheld by force. The committees thereupon got up the courage to bring out onto the floor for debate, bills for a Riot Act and a suspension of the Habeas Corpus."

Blair continued. "Well, the debates were acrimonious, as you can imagine. Passage was certain in the Senate. But the Tories faced defeat in the House. Then Daniel Shays tossed out this bombshell."

He pawed over his desk, found a paper and handed it to me. It was dated at Pelham on the 23rd of October.

"Gentlemen:
By information from the General Court, they are determined to call all those who appeared to stop the court to condign punishment. Therefore I request you to assemble your men, to see that they are well armed and equipped with 60 rounds to each man and to be ready to turn out at a minute's warning: likewise to be properly organized with officers.

DANIEL SHAYS."

I whistled softly. "Then, what happened?"
Blair shrugged. "What any damn fool would have predicted. Here was a threat of armed rebellion, a defy to the sovereignty of the Commonwealth. The waverers swung over. The Riot Act was passed. The Habeas Corpus was suspended."

341

"Just what is this Riot Act, Mr. Blair?"

"It prohibits illegal assemblies. If a mob gathers, the Sheriff or other peace officer is directed to read them the Riot Act, calling upon them to disperse. If they haven't dispersed in two hours, the offenders are arrested. The punishments would then be: confiscation of all property, the infliction of 39 stripes and imprisonment for one year with 39 stripes every three months."

"Good Lord!" The severity of the punishments took my breath away. "And how is a mob defined?"

"There's no precise definition. That's left up to the judgment of the Sheriff."

I sat very still for a moment. "That's tyranny of the worst sort. County conventions could be suppressed. Discussions of political issues in our taverns would become a crime. That's the end of free speech."

Blair frowned. "As I said before, we're in for more trouble —more serious trouble."

"Wasn't anything constructive done?" I asked.

"Oh, yes, a little. The General Court passed a total of sixteen bills. You can read them in your newspaper if you want the details. Of the sixteen, just three had a bearing on a redress of grievances. One is designed to cheapen law suits by beginning all law suits before a Justice of the Peace. Since all law suits are appealed, that adds another step to the process. So, the bill, instead of cheapening law suits, makes them more expensive."

Blair chuckled as he saw my speechlessness.

"The second bill seems better. It provides for the payment of back taxes in commodities, in flax, wheat, corn and so forth, and including manufactured goods, such as cloth and nails. The expense and bother will make that mode of collecting the tax unprofitable. Besides, only the taxes for the years 1780 to 1784 can be paid that way. The great bulk of the unpaid taxes are from '85 and '86 when the depression really set in. So, you see, my boy, that bill is virtually useless, too."

"That's amazing," I managed to say.

"The third of the bills has some value. It's a Tender Act. A debtor can pay off in real estate. But the creditor isn't compelled to take the land. The bill only runs for eight months, so all the creditor has to do is sit tight and wait until the law expires. But at least the debtor has eight months respite."

Blair smiled thinly. "Of course, there is one bright note. The Government magnanimously pushed through an Act of Indemnity. All rebels who take the oath of allegiance and promise to behave in the future will be purged of their crimes. The offer stands to January 1."

"Now isn't that generous of the Government," I said sarcastically.

Blair nodded. "Your fellow insurgents agree with you there, Warren. Not one has asked for a pardon."

"There's going to be trouble," I predicted.

"You haven't heard it all yet, Warren. The Supreme Judicial Court sat at Cambridge on October 31st. That was while the Legislature was still in session and before the Riot Act was passed. Everybody still hoped something would be done to rectify the wrongs, so no one appeared to stop the court. What happened? The court proceeded to indict Job Shattuck, Oliver Parker and Nathan Smith for treason, and Benjamin Page for sedition."

"So, they're in jail?"

"Not yet. The Governor knows that the moment he puts the warrants into the hands of the sheriff, the Regulators will be up in arms." Blair's thin lips tightened. "We'll see what he does on the 28th of this month. A court is due to sit at Cambridge. Seven regiments of militia have been ordered to stand by to support the court. Joe Shattuck is sure to lead a party of Regulators in. From all I hear of Shattuck, he's a fireeater—something like Luke Day. Shattuck won't be in a good mood, either—not with a treason indictment hanging over his head."

"My God! Can't we do something?"

Mr. Blair leaned back in his chair, his fingertips touching. "Possibly. You may be able to do something."

"Me? I'll do anything. . . ."

"Not now," Blair broke in. "We'll see how the situation shapes up. Perhaps in a day or so."

"How about interviews with Hancock and Adams?" I asked.

"I'll try to arrange them, but I assure you they won't do you or your cause any good. Hancock is out of politics. He's

343

waiting to see how the cat jumps. Then he'll jump and reap the rewards of being on the popular side."

"That's despicable," I said hotly.

"That's politics," Blair returned blandly. "I really believe John Hancock doesn't realize just how serious the troubles are. Anyway, you can talk to him—if I can arrange the interview. As for Sam Adams, he's on the government side. But you can try, anyway. Maybe he'll switch over. Though I doubt it."

Blair clapped his knees. "Now, let's forget politics for a while. How about having supper with me tonight?"

"I've been invited to a supper and card party given by Mr. Lang. Do you know him? I was told I could bring a guest, if I liked. Would you come with me? Please do."

Blair considered for a long time. "I know Lang slightly. I— all right, I'll come with you. What time?"

I rose. "I'll be here for you at six-fifteen."

It was in a somber mood that I walked from State House over to Dock Square. I couldn't quite understand why the conservatives had acted so foolishly. Could it be that the merchants wanted to enslave the farmer, the rich make serfs of the poor? These were answers too glib to satisfy me. Yet, I knew well that the demagogues in our ranks would exploit these sinister reasons to the full. It was my duty, therefore, to probe deeper, for I did have some small influence which I could exert on the Regulators, especially on men like Dan Shays.

Mr. Fitch, with all his personal limitations and prejudices, reasonably could be considered as representative, in viewpoint if not in specific opinion, of the small merchant class. Accordingly, I believed he could help me.

Not until I turned into Dock Square did I realize how cold it was getting. I regretted now that I had allowed Jason to take my greatcoat to the Burdicks'. Bonfires had been lit here and there over the great, wind swept square and farmers and fishermen stomped about near the blazing fires, chattering and chatting and scooting away now and then as a bundled up housewife stopped by their stands to make a purchase. It

344

wasn't freezing, exactly, but the nip in the air promised that winter's snows would soon be upon us.

As I ducked into Mr. Fitch's grocery store, I bumped into a stocky man who was just emerging. I apologized and headed straight for the Franklin stove, the group of idlers giving way for me. The stocky man, I noticed, had not acknowledged the apology, but had paused and was looking back at Fitch in a most miserable fashion. Fitch was scowling over his ledger on the counter.

"All right, all right, Jeremy," Fitch called in a tone of disgust. "Come on back."

The men grouped around the stove suddenly found the hot ironwork extremely interesting. No one turned as the stocky man closed the door and came back to the counter. Fitch, grumbling to himself all the while, brought out a sack of flour, some sugar, some tea, and some oatmeal. Then, as an afterthought, he sliced off a big chunk of cheese and put it with the rest of the goods.

"It ain't decent, a man like me beggin'," the man said in a low, bitter voice.

"You ain't beggin'," Fitch said churlishly. He tapped his finger on the ledger. "You're going to pay me every farthing." He spied me and the harassed lines dropped from his mouth. "Why, it's Mr. Hascott . . . Go on, git, Jeremy. And don't go on starvin' them young 'uns any more." He was beaming as he came over to me. "I'm glad to see you again, Mr. Hascott. I've been dying to talk to someone with sense." He gave a contemptuous look at the men standing around the stove. "See them fellers, Mr. Hascott? Rebels, they'd be, if they were outside of Boston. This is Mr. Hascott, boys. A friend of mine. And he's got sense, too."

The men grinned and greeted me without animosity, showing they did not take Mr. Fitch too seriously.

"Come inside, Mr. Hascott. Amy has Mistress Crane settled by now, I imagine." He paused abruptly, turned back. "Sam, think you can find that feller who was in here a while ago? I'd like for Mr. Hascott to talk to him."

"Would he be interested?" Sam asked.

"Scoot, just fetch him. He ought to be in the tavern down the street." Mr. Fitch opened the door to the rear apartment

345

for me. "You'll be interested in that feller. Took me a while before I got wise to his game . . . Amy, here's Mr. Hascott."

Beulah and Amy had already become friends, that was evident. Beulah was in her older homespun dress, her arms white with flour, hard at making dried apple pies.

"Are you sure you can't stay for dinner, Mr. Hascott?" Amy opened the Dutch oven and a delicious aroma poured forth. "See what you're going to miss?"

"I'm devastated. My favorite pie, too. If Ethan weren't going to marry you, I'd be tempted myself."

"Oh, I didn't make them," Amy said quickly. "Beulah did. If you want someone who can make good pies, there she is."

Beulah sighed with mock resignation. "I'm afraid I'd be an old maid if I waited for him, Amy. He wants a lady."

"If a lady is one who can't make pie," I said dryly, "I deny the libel."

Amy craned her neck as her father went out to wait on a customer. "Beulah tells me she went to a theatre," she whispered.

I smiled. "It isn't as sinful as you may believe."

"Don't tell me!" Amy cried. "Let me think it's wicked, anyway, Beaulah's going to tell me all about New York."

"If she tells all," I assured her solemnly, "you'll know New York is a very wicked place."

"Must I tell all?" Beulah asked slyly.

I felt like a fool when Beulah laughed. I was blushing. I was glad enough when Fitch called me outside.

He met me at the door. "You let on you're in need of work. Fend him off after he makes his offer."

He winked and, slightly puzzled, I followed him out into the store to face a rather angular fellow with bright, serious eyes.

"You don't look as if you need employment, sir."

"I just lost my berth, mister. I was mate on a coastwise schooner. God knows when I get a berth again."

"Have you ever considered joining the Continental Army?"

"The Continental Army? Why, no. I thought the army had disbanded after the peace treaty was signed."

He looked at me sharply. "Then you must have been at sea ever since the war. The truth is, sir, Congress is raising a new levy for service on the frontier. The Indian menace is growing graver by the hour."

"Yes, I heard about it while I was in New York. The news in the papers there was that the British were stirring up the Indians against us. The Wabash and the Shawnees were said to be joining with the Six Nations in plans for attacking the frontiers."

The man turned quickly, triumphant. "There! You see? You all thought I was lying."

"I still think so," one of the men growled.

"But it's true, gentlemen. Fifteen hundred men from Kentucky, under General Clark of Virginia, have marched against Big Knife and the Wabash tribe. It's true, I tell you." He turned to me in desperation. "I can't convince these men. You, sir, have heard the news, haven't you?"

"From the newspapers," I answered cautiously.

"Well, no matter. If they won't believe, they won't believe. Would you be interested in service, sir? You will have your food, clothing and twenty shillings a month. Besides, you will get a bounty of twenty pounds for signing up."

"In Continental money?" I asked.

Everybody laughed and the agent flushed. "In cash, sir."

"I can't reply at once, mister. I need work, yes. But I haven't considered the army. Can I have time to consider?"

He nodded briefly. "If you decide to join, sir, you'll find me at Sun Tavern any time after eight. Good day, sir."

As soon as he was gone, Fitch turned to me. "Well, what did you make of it?"

I thought immediately of the agent who had tried to recruit whalers at the Two Palaverers, but this didn't seem like the same sort of scheme. I shook my head.

"He doesn't understand," Fitch announced.

"Be fair, Mr. Fitch," I protested. "I've been out of the state for the last month or so."

"That's right. I forgot. Well, Mr. Hascott, why do you suppose Congress is recruiting an army?"

"To fight Indians," I answered. "I know Massachusetts has just concluded a treaty with the Penobscots, and I heard that Georgia has signed a treaty with the Creeks. But the Kentucky reports are true. I'm certain of it."

"Do you believe Congress would recruit soldiers here in Massachusetts for service in the Ohio Territory?"

"Why not? Soldiers are hard to find these days."

Fitch threw up his hands. "Dammit, the answer's right under your nose." He wagged his finger in my face. "Them soldiers are being raised to put down the Regulators!"

My eyes widened. "Why, I never thought of that. It's possible, isn't it?"

"Possible? Dammit, it's true! General Knox is afraid the Regulators will seize the stores at Springfield."

I nodded slowly. "That may be. Shepard occupied the Springfield Arsenal after the court adjourned. I remember talk about seizing the stores. How many men is Congress raising?"

"Six hundred from Massachusetts," Fitch supplied. "But if that feller is telling the truth, Congress won't get fifty out of the whole state. He's pretty discouraged already and he's only started. You can guess how many he'll sign up outside Boston."

"None, if that story circulates. Not even our enemies would join up to put us down."

"Say, are you a Regulator?" Sam asked.

I couldn't deny it and was immediately swamped with questions about the court stopping affairs. One thing bothered me, though—Mr. Fitch's attitude.

"The last time I talked to you, Mr. Fitch, you were against us. What made you change your mind?"

"I don't know," he grumbled. Then quickly, "I'm not with you, mind. I'm neutral."

"How about you gentlemen?" I asked of the others. "Why haven't you organized to protest as we have in the country?"

Sam shrugged. "There ain't enough of us. The minute we tried anything, the militia'd be out. Even Fitch would turn out, and he's friendly to us."

"Yes, I would," Fitch affirmed. "I don't believe in letting anybody tear down the Government. Maybe the General Court ain't so fast, but in time everything will be all right."

This led us into an argument over the work of the special session, Mr. Fitch holding that enough had been done, the rest of us saying that nothing had been solved. Mr. Fitch was not very successful in his defense of the General Court and, as his views unfolded, it became all too clear that he was horribly confused.

And so the afternoon passed quickly. Six o'clock came all too soon, for—as you have probably noticed—I am endeared of a good hot argument, though I trust not merely for the sake of hearing the sound of my own voice. Regretfully, I had to take my leave. Before I did, however, I went in to see Beulah.

"I hope you won't have too dull a time of it, Beulah."

Beulah went on with setting the table. "You'll be staying at the Burdicks', won't you?"

"Well, I couldn't refuse. After all, Burdick has helped me a lot. And that business deal isn't completed yet, either."

"I know." She moved away a bit. "I suppose you'll be going to the Rout they're having tomorrow night."

"A Rout? I hadn't heard about it. But if they're having a party I don't suppose they'd put me out." I turned her around and lifted her chin with my forefinger. "Judith doesn't know you're in town. As soon as she does, she'll send you an invitation."

"It's all right, Warren. I really don't want to go. Honest. I have to get up early the next morning, you know."

She was a delightful little liar. The very fact that she mentioned it showed she would like to go. Whether she wanted to go, in the sense of having the courage, that was another matter.

"I'll call around in the morning," I promised.

349

Chapter 25

I DIDN'T see Judith until the next morning, and then only for a brief moment. The ladies had retired by the time Mr. Burdick and I got in, and they were still abed when we arose and came down to breakfast. We had to be at the inquest at nine and Mr. Burdick had to stop at his counting house first, so we had to get out early, which was lucky for us. Preparations were already under way for the Rout the Burdicks were holding that evening. In the afternoon, Burdick told me, Judith was having some friends in for tea. Thus, when I saw Judith, I knew my cues. Just as we were leaving, she came out on the upper landing. Her hair was down and she was wearing a frilly pink chintz dressing gown, a lovely picture.

"Warren!" she called. "Will you be back for dinner? I wish you would."

"I'm sorry. I'll be busy all day, Judith. I'll see you this evening. Save the first dance for me."

"No." Judith pouted. "Not unless you come back this afternoon. I want to show the girls a real live Regulator."

Burdick grinned and opened the door. "This way to the exit, my boy. Better not count on him, Judith."

She crinkled her nose. "Jothan gets the first dance."

But not even that threat could tempt me to set foot in a house filled with chattering females. As for the dancing, perhaps I'd be better off not attempting to show my skill, for it had been many many years since I set foot on a ballroom floor.

I shall not detail the proceedings at the inquest. It was a tedious affair, enlivened only by the crowd that had come to drool over the testimony. As we suspected, the coroner was angry when he learned Joe had been allowed to sail, but nothing could be done about it. After Burdick and I and the constables had testified, the Jury retired and deliberated. They brought in the verdict that Spencer had been shot and killed by one Kimble, whereabouts unknown. It took them almost three hours to bring the proceedings to that brilliant conclusion.

Mr. Burdick and I dined at the Golden Bull on Merchant's Row, which proved to be a bad choice, for we were constantly interrupted by gentlemen who had done business with Spencer and wanted information about his financial status. No one had definite information, but it seemed fairly certain that Spencer had died a bankrupt. I fell into a sweat every time I thought of what my position would be had Kimble killed Spencer prematurely.

It was after two o'clock before I managed to break away and go over to the Fitch's to see Beulah. I planned to spend the afternoon with her, either showing her Boston or taking her across the new Charlestown Bridge to visit the Bunker Hill battlegrounds. I was surprised to find that Beulah was not in. Amy was a little excited when she told me about it.

"She went over to the Burdicks' for tea. They sent a coach for her. Beulah didn't want to go at first . . . the silly."

"Well, I suppose she thought she wouldn't fit in."

"Why not?" Amy flared. "Beulah's just as much of a lady as any of those rich snips." She giggled. "She didn't even change her dress. She went in that brown homespun."

I smiled. "Homespun or not, that's a handsome dress."

"Yes, isn't it marvelous? I wish my mother could sew like that." Her smile faded and her blue eyes grew very round. "Will you be at the Burdicks' rout tonight?"

"Uh huh, and I'll try to get Beulah to come, too."

Amy pouted. "You know, Ethan's going. He has to escort Abigail Overton. She's awfully rich, I hear . . . her folks, I mean. Mr. Blair wants Ethan to marry her."

I laughed. "I wouldn't let that worry you, Amy. I'm sure Ethan will have a miserable time."

Amy gave me a grateful smile.

I hung around the store for an hour or so, talking to Fitch, then left to do some necessary shopping. I had to get a few items to fill out my attire for this evening. I couldn't have clothes made to order on such short notice, nor was I particularly anxious to do so, for it would be squandering money on finery I'd use infrequently, if at all, after tonight. So, I prowled through the used clothing shops, of which there were many in that section of town, searching for suitable pieces at reasonable prices.

The stores around Dock Square and along Ann Street were not to my taste, for they catered mostly to the seafaring trade. Up on Hanover Street, I picked up a pair of light tan breeches and a waistcoat to match, both in good condition, for twenty-two shillings. At another place on Queen Street, I got a good silk shirt with ruffs down the front for ten shillings. I haggled quite a while with the old man before I snared a set of knee and shoe buckles of paste for eight and a half shillings. I had a clean lace neckcloth with me and I would wear my plum colored broadcloth coat, so I felt sure I wouldn't be conspicuously ill dressed at the Rout. Thus, around five o'clock, I bore my loot back to the Burdicks'.

Polly opened the door for me and I tried to get across the hall unobserved, for the giggling and chattering told me the tea party was not yet over. But I couldn't resist the temptation to peek in and see how Beulah was enjoying herself. And I was caught. Judith spied me and called me in. I made motions to indicate I wanted to go up and change clothes, but she wouldn't hear of it. She came out and got me. With some misgivings, I gave my packages to Polly and asked her to take them up to my room.

Judith shook my arm with amusement. "Don't look so frightened, Warren. They don't bite. They scratch sometimes, but bite . . . never."

"I've heard of men dying from scratch wounds," I said ruefully. "So, if I perish, you know I have sacrificed myself on the altar of my devotion."

Judith laughed. "What a lovely thought."

There were about fifteen girls, all grouped around the big secretary in the far corner. The moment they saw me, they broke away and engulfed me. Judith introduced me around, but I got only a few of the names. There was Mistress Delia Graham, a niece to the Graham I knew and disliked. She was a mousy little thing with shining black eyes, a rather sullen sort. Then there was a Mistress Bassett, a brassy blond, rather big in the hips and thin in the mouth and nose; a Mistress Susan Locke, quite attractive, despite her large nose and big, toothy smile. Mistress Abigail Overton interested me, for she was the one Ethan was supposed to be escorting to the Rout tonight. She was a sultry, sloe eyed girl with olive skin and a soft, well rounded figure calculated to make a male's fingers itch. She was a little too loud, however. I searched everywhere for Beulah, but it was quite evident that she had already abandoned the party.

The murder of Spencer was common gossip by now and everyone wanted me to give all the gory details. I tried my best, but it was hopeless to keep up with the rattle of questions. When someone mentioned that I was a Regulator, the conversation veered sharply. The comments led me to believe these girls thought the Regulators were either 1.) thrilling adventurers, or 2.) misguided knights, or 3.) just plain damn fools.

"Should we get him to sign?" the Overton girl asked.

Mistress Locke, she of the big teeth, fingered the cloth of my lapel. "Imported, I'd say, wouldn't you, Beatrix?"

"Undoubtedly," the blond Bassett answered. "Make him sign the pledge."

I was puzzled. "Have I stepped into a temperance meeting?"

The shrieks that greeted that remark told me that I was wrong. My nose confirmed it. Some of these girls—that Overton lass particularly—hadn't been drinking tea exclusively.

Judith smiled. "This was no useless tea party, Warren. We've met to form a Non-importation Committee."

"Show him our circular letter, Judith," the Locke girl suggested.

"Don't tell me you're worrying about the state of public affairs," I said in mock horror.

Judith's brows went up. "And why shouldn't we? We live in the Commonwealth, don't we? And live very well, thank you. We'd like to continue living that way without civil war to upset our nice, pleasant existence."

"If you'll pardon an ignorant male," I said with a slight bow, "just what do you think you can do?"

One of the girls pushed a paper into Judith's hand and she passed it on to me.

"This is the pledge we're taking. We're sending letters all over the state to enlist the support for our movement."

The circular letter held, in effect, that the women of Boston were conscious of the calamities which have descended upon our state and were sensible that many of them were occasioned by luxury and extravagances. Thus, they were pledging themselves to retrench all unnecessary expenses while the men sought a solution for the problems besetting the country.

Accordingly, they promised the following: First, they would not, for the space of one year, buy any gauzes, ribbons, laces, silks, muslins and chintzes, except for weddings and mournings. Second, they would dress plainly, encourage industry, frugality and neatness, giving due preference to manufactures of their own country. Third, when they made visits and entertainments, they would avoid all unnecessary expenses, especially in foreign articles. Fourth, during this year, they would try to form more systematic and extensive methods of domestic economy.

I clucked my tongue. "Ladies, my condolences. I'm sure these sacrifices will be hard to bear."

"He thinks it's a joke," Betsy Bassett said with a sniff. "What can you expect from a. . . ."

"That will do, Betsy," Judith broke in. "This is not a joke, Warren. Sixty members of the Legislature, including Judge Ward, have signed a similar pledge to refrain from extravagances, the use of foreign luxuries and promotion of our own manufactures."

"Over a hundred of the First families of Connecticut have signed similar pledges," Delia Graham added, her tone a bit sharp and belligerent.

I smiled wryly. "I'm sure only the first families could afford to, Mistress Graham."

"Don't mock us, Warren," Judith said. "We're serious. Haven't you noticed anything about us?"

I stepped back and eyed them critically. "You're all very charming. Yes, very charming."

There were shrieks of laughter and howls of "Flatterer."

Judith was annoyed. "Look harder. Our dresses."

I lifted my hands, laughing. "Please. I'm only a poor, unobservant male."

"We're all wearing homespun," Judith said firmly.

I looked closer and my smile faded slowly. Brown and dark

354

blue predominated among those dresses, though there was one of scarlet and another of a lovely light blue. After some thought, I decided Judith was indeed telling the truth. These girls were really wearing homespun. But the dresses were cut and sewed as few were made in the country districts—with the possible exception of Beulah's. Then, I spied a silk collar on one of the dresses. Judith, too, had a blue silk ribbon about her waist.

I fingered the bow. "Excellent homespun."

"Excellent," Judith echoed evenly. "I'd have you know, Mr. Hascott, that this piece of silk was grown, spun and woven right here in the Commonwealth of Massachusetts."

My jaw dropped. "No!"

"It's true, Mr. Hascott," the Locke girl put in. "My father bought it from the man who made it. He's interested in helping the man establish a silk industry here."

I was properly squelched. "My apologies, ladies." I frowned at the circular letter for a moment. "This may not be such a bad idea, after all. Out where I live, the people complain a lot about the extravagances of the people of Boston. If you truly lived up to those four points, you'd do much to help the situation. If nothing else, you'd lessen resentment and envy and deprive some of the more violent orators of their best ammunition."

"We'll live up to the pledge," Judith promised.

I returned the paper to her. "If you'll excuse me now, I'll leave you to your work. It's getting late."

The Bassett girl started. "Mercy, it's after five! I have to get home and dress."

The other girls took up the cry and there was a rush for hats and coats. The girls swept past Judith and me, leaving us alone for a moment.

"I heard you had Beulah over," I ventured.

Judith nodded soberly. "She left early. She . . . she was a little angry." She snorted. "That Bassett wench! I could have choked her. She started bragging about her family . . . a long line of distinguished jurists and rulers," she mimicked. "Beulah took it very well until Bassett made some remark about how amusing it was that these farmers should try to tell their betters how the country should be run."

I winced. "What did Beulah say—or do?"

355

Judith crinkled her nose. "What would you suppose she'd say? She told them if this was the way our distinguished families ruled us, it was about time honest men took over. That started it. Some of the girls ganged up on her. I tried to stop it but I was helpless. Beulah finally got up and walked out."

"Well, as long as she didn't start any hair pulling."

"I assure you I would have helped her." Judith frowned. "Some of the girls are insufferable when they get on the subject of how inferior other people are. I only have them here—that Bassett woman, for instance—because of Papa. He's a businessman, you know. We have to be practical, too."

"I think I'd better go over there and—"

"No, don't," Judith broke in. "She'll be here tonight. I made her promise. I've asked Jothan to bring her. He dropped in a little while ago. That ought to be a nice slap in the face for Betsy. She's been after him for years."

"Well, if you think it's all right. . . ."

"Yes, I think she understood my position. She'll be here tonight, if I judged her rightly. And I'll take care of her, if she can't take care of herself, don't you worry about that."

Judith gave me a broad wink and went out to speed her guests on their way. As I crossed the hall, Polly intercepted me.

"Mr. Burdick is home, sir. He's in there." She pointed to the library door. "He said he'd like to see you."

Mr. Burdick, his short legs stretched out, was sitting in an easy chair, sipping a glass of Madeira. He grinned and lifted his plump hand as I closed the door on the shrill gabbling.

"Seems we're marooned, eh, Warren?"

"Only for a few minutes, sir. They're all going."

Burdick sighed. "I'm marooned, anyway. My wife is upstairs with the seamstress and hairdresser." He took a paper from his pocket and handed it to me. "Here's an accounting of your transaction, Warren. A tidy profit, there, very tidy."

Tidy was the word for it, all right. After deducting the freight charges and Mr. Burdick's ten percent, the total due me was one thousand and seventy-six pounds. Of that, I had to pay out five hundred and ten pounds to my father and neighbors, leaving me a net profit of five hundred and sixty-six pounds. Not bad for a deal swung without the investment of a farthing of my own.

"You'll have to wait a while to collect the full amount, Warren. But I'll advance you any part you wish."

"Thank you. I'd appreciate about twenty-five pounds cash for pocket money. And if you can, I'd like to have about five hundred and twenty-five transferred to Gerson in Northampton. I have to pay off the notes I gave to my father and my uncle and the rest. I imagine they'll want to pay their taxes and other debts." I folded the paper and put it in my pocket. "You may not believe it, but I'm happier that I can give them the money than I am to have such a big profit for myself. I was worried, taking their crops."

"I daresay much of the crops would have rotted in the fields if you hadn't taken them off their hands." Mr. Burdick shook his head. "I thought the amount of God's good produce that rotted last year was enormous. This year the amount will be even greater. Not half of the normal amount has moved to market."

"I heard the Hessian bug destroyed a lot of wheat in Connecticut and New York this fall. And rains in Pennsylvania cut down their wheat harvests."

"I know, but it didn't open much of a market there. They had excellent crops of Indian corn. Instead of living on wheat, the people will eat corn bread this winter. Markets all over are dull except in the West Indies. And we don't dare send our ships down there. But mark me, Warren, I have a feeling the British will come to terms by next year. The English ministry is just begging for a famine in those colonies." Burdick closed his fist. "Then we'll squeeze them, never fear."

"That doesn't help the present situation much," I remarked. "It seems strange that the Legislature doesn't do something. If they don't want to use our suggestions, why don't they use their own ideas in trying to solve our problems? Or maybe they have none."

"Oh, there are plenty of constructive ideas on the other side," Burdick assured me. "The papers are full of articles on methods of redressing grievances. If you care to, sometime, take a look, especially at the articles written by 'Democratus'. He's put forth a sound, sensible plan for cheapening and quick-

357

ening the processes of law suits. He had an analysis of our financial troubles and suggested remedies for our confused fiscal policies. He had another article on paper money—a proposal to start a state bank like the Bank of England, issuing paper money backed by gold and redeemable at par. He even urged the adoption of a bankruptcy act. Yes, my boy, there are sound, constructive ideas in circulation."

"Then why in Heaven's name doesn't the Legislature put some of them into effect?"

Polly knocked and came in and informed us we would have to take our supper here, for the tradesmen were already arriving and the buffet was being set up in the dining room. That was no hardship. We were glad enough to be out of the way, secure in our den while the tradesmen tramped up and down the stairs to the large ballroom on the top floor. As I could understand it, there were to be two buffets, one up in the ballroom where there was to be dancing and another downstairs for the older folks who would want to sit and talk or play cards.

Eight o'clock came all too soon for me. I could hear coaches drawing up to the door and shrill laughter and chattering and the rustle of silks passing my door. I dressed deliberately, lingering, feeling a bit nervous, for many important personages would be on hand and I wanted to make a good appearance. Bracing myself, I blew out all except one of the candles and ventured out into the hall.

As luck would have it, I reached the stairway at the same moment as my friends, Mr. and Mrs. Ormond B. Graham. Mrs. Graham gave me a stiff, absent nod as she went by. She paused at the stair rail and turned back, her nose lifting slightly.

"Why . . . why, it's the farmer boy."

I bowed politely. "Your provisioner, M'am."

Someone in back of me snickered and she glared over my shoulder. With a slight snort she continued up the stairs.

"We do meet such a variety of people, don't we, Mister Graham?" her voice floated back.

Mr. Graham gave me a cool stare. "Good evening, sir."

I couldn't help but chuckle. This evening had started well. The ballroom was magnificent. It was every bit as big as the assembly hall at Col. Murray's Tavern in Northampton. There the resemblance ended. The ceiling was covered to form an arch overhead. The plaster was painted blue and studded with small silver stars to resemble the heavens. The walls were painted—no, again I was fooled. They were covered with rich imported wall paper, on which were depicted soft, moonlit landscapes. Four brilliant crystal chandeliers sent a shower of sparkling light over the dark, polished mahogany floor.

Down at the far end of the room were the musicians, seated on a small dais, flanked with huge tables loaded down with all sorts of delicacies, cold meats, pickled fishes, cold creamed lobsters, jellied sausages, brandied preserves, tarts and blanc manges and every variety of small cakes and confections. On each table was a big silver punchbowl and a vast assortment of liquors. Truly, it must have cost a small fortune to set those tables.

Someone accidentally jostled me, and I moved on to where my host and hostess were receiving. Mrs. Burdick was quite cordial, amused and pleased by my evident awe. I felt no less awed as I moved into the crowd. On every hand were silks, velvets, damasks, cloths of every hue in the rainbow, not to mention the jewels and gold ornaments on the men as well as the women. If ever evidence was needed to convince me the farmers' complaints about lavish luxury had foundation, here was the place to come.

My awkward feeling eased away as I was greeted on every hand by friends and acquaintances I had made. Mr. and Mrs. Lang, Mr. and Mrs. Trowbridge, Mr. and Mrs. Goulding—I was introduced to the latter—all greeted me warmly. General Ward and his lady remembered me, though General Ward was a bit cool, for he had heard of my participation in the affairs of the Regulators.

"You'll be interested in meeting this gentleman, Mr. Hascott . . . General Lincoln, may I present a young friend of Mr. Burdick's, Mr. Hascott. I suspect he's a Regulator."

General Lincoln chuckled as he shook my hand. "An odd place to find a Regulator, I must say, Mr. Hascott."

General Lincoln listened with amusement as General Ward

told his experience in Worcester. He was a rather short man, roundish, his face moonlike and his forehead given the illusion of broadness by his receding hairline. His hair was long in the back, a silky brown. He certainly was an unmilitary looking sort to be the Commander-in-Chief of the Commonwealth's Militia Forces.

"You'd better be careful, Mr. Hascott," he warned in a half serious tone. "If you don't behave out in the country districts, I may have to come out there and teach you respect for the Government."

I smiled. "We've had fair warning, General. Thank you."

Passing on, I was soon absorbed into the younger crowd. Miss Betsy Bassett, whose blond locks were now covered with a white wig, introduced me to her escort. I didn't catch his name, but he looked foppish. That Bassett woman fascinated me. She had generous hips to begin with, so her pads made her seem as if she was wearing a balloon from the waist down.

A small hand slid under my elbow and I turned to find Judith at my side. Then, as I saw her escort, my brows went way up.

"Mr. Salderman! I thought . . ."

"She spurned me, Mr. Hascott," he said with mock dolor.

"Oh . . . so, she wouldn't come."

"Oh, yes, she insisted she was coming. She said she had found another escort." He sighed. "I must be getting old."

I was a little puzzled until I remembered that Mr. Blair, the elder, was invited and was due alone. I supposed she'd feel more at ease with him as her escort.

The voices grew shriller and I saw that Miss Abigail Overton had arrived. The young gentleman at her side also had slanted eyes, so I gathered he was her brother. She spied me and, with a small squeal, disengaged herself from her brother and took possession of me.

"The punchbowl is that way, Lud," she said, pointing. "Mr. Hascott will take care of me, won't you, Mr. Hascott?"

Salderman winked. "Think twice, Mr. Hascott. Then put a ring in her nose for safety."

A chord from the music broke it up. The babbling died down and the maestro announced that dancing would begin. There was applause and a general shuffling of the crowd, the elders moving out to the sides, the younger people moving onto the dancing space which opened up. I was panicky as Abigail Overton moved me out to take a place on the forming lines. The first dance was to be properly staid, a minuet, and the steps whirled through my mind as I tried to remember them. I had learned many, many years ago, but the memory was all but obliterated. I hung back a little.

"I'm afraid you'll have to excuse me, Miss Overton. I— I've been out of the country so long, I don't remember . . ."

"Tush. It's simple, really. It will all come back to you. Just follow along."

I was sweating under the collar, desperately looking about for some young man to whom I could turn her over. But no one I knew was in sight. All the young gentlemen I had met were on the floor with partners. If you have ever been in a comparable position, you know my agonies at that moment. I kept mumbling apologies for what I knew was coming, and feeling very foolish.

Judith was at the head of the line, looking very lovely and radiant. She crinkled her nose at me and nodded to her partner, Jothan Salderman. I was tickled to death not to be her partner, for most attention was naturally on her.

The slow, stately music began and I felt myself moving. My feet were big as bowsprits and twice as hard to maneuver. The notes kept pounding through my head . . . By Gosh, it wasn't so bad, after all. Anyway, my courtly bows were as good as any gentleman's to the right or left of me. I was going along fine until I caught a comment from the sidelines.

". . . but of course he's a farmer."

And I tripped and almost fell flat on my face. I went flaming red and only by vast will power did I keep my mind on my steps. The comment had come from the Graham woman. I could have choked her without putting on white gloves.

At long, long last, the music stopped—with me one step still to go. I applauded a bit too hard, too. Then I noticed Betsy Bassett was next to us. She was whispering and giggling to her escort, Gail's brother. Gail Overton herself didn't seem too displeased. She smiled and patted my arm.

"I expected much worse, Mr. Hascott," she said, loud enough for the Bassett woman to overhear. "For one who's been imprisoned in Algiers for seven years, you're a remarkable dancer."

Which was rather a hind side compliment, but acceptable none the less. "Would you care to stay the next one out? I feel the need of refreshments."

"The one after is a quadrille," Abigail said tentatively.

I grinned. "Say no more, I'm on firmer ground there."

I got a cup of punch for my partner and one for myself and we stood there chatting until the next dance should start. Abigail Overton had her faults, perhaps, but she wasn't so bad. And that red, kissable mouth of hers was very intriguing.

A stir suddenly went through the ballroom and the drone of conversation slowly receded, like the gradual shutting off of a gurgling waterfall. The sound trickled away and died. The scruff of feet and an occasional cough rose to fill in the long hush. All the women about me were craning their necks to see who had just come in. Then, with sinking heart, I caught sight of Ethan. I couldn't see all of the girl he had brought, but I knew.

The woman who was blocking my line of vision bent her head to whisper to her husband. I got the shock of my life. Beulah was a mess.

She was wearing a white wig, ornately curled, not much higher than some of the wigs in the room. But she had forgotten to tuck in her brown hair at the back. Her face was a horror, thickly covered with pomantum, giving her the appearance of having dipped herself into a flour barrel. Her cheeks and lips were hideously reddened with carmine. She wore large brass earrings that jangled when she moved. A big paste broach flashed from her bosom, which was bared and uplifted to show an indecent expanse of flesh. Her smile was hard and fixed, but she showed no sign of being aware of the outraged whispers and scowls of disapproval.

Ethan was very red, his face set in sullen defiance as he presented Beulah to Mr. and Mrs. Burdick. Mr. Burdick greeted her politely, albeit bewilderedly. Mrs. Burdick looked as if ready to curl up and die and she glanced from side to side in desperate appeal for help. A mechanical smile broke her stiff face and she bowed slightly as Ethan introduced Beulah. As the two moved off, she said something sharply to Mr. Burdick. But Burdick only shrugged. Mrs. Burdick was furious.

"She looks like a whore, painted that way, doesn't she?" Abigail commented in an amused drawl.

The tittering about me brought an angry flush to my face. "Before I made a remark like that," I said as evenly as I could, "I'd look at my own face in a glass, Miss Overton."

Abigail Overton gasped and turned to her brother. Lud Overton just chuckled. He ran his fingers across his sister's cheek and stared at the white stuff he had removed. Abigail burned. From the corner of my eye I caught her trying to pull up her gown a bit more.

Beulah and Ethan were headed this way, and I excused myself to hurry to her side. Despite her horrible getup, she was a strikingly handsome woman and I thought if I could only get her downstairs for a few minutes and get some of that stuff off, the situation could yet be saved. But I never reached her.

Ethan was suddenly finding himself very popular. From all parts of the ballroom, men were swarming over to be introduced—the younger, unmarried men, mostly, but some of the older bachelors, too. Many of the staid, married men would have gone to her, but their grim wives forbade it. Even Salderman was attracted, leaving Judith's side to push in and gain Beulah's left. She was like a queen bee, sought after by a swarm of drones.

Jothan Salderman had taken over completely. Beulah was laughing and chatting gayly, so absorbed in him that she was oblivious to the mounting chatter of furious tongues. A few of the elders were shocked to the point of leaving the party. Mrs. Burdick tried desperately to keep them, then cornered Judith and, by her motions, I could see she was begging Judith to do something. Judith just shook her head and walked away.

By the time they reached the musicians, Ethan had disappeared and left Beulah entirely to Salderman. Half a dozen young men were begging her for the next dance. Salderman fended them all off. He spoke to the musicians and they struck a chord. The crush eased off a little and the director stood forward.

"The Quadrille, Ladies and Gentlemen. Choose your partners."

Dead silence. Slowly, the younger men backed off and sought out their partners. On every hand, the young women shook their heads firmly. Salderman and Beulah stood facing each other at the head of the line. But no line formed I glanced about quickly for someone I knew, but found no one. Abigail Overton was gone. Then I spied Judith and started toward her. Judith, at least, would have the decency to help me back Beulah up. But before I could get to her, the fiddles broke forth in a loud chord. The swinging, feet tapping rhythm of the quadrille sawed out.

Salderman and Beulah executed the first set without difficulty, Beulah never missing a step. She did the brisk, hopping steps with as much gaiety as if the floor was filled. Neither of them were a bit fazed at the order to change partners. They merely swung about swiftly, stepped around and faced each other from the opposite sides and went the various convolutions, the turnings and sidesteppings and bowing without the least difficulty. It was astonishing. And, more, they looked as if they were thoroughly enjoying themselves.

I laughed aloud as the moment came for the men to make a bridge. Salderman blithely put up his arms and Beulah ducked low and went under, in perfect time to the music. She scurried back and held up her arms and Salderman solemnly ducked and went under. Then as he straightened, he caught her hand and swung her around, without missing a beat. A titter went through the crowd and a small burst of applause, which was quickly squelched by the ladies. Poor Beulah was taking quite a tongue lashing. But she didn't care. Her eyes were shining and her head was thrown back and she was enjoying every minute of the rather strenuous dance. Salderman was the perfect gentleman. He was oblivious to all but his partner.

The music gave a quick bump bump and stopped. The two bowed solemnly to each other, then laughed and hooked arms. One or two of the gentlemen, already in their cups, cheered lustily until sharply hushed. Beulah and Salderman headed for the refreshments. Again and again, people deliberately turned their backs to them. Neither noticed, absorbed in their own conversation. Then, I saw they were going to the wrong

364

table, for Mrs. Graham, like a stern and righteous pouter pigeon, stood directly in their path, as if waiting for them.

Before I could get to them, they had been stopped. A group of the younger set swiftly gathered around and blocked their way to the refreshments and noisily complimented Beulah on her dancing. They were too effusive, too generous in their praise. They were like calculating vultures, sharpening their claws in pleasurable anticipation of tearing her to shreds.

She spied me and waved ostentatiously. "Warren! I've been looking all over for you!" Her eyes held mine only for a moment, then, with a delighted start, she saw Judith. "Oh, Judith, darling, it's such a wonderful party, simply wonderful."

Judith smiled. "I'm glad you're enjoying yourself, darling. I believe you know the girls. . . . This is Mr. Halsey, Mr. Pierce, Mr. Overton, Mr. Winton. . . ."

Beulah gave Judith a quick glance, then inclined her head in acknowledgment. The gigglings faded and the smiles became fixed and malicious. Then, with a sudden sinking sensation, I realized Beulah had committed the crowning sin. She positively stank of perfume.

Betsy Bassett was sniffing pointedly. "My, what an unusual scent. Did you have it made up special?"

"Oh, yes," Beulah replied eagerly. "I got it at Mrs. Greely's —the place you said you bought yours. She assured me it was the same as yours." She sniffed loudly. "Awful, isn't it. But it's necessary in the city, isn't it? At home, we bathe once in a while."

Betsy Bassett flushed angrily and I thought for a moment she was going to slap Beulah's face. I couldn't help smiling. Beulah was right. I hadn't been close enough to her before, but I was now aware the hippy Miss Bassett did have a strong body odor.

Beulah was conscious, from the snickering, that she had said something wrong and she glanced about bewilderedly. The moment was saved by the arrival of Harry, bearing a huge tray of cups with punch and crystal mugs of stronger liquors. The men handed cups to the ladies and took mugs for themselves. Beulah reached for a mug and Salderman slapped her wrist playfully.

"You musn't, Beulah. It's not for little girls."

"I don't see why not," she said pettishly. "If Abigail can drink gin, why can't I?"

Abigail Overton gasped and almost fainted from chagrin. The other girls almost choked with the effort of holding in their derisive laughter. So, it was gin I had smelled on her this afternoon. Only Lud, her brother, had the indecency to guffaw outright. He whisked a glass from the tray and with an elaborate bow handed it to Beulah.

"The other is punch, Miss Crane," he said slyly. "The only difference is you have to drink more to get the same effect."

"Oh, no, thank you just the same. I see I made a mistake. Ladies don't drink gin . . . in public."

A snort came from the edge of the crowd. Beulah glanced about slowly, a hurt look crossing her face as she saw Mrs. Graham glaring at her.

"Ethan!" she called.

"Right here!" Ethan replied, coming into the circle.

"Ethan," she said in a meek tone, "I don't believe I met that lady." She pointed to Mrs. Graham.

Ethan cleared his throat and in a bold, loud voice, "Miss Crane, may I present Mrs. Ormond B. Graham."

Mrs. Graham stiffened, shocked. Her voice was low and harsh, "Young man, have you forgotten your manners?"

"Why, no," Ethan replied slowly. Then he pushed his fists deep into his pockets. "No, I don't believe I have."

Mrs. Graham looked as if she'd make an issue of it. But the situation was bad enough without highlighting this almost unforgivable breach of etiquette. An inferior must never be presented to a superior, always the other way around. I caught Judith's eyelids drooping very slowly, very thoughtfully. My reaction was just the opposite. My eyes widened.

"Graham," Beulah murmured. "Why, of course, you must be Delia's grandmother. Oh, my pardon, her mother."

"Her aunt," Mrs. Graham corrected grimly.

"Oh, then you must be a Pyne. Delia told me so much about your side of the family, Mrs. Graham. The Pynes were one of the first families in America, weren't they, Mrs. Graham?"

Mrs. Graham softened a bit. "Since 1650."

"Yes, I know. I'm so interested in those things. I asked about your distinguished forebears, the three Tories now in

Halifax. But you must be from one of the other branches. Was it the Acton branch—farmers?"

"Certainly not," Mrs. Graham replied indignantly.

"The Boston branch—tailors?"

Mrs. Graham went pale. "My father was a merchant."

With a long, haughty look, she turned and stalked off, oozing dignity.

"Well, it could be true," Betsy Bassett said softly. "I heard they never had anything until the war. I'll wager she knows the inside of a kitchen."

"That's not so!" Delia Graham flared. "The Pynes were always of the gentry." She humphed. "You should talk. Your uncle's in jail for debt right this minute."

Betsy Bassett lashed out. The slap left vivid red fingermarks on Delia Graham's white cheek. Delia swore in a most unladylike fashion, snatched Betsy's wig off and trampled on it.

The two rushed at each other, tooth and claw, shrieking and yelling and tearing at each other's clothes. Several gentlemen called for them to desist and tried to pry them apart. They got scratched for their pains. A few of the men, like fools, cheered them on. Horrified elders came running from all parts of the ballroom. This time, Mrs. Burdick did faint.

The battle was brief, but exciting. I watched with a curious detached amusement. Judith didn't lift a finger to stop it. Finally, the two were pulled apart, screaming and swearing at each other. I learned two new words. Betsy Bassett learned never to fight in a tight evening gown. One of her breasts had popped loose. She ran shrieking for the stairs.

The ballroom quickly quieted and the curious broke up into small, whispering groups. Many of the guests were chuckling, some were indignant, all were condemning the unmannerly conduct of the two ladies. One elderly dowager snorted that they were no better than Beulah, with which I could heartily agree.

Beulah was yawning. "I'm afraid I must go."

Judith smiled slowly. "Nonsense. The evening has just begun. You won't want to miss the rest of the fun."

Beulah stood very still for a moment, a puzzled look in her eyes. "No, I guess I've had my fun." She took off her wig and shook out her brown hair. "Showing them up was easier than I thought. I guess I gave them credit for more brains than they have."

Judith nodded. "For all the good it will do. The Grahams will always be the Grahams. You're sure you won't stay?"

Beulah shook her head slowly. "No, I must go. I have to be up early tomorrow morning. Thank you just the same."

"As you wish." Judith glanced at me. "Warren, you see her home. Ethan, you'd better talk to your father before he erupts."

I saw Blair standing over by the musicians, his wrinkled face red. He looked ready to explode. I determined to talk to him, too, when I got back. We stopped by to say goodnight to Mrs. Burdick, who was now recovered. Beulah was a bit timid.

"I—I hope you don't think too badly of me, Mrs. Burdick. I know I was rude. But I didn't mean to upset things."

Mrs. Burdick managed a frosty smile. "Judith told me what happened this afternoon. We understand."

Beulah took it very well. She curtsied to Mr. Burdick and I followed her downstairs. She held herself together until we were outside. She tried not to show me, but as we walked down the street I could see she was weeping very softly.

Chapter 26

THE ground was quaking under our feet and yet we laughed and danced and drank far into the night. I should have known something serious was afoot when both General Lincoln and General Ward left early. Mr. Blair hinted to me that soon I would be called upon to act for my cause and my country. The Concord court had met that day. The news from there was neither good nor bad. But the situation was desperately dangerous. The court had opened. No militia was on hand. No Regulators had made an appearance. Yet both were mobilizing. The fuse was sizzling. Still, we laughed and danced and drank far into the night.

Beulah didn't go home that Wednesday, the 28th of November. She decided to go to Attleboro, justifying herself by saying it would be better if I arrived home first and she brought positive proof of having actually been to her grandfather's. I tried to argue her out of it. I thought she feared that the news of her having been at the Burdick's party would get back and I told her she could explain by saying she had accidentally met Judith while in Boston, a credible enough coincidence. I could see that she didn't give a hoot what people would say, a feeling she'd get over quickly enough once she got home. But right now her mind was on the 4th of December. She was determined to be in Worcester that day, the day the court was due to sit. That situation might prove even more touchy than the one at Concord.

But I had hardly given these matters a thought until I started out to see Beulah on her way. I didn't have to rise so early, for the Providence coach, which passed through Attleboro, didn't leave until seven-thirty. Even then I was still sleepy when I arrived at Pease's Tavern on Common Street. Beulah was in the taproom, seated at a table with Amy, chatting over cups of coffee. Amy rose as she saw me coming over.

"Well, I must be going, Beulah," she said quickly. "Good morning, Mr. Bassett."

" 'Morning, Amy. You don't have to run away just because I'm here, do you?"

"Well, no . . ." She laughed. "I mean, I must hurry along. I expect Mama home this morning and I have a million things to do. Goodby, Beulah. Have a good trip." The two girls kissed. "And do stay with us if you're ever in Boston again. You can always be sure you're welcome at our house."

"Thank you, Amy. You've been good to me. I hope I'll be able to repay your kindness some day."

Amy hushed her and said goodby to me and left.

I seated myself and called for a cup of tea. "How long do you expect to be down at Grandpa Crane's?"

"A few days," Beulah said. "I'll be back maybe Saturday. I'll take the morning coach home Monday."

I nodded. "You'd better not stay over at Worcester for the court, Beulah. Blair tells me the Governor may adjourn it."

"What was the news from Concord?" Beulah asked quickly.

"Something's afoot, that's sure. But Blair didn't know. Nothing happened there yesterday. The court opened without any trouble. I'm going to see him this morning." I lifted my finger. "You're not missing the coach on that account."

"All right." She made aimless circles on the table. "Was it very bad when you got back last night?"

"There was some gossip, of course," I replied frankly. "But it wasn't so bad. The elders were more outraged by that squabble between the girls. Not many knew you started it. But you shouldn't have done it, Beulah. It wasn't nice."

"I know. It was just . . . well, I got so mad at those snobs. Just because their fathers have a little money they think they're better than everyone else."

I smiled. "You'll find that kind everywhere, Beulah. Just think of Lucella Morse back home. Just because her father has four more pigs than anyone else, she thinks she's just it."

"I know, but sometimes it's infuriating, just the same."

The coach driver stomped into the taproom. "Everybody for the Providence stage, outside. Time to start soon."

I picked up Beulah's box and gave it to the servingman who carried it outside. Beulah held my arm tight as we walked out to the coach. Several gentlemen passed us and got in, staring back at Beulah with upraised brows.

"Will you still be here Saturday?" Beulah asked.

"Why, I don't think so. What makes you ask?"

"Well, I was just thinking. . . ." She smiled slyly and brushed a speck of lint from my collar. "I don't believe I ought to impose on Amy over the weekend. I noticed a little inn up on Hanover Street—the 'Good Woman'. I thought I'd stop there."

Her eyes held mine for a long moment.

I grinned. "I'll inquire for you there."

Beulah waved as the coach door slammed. I was impatient for it to come back Saturday.

The corridors of State House were tense. I could feel the air of subdued excitement the moment I entered. The clerks were not working, but whispering among themselves. They jumped up and glanced sharply at me as I passed by. Upstairs, at the head of the circular stairs, was a knot of buzzing gentlemen. Among them was my friend Mr. Graham. He gave me a long suspicious glance, a jerky nod, then resumed his conversation. I noticed he was watching me furtively as I went into the office by the House chambers.

Mr. Blair was standing by the window, glowering at nothing, his wig more askew than usual. He started as I entered, turned and stared at me thoughtfully. He looked sleepy and grouchy and troubled.

"Hell's ready to break loose," he whispered sharply. He craned around the corner of the door, then added softly, "The Regulators have marched."

"And the militia. . . .?"

Blair shrugged. "The Governor hasn't made up his mind yet. The Council meeting's called for nine o'clock." He shook his head. "Those seven regiments are still standing by."

"Just what did happen at Concord yesterday?" I asked. "Have you had further news? What I don't understand is why the militia didn't march Monday. I've been so busy with personal affairs. . . ."

"I know. Well, here's what happened. Oliver Prescott—he's a Groton man, about the richest man up there—begged the Governor not to send the militia until he had a chance to negotiate a peace between the Government and the Regulators. Prescott got Job Shattuck to promise that the Regulators wouldn't march. In return he promised that the Government wouldn't call out the militia to support the court. The Governor kept his part of the bargain. The Regulators reneged."

"That doesn't sound like Job Shattuck," I commented. "From people who know him, I've heard he's a pretty hot-headed sort but a man of his word."

"Oh, he's a man of his word, all right. He's still in Groton. Oliver Parker and Ben Page are leading the Regulators. We had a report from Worcester a while ago. Our informants say that the Worcester leaders at a secret meeting made the decision to overrule the agreement between Job and the Government. So, Job's only paying lip service to the agreement." Blair waved impatiently. "But that isn't important—not so very, anyway. The important thing is this: Prescott has just sent in a formal request to the Governor that warrants be issued against Job Shattuck, Oliver Parker, Ben Page, Nathan Smith and John Kelsey. Prescott certifies that those men have been active in the late rebellion and in stirring up the people against the Government, which makes them dangerous persons."

I whistled softly. "And have the warrants been issued?"

"Not yet. That's the important business the Governor and his council will discuss." Blair's thin, wrinkled face became very grim. "Warren, if those warrants are issued, will you ride to Groton to warn Job Shattuck?"

I was shocked and I thought a full minute before I could answer. "That seems like outright spying to me."

"Bah! Don't be a fool. I'm not doing this to help the Regulators. I'm doing this to stave off disaster. Don't you see? The moment Job Shattuck is thrown in jail he'll become a martyr to the cause and any chance for a compromise is gone." He shook a skinny finger under my nose. "Throwing Job in jail is tantamount to declaring war. And war means killing, remember that. It will be civil war."

I shifted uneasily. "Well, I'm not so sure."

"I am," Blair snapped. "I'll let you in on another secret. It

372

will be all over town tomorrow, anyway. General Lincoln is urging the Governor to raise an army—an army outside the militia. He's ordered the Quartermaster-General to seek out all the muskets and powder available. There's a lot of old British equipment lying around in warehouses in this country. Call that spying, too, if you like. My conscience is clear."

I scratched my head. "Will Shattuck's escape really be a good thing? If he gets away, won't he rush out to Worcester or Berkshire and be free to stir up more trouble?"

"That's possible, but then he'll only be an ordinary Regulator, not a martyr. You must do your best to persuade him to get out of the state—into New Hampshire. Put it on this basis: If he stays in the state, he lays the rest of his friends open to the same indictment—treason. The penalty for that is hanging. I know Job Shattuck. He won't jeopardize his friends' necks if he can help it. He'd be hindering the cause, not aiding it."

"Well, I'll do my best, Mr. Blair."

"Fine. Now, get out of here. Your face is becoming known. Wait at the Bunch—No, that place is too expensive. Wait at the Crouching Dog up on Queen Street, right near the jail."

"A nice handy place to wait," I said wryly as I got up to go. "Oh, by the way, how about those interviews with John Hancock and Sam Adams?"

Blair shook his head. "Hancock won't see you, as I predicted. Adams may. If he does, be discreet."

"I surely will, sir," I replied.

The day proved irksome and tiresome. Hour after hour I sat in the Crouching Dog, waiting for word from Blair, wondering if the Governor would dare issue those warrants. He must know the consequences. Heretofore, he had receded, step by step, because he knew the Regulators had right on their side.

At one o'clock, Mr. Blair came to the tavern and we had dinner together. The taproom was very crowded with lawyers and bailiffs and such, so he had to throw me the news in snatches. The Council was still in session. No decision had been reached. The split evidently was serious, for merchants and military men were being called in to help. The meeting promised to last all day. After dinner Blair left to return to his office and I was left to wait.

The minutes spun out into an eternity. Two o'clock and no word. Three o'clock, then four o'clock and I was practically bloated with tea, for I had chosen to dawdle over such a drink rather than anything stronger, for fear my head would not be clear if and when my moment came to act.

At half past four I thought the moment had arrived. A young man I had seen around State House entered the taproom and stood in the doorway looking for someone. He was looking for me.

"Are you Mr. Hascott? . . . Mr. Blair's compliments, would you please step over to his office?"

Would I please? I outdistanced the young man to the door of State House. Before entering, however, I tried to compose myself. It would not be well for one such as I to show excitement within these walls.

The moment I stepped into Mr. Blair's office, I saw I had been summoned for a different reason than I had anticipated. A stocky, elderly gentleman, his greying hair slightly disheveled, was sitting in the chair next to Mr. Blair's desk.

"Oh, there you are, Warren! I'm glad you hadn't left. Mr. Adams, may I present my friend, Mr. Warren Hascott."

Sam Adams stared up at me with cold grey eyes. "Mr. Blair tells me you're one of the Regulators."

"In a manner of speaking, yes, sir," I responded uneasily. "I believe the weight of justice is on their side."

"And what is it you wanted to see me about?" Adams asked gruffly.

I rubbed my hands on my thighs, my mind suddenly blank.

"Come, come, young man. Speak your piece. I'm not going to have you arrested—yet."

"Or ever, sir, if you believe in justice." I licked my lips. "Mr. Adams, you have always been for the common man. We—that is, the people of the country districts—have only sought a redress of grievances. We believed, in view of your well known championship of the cause of liberty and justice, that you would support our cause."

Adams' brow went up. "To subvert the Government?"

That was exasperating, and unexpected from a man like him. "No, sir. To seek a redress of grievances."

"And what do you consider just grievances?"

"Well . . . at this late date. . . ." I floundered a moment.

"You must know them, sir. . . . The lack of a circulating medium, for one thing. Many of our farmers couldn't sell their crops this year. They let them rot in the fields. Then, there's the burden of taxation, the pernicious practices of lawyers, the high cost of law suits, and other injustices. Surely, sir, you've seen our petitions? Surely, sir, you cannot hold that we were given adequate relief at the last session of the Legislature."

Sam Adams slumped in his chair, blowing on his fingertips, his worn features profoundly thoughtful. I was feeling good. I spoke only the truth. There could be no answering the truth. So, with rising confidence, I went on with what I believed would be compelling arguments to swing him to our side.

"You were one of the first to cry out against the tyranny of England, sir. You lifted your voice for the freedom of the common man. Your name will always be honored for the services you rendered to our Revolution. The Revolution is over. But the fight for liberty is not yet done. Surely, sir, you would not stand idly by and see those liberties you fought for trampled upon. Examine the facts. Freedom of the press is being choked by a pernicious tax; our soldiers, returned destitute from the war, are being thrown into prison for insignificant debts; our people who had the right to vote under King George—those same people are denied the right to vote because property qualifications have been doubled. Is that the democracy we fought for? Look about you, sir—right here in Boston. The mechanics, those men who made you their idol because you fought for them, those mechanics have no vote, no employment, no hope. They cry out for someone to lead them to the freedom they were promised—to the freedom you promised them. Would you see them crushed under a tyranny that masquerades as democracy? Would you spurn their plea for a voice in the government you told them would be theirs? Would you abandon them to the wolves of wealth?"

I paused, sure I had scored and unwilling to spoil the effect of my words. Sam Adams was moved. His aging, sagging, features seemed very weary, as if his defenses were crumbling. But his slow smile made me wonder if he was completely convinced.

He cocked a grey brow at Blair. "He gets better as he

warms up, eh?" Sam Adams chuckled. "You should enter politics, young man. You'd do very well at it."

Then his smile was gone. He rose slowly and stepped to one side of his chair, setting his foot on one of the rungs.

"I think, Mr. Hascott," he began slowly, "that you should be given a few fundamentals. Perhaps you do not know exactly what liberties we fought for during the late war. I agree that the present restraints on the press are wrong. I agree there is a measure of justice on the side of your fellow farmers and mechanics. Yes, much right. But I cannot agree with the methods you have chosen to obtain a redress of those wrongs."

"We have petit. . . ." I began.

"Please!" Adams broke in softly. "I know you have petitioned. I know those petitions seemed to have been ignored. We shall not concern ourselves with that at the moment. Let us examine the broader concepts of liberty." He began pacing with deliberation. "There are two kinds of liberty, Mr. Hascott, natural liberty and civil liberty. Natural liberty is the right of a man to do exactly as he pleases. I please to destroy a tree. May I? By natural right, in a wild and uncultivated forest, completely unoccupied and unknown to other men, I may destroy what I please. You cannot find that kind of liberty within any society. Civil liberty implies the necessity of giving up some of my natural rights as the price for living within a society. In return, a man receives security of his person and property. Thus, natural right and civil right are inconsistent with each other. If every man could do exactly as he pleased, no man would be secure. Might would be right."

Sam Adams stopped pacing and pointed. "Observe, Mr. Hascott, he who is compelled to do more or less than the law allows is being deprived of his civil liberties. You have stopped the courts from functioning. In so doing, you are denying the right of all men to the protection of the court. Thus, you are acting in a tyrannical and oppressive manner. Imagine, sir, if every time a man disliked a court and a law and resorted to violence, where would violence end? If the constitution was changed to fit insurgent ideas would everyone like it? What sort of redress would dissenters have? A resort to arms? In that case the country must be kept in a state of perpetual confusion and anarchy. Did we fight our Revolution for that, young man?"

"No, sir." I felt chastened, like a schoolboy, he was so infernally right.

"I have heard," Sam Adams went on, "that British agents are behind this affair. True or not, it makes no difference. This is incontestable! Britain alone can gain from a civil war here. If we fight among ourselves we lay ourselves open to losing all we have gained through seven years of war. British troops still occupy our western posts. France will not help us again, for France has pledged her neutrality in another war against us. Must we again become a part of the British Empire? Must we again squander our sons in all of Britain's wars? Would you exchange our debt for a quota of the British debt? Do you think Britain would accept us with less contempt than before? No, no, young man. We must guard what we have won."

Sam Adams clasped his hands behind his back. "Go back to your friends, young man. Tell them we must not be a divided people. Tell them we must not resort to arms every time government displeases us. If the majority want the measures you favor, then you shall have them. If only a minority favors them, then, under our system, it must submit until it can persuade the majority. The right of persuasion is inalienable to the minority. The right of violence can never be recognized by our Government." He smiled and put his hand on my shoulder. "You have listened like a man with an open mind. Can I hope I have persuaded you?"

"Yes, sir," I replied huskily.

"Then, I can hope you will do all you can to persuade your friends to lay down their arms?"

"I will do all I can, sir."

"Good." He gave my shoulder a satisfied pat. "Now, you understand why I must vote for measures upholding the Government."

Without another word Sam Adams left us and returned to the Council Chamber.

It was some minutes before either Mr. Blair or myself stirred. Both of us were deeply moved by the force of Sam Adams' logic. Finally Mr. Blair cleared his throat.

"I think," he ventured, "that it's more necessary than ever to warn Job. Don't you?"

"Of course. His capture would inflame the Regulators, I'm sure of that. Reason wouldn't be very acceptable to them after such action." I slumped and scowled at my shoes. "Shays would listen to me. I think Wheeler would, too. Luke Day wouldn't, but he has less influence than the other two." I sighed and got up. "Yes, perhaps I could do something to stop the movement."

"Fine. Then go back to the Crouching Dog. It's almost five o'clock now. I'm sure the council will come to a decision soon. As soon as I know, I'll either come myself or send someone."

Daylight was almost gone when I plodded back up Queen Street to the tavern. Something was troubling me. The weather? No, that wasn't it, though the sky was sullen and an icy wind was whipping in from the harbor. No, it was something about those words Sam Adams had spoken that didn't ring quite true.

When I sat down again at my table by the window in the Crouching Dog, I mulled over his argument, point by point. I ordered a rum flip to chase my chill and, after a time my mind seemed to thaw. Gradually, the magic of his personality, the precision of his logic, his quiet sincerity, all dissolved and I could finally see what he had done. He had fallen into one of the commonest of logistic errors, the *Ignoratio Elenchi*. Yes, Sam Adams had refuted the wrong point.

The more I thought of it, the more I became convinced that I had discovered the blind spot in men of his caliber who were supporting the Government. I had argued from facts and reality. Sam Adams had argued from wish and theory.

In all honesty, could I go back to those men and ask them to lay down their arms? If we laid down our arms, our chances would be nil. The Tories would say we had bowed to the might of the Government. They would shout that a vote for the Tories and Bowdoin was a vote for law and order. The forces of reaction would be triumphant. The rule of money would be secure. And we who had hoped for justice would face the grim possibility of murderous witch hunting, treason trials and hangings.

On impulse, I called for paper and quill and wrote a letter to Sam Adams, respectfully pointing out the error of his position and begging him to work rather for another special session than more repression. The issues, as set forth in our petitions, were compromisable. But I warned him that if the issue were drawn as a choice between submission to the tyranny of the Tories or war, the Regulators could only, in honor, choose war.

I looked up suddenly and found Mr. Blair standing at my side. The glow of the candlelight falling from above on his hat brim cast a dread shadow over his thin, wrinkled face. His eyes were hard, his lips tight.

"Is it all over?" I asked in a whisper.

Blair nodded curtly. "Sheriff Baldwin and Colonel Hitchburn have just been handed the warrants. It's Job they're after, as I suspected they would be. They start in the morning."

"Then I start this very minute."

Blair nodded and, as I pulled on my coat, he moved over to keep his back to the room, lest he be recognized. "Go to Todd's Livery Stable on Leverett's Lane. Say you're a friend of Burdick—not me, mind. I suppose they'll suspect me if Job gets away, but I don't care. Todd will give you a good horse. Need money?"

"No, I have ample."

"If you don't return to Boston, send the horse back with one of Job's sons. Tell him I said so. Good luck, boy!"

He gave me a heartfelt handclasp and I hurried out.

I had trouble with Todd. The night was growing colder and promised snow and Todd didn't want to risk his horse outside of Boston. But I gave him an extra Spanish dollar and said I was only going as far as Cambridge, so he finally agreed and saddled up a bay gelding, a good, strong, sure-footed beast.

I couldn't leave Boston without stopping by at the Burdicks'. Accordingly, I rushed over there. As soon as Polly opened the door, I brushed past her and strode into the parlor where Judith was playing softly on the spinet.

Her hands struck a sharp discordant chord as I entered. "Is there something wrong, Warren?"

"Nothing alarming," I replied, trying to appear casual. "I've been called out of Boston on business. I'm sorry to rush away like this but I must. Would you send my baggage through to

Amherst on the Albany stage with orders to deliver it at Clapp's? Attach a note, asking Clapp to send it to my home."

"Of course, Warren." She got up from the spinet, her eyes round and solemn. "Has open warfare broken out? I know it must be business concerned with the Regulators."

"No, no war. My job is to prevent. . . ."

A sharp banging on the front door made me pause. For a full minute we stood motionless, scarcely breathing. Then footsteps pattered out from the kitchen and Polly appeared in the parlor doorway. She was white-faced, nearly fainting with fright.

"Th—There's m—men in the back. They g—got guns."

I whirled, wondering if I could get out the side window. The banging resumed on the front door. A harsh, muffled voice cut through the shocked stillness.

"Open in the Name of the Law!"

Chapter 27

I BLEW out the candles on the spinet and ran over to the window. Two men were standing back in the gardens, watching the house. One of them caught sight of me, pointed and shouted something, and the pounding on the door became more insistent. I knew it would be suicidal to attempt an escape, for those men were armed and I was not. With a shrug, I decided to accept the inevitable lest a futile fight cause embarrassment and scandal to the Burdicks.

"Polly, let them in, please," I said.

"No!" Judith blurted. Her eyes showed deep concern. "I'll send them away."

I shook my head. "No use, Judith. They know I'm here. My horse is hitched outside. They'll search the house. Maybe we can put them off, maybe not. If not, send me a lawyer, will you?"

Judith sighed. "All right, Polly. You'd better open the door before they break it down."

I smiled wryly. "You actually look worried about me, Judith."

Her chin quivered. "Well, after all, you are a friend."

"Just a friend?" I asked softly.

Judith was saved from replying by the stomping in the entry hall. It sounded more like horses than constables. Polly's fright was overcome by her indignation, but her demand that they go outside again and scrape their shoes was ignored. I composed myself, trying not to show my anger and disgust at having my mission frustrated even before I could get out of Boston. I wondered idly how the authorities could possibly have learned of my purpose.

Polly, still giving the constables a tongue lashing, stopped them in the parlor doorway.

"These creatures say they're from the Sheriff's office."

A small man with a cocky grin hustled her to one side. Two taller men were at his back, their pistols out and ready.

"Mr. Hascott?" the little man demanded shrilly.

Judith drew herself up. "How dare you? Remove your hats."

The little man hesitated, glanced up at his two comrades, then took off his tricorn with an abashed grin. The other two glowered as they reluctantly uncovered.

"Whatever your business," Judith went on coldly, "you may state it to my maid—outside on the steps. Now, get out!"

The little fellow grew red. "Damned aristocracks," he mumbled. Then, in a bold, high voice, "M'am, we come for a rebel an' we aims to get him. Here's the warrant."

Judith's manner was supremely haughty. "You are fool enough to seek a rebel in this house, the house of Moses Burdick?"

The constable squinted up at his companions. "She's funnin', ain't she?" He rubbed his button nose, then raised his voice. "Hey, you out there, is this the feller?"

The taller constable stepped to one side and a solid, well dressed gentleman came in. I was a bit shocked, but not too surprised, to see my well-beloved friend, Ormund B. Graham.

Judith gasped. "So, you brought them here."

The cleft in Graham's square chin deepened as he tried to hold back a smile. "I assure you, Miss Burdick, this is a co-incidence. I came to see your father. Is Mr. Burdick at home?"

"You swore out the warrant," Judith accused.

Graham shrugged. "That's a matter of no concern to you, M'am." He took a paper from his inner coat pocket, unfolded it and held it up. "This, my dear Mr. Hascott, is a bill of exchange for the remainder of my debt to Mr. Burdick. I've completely pulled out of my hole since we last had business. I thought you'd like to know. You can save your bluster."

Judith grew angry. "After all my father's done for you, I should think . . ."

"Let it go, Judith," I interrupted. "That won't do any good. You men get out of here. I want to talk to Graham alone."

The constables looked to Graham for their cue.

He stared at me, fingering the cleft in his chin, then nodded. "He can't escape. Leave us, please."

The constables filed out reluctantly, the smaller one glowering over his shoulder and muttering something about "aristocrats."

I gave Graham a bland smile. "Perhaps you and I can come to another understanding, Mr. Graham. Would you withdraw your charges for . . . ah . . . for a consideration?"

Graham bristled. "If you think you can bribe me to forget my patriotic duty. . . ."

"Please," I cut in wearily. "No speeches on patriotism. I can show you how to make some money—a lot of money."

Graham was silent a long moment. Then, "I'm listening."

I glanced at Judith. "Can I trust him to carry out his part of the bargain?"

"Get his word," Judith suggested. "I think it's good."

Graham frowned quickly. "I may have made a mistake, Mr. Hascott. My word I'll withdraw the charges if . . . ."

"That's good enough for me. Here's some advance information. It will be public in a few days, but you can make a big profit if you act fast. Lincoln has ordered the Quartermaster-General to buy up equipment. I understand there's a big supply of English muskets still in the country, in New York, left there when the British evacuated at the end of the war."

"Yes, I've heard of those stocks," Graham said slowly. His eyelids drooped. "That sounds very good." Then, sneeringly, "A fine rebel you are."

I shrugged. "I'm not admitting I'm a rebel. But even if I were, we wouldn't have the time or the money to pick up those stocks. Is it a deal?"

"If your news is true," Graham said. "It's a deal."

"It's true. Now, call off your dogs."

Graham shook his head. "I'm afraid I can't, Mr. Hascott. You'll have to go with them. They have the warrants. I'll tend to quashing the charges in the morning."

"But listen!" I blurted. "I can't go to jail tonight. I've got to go to—I mean, I have an urgent appointment."

383

"Sorry," Graham said curtly. "I can't do anything now. I assure you, I cannot do anything until tomorrow morning."

I groaned inwardly, but I was helpless. "All right. Judith, I may need that lawyer after all."

"I trust you won't," Judith said coldly. "I'm sure Mr. Graham will rectify his mistake in the morning."

Graham bowed. "Of course. This was a mistake, a ghastly mistake . . . if your news is true."

The new stone jail on Queen Street was a commodious three-story brick building, entered through three strong doors at the front. The third story, by far the most populous, was reserved for debtors. As recently as it had been constructed, the place had already acquired the usual jailhouse odors of stale sweat, body wastes and urine, a stench most disagreeably evident in the offices and receiving pens which were heated by roaring hearths. Upstairs the air was more bearable only because a bitter chill clung to the stone corridors and sheet iron doors.

Being a political prisoner I was given the dubious honor of a cell to myself on the second floor. It was furnished with a straw pallet in the corner, a three-legged stool and a pot for my convenience. There was no heat. For light I had a single sperm candle which I could either keep on the floor, and risk setting fire to my bed, or keep on the windowsill where the draught from the loosely fitting window was wont to blow it out.

I spent a horrible night. For a time, I was restless and angry and tried pacing up and down to relieve my feelings. The cell was too damn small to pace with comfort. When I wearied I considered the matter of sleeping. I dared not sleep on the straw, for I feared it was verminous. Accordingly I placed the stool in the corner nearest the door and, resting my shoulders against the wall, settled down for the night. The cold bit through my greatcoat as if it were summer linen.

Around midnight I awoke to find snow seeping through the cracks in the window. I was mightily cheered. Perhaps, if I were released early in the morning, I would still have time to get up to Groton to warn Job Shattuck. I doubted strongly if the Sheriff would ride through the snow. Since he would also have to spend some time gathering the militia, it was unlikely that he could reach Job Shattuck before nightfall. Even if I left as late as nine o'clock I felt I'd still have a good chance of beating the sheriff to Groton.

Thus relieved, I settled back on my stool again. My sleeping strategy had not worked. The sharp pricklings under my arms and in my crotch told me I was lousy. In disgust I flung myself down on the straw certain I wouldn't sleep a wink. I wasn't far from right. I dropped into a troubled doze and dreamt I was swinging from the scaffold, a very peculiar sensation, especially around the throat. The next time, I promised myself, I'd remember to open my cravat before trying to sleep.

The morning was bright and clear and the snow was almost gone. The roads would be in good condition. I was impatient to be on my way, so I banged on my door until the jailer came. I asked him if the order for my release had come through, but it had not. He got my breakfast from a nearby tavern, charging me three shillings for a ten pence meal. He told me then that a young woman had called but had not been allowed to see me. I was being held incommunicado.

Not until nine o'clock did I really start worrying. Every minute lost from then on cut down my chances of reaching Groton on time. By ten o'clock, I was raging. What the hell had happened to that man Graham? I called for the jailer again and demanded that I be permitted to send out a letter. No, I could not send out notes. I showed him a shilling, a half crown, a crown, a golden guinea. He was sorely tempted, but would not succumb. Perhaps it was as well that I couldn't write that note. The words would have burned the paper to ashes.

Twelve o'clock and still no sign of Graham. I hollered for the jailer again and demanded that I be taken to the warden. That was impossible. I demanded to see my attorney. Regretfully he told me I could not get in touch with him. I cursed him from pillar to post, but all I got out of that was a bit of relief.

By three o'clock my fury had exhausted itself. The keys rattled in the lock of my cell door, but I didn't get up. I was too tired from pacing and swearing and thinking of all the changes I'd make on that handsome face of Graham's the next time I saw him. As the door opened, I leaped up hopefully. No, it was not Graham. It was Jothan Salderman.

"I'm sorry I couldn't get here sooner," Salderman apologized. "I tried three times this morning."

I nodded numbly. "I suppose you heard from Judith what happened. Where is that bastard Graham?"

Salderman shrugged his shoulders. "He took the New York stage early this morning."

"He'll regret it," I promised. "Can you get me out?"

"I'm afraid not, Mr. Hascott." Salderman's long face was mournful. "You're being held incommunicado. Graham certified you as a rebel, dangerous to the Commonwealth's safety. And since the Habeas Corpus has been suspended. . . ."

I sank down on my stool. "How long do I have to sit here?"

"Indefinitely, unless we can pull the right strings."

I grunted. "I don't like this, putting my friends to all this trouble, I mean. Yet. . . ." I smiled and spread my hands. "I don't want to spend the rest of my days here."

Salderman chuckled. "Naturally not. We'll do all we can. Meanwhile, Judith is sending over some blankets and things you'll need. That's why I came, really—just to let you know you haven't been forgotten."

"That's some comfort. And thank you for coming, Mr. Salderman. Send over my razor, will you?"

"I'll do that. If you want anything else, you can ask the jailer. He has orders to see to your comfort."

I thanked him again and he departed. For some minutes after he was gone I considered writing a note to Mr. Blair. I finally decided against it. If I communicated with him he might get in trouble and wind up in the cell next to mine. I was fairly certain he'd hear of my plight soon and, if he believed it safe, he would get in touch with me.

Later in the afternoon, Judith sent in some necessaries, blankets, soap, my razor, a bottle of brandy, some confections and some dried and preserved fruits. But she had not been permitted to come to see me. Nor did I hear from Mr. Blair.

And so passed Thursday, the 29th of November.

My worst lack was reliable news. I could sense that the jail was seething with rumor and, for a small fee, I learned from the jailer that everyone had heard of the Governor's action in issuing the warrants for Job Shattuck and the other rebels. Everyone, criminals and debtors alike, was praying that Shattuck and the others escaped the net of the militia.

How the news managed to reach the jail so quickly, I shall never understand. It seemed that the reports got here faster than anywhere else in Boston. But it was exasperating to attempt to separate fact from fancy. It wasn't until Saturday afternoon that the situation clarified. Late that afternoon, Oliver Parker and Ben Page were put in cells down the corridor from mine.

The story, as relayed to me by the jailer, made me groan. The sheriff hadn't gone directly to Groton. With the militia, he had struck first at Weston. Oliver Parker and Ben Page were quickly taken, but Nathan Smith and John Kelsey had escaped the Government trap. The Regulators, who had gathered there with the idea of breaking up last Tuesday's court at Cambridge, were effectively broken up themselves. Most had scattered to their homes. A few had departed hastily for Worcester, where they would aid in the attempt to stop that court which was due to sit there next Tuesday.

The militia hadn't arrived in Groton until very late on Thursday night. They went directly to Shattuck's house, but someone had warned Job and he was gone. It snowed that night so the militia abandoned its search.

Early the next morning the Light Horse regiment got word that Shattuck was hiding in the house of Samuel Gragg, who was Job's next door neighbor. The Horse rode there at once. Gragg denied that Shattuck was there, which was true. Shattuck had gone out the back way a few minutes before. Shattuck's footprints were as plain on the virgin snow as though he had signed his name. The Light Horse immediately started after him.

Within a few minutes they came upon him near his own house, where he was headed to get a horse. Shattuck was armed and determined to sell his freedom dearly. Lt. Varnum, the first to reach him, drew his sword and the two clashed. Shattuck inflicted a slight wound on Varnum's cheek, but in doing so he slipped and was thrown off balance. Varnum lunged forward. He slashed a deep cut in Shattuck's knee. Shattuck fell. A moment later he was disarmed.

That much of the story was clear and true. The many embellishments were later proven false. One report had it that the Light Horse had broken into Shattuck's house, torn the breast off Mrs. Shattuck and gouged the eyes out of two of her grandchildren. There was a rumor that the militia burned down Shattuck's house but later I found that it was Aaron Brown's potash works that were burned out. Brown was one of the constables who had served the warrant on Job.

As for Shattuck himself, his treatment was indecent. He was variously reported to have had his throat cut, his arms hacked off and his stomach laid open. His real wound, a bad gash on the knee, was serious enough. Lt. Varnum had been sent directly to a doctor for the scratch on his face. But Shattuck, instead of being given medical attention, was flung into jail.

Government supporters excused Captain Sampson Reed's treatment of Shattuck on the grounds that Reed had more urgent business. As soon as Shattuck was safely in jail, Reed headed for Holden to get Adam Wheeler and possibly Dan Shays, both of whom were reported there, getting ready to move in to Worcester. There was some doubt that the Light Horse could legally cross the county line into Worcester, but the militia wasn't standing on the strict letter of the law at a time like this. It was with impatience and dread that I awaited further news of the Light Horse's expedition to Holden. If Adam Wheeler and Dan Shays were caught, the Regulators would be finished.

Mr. Blair didn't come to visit me until late Saturday afternoon. He seemed worn and haggard and his thin face was more wrinkled than ever. I was delighted to see him, but I refrained from showing it until after the iron door clanged shut and the lock clicked over.

"So, you got yourself in jail," Blair said churlishly.

I shrugged. "It was that louse, Graham. He was hanging around State House when I came. I guess I shouldn't have come to your office. I wouldn't have, had I known what I was to do later."

Blair waved a thin hand. "Water over the dam. I heard about your arrest an hour after it happened. I sent someone else up to warn Shattuck." He grunted. "Not that it did any good. I'm sorry I couldn't get to see you sooner. I have to be careful. You'd better communicate with me directly from now on." He eyed the blankets, my line of bottles and shaving materials on the window sill. "You don't need anything special, I see."

"No thanks. I just want to get out of here."

"Your young lady, Miss Burdick, has Mr. Lang on the job. Lang's the best lawyer in Boston. And he can't do a thing." He gazed at me thoughtfully. "But I can get you out."

"How?" I asked eagerly.

"You can sign the oath of allegiance and avail yourself of the Amnesty Act."

I shook my head. "Nothing doing. I won't tie my hands that way. How many have signed so far?"

"Not one," Blair replied, smiling. "But they're on the outside. You'll be tried sooner or later."

"I doubt it. I have a feeling that Graham will release me as soon as he gets back from New York." I scratched my head. "I'd like to get out before, if I could. Look, Mr. Blair, do you think Sam Adams would help me? Remember I said I'd try to get the Regulators to lay down their arms. That wasn't a hard and fast promise, but you know I'll work for peace. And I do have some influence among the leaders. Perhaps Sam Adams could be persuaded I'm more valuable to the Government out of jail than in."

Blair crackled mirthlessly. "It's something to try, Warren. It may work. I think Sam Adams liked you."

"You can tell him this is spite work. Tell him how I forced Graham to settle my father's debt at a third off. He may have heard the story. It's been around."

Blair patted my shoulder. "You'll be out of here by Monday . . . and without committing yourself." He straightened his wig. "I'll see Adams right away. Maybe you can be out tonight."

"I hope so. At any rate, I hope to see you Monday."

Blair shook his head. "No, as soon as you're released, get out of Boston. You'd better not communicate direct with me again. If you come to Boston, get in touch with me at the Two Palaverers. If I'm not there leave word with Rhodes. He's safe. If you write, send your letters through Robert Ashton of Worcester. He's a commission merchant, dealing in grains. Goodnight, boy."

He left me with high hopes. I really didn't expect to get

out the same night, so I wasn't disappointed when my release didn't come through. But I could hardly sleep for impatience.

Then, just as I was dozing off, a new thought brought me up sharp. Beulah! Good Lord, I was supposed to meet her earlier this evening. I cussed myself out for not remembering to send a note over to the Good Woman earlier in the evening. I wondered what she was thinking.

The Sabbath was exasperating. No word from Blair. No word from Judith. Not even a new rumor cropped up that day. I sent a note over to the Good Woman, but the messenger returned and reported that no one answering to the name of Beulah Crane was there. Indeed, no young woman had taken residence at that place on Saturday. I spent the rest of the time counting the minutes, an occupation calculated to drive a man slowly insane.

The sky was just getting grey when the key jangled in the iron door and the lock clanged over. Monday morning. I jumped up eagerly as the cell door squealed back. The jailer was standing there, grinning lopsidedly.

"Guess you can go now," he said. "There's an order for your release downstairs."

"Yes, sir!" I stuffed my razor into my pocket. "The rest of the stuff is yours. The bottle is half full. Watch out for the blankets. They're lousy."

The jailer chuckled. "Me old woman's used to 'em."

I fled from the cell as if from a plague. In the office downstairs a fat deputy informed me that the order for my release had come through late Saturday night but no one in authority had been on hand to order my release. I almost choked him when I heard that, but I was thankful enough to forgive. I signed all the papers set before me and headed straight for the nearest barber for a shave and a delousing.

It was not quite seven when I got over to the Burdicks. Burdick had already gone to business and the ladies had not yet come down to breakfast. I tried not to show how pleased I was.

"You tell Miss Judith I've been released from jail, will you, Polly? Tell her I had to rush away on important business."

390

"Yes, sir," Polly frowned. "But won't you stay for breakfast, sir? Miss Judith is awake, I think."

"No thanks, Polly. I'm in a rush. Thank her for what she's done for me and say I'll see her soon again. And give her this for me." I kissed her cheek. "Don't forget!"

Polly giggled. "I won't, sir."

I took my portmanteau and rushed right over to the Good Woman. The landlady informed me that a young woman had come there on Saturday, but she had left later in the evening. I thought she might have gone over to the Fitch's. And the chances were that she had taken the stage for Worcester this morning. Inquiry at Pease's on Common Street established that a young, unescorted woman had indeed gone out this morning. So, I hired a horse at Pease's and started out for Worcester, hoping against hope that I could overtake the coach along the road.

One advantage of hiring a horse from Pease, though his rates were higher, was that I could change horses at any of the stage stops along the way without any question. Since my stops were frequent, I always had a fresh horse. And I was told the short ways so that I made remarkable time on the road to Worcester.

By hard, fast riding, I finally caught up to the coach at Marlboro. The passengers were having refreshments in Howe's Tavern while the horses were being changed. I hurried into the taproom and looked around. There was an unescorted woman among the passengers, all right. She was a hawk-nosed, stern young lady of eighteen. She bore not the slightest resemblance to Beulah.

Puzzled, I turned my horse over to Landlord Howe and ordered a fresh one. What could have happened to Beulah? I could only conclude she had stayed with the Fitch's. I acted upon that assumption and sent a note to the Fitch's, which Landlord Howe assured me would catch the stage for Boston due to pass this way within a short time. I was thus confident that Beulah would turn up in Worcester on the very next coach.

I would have gone back, but I had heard that General Warner had ordered the Worcester town militia to mobilize this afternoon. If I hurried, I figured, I might be able to get there in time to see what happened when the two forces met.

Accordingly, I skirted Westboro and rode on faster than ever and made Worcester by four o'clock.

I went to the Hancock Arms and settled myself in my room. I had hired a room just in time. A good number of the Regulators were billetted in the courthouse, but the overflow went into the Hancock Arms. By nightfall every room was taken.

Since the taproom was jammed to capacity, I decided to have my supper down at the U. S. Arms Tavern where the Regulators had set up headquarters. Ben Convers, Abe Gale and several other officers were taking their dinner with Adam Wheeler. As I approached, Wheeler glanced up. The broad smile breaking on his ruddy features assured me I was not to be unrecognized.

He stood up and held out his hand. "Warren Hascott! It's been a long time, my boy."

I grinned and took his hand. "I was afraid you wouldn't remember me, it's been so long."

"Well, Dan's been telling me so much about you, I've been expecting to run across you." He squinted critically. "Besides, I'd know you anywhere. You haven't changed much. Maybe you've filled out some—especially around the shoulders—but that's all." He turned to the others. "I guess you remember the schoolmaster, Abe. The last one we had before the war broke out."

Abe Gale chuckled and shook hands with me. "I guess I remember. I was courting Freda at the time. I remember I hadda kick him outta the parlor one night."

"Ben, pull up a chair for Mr. Hascott," Wheeler ordered. "He'll have supper with us. . . . Dan told me you took some of his crops to sell. I wish you could have taken some of mine. I had to leave one whole apple orchard go to rot this year."

"A shame, I say," Convers commented, drawing over a chair for me. "There's going to be a cider shortage this year, I think."

"Weren't you the man who was a captive in Algiers?" Captain Clark asked.

I admitted I was and, over my supper, had to relate some

of my adventures. It was gratifying to see how quickly I had been accepted into the circle and treated as a friend. Captain Wheeler made me slightly uncomfortable by calling me "Mr. Hascott," but that was more or less habit. While I had lived with him, he had been careful to help me maintain my budding dignity. To him I was still the schoolmaster.

All during the meal there was practically no talk of the present troubles, for we had plenty else to occupy our tongues, mutual friends, adventures, war experiences, farm gossip, the state of trade. These men, I found, were more commerce conscious than the people out in my section of the country.

"It's snowing," Abe Gale interrupted suddenly.

The conversation died abruptly and everyone turned to stare at the windows. It was snowing hard. The wind had risen and savage gusts splattered the snow like grapeshot against the glass. For some minutes, no one spoke. This was serious. Hundreds of our men were on the road, many of them without adequate clothing. This looked like a real storm, one which would block the roads and keep our comrades from joining us. No one was worried about being reinforced. The Regulators had plenty of men to keep the court closed. And if the Insurgents couldn't be reinforced, neither could the militia. But those men on the road—they were in for it.

About half past nine, Captain Holman of Templeton, who had commanded the picket line to the east, came in and joined us in the taproom of the U. S. Arms. His plump face was as red as a boiled lobster and his brows were rimmed with ice. He shucked his coat, downed a sizzling rum flip and sat down with us.

"Any sign of the militia?" Gale asked. "We heard that General Ward sent orders to General Warner to have the militia come in by tomorrow morning."

"They won't be here—not in this weather." Holman dug into his pocket and tossed a purse on the table. "The only one who came in was this feller from Boston. Says he's a sympathizer and wants to help. Balderdash, I think he said his name was."

"Salderman!" I half shouted. "I know that man. A sort of horse-faced fellow?"

"That's him. Had his own private coach. Is he square?"

393

I smiled. "I'm biased. He's courting someone I like. Anyway, he supplied us with some money at Springfield."

Wheeler chuckled as he finished counting the money. "Ten pounds. The way we need money, we won't be finicky about who he is."

I got up. "Where is he stopping, do you know?"

"Sun Tavern, most likely," Holman answered. "The rest of the public houses are full up with our men."

"It's getting late. I think I'll stop over there, then go to bed. See you in the morning, gentlemen."

Wheeler and the others bade me a "goodnight" and I left.

The snow was knee deep by this time and I wished mightily for splatterdashes. My stockings were soaked long before I plowed my way through to the Sun Tavern. That public house was only a short distance down Main Street, but I almost turned back once.

The taproom of the Sun Tavern was virtually empty, for the Regulators had left this place to travelers and the people of the town. Salderman was nowhere in evidence. I asked the landlord if my friend had come here and was assured he had. Salderman had gone directly to his room and had taken his supper there. The landlord hesitated to give me directions to his room, saying he believed Mr. Salderman wouldn't want to be disturbed. I assured him it would be all right and went upstairs.

The light was shining through a crack in the door so I knew Salderman was up. I knocked. The door opened a crack and he peered out. "I gave orders not to be dist. . . ." His eyes widened and the door opened a trifle more. "Why, it's Mr. Hascott."

"I'm sorry to disturb you, sir." I caught a glimpse of a petticoat on the chair next to the bed. "I am sorry, sir. I'll come back in the morning and. . . ."

The rest froze in my throat as I spied a brown arm. Salderman growled deep in his throat and started to close the door. I stepped forward and flung my shoulder against the panel. Salderman staggered away and I got a clear view of the woman sitting up in bed.

It was Beulah.

For long moments I just stood and stared and tried not to believe my eyes. The room slowly receded until only Beulah's

394

flushed, resentful face remained. Then her features were swallowed in the furious red mist swirling about me.

"Now, Mr. Hascott," Salderman said soothingly, "there's no need to be. . . ."

He never finished. I pivoted and my fist snapped up. Salderman's long, horse-like face faded backward. He crashed against the wall and sat down hard, his eyes glazed and stupid. I turned on my heel and walked out.

Then Beulah called sharply. "Warren!"

I did not look back.

Chapter 28

I WAS exhausted, physically and mentally, when I finally reached my room in the Hancock Arms Tavern. Vaguely I remembered plowing through waist-deep snowdrifts and almost tumbling right into Paine's Brook. Why I didn't get lost and wander in circles all night, I'll never know. I wouldn't have cared. But my anger was gone by the time I crawled into my bed. I was wondering if I had the right to be resentful. I was wondering if I could blame anyone but myself. I had this coming to me.

Loud cheering awakened me. I jumped out of bed and immediately regretted it. Glory, how cold that room was! I slipped into my shoes and went over to the window. A detachment of about fifty men was struggling up a half-formed path to the courthouse. The amount of snow that had fallen was astonishing. I had almost forgotten our New England skies could debouch that much. The newly arrived contingent couldn't have come from the north, from Holden, for that road was completely unmarked. Huge snowdrifts, like lumpy white barriers, were stretched across the road. Those new men must have come from the east, from Shrewsbury. And that meant that Dan Shays had not yet arrived.

I jumped into my clothes, hurried downstairs and sought the warmest spot near the hearth. The taproom could have done with some fresh air. The stench of stale tobacco smoke and sour beer, damp clothes and unwashed bodies was almost enough to make me skip breakfast. Almost. I found, remarkably, that I was as hungry as a horse. But curiously, my corn meal pudding tasted like straw. The memory of what had happened last night returned again and again, no matter how hard I tried to cast it from my mind.

It was queer, in a way, how I was defending and excusing her to myself. I had no claim on her. I remembered how delighted and relieved I had been when she put no overt claim on me for the intimacy between us. I still wasn't sure I wanted to marry her. And, after all, she had to look out for herself. Salderman was a rich man. I was not. True, I doubted she'd have a chance to compete with Judith for him. But then, I myself had taken him lightly when Judith told me she was going to marry him. I winced as I remembered how blithely I had assumed both were mine. That confidence was gone. Perhaps it was a good thing.

A large group of babbling men was crowded about the roaring fireplace in the taproom of the U. S. Arms. Abe Gale gave me a hearty "good morning" and introduced me to Reuben Taft of Uxbridge, who commanded the newly arrived detachment. I shook hands with him, asking him the condition of the roads. Terrible, was his answer. He and his men had to fight drifts all the way in. However, the farmers were out with their oxen, hard at work breaking open the highway. So, we could expect that many of our men would eventually be able to get through to us.

Adam Wheeler was composing a petition to the judges. It was the usual request that court adjourn. As soon as it was completed, a messenger was sent to the Sun Tavern with instructions to place it in the hands of Judge Ward. The messenger also took along a petition which had been sent in by the town of Sutton, requesting that the court adjourn until March. We didn't care if the court adjourned without setting a definite date or until sometime in March, as long as it was adjourned until after the Legislature met. With the messenger on his way, we all relaxed. There was no sign as yet that the militia was gathering. It was now close to ten o'clock.

Not fifteen minutes later, the messenger returned. He took off his hat and whooped.

"Court's adjourned! Ward adjourned the court!"

The notice of adjournment passed from hand to hand and everyone shouted with glee and hugged each other. I myself felt very good, for this was vindication of our methods. Yes,

I was feeling confident that the matter could be handled exactly as before and again give us victory without violence.

Only one man did not seem happy about the adjournment. Adam Wheeler scowled over the notice a long time and the rest, noticing how quiet he was, became quiet, too.

"God damn that man," Wheeler burst out suddenly. He held up the notice. "Didn't you see it? He adjourned the court until the 23rd of January."

"Well, what of it?" Gale asked.

"Just this," Wheeler said in a low, angry voice, "we asked him to adjourn without day so the court wouldn't be in session again before the Legislature meets at the beginning of February. We'll have to keep our men together until then—those who can't keep themselves. And, remember this, every time we stop a court, we lay ourselves open to starting riots and hurting some innocent people. One of these times, we're likely—maybe through no fault of our own—to do something to alienate our support among the neutrals." He threw up his hands. "I don't know. Maybe they're forcing us to keep turning out in the hope that something like that will happen."

A gloomy hush fell over the taproom.

"Maybe we ought to march on Boston," Reuben Taft said nasally. "Make Bowdoin call the Legislature now."

"Yeah," Abe Gale agreed. "And maybe we ought to get Job Shattuck out of jail."

"Don't talk like an idiot," Wheeler snapped. "We can't do anything ourselves, anyway. We'll keep our men on the ground until all the others get here. Shays ought to come in today. So may Luke Day and Eli Parsons. This isn't a local affair any more. Any decisions made should be made by representatives of all parts of the state."

This was agreeable to everyone, for those who favored moderation believed that in a full dress debate, their views would prevail. The others were equally convinced that men like Luke Day and Eli Parsons would swing the movement toward forceful, decisive action. Within a few moments, the taproom was nearly empty, the officers drifting out to inform their men of this new development and see that none departed for home. Holding the men together was no great problem. The destitute had little stomach for returning to the charity of their friends and neighbors. Those who had property had few chores, now that winter was upon us, and most had sons or wives who could take care of their livestock.

After a time, Wheeler was left alone and he ordered his breakfast, only now remembering he had overlooked it. While he ate, Wheeler told me there was much to his liking in the present situation. Many citizens were rallying to our cause. Colonel Flagg, one of Worcester's leading men, had come out for the Regulators. He had sent a contribution of two barrels of rum and promised more aid later. Many of our former supporters had veered over to the Government, but not as many as Wheeler had figured would eventually do so. As for Ward's action in adjourning the court to the 23rd of January, Wheeler wasn't surprised, but he was hopeful.

"Our cause must prevail, Mr. Hascott," he said earnestly. "We have justice on our side. Ward knows it. Bowdoin knows it. That's why they keep bowing to our demands to close the courts."

"They took Shattuck," I pointed out.

Wheeler waved his fork impatiently. "Job was too loud mouthed. He's something like Luke Day."

Wheeler stared into space a moment. "Well, it's a good thing we're going to have a full discussion of our future course. Oh, there's somebody you ought to know just came in, Mr. Hascott."

Expecting it would be Salderman, I threw a sour glance over my shoulder. I swung about sharply, astonished. The newcomer was the one person whose face I did not expect to see here. It was Beulah.

She stomped the snow from her shoes, threw her hood back and came brazenly over to where we were sitting. I was even more astonished when she smiled and waved greetings. Her cheeks were glowing and her eyes were clear. She was perfectly composed, absolutely without remorse or shame.

Wheeler thought my surprise referred to his knowing her. "Joab served under me in '77," he explained in a low voice. "I been to see him a couple of times since the war."

Then Beulah was upon us. "Good morning, gentlemen."

"Good morning," Wheeler returned. "I'm sort of surprised to see you here in Worcester."

"I've been visiting with my grandfather," she said blandly.

"I just happen to be passing through." Then she added with a smile, "The coach didn't go out this morning."

Wheeler evidently sensed something was wrong between us, for he gave me a quick, puzzled glance. Beulah brought out a bag of money and tossed it onto the table.

"Fifty pounds. For the cause, gentlemen."

Wheeler made no move to pick it up. He was still watching me. I eyed the bag with distaste.

"I don't think we can use that," I said coldly. "We're not stooping yet to collecting from whores."

Beulah gasped, straightened, stood very still. Then stars exploded before my eyes. I rubbed the spot where she had slapped me. I did not look up at her.

"I never expected you to be stuffy," she said evenly. "Or perhaps you think I'm a stupid child. You don't think you can—" She broke off angrily. "Captain Wheeler, there are men to be fed and clothed. Whatever he says about me, remember that."

She gave me a look of supreme contempt and turned away. But she paused at the door and glanced back. She was curiously pale.

I was too astounded to move. She evidently thought I was no better than Salderman, which was fair enough. But her attitude toward herself completely baffled me. When I disapproved of her indiscriminate relations, she thought I was stuffy.

Wheeler took a long draught of his cider pot. "I don't want to pry, Mr. Hascott, but I own I am curious."

I scratched my head. "I'm curious myself, Captain. Maybe you can understand it. I can't."

And I told him what had happened the night before. I might have hesitated to confide in someone else, but he was a man of over sixty, older than my own father, and, since he was only a casual friend, I could feel less reticence in matters of this kind than I could toward my father.

Wheeler was silent a long time after I finished. He turned the cider pot around and around between his big brown hands.

"You know, Mr. Hascott," he said with soft deliberation, "back home I'm a deacon in the church. I suppose I should be one of the first to condemn a girl like that. Deep in my heart, I can't. Before the war I wouldn't have doubted. It's different now. I keep remembering the first time I went into battle—that was at Bunker's Hill. I shot a man right between the eyes. And you know what I was thinking at the time? 'Thou shalt not kill'."

"Well, in war . . ." I objected feebly.

Wheeler sighed. "I'm not questioning the rightness or wrongness of shooting that soldier. After a while, I got myself to believing that I wasn't killing men, but an evil idea . . . that is, before or after battles," he added with a smile. "I never did bother to think while fighting. But my point is this: You and I and all the rest of us came out of the war with a different set of moral values. So you see I can't condemn that girl. I wouldn't encourage her in her wrongness. But I wouldn't say she's immoral. Rather I'd say she was unmoral."

Which put the matter on a high academic plane. More practically, I wondered if that louse Salderman had told her I was in jail. I wondered if she hadn't become furious when I didn't show up and concluded that I was deliberately avoiding her.

Throughout the day, more and more men poured into town. The arrival of so many men—there were some eight hundred in town by nightfall—posed a ticklish problem of housing them. Every tavern was filled to capacity, and still there wasn't enough room. The weather was too inclement even to consider having them camp out of doors. Accordingly, the officers made a house-to-house canvas, asking the people if they would be willing to accommodate some of our men. I did considerable of this work myself, for I was dressed better than most and thus was more easily able to gain confidence.

On Wednesday, Dan Shays finally came in. He was not destined to slip into town unnoticed.

The first inkling we had of his arrival was a commotion outside of the U. S. Arms Tavern. Captain Wheeler, Reuben Taft and I had just sat down to have dinner. Immediately we concluded that disorder had broken out. We had half feared, half expected trouble, for the men had been so phenomenally well behaved, despite being so bored with inactivity. As we were rushing to get outside, a man burst in, shouting and dancing about with excitement.

"Shays is coming in! Dan Shays is here!"

A wild cheering broke out and everyone stampeded for the door. Wheeler was calling out to various officers to gather their men at North Square. They gave Shays a rousing welcome.

After acknowledging his welcome with smiles and bows Shays decided he'd better round up some of the men, mostly the destitute, and take them back to the Rutland Barracks and maintain them there. Anyone who could afford to stay on would wait for Luke Day and Eli Parsons.

It was evening before Shays' men were billeted for the one night they'd be in Worcester. But it was a good hour or so later before Shays finally showed up at the U. S. Arms Tavern. He was acting very strangely. He took practically no part in the usual committee meeting, which this time merely decided that a letter explaining our actions should be drawn up and sent to the towns and the newspapers. Dan seemed nervous and uneasy, as if he momentarily expected disaster to befall him. I tried to corner him and find out what was his trouble. Beulah, too, who came in later, tried to get a word with him alone. But he made sure he was always in a crowd. He excused himself early, for he was staying with Colonel Flagg, one of Worcester's leading citizens who had come out for us. Some of us followed Dan outside to try to have a word with him. He rushed off, on the absurd excuse that his appointment with Flagg was urgent.

We stood about, chatting and went back inside to have a nightcap. I made it a point to ignore Beulah. But when I said goodnight to all and started to leave, she decided to leave, too. She asked me outright to see her back to the Sun Tavern. I could hardly refuse, though it did occur to me that Salderman was no longer there. We hardly spoke two words on the way down Main Street.

Finally, "Are you still angry with me, Warren?"

"No . . . I guess not. I don't know. I'll get over it."

"He's a rotter, isn't he—Salderman, I mean. He never told me you were in jail. I thought. . . ." Her voice trailed off. "I thought you . . . you didn't want me."

I didn't answer, but I could understand how she must have felt. And people with wounded pride do strange things.

"Anyway," Beulah went on. "That's not why I wanted you to walk with me. Did Dan tell you about Putnam?"

"Putnam? No, who's he?"

"Putnam—General Isaac Putnam. He's in town. He asked Dan to call on him. His room's right next to mine. I overheard everything they said. He offered Dan a pardon."

I swung around aghast. "No! What did Dan say?"

"Well, Putnam didn't really offer him a pardon. He put it this way: 'If you had the opportunity, would you accept a pardon and leave these people to themselves?' And Dan answered, 'Yes, in a minute'. Now, wait until I finish. Dan went on to say he had decided to have nothing more to do with stopping courts. He denied he was the leader of the Regulators. But, he added, if he couldn't get a pardon, he'd gather a force and fight to the last extremity rather than be hanged."

"My God, that sounds as if he's getting ready to quit."

Beulah nodded soberly. "You'd better talk to him as soon as you can. I'll talk to him, too. And so will Tom."

I promised I would—at the first opportunity. If Dan Shays quit now, the movement was sure to collapse.

Chapter 29

O N FRIDAY morning, Dan Shays was so busy that I decided to postpone talking to him until I could get him alone at home. He certainly didn't act or talk like a man preparing to abandon our cause. But Beulah, despite her faults, was no liar.

As was inevitable, more and more of our men left town to return home that day. We had word, early in the afternoon, that Luke Day was definitely on his way and might possibly arrive by nightfall. So we spent the afternoon in copying, lightening that tedious task with much banter, as you may imagine. By six o'clock we were all through and messengers were dispatched with letters to the surrounding towns. One post rider took a whole sheaf of them, promising to pass them out in Hampshire and Berkshire.

One piece of business was left to be done—drawing up another petition to the Governor, asking for a special session. Since so many had determined not to wait for Luke Day, we drew one up that very afternoon. I would not sign, for it contained more than the usual number of rebel exaggerations about the violence done to our members. Norman Clarke signed it and sent Obediah Cooley to Boston with it. Mr. Cooley didn't like the assignment at all. He was sure the governor would toss him into jail the moment he read that flaming document.

Now that most of the excitement was over, Beulah became more conspicuous. The Government supporters were circulating a story that the Regulators were attended by a number of lewd women. As soon as Beulah heard it, she decided it was time for her to stay away from the U. S. Arms Tavern entirely. Adam Wheeler agreed that it was best. Accordingly, she took her supper at the Sun Tavern, in the ladies' dining parlor, with only me for company.

The tension between us had almost completely gone, for I decided her action was her own affair and persisted in taking the brighter view that she may not have had any relation with Salderman after I had barged in. I had heard that Salderman had gone on to New York, but we didn't mention his name. Our conversation held to inconsequential topics, bits of gossip about the movement and discussion about incidents occurring around the dinner table. After we had been served our pie, a long pause fell on the conversation.

"I suppose we'll have to go home soon," I said finally.

Beulah nodded. "I hate the thought of it. It's almost like going back to prison. But we can't have what we want forever."

"No, I guess not." I frowned at my pie. "This is one thing my mother can make better than town cooks. I guess we'd better take the sleigh-stage out tomorrow morning. I understand stage service goes on a winter schedule next week."

Beulah concentrated on her pie. "The next one would be Tuesday, wouldn't it? A few days more or less. . . ." She raised her eyes slowly to mine. And she smiled. I smiled back.

Then I swore softly. The setup was perfect, but I couldn't take advantage of it. I took out my store of money to make sure. Beulah had gotten some from her grandfather and we compared notes. If we stayed over 'til Tuesday, neither of us would have stage fare home. As it was, she had to lend me a shilling to cover my bill at the Hancock Arms. There wasn't any possibility of borrowing any money, despite the number of people I knew. They were as stony as I.

But we did have one night together. And a glorious night it was.

Beulah and I caught the morning sleigh-stage, a mode of conveyance much better and speedier than the coaches. At Western, we parted, Beulah hiring a sleigh to go directly home while I would go on to Northampton and come home from that direction. Our holiday was over. I intended to get more money at Northampton, but that didn't help any, for I was too well known in that town. So, we both agreed there would be no point in spoiling everything, especially by returning to Pelham together and allowing the gossips to add one and one to get the correct answer.

It snowed quite heavily that afternoon, so I didn't reach Northampton until late, too late to see Gerson. Accordingly, I was forced to spend the night there. Since I now had a bill to meet and not a farthing in my pocket, you can be sure I was at Gerson's counting room very early the next morning.

Gerson was surprisingly uncordial. "If it's money you're after, sir, don't sit down. I can advance you no more."

My brows went up. "Hasn't Mr. Burdick's letter come?"

"It has," Gerson replied churlishly. "He has given me specific instructions not to advance you any more."

I was stunned. "Why?"

Gerson lifted his shoulders. "Because you're a rebel, I suppose. Oh, I've heard of your activities, sir."

I felt my anger rising, but I held my tongue in check. "There must be some mistake. Burdick owes me a thousand pounds."

Gerson stared at me, fingered a letter on his desk. Then his eyelids drooped shrewdly. "I might be able to advance you a small sum—say, thirty pounds. At a slight cost."

The cost was a mere five pounds—which also irritated me. I objected, but only feebly, for I needed the cash too badly. So, I agreed to the usury.

While he went for the money, I sat down and looked around for Burdick's letter. I found it and read it over carefully. The letter merely stated that I would undoubtedly be coming in and asking for money. Mr. Burdick regretted exceedingly that he would not be able to honor any note of mine at this time. No reason was given for the action. I dipped the quill into the ink pot, drew a piece of notepaper to me and ordered my thoughts for a blistering reply. I wrote at white heat, telling him what I thought of him for withholding my money because of my political activities. I used all the invective at my command. When the letter was finished, I felt a lot better. I tore it up.

I was no fool. Mr. Burdick had a thousand pounds of mine and I had no written proof of it. In the shuffle I'd even lost that accounting he'd given me. I was sure I could prove my case in court, but that would be an expensive and unpleasant business. I decided to suspend judgment until Mr. Burdick had the opportunity to explain himself. In that tone, I wrote a second letter.

Whatever his reason for holding up my money, I begged him to release five hundred pounds in order that I might pay off my father, my uncle and my other friends. I also asked him to pay Mr. Gerson his thirty pounds. I let Mr. Gerson read the letter. Mr. Gerson approved and assured me he'd be only too happy to make certain that the letter got to Boston promptly.

I arrived home just in time for dinner. Nobody seemed very surprised to see me, though mother flew to me and gave me a hug and a kiss the moment I came in. Pa acted as if I'd just been down to the tavern for a while. Increase gave a good imitation of being phlegmatic, too. Then I noticed my place set for me at the table.

"We figured you'd be here today," Pa explained. "Beulah dropped in yesterday."

Without thinking, I said, "Oh yes. How is she?"

"For goodness sake's. Warren," Mother returned, "you saw her in Worcester, didn't you? She said she saw you there. That's how we knew you'd be here."

I felt a little foolish. "Oh. I forgot. I didn't see very much of her. I was too busy."

"Did you look at cloth while you were in New York?" Increase asked shyly.

I grinned. "I saw a fine piece—twenty-two shillings a yard. You'll have to wait for what I owe you, though. I haven't collected my money yet. How are you fixed, Pa?"

Pa smiled and spread his hands. "I got a shilling piece to bite. I won't need more 'til spring. Oh, and that reminds me, I gave your note for taxes. They let me vote at the last town meeting."

Over the dinner table, I had to give an account of my experiences during the trip to New York.

"Then you really did go to New York," Mother remarked when I'd finished. "I'm so glad."

"What makes you think I didn't?"

Pa scratched his chin. "Well, I happened in to Dr. Hynds'

yesterday afternoon. Some of the fellows said it looked suspicious, you and Beulah coming home so close together. I told them I expected you home today."

I became angry. "To hell with the gossips. Let them say what they like. I'm through worrying about them."

Pa laughed. "That's exactly what Beulah said when I told her."

After dinner, I decided to go down to Conkey's, for I was anxious now to have that talk with Dan Shays. The roads had all been broken out, but there hadn't been much traffic to pound it down. In some places I almost sank to my knees in soft snow. As I passed Dr. Hynds' I thought of going in and facing Dr. Cameron and putting an end to the gossip. I was afraid, however, that I'd merely make matters worse. Mr. Gilman was standing in the window and I waved to him. So, now they all knew I was home. Let them make the most of it.

The warm air in Conkey's taproom was loaded down with the smell of steaming clothes and cider and good New England Rum. As soon as I unbuttoned my coat and showed my full face, the boys gave me a rousing welcome. Even Dave Corbett gave me a shy grin. I was rather surprised to see him here and wondered if he had joined up with us. Anyway, he wasn't sore at me any more.

"Dan's in the sitting room," Conkey told me. "How was the trip? I heard you helped catch a murderer."

"I'll tell you about it later," I promised.

The door to the front chamber was open, so I assumed Dan wasn't engaged in any private business. I walked right in. The big oval table was almost covered with papers.

"Warren!" Dan threw down his quill and rose to shake my hand. He grinned and waved at the papers. "Look! Letters from all over the state—most of them approving our stand."

I took off my coat and threw it on the chair. Then, I carefully closed the door. Dan frowned at me, puzzled.

"Dan, I heard you saw General Putnam."

"Oh." Shays was silent a moment. He turned away and walked over to the hearth. "So, you heard about it, too. That makes three, so far—you and Tom and Beulah. Who else knows?"

"Nobody else, as far as I know. But as soon as the General reports back to Boston, that story will be in circulation. I suppose you know that."

Dan gave me a quick look. "I never thought of that."

I shrugged. "I want the truth, Dan. If the Government offers you a pardon, will you accept?"

Dan Shays turned back to the fire and a slow flush crept over his smooth cheeks. He fidgeted a moment, went back to the table, fingered the papers nervously.

"I'll be honest, Warren," he said in a low voice. "I don't know."

His lips tightened and I could see he was struggling with himself to provide his own answer, so I kept quiet. After a while, he walked to the window and stared out over the bleak, white fields.

"Read those letters, Warren," he said heavily. "Over ninety percent of them approve of what we've done. But over half of them are from men who've been in this thing from the beginning. They're worried—worried for themselves and their families. We're all playing with treason. We're all subject to indictment for sedition. We're all liable to hang."

"I've known men to risk the noose for freedom."

Shays whirled from the window. "Good Lord, Warren, you don't think I'm afraid for my neck, do you? If I believed we could win by such a sacrifice, I'd make it willingly. No, no, I'm not thinking of myself. Look what's happened to us—all of us. We stopped the court at Northampton. That was the beginning. Then it was Worcester, Taunton, Great Barrington, Concord, then the Supreme Court at Springfield. We won, didn't we? We got the Legislature into session. Did we get satisfaction? No, we got more suppression. We've lost control of the situation, Warren. Now, it's no longer a matter of choice. We must stop the courts again and again and again. Where will this end? Lincoln and Shepard—and even Knox—are urging the Governor to take firm measures. Suppose Bowdoin stops dilly-dallying and raises an army? That means civil war. God help me, Warren, I would never want it on my conscience that I was instrumental in bringing on a bloody war."

"Dan, do you believe we have right on our side?"

"Certainly, yes." Shays returned promptly.

"If we were crushed, would there be a danger of us all losing more of our freedom?"

Shays was slower to answer this time. "Yes . . . possibly."

"Let's put it this way: If we were crushed, how many of us would be persecuted and sent to the gallows? The leaders, surely. And the people? Would they get less oppression or more?"

Shays gripped the back of his chair. "Am I the only man who must lead this? I didn't ask to be made commander."

"Whether you asked or not, Dan, you are the commander. The men have faith in you. You can't betray them now. You're in too deep. You'd better face it." I gripped his shoulder. "Just think what your betrayal would mean. At best, our movement would go on with another leader. Who would take command? Who covers the power you would spurn? Don't you think Luke Day would like to take over? And what will happen if a man like Luke Day gets the power? Do you think moderation would prevail? Do you think we'd have a chance of compromising and playing for time until the Legislature is in session? You'd exchange the possibility—and a remote one, I believe—of civil war, for the certainty of war."

Shays was thoughtful. He was silent a long time after I had finished. His gaze held to the mass of letters covering the oval table. Then, he smiled slowly.

"It's odd, isn't it," he said softly. "A lot of these men fear for their lives and the safety of their wives and children. Yet, not one has taken advantage of the Amnesty Act. Not one has suggested we abandon the fight for liberty and justice."

The doubts seemed to slip from Dan's shoulders. "I'll be offered a pardon, all right. I shall accept—if our demands are met and a pardon issued to all of our followers."

"About that story, Warren, what shall we do?"

"Spread it around—now before the Government gets it into circulation. Tell everybody you spurned the pardon and that you won't quit until we've won."

The story was duly thrown into circulation. Government supporters tried to get their version to prevail. But ours went out first and thus took the sting out of the Tory tale. As I expected, our followers became more loyal and the neutrals

410

more impressed by Dan's sincerity, even if they weren't ready to swing our way.

Practically all of Pelham was to meeting on Thanksgiving morning. Everyone was dressed in his or her best—which all too frequently was rough homespun, a sure indication of hard times. Our early arrival in the hope that meeting would start early was a waste. But it did give us a chance to greet old friends and talk about last fall's crops and the rebellion and taxes and congratulate our friends on their latest calves and babies.

I hadn't seen Beulah since I had come home, believing discretion the better part of desire, so I looked around for her in the crowd. The Cranes' ping was in the shed, but they were nowhere in sight, so I concluded they'd already gone inside. Rather than go inside myself, I joined a group which included such men as Caleb Keith, Dr. Cameron, Dr. Hynds, Tom Dick, Eb Grey and other substantial citizens of the town. Tom Packard was standing over in a group with Dan Shays and Tom Johnson and other rebels. He had a broad grin on his long, bony face. His ostentatious wink told me he knew why I had chosen this company.

Dr. Cameron shook my hand limply. "You had a successful journey, I hear, didn't you, Warren?"

"Yes, quite successful, thank you. In a month or so, I'll be able to pick up those notes my father and others gave for taxes."

Matt Clark chuckled dryly. "I told 'em you would."

Some of the other selectmen shuffled uncomfortably. Dr. Cameron changed the subject quickly to cover the embarrassment.

"I understand you had adventure, too. A friend of mine in Boston wrote and told me about the Spencer affair. Shocking, wasn't it?"

A lump formed in my stomach. "Very shocking. Though, Mr. Spencer only got what he deserved."

"God's will be done," Dr. Cameron pronounced. "Do tell us about it, Warren."

With considerable uneasiness, I gave a brief account of the affair, watching Dr. Cameron to see if his friend had said anything in his letter about a woman being aboard the schooner. Evidently not, for his questions seemed to indicate he had no idea that Beulah had been along on the trip. Nevertheless, I was not sorry when the time came to file into church.

Our supplier was a young man whose name escapes me. He was surprisingly good—if you like preachers who can tear the hide off the Devil while giving a history of the Pilgrim Fathers. He was astonishingly brief, his sermon lasting only an hour and three quarters. Caleb Keith, our tithingman, only had to wake me up once, though if he had knocked my skull just a trifle harder I wouldn't have awakened at all. Brief as the sermon was, I suffered throughout and I envied my mother and Aunt Hattie, who had footstoves along to keep their feet warm. My own were blocks of ice.

At long last, the services were over and we trooped out like children released from school. Again, everyone gathered into chattering knots—this time families, mostly, grouping for the journey to one of their relation's homes. Uncle Enoch, who had come to our church for the occasion, finally emerged with his sons and daughters-in-law trailing after him. This was the first time I had seen my other cousins since my return home. Cousin Jesse's wife, Emeline, was a formidable looking woman, but Cousin Saul had picked a cute little trick who looked as if a good wind would blow her away. Jenett may have looked like a sparrow, but you should have seen her eat! I noticed Cousin Anzel had forgotten to take the hemlock sprig from his hat.

"How do they stand, Anzel?" I asked, indicating my other two cousins.

Anzel frowned. "Jesse's not on our side. Saul just don't give a damn about neither. Maybe you and me can swing him over, Warren. But if Jesse goes Tory I'll never talk to him again as long as I live."

I winked. "We'll try after they're full of food."

Our house bulged with the number of people who crammed in that day. No one minded the resulting confusion, but the menfolk kept grousing and wondering if the women intended to starve us to death. It was a wonder that none of us collapsed, those odors from the kitchen were so overpowering.

We discussed politics in a desultory fashion, none of us being very rabid for such talk with more important business in the offing. Oddly enough, Jesse seemed to lean more on the Tory side than I expected. Jesse had been at Northampton, but hadn't participated in the movement since then. He was questioning the wisdom of our course, for which I couldn't blame him much. Many of us were wondering whether we could achieve our fond hope of "victory without violence." Increase had only one interest in life at the moment, and it wasn't politics. Mr. Pennington and Uncle Enoch got into a good rousing argument over the best method of castrating lambs.

Finally we were called to dinner. With whoops and shouts, we stampeded to our places, vowing mayhem and utter destruction to those luscious geese and chickens and hams. My father asked Uncle Enoch to say grace. Uncle Enoch uttered the usual familiar sentiments, but they meant just a little more to us on this day. Truly, my mother and father, Increase and I, all had much to thank the Lord for.

The Groaning Board was no idle term that day. Two huge tables had been set, one for the elders and one for the younger people. As host of the younger set, I presided over the second table and was required to carve. At our table alone, we had two tremendous geese, two chickens and a fifteen-pound ham, not to mention the turnips, squashes, potatoes, cranberries and apple sauce, pickled carrots, beets, radish pods and so on ad infinitum. Then, of course, came the pies, mince, apple, pumpkin and cherry. Mother had the nerve to apologize for not having tarts and blanc manges. By that time, we hardly had the strength to accept the apology.

This being the time for celebration, we were given two momentous announcements. The engagement of Increase and Hope was officially proclaimed amid much cheering and toasting in cider. Amid the giggling and joking about the possible issue, Saul was moved to reveal that his wife Jenett, was with child. The women had all known it for a long time, but now it was official. Now, we could openly toast her and hope for a girl, for she only had one girl among three boys. Jenett laughed and assured us Saul would much prefer another boy who could do chores. Personally, I marveled that such a wisp of a woman could produce such a strong, healthy brood.

After dinner Anzel and Jesse got into an argument that almost ended in blows. We knew it was hopeless. Jesse would fight against us.

"Well," I said soothingly, "there's no use in becoming unfriendly about it. The whole affair will blow over soon."

Anzel gave up the argument in disgust. He turned to me and said, "Warren, yesterday our company got together and elected Joel Billings as captain. Step by step, we came to that point. Joel tells me the next step is to get up regular enlistment forms and sign our names to them. We can't turn back unless the Government yields. Will Bowdoin yield? Wake up, Warren. It's fight or hang. And you can be sure, it will be fight—it will be civil war."

Chapter 30

Two weeks remained before the expiration of the Amnesty Act. Two weeks remained to make peace with my conscience or switch my allegiance. I had been shocked out of my complacency, blasted loose from the belief that I could maintain a position of limited liability. With frightening clarity I now saw that the Government, though it had vacillated and hesitated, had never once made the slightest effort to recede from its entrenched position. Peace was still possible. War was probable—civil war. And in war, neither friendship nor sentiment could count. A man's choice of side must depend wholly on his convictions in the rightness and justice of the opposing causes.

Because I was seeking calm and dispassion to help me in my appraisal of my position, I did not go to Springfield on the 26th of December. I didn't miss much. As usual, the Regulators marched in and seized the courthouse. As usual, they sent in a petition to the judges, demanding that the court adjourn. The court bowed and adjourned without fuss or bother. Then the officers of the Regulators met in consultation. From that conference emerged a committee to recruit soldiers. An enlistment form was drawn up. Privates were to be enlisted for three months at wages of 40 shillings a month, plus a large bonus—if they got the day.

That last qualification was ominous. It brought forth pictures of loot and pillage, public and private. Shays, when he got home, defended the enlistment form vigorously. He argued that, since everyone knew we had no cash on hand, we must show the men where we expected to get the money to pay them. He shrugged off my argument that this meant either we would have to loot the public treasury or confiscate the wealth of the rich. Tom Packard merely grinned when I spoke to him about it. He wanted to know where I thought the movement had been drifting all along.

Yet, although the enlistment form had been drawn up and distributed to all the officers, recruiting had not actively begun. Shays insisted there would be no overt recruiting unless and until Governor Bowdoin raised an army against us.

The neutrals were more stubbornly neutral. Few still clung to the hope that the storm would blow over harmlessly. Most had not the slightest doubt that a clash was coming. No one wanted it. Everyone feared it. But the issues were so confused, there was so much right and wrong on both sides that the neutrals wouldn't even try to take a stand. They could afford to wait until violence had clarified the situation. I could not wait. Unless I decided to apply for a pardon before the Amnesty Act expired on January 1, I would be irrevocably in the camp of the Regulators.

The first of January passed quietly. I had come to my decision. I had not applied for a pardon. I had taken my stand in the ranks of the Regulators.

Peace or war, we would have our answer soon. The last test before the opening of the General Court would come at Worcester on the 23rd of January. It would be the irony of ironies if Bowdoin, after so many months of inaction and hesitation would suddenly come to life and act at the very worst moment.

On the eighth of January our doubts were finally laid to rest. Tom Packard, Beulah and I were in Conkey's front chamber, writing some letters, when a guard burst in.

"Sleigh coming, sor!"

"If it's only one sleigh," Tom drawled, "we got nothing to worry about."

A moment later, the sleigh pulled up at the door and the guards challenged him. We kept a heavy guard around the tavern whether Shays was here or not, for we kept our records here. After a moment, a slight, bristly man came striding in.

"Mr. Hascott?" he asked. He saluted as I acknowledged my name and handed me a dispatch. "From Boston, sir."

I snatched it from him. "Hank, see that this gentleman is given refreshments. He looks cold."

The handwriting told me immediately that it was from Mr. Blair. My heart was pounding as I opened it.

"Dear Warren:

The die has been cast—for war. Enclosed is the text of the proclamation Governor Bowdoin has just sent to the printers. It will be issued on January 10th. The Governor has, as you will notice, found it necessary to justify his regime—in a most unconvincing manner, to my mind. Notice, he says he is raising an army, pretending he is merely calling out a portion of the militia.

General Lincoln has almost completed his preparations. According to the latest information, the army will be raised as follows: 700 from Suffolk County, 500 from Essex, 800 from Middlesex, 1200 from Hampshire, 1200 from Worcester, four thousand four hundred men in all.

The Quartermaster-General and the Commissary report there is no food and equipment on hand and no money to buy any. However, Lincoln has received pledges of twenty thousand pounds sterling to equip and victual the army. This, after the Council advised him to borrow no more than six thousand pounds!

I have heard that General Shepard is to be ordered to seize and hold the Springfield Arsenal. It is believed he can do it with three or four hundred men. The rest are to be sent to Worcester to assist Lincoln in upholding the court due to open there on the 23rd of January.

A number of liberal minded gentlemen of this town have been striving desperately to evolve plans acceptable to both sides to stave off disaster. They have made repeated representations to the Governor to call a special session this month, instead of waiting until the first of February. The Governor has flatly refused. He seems now to be under the influence of the most reactionary of the mercantile elements, which is thoroughly alarmed and demanding an end to the threat to their security and their ever beloved "happy constitution." Poor fools! They ask that their own throats be cut. The liberals have given up in disgust. Their plans are no longer debatable. The action is in the hands of the military. Pray God your officers can rise to the occasion.

I am still hanging on here, though my position becomes more difficult day by day. However, you can be sure I have made arrangements to maintain my information should I be forced to flee to Hubbardston or farther west.

Yr friend and ob't s'v't

Boston, January 6th, 1787.   AMOS BLAIR."

The Governor's Proclamation, dated the 2nd of January, was an insult to our intelligence. It was an outrageous denial of every grievance, every failure of the Government, every attempt of the Regulators to obtain justice without the use of violence. Yes, it was a masterpiece of demagogery. It was an outright provocation—perhaps deliberate provocation—to civil war. Could any decent, self respecting Insurgent soften in the face of this mixture of arrogant falsehood and implied threat:

"It has now become evident that the object of the Insurgents is to annihilate our present happy Constitution, or to force the General Court into measures repugnant to every idea of justice, good faith and national policy: And those who encourage or in any way assist them, either individually or in a separate capacity, do partake of their guilt and will be legally responsible for it."

There was an attitude to encourage peace! There was an attitude to encourage us to lay down our arms and throw ourselves upon the mercy of Government! I would not directly accuse Governor Bowdoin of wanting war or being a catspaw to those autocrats who sought to betray our revolution and set up a dictatorship. I can only hold that, if his motives were innocent, he was a blind, incompetent fool.

Tom Packard noticed my rising anger and took the proclamation from me. "You'll bust a blood vessel if you don't watch out, Warren," he said with a chuckle.

"Look to your own blood vessels after you've read it," I

418

growled. "Beulah, get out those letters we prepared—the ones telling the officers to start enlisting their men."

Beulah was very pale. "There's no more hope?" she asked fearfully. "No hope of peace?"

"None whatever," I replied flatly. "The Government has chosen war."

For a long moment, no one stirred. Joe Ranken blinked and his voice shook.

"Is—is it . . . fight?" he asked huskily.

"Yes, it's fight," Tom answered harshly. Then, "I'm sorry."

Joe closed his eyes and tears forced through the lids. "God help us! My Tommy's for the Government."

A sympathetic rustle went through the taproom. Not a man but knew how Joe felt. Not a man but would have a friend or a relative in the firing line opposite him.

Within fifteen minutes, Conkey's Tavern was virtually deserted. Messengers were riding to every point of the compass, all spreading the long awaited, long dreaded command—enlist!

When we were alone, we found we could laugh again and relax and think. Horrible as the news was, it had not been unexpected. We had known, in our hearts, that it must come. Now that it had come, we were vastly relieved. There was an end to waiting and wondering and talking. The time for argument was over. The matter was now in the hands of our military leaders.

"Conkey!" Tom shouted. "Bring us a drink. We need one." He pawed among the papers littering the table. "Looks like it's time for me to enlist, too." He picked up the quill, dipped it carefully into the inkpot and signed his name with a flourish. "There. You, Warren?"

I signed my name under his. "Well, I'll see you on the firing line, Tom."

"Or on the gallows."

Chapter 31

T
HE next morning before I was out of bed, I heard a
sleigh jingling up the lane. Both Increase and Pa were
already at their chores, so I figured one of them would
take care of whoever the visitors were.

Heavy footsteps pounded up the stairs and my door banged
back. I lifted my head over the covers, shivering, for the room
was horribly cold. Dan Shays was standing in the doorway,
holding up a candlestick. He looked very tired, very pale,
very frightened.

"Warren, is it true?" He asked hoarsely.

I yawned. "If you mean, is Lincoln raising an army, the answer is yes—definitely yes."

"My God." He stood very still for a long moment. "That
means war—civil war."

"Well, now that it has come, your job is to lead us to
victory."

"Wait!" He jumped up. "All hope isn't gone. Listen! Remember that petition you drew up in Worcester after I left—
the one signed by Norman Clarke? Well, it was never delivered. The messenger—Cooley, his name was—lost his nerve.
That's why Bowdoin was so angry about it. It was published
in the papers, but he never got a copy. Warren, we want you
to take it to Boston."

I sat up, angry. "Now, listen to me, Dan. This has been
coming on for a long time. We did everything in our power
to stave it off. For Heaven's sake, be a man. Don't turn to
jelly on us."

Dan slumped into the chair, scowling. "I know, I know I
sound like a coward." He rubbed his hands together nerv-

ously. "You won't take the petition to the Governor? There may be hope . . . a chance for peace . . . slim, maybe, but still a chance."

"There is no hope for peace," I said flatly. "I have no influence in Boston. You know that as well as I do."

"Well . . . maybe. But go, anyway—for me. I'd never have a clear conscience if I led troops into battle knowing I'd neglected the slightest opportunity. Please, Warren. Set my mind to rest, if nothing else."

I threw the covers back. "All right, if it will make you feel better, I'll go. I'll talk to everyone I know in Boston. I'll see the Governor himself. I'll do everything possible."

"Fair enough." Dan's lips tightened. "If you fail, you've lost nothing. And you've helped me."

I grabbed my clothes and ran down to the warmth of the kitchen to get dressed.

On this journey, I made the fastest time to Boston of any of my trips. And the cheapest. That was one of the advantages of being on official business for the Regulators. I hadn't realized what an efficient, if informal, courier service had been set up throughout the state for our convenience.

My first stop in Boston, quite naturally, was not strictly in the line of Insurgent business. I gave myself the excuse that I was calling on the Burdicks to fill my purse, which was getting low again. But I knew my interest was not entirely in Mr. Burdick and money.

For the first time Polly wasn't so cordial in her greeting to me. She opened the door only part way and a flush was creeping over her plain features.

"Miss Judith ain't home, Mr. Hascott," she said timidly.

I grinned. "My business is with Mr. Burdick, Polly. Is he home?"

Before she could answer, a voice came from the back of the entry hall. "Who's there, Polly?" Polly opened the door a trifle more to reveal Mrs. Burdick in the parlor doorway. "Oh, it's you again." Her thin lips pressed together as she came over to me. "Judith isn't here. She's gone to Amherst."

My brows went up. "Amherst?"

"For a trip—to visit with the Dobsons. She insisted upon going." Mrs. Burdick's features lost some of the sternness. "Is

421

it true war may come at any moment? I'm worried about her."

"She's safe enough for a while yet," I answered. "There won't be any trouble until the 23rd of this month, at least."

Mrs. Burdick humphed. "I'm worried just the same. You and your Regulators. Why can't we have peace? Wasn't one Revolution enough?"

"I've asked that question a thousand times, M'am. And I've come to Boston to ask it once more—one last time."

Mrs. Burdick became nervous. "Perhaps you shouldn't be seen here, young man. Why that daughter of mine had to go out there to see you. . . ." She caught her breath sharply and then said:

"Well, come in. You may as well stay for dinner."

I started. "Oh, no, thank you just the same. I really came to see Mr. Burdick—honestly, I did."

"Well then, come in. He's home for dinner today—for a wonder. It's not often he keeps his promises."

I was still slightly dazed as I was ushered into Mr. Burdick's den. Absently, I took his outstretched hand.

He gave me a sharp look. "You wanted to see me, Warren?"

"Oh! Oh, yes. Sorry. I was thinking of something else."

Burdick chuckled. "I daresay, you'll catch her in Amherst if you start back tomorrow. She said she'd be staying there a week or more. She has a lot of old friends to visit—to make the trip seem reasonable, you understand."

I grinned. "I hope I do. But I do have business, sir. Could I possibly have some money, sir?"

"A hundred pounds be enough? I can manage that amount. I'm strapped at the moment. That's the honest truth, Warren. In another month, your money will be transmitted to Boston and I'll have it for you."

"A hundred pounds would be fine."

Burdick poured glasses of Madeira for us. "Tell me, what's the situation out in the west?"

"Warlike, sir." I told him my mission to Boston. "I expect the Governor was angry when he saw the petition in the press and had no copy of it delivered to him."

Burdick shrugged. "I doubt if it would have made any difference. Bowdoin is now under the influence of those men who want him to use strong measures. He believes he has

422

done the best he can and has shown extreme patience toward the Regulators."

"If he had worried more about settling domestic issues and less about us, we'd have laid down our arms long ago." I finished my wine and got up. "I really must hurry along."

Mr. Burdick opened the chamber door and escorted me into the hall. "Drop by later at the counting house for that money. And good luck in your mission, Warren." He hesitated, a bit embarrassed. "About the rest of the money—don't worry about it. You'll get it, no matter what happens." He put out his hand. "I hope we'll be friends always, war or no war."

I said nothing about his letter to Mr. Gerson. Neither did he.

I did not hesitate when I reached State House. I was aware I was again liable to arrest as a rebel, but I felt sure I wouldn't be jailed until after I had seen the Governor. Since hostilities hadn't yet opened and my mission was peace, I could hope that I would receive some sort of a reply to take back and thus assure myself of momentary immunity from prosecution.

As I came up the circular stairway to the second floor, I spied Mr. Blair standing outside his office and chatting with a distinguished looking gentleman in a tan broadcloth coat. Blair started as he saw me, quickly excused himself and hurried over. For once, he was not glad to see me.

"What are you doing here?" he demanded in a hoarse whisper. "Are you crazy, Warren? The Governor's Council is sitting in there right this minute. They're drawing up a list of Insurgents to be arrested. Do you want your name on it?"

"It's probably there already," I said dryly. I took the petition from my pocket. "Do you remember the petition we drew up at Worcester on December 5th or 6th? It was published in every paper, but the Governor never got a copy. Here it is."

Blair grunted and straightened his wig. "Useless, totally useless. They won't listen to you. It's too late."

"I promised," I insisted. "I must deliver it. Take my word, it's important to the cause."

"All right. You're a fool, but. . . ." His thin shoulders lifted. "Let me have it. I'll take it in to the Governor."

"I'd rather see the Governor myself, if I may."

Blair scowled at me, then spread his hands. "If you insist. It's your neck."

A ten pound cannon ball suddenly felt as if it was settling in the pit of my stomach. My knees were not quite steady as I walked by Mr. Blair and entered the Council Chamber.

Governor Bowdoin, a stern, stocky gentleman, was seated at the speaker's desk. He wore a cued white wig, a claret broadcloth coat, a cravat of fine Holland lace. Over to one side was another desk, at which John Avery, the Governor's Secretary was seated. The councilors were seated along the front row, their faces turned to me, and I recognized some of them—Thomas Cushing, the Lieutenant-Governor; Samuel Phillips, the president of the Senate, and Spooner, a wealthy merchant. Also present, but seated to the left were Sam Adams, General Lincoln and General Ward. It was a gathering likely to awe a better man than myself.

The door thumped behind me and I felt horribly alone. The hostile faces did not give me an overweaning confidence, either. The Governor motioned me to come forward and I did. My legs felt curiously wooden.

I brought out the petition and dropped it on his desk as if it were hot. Behind me someone was snickering.

"Another petition!"

A retort leaped to my lips as I swung around to see who had made that remark. I kept my peace. Governor Bowdoin was smiling as he waved to his secretary.

"Read it to us, John."

Mr. Avery took the petition—which was pretty bedraggled looking, another cause for embarrassment to me—and, holding it gingerly as far away from him as possible he read it out. He had some difficulty with some of the sentences, which were not very grammatical, and with some of the words, which were not very legible. The snickers made me angry, however, for I knew the writers had been sincere—if a bit crude.

There was a postscript, explaining that the messenger originally sent had failed of his duty in delivering the petition. The explanation ended thusly:

". . . However, we now beg leave to present said petition to Your Excellency and your Honours in full confidence of its meeting your kind reception and wise consideration and deliberation therein, and that we may have a kind and gracious answer to the prayer thereof. . . ."

Since the postscript also asked the council to deliver its answer by the bearer, I waited patiently until Mr. Avery was finished. From the scowls, I had little hope of a favorable reply. Only General Lincoln's round face was perfectly placid.

When the secretary was through, Lincoln leaned over. "Young man, I'd remove my hat if I were you. I don't think these gentlemen quite approve of the badge of rebellion you're wearing."

I turned crimson and snatched the hat off my head. "I'm sorry. I didn't realize. . . ." Had I tried to act the country bumpkin, I couldn't have succeeded better.

"If you'll step outside, young man," Bowdoin suggested, "we'll consider the petition at once. Your friends seem in a hurry for an answer."

Mr. Blair was waiting for me in the other hall. But he wasn't alone. He was talking to a worried looking young man.

"Warren," Blair said, taking my arm, "I want you to meet Job Shattuck, junior. He's trying to get bail for his father. . . . Mr. Hascott's a rebel, too, as you can see from his hat."

I grinned. "The Governor saw, too—and was not favorably impressed. Glad to know you, sir. How is your father—his wound?"

The younger Job shrugged. "Pa had a pretty bad time of it for a while. But the wound's healing and he's well enough to be hungry again. They're giving him a tonic of bark and wine but no spiritous liquors and no meat." The boy grinned. "I can't figure which denial bothers him most."

Just then a bell tinkled and the attendant opened the door a trifle and poked his head in.

"Send that young man in, Mike," the Governor called.

The guard opened the door wide and I walked down the aisle, my heart thumping wildly. One or two of the councilors turned to stare at me, the rest were absorbed in their thoughts. As I stopped before the podium, the Governor folded his hands before him, his lips tightening.

"After due deliberation and by advice of Council, I regret I must reject the petition in its entirety."

I bit my lip, making no effort to hide my disappointment. "You're making a bad mistake, Your Excellency."

Someone behind me snorted. "Why, the impudent puppy! When we want your advice, we'll ask for it."

I whirled. "Impudent, am I! I'd rather be impudent than stupid! You're a pack of fools or else traitors to your country. If you had one lick of sense. . . ."

The Governor's hand slapped the table, cutting me off short. "That will be all, Mr. Hascott," he said coldly.

"All!" I half shouted. "You dismiss me like a servant, like a two-year-old idiot. I'm not pleading for my neck. I'm pleading for the Commonwealth you've sworn to uphold, for the homes that will be ruined, for the soldiers who will be killed, for the misery and devastation. . . ."

"Enough!" the Governor roared. His hands were trembling a little and it was with an effort that he held his voice low. "You and your pack of profligates are in rebellion against the duly constituted Government. I am determined to uphold that Government. If violence ensues, the blame is yours and yours alone. Any further dealings you have with Government will be through General Lincoln. Now, get out!"

I was calm, icily calm. "I want you to remember this, gentlemen, and remember it well: Never has a rebel—so called—found it necessary to explain himself to the people. Not one of our side would lower himself to accept amnesty from a tyrant. We asked for justice. We asked for peace. You denied us both. I see I bore you. My humble apologies. Indeed, Your Excellency, do send General Lincoln to Worcester on the 23rd. We will surely deal with him there—with lead."

Once in the open air, I lost my rage and a mood of depression fell over me. I shouldn't have lost my temper. Those dramatics had done neither me nor the cause any good. I should have tried to reason—I grunted sourly. Reason! Those asses didn't know the meaning of the word.

I turned up Kilby Street before I was fully aware of my next destination. This was the way to the Burdicks, but I wasn't going there. Then, as I turned into Battery Marsh

Street along the waterfront, I realized that the one man I wanted to see now was Jothan Salderman.

The very idea of talking to that man made me sick to my stomach. But I would not be visiting him on personal business, so I had to forego the pleasure of beating his head off. I had to admonish myself to remember to hold a check on my temper. It was going to be hard. But it was for the cause. Verily, I was going through a lot for the cause.

The tide was half out and the vast expanses of Dorcester Flats were exposed, but it was so cold that I couldn't smell the mud. By the time I reached Salderman's Wharf, I was so thoroughly chilled that I would have welcomed the prospect of a good tussle with him. The wharf was empty and, from the look of the warehouse, it seemed his business was closed down for the winter. But his door was unlocked, so I walked in. I headed straight for the fire, giving myself one last reminder to hold my temper. Salderman's ancient clerk slid off the stool and asked me my business.

"Inform Mr. Salderman that Mr. Hascott would see him."

The clerk bowed and went into Salderman's office. He was out in a moment, inviting me in. I entered and closed the door behind me. Salderman was coming around the desk, stretching out his hand, showing no embarrassment or memory of our encounter. With relief, I found I held no anger toward him, only contempt.

"Mr. Hascott! I didn't expect to see you in Boston. Sit down, sir, sit down." He poured brandies for us. "I suppose your're here on rebel business?"

"I've just been to see the Governor with a petition."

"Another one?" Salderman smiled and shook his head. "I can read the Governor's answer in your face, Mr. Hascott." He handed me a glass. "Shall we drink to open insurrection?"

"We may as well. It's coming—on the 23rd of this month, I believe. To the Regulators, sir!"

Salderman lifted his glass to the toast and we drank.

I sat down. "The matter's too far gone to talk about any possibility of peace, Mr. Salderman. That's dead. So, suppose we get down to business. We'll need money."

Salderman leaned back in his chair and twirled the glass stem in his long fingers. "Any idea of how much to start?"

"No, I've made no accurate survey. We'll need powder,

muskets, blankets, tents, and all the rest of the equipment necessary to maintain an army in the field."

Salderman frowned into his glass. "I could offer you money —say, about five thousand pounds. But the money wouldn't be of any value to you. You couldn't buy a musket or a grain of powder here in Boston. I doubt if you could get them in New York. Lincoln's bought up all the arms and ammunition in town and he's contracted for a store of military equipment the British left behind in New York."

"We're desperate for powder and ball. Any powder mills within easy reach of our part of the country?"

"I think there're one or two in Connecticut," Salderman answered. "There's a supply of arms and ammunition much nearer, though. And it's yours for the taking."

I looked up quickly. "Where?"

"The Springfield Arsenal."

I nodded. "I can safely predict we'll try to seize the arsenal. Shepard's planning to seize it, too, I've heard. Luke Day's watching the place. We won't have much trouble there." I spread my hands. "But we'll need money, too."

Salderman smiled. "Of course. I can let you have two hundred and fifty pounds now—more later. I'll deposit two thousand in gold with Mr. Flemming in Springfield by . . . by . . . shall we say the 27th of this month?"

I saw through his scheme at once. By the 27th, we would have had our first encounter with Lincoln. The result would be known. If we inflicted a decisive defeat on him, we'd get the money. If we were beaten decisively. . . .

I got up and put on my hat. "Fair enough."

"One thing more, Mr. Hascott." Salderman rose languidly, pursing his lips and looking into the fire. "You'll need a lot more arms—ultimately—than you can get from the Springfield Arsenal. You may have to accept help from obnoxious sources —especially if the Government holds the seacoast."

I hadn't thought of that. And the idea disgusted me a little. Then, I shrugged.

"Let's not be coy, Mr. Salderman. You mean we'll have to get arms from Canada—from the British. Well, in war, men are willing to accept help from the Devil himself. You can be damn sure, however, we will not embrace the Devil. We'll be damn careful the Devil doesn't worm himself into our confidence."

Salderman lifted one brow. "I trust Dan Shays is as much of a realist as you are, Mr. Hascott. I'd be afraid to send an agent to him. Be on the lookout for him, will you? A man named Jaeger, a German."

"I'll be watching for him. And please keep this in mind, Mr. Salderman: There must be no question of sending British troops to help us—supplies only."

"Naturally. I daresay your men would mutiny if British troops joined them. Supplies only." Salderman smiled crookedly. "We wouldn't want the British to get the fruits of our victory, eh?"

I merely shrugged. Once we accepted British supplies, it would be hard to fend off British influence in our councils. I feared that less, however, than the influence Salderman and men of his ilk would attempt to exert once the war was under way. I was well aware Salderman was not interested in justice or in winning the next elections or our democratic form of government. He wanted a military dictatorship—with Jothan Salderman manipulating the puppets Shays and Luke Day and Adam Wheeler. I was confident that he was vastly underrating their intelligence.

Salderman left the office briefly and came back with a purse of two hundred and fifty pounds in hard money. I thanked him and assured him the money would be put to good use. He was in high good humor as he saw me to the door.

"Secrecy is the watchword, Mr. Hascott," he said as he shook my hand. "No hint of Yeager's British connections must leak out. There are Americans who are squeamish about accepting the Devil as their ally. . . . Good luck, sir."

I thanked him and hastily departed. I felt unclean and squirmy, as if I had passed through a louse-infested barn.

At Long Wharf, I stopped in at Mr. Burdick's and picked up that fifty pounds, then decided to subject myself to one more unpleasant encounter before leaving Boston for what might be the last time. Again, the very thought of coming face to face with an even lower specimen than Salderman made my knuckles itch. Again, I admonished myself to keep my temper in check. Again, it was for the same cause.

Mr. Ormund Graham was surprised to see me. His churlish

protest at this rude interruption died in his throat. He became quite pale around the gills, his mouth opening and shutting like a fish gulping for air. I kicked the door closed behind me and sat down in the chair facing him.

"Well, it's Mr. Hascott!" he finally blustered. He got up from his desk, came around to me and held out his hand. "I do owe you an apology, sir. I tried to arrange your release from jail that morning, but I found it would take another day. Naturally, that business in New York couldn't wait. And when I got back. . . ."

"We can dispense with explanations, Mr. Graham," I broke in. "I'm not here for apologies. I'm here on business."

Mr. Graham retired into his dignity. His mouth regained its sullenness and he dropped his hand awkwardly to his side. With a stiff nod, he went back behind his desk and sat down.

"Just what is your business?" he asked coldly.

"We'll waste no time sparring, Mr. Graham. War is certain to break out within the next two weeks. The Rebels need guns. How many can you get for us?"

Mr. Graham straightened slowly. "You expect me to have dealings with that scum? Me, an upholder of good government."

"We'll pay cash," I said abruptly. "In gold."

Graham's mouth remained open for some moments. Then, he closed it, leaned back, his eyes narrowing.

"Well . . ." he drawled.

"One and a half joes, gold, per musket."

"I'm paying eighteen Spanish dollars and you offer me twenty-two? Don't be ridiculous. The Government's willing to pay me thirty. As a special favor, Mr. Hascott, you can have them for fifty dollars each."

"Deliver them in Pelham and we'll pay you forty."

"In gold?"

"In gold."

Graham's thin, patrician fingers drummed the desk. "Payable in advance . . . here in Boston."

"I'll meet you halfway, Mr. Graham. Payable on delivery in Shrewsbury on the 30th of this month."

"It's a deal." Graham pulled the stopper from his brandy bottle. "A drink on it?"

"No thanks. I've had enough for a while today. How about powder and ball?"

"I know where I can lay hands on a store."

"We'll buy all you can lay hands on. Let me know how much you can deliver, muskets and ammunition, and we'll have the money ready for you. We have ample backing—not British."

Graham's lips tightened. "German?"

My head cocked and I wanted to ask him where he had gotten that idea, but I thought it best not to press the matter.

"All right, I'll send a man out to see you," Graham said. "He'll settle the details. Watch for him in about two weeks."

I nodded curtly and walked out.

It didn't take me long to decide which of those two men was the most contemptible. Jothan Salderman was ambitious, with delusions of becoming another Caesar. Ormund Graham sought only to become another Judas.

All in all, however, I felt well pleased with the results of my trip to Boston. True, I would have been happier if some good had come from my interview with the Governor. But I hadn't expected anything from that direction. Having laid the groundwork, we now could be assured of desperately needed supplies. I had no doubt that I would be able to pay Graham for every pound of powder and every musket. The Regulators must only win the first battle.

On reaching the Salvation Inn, I found that Mr. Blair had not come to meet me, but had sent a note. He urged me to quit the town just as fast as possible. The Governor and his council were now drawing up a list of Rebels to be arrested. Shays was on the list, as was Wheeler, Luke Day, Eli Parsons, and everyone else who had been prominent in the movement. Blair promised to send me the complete list just as soon as one was available.

I wasn't a bit annoyed to hear that warrants were about to be issued against us. Indeed, I was glad. More than anything else, a warrant in the name of Dan Shays would put real stiffness into his spine.

Chapter 32

I ARRIVED back in Pelham at dusk of the following day, having been relayed from town to town by the Regulator couriers. Conkey's Tavern showed lights from every room, for Shays had now taken residence there, along with his bodyguard of some thirty men. The taproom was very crowded, since it was suppertime. But everyone lost interest in food the moment I walked in. Everyone set up a clamor for news.

Shays came running from the front chamber and pushed his way through to me, trying to quell the pandemonium. He was successful, too. It was remarkable how quickly the men obeyed. Truly, they had accepted him as their Commander-in-Chief.

As soon as he got a semblance of quiet, he asked eagerly, "What happened, Warren? Any hope at all?"

"Not the slightest," I replied. "And this is official. I saw the Governor himself, and the Council."

I repeated word for word, as closely as I could remember, what had transpired in the Council chamber. I modestly toned down the useless speech I had made at the end of the interview. When my tale was finished, the men were growling and they quickly melted away, returning to their food and discussing the news in angry tones. Most were resigned to war. Some were eager. Only a few showed signs of weakening. And among those few was Dan Shays.

"I have one more bit of news of personal interest to you, Dan. The Governor's issuing warrants for our arrest. Your name is at the top of the list."

As I expected, Dan grew pale. But after a moment, he lifted

his shoulders and smiled. "I could have expected that. Well, I guess we're in to the bitter end."

I gave Dan the purse. "Here's something to keep us going for a while."

He hefted the purse and whistled softly. "Salderman? If that man thinks he can buy me, he's mistaken."

"I'm damn glad to hear that, Dan." I slapped his shoulder. "I'll be back in a little while."

I thought of going right over to Amherst to call upon the Dobsons—and Judith. But, as I came over East Hill, my enthusiasm for that idea oozed away. It came to me with an unpleasant shock that I was in a pretty mess. I was in love with Judith, there was no doubt of it in my mind. Yet, now that war had come, a barrier had been set up between us. Judith was no Tory by any means. But she was tied to the Tory cause, both by family and her way of life and thinking since the Revolution. Before, compromise had been possible. Now, there was none. Passion wouldn't be enough to keep our marriage happy. If we disagreed fundamentally on political issues, we would face growing bitterness, suspicion and hate. Not even the end of the war would wipe that out. Strange that politics should be a factor in marriage. Yet, I knew full well that it would be a vital factor.

And inevitably, my thoughts turned to Beulah. Beulah and her luscious charms and vigorous body, her strong mind and her generosity, her honesty and her almost contradictory feminine illogic. Beulah would make me a good wife, one on whom I could always depend to stand by me in trouble or trial. Yet, I now knew I had never seriously considered tying myself to her. She lacked something indefinable.

This was one of the few times of my life I ever suspected myself of clairvoyance. As I came up to the house, I noticed that the light shining from the window seemed brighter than usual. I concluded at once that we had company. I knew immediately that Judith was there. Then, with a sinking sensation, I saw we had other guests, among them Beulah.

The greetings to me were subdued as I came in. My Uncle Enoch and Cousin Anzel were there, too, obviously come over to get the news. I was glad they were here, for I sensed they'd serve more or less as a shield between me and my other two guests. Mother got up and kissed me.

433

"We waited for you," she said. "We didn't think you'd come any later tonight."

"I had to stop at Conkey's," I explained. I shucked my coat and gloves and hung my hat up, then went directly to Judith. "I stopped by at your house, Judith. Your mother told me you'd come out to Amherst for a visit."

Judith's lips pressed together. "I thought I'd come once more before . . . before the war broke out."

I caught myself staring at her a bit too hard. She was certainly a handsome woman. She was wearing a beautifully tailored brown traveling dress of fine broadcloth. I started, smiled, and winked at Beulah.

"Anything happen while I was away?"

Beulah smiled back. "You had company, that's all."

Everyone laughed politely and I shook hands with my uncle and cousin. Uncle Enoch looked terribly tired. There were dark rings under his deep, brooding eyes.

"Is there hope, Warren?" he asked huskily.

I shook my head. "I'm sorry to say, no. I saw the Governor himself. I'm about ready to believe all the stories I've heard about him. The only petition he would have entertained was complete surrender."

Judith put her elbows on the table, clasping her hands. "Perhaps that would have been better than war."

Beulah sniffed. "We'll surrender our liberties only to superior force. Any other course would be cowardly."

"How are the Dobsons, Judith?" I asked quickly.

"Fine." She didn't even look at me. "I suppose you'd say this was inevitable—that there must be killing."

Beulah frowned. "People who aren't willing to die for their freedom don't deserve it."

I dawdled with my food, tried again to turn the conversation. "How are things with you, Uncle Enoch?"

The look of pain that crossed his heavy features told me at once that I'd taken the wrong tack.

"Saul and Margery have separated."

My mouth dropped open. "No!"

Uncle Enoch nodded slowly. "Saul's decided to turn out for Government. Margery's brother and father have joined your ranks, so she went home to them."

I suddenly wasn't hungry any more. "I suppose Jesse hasn't changed his mind."

Anzel grunted. "I think he was the one who got Saul over to the Government."

"Wife against husband," Judith said softly, "brother against brother. And you talk about dying for liberty."

"God help us all," Uncle Enoch rumbled.

A gloomy silence fell over the table. I ate absently, vaguely surprised to find my plate almost empty. This was a rotten situation from beginning to end.

"We'll know how we all stand after the 23rd," Anzel commented. Then added, "I wish it was over."

"So do I," my mother said. She was standing beside me, absently wiping her hands on her apron. "I went through one war. I prayed God I'd never see another. I lost one boy as a result of the Revolution."

"Shucks, Ma," my father said in a too hearty voice, "Warren's safe enough. If the Turks couldn't kill him, I guess Bowdoin's bullets won't harm him. Why, come spring, him and Beulah will be all married and settled."

I winced. Pa noticed it and his eyes widened, realizing his mistake. I had thought about it and resigned myself—no, not exactly to marrying Beulah, but to drifting along until caught. I had drifted. I was caught.

Pa coughed. "Well, not exactly marrying her," he said with a nervous laugh. "It ain't all settled yet. You know how gossip is. We all figure. . . ."

Pa gulped. And my mind had to pick that precise moment to go blank. I said nothing.

"Well," Judith said finally, in a small, breathless voice. "I didn't know. Congratulations, Warren—and Beulah."

Beulah was watching me with half-closed eyes, her face showing nothing. Then, "As Mr. Hascott said, nothing's really settled yet."

Then, Ma had to put in her t'pence worth. "Pa and I even got a piece of land picked out for you—if Warren wants to stay."

Inwardly, I groaned. I really couldn't blame my mother—or anyone else, except myself. I couldn't think of a damn thing to say that wouldn't make matters worse. I had to think of Judith's feelings, too. She wasn't aware I knew why she had come here. There was only one thing I could do—keep my mouth shut and pray I could get her alone a moment before she left.

Pa made a feeble attempt to resume the conversation. Neither Uncle Enoch nor Anzel seemed aware that anything was wrong. They had shown no surprise and had not bothered to congratulate me, thank Heaven! But it was disconcerting to know they had taken it for granted. This was the only time my mother's pie tasted like straw. Never did I dream that I'd experience nostalgia for the simple tortures of the Algerian galleys.

A decent interval passed before Judith got up from the table. "It's been a very pleasant visit. I must go now."

Pa jumped up. "Shucks, don't run off like this," he said politely, then turned, "Hey, Harry!" Judith's negro servant came from the parlor. "Miss Judith wants to go. Have enough to eat?"

"Yes, sar. Yes, indeed, thank you, sar." He bowed. "I fetch the sleigh immediate."

"I'll help you hitch up," Pa offered.

"No, sar, thank you, sar. I kin do hit myself."

Pa gave him a lantern and he thanked my mother for the meal, then shuffled out, shaking his woolly head. Harry must have thought my family crazy, putting him in the parlor while we ate in the kitchen. I was only surprised that they hadn't set a place for him at the table with us, for out this way a servant was a hired man. Color of skin didn't mean much to folks in the country districts.

My father helped Judith on with her cloak. Beulah eyed the garment, torn between envy and resentment, understandable enough. It was a very expensive cloak, made of heavy black velvet lined with red flannel. Judith tucked her curls under her hood, then kissed my mother and thanked her for her hospitality.

She extended her hand to Beulah. "Goodby, Beulah. I hope I see you again soon—after the troubles are over."

Beulah took her hand boldly. "Soon. If—when, I mean, we win, maybe we'll live in Boston, too—in a house like yours."

Judith smiled. "If we have to flee the country, perhaps you can get our house."

"Like you got it—from a departing Loyalist?"

436

Judith was the only one who didn't show embarrassment. She laughed lightly. "Exactly—at a fraction of its cost."

Judith said goodnight to Uncle Enoch and Anzel, then offered me her hand. I refused it, taking her by the elbow and escorting her outside. No one followed us.

"Look, Judith, there was a misunderstanding . . . that talk of marriage. You know how it is in a place like this, you talk to a girl once or twice and the gossips immediately take the dark view."

Judith's brows went up. "Why, Warren, don't tell me you've been playing with that girl's affections. She may not say so, but she thinks everything's settled."

I waved impatiently. "Nonsense. Beulah's a sensible girl. She doesn't believe that just because people talk it means we must marry. That's why I kept my mouth shut in there—to spare everyone's feelings. The old folks don't understand."

"Understand what, Mr. Wiseacre?" Judith shook her head slowly. "You take a peculiar attitude toward women, Warren. They weren't made to amuse you. They are human beings—with hearts as well as minds. Spare everyone's feelings, indeed! You haven't thought of anyone but yourself since you came home."

She turned away quickly and walked over to the waiting sleigh. I caught her as she was stepping in.

"Judith, it's you I want to marry. I know it's impossible now, but in a little while. . . ."

Judith's brows arched. "I've heard that before, I think."

"Dammit, you know it's impossible—with this war coming on." I seized her arms, turned her around. "There is a way out of the dilemma—if you have courage. We can go west. There's land out there—opportunity."

Judith giggled. "I heard you gave Ethan Blair some advice along that line." She patted my cheek. "Stop thinking, Warren, you're losing your mind. And remember, I've already decided to marry Jothan."

I scowled. "You're not going to marry him."

"And why not, pray?"

"I can't tell you. But unless I've misjudged you, you're not going to marry him—not after you find out. . . ."

I closed my mouth before I said too much. It wouldn't be

well to reveal Salderman's activities in our behalf, even to Judith. This was no longer a personal matter. This was war.

Judith didn't press me, which oddly enough irritated me. Then my mother came out with Judith's footwarmer, ending my last chance to say all those things I had in my heart to say. Perhaps it was just as well that I didn't have the opportunity to make more of a fool of myself. I tucked her into her blankets and, as I leaned over her, I came within an inch of kissing her ripe red lips. Her head drew back with mocking deliberateness.

"Goodby, Warren. Be sure to drop in on us if you ever visit Boston again." Her tone revealed her doubt. "Goodby, Mrs. Hascott. . . . And I wouldn't worry about Warren if I were you. God always takes care of mothers' little boys."

That stung. She crinkled her nose at me and gave the order to Harry. I scowled at the sleigh until it turned out into the road. She was angry, all right. I would have felt better if she had given a sign of it. She hadn't even looked back.

I wasn't very good company after I returned inside. I tried hard to keep my grouch covered, but Beulah noticed. She kept the conversation going by asking Anzel who and how many would turn out from Amherst. Anzel didn't know, since he had already left home and was staying at the Rutland Barracks. He was home on leave and returning tomorrow morning. Listening to him and watching my Uncle Enoch, I realized my troubles were trivial and unimportant. That didn't make them any less annoying. I was glad when Anzel and Uncle Enoch decided to leave. Beulah got up, too, and put on her cloak.

"Hitch up, Anzel," my uncle ordered. "We'll take you home, Beulah."

"Thank you just the same, but I'd like to walk. It isn't far. And that hill is terribly slippery. You might get stuck."

I got into my greatcoat. "I'll see you home, Beulah."

I didn't feel much like talking, so we walked along the frozen road in silence. The moon was over the horizon, giving the hushed white countryside a lovely metallic sheen. The gaunt, ice-trimmed trees and the glistening, snow-covered fields seemed particularly beautiful and peaceful this evening. Here was none of the dirty slush of Boston's streets. Here was none of the ceaseless bustle and endless scheming and matching of wits with the lords of the counting houses. Here God, not Mammon, ruled. There was room for me here, not necessarily as a farmer, if I would but give up those grandiose dreams of trading with and beating the world.

I held Beulah's arm tight as we went down the steep, slippery hill that curved past the Crane place. Her nearness again stirred my pulses and filled me with that vague, warm discomfort I knew so well. As we came into the barnyard, I could hear the eternal tap tapping of Joab's hammer. Irrelevantly, I was thinking that Pelham was only two days from the sea.

At the door, Beulah tried to move away. I held her arm tight, turned her to me. I tried to sound casual, but my voice was clumsily gruff.

"Maybe we ought to settle it now, Beulah. Do you want to publish the banns now or in the spring?"

Her grey eyes widened. "I . . . I don't know."

"Maybe the spring is best. We'll get married at the same time as Increase and Hope. The troubles should be over then."

I must have sounded a bit irritable. That's how I felt, not toward her, but myself. I could feel myself flushing. Again I was seeking a postponement of the inevitable.

"Well?" I asked impatiently.

Beulah didn't resist as my arm went about her waist. She trembled slightly and, like a small, frightened child, she clung to my lapels. Lord, how I wanted that woman. I pressed my lips against hers, gently, pleadingly. Slowly, her arms crept over my shoulders. She was mine.

Our lips parted and her head drew back slightly, as if waiting for me to say something more. Then, she shivered.

"I . . . I don't know, Warren. I don't know."

She slipped from my arms and half ran to the house. As the light from the opening door flooded over her slim figure, I took an impulsive step forward. I stopped short, startled. I could have sworn that girl was crying.

It was some moments before I recovered from my astonishment.

Dr. Cameron went out of his way to be pleasant to Beulah on the Sabbath and, when he passed a remark about setting a date for her marriage to me, she was non-committal. How swiftly news traveled in our town! Anzel had mentioned it in Conkey's after leaving our house that evening and, lacking denial from me, everyone accepted it as true. I had given up the struggle. Beulah had said nothing about it since that evening. The decision was in her hands.

To show my own attitude, I made a point of walking home from church with her. We confined our talk mostly to the cause, since she hadn't been around to Conkey's since Friday and she wanted to know if anything happened. Somehow, she managed to drag Dave Corbett into the conversation, telling me what a fine fellow he was. It annoyed her considerably when I agreed. She thereupon castigated poor Dave for refusing to enlist.

On Monday, the 15th of January, the officers came in for the general strategy meeting which Dan had called. Beulah came in around nine o'clock, for Mr. Conkey had asked her to help Mrs. Conkey with her bar duties that day. The bar became quite an attraction with Beulah behind it. I hardly got three words with her, she was so busy filling orders and fending off lotharios. The age of some of the gentlemen seeking her smiles was evidence that youth had no monopoly on the roving eye.

Dan Shays came down shortly after the dinner dishes were cleared away. Everyone stood up and gave him a resounding ovation. Dan flushed with pleasure at this demonstration of confidence in him. He was well turned out in his best uniform coat and white breeches. He carried a map rolled up under his arm. I have often been puzzled by the lack of jealousy shown toward Dan's assumption of command. Lord knows, there was bickering enough among the officers over minor prerogatives and commands. Perhaps it was that Dan didn't really care about leading the Regulators. Everyone knew he would gladly have stepped down had anyone so requested him.

Dan slowly made his way to his table—the big center table near the fire, of course—shaking hands and having a word with practically everyone along the way. Conkey promptly brought him a mug of cider, urging him to try it. Dan thanked him politely and picked up the mug.

"To the Regulators, gentlemen!" Everyone was on his feet.

"To victory!" Luke Day added in a booming voice.

Dan put down his cup carefully and spread out his map. "If you don't mind, gentlemen, I'll act as chairman of this meeting. The chair is open to suggestions. As you all know, Lincoln will move from the vicinity of Boston on the 19th or 20th and march in to support the court at Worcester on the 23rd. Shepard, I understand, is to hold the Springfield Arsenal with a small force and send the bulk of his levies to Worcester to aid Lincoln. It is obvious, therefore, that Lincoln expects us to attack him at Worcester and try to close down that court. The question is: Shall we do the obvious?"

A respectful, and somewhat puzzled, silence held the room. Finally, Day grunted. "Got a better idea, Dan?"

"I've been considering the whole matter," Shays went on. "It seems to me, if we mobilized first and moved into Worcester, that place would be hard to defend. The terrain favors neither side—neither attacker nor defender. We could certainly stop the court from sitting. But suppose the judges decided to hold the court behind Lincoln's lines—say at Leicaster. The court would do little business, but the moral effect on the people would be considerable. Whatever business was transacted would constitute a defeat for us. And, at the same time, we would be trapped in Worcester. Lincoln would surround us and smash us by attack or starve us out by siege. Either way, we lose."

Shays paused and stared into space, as if visualizing the map. "On the other hand, we could wait until Lincoln took over Worcester, surround him and either try to smash him by attack or starve him out by siege. With us, only the former alternative is feasible. We would have to attack—and that, gentlemen, would be bloody business. Not only would we lose half our army, but we would be likely to lose the people. We would be held up by the Government as the aggressors."

"How about siege?" Gale put in. "We could starve him out. The people of Worcester would support us with provisions."

"Yes, we could do that," Shays agreed. "But we'd be vulnerable. If Lincoln chose to sit and wait, Bowdoin could raise another army in the east and send it against us to lift the siege. Again, we'd be in for a bloody time."

Luke Day snorted. "After all, Dan, you can't expect to run a war without somebody getting hurt."

Shays smiled wryly. "Perhaps not, Luke. But I would like to settle the matter as quickly and bloodlessly as possible. And. . . ." he lifted his finger ". . . as far from Boston as possible."

"How do you figure, Dan?" Wheeler asked.

"Here's the plan, in broad outline. Instead of us going to meet Lincoln, we should make Lincoln come to meet us. I suggest we stay in Hampshire County with as great a force as we can muster right now—three thousand would be enough, even if Lincoln raised his full force of forty-four hundred. The farther from Boston Lincoln gets, the longer become his lines of communication. He'll need supplies from the coast—powder and ball and rum, especially rum. In this weather, rum is a necessity for an army. I understand Shepard's already begging Bowdoin to send him rum. He can't buy enough for the men he intends to muster."

"He'll need provisions, too," Billings put in eagerly.

Dan shook his head. "No, let's not deceive ourselves on that score. There are enough Government supporters out this far to keep him supplied with food. What he can't get by contribution, he can buy. My point is this: If we can lure him into mountainous terrain, we can cut his army to pieces without destroying civilian property. That's very important, gentlemen. We must do all we can to retain and get more civilian support. And, of course, with Lincoln chasing us, the civilian population will assume that he is the aggressor, not us."

Dan stopped and let the hum of discussion rise. It sounded like a very good plan—if it worked. As you could expect, Luke Day and Norman Clarke and a few of their nature objected on the grounds that the campaign would be dragged out too long. Luke Day suggested cutting behind Lincoln's Army at Worcester and making directly for Boston. The town of Boston was virtually undefended, since all the fortifications had been torn down after the siege and few replaced, those latter being removed after the war. Strike hard and fast, Day held, release Shattuck, Page and Parker, seize the Governor and have the main army retire. A small force, with the mechanics of Boston, would hold the town. With our army in the field and the Governor in our hands, Lincoln would quickly sue for peace. It was a bold plan and a good one, but extremely risky. Shays objected to it on the grounds that transportation in this cold weather was too difficult. If we had cavalry, a swift raid might accomplish that purpose, but moving three thousand men would present too many obstacles to the success of the movement.

After a lively debate, opinion veered back to Dan's plan.

"Just one thing bothers me," Wheeler said, at length. "Does this mean we make no move at all on the 23rd? That would look bad—as if we were afraid of Lincoln."

Shays smiled. "Yes, I thought of that. We'll have action around that time. We'll hit Lincoln at his weak spot. We'll attack the Springfield Arsenal."

A spontaneous cheer went up. Shays didn't have to explain the advantages of that move. Shepard would be holding the arsenal with a small force. He might—if he were sensible—surrender without firing a shot. We would be getting sorely needed muskets and ammunition. The magazine was reported to contain a good store of unspoiled powder. There was little further debate.

Luke Day lifted his hand. "Do we need a vote, gentlemen? All in favor—"

The "ayes" shook years of dust from the rafters.

Shays took a paper from his pocket. "Thank you, gentlemen. Here are your marching orders."

A general laugh went up and everyone burst into applause. That was the kind of a commander we wanted—a man with confidence in himself! Shays flushed, but he wasn't displeased.

Dan Shays had also laid the plan of attack, viz: Luke Day would hold West Springfield. Eli Parsons would move from Pelham back to Hadley and down the river road to Chicopee, thus cutting Springfield off from the north. Shays, coming down from Rutland, would meet Clarke at Palmer, straddling the Boston Road and cutting Shepard off from help from the east.

"I'm going to Rutland to see my men in the morning," Shays told me later. "Want to come along, Warren? Tom's staying there. He'll serve under Parsons—courtesy, you know."

Beulah overheard him. "Take me along, Dan? Please?"

"The answer is no," I said firmly.

And that settled it, I thought.

443

Chapter 33

NEVER having visited the Rutland Barracks before, I expected to find a few dilapidated sheds and little else, for the poverty of Congress during the war, as I believed, would have precluded a more elaborate establishment. I was therefore astounded to find an extensive military reservation comprising some seventy acres, completely fenced and exceedingly well kept.

The guardhouse contained only two rooms on the ground floor, the front chamber very large, the smaller rear chamber being used as Dan's living quarters and personal office. I was assigned a room upstairs—nominally a cell. My position was rather obscure, though I had been commissioned a lieutenant and considered by the other men as an aide-de-camp to Commander Shays. I was quickly put to work handling the more important correspondence. I had ample clerks to help me. I would have preferred to fight by the side of Tom Packard and my Pelham friends, but I was not sorry I was to be denied that arrangement. I suspected Dan had brought me along more to have a friend at his side than an aide, for he constantly consulted me on the most trivial matters. I could read the signs plainly. Dan Shays was getting shaky.

We were beginning to have a little trouble with the men, too. The news of the impending action had set off a lot of pent up exuberance. Half a dozen times we had to break up fights and, by night fall, we had ten in the blockhouse gaol, seven for drunkenness, two for brawling, one for attempted theft. Not a bad record, all things considered, though we could have incarcerated a lot more if we had wanted to clamp down tight on the boys. Some pious bluenose insisted we

444

ought to deny the men all spiritous liquors, a perfectly asinine suggestion, since only seven of the whole army had to be confined for disorderly drunkenness. We did the sensible thing. We doubled the guards at the gates and let none of our soldiers loose to annoy the civilians of Rutland.

Messengers came over from Pelham with the news that the Hampshire men were already gathering there. Dr. Hynds' was overcrowded, Bruce's was filled up. Many of the troops were being billeted on our people; willingly, I may add. Here at Rutland, our numbers were rapidly swelling.

Around eight o'clock Anzel came in. I thought Anzel had some news or dispatch for Shays, but Dan was sitting at the head of the table, plain as life and Anzel kept searching about the smoky circle. Finally, he spotted me and hurried over to where I was sitting. There was a deep flush on his face, much deeper than could be accounted for by the cold outside.

"Anything wrong, Anzel?" I asked quickly.

"Well, yes, a little." He rubbed his cold nose nervously. "Can I see you outside—alone?"

Shays had risen and come around the table. "Is there something wrong, Anzel?"

"No, sir." Anzel shifted awkwardly. "Nothing wrong. Honest. It's—ah—a personal matter for Warren."

Dan looked at me. I looked at Dan. The answer flashed over us both at the same time. I jumped up. Dan's brows lifted.

We grabbed our coats and followed Anzel outside.

"Where is she?" I asked as soon as the door closed.

"By the gate. Hank McCullock was on duty with me. He's holding her." Anzel shook his head. "She tried to sneak in. Golly, Warren, that woman must be cra. . . ." He caught himself. "Sorry."

"Don't be," I said gruffly.

There was a small knot of men gathered about the half open gate. Beulah was standing behind Hank, who was guarding her from the others, two of whom were trying to paw. I couldn't blame them much, since they'd been virtually shut up in here for over a month. She was wearing a uniform, complete with greatcoat, and I must say the uniform fit almost perfectly. Almost. Not even that baggy coat could hide her womanly hips and breasts. By the time we reached them, I was burning mad.

445

"All right, men," Shays called crisply, "back to your posts." Some of them moved, but a few lingered, leering. "Back to your posts!" Shays ordered sharply.

They moved a lot more quickly then. Soon we were left alone, except for Anzel and Hank.

"You, too, Hank," Shays said. "Anzel, run back and give Captain Holman my compliments. Ask him to meet us at Hitchcock's. Don't mention this."

"And no gossip, boys," I added.

Both assured me they'd keep absolutely mum.

Beulah looked very scared as we took her out and headed her into Rutland. Neither of us said a word during the whole of the mile walk.

We went into Hitchcock's by the back way, for the taproom was crowded with elderly gentlemen arguing vigorously whether or not to support us. Shays asked us to wait in the kitchen, went into the taproom and came back a moment later with Mrs. Hitchcock.

"This is Mrs. Hitchcock—Lt. Hascott. Mrs. Hitchcock will show our guest to a room. I'll wait down here for Holman. He'll be able to get her a dress."

"I'm sorry, Dan," Beulah blurted.

Shays shrugged. "You're lucky Anzel and Hank were on duty, that's all. Otherwise we might have had a rape murder on our hands."

"I didn't realize," Beulah said in a small voice.

"Well, you should have," Shays said sternly. "There're almost a thousand men in there. You'd have tempted the most decent of them." Shays sighed. "Well, never mind. I think I understand. Go up with her, Warren. I'll wait here for Holman."

Mrs. Hitchcock took us up the back stairs and put Beulah in the front chamber, lighting a fire then retiring with a sniff. I was still so angry I couldn't talk.

Beulah took off her coat wearily, tossed it on a chair and walked over to the fire and warmed her hands. She bowed her head fearfully, then coyly looked around.

"Please, Warren, I didn't mean any harm."

I was in no mood for coyness. "You ought to be spanked. Haven't you any sense at all?"

"I thought it would be all right," she replied meekly. "I . . .

446

I thought everybody would take it the way I meant it—as a joke. Wouldn't the men feel better if they had a m—mascot like m—me along?"

"Beulah, this is not another one of those court-stopping expeditions. This is war. It's serious business. We have trouble enough combating the government propaganda painting us as licentious scoundrels. If you came along, they'd say every second member in our ranks was a whore. We'd lose every neutral in the state. Now, I don't want to shout or rave or even point out that you might have made me the laughing stock of the army. That won't help you or me. But if you want to do me—and the cause—a service, then go home."

Beulah's lips trembled. "Can't I stay? Can't you make Dan let me stay?"

"No!" I half shouted. "God dammit, what have I been talking about? You go home in the morning."

"But I think I can help! I must stay, Warren." She put her arms over my shoulders. "Warren, can't you see it? Dan's weakening. We mustn't let that happen."

"Am I blind?" I asked indignantly. "I've seen it. And I can take care of him—with help, not from you, but from men he'll listen to." I pulled her arms down. "Now, promise me you'll go home."

Beulah's eyes clouded with defiance and she shoved her fists deep into her pockets, turning her back to me and frowning into the fire. I had to struggle with my impulses to remain stern. Those breeches were skin tight.

"All right, that finishes it. Goodby, Beulah."

She whirled, caught me at the door, clung to me. "I'll go home . . . honest I will." Her voice was a husky whisper. "Don't leave me . . . not now. I—I've been so worried. Can't I stay . . . just for tonight?" She kissed the point of my chin. "Warren, don't be so stupid."

I would have been if I couldn't see through that tactic. But I couldn't draw away. Her warm breath against my cheek, the musky sweetness of her hair, the softness of her pressing against me, her sensuousness unraveled my resolution and roused my hunger for her. Her eager lips sought mine and I held her very close. She wore nothing beneath her shirt and breeches.

447

Somewhere in the distance, a board creaked. I stiffened, disentangled myself and stepped away shakily.

"Dan's coming," I said breathlessly. "I can't stay tonight, Beulah. This place isn't like Worcester. The gossips would have the news in an hour. Just as soon as I get back to Pelham, we'll be married. You will marry me, won't you?"

She nodded very slowly. "Yes, Warren."

I could hear footsteps coming down the hallway and we drew farther apart. We were both composed when the knock came. It was Dan, right enough, with a woman's dress for Beulah to wear instead of the uniform. He gave us a sharp glance, noticing how flushed we both were.

"I had a bit of a struggle convincing her," I said hastily. "She's going home tomorrow morning."

Dan nodded soberly. "Yes, that's best. I'll send Sam Baker around for you in the morning, Beulah. He has to take dispatches to Pelham. He'll take you right home." He gave her a kindly, apologetic smile. "I know you want to help somehow, Beulah. But you'll have to leave this to us. War is man's business."

"Yes." Beulah's eyes were filling. "Goodby, Dan. Goodby, Warren. God keep you both."

I hustled Dan out. I knew Beulah wouldn't want either of us to see that she was crying.

The tale naturally got around the camp, but no one except Anzel and Hank knew the identity of the woman. As far as I could discover, neither of them had talked. The men thought she was one of the many sluts who inevitably turned up and tried to gain entrance. So, Beulah's reputation was safe—for the moment. I shuddered every time I thought of how blithely and naively she took conventions. I hoped she'd forget, after we were married, those silly notions about women being free and entitled to do as they pleased.

On the following day, the 19th of January, it became more and more manifest that Dan Shays was building up to a mental breakdown: He became snappish and moody and confined himself to his room, where he sat by the table, hour after hour, staring into the fire. The arrival of a messenger from

Luke Day did nothing to cheer him. The letter informed us that Shepard had fully occupied the arsenal the day before with a force of about four hundred men. The news seemed to come as a profound shock to Dan, as if he had never believed, in his heart, that the Government would dare mobilize forces to oppose us.

At long last, that evening, the headquarters office emptied and Captain Wheeler and I were alone with Dan. We had outstayed everyone, waiting for the opportunity to thrash out Dan's attitude with him. But Dan was determined not to give us the chance. The moment the last of the officers had drifted out, he got up abruptly and went into his chamber. He didn't go to bed. We could hear him pacing up and down, up and down.

I scowled at Wheeler. "Should we break in on him?"

Wheeler shook his head. "Whatever happens, he won't run out on us. Let him think it out for himself."

"My God, Captain, the time for thinking is past."

Wheeler smiled slowly. "He'll realize it soon."

He got up and went over to the guard at the door, ordering him to rouse him if Shays should leave the building. After that, we went upstairs to bed. I was getting sleepy, too, so I followed him. Dan's chamber was right below mine and I could hear him pacing, six paces up, six paces down, six paces up, six paces—I dropped off to sleep with the sound beating in my ears like the steady ticking of a clock.

From the vast distance, the slow, regular pounding of footsteps returned to my consciousness. I lay in my bunk for a considerable time, listening to that regular rhythm.

Finally, about dawn, I couldn't stand that pacing any longer. I got up and dressed myself and went down the hall to Wheeler's room. My knock didn't awaken him, so I went in and shook him. His eyes snapped open and he stared up at me, fully awake and alert.

"Listen!" I whispered.

Wheeler hauled himself on his elbow, listened intently a moment, then sighed. "Looks like Dan needs a little help making up his mind to fight. I'd hoped he'd see the light himself."

He dressed himself hurriedly and we went downstairs. Wheeler had to knock twice before Shays invited us to come in.

449

Dan looked haggard and pale in the sickly yellow light of the lone, burnt down candle. He stared at us a moment, as if trying to remember where he had seen us before. Then he grunted, slumped down into his chair, scowling at his outstretched feet.

"All right, say it. I'm a coward."

"I ain't saying nothing, Dan," Wheeler returned. "It's after five. We've got to get ready to march."

Shays rubbed his eyes. "Adam, I–I can't go through with it. I can't."

"You must," Wheeler said stolidly. "A thousand men are depending on you. Our lives are in your hands, Dan—our lives."

Dan groaned and buried his face in his hands. "Adam, I can't go on, I can't. I never wanted to get into this. It's not right. It's civil war. We have no right to plunge the Commonwealth into civil war."

"The Governor chose this course, not us."

"I know, I know. But the killing . . . the maiming. . . ." He jumped up. "Adam, there's still hope." He fumbled feverishly among his papers and found the one he wanted. "Here—we've got to try this. I—we—a small group of us got together and drew it up a few days ago. I hesitated to send it out without a general vote."

Wheeler's face was stony as he accepted the paper and read it. He passed it over to me. It was another petition.

It said that the Regulators had agreed not to obstruct the courts at Worcester on the 23rd of January, provided that the Government would withhold its troops from marching. Further, the Government must agree that all who had taken an active part in the rising would have safety in person and property. It concluded by stating that the Regulators were certain that the General Court would redress all grievances at the next session and so restore peace and harmony to the Commonwealth.

I shrugged. "Send it. It can do no harm."

Shays brightened. "You agree there's still hope?"

"No, Dan," I answered flatly. "There is no hope."

"There is hope," Shays insisted desperately. "It's never too late to compromise. Suppose Bowdoin really does believe in the democratic principle? Suppose he's only stupid? We will

450

be leading our people into a useless war—a civil war. We will be killing and maiming our friends and brothers without purpose. It's senseless, Adam. It's wrong."

Wheeler's heavy features were placid. "Dan, sit down, please," he said gently. "I could answer you by reminding you that you and I have no choice—except treachery. If we negotiate for a pardon, we save our necks, but earn the contempt of all, our friends and our enemies. If we surrender, we face the hangman. It's too late to turn back. We must go on."

Wheeler put his hand on Shays' shoulder. "Dan, search your soul. It is not given to every man to grasp greatness. A small man closes his mind and his heart to his destiny. Only the unthinking fool is wholly without fear. You have a right to be afraid. You have a right to hesitate to rush blindly into the valley of darkness. You have the duty to think twice about the lives Fate has placed in your hands. But don't close your eyes Dan. Don't stare straight into the darkness. Look up, Dan. Fate has placed a star in the sky for your guidance. And the name of that star is Freedom."

Shays sighed deeply, got up from his chair and walked slowly to the window. He threw it open and stared out into the cold, bleak dawn. The morning hush was broken only by the crowing of a distant cock, the gribbling of awakening birds, the brittle laughter of men splashing each other at a nearby well. The crisp, icy air cut like a sharp knife through the heavy, stuffy warmness of of the disheveled room.

"It's daylight," Dan said gruffly, his lips tightening. "You'd better awaken the men, Adam. Send in an orderly with my breakfast and some hot water. I must shave and dress."

The drums began beating just as I was shaving my adam's apple. The sound was so startling that I almost cut my own throat. The camp was soon in a fever of preparations. Shays confined himself to his chamber, leaving his door open. He acted very assured and polite to anyone who came in with a problem for his attention. He gave me the petition to the Governor and I passed it on to a messenger who was going east this morning. He was superbly calm with those officers who came storming in with complaints about conflicting orders or demands for more sleighs.

At a quarter to eight the drummers sounded assembly.

Being ready, I hurried out to join the group of officers gathered by the front gate. The moment I showed myself, they swarmed around me, clamoring for news, for all the morning dispatches had passed through my hands. Nothing important had come in. The portion of Lincoln's army that had gathered in Suffolk and Middlesex had marched late yesterday afternoon, but they had only gone five miles toward Worcester. That would put them five days, at least, behind us. We would have struck at Springfield and be gone long before he could possibly catch up to us.

At length, all of the companies were in position, forming a huge three-sided square facing the front gate. Our colors and drums were massed inside the open square. Our numbers were quite impressive. Our army now stood at eleven hundred men, imperfectly trained, but imbued with a belief in our cause and enthusiasm for our leaders.

Chapter 34

BOTH Captain Wheeler and I urged Dan to travel in one of the sleighs, but Dan was adamant. The bulk of the men must march on foot. Dan would share their march. That he had not slept and was dog tired made no difference whatever. In a way, this attitude was foolish, yet I couldn't help admiring it. The men never noticed or commented upon his sacrifice of comfort, accepting it as the natural thing to do. Yet, had he chosen to ride, I am sure there would have been grumbling and a consequent lowering of morale.

Not having had extensive army experience, I had no idea how many delays could develop along the line of march, especially when encumbered by a baggage train. We stopped to rest at frequent intervals, but more frequently to entangle a pile-up caused by a sleigh breaking down. Sometimes we had to wait for stragglers to catch up to us. Once a horse died on us, which necessitated transferring the baggage to another sleigh. And several times during the day, we were met by dispatch riders.

The news was good. Luke Day sent another letter, reporting that he now had about four hundred men and was expecting more. Shepard had seven hundred in his garrison, with more arriving hourly. That news was balanced by the intelligence that many of the units he had expected had sent word they could not—or would not—march because of the hostility of the townspeople. Shepard was in dire straits. His men were badly equipped—for a very odd reason. He hadn't received permission from the federal government to equip his men from the arsenal stores. That news gave us all a hearty chuckle.

In a later dispatch, Luke Day further reported that Shepard

453

was having trouble with his soldiers, too. Shepard was begging Lincoln to send money for food, rum and wood. Lincoln hadn't sent him a farthing of the money collected in Boston. Shepard had tried to raise two thousands pounds in Springfield, but no one would lend it to him. One of Shepard's original dispatches fell into our hands, from which I quote:

". . . The men cannot be held together, especially in this season, without a daily allowance of spiritous liquors. It will be very disagreeable to me to be defeated by such a wicked banditti when I am guarding the arms of the Union and and when I have no arms to defend myself even from insult. . . ."

We reached Ware on the 22nd of January and on the 23rd we marched into the town of Palmer. Each night, upon entering a town, we billetted our men upon the inhabitants, in houses and barns, for it was too cold for the army to bivouac in the open. We had surprisingly little trouble, most of the people gladly opening their homes to our soldiers. I must confess we did have a little trouble with petty thieving, but not as much as might be expected. We caught four men during those two days and gave them prompt punishment. They were lashed and forced to wear a sign with a big "T" on it pinned to their backs for the next two days.

Upon reaching Palmer, we set up our headquarters at Scott's Tavern, where we had expected by this time to have been joined by Captain Taft and the South Hampshire group.

The news from the west was good. Luke Day reported he now had five hundred men. Eli Parsons had marched from Pelham with four hundred and was awaiting further orders at Chicopee. Shepard was now cut off from the north, south and west. We straddled the main highway, so there was little chance that he could get reinforcements from the east. Parsons reported, too, that he had intercepted a sleigh train loaded with provisions destined for Shepard's armies. Poor Shepard!

Lincoln, according to dispatches intercepted from his messengers trying to get through our lines, was having his own troubles. He, too, lacked money. True, he had received pledges of some twenty thousand pounds from the merchants of Boston, but collecting on the pledges was an entirely different matter. Lincoln was bitter in his complaints. The merchants of Worcester wouldn't lend a penny on the Government's credit, it had fallen that low. Only by pledging his own personal credit was he able to get money to feed his army.

At dawn the next morning, the 24th of January, we decided to push on to Wilbraham and there await the arrival of the other contingents from lower Worcester and Middlesex. Wilbraham was the last town before Springfield and, to us, it held considerable strategic value. The town lay two miles south of the main highway. Thus, Shepard could send his messengers through that town, thence south in a wide circle, swinging back to hit the main highway behind us. With our troops in possession of that crossroads, we would pinch off Shepard's last avenue of communication with Lincoln.

The populace had ample warning of our coming. When the column turned south from the main highway, our fifes and drums struck up a lively tune, loud if not so very good. Our men were in exceedingly good humor this morning, for they had been told they'd only be marching to Wilbraham and we would not be attacking Springfield this day. Their enthusiasm for the cause was as high as ever, but their enthusiasm for the heavy business of fighting was growing considerably less the closer we came to our goal. Everyone dreaded the thought of bloodshed. Practically all had some relative or friend who might be in the ranks of General Shepard.

Captain Nutting, with seven large sleighs and seventy men, arrived from Middlesex shortly after one o'clock. They had made excellent time, for they had traveled all the previous night to be on hand for the anticipated battle. They were grateful that they wouldn't be required to fight this day, but could catch up on their sleep. Nutting had brought along extra provisions, too, which were added to our reserve. He said he could have raised more men, but he thought it best not to call them out until our need was greater.

Around four o'clock, we received dispatches from Worcester. The news was bad. Lincoln had protected the opening of the court the day before, the 23rd, and the court had done some business, enough to give a semblance of a session. The court had adjourned the same day. Lincoln had immediately put his troops into motion. He was on his way here to relieve General Shepard.

"We'll have to move fast," Wheeler commented. "Lincoln will take three days, at least, to get here. If we strike tomorrow, we can be on our way north with the powder and ammunition before darkness falls."

Shays crumpled the dispatch. He was pale and his voice was strained. "We'll have to strike soon, that's certain."

It hadn't occurred to me that we might have struck sooner, since we had been dawdling on the excuse that we were waiting for Nutting and Taft. Yet, we could have sent word to have them meet us wherever we intended to go after striking at the arsenal. Had Shays been purposely postponing the inevitable? Dan caught Wheeler and me eyeing him and he flushed.

"Don't be foolish," he growled. "I mean, don't worry about me. I'm not thinking—you know what." He avoided our eyes. "I'm tired. I'll be in my room if you want me for anything."

Wheeler and I exchanged a scowl and watched Dan go slowly up the stairs. His hand was trembling on the stair rail.

Abe Gale came over to us. "What's wrong with Dan?"

"Huh?" Wheeler's head jerked around. "Oh, nothing. He's just tired. Like the rest of us."

"Like the rest of us," Gale repeated, rubbing his palms together. "I'm damned good and scared, I don't mind telling you."

Wheeler frowned as Abe Gale walked away. "If Dan was scared that way, we wouldn't have to worry."

The rattle of drums made me jump. Half of the men in the room also gave a jerk, as if stabbed with pins. We relaxed sheepishly. Lincoln certainly wouldn't announce his coming with drums. A moment later, the guards told us it was Captain Taft and the long awaited contingent from lower Worcester. Ben Convers came in a little later and told us Taft was bringing in four hundred men. Our total now was sixteen hundred, twice Shepard's strength.

Captain Wheeler alone did not grab his coat and go out to meet Taft. I had mine on, but I hesitated. Wheeler was watching the stairs, waiting for Shays to come down.

"Think we should go up?" I asked.

Wheeler nodded and I took off my coat and followed him. Dan had the best room in the house, the front chamber. As we came down the hall, the silence told us Dan wasn't pacing the floor, which was some consolation.

Wheeler knocked. "Dan, Rube Taft is here."

"All right, all right. I'll be down in a minute. Come in if you like."

We found Dan sitting by his desk, quill in hand. He grunted, threw the pen down and got up, walking to the window. Wheeler, his thumbs hooked in his belt, sat down in the chair Dan had vacated and glanced at the paper.

"Go ahead, say it." Dan's voice was bitter. "Another petition! Adam I can't help it. I keep thinking. . . ." His jaws clamped shut and he reached for his sword and buckled it on. "What's the use? I know it's foolish. I know I can't back out. You can skip the lecture this time."

"You know, Dan," Wheeler said slowly, as if he hadn't heard, "I've been thinking about tomorrow. Seems to me there's no need for bloodshed."

Dan's mouth dropped open. "Say that again."

"It's common sense," Wheeler went on in a thoughtful voice. "We'll be moving to the arsenal from this direction, Luke and Eli Parsons will be coming from Shepard's rear. There'll be sixten hundred of us and about a thousand in Luke's and Eli's forces. We'll have Arsenal Hill surrounded. Do you think it's likely Shepard will commit suicide?"

"He may," Dan said glumly. "He's that kind of a man."

"Maybe. But will his troops be willing to die to the last man? Or even fight against such odds? It would be useless sacrifice of life if Shepard fought us. His men will know it. Maybe they'll persuade him to surrender."

"Maybe . . . and then again, maybe not."

"Shepard knows we're here. His men know our strength. They must be talking about it right now. We'll give him a chance to surrender. But if he refuses, I think we can walk right in and take the arsenal without firing a shot."

Dan's eyes narrowed. "Maybe." Then he grunted. "Adam, you don't have to lull me into feeling we can get the arsenal without fighting. If I lead my men to the arsenal, I lead them to fight. If we can avoid bloodshed, fine. If not, well, I hope our casualties—and theirs—will be as few as possible."

Wheeler smiled. "We'll rout him, never fear."

Shays reached over his desk. "We won't need this."

Wheeler pounced on it first. "Don't tear it up. We're send-ing it out. Sign it." He got up and opened the window. "Howdy, Captain Taft. Billet your men. We'll be down in a minute. Abe, show Captain Taft where his men belong. . . . Johnny! Oh, Johnny! Come up here a minute." He closed the window and rubbed his hands. "We're going to need all the time we can get. Maybe that petition will delay Lincoln."

Shays' brows went up. "That's an idea. Why not send War-ren? He knows Lincoln."

Wheeler shook his head. "Not after what happened last time he was in Boston. Lincoln was at the Council meeting, wasn't he?"

I nodded. "Lincoln would probably arrest me on sight. I wasn't as humble as I might have been."

Being curious, I asked to see the petition. It stated that Shays, being unwilling to shed blood and being desirous of promoting peace, would consider surrender under certain conditions. He proposed that Lincoln disband his troops at once, that all the Insurgents be indemnified until the next sitting of the General Court. Persons already taken by the Govern-ment—meaning Job Shattuck, et al—should be released without punishment. These conditions must be made sure by a procla-mation from the Government. The Insurgents then would return to their homes and await constitutional relief from the insupportable burdens under which they now labored.

Hope died hard in Dan Shays' breast. "Do you think he'd entertain a petition like that, Warren?"

"Certainly not. In the first place, I doubt if he'd have the authority to promise those conditions. And then, his men are enlisted for thirty days or less. That means some money has been spent for the army. We could disband and reorganize within a few days. Not Lincoln. He'd have to go to the Legislature to get authority to raise a new army. Then he'd have to get more funds. The debates would take weeks—if not months. No, Dan, Lincoln will try to smash us now, while he's only responsible to Bowdoin."

Shays nodded gloomily. "You're right, of course. But it seems to me Lincoln isn't doing things in a democratic way." Then he added, "There may be something in this stuff about Lincoln and Bowdoin trying to set up a dictatorship."

A moment later, a knock came at the door and Johnny

Wheeler, Adam Wheeler's cousin, entered. He was not alone. Right behind him was a tall, skinny man, elegantly dressed. His greatcoat was of a heavy dark blue woolen material, the buttons of brass and the lapels faced with blue velvet. His nose was hooked and on his sunken cheek was a mole sprouting a tuft of grey hair.

John Wheeler jerked his head at the man. "The patrol picked him up on the Chicopee Road. He says he wants to see Shays."

Shays and Wheeler exchanged a quick glance. The smile tugging at the corners of Shays' mouth showed he was hoping this was an emissary from Shepard. I was wondering if our visitor was the man Jaeger Salderman was sending. But then, Jaeger would have asked for me.

"General Shays?" the man asked in a raspy voice.

"Captain Shays," Dan corrected coldly.

"Ah, yes, my apologies." He cocked a brow at Wheeler and me. "May I see you alone, Captain Shays?"

"Johnny, wait downstairs, will you? Close the door as you go out." When John Wheeler was gone, Shays clasped his hands behind his back. "These gentlemen are my trusted aides. You may speak freely before them. Your name, sir?"

"Cottle, Phineas Cottle." He gave Wheeler and me a sour look, then shrugged. He opened the door, peered down the hall, then closed it again. "We can't be too careful these days, can we, gentlemen?" He laughed harshly.

Dan was getting impatient. "We are busy men, Mr. Cottle. Please state your business as quickly as possible."

Cottle took out a snuffbox, took a pinch, breathed deeply. He did not sneeze, which gave me great wonder.

"Ah, yes, business. For my humors—very bad in this weather." He snapped the snuffbox shut. "Gen—Captain Shays, I daresay you'd be interested in obtaining more troops?"

We all straightened. This man was not from Shepard. And he evidently had not come from Salderman or Graham.

"How many?" Shays asked.

"Ten thousand, fully equipped, with artillery and a supply of powder for your own army."

The man's dry, crackling voice hung on the dead silence. For long moments, none of us moved. Then Wheeler glanced to me, a small smile breaking over his heavy features.

"English troops, Mr. Cottle?" he asked softly.

"Certainly not!" Cottle returned with the proper amount of indignation. He spread his hands. "Perhaps their speech might suggest Wales or Ireland, but there are many in America with such accents—especially since the conclusion of the late war."

Shays eyes grew cold. "What do we do for these troops?"

"Nothing, nothing at all. They will serve your cause for —ah—shall we say, love of country?"

Shays was getting mad. But Wheeler was amused.

"If the struggle goes on," Wheeler said easily, "we shall certainly need help. And we can't be too choosy, eh, Mr. Cottle? Whom will we be dealing with?"

Cottle's deathlike features cracked in a smile. "That's the sort of talk I like to hear, gentlemen. You're realists, I see. Well, gentlemen, the moment you want those troops, send a man to General Sir Henry St. John in Montreal."

Wheeler stepped forward and opened the door. "That's what I wanted to hear, all right. Get out!"

Cottle's mouth dropped open. "You just said . . . I've heard from everyone you would welcome English help. This is. . . ."

"You'd better go quickly, sir," I said quietly. "And next time don't believe all you hear about us."

Shays gave Wheeler a frantic wave. Wheeler winked. He deliberately knocked Cottle's hat off. Cottle glared at the Captain, stooped over to pick up his hat.

Shays hop-stepped and his toe arched. Mr. Cottle went flying out of the door, butting his head against the opposite wall. Wheeler slammed the door and he and Dan shook hands, grinning like pleased kids. It was all very enlightening to me and gave me a guide for the time I would be negotiating with Mr. Jaeger. Once the war was in full swing, I knew, neither Dan nor Adam Wheeler would feel the same about accepting obnoxious help.

John Wheeler returned as soon as Cottle was gone. "Say, he looked real mad. What happened?"

"Nothing for you to worry about, Johnny," Adam Wheeler told him. "Now, look here, Johnny, we have a job for you. You're going to deliver this letter to General Lincoln. Read it over."

John Wheeler read it carefully. "Say, this would be all

460

right if it worked. None of us feel much like fighting. But I don't think Lincoln would—"

"Neither do we," his cousin broke in. "It's a fake. Your job is to dicker with Lincoln and delay him as long as possible. Ride all night. I think you can get to him by morning. When you run into Lincoln's pickets, be sure to tell them the contents of this letter. We want his men to know about it."

"I don't see. . . ." John began.

Adam Wheeler waved impatiently. "If Lincoln's men know we want peace and Lincoln refuses to negotiate, some of them might desert or make a fuss. Anyway, it might delay him."

John Wheeler smiled broadly and put the letter in his pocket. "I'll do my best. Maybe I can keep him on the road an extra day, at least. Where shall I meet you? You won't be here when—and if—I get back, will you?"

"No," Shays spoke up. "Meet us at Pelham. We'll head in that direction and stay over there a few days, anyway."

John Wheeler snapped to attention, saluted and, chuckling, hurried about his mission.

"We'd better get downstairs," Shays said.

The taproom was very crowded when we came downstairs. All the officers had come in, expecting a consultation. Most were grouped around Reuben Taft and his officers, asking about Lincoln's forces and how far he was from us. Everyone gave way as Shays, now perfectly assured and smiling, came through to welcome the arrivals. Besides Taft, the newcomers included Dan Gray, Gardner Maynard, Moses Smith, and many others whom I had met before.

As soon as the greetings were disposed of, Dan called for paper and pen and sat down at the big, oval table in the center of the room. He rapped for attention.

"I expect we all are aware what our next move must be," Shays began in sober tones. "We must strike at Shepard within a very short time. Lincoln is already on his way to relieve him. I believe we must strike no later than tomorrow morning."

A rustle of resignation went through the assembled men.

"Colonel Day is at West Springfield," Shays went on, "Colonel Parsons stands at Chicopee. Our troops here at Wilbraham give us an overwhelming force. We should be able to storm the arsenal with little loss to ourselves. To achieve success with the least cost to ourselves, our combined forces

461

must strike together. I therefore suggest we send messages to Colonel Day and Colonel Parsons, informing them of our intention of attacking tomorrow morning, the 25th of January, at 10 o'clock."

There was no opposition.

Shays wrote out the message, sealed it and called for a messenger. Abe Gale fetched one of his men, a fellow by the name of Tom Grady, a resident of Longmeadow.

"Be sure to avoid Shepard's pickets, Tom," Shays instructed him. "Ride south as far as you feel it's necessary before swinging back. Wait for a reply, Tom. Be careful. Our lives may be in your hands."

The messenger saluted and hurried to the stables. Shays smiled with genuine relief.

"The die is cast, gentlemen. By your leave, I shall buy a round of refreshments. We must drink to victory."

"To victory!" came the low, solemn echo.

Chapter 35

ⵀⵀⵀⵀⵀⵀⵀⵀⵀⵀⵀⵀⵀⵀⵀⵀⵀⵀⵀⵀⵀⵀⵀⵀⵀⵀⵀⵀⵀⵀⵀⵀⵀⵀ

A STRANGE calm fell over the town of Wilbraham. At long last, the facts had been faced and accepted. The officers talked in subdued tones, walked with lighter steps, fell into long, thoughtful silences. The barns resounded with no cheery songs that night. The men indulged in no light-hearted horseplay. A vast number of the men wrote letters home or, a grimmer note, made out their last wills. This was no time for argumentation, no time for doubt. This was the time for every man to search his soul and assure himself he had the courage to face the morning.

I was up shortly after five o'clock, feeling more refreshed than I had in many months. Poor Landlord Bliss was up, too, when I came down to breakfast. He told me he hadn't been able to get to bed before two o'clock, for everyone had waited until then for the messenger from Luke Day. Cal Morse hadn't returned by two. He hadn't returned by dawn.

Dan Shays came down at half after eight and scolded us for allowing him to sleep so late. The extra hours in bed had done him a lot of good. He looked fit, clear-eyed, eager to be about the job at hand. He was freshly shaved, his shoes were blacked and he wore a new red silk ribbon on his queue. He was disappointed to hear that Cal hadn't returned from Luke Day, but he merely shrugged and settled to breakfast. He gave the order to assemble, confident we would be moving within an hour.

The army did not move within the hour. Dan came out and inspected the troops and gave them a short snappy speech about how much the country and the people were relying upon their courage. He promised them they would march soon. At half past ten, they were still waiting restlessly and impatiently for the order.

By this time we were becoming thoroughly alarmed. What in heaven's name had happened to that messenger? Had he been intercepted? If so, when? On the way to West Springfield or on the way back? Had Shepard made a surprise attack on Luke Day? What about Eli Parsons? We hadn't heard from him, either. Our pickets had reported no movements at all on the roads.

The men had a trying time. The sun shone all morning and there was no wind, but just standing around on the snow made it hard for the men to keep their feet warm and dry. After a while, the whole army was stomping about like a tribe of Indians indulging in a sullen war dance.

At eleven o'clock, the officers gathered in the tavern for a consultation. But to what purpose? The messenger hadn't arrived. We didn't want to attack without support. Our whole strategy depended on simultaneous appearance at the arsenal in order to overawe Shepard and possibly win a bloodless victory. If we marched in alone, Shepard might well consider his thousand men, fortified on Arsenal Hill, the match of our sixteen hundred.

"Maybe Cal got lost," Lt. Phelps suggested.

It was a possibility, though hardly likely. What we feared most was that the messenger either had been taken by Shepard or had turned traitor.

Abe Gale was emphatic in rejecting the latter. "I've known Cal Morse all my life. I'll swear by his honesty."

Shays sighed heavily. "There's only one thing to do, gentlemen. We'll have to wait a while longer. It's almost noon. I suggest you see to the feeding of your men. They're restless enough as it is. Food will at least keep their spirits up."

The knowledge that General Lincoln was on his way made many of the officers nervous and jumpy. Wheeler assured them that Lincoln couldn't possibly arrive before the day after tomorrow, the 27th, and then only by making a forced march. That wasn't very cheering, anyway. Each hour lost here was an hour taken from our contemplated retreat from Springfield. Each hour spent in idleness here was an hour wasted from our plan to fortify ourselves in the hills. And if Lincoln could catch us on the march, we might face disaster. He had

464

cavalry. We had only infantry. He might be able to swoop down suddenly and cut us to pieces.

During the dinner hour, a new and more troublesome thought came out. Captain Maynard suggested that Cal might be on his way back, but, taking such a long roundabout way, might not arrive until nightfall. Meantime, Day and Parsons, having set a time for attack, might be marching on Springfield with the full expectation of meeting and being supported by us.

That idea gave us the chills. Unless Parsons and Luke Day arrived at exactly the same time, Shepard might get the chance to take them on separately. Shepard we had learned, had some artillery. Lord, what a shambles he could make of those two detachments if he could get them one at a time. He'd knock them out of the battle for good. After that, he'd have no fear of our sixteen hundred. He could just sit tight and accept a siege, knowing that Lincoln would lift it two or three days hence.

The idea soon became an obsession. Day and Parsons faced destruction if they attacked without our support. The terrain favored the defenders. Using artillery, Shepard's men could mow down Day's and Parson's eight hundred more thoroughly than we mowed down the British at Bunker's Hill. There wouldn't be enough of the Regulators left for a second charge. If, however, our men attacked on the other side, Shepard's lines would be spread so thin that nowhere would he be able to make an effective resistance.

One o'clock passed and still no word from Luke Day. Shays was nervous and snappish and paced constantly before the hearth. Wheeler and I knew Dan was not thinking of retreat or surrender. He was thinking of the horrible slaughter that was certain if Luke Day and Eli Parsons attacked alone.

"I say march—now!" Shays burst forth suddenly.

"We must march," Shays said fiercely. "Good God, we can't let Day and Parsons meet Shepard alone. Gentlemen, we set the time of attack for ten in the morning. Had he attacked, we surely would have had word from Springfield. Our pickets, who have stopped travelers, have reported no battle in Springfield. From that, I must deduce that a morning attack was not convenient to Luke Day—possibly because the messenger didn't arrive in time. Therefore Day must have decided to attack this afternoon. What has delayed our messenger, we may never know. But we can't take any chances. You may ask, suppose the messenger never reached Colonel Day? Suppose neither Day nor Parsons will be there to join us in the attack? I answer, we are sixteen hundred to less than a thousand of Shepard's. We alone can lick Shepard. Day and Parsons alone cannot. Again, I say, we must march—now! All in favor . . . . !"

The drums sounded assembly and the men who had scattered to find a place to rest rushed back to their units. News of our decision spread rapidly through the ranks. The men were as uneasy as their officers. There was no use trying to lie to them by telling them the messenger had come. They knew the truth. They knew, too, that the plan of a threefold, simultaneous attack would not only give us certain victory, but perhaps even a bloodless one. They didn't like the idea of moving without being sure our full strength would be thrown against Shepard. But they were now soldiers. They could not protest. They must only obey.

The last of our pickets were drawn in and Captain Holman was put in charge of the baggage train. Our baggage train would move to East Springfield and there await the outcome of the battle. They'd join us in Springfield as soon as we had the barracks. Captain Holman didn't relish the assignment, for he wanted action. I daresay, there were a number of the officers who would gladly have taken his place had they the nerve to ask for the transfer.

At two o'clock all the companies were in position. Shays gathered the officers around him and went over the plan of attack, drawing a map of the arsenal on the snow with the point of his sword. Everyone was quick to notice that the men would be deployed as if we expected no help from anyone but ourselves. The orders given, Shays shook hands all around and we wished each other good luck. The officers hurried back to their companies.

The drums gave a sharp roll and the men snapped to attention. Shays gave his men a long, tight-lipped look. Then he turned and lifted his sword. It swung downward. The drummers broke into a defiant crackling, then settled to a regular thumping. One by one, the companies swung into place and the army of the Regulators marched east toward Springfield, toward that inevitable moment long since ordained by destiny.

The column had barely formed when those of us up front saw a horseman come out of a barn a half a mile up the road. He was cutting across the field to reach the road ahead of us.

"That's Aspath King!" someone behind us shouted.

Immediately, the front line surged forward. Shays barked the command and they retired to their places.

"He'll warn Shepard!" Hank McCullock called out.

"Let him!" Shays snapped. "Shepard can't be surprised, anyway. He's been expecting us since yesterday."

I was inclined to question Dan's judgment. We still had time to intercept the sheriff. King wasn't making very rapid progress across that field. The snow was deep and there was a hard crust of ice over the surface. The horse had to be spurred until his flanks bled to force him to break a path. At times the beast hopped like a jackrabbit to make progress. King broke out to the road a scant quarter mile up ahead of us, wheeled and dashed up the icy road at a reckless pace. The horse evidently had cut his shins badly, for the road was flecked with blood. At any moment, we expected King to be thrown. Luck was with the sheriff. The last we saw of him, he was spurring his mount on faster.

The incident further depressed our men. Those in the rear who hadn't seen it heard about it quickly enough, for the word was passed down the line. Almost everyone agreed we might have caught him if we had tried. It didn't matter whether or not the news would be of value to Shepard. But it was certain now that Shepard would be drawn up to meet us. Shepard was being warned.

The march to the Springfield Arsenal was made in two hours. As we entered the outskirts of Springfield proper the men looked to their weapons, assuring themselves that their muskets were charged and primed and ready. The ground became more level, and, as we came over each of the short hills, all eyes searched eagerly, desperately, for a sign of Eli Parson's men on the Chicopee Road to the northwest. Except for one lone sleigh ambling leisurely along that road, we were alone.

Our column joined the main Boston highway and we turned slightly southwest toward the town of Springfield. As the woods thinned on our left, Arsenal Hill came into view. A nerve wracking sigh rippled down the line, then our soldiers grew tenser. The highway swung around to the left of the hill, then cut straight into town to meet Main Street. There were a number of houses and shops on either side of the road as it curled around the arsenal, but there was plenty of open space to deploy our troops for the assault on the barracks at the brow of the hill.

Lord, what I wouldn't have given just then for a sight of Luke Day's troops coming out the Arsenal Road from Main Street. There wasn't any question that Day would have been able to go through the town unmolested. The townspeople were with us almost to a man. Shepard had complained of that fact in his letters to Lincoln. But as more of the road came into view, my heart sank. Now, we could see more clearly the brow of the hill. Shepard was drawn up in front of the barracks. There was still no sign of Luke Day or Eli Parsons. It was almost four o'clock. We were going to make the attack alone.

I happened to glance at my cousin Anzel, who was in the front rank. Anzel was white, almost numb with fright. I knew how he felt. He had never been under fire before. I dropped back a little to see if I could get him to relax.

"Steady, Anzel," I said in a low voice. "They're as scared as we are. Man for man, we're better than Shepard's men will ever be."

Unconsciously, my voice had risen a trifle, so Hank McCullock overheard the latter part of my remarks. He snorted.

"They got artillery, Warren, and we ain't."

That would better have been unmentioned. I tried to spit, but couldn't. Facing artillery wasn't going to be pleasant. Our only hope was to rush up the hill so fast they wouldn't have the chance to reload. We were within a half a mile of the Arsenal now and we could see the artillerymen, standing at ease by their guns. A dozen pieces were lined up, aimed at the ground we would soon be covering. I could hear the word rustling down the whole length of our column.

Step by step, yard by yard, the Regulators moved relentlessly closer. The men were very quiet now, their eyes held straight ahead. Adam Wheeler and I exchanged a grim smile. He glanced back over the troops, shrugged expressively, then turned his eyes front again.

Two men suddenly came running down the hill. A shudder

468

of hope went down the line. Shepard was sending emissaries to treat with us! Shays lips held a hopeful smile as he turned.

"Adam, go out and meet them. Take Simon and Warren." He lifted his sword. "Company . . . Halt!"

As the column shuffled to a halt, Captain Wheeler, with Lt. Phelps and myself a step behind, moved forward to meet the two officers from Shepard's army. We were close enough now to see Shepard's men quite clearly. They were exactly the same as our own men, the same faces, the same clothes—a few in old war uniforms, the rest in smocks or homespun suits. And they had the same nervousness. But I could sense these men, holding more protected positions, had more confidence.

Captain Wheeler walked slowly, with almost casual insolence. The two officers were puffing as they came up to us. One of them started to give us a military salute, then checked himself.

"What do you men want?" the taller of them demanded.

Wheeler grinned and scratched his head, shifting his tricorn a trifle to show his pine tuft more clearly.

"Now what do you think of that? I plum forgot to ask Captain Shays what we came for. Lt. Phelps, will you be good enough to run back and ask Captain Shays what we want?"

Phelps suppressed a grin, saluted, turned stiffly and marched back to Shays. The two officers shifted uncomfortably and glanced at each other, as if wondering if they were dealing with madmen.

Lt. Phelps spoke to Shays, marched back briskly and saluted "Compliments of Captain Shays, sir. He says he wants the barracks and the barracks he shall have."

Wheeler lifted his palms. "I guess that's your answer, gentlemen," he drawled.

The officers scowled. The taller one, whom I later learned was Captain Buffington, leaned over and whispered to the other, Captain Woodbridge. They straightened.

"You'll purchase them dear," Woodbridge warned.

Wheeler shrugged and turned away. "We're wasting our time, gentlemen. Let's get back to the column."

The two officers hesitated, then turned and hastened back to their lines. We rejoined our companies and Wheeler reported

469

the conversation to Shays. Shays just grunted and gave the order to march again.

The column wrenched into motion, like the long articulated body of a snake, reluctantly pulled forward by the eager head. Shays was impatient and cursed Shepard for forcing us to storm that hill. Many of the officers prodded their men on faster, as if they wanted to get the distasteful business over. On the hill, Shepard's soldiers waited impassively. Not a man of them moved. I caught a blob of red bobbing up and down and, as we came closer, I saw it was a small boy on the back of a horse, almost beside himself with excitement. One of the men commented that it was an inexcusable disregard for the boy's safety. I was inclined to believe it was evidence that Shepard's men were of the same unrealistic, wishful mentality as ours. Those men, too, could not make themselves believe we actually intended to fight.

Within two hundred and fifty yards of the arsenal, Shays halted the army and shouted orders to the officers to deploy the men. Quickly, the companies assigned to the flanks broke from line and took their positions. Before the maneuver was complete, we saw two more officers come racing down the hill. Again hope leaped into our breasts. Perhaps Shepard realized his predicament, since he was outnumbered nearly two to one. Again, Shays sent Wheeler, Phelps and myself out to meet them.

Within a hundred yards, we stopped and waited for them. Wheeler was praying as hard as any of us that those officers had orders to negotiate. But he wouldn't give them the satisfaction of showing anxiety. He hooked his thumbs in his belt and glowered.

One of the men was Captain Woodbridge, the other was Major Lyman, Shepard's aide-de-camp. It seemed a good omen that Shepard had sent a ranking officer. But, close up, the mouths of those cannons looked horribly ominous, grimly ready for business. And our incipient elation died the moment Major Lyman spoke.

"You there!" he called sharply. "I warn you, come no closer with that rabble or we'll shoot! The militia is posted here by order of the Governor and Congress."

Wheeler lifted his shoulders and turned away. "I guess that's all we want to know," he said quietly.

We trotted back to the army, any moment expecting to hear the rattle of muskets and the punch of bullets in our backs. We didn't report the Major's words. Shays had heard them. He gave the front ranks a sweeping glance, raised his sword.

"Forward . . . March!"

The broad, wavy line surged forward. The Government line stiffened up and the click of flintlocks was audible even over the steady tramp of our boots. I was suddenly conscious of a chill breeze on my damp brow. I gripped my sword tighter. I was fascinated by the faint wisp of smoke curling up from the end of the artilleryman's slow match. General Shepard alone was moving about, soothing this one, joking with that, pausing to give orders to the artillerymen. No longer could there be any doubt. General Shepard didn't have the slightest intention of yielding.

Fifty yards . . . sixty . . . seventy . . . a hundred. And now we reached the base of the hill. A hundred and fifty yards to go. The faces of the Government soldiers were plainly visible. They were hard and expressionless. Another twenty yards . . . thirty. Shepard's voice barked an unintelligible order. Four of the artillerymen jabbed their matches at the touchholes.

Four cannons bellowed. Four balls whistled over our heads. Somewhere in the rear, a man cried out hoarsely. No one was hurt. Our line held firm and the relentless rhythm of marching feet did not falter. The artillerymen were working feverishly to reload. The Government troops were shifting uneasily, glancing nervously toward General Shepard. The General was watching Shays, his face impassive, his eyes grim. We were now within fifty yards. The Government line had become very quiet.

"Fire!" Shepard roared.

Four cannon spat searing flame in our faces. The balls ripped squarely through the center of our ranks. A shrill, agonized shriek clawed at my eardrums. A half dozen of our men stumbled and sprawled out in the choking acrid dust.

The line buckled and convulsed and a rumble of terror swept through our army. In an instant, our front lines drove ten yards back, as if pushed by a giant hand. Then, order exploded. The lines swirled and dissolved and broke into knots of blind, frenzied panic. Screaming, cursing, bawling, screeching like wounded animals, our men slugged and kicked and clawed each other to get away from those horrible, smoking cannon. I was stunned. Like a fool, I just stood there, my back to the cannon, watching the writhing mass receding like an ugly black tide.

Shays was belaboring the men with his sword, swearing and crying and begging them to turn and go back up the hill. Wheeler, too, was fighting his own men, cursing them, bellowing insults, ordering them to turn and fight. Then, I remembered my own duty, I flung myself down from the hill, waded into that chaos, swinging my sword and yelling unintelligible orders. That was a sight I shall never forget—those fear-twisted faces, rolling eyes and drooling mouths, those friends fighting each other, those heedless feet trampling over quivering bodies, those frightful snarls, those grown men sobbing like tortured children.

I punched and kicked and cracked heads until I was exhausted. I hollered meaningless commands until I was hoarse. I remember hitting my Cousin Anzel. I saw him fall, weeping bitterly. Vaguely, I saw blood coming through his fingers which were clutching his side. Nothing registered deeply. I remember thrusting him aside and throwing myself again into that melee.

It was no use. Nothing on God's earth could have stopped that stampeding mob. The knots unraveled and the men scattered like grapeshot, fleeing across the fields and stringing out along the road. I stumbled with abject weariness, crawled on my knees after them, shouting wild oaths into their wake. Then I realized I was weeping, too, weeping with rage and disappointment.

I felt a strong hand under my armpit and, with its aid, climbed to my feet. As my eyes cleared, I saw Adam Wheeler at my side. His heavy features were sagging with bitterness and he stared like a man bewitched at the rampaging rabble that had been an army. I caught sight of Shays down the road, still stopping men and shouting at them and trying to rally them for another charge. If Shays hadn't lost his own mind, he would have known that the task was hopeless.

"Well, Shays didn't fail us, anyway," Wheeler said softly.

"That's small consolation," I remarked. I rubbed my tired eyes. "I had a feeling something like this would happen."

Wheeler shrugged. "The men licked themselves before we started. But there's no use crying about it now. Maybe it was a good thing. Next time, they won't be so scared of gunpowder."

I nodded gloomily. "I hope so. I suppose they'll be ashamed of themselves when the panic wears off. Tomorrow—" I broke off sharply. "Anzel! Oh, my God."

Wheeler caught me as I was turning to go back. "Hey, wait a minute. What's up?"

"Anzel—my cousin. He was wounded. I saw him fall back there. He was bleeding in his side."

Wheeler's grip tightened. "You can't go back for him, young fella. Look!"

Shepard's men had come down from the hill and were carrying the bodies to the barracks. I was astonished to find how far away they were—fully a mile and a half. They had made no effort to pursue the disordered army. Had they sallied forth, they could have slaughtered us like bewildered pigs. Wheeler was right. I couldn't go back there now.

"We'd better be getting along," Wheeler said. "Shepard will be putting out his pickets again. I'd hate to get caught now. We'd hang sure."

Captain Wheeler and I traveled as fast as we could, but the faster we went, it seemed, the faster and farther the army retreated. We almost missed the army completely. The main body had struck north off the main highway in the direction of Ludlow. We were amazed to find the distance our men had fled. Those fear-crazed men hadn't stopped until they reached Ludlow, ten miles away.

It was getting dark when Captain Wheeler and I finally reached Ludlow. The last of the stragglers were coming in and the officers were herding their companies like irritated collies. Shays was pacing up and down in front of the tavern, his face white with fury. He whirled angrily as we approached, then relaxed.

"Oh, it's you." He grunted and went on coldly. "Not a musket fired. Not one musket fired on either side. Not that Shepard's men needed muskets. All they needed was a loud noise." He seized my lapels. "Do you know how many men fell? Four—just four! I counted them myself. If these cowards hadn't turned tail, we'd have broken Shepard's lines like kindling. But no, they ran. They ran like goddam mice."

He waved us away and returned to his pacing. His pride as a soldier was hurt, which was easily understood. This was a humiliation that might make us the laughing stock of the state. Worse, the disgrace might cost us the support of the neutrals.

Our baggage train had come in from East Springfield and was stretched out in a long line on the road north of the green. Most of the companies had formed again. Everywhere the men avoided my eyes and the eyes of their comrades. All were deeply ashamed. Only a few argued noisily, placing the blame on someone else. I saw one such knocked down by one of his comrades.

I dreaded rejoining my own company. My heart sank as I saw Hank McCullock without Anzel at his side. As I approached, Lt. Phelps bounded over to me, seized my hand.

"I thought you had fallen. Thank Heaven you're safe."

"Have you seen anything of my Cousin Anzel?"

Phelps' eyes turned away. "Yes, we brought him back. He—he is badly hurt—in the side. He must have been right in front of the cannon. It fired grape. Shays sent him home already in a sleigh. Some doctor around here bound him up and said it was best he go home."

I felt relieved, yet worried. Either that wound was light enough to make it safe for him to be moved or he was being sent home to die. I shuddered. Poor Rowena—and the twins. I wondered, too, how Uncle Enoch and Aunt Hannah would take it.

Daylight was almost gone. The men were moving about restlessly, watching Dan Shays, who was still pacing up and down. They knew what he was thinking. And, when he stopped and faced them, they braced themselves for a blistering lecture on courage.

"We're not staying here tonight," Shays began, his voice curiously calm. "We're going back to East Springfield. We're going back to within striking distance of General Shepard. We're going to attack again tomorrow morning."

An uneasy stir went through the ranks.

"Oh, you don't like that," Shays said in a sneering tone. "You, the Regulators, the Soldiers of Liberty. You who were to crush tyranny and re-establish government by the people.

474

You, you spineless halfwits, you hear a loud noise and run away." He shook his fist at them. "By God, you're going to hear more loud noises. You're going to smell more powder. Tomorrow, you're going to fight like men, not like jellyfish. I warn you," and he shook his finger angrily, "if one man breaks tomorrow I'll see that he hangs. I could pick out a hundred of you right now whose faces I remember. I won't brand you cowards—not this time. Tomorrow you'll get your chance to redeem yourselves. You'd damn well better take your chances against Shepard's bullets because tomorrow cowards hang."

That was sheer bluff. If the men went into another panic the whole army couldn't be hanged. Certainly, in the confusion, no one could say who broke first. But the threat was sobering. And I felt it was not wholly necessary, for every man would be striving consciously to wipe out the memory of his disgrace—for the sake of his own conscience if not for the movement.

"All officers will billet their men in East Springfield as soon as we arrive. I shall set up headquarters at Chapin's Tavern. We will discuss our plans for the morning there. That's all." He motioned to the drummers.

The men were exhausted, emotionally and physically, from their experience. But there were no protests, no grumbling, as we started back to wipe out this shameful defeat.

Chapter 36

~~~~~~

S OON after headquarters had been set up at Chapin's Tavern
in East Springfield, we were besieged by friends and relatives who came to inquire about the missing. From the
number of inquiries, the casualties would appear to be over
a hundred, which was ridiculous. Shays insisted no more than
four or five had fallen. But an accurate check was impossible,
for our troops were scattered in barns and farmhouses all
over the countryside. Most of the missing, we knew, were de-
serters. We were positive of only one casualty, Jeremiah Mc-
Millan of Pelham. Tom McMillan said he had seen his brother
fall, but he had been swept away by the mob and couldn't
get to him. We believed Tom, for we had known both of
those boys all our lives. We were certain Jerry wasn't a
deserter.

In an effort to learn our casualties, Shays sent Lt. Williams
under a flag of truce to General Shepard, asking that our dead
be sent back. General Shepard's reply was unnecessarily brutal.
He informed us he had picked up four of our men from the
battlefield, three dead, one not yet dead. Then he added that if
Shays attacked again, he would be pleased to furnish him with
as many dead rebels as we would desire.

Later, however, he softened his tone. He sent us a casualty
list and said that if the friends of the dead would apply in
their names, he would release the dead to them. He gave the
names of the dead as follows: Ezekial Root of Greenfield,
Ariel Webster, also of Greenfield, Jabez Spencer of Leyden,
all dead. John Hunter of Shelburne was wounded, but was
expected to die. No one had the heart to rout out the friends,
since it was very late when the messenger finally returned from

Shepard, so we decided to leave that distasteful duty until morning.

As soon as everyone was settled we held the inevitable conference to plan for the morrow. Shays was still insisting upon an attack at dawn. He was still burning with rage and humiliation. But the other officers, including Adam Wheeler and, surprisingly, Captain Norman Clarke, usually a fireeater, had cooled to the idea. Many believed that the men might still be too shaken to be dependable if they acted alone again. General Shepard's troops would certainly have high morale. Another fiasco like today might be fatal to our cause. Thus, almost everyone agreed, it would be much better to revert to the original plan of striking Shepard from three sides with our full strength.

"Look at it this way, Dan," Wheeler reasoned. "We're running a war. We don't want to punish the men. We want to win. Even if our men didn't crack—and I don't think they would—taking that hill by ourselves would be bloody business. Both sides held their fire today because neither of us were sure that the other would really fight. We know now they'll fight. They know we'll fight. Shepard won't wait so long before giving the word to open fire. On the other hand, if Day and Parsons act with us, Shepard might reconsider and give us the bloodless victory we're hoping for."

"That's good sense, Dan," Abe Gale put in. "What happened today could have happened to any body of green troops. It happened lots of times during the war. And, God knows there weren't many cowards in the Continental Army. Our men really aren't cowards. If I thought so, I'd quit right now and go home. Our business is to win our objectives at the least possible cost. Let's not worry about what our men did this afternoon."

"All right," Shays replied with a sigh. "We'll send another messenger to Eli Parsons and Luke Day. This time we won't move until we're sure of their support."

Shays thereupon sat down and wrote letters to Parsons and Day. There was no question this time about our line of communication. Shepard's pickets wouldn't be likely to be out this far. It was only five miles or so to Chicopee and another eight miles south to West Springfield. Thus, Shays felt justified in demanding a reply from both Parsons and Day the same night.

Shays set the new time for the attack at ten o'clock the next morning.

Within two hours, our messenger returned from Chicopee. We were relieved to learn that Eli Parsons actually was there. Parsons had sent back no written reply, merely informing our messenger that he would consult Day and then answer. He admitted to our messenger that he had received our letter of the 24th, but gave no explanation why he had not been on hand to support us this afternoon. Though we had no positive evidence, we felt strongly that Parsons and Day were hatching something between them for their own advantage, not ours.

The evening dragged on and on and on. Everyone was very tired and our bodies cried out for a bed. But we all awaited the word from Luke Day. Midnight and no messenger. Shays was disgusted. He stomped off to bed, leaving word to be awakened the moment the messenger arrived. One by one, the rest of us gave up hope and sought our couches. I didn't turn in until nearly two o'clock. And a tedious refrain was going through my head: "No word from Luke Day."

The morning gave us no relief. We were becoming more and more annoyed with those two men. Hours, precious hours, were slipping by. A messenger from the east had come in and reported that General Lincoln was approaching Brookfield. Lincoln could be expected tomorrow, the 27th, or the following day, the 28th, by the latest. We needed every minute we could get if we expected to crush Shepard and retreat beyond Lincoln's reach. Our messenger reported that Lincoln's army was about twenty-three hundred men, plus several companies of Horse. He had artillery, too. To stand and fight in these regions would be suicidal.

Seven o'clock and still no word. Shays was furious. Indeed, there wasn't a man among us without murder in his heart. If we had had the slightest inkling of what had gone wrong, if anything, the strain would have been bearable. But the absolute silence wore like acid on our nerves. We sent another messenger. By nine o'clock, that man hadn't returned. That was the last straw.

"Sound assembly," Shays snapped. "We're going over to Chicopee and see for ourselves what's happened to them."

As soon as our drums began beating, our men poured onto

the common from every direction. They were in better spirits than we were. They were rested and chastened and determined to wipe out the shame of yesterday. I do believe that if we had decided to attack without Day and Parsons they would have taken on the task with grim enthusiasm and given a good account of themselves.

At nine-thirty we marched from East Springfield. At eleven o'clock we reached Chicopee. We met Parsons' pickets about a mile east of the meeting house, but there was no sign of the rest of the men. They were snug in their billets, the pickets told us. Except for a handful of men guarding the tavern, the town was quiet. It had been suggested that our messenger possibly couldn't get through to Luke Day because the Connecticut River wasn't frozen hard enough. That proved untrue. The river was frozen solid, the ice firm enough to support a horse and sleigh.

Shays was so impatient that he didn't wait for our troops to be established on the common. He stalked on ahead. Captain Wheeler and myself went along with him, fearful that Shays might do violence to Parsons unless he had a good excuse for not replying to our dispatches. Shays was so angry he didn't acknowledge the salutes of the guards at the door. He kicked the door open and strode in. Eli Parsons was seated in a big easy chair by the fire, calmly getting himself shaved.

Dan Shays almost burst a blood vessel. It was many minutes before he could find his voice. Parsons greeted us pleasantly, with no show of surprise and little real interest. Dan's voice was low and level, but it quivered with anger.

"You seem to have it comfortable here, Colonel Parsons."

"Tolerable," Parsons replied coolly. He waved to his barber. "Finish up, Sam. Captain Shays won't mind waiting."

I thought Dan would hit the ceiling.

"Did you get our note day before yesterday?" he asked in that same level, strained tone.

"I got it," Parsons admitted.

The scrape of the razor rasped through the tightening silence. Shays' knuckles were white. He held them firmly at his sides in an effort to control himself.

"And Luke Day got my note, too?"

"Uh huh . . . Easy there, Sam. You nicked me that time."

Some of our officers were coming in by then. They sensed

479

the delicacy of the moment and practically walked on tiptoe to avoid startling our leader into doing something rash. Not that there weren't many among us who would have been glad to give that barber's elbow a jab as he scraped Parsons' prominent adam's apple.

The barber wiped off the soap and combed out Parsons' long, bobbed hair, then retreated nervously. Parsons grinned and got up, stretching himself languidly.

"Luke Day got my dispatch of the 24th?" Shays repeated.

"I told you he did. Matter of fact, I went down to West Springfield and consulted with him. We decided not to attack on the 25th. Didn't you get our letter?"

"I did not," Shays replied coldly.

Parsons frowned. "Well, we sent it—early yesterday morning. So, that's why you attacked yesterday." He grinned irritatingly. "We heard what happened."

Shays' lips tightened. "And why did you decide there would be no attack yesterday?"

"We figured we'd give Shepard time to surrender," he fumbled in his coat, which was hanging over the back of the chair. "Here's a copy of the letter we sent you. I took it for my records."

Shays accepted it without changing expression. He read it over, then passed it on to us.

"West Springfield, January 25th, 1787
Sir:

I have dispatched Captain Walker with my resolution. Have ordered Colonel Parsons to treat with General Shepard and in case General Shepard rejects the terms, shall put my troops under my command into motion to support my demands; precisely four o'clock is the time prefixt. But shall not expect them to come into action this day.

LUKE DAY.

To Captain Shays."

Parsons shifted nervously as he saw the hostile faces all around him. "For Chri' sakes, you're not blaming me for what happened yesterday, are you? Here. . . ." He dug into his pockets again and came out with another note. "Here's the letter we sent to Shepard. Luke drew it up, not me."

In cold silence, Shays read it, then passed it around.

"Headquarters, West Springfield, January 25th, 1787.
The body of people assembled in arms, adhering to the first principles of nature—self protection—do in the most preemptory manner demand that 1. The troops in Springfield lay down their arms. 2. The arms to be deposited in the public stores under the care of proper officers, to be returned when this affair is over. The troops are to return home on parole.   LUKE DAY."

"Those were the terms you expected Shepard to accept?" Shays asked in a tight voice. He was struggling desperately for control. "And what, pray, did the General reply?"

Parsons glowered defensively. "He said he'd think about it. That's why Luke Day decided not to attack at four o'clock." He was sweating a bit now. "Don't you see? We wanted to settle this without bloodshed. That's reasonable, isn't it?"

Shays turned away without replying. "Frank! Come over here. Fetch me pen and paper for Captain Stone. . . . Sit down, Frank. Take this letter to Luke Day."

Francis Stone, one of the officers in Parsons' army, settled at the table and pen and paper was brought to him.

"Sir," Shays said in a harsh voice. "I have arrived at Chicopee and have been informed you took the authority to treat with General Shepard. Be informed that, by mutual consent, I was chosen to command our armies. I therefore expect strict obedience to my orders from my subordinates. Our armies shall be set in motion at precisely four o'clock this afternoon. I direct you to reply to this dispatch at once since I shall be returning to East Springfield to strike from that direction. Signed: Daniel Shays. . . . Lt. Phelps, take this directly to Colonel Day. Wait for a reply. Captain Holman, issue a half pint of rum to our men. They'll need something to keep them warm while we await Colonel Day's reply."

Shays was so angry he didn't trust himself to say anything more to Eli Parsons. We hustled him upstairs to try to get some sleep, for we knew he hadn't slept at all last night. We ignored Parsons completely. Parsons made it hard for us, for he made several remarks about the courage of our men and

481

sneered at our conduct in yesterday's encounter. With great effort we refrained from punching his nose. After a while he gave up and retired to his room, there to sulk in solitude.

We decided to utilize the rest of the morning in making a complete check of the men. Our checkup gave us better results than we anticipated. We still had fourteen hundred, only two hundred having deserted. We felt well rid of them, for they would be the most likely to crack the second time. Many friends of the missing men kept insisting that they had fallen in battle. But we had the names of those from Shepard, so we could dismiss such claims. True, there were a few who had been wounded, like my Cousin Anzel, and had been sent home last night, but that number wasn't more than about ten.

We left until the very last the distasteful task of releasing the casualty list Shepard had sent us. But it had to be done. The nearest of kin of the dead were detached from duty and given permission to go to the arsenal to claim the bodies. To hold to the letter of Shepard's promise they had to present a petition. That was a heartbreaking moment. The four involved were so grief stricken that I took it upon myself to help them, writing as they dictated and leaving the wording as they gave it to me. A fifth name, Jeremiah McMillan of Pelham, was added, for we had no word of Jerry and surmised Shepard's men might have picked him up later. We all hoped that, as Tom claimed, Jerry had merely been wounded.

Here is the way the petition went:

"Chicabury, 27th January, 1787.
Honoured sir:
By the flag that was sent to your Honour yesterday, you informed us that if the friends of the dead in custody sends after them, the bodies shall be resigned. We the friends here offer subscription for each dead body, humbly pray that the present flag may have leave and liberty to fetch the whole number of the dead with them.
Greenfield: Ezekial Root—Solomon Root, brother.
Greenfield: Ariel Webster—William Webster, brother.
Shelburn: John Hunter—James Anderson, friend.
Leyden: Jabez Spencer—Thomas Crawford, father-in-law.
Pelham: Jeremiah McMillan—Thomas McMillan, brother.
(Wounded and missing)"

These were the first who had given their lives for our cause. We prayed that their sacrifice would not be in vain.

We expected Lt. Phelps would return from Luke Day by noon or shortly thereafter. We were annoyed, but not surprised, when one o'clock passed without a sign of him. We began to believe Luke Day was a myth, a remote and unreachable sphynx. Tom Packard made a shrewder guess. He thought Day was getting too big for his britches.

Lt. Phelps finally arrived at two-thirty, the last possible moment if we were to get back to East Springfield and strike from there. We sent the note directly up to Shays and thawed Phelps out. Dan's roar of rage, plainly audible in the taproom, gave us a hint of the contents. Dan came storming down the stairs, his shirttails flapping, his face red.

"You go back there and tell that goddam louse we march today—today!" He waved the paper excitedly. "You know what he says? He says he expected to have Shepard's surrender in his hands by night fall. If Shepard doesn't surrender, he'll attack tomorrow—tomorrow!" Shays nearly screamed.

"Well, what's wrong with that?" Parsons asked.

Shays whirled and watched Parsons come down the stairs and join our group. "Now listen to me, Parsons, Shepard hasn't the slightest intention of surrendering. He's stalling, hoping to keep us off until Lincoln arrives the day after tomorrow."

Parsons lifted his shoulders. "So? we've got plenty of time. Tomorrow's time enough. If Shepard surrenders in the meantime we don't lose any more men. That's what we want, isn't it—a bloodless victory?"

Shays glared at Parsons for a long moment, then turned to Phelps. "How long did it take you to get here?"

"Almost two hours," Phelps replied apologetically. "The roads are in bad shape. I couldn't travel fast. If I went down through Springfield, maybe I could do it in less time."

"You'd probably be caught by Shepard's pickets." Shays chewed his lips. "How about it Parsons? March today—with me and without Luke Day? We can't get word to him in time any more."

483

Parsons scowled. "If Shepard's ready to surrender. . . ."

That argument had just enough weight to make Shays pause before ordering Parsons to move. Two hundred of the five hundred under his command were Berkshire men. Luke Day had a large personal following. Shays was furious, but not so foolish as to assume a dictatorial attitude—yet. He realized if we started quarreling among ourselves now, Parsons and Day might pull their contingents out. We might also lose the neutrals, for desertions from our ranks could be twisted to appear as proof that Shays wanted to be a dictator.

Shays finally shrugged. "All right, tomorrow."

Shays sat down and wrote another note to Luke Day. I thought the paper would curl under Dan's sizzling pen. With that note sent out, we went about quartering our men for the night. Our men grumbled with disappointment when told they would not meet Shepard's men today. They were eager to get the chance to wipe out the memory of their humiliating defeat. Many of us thought it might have been better if we had marched alone again.

Around suppertime, our messenger returned with a nasty note from Luke Day. In effect Day said that if Shays insisted upon attacking before all avenues of peace were closed, he would have nothing further to do with the movement. That from Luke Day! He further stated that he had arranged for another conference with Shepard in the morning. If Captain Walker brought back an unfavorable reply the attack would be at four o'clock in the afternoon. For the sake of unity, Shays yielded and informed Luke Day that such an arrangement was satisfactory. It was becoming obvious to some of us that Luke Day was attempting to supersede Dan as commander of the Regulators.

The following day, the 27th of January, was colder, if possible, than the day before. We had another dispatch from Luke Day, informing us that General Shepard had asked for more time to consider the terms of surrender. However, Day now suspected that Shepard was insincere. Oh, glorious dawn! Accordingly, we would attack at the scheduled time, four in the afternoon. Whatever else we were thinking about Luke Day, we certainly were relieved that, at long last, we were all agreed on something. Today's attack, everyone vowed, would be different from the one on the 25th.

484

At two o'clock, our drummers sounded assembly. Our men came running from all directions, joking and laughing and jeering at each other as cowards who would flee as soon as they heard another cannon. That was a very good sign. They were rested and well fed and, underneath their banter, determined that they would have their revenge and vindication.

Within a half hour, our men were all lined up and ready to march. Parsons' detachments were lined up along the road, ready to muster on the common as soon as we left. Tom Packard suggested that I rejoin the Pelham company, but I decided not to. If I left my company now, others might want to do the same, which would result in a lot of unnecessary confusion. Besides, I wasn't very eager to serve under Parsons, even though I knew that our men would take the brunt of the fighting. Our men had tasted fire. They had reason to fight hard. I had no such confidence in Parsons' army.

Shays and Parsons had buried their differences and, since Shays had yielded, the rancor between them had practically disappeared. Shays gave Parsons detailed instructions of the strategy to be used and Parsons listened carefully. Parsons seemed to be in a cooperative mood. His long, square-cut hair and mild blue eyes gave him the look of a pious Quaker.

We were just about ready to go when we saw a sleigh racing up from the direction of Springfield. The driver was standing up, shouting and waving his hat excitedly. It was too much for our men. They had to turn around and look. They tensed, gripped their muskets hard, ready for any eventuality.

"Lincoln!" the man shouted. "Lincoln's here!"

"That can't be," Shays whispered hoarsely.

The driver yanked on his reins and the horse's legs nearly slipped out from under him. The sleigh was still skidding around in a slow circle as the driver flung himself down and ran over to us. He saluted Shays.

"Lincoln's arrived in Springfield, sir! He's at the arsenal. He's striking at Luke Day first."

Shays was still unwilling to believe it. "You're mad. Lincoln can't get here until tomorrow at the very earliest."

"He's at the arsenal!" the man half shouted. He danced up and down excitedly. "I seen him myself. He made a forced march. He's gonna clean up Luke Day first, then head this way!"

485

The news spread like a flash of lightning. The way in which the news was received was indicative of the morale of our troops. Parsons' men were silent and apprehensive. Our men were defiant and we heard loud curses and shouts of: "Let 'im come!" "We ain't worried!" "Give us a crack at him, Dan!" Dan Shays smiled slowly, considered that course, then frowned and turned to the circle of officers surrounding him.

"The cost would be too high. Captain Holman, put the baggage train in motion at once. Head for Pelham. Billet your men there. Headquarters will be at Dr. Hynds' Tavern." Shays turned to the messenger. "Does Colonel Day know of this?"

"Yup, we got a man across the river to him."

Shays rubbed the hilt of his sword a moment. "Phelps, get down there at once. Warn Colonel Day not to make a stand. He might be fool enough to try. Tell him to proceed to Pelham by the best possible route. We shall need every man we can get. Impress upon him that he must not accept battle with Lincoln." He returned Phelps' crisp salute. "Colonel Parsons, your men will head the line of march, if you please."

A groan of disappointment went through our army as the news spread. Captain Holman and the baggage train went out first. Parsons' army lost no time in swinging into line and following. The drums were silent as our men took their places in the column. They were looking back, angry that they were to be denied the opportunity of meeting Shepard again. But they vowed to give Lincoln a hot reception when he came to Pelham.

A dozen times during the four hours we marched, alarms swept up from the rear ranks. Each time, we had to make sure that Lincoln really wasn't right behind us. The last time, the army almost stampeded, for a horseman came riding up the road and the cry went up that Lincoln's cavalry was on us. The cavalry proved to be Lt. Phelps, returning from West Springfield. His horse was in a lather and the snow on the beast's flanks told us he had slipped and fallen in a ditch along the way.

Phelps threw himself from the saddle and saluted. From his expression, we knew instantly that he didn't bring good news. In fact, he drew us out of earshot of the men.

"Day has been routed from West Springfield," he said in a

breathless voice. "Lincoln caught him unawares at three-thirty."

"Unawares?" Shays almost shouted. "Why goddammit, he should have been marching on Springfield at that time."

Phelps scowled. "I don't understand it, either, Captain. All I know is that his men were caught in their billets. A small squad was holding the ferry house. Lincoln's troops were halfway across the river before they saw them. They fired a volley into Lincoln's forces, then broke and fled. The rest of them went into a panic. They left their food and baggage and fled up the road toward Southampton. It was pretty bad—as bad as what happened to us. They threw away their guns and packs and everything in their rush to get away. I saw part of it."

"Wait 'til I get my hands on that man," Shays growled. Then, he laughed shortly. "Well, he won't be able to sneer at us, if that's any consolation. How many men did Lincoln put across the river?"

"I didn't get close enough to see. I was told he sent four regiments with four pieces of artillery."

"And he continued to Southampton?"

"I think so. I know the biggest part of his army is heading this way. They weren't moving fast, though."

Shays swore. "How about Shepard's men?"

"It was Shepard's men who went across the river. They're chasing Colonel Day, sir."

"All the better. Shepard's men are fresh. Lincoln's troops must be near exhaustion. They'll have to stop at Chicopee tonight. We'll get away, all right. Thank you, Lt. Phelps. Ride on ahead and join the baggage train. You'll probably find it at South Hadley. We expect to stop there tonight."

As soon as Phelps had gone on, Shays passed along the word that Lincoln had struck at Luke Day, giving the impression that Day was luring Lincoln out toward Southampton to give us time to escape. But the men at the rear were still jumpy and raised false alarms several times more before we stopped for the night. The men up front, however, refused to pay any more attention to the alarms. The officers were fervently hoping that we wouldn't be caught like the shepherd who had heard the cry, "wolf", once too often.

Darkness overtook us before we could reach South Hadley, where our baggage train had stopped. We had to put over at a small settlement in the most southerly district of the township, a place now known as Willimansett. There were just enough houses and barns to give shelter to our men. There wasn't enough food. The people contributed to their limit. But there were some two thousand of us. We did the best we could, dividing the provisions equally, with the inevitable result that no one really got enough. There wasn't enough rum, either, though we cleaned out the tavern of its supply. Worst of all Shays informed us our money was getting low.

Our army was on the road again at dawn. Until this time, there had been no disorders and no incidents worth noting. That was too good to last. The rowdies were getting harder to manage, especially since their bellies were getting emptier. Shays, Wheeler, myself and several other officers ranged up and down the line, assuring the men that they'd get food as soon as we could reach South Hadley and buy some. The wails were growing louder.

If there had been a way to avoid passing the house of Major Goodman, which was on the outskirts of South Hadley, we would have taken that route. The night before we had been told that Major Goodman had a considerable store of rum. The townspeople told us that Shepard had been up here several days before and begged the Major to sell him the rum for use by the government troops. Goodman flatly refused and not because he was a rebel sympathizer. That rum was for his own use only and he wouldn't part with it. The rum was still there. Our men were cold and hungry and some had talked about trying to get at that rum. We expected trouble. We got it.

I happened to be up near front, talking to Joel Billings, when the men broke loose. First I knew of it, I heard shouting behind me, then saw men streaming across Goodman's front yard. Instantly, and according to previously issued orders, the officers halted their men and forbade them to leave the line. Not many disobeyed, especially in those companies whose officers were townsmen of the soldiers in the ranks. But many of the men who had stayed the month at the barracks in Rutland were commanded by strangers. Those were the men who broke loose.

Shays, Wheeler, Billings, myself and several others who had been assigned the task, rushed out from line and ordered the men back, threatening them with court martial. Several did go back and it looked for a moment as if we'd regain control. Then the front door splintered and the cry "Rum!" went up. More men broke from line. A hundred tried to get into the house at the same time, fighting madly to get to the barrels before the rum was all gone.

Window glass tinkled and several gained entrance to the house that way. Inside, there was a horrible splintering and crashing. We officers threw ourselves at the mob, cursing and flaying and pulling them back from the door. There were too many of them. Inside a discordant crackling and thumping told us that a spinet had been smashed into pieces.

A wild animal-like cheer broke loose in the kitchen and a shaggy, unshaven brute emerged with a keg on his shoulder. Another man came out with a barrel. Instantly, the heads were knocked in and the men closed about the barrels, waving pewter cups and ladles stolen from the house. Shays tried to get through, but was knocked aside and almost trampled. Ben Convers and I had to charge into them and scatter them to give Dan room to get up.

The three of us battered our way in. As we broke through, a scrawny little fellow laughed and cheered and thrust a cup of rum into Dan's hands, slopping rum all over him.

"Hurray for General Shays!"

Dan knocked him flat, whether for looting or calling him "General," I couldn't be sure. Ours was a hopeless task. We gave up after a while and Shays moved out into the yard. He told Ben Convers to make a list of all the men who had broken from line. Most of our men were standing along the road and watching their comrades in disgust. Ben made a pretense of taking the names. He carried writing materials in a pouch at his side. Unfortunately the ink was frozen.

The rowdies made a thorough job of looting Major Goodman's home. They trooped back to the column, jubilantly bearing plate and silverware, clocks, clothing, even pots and pans from the kitchen. And, of course, the rum. Those who remained in the line, either from decency or fear of the consequences, had no compunction in sharing the rum that had been stolen from Major Goodman's cellar. I must say the liquor was of excellent quality.

The house was a wreck. But no one had been hurt. The

Major himself and his family had been absent at the time. There was only a hired hand to protest. The hired hand stormed and cussed and begged and vowed that the Major would have us all hanged for this. We needed a good laugh at this point. Shays informed him that the Regulators would pay for the damages—all except the rum—if a reasonable bill were presented. As for the threats, no one worried. After the way Major Goodman had treated General Shepard, he could expect damn little sympathy from any side.

It was more than an hour before we could go on. When we got into South Hadley, Shays bivouacked the army on the common and rustled around to get food. Our baggage train, we found, had gone on ahead. This was all right with us, for we knew we would be needing that reserve of food when we got to Pelham. The people of Pelham couldn't be expected to feed the army. For the present, Shays managed to round up some pork, two sides of beef, a quantity of flour and maize and some bread. But we never did get to cooking and eating our meal.

Just before our commissary committee, headed by Perez Hamlin and Joel Billings, were ready to distribute the food, a sympathizer rode in, his horse in a lather. His news brought us upright. Lincoln had reached the town limits of South Hadley. Within five minutes, we were in motion, marching hard and fast to get out of reach. Not a man complained of hunger all that afternoon.

Chapter 37

※※

WITH Lincoln's army practically trampling on our heels, we had considerable difficulty in keeping the retreat from becoming a rout. The recurring false alarms nearly drove us to distraction. Shays finally resolved that situation by forming a rear guard of a hundred picked men, all seasoned soldiers, under the command of Lt. Hamlin. Thereafter we rapidly widened the distance between ourselves and Lincoln's forces, for we were unencumbered and Lincoln was burdened, not only with a baggage train but with artillery as well. Yet we didn't have an easy moment during the whole of the march. Had Lincoln sent his cavalry to hit our flanks, fifty horses could easily have scattered and broken the two thousand that constituted the bulk of the army of the Regulators.

Not until we reached Amherst did we dare stop for the night. Shays set up Headquarters at Clapp's Tavern and the troops were quickly billetted on the inhabitants. At the tavern we received two pieces of news, one good, one bad. Ten sleighloads of provisions had arrived from Berkshire and were waiting for us in Pelham. Then the bad. Luke Day had passed through Amherst just before dusk. He had about two hundred men with him. Shay's expression when he heard this gave sure indication that the meeting between the two on the morrow would not be cordial.

Our own baggage train was sent directly to Pelham and most of our boys, including Tom Packard, went along to sleep in their own homes that night. I passed up the chance to go. I was anxious to visit my Uncle Enoch and see how Anzel was getting along. I arranged to take Captain Hinds and ten of his men with me, for I preferred to have the better grade men billetted on my uncle.

Captain Hinds and his men waited in the barnyard while I went in to make the arrangements. Uncle Enoch evidently had heard us coming, for the door opened as soon as I knocked. He didn't smile or say anything. He merely nodded and widened the door. Aunt Hannah was rocking herself by the fire, knitting a new pair of socks. She stared unseeingly at me for some moments. Then she put her knitting aside and came over and kissed me. She looked terrible. Her usually plump red cheeks were wan and she seemed to have lost weight. Her eyes were red rimmed from crying.

"How's Anzel?" I asked huskily.

She shook her head. I looked to my uncle for the answer.

"The doctor says he's got a chance." Lines of worry were etched deep into his weathered face and dark pouches hung under his brooding eyes. "The doctor says he's got a chance," he repeated dully. "The doctor says a piece of shot passed through his left kidney. He's passing blood in his water."

I shuddered. Words of sympathy stuck in my throat.

"Who's that outside?" my uncle asked finally.

"Captain Hinds and some of the Greenwich boys. We'll billet them elsewhere if you think. . . ."

"No, it's all right." Uncle Enoch took a lantern from the mantel. "You can go up and see Anzel if you want to."

Aunt Hannah didn't offer to come up with me.

The house seemed awfully quiet, so quiet I could hear my cousin's slow, labored breathing as I came softly up the stairs. A candle was burning on the side table, which was littered with salves and tonics and bandages. The moment I stepped into the room, the faint sickish-sweet odor of pus swirled about my head like an evil, miasmic fog.

Rowena was sitting by the table, her hands folded in her lap. She looked like a tiny, bewildered sparrow, her shining black eyes never leaving her husband's pale, shrunken face. Anzel seemed lost in the deep feather mattress. His bare arms, stretched over the patchwork quilt, seemed terribly thin and wasted away.

I scruffed my foot gently to attract Rowena's attention and her gaze turned reluctantly from her husband. A small, wan smile touched her lips and she got up and bent over the bed.

"Anzel, Warren's here," she whispered.

My cousin's eyes slowly opened and he stared blankly at the foot of the bed. I moved over into his line of vision. His lips quivered and his hand lifted heavily and dropped.

"For God's sake," he whispered hoarsely, "I'm not dead yet." His hand edged over in an effort to gesture. "Sit down, Warren. How—how are—how are things?"

A lump in my throat made it hard to reply. "Pretty well."

He frowned. "Did—did you meet Shepard again?"

"No, Lincoln arrived, so we decided to make our stand up here. In another week the war will be over."

Anzel stared at me a moment, then stared up at the chintz canopy over the bed. The fire crackled mockingly in the momentary hush. His eyes slowly closed.

"I wish . . . I wish I hadn't run away."

"Don't talk nonsense, Anzel," I said quickly. "How could you run away? You were wounded—facing the cannon."

His head moved from side to side. "I never felt it, not . . . not until a long time afterwards. I . . . I lost my head . . . just like the rest. If only . . . if only. . . ." Tears oozed from the corners of his eyelids. "I'm a coward . . . a coward."

"Don't be foolish, Anzel. Anybody's likely to run away the first time under fire. I almost did myself at Bunker Hill. I guess you heard the story—how Jonathan had to knock me down to keep me from running when the British started bombarding us from the ships. You get used to the noise after a while and don't pay any attention to it. You'll see."

"I hope so. . . . I hope so."

"Hope nothing," I returned with more heartiness than I felt. "You'll be back with us in a couple of weeks at the most."

Rowena sniveled, clapped her handkerchief to her mouth and ran from the room. I was acutely uncomfortable, but Anzel was smiling, a small and wistful smile.

"Women don't understand," he whispered. "There are some things we value as much as their love—liberty, ours and theirs and the liberty of our children."

I squirmed in my chair, then got up. "I musn't tire you, Anzel. I'll . . . I'll be back later."

I couldn't get out of that room quickly enough. Rowena was standing in the hall, recovered from her tears; her shoulders drooped with weariness and despair. She was so tiny and forlorn, I couldn't help but put my arms about her and try awkwardly to comfort her.

"Don't you worry, Rowena," I said softly. "He'll be all right. And he won't have to go back. The war will be over in a week—two at the most."

Her shining black eyes lifted slowly. "The Revolution lasted eight years, Warren." And she returned to her husband's side.

I was profoundly shaken. For the first time, I was wondering if there was so much right in our cause that we must again inflict this hell upon our people.

Our detachment marched from my uncle's place at dawn the next morning. At Clapp's we heard that Lincoln had reached only as far as South Hadley, where he had been forced to stop and rest his men. Thus there was no chance that his army could reach us before we were behind the hills of Pelham. A few stragglers from Luke Day's army had come in, too, and given a report of what had happened at West Springfield on the afternoon of the 27th. That was a doleful tale.

Lincoln's men had struck so suddenly that Day's troops had to abandon everything they owned, food, clothing, ammunition, some even their muskets. Half of Day's men fled due north, up the river road, the other half struck northwest. A small detachment of Shepard's men pursued this latter group. At Southampton these Regulators turned on the Government troops and captured practically all of them. As soon as Lincoln heard about it he immediately dispatched the Brookfield Volunteers under Colonel Baldwin, and a hundred horse under Colonel Crafts. The Regulators, by this time, had reorganized under Captain Luddington and quickly withdrew to Middlefield, where they were overtaken by the Government troops which had been sent in fast sleighs.

Captain Luddington and a considerable number of his men retired to a farmhouse and vowed to fight to the death. The Government forces prepared to lay siege to him. But it happened that General Ben Tupper was along. Luddington had served under Ben Tupper as a corporal during the war. Ben Tupper walked boldly up to the door of the farmhouse

494

and ordered Luddington out. Captain Luddington obeyed. The men who told us about this seemed amused that Luddington should be overawed by the voice of authority. None of the rest of us shared their amusement. If Government continued to win such cheap victories, our cause was as good as lost.

While our troops gathered on the Amherst Green Shays held a conference of the officers in Clapp's Tavern. But there was no conferring. Shays presented full plans for manning the hills and gave orders for the disposition of the troops as soon as we reached Pelham.

Parsons and his Berkshire men were to defend East Hill. Wheeler and a mixed regiment of Hampshire and Worcester men would defend West Hill, the danger spot. Other companies were to be posted in strategic positions to the north and south and pickets would be keeping a constant patrol beyond our lines to guard against a surprise attack. With that settled we prepared to march into Pelham, each officer knowing approximately where he and his troops would be stationed and billetted.

At precisely eight o'clock the army of the Regulators issued from Amherst with drums beating, fifes playing and our flags flying. The men were cheerful and confident, not only because they were rested and full of food but also because they knew the terrain would be easily defendable. This time, the Government troops would have to storm our positions. Lincoln's cavalry would be useless and his artillery of little value unless and until we were driven from the hills and into the hollow. Such a possibility was unthinkable.

When we arrived at Bruce's Tavern Shays shook hands with the southern commanders, Elijah Day of West Springfield, Captain Colton of Longmeadow, Gad Sackett of Westfield, and Captain Fisk of South Brimfield, all of whom had escaped from Shepard's forces. There was no sign of Luke Day.

Tom Packard winked as Dan gave him a quizzical look. "I guess the Colonel is what you might call indisposed. He—ah—imbibed too much last night. He's having his breakfast."

"I'll take care of him later," Dan promised grimly.

The selectmen, headed by Dr. Cameron, came over to extend the town's welcome and Dan barked the order which snapped the army to attention.

Dr. Cameron put out his hand. "Welcome home, Dan. We can't honestly say we're glad to see you, my boy, but we'll do our best to make your men comfortable."

"Thank you, sir. I've given strict orders to the men to conduct themselves properly. Don't hesitate to report anyone who commits a nuisance. We're anxious to cause you as little inconvenience as possible. Now, gentlemen, I have work to do. I expect General Lincoln will arrive later today. I must have my men placed. Would you care to assist me in assigning billets?"

The selectmen would and did.

While Shays and the elders were arranging those matters I looked around for Beulah. She was standing discreetly back in the crowd, talking to Hope and Mrs. Pennington. I saw nothing of my own family and so concluded they hadn't bothered to come. At Beulah's side was a tall, blond young man and I must confess I felt a slight pang of jealousy until I looked again and recognized him. That blond young giant was Joe Crane!

I really shouldn't have left my company just then, but I knew Joe would have the latest news from Boston, so I quickly called Lt. Phelps over and, asking him to assume command of the company, I hurried over to my friends. Joe saw me coming, waved cheerfully and gave his sister a poke. Mrs. Pennington and Hope said "howdy," then graciously moved off to leave us alone. Beulah looked very solemn and sedate and she gave me a timid curtesy in greeting. Her use of such a feminine and deferential gesture almost bowled me over. Joe cocked a brow.

"You've been beating her," he accused. "Let me be the first to tender my condolences. Your mother told me you and Beulah will be publishing the banns soon. But don't let her deceive you, Warren. She's just playing at being tamed." He winced as his sister kicked him. "See what I mean?"

I grinned. "No, I'll have to find out for myself. How are things in Boston, Joe?"

"Fairly quiet," Joe replied. "Everyone's talking about what's going on out here, of course. But no one's ready to do anything about it—yet. Win a few victories, though, and you'll get a lot of recruits from Boston. The mechanics will be with you almost to a man. You'll get a lot of support from the sea-

496

board, too. Lincoln had a hard time recruiting in places like Salem and Lynn." Joe scratched the point of his chin. "Things haven't started off so good for you, have they?"

"We had a misunderstanding," I replied uncomfortably.

"Luke Day, wasn't it?" Beulah put in.

I nodded. "It was his fault, all right. Dan will have it out with him, though. He'll be put in his place."

"Oh, that reminds me," Joe said quickly, "I heard Anzel was hurt. How is he?"

"Bad. We're not sure he'll live."

Joe shook his head. "Jerry's low, too."

"Oh, did he get home? He's been missing. How is he?"

"He's going to live," Beulah put in hastily.

Joe snorted. "He hasn't much chance. Grapeshot tore a big hole in his shoulder. It pierced the lung. At best, Jerry will never use his left arm again."

"We can't think of that now," Beulah said in a flat voice. "I feel sorry for Jerry, but . . . well, it can't be helped."

"I guess not." I shifted awkwardly, trying to think of something less depressing. "You didn't happen to see Burdick while you were in Boston, did you?"

"Now that you mention it, yes. He told me he has your money. He's holding it for you. He says he doesn't like to send it to Northampton in times like these."

"I'll get it just as soon as I can. We're running short of cash."

"You don't have to take it all at once," Beulah murmured.

Joe guffawed and slapped my shoulder. "You're hooked, Warren. When a woman starts worrying about a man's money. . . ." He pulled his finger across his throat. ". . . Goodby, freedom."

Beulah gave him another kick and I laughed.

"Don't pay any attention to him Beulah," I said. "I don't mind having an economical wife, honest. I have to get back to my company. I'll see you later."

As soon as the men had been dispatched to their posts on East Hill, the officers began drifting down the road toward Dr. Hynd's Tavern. Dr. Hynds was at the window, watching for us. He wasn't too happy about having our patronage, even though he would be paid for it. He was one of the town's biggest property owners and, if we lost, the very fact that his tavern had been our headquarters might bring reprisals down on his head. Like the rest, however, he had to make the best of it, take our money and hope we'd win.

Luke Day was seated over by the fire and, from the pile of dishes at his elbow, he must have consumed an enormous breakfast. His face was red and his eyes were heavy, but he was freshly shaven and well groomed. He turned as we filed into the taproom and waved with exaggerated heartiness, but he didn't rise.

"Glad to see you, gentlemen!" he boomed. "Hynds, refreshments for my friends."

Shays was scowling as he came over to Luke Day's table. "Refreshments can wait. I'm much more anxious to hear what you have to say, Colonel Day."

Luke Day's big head cocked. "Me?" he asked innocently. "What can I say? I was caught by surprise, that's all. I thought I was dealing with a gentleman. Not an hour before, Shepard had sent a messenger to discuss terms of surrender."

"I see. You believed he'd surrender to bluster?"

"Look here, Dan," Day said in a deep, growling voice, "There's no call for insults. I was caught unawares and forced to retreat, that's all there was to it."

"Retreat?" Dan repeated in a hoarse whisper.

Day flushed. "Retreat," he insisted. "If Captain Luddington hadn't taken it upon himself to lead his troops up the Southampton Road, I would have been able to bring the whole army out intact. As it was, I got half of them away. Most of the others will rejoin us later." He leaned back and scowled blackly. "I don't like your attitude, Dan. You have nothing to boast about after what happened at the arsenal Thursday."

"Ah, yes," Dan said quietly. "I was coming to that. Suppose you explain why you weren't on hand to support me."

"That's obvious, isn't it?" Day replied airily. "I sent you a letter, informing you I wouldn't attack until the 26th. The messenger was captured on his way back to you. You can't blame me for that, can you? I was negotiating with Shepard for his surrender. Ask Parsons . . . or any of my officers."

Shays held his voice level. "Luke, I think it's about time we came to a decision. Only one man can command our army. It's between you and me. Shall we put it to a vote?"

Day jumped from his seat. "Now, look here, Dan, you're

making it look like I've done something wrong. Since the very beginning our object has been to obtain our ends by peaceful means. On your head lies the blood of those who fell before Springfield. You insisted upon precipitating war before the last avenue to peace was closed."

Dan started to swing. Adam Wheeler grabbed him and held him back. Dan shook Adam off and just stood there, shaking with rage. It was a long time before he relaxed.

Elijah Day cleared his throat. "Luke's right, ain't he? About peace being our object? Maybe—begging your pardon, Dan —maybe Shepard would have surrendered if you hadn't marched."

"Shepard would have surrendered only to a vastly superior force," Shays said flatly. "We knew it. You found it out. He stalled and stalled until Lincoln came. That was his game all along and you're a goddam fool if you couldn't see through it."

"Peace was my objective," Day insisted sullenly. "As long as there was a chance to avoid bloodshed, I believed it my duty to attempt negotiations."

Not many of us were fooled by Luke Day's pious mouthings of "peace." All remembered he was the man who held out for a march on Boston and the leveling of State House, if necessary, to attain our ends.

The argument went on from there, growing more heated and less logical. "All right, all right," Shays shouted finally in exasperation. "This gets us nowhere. I still must insist you were insubordinate in attempting negotiations without my permission. Would you contest my right to supreme command?"

Day glared about him a moment, but no one rallied to his support. "No," he said, reluctantly.

"Very well. The past is past. We both suffered defeat so we're on equal footing there. Hereafter, however, my word is final. You agree to that?"

Day shrugged his shoulders. "I suppose so."

"There is no supposing," Shays said coldly. "Either you agree or you don't. And let me remind you, Colonel Day, that one more such act of insubordination and you make yourself liable to court martial proceedings."

"Goddamit! It wasn't my fault that the messenger got captured, was it?"

"That's over and done with. Forget it. No one will suffer for the accidents of war, only for disobedience. Remember that. And remember, we're in rebellion against a duly constituted Government. If we quarrel among ourselves we court defeat. If we lose we hang. If we stand together and bury our differences we will have victory. From this moment forward let us not forget for one minute that we have a war to win. My hand, Colonel Day."

Luke Day was pouting, but he took Dan's hand without hesitation.

"Dan," Joel Billings ventured in a small voice, "does this mean there's no hope of peace? We got to fight it out?"

"We must fight it out," Dan returned promptly. "As far as I can see, there's no hope of peace—unless we surrender. Does anyone suggest surrender?"

Not a voice lifted in the momentary silence.

"Lincoln ain't so anxious to fight," Joe Hinds put in. "Suppose . . . suppose. . . ."

"If Lincoln wants to negotiate peace," Shays assured us, "I shall be happy to accommodate him. If we can get honorable terms we would be fools to fight. But let us not delude ourselves."

The tension between our officers and those under Parsons and Day had almost completely disappeared. But the argument between Day and Shays had left its mark, even on Shays himself. Dan was again lapsing into those familiar, thoughtful silences. His uncertainties and fears were returning. This time, Adam Wheeler showed he might not be on hand to bolster Dan's waning moral courage. He, too, was thinking hard. Two of his sons were in the ranks. . . . Wheeler caught me eyeing him and flushed.

"Sure, I'm thinking about . . . about putting an end to this. If Lincoln would offer good terms. . . ."

Luke Day grunted. "I'm glad to hear someone has sense around here. Maybe you understand now why I acted as I did —trying to negotiate with Shepard, I mean."

Wheeler snorted. "You wanted 'peace.' We know."

"It's the truth, Captain Wheeler," Luke Day said, keeping his voice as low as possible. "Can't you see it? You and your mouthings of 'peace' have near ruined the army. You don't want to fight. And the men, consequently, don't want to fight.

You can't build fighting spirit in an army by doubting. You can't inject fervor into a soldier by letting him examine all sides of the truth. The other side must be all black. Your side must be all white. Look at what the Government has done. Never once has it admitted for a moment that there might be some right on our side. Never once has it doubted that it was upholding constitutional Government. Is that the truth? Certainly not. But the Government troops believe it. They're willing to die for 'Constitutional Government'. Our men doubted because we have sought compromise. That's why they broke. That's why they went into a panic—not because they're cowardly. For God's sake, get rid of those moderate ideas. Give the men slogans and half-truths and simple principles they can understand and fight for. You're not lying to them. You chose our side because you believe there is more right in our cause than in the Government's, not because we have a monopoly on truth or justice. Forget the shadows. Concentrate on the one issue the men can understand: A Government victory means enslavement of the common man. They'll fight to prevent that. They'll die to hold their liberty."

My eyes were widening. Luke Day was showing himself a shrewder, smarter man than I thought—and a more dangerous man.

Adam Wheeler shook his head and sighed. "It's hard for a man who believes in truth to fight for a half-truth. But you're right. Our army is brittle. Our policy of moderation and the Government's intolerant propaganda have made it so. To win, we'll have to fight fire with fire." Then he added ruefully, "But I sure would like to see Lincoln's terms. He's a soldier, not a two-faced politician."

Chapter 38

I HAD never before fully realized what it meant to the people to have troops billetted upon them, for whenever the army had stopped at a town for a night or longer I usually stayed at one of the taverns. Now I was learning that housing our soldiers meant all sorts of petty irritations. The ten Berkshire men who stayed at our place, two in the house and eight in the barn, were decent fellows on the whole and tried to make as little bother as possible to my mother and father. Yet their personal habits and differences often raised annoying problems.

Neither Pa nor Increase had to chop a stick of wood while the soldiers were with us, for they were most eager to show their appreciation for being housed and fed. They also helped Pa with many of the chores, being farmers themselves. But they sometimes complained about my mother's cooking, sounding off at great length on the skill of their own wives. They sat around the kitchen to all hours of the night, using up our precious supply of sperm candles. They smoked their pipes incessantly, making the air in the house insufferable. They borrowed Pa's knives to whittle and littered up the floor, which nearly drove Ma wild. And some of them left their dirty clothes wherever they happened to drop them, half expecting my mother to delouse and launder them.

The worst offender was a fellow named Ruluf, whose last name I gratefully cannot remember. Ruluf was, without a doubt, the best of the story tellers, for he had fought on the frontier and lived a year among the Indians. I rather suspected some of the tales of his own prowess, but I certainly enjoyed his hair-raising accounts of cruelties inflicted upon prisoners and the customs and primitive ways of living of our red-skinned brethren. His descriptions of his adventures with coy Indian maidens, told only when my mother was not present, were also highly interesting. But his habits were every bit as crude as the most barbarous buck's.

We didn't mind his deep-bellied belches and his spitting out small bones on the floor. We got used to his awful, animal-like odor, which was particularly high after coming in from patrol and sitting by the fire awhile. Ruluf was on the early evening picket line, a time when the cold seemed bitterest and he bundled himself up like a mummy. As soon as the heat got to his clothes, they practically crawled out from the corner where he usually tossed them. But when, rather than braving the icy night, he did his business in the corner of the hearth, that was too much. You allow that from children, but not grown men. I made him clean up the mess and banished him to the barn for the rest of his stay.

I didn't have very much free time during those days, for I was assigned as one of the officers who roved ceaselessly to make sure our pickets were on the job. The pickets found work to do the very first night. Lincoln's army arrived in Amherst near nightfall of the 29th of January, the day we arrived in Pelham. He immediately set out pickets to reconnoiter our positions. Not all of them returned to report to Lincoln. Before midnight our men had captured ten of them and brought them in triumph to headquarters. No shots had been fired so no one had been hurt. Our pickets had merely surrounded the Government soldiers and forced their surrender.

What to do with the prisoners was a problem. Shays talked it over with the officers and we decided to release them and send them home. We believed that showing moderation would have a favorable effect on the neutrals. We merely asked the prisoners to sign a pledge that they would not bear arms against the Regulators or assist the Government in any way unless later exchanged. Most of the prisoners, we found, were veterans of the late war and could be trusted to observe this military convention. It was notable that neither we nor our prisoners showed hate or bitterness for the other.

On the afternoon of the 30th I happened to be in Dr. Hynds' swapping lies with the boys when a shouting outside brought us all to our feet. We made a rush for our coats and hats, certain that Lincoln had begun his expected attack.

"No attack!" Billings shouted from the window. "It's better than that, boys. It's a flag from Lincoln."

The door was opened promptly when the messenger arrived and we all but put out the red carpet for him.

"General Shays, sor?" the messenger asked uncertainly.

"Captain Shays," Dan corrected gruffly.

"Yes, sor." He pulled a letter from under his coat. "Compliments of General Lincoln, sor."

He started to back out, but Shays stopped him. "There may be a reply. Be good enough to wait in the barn. Dr. Hynds, will you furnish this man with refreshments?"

A tense hush fell over the taproom as Dan tore the letter open and read it. Our hearts sank as a scowl slowly settled over his face. He must have read it over five times. The impatient shuffling and clearing of throats became louder and louder. Finally, he handed the note to Frank Stone.

"Read it out, Captain Stone," Shays ordered.

Stone glanced over the letter, then read it aloud:

"Hadley, January 30th, 1787.

To Daniel Shays and others in arms against the Government:

Whether you are convinced or not of your error in flying to arms, I am fully persuaded that, before this hour, you must have the fullest conviction in your minds that you are not able to execute your original purposes.

Your resources are few, your force is inconsequential, and hourly is decreasing from disaffections of your men; you are in a post where you have neither cover nor supplies, and in a situation where you can neither give aid to your friends nor discomfort to the supporters of good government.

Under these circumstances, you cannot hesitate a moment to disband your deluded followers. If you should not, I must approach and apprehend the most influential characters among you. Should you attempt to fire upon the troops of the government, the consequences must be fatal to many of your men, the least guilty. To prevent bloodshed, you will communicate to your privates that if they instantly lay down their arms and take and subscribe to the Oath of Allegiance to the Commonwealth, they should be recommended to the General Court for mercy. If you should either withhold this information from them or suffer your people to fire upon our approach, you must be answerable for all the ills which may exist in consequence thereof.

LINCOLN."

Stone's voice faded into a disappointed silence.

"Peace, he wants," Abe said disgustedly. "Yah, peace on his terms—abject—surrender for us."

Luke Day snorted like an outraged bull. "I'll rot in hell before I yield an inch to that man."

"Dan," came Parsons' grave voice over the tumult, "you ain't gonna read that to the privates, I hope. Some of them fools will think Lincoln's offering them a pardon and desert to him."

The angry voices grew in volume and shouts of "Don't read it!" came from all parts of the room. Then, slowly, bewilderedly, the noise faded away to a restless murmur. Soon every voice was still. Every eye was fixed on Dan Shays. He was standing very straight, gripping the back of his chair. He was very pale.

"Gentlemen," he said in a low, strained voice, "I'm heartily sick of this whole business. I've been sick of it for a long time. I say it's time to quit."

Pandemonium set the rafters to shaking, and cries of "Traitor!" and "Coward!" lifted above the uproar. Yet there was a goodly number who said nothing at all.

"Please, gentlemen!" Shays looked pained and surprised by the demonstration. "Gentlemen, I am neither a coward nor a traitor to the cause. I merely expressed an opinion. I say it's time to quit—before we unleash a devastating and bloody war upon our people."

"Quit now and lose all we fought for?" Captain Sackett asked indignantly. "You have damn little faith in our cause, sir. The man who won't fight for freedom doesn't deserve to be free."

"You're mistaken, Captain Sackett," Shays said. "I have the utmost faith in the justice and rightness of our cause. But consider the consequences—ruined homes, families torn asunder,

505

friends and neighbors killed and maimed, our country devastated."

"What the hell, Dan," Stone said mildly, "if we thought that way in '75, we'd still be ruled by the British. If we quit now, we'll be ruled by the aristocrats. We begged for peace and what do we get—this! A threat. Free men can't be threatened—not while they have the strength to fight."

A cheer of approval greeted his words.

"Please, please, gentlemen," Shays begged. "Let us stay calm. I fear you've mistaken my meaning. I'm not urging surrender. I swear to you, gentlemen, I will be the last to surrender. I wish only to stop the war, to prevent it from flaring up and ruining us all, friend and foe."

A puzzled quiet came over the room.

"You'd better explain, Dan," Captain Hinds called. "I don't get it. You quit without surrendering. You lay down your arms without giving up the things we flew to arms to get."

"Yes, exactly. I believe we have already won. I believe the people of this Commonwealth are with us now. I am convinced that the people will support us in the next election but the moment we fight, we lose their support."

"I don't see that," Gale said doubtfully.

The officers fell to a discussion of the matter and the room buzzed with argument. But the majority of the men had been swayed, possibly more because of their fervent desire for peace than because of the strength of the logic.

"Just a minute!" Luke Day roared. "You mean we're to lay down our arms and go home? Why, dammit, gentlemen, every last one of us will be jailed and hanged."

"No," Shays said quickly. "I don't propose to lay down our arms—not right away. I propose we send a petition. . . ."

"Petition!" Day snorted.

"For God's sake, Dan," Tom Grover groaned, "did you have to beat so far around the bush just to get to a petition?"

"The Legislature meets on February 1," Shays went on, "two days from now. We shall ask for a full pardon for all who have participated in this affair—all. Remember, gentlemen, we have kept the courts closed, as we intended, until the General Court convened again. We can afford to disband if we all get a pardon—all," he emphasized.

Adam Wheeler cleared his throat. "I'd like to say, gentlemen, that I favor Dan's proposal. As I pointed out to Dan once before, we're in a strategic position. If we disband now —with full pardons, of course—we can quickly mobilize again if the General Court acts in a tyrannical manner. Once Lincoln's army is disbanded, he'll have to go before the Legislature for authority to raise another. If the Legislature authorizes an army and we're not mobilized, then we'll know the Government intends to set up a dictatorship over us."

"I don't like it," Parsons said vehemently. "Suppose the General Court rejects the petition like all the rest?"

"Then we're no worse off," Shays answered. "In fact, we're better off. The people will then have evidence that we wanted peace to the very last, that we resorted to arms only against an established tyranny. I believe the people will stand behind us if our final appeal is arbitrarily spurned. One way or the other, gentlemen, we shall be assured of victory."

The last resistance crumbled and the officers quickly selected a committee to draw up the petition. Captain Francis Stone was chosen chairman. Practically everyone took an active part in settling the content of the message.

Our final appeal for peace with honor follows.

"COMMONWEALTH OF MASSACHUSETTS

To the Honourable Senate, the Honourable House of Representatives, in General Court Assembled at their next session.

A petition of the officers of the Counties of Worcester, Hampshire, Middlesex and Berkshire, now at arms.
Humbly sheweth,

That your petitioners being sensible that we have been in error in having recourse to arms, and not seeking redress in a constitutional way, we therefore pray your Honours to overlook our failings in respect to rising in arms; as your Honours must be sensible, we had great cause of uneasiness, as will appear by your redressing many grievances at the last session. Yet, we declare that it is our heart's desire that good government may be kept in a constitutional way, and as it appears the time is near approaching when much human blood will be spilt unless a reconciliation can immediately

507

take place, which scene strikes us with horror, let the foundation cause be where it may.

We therefore solemnly promise that we will lay down our arms and repair to our respective homes in a peaceable and quiet manner and so remain, provided your Honours will grant to your petitioners and all of our brethren who have had recourse to arms or otherwise aided in our cause, a general pardon for all their past offenses.

All of which we humbly submit to the wisdom, candor and benevolence of your Honours, as in duty bound shall ever pray.

FRANCIS STONE, Chairman of the Committee for the above Counties.

Read and accepted by the officers
Pelham, January 30, 1787."

Someone remarked that this was the first time the Regulators had ever admitted we had been wrong in taking up arms against the Government. Everyone agreed it was a tentative admission, contingent upon the reception of this, our last, petition. It would be true only if the Government finally came to its senses.

Shays asked me to take the petition to Boston. I declined, though I had ample reason for wanting to visit Boston. But my connections with the inner councils of the Regulators were so well known, that I felt sure I'd be seized on sight and tossed into jail. We sent Hank McCullock and Sam Baker, men we knew would make the trip as speedily as possible.

As soon as Hank and Sam had been sent on their way a note in reply to General Lincoln's was drawn up. We informed him that, although we would admit no wrongdoing, we wished to avoid bloodshed and would lay down arms if a general pardon were granted. We therefore asked General Lincoln to suspend hostilities until our message could be delivered to the General Court and an answer returned. In the meantime, both armies would remain at their posts.

We received numerous reports from Amherst, mostly from Clapp, on the situation in the Government camp. Lincoln was nearly as worried as we were. His food supplies were not ample. His money was low. The men in the ranks, and even his officers, were extremely reluctant to fight against us. The people were not friendly to his army. In a letter to the Governor, which fell into our hands, Lincoln demanded that the General Court proclaim a state of rebellion to discredit and outlaw us. He acknowledged to the Governor that we were hourly getting more supplies. He had only one advantage over us: his army had powder and ammunition. We were afraid he might decide to use that advantage and try to crush us before the Legislature had a chance to act.

Accordingly, we drew up another letter to him, an effort to smoke out his intentions.

"The Honourable General Lincoln
Sir:
As the officers of the people now convened in the defense of their rights and privileges have sent a petition to the General Court, for the sole purpose of accommodating our present unhappy affairs, we justly expect that hostilities may cease on both sides until we have a return from the Legislature. Your Honour will therefore be pleased to give us answer.

Per order of the Committee for Reconciliation

FRANCIS STONE, CHAIRMAN

Daniel Shays, Captain

Adam Wheeler

Pelham, January 31st, 1787."

We sent a delegation of three men over to Hadley with orders to deliver the letter into the hands of General Lincoln and no one else. They were back in three hours with a reply:

"Gentlemen:
Your request is totally inadmissible, as no powers are delegated to me which would justify a delay of my operations. Hostilities I have not yet commenced.

I have again to warn the people in arms against the government, immediately to disband, as they would avoid the ill consequences which may ensue should they be unattentive to this caution.

B. LINCOLN

To: Francis Stone, Daniel Shays, Adam Wheeler
Hadley, January 31st, 1787."

Lincoln's attitude stiffened morale and our pickets were more alert and vigorous in their patrols. In two days over forty of Lincoln's men had been captured. It was God's wonder that no one was hurt in these encounters. Our prisoners confirmed our belief that the people were with us, for they told of Lincoln's difficulties in getting supplies of food from the countryside. He had to pay spot cash for everything he got. The attitude of Lincoln's troops was revealed in the eagerness with which they signed the pledge to go home and not fight against us.

Our soldiers kept order beyond our fondest hopes. No rape was reported. Very little thieving went on. The decent elements in our ranks were determined that the rowdies would not repeat the shameful performance at South Hadley. And, lest you believe the Government stories that our army was composed of the dregs of humanity, let me point out that there were dregs in Lincoln's army, too. Seven of his men were courtmartialed for thieving. They were convicted and condemned to march before the army with signs pinned to their chests bearing the legend: "FOR PLUNDERING."

On Friday I didn't get back to Dr. Hynds' until well after four o'clock. I thought I really should go over to the Cranes' to see Beulah and Joe, whom I had visited only once since returning home. Beulah and Joe had dropped in at headquarters several times in the last few days, but I had always been out on patrol at the time, so I missed them. Beulah, I may add, avoided hanging around the tavern, for Dr. Cameron was there almost all the time and Joe's return home had reawakened the doctor's antagonism toward the whole Crane family. I suppose I should have been glad I was getting a woman with that much sense. But I was too concerned about the cause to be enthusiastic about anything at the moment.

It was almost laughable to see how everyone perked up when I came in, then relaxed when I was recognized. I didn't stay in the taproom to share their grim silence but went upstairs to the corner room Dan used as his personal office. He was so exasperated with his officers that he didn't even want to be with them. Personally, I thought he was sulking because Luke Day and his crowd blamed him for implanting the thought of surrender in the men. Luke Day only mentioned it once—and almost got his head bashed in for it—but the tension had really never eased.

Dan wasn't alone. Joel Billings was lying, belly down, across the bed, a mug of cider in his hand. Adam Wheeler was sitting over by the window where he could watch the door. Tom Packard grinned and waved me over to the fire to get warm, which invitation I accepted as soon as I had my coat off. Dan was hunched over his desk, whether writing a letter or drawing up another petition I never did get to learn.

"Nothing yet, eh, Warren?" Tom asked.

"Nothing yet," I replied. "It's getting colder, that's about all."

"I hope it snows," Joel said sleepily. "That would keep Lincoln indoors. How is it out on the lines?"

"Quiet. Clapp tells me Lincoln's about set to march. He may attack tomorrow."

"Rumors." Wheeler grunted. "I wish he'd attack and get it over with. If he'd only start something, we'd have an end to this goddam waiting."

Shays turned from his desk. "You know what I think? I think the Legislature's going to stall—the senate, anyway, and look how our army is shrinking. Soon, we'll be so weak Lincoln will be able to walk through our lines and take us without firing a shot."

"Bosh, Dan," Billings said lazily. "It ain't that serious. More men are coming in every day."

"Less are coming in every day," Shays countered. "We lost sixty men yesterday. We got fifteen recruits, a net loss of forty five. All right, the situation isn't serious yet. But suppose we sit here a month or more?"

Tom shifted his rump from the fire. "I'm comfortable. Or maybe you got some suggestions, Dan."

Shays brushed his chin with the quill. "Well. . . ."

"We could keep marching," Wheeler ventured.

"We certainly could," Shays agreed quickly.

"In this weather?" Joel asked incredulously. "Golly, it was so cold last night, the wolf knocked on my door and begged us to let him come in by the fire."

Shays waved impatiently. "We could stop every night.

Look, suppose we drew Lincoln deep into Berkshire. The people out there are hostile to Government, not just luke-warm like the people around here. We could get food along the way and he couldn't. We'd wear him out. All we'd have to do is avoid a clash, not only because we haven't enough powder to fight him but because we don't want any killing, anyway. That way, I think we can keep the support of the neutrals until the elections."

Wheeler frowned. 'You can't keep marching three and a half months. That's crazy, Dan. The men would desert right and left. Half the men would be gone in a week."

"All the better," Tom drawled. "We wouldn't have to feed them." He straightened suddenly, his long jaw dropping. "Say, maybe Dan's got something there. We'd only have to march three weeks. Lincoln's men only enlisted for a month. The Legislature will have to act by then or Lincoln's army will dissolve."

"See?" Shays asked eagerly. "It's practical."

Tom grinned and scratched his head. "Queer sort of war, ain't it? Both sides sweating over how to avoid fighting."

"I think we're fooling ourselves again," I put in. "Maybe the Senate stalls and maybe not. Suppose the Legislature out-laws us as Lincoln wants them to?"

Dan shrugged. "We'll fight rather than hang, of course."

"I've been thinking about that," I said slowly. "Would you plunge the country into civil war to save your own neck?"

Everyone gave me a startled look. Shays pouted a moment, then smiled ruefully at Wheeler.

"Is it you and me against Warren this time?"

Wheeler didn't answer for a long moment. "I don't know, Dan." He stared out the window. "To tell the truth, I've been thinking along those lines myself."

Shays nodded soberly. "I guess we all have. Frankly, War-ren, I don't know what to do. I don't seem to be master of my own soul any more."

Wheeler rubbed his knees thoughtfully. "For the sake of argument, Mr. Hascott, we'll assume Bowdoin doesn't aspire to dictatorship. We have no certain evidence on that —yet. Now, we have the neutrals. So, it looks like we ought to disband. There's only one hitch. How are we going to prevent the Government from taking vengeance on us, hanging us for treason, confiscating our property, then setting themselves up as the party of law and order and winning the next elections? Answer me that and I'll lay down my arms this minute."

The slam of the door downstairs abruptly broke off our discussion. Our hopes gave a bound as an excited babbling went up in the taproom below. We all rose, but none of us made a move to leave the room, for we had been fooled too often. Then, we heard footsteps pounding down the corridor. Joel flung the door back before the newcomer could knock. It was Sam Baker.

"Sam!" Joel cried with delight. He seized the man and dragged him inside, closing the door. "Do we get our pardons?"

"I dunno, Joel," Sam replied uncomfortably. He struggled with his coat and brought out a letter from an inner pocket. "The legislature ain't acted yet." He drew the letter away from Dan's outstretched hand. 'It ain't for you, Dan. It's for Warren, here."

I snatched it from his hand, glanced at the handwriting to confirm what I already guessed. The letter was from Blair. I tore it open. It was brief and to the point.

"Dear Warren, The latest petition of the Regulators was received here today and, from indications, will be acted upon no sooner than the end of the week. I have counted noses in the House and find sentiment nearly equally divided. However, if Lincoln can inflict a defeat upon you before the petition comes to a vote, the Government will be able to defeat any bill offering you a pardon and put through a bill declaring a state of rebellion. I trust this word to the wise will enable you to take the proper precautions.

Hastily,
A. B."

I gave it to Shays, who read it and passed it around.

"We'd better try that plan of yours, Dan," Wheeler growled.

"Yes," Dan replied, with relief. "We march tomorrow." He glanced at Sam. "Not a word of this, Sam. There was no news, as far as you're concerned. This must remain absolutely secret until tomorrow morning."

Chapter 39

U NEASINESS was my first reaction to the decision to march
and keep marching, retreat and constantly avoid battle
and bloodshed. The plan was good. Dan Shays was
absolutely sincere in his intentions. Unfortunately, our plans
and good intentions had been uniformly upset by some im-
ponderable, some unforseeable circumstance that confounded
all reasonable expectations. If some mischance brought the
two armies together, Shays would be forced to stand and
fight. The countryside might then flare up and the dreaded
civil war become a stark reality.

I decided to withdraw from active participation in the
movement. There was nothing dishonorable or treacherous in
this decision. I knew I would not be alone in taking this step.
I admit I was swayed by personal considerations, but I saw my
services were no longer needed, at least for the present. I was
determined, however, to rejoin the army if the plan failed and
real war broke out.

It was Tom Packard who had suggested my line of reason-
ing. The longer the army marched, the more it would shrink.
Some would become disheartened and would go home. Some
would escape to the frontier. The farmers would surely drop
out as soon as the time came for spring planting. This was an
advantage rather than a disadvantage, for the army would
gradually become more mobile, less food would be required,
the stocks of powder would stretch farther. At least six hundred would remain, the men without property, those burdened by insufferable debts, those with no place to go and no
hope except in the readjustment of their debts and the return
of prosperity. Thus, Shays could well dispense with some of

us, secure in the knowledge that we would all flock back the moment our services were necessary.

I made no mention of this around headquarters, principally because I didn't want to explain my personal motives. One man I did have to tell was Dan Shays, lest my departure be misunderstood, but I postponed that chore until I should have a chance to see Joe. I had written to Burdick, asking him to turn my money over to Blair who would see that it got to me. Actually, Blair was holding it for me until I could get to him, either in Boston or at Hubbardston. I had a vague idea for a little deal from which I could pick up a few pounds. But before I saw Joe I attended the last meeting in Pelham of our officers, which had been called for dawn of the 3rd of February.

There was a lot of grumbling when Shays explained the new tactics. Yet everyone agreed it was the only step left, short of open warfare. That the issue would be settled, one way or the other, within three weeks at most, mollified Day and Parsons and the other advocates of vigorous action now. Poor Luke Day was in a tight spot. He had shouted so loud and so long for "peace" that he could not now reverse himself or advocate war while there was a shred of hope left that we could win without fighting.

The meeting broke up in a mood of suppressed excitement and relief. Five days of sitting around had made everyone eager for action, even if the action was only marching. Dr. Cameron, whom we had not dared bar from our meetings, gave only grudging approval to the plan. He believed we were merely postponing the inevitable. Only a few disagreed. Then, surprisingly, I learned Adam Wheeler was relinquishing his command.

He smiled as he caught my startled look. I'll be back if I'm needed. I'm over sixty, you know. I don't think I could stand such a march. It will be a long one, I hope. Abe Gale will replace me. He's my son-in-law, you know. The men have confidence in him, so I guess it will be all right."

"Strangely enough, Captain," I said, smiling, "I've been planning to take a leave of absence myself. I have some money to collect in Boston. I'd like to do it before it's too late."

Wheeler's brows went up. "Boston will be a dangerous place for you to visit right now, won't it?"

"I suppose so. But I have friends. I'll manage. That money may come in handy a little later."

Shays overheard us and came over. "Please, not so loud, gentlemen. Some of the other men heard about your leaving, Adam, and are thinking of doing the same. If that idea becomes general. . . ."

"In that case, I'll stay," I assured him.

Shays looked around quickly. "Well, I'll tell you, Warren, you can do us a service. You go along with Joel and Adam. They're going over to Hadley later to confer with Lincoln. They're really going to spy. If word of our leaving gets to him prematurely, they're to try to persuade him it's an idle rumor. If they fail, they're to ride back and warn us. Otherwise, they can leave the army and go on home. Adam will, that is. Joel is going to rejoin the army at Petersham. Will you go along, Warren? If Lincoln marches today, one of you will have to get through to us."

"You can count on me, Dan. Do I have time to go home?"

"Be back around ten o'clock, Warren."

I stopped by at the house to change to my good clothes, for I wouldn't be able to take along a portmanteau. I couldn't even have my folks send my clothes on to me in Boston. I would be a virtual fugitive and would have to keep out of sight as much as possible. My money would do neither me nor the cause any good if I wound up in a cell next to Job Shattuck.

"How long do you figure on being gone?" Pa asked.

"A month, maybe two. That depends." I pulled on my greatcoat. "I'll be back sooner if the war breaks out."

Pa chewed on his lips a moment. "Increase has decided to join up with the Government if war comes."

I whirled. "What?"

Pa nodded soberly. "Hope talked him into it." He smiled weakly. "A boy's folks don't count much when he's in love."

My mother was on the verge of tears and I put my arm around her. "Now, don't worry, Ma, there's not going to be any war. Dan will see to that. You can trust Dan Shays."

My mother dabbed her eyes with the corner of her apron. "I know Dan's a good boy. But it may not be up to him."

Pa nodded soberly. "Lincoln's a hard man, son."

I grinned. He'll have to catch us first. And we're experts at running away." The joke fell very flat. "Well, I'll be getting along. If I can't get anyone I trust to bring back that money I owe you I'll come back myself."

My mother gave me a hug and a kiss and told me not to worry about the money. Both Ma and Pa tried not to show how pleased they were that I'd be out of harm's way for a month, anyway. I knew Pa would be with Shays the moment serious fighting broke out and he would expect me to be at his side, but still there were times he thought of me as just his boy. Had I the time, I would have taken that brother of mine into the barn and knocked some sense into him.

My feet seemed strangely heavy as I went down the long, winding hill to the Cranes' place. I almost turned back on the excuse that it was too early to be visiting. The fresh white spume curling up from their kitchen chimney knocked those hopes awry. As I turned into the lane, I happened to glance up the river road and noticed a squad of soldiers marching northward to their posts. They didn't know yet that they would be pulling out. I wasn't quite sure I was happy that I was to get a chance to talk to Beulah in comparative privacy.

The muffled, monotonous tapping told me that Joab was already hard at his shoemaking. I knocked and Joe's deep voice bade me come in. Joe was rocking himself by the fire, his feet propped up on a stool. Beulah was cleaning up the remains of a dozen or more breakfasts from the table. She seemed pale and weary and her hair was bedraggled, as if she no longer cared how she looked.

"You're working too hard, Beulah," I commented.

She shrugged. "Mrs. Lowry's been ailing. Mother's not feeling so well this morning, either."

"Well, cheer up, you'll have less work to do after today. The army's moving out this morning."

Joe's feet thumped to the floor. "No! What happened?"

Nothing—yet. We're moving out to prevent a clash with Lincoln. Dan plans to keep marching until we get word from the legislature. That should be three weeks at the most. This is a deep secret. Don't breathe it to a soul."

"Sure, you can trust us, Warren."

"You're going away, too, aren't you, Warren?" Beulah's

voice was listless. She didn't look at me as she added, "You haven't been around much lately."

"Well . . . you know how it is. I've been busy . . . very busy." I shifted uncomfortably. "When are you leaving, Joe?"

"In a few days—Monday, I guess." He gave me a broad wink. "I'm getting a little fed up around here."

Beulah turned quickly. "So are we."

Joe stuck out his tongue. "Bah, to you, sweet sister."

I tried to smile. "I . . . ah . . . I expect to take a little trip to Boston, Joe. I thought maybe you and I could get together on a little deal."

A plate rattled on the table and Beulah stood very still. Joab's incessant tapping rose to fill the momentary hush.

"You're surrendering," Beulah breathed.

"Don't talk nonsense," I returned gruffly.

But I could feel a flush creeping up my neck. Joe swung one foot up onto the stool, leaned back, his eyelids drooping.

"Warren's getting some sense," he said softly. "I'm sure you and I could make some money together, Warren."

Beulah straightened very slowly, rubbing her palms on her hips. Two red spots burned on her sallow cheeks. "Warren, you can't surrender now, not after—after what's happened."

"I'm not surrendering," I insisted, with some irritation. "I'm just leaving the army for a while. Dan's going to be retreating day after day for about a month. A lot of the men will drop out. We'll all come back when and if we're needed. In the meantime, I can be making some money. I'll certainly be needing some extra money, won't I?" I added with feeble gaiety.

The color drained from her cheeks and her faded tan became almost yellowish. She just stared at me, her lips half parted, her eyes misting. She gripped the back of the chair hard. Her knuckles were a dead white.

"You won't be coming back, will you, Warren?" Her voice was low and frightened. "Warren, be honest."

I shoved my hands deep into my pockets, turning away. "I said I'd be back, didn't I?"

"You're running away, Warren." The accusation was cold and harsh. "You're going to Boston, to your fine friends, to your kind of people. Don't deny it. You're not one of us and you never were. You never saw things the way we do. You never thought the way we do. In your heart, you're as much

519

of an aristocrat as any of those satin and silk-clad fops. Damn the cause if it suits your purposes to run out on it. Damn the people if helping them means keeping you from your legal thievery you call trading. You talk about liberty and the plight of the poor, downtrodden common man. Then you consort with our enemies, long for their company, try to ape them—yes—and maybe you've even been spying for them."

She paused, her breasts heaving, her mouth twisted in dry, ugly anger. My fists dug deeper into my pockets. I no longer feared to meet her eyes.

"You're being too absurd to hurt me, Beulah. But if it relieves you, I'll listen. Go right ahead."

"Get out of here." Beulah leaned forward, groping for a heavy mug. "Get out of here! Go to your precious Judith and be damned to you. Go to that empty snob—yes, snob! She's a snob, for all her affected modesty, her and her silks and furs and fine servants and imported geegaws. You'll make a fine pair, you—you—I hate you!"

She threw the mug. I dodged it easily. Joe guffawed. She turned on him angrily, but she said nothing. Soon, she was calm again, her mouth a straight red line. Slowly, she relaxed, her brooding grey eyes fixed on me.

"You don't understand what I'm talking about. But you will—someday you will. This is only the beginning. Dan may not know it, but the fight's going on without mercy or pause until you and your kind are wiped from the face of this earth, until every last money grubber molders in his grave. Someday the land and the power to rule will belong to us, to the people who rightfully deserve to rule."

The last spark flickered in my breast. "I'm not sure you know what you're saying, Beulah, but I think you believe it. I'm sorry. There's nothing more to say, except goodbye."

She gazed dully at my outstretched hand, then turned as if dazed and walked over to Joab's room. The tapping had stilled and only the hiss of hard linen thread drawing through leather broke the flat silence. At the doorway Beulah paused and looked back, her features stiff and expressionless.

"I'm a woman. I can't do much and I know it." Her fingers felt at her waist. "But he will fight my fight. God will give me a son."

Instinctively, even before the full import of her words had

seeped into my consciousness, I was moving toward her. She shrank back, tried to close the door in my face. I gave a bound, knocked the door back, seized her shoulders and shook her hard.

"Beulah, what did you mean?" I released her as she whimpered. "You're with child," I whispered huskily.

"Y—yes," she replied shakily.

"Whose?" Joe called jeeringly.

Beulah cried out, brushed past me, swept a heavy brass candlebranch from the shelf over her head and hurled it with all her might at her brother. Joe ducked in plenty of time and the candlebranch bounded off the side of the hearth. She screamed a curse at him, sprang like a snarling wildcat. I grabbed desperately, caught her around the waist and swung her around.

"Let go of me!" she shrieked, pummeling my face. "Let me go!" Her shrill voice tore through my nerves, but I didn't relax my grip. "God damn him! God damn. . . .!"

I clapped my hand over her mouth and she bit me. Her small flailing fists stung my cheeks and forehead, but I finally caught one of her arms with my free hands and pinned it to her side. Her blows became more and more feeble and she slowly went limp, as if the last of her fury was draining from her body.

"Warren!" she called in a small, anguished voice. "Warren, hold me tight. I . . . Oh, God help me. I'm frightened . . . so frightened."

Her head dropped against my chest and she was a dead weight in my arms.

I gulped. "She—she's fainted."

"So she has," Joe conceded blandly.

I swore at him. "Get a doctor, you fool! Quick!"

I carried Beulah into Joab's downstairs bedroom and laid her on the bed. Her breathing was hard and rasping, as if she were suffocating. I was scared, badly scared. There was no color at all in her face. Her breathing became more choked and for minutes at a time, it seemed, she didn't breathe at all. Her limbs were as loose as if she were dead. I didn't know what to do. I rushed out into the kitchen.

I stopped abruptly. Joe was still sitting by the fire, calmly rocking himself. He hadn't made the slightest move to call the doctor. I felt my temper slipping and I made for him.

His feet came down from the stool with a bang and a long, ugly sheath knife appeared in his hand. The point was touching my belly before I stopped. Joe smiled easily.

"Later, Warren. We'll talk later." Our eyes locked for a long moment, then he repeated, "We'll talk later. If you insist on having a doctor, send Reuben. He's out in the barn."

I only half remember stumbling across the ice-encrusted barnyard and babbling to Reuben that his sister was sick and he should run for the doctor. I was calmer when I got back to the kitchen. Joe was rocking himself again, studiously cleaning his fingernails. During all this time, Joab hadn't paid the slightest attention to us. He acted as if struck deaf and dumb. Now he was holding up a completed shoe, rubbing the toe to give the leather a semblance of a polish. I cursed them both and stormed into the bedroom.

Mrs. Crane was there, an unbleached wrapper over her nightdress making her frail figure seem preposterously bulky. She smiled vacantly, placed only a bony finger to her bloodless lips. I listened intently. I could not hear Beulah breathing. She was lying as still as a corpse, her eyelids partly opened, a horrible waxy sheen on her yellowish features.

"I shan't need you, boy," Mrs. Crane said gently. "I can take care of her. Yes, indeed, I can."

A sudden stifling sensation came over me as I tried to speak, but I could not ask the question burning on my tongue. Then, I saw Beulah's hand move ever so slightly. The cold fear in my heart slowly eased away. I was reluctant to withdraw, but Mrs. Crane kept smiling stupidly at me, as if waiting for me to go. I stepped outside, pulled the door closed, wiped my moist palms on my coat. Irrelevantly I wondered how Beulah had kept her sanity all these years.

Somewhere in the house a clock loudly ticked away the endless minutes. Joe gave his full attention to the delicate task of paring his nails with that vicious looking blade. The sharpness of the edge was impressive. Joab's knife was even keener. The big, brutish man was hunched over his workbench, carving out a new last. The blade made no sound at all as it cut through the thick leather. I tried to think of something else.

An eternity dragged by without a sign of Reuben or the

doctor. I tired of pacing and glancing out of the window, yet I found I couldn't sit still. All at once, I was aware that I was sweating, then realized that I had forgotten to take off my great coat. The house was very quiet. I could hear Mrs. Crane's small feet pattering across the bedroom floor. Several times I thought Beulah spoke. It was only the old lady, mumbling to herself as if incanting a magic litany to dispel the powers of darkness.

The drumming of hooves in the distance sent me bounding to the window. A sleigh was coming up the river road. That puzzled me a moment until I remembered that no sleigh could possibly come down the long hill in this icy weather, but had to take the long route around where the hill wasn't so steep. The sleigh skidded almost in a circle as it turned into the lane and the horse had to paw wildly to hold his feet. I caught sight of a white, oval face behind the driver. Never before had I been so glad to see Dr. Cameron.

The doctor was out of the sleigh almost before it stopped and I opened the door. Dr. Cameron waddled in, his small eyes darting from side to side. The driver, a huge man, was right behind him. It was Dave Corbett, deep concern fixed on his ruddy face.

"Where is she?" Cameron asked abruptly.

"In the. . . ."

The word stuck in my throat. The bedroom door was open and Beulah was standing there, white-faced, her lips pressed together, her hands clasped tightly together.

Dave brushed past us. "A—are you all right?"

Beulah waved him off. "I'm all right," she replied weakly. "I—I just had a f—fainting spell. I'm all right." She emphasized the words, clasping and unclasping her hands nervously. "Thank you for coming, doctor. I'm sorry I troubled you."

Dr. Cameron's fleshy lips pouted and his egglike body rocked back and forth. His heavy eyelids drooped as he gave her a searching look from head to foot.

"You recovered quickly, my dear." The doctor's voice was soft, yet strangely malevolent. "May I see the child?"

I gasped. "Child?"

Dr. Cameron's pale blue eyes fixed on me. His lips twitched and he patted Reuben on the shoulder. Reuben was open-mouthed, appalled.

"I—I—He—he said. . . . I thought. . . ." There was deep pain in his young eyes. "Gosh, Warren, I thought you meant. . . ." He gulped and stepped back, shaking the doctor's pudgy hand from his shoulder. "I guess I made a mistake."

Dr. Cameron shook his head slowly. "Indeed not. You made no mistake, my boy." His head lowered and he stared at Beulah for a long time. Then, a knowing smile touched his flabby lips. "Beulah, my dear, I wish to talk to you in private. Please go into the bedroom."

He took a step forward. Beulah flattened herself against the doorjamb, terror distorting her throat muscles and clawing at her eyes. Her lips twitched in a silent scream.

"D—don't come near me," she breathed breathlessly. "Don't you t—touch me."

Dr. Cameron walked slowly toward her, step by step. Like a grey wraith, the old lady suddenly materialized in the doorway. She gave the doctor a timid smile and bowed jerkily.

" 'Evening, Doctor." Her eyes widened a trifle as she looked around. "Is there something wrong?"

The doctor did not answer. No one spoke. Mrs. Crane glanced from one to the other with bewilderment.

"Is something wrong?" she asked again in a thin, reedy voice. "You mustn't worry about Beulah, you know. She's fine, perfectly fine." Her head thrust forward and she whispered stagily, "She's just upset, Doctor. Her period . . . almost over."

Beulah cried out. An exploding bomb couldn't have stunned me more. Dr. Cameron turned and gazed at me. His lower lip was protruding, quivering with rage. Joab grunted and threw down his knife and turned from his workbench. His sullen eyes clashed with the doctor's but he did not speak.

The doctor's voice was silken. "It has been many years since the scarlet letter has been branded upon a woman's shoulder in this town." His fleshy face became thunderous. "Go in there, Beulah. Go in, I say!"

Beulah's breasts were heaving and her eyes darted from side to side, as if seeking escape from the terrible trap. I could not ignore her silent, anguished appeal. I started for her and a huge hand clapped on my shoulder. I felt myself spinning around, slamming against the wall, the breath knocked out of

524

me. Dave Corbett held me pinned to the wall, his other fist cocked.

Beulah slid away from the jamb. She took one step back . . . then another . . . then another.

"You keep away from me. Keep away from me!" Her voice cracked. "I—I'll kill you!"

She stumbled back, tried to close the door. She wasn't quick enough. Dr. Cameron strode straight through, knocking the door back, then closing it carefully behind him. I struggled to get loose from Dave, kicking out and forcing him to give ground. But Joe slipped out of his chair, catching my arm and shaking his head.

A long, painful hush fell over the kitchen and all eyes fixed on the solid oaken panels. Inside, Dr. Cameron was laying down the law in a deep, pontifical voice. His words were muffled and indistinct. Then, silence. Beulah did not reply.

A shot thundered through the stillness and the ball crackled through the brittle plaster. We waited breathlessly. There was no other sound.

The door creaked open and Dr. Cameron came out. He stood there a moment, his lips half parted, his pudgy fists clenched.

"She shot at me," he said incredulously. "She dared shoot at me."

As if in a daze, he walked to the back door. There he paused and glared at Joab.

"I expect she will be gone from this town by next week. By next Saturday." He rocked back and forth a moment. "The penalty for disobedience will not be pleasant."

The back door slammed angrily behind him.

My soul seemed to shrivel inside of me. I knew what he meant. Unless she left, she would be read out of the church and cruelly branded. That barbarous practice was not yet dead in our enlightened country. Sooner or later, she would be forced to go, anyway. But where could she go? No other town in the state would allow her to settle within their bounds without a clean bill of health from the selectmen here. She would be hounded and despised and inexorably driven to whoredom.

Angrily, I broke away from Dave. I could see Beulah, lying

face down on the bed, burying her tears in the pillow. This was all my fault. If I hadn't momentarily lost my head and sent Reuben for the doctor, this wouldn't have happened. I couldn't walk out on her now.

Dave caught me at the bedroom door. "You did that to her."

I shook loose again, shoved him away. I slammed the door in his face and gave the key a savage turn.

I sank down on the bed beside her, pulled her up and turned her toward me. Her shoulders were racked, but her eyes were dry. She stared blankly at me for a moment, then pressed her cheek against my chest and sobbed. I let her cry herself out.

She relaxed with exhaustion and I lifted her face to mine. I brushed my lips over her moist eyelids, then kissed her hard.

"I'll be back early next week," I told her. My voice sounded strangely harsh. "We'll go over to Northampton and get married. We'll go to meeting the following Sunday. Then, let him do his damndest."

Her arm crept over my shoulder. "Don't leave me, Warren," she said in a small, frightened wail. "Don't leave me—ever." Her whisper was fierce, desperate, "I do, I do love you."

I kissed her again. "After next week, I'll never leave you again . . . never. We'll live in Boston—or New York, if you prefer—anywhere, as long as we're away from here."

"Yes, Warren." She pressed herself against me. "Anywhere, as long as I'm with you."

Her lips burned the promise into my heart.

Chapter 40

A FIST pounded on the panel. "Warren!" It was Joel Billings. "Warren, come out of there!"

I untangled myself from Beulah and got up. "I have to go, Beulah—army business."

"Our army?" she asked quickly.

I grinned. "Our army. Joel, Adam Wheeler and I are going on a special mission." I kissed her again. "I'll be back by next Saturday without fail."

Beulah had recovered most of her assurance, but some of her fears were returning. "You . . . you can't stay?"

"Would you want me to? . . . If I was needed?"

Beulah hesitated only a moment. "No."

Joel pounded again. "Come on!"

I opened the door and saluted. "At your service, sir. I had some unfinished business to attend."

"A helluva time to be making love," Joel grumbled. He jerked his head. "Adam's waiting outside."

I pulled on my greatcoat. "Joe, will you be here next week? Beulah and I will be going to Northampton. You can stand up for her, if you will."

Joe didn't look at me. "I'll be going to Boston. I'll leave Monday at the latest." He gave me a sidelong glance. "But I won't be sailing for another two weeks if you change your mind."

"No chance, Joe. Not any more. Maybe I'll see you anyway . . . Goodby, everybody." I gave Dave Corbett an amiable poke. "Everything's fixed, Dave. You can stop worrying now."

"Maybe so, maybe not," Dave rumbled.

A shout outside made me run. I was feeling peculiarly light

headed, almost as if intoxicated. I climbed into the sleigh and settled with a "whoosh" beside Adam Wheeler. Maybe the situation hadn't turned out as I had secretly hoped, but the mere fact that everything was at last settled was a profound relief.

"What was going on in there?" Joel asked. "It looked almost like a funeral."

"It was—in a way—mine." I smiled wryly. "Looks like I got me a wife."

Wheeler grunted. "Maybe that won't be such a bad thing for you, young feller."

Maybe not. Slowly, the exhilaration ebbed away and a wave of regret flowed in. Somehow, the grass seemed greener in Boston. Now that everything was over, I was beginning to feel sorry for myself. I was sure I could have been happier with Judith.

Our driver was Lon Joplin, a neutral, who was to take us as far as Amherst where we would get horses. Wheeler told me that a messenger had come in to headquarters with the news that Lincoln had been informed of our plan. Lincoln was said to have scoffed at the idea. Our job was to get to him as quickly as possible, before he decided the reports of our troops leaving Pelham were true and ordered his troops to mobilize and march.

The weather was on our side. The air was growing warmer and the heavy masses of low hanging clouds were pregnant with snow. The threat of a storm undoubtedly moved Lincoln to discount all the reports of our troops marching. If the snow held off until nightfall, Dan would gain an extra day or more to move farther out of reach. It wouldn't be so good for our troops, however, if the snowstorm broke during the afternoon while they were on the road.

As we skimmed through the town, we passed column after column of our troops, all heading for the road north which ran along the inner edge of East Hill. They were singing as they marched, most of them by now aware of their destination, for that couldn't be kept a secret forever. After we passed over West Hill, we ran into a squad of our pickets, who recognized us and waved us on without stopping us.

At Clapp's, we wasted no time. Joel rushed inside to get Clapp while Wheeler and I hurried to the barn to saddle up our mounts. I picked myself a nice bay mare I believed would be surefooted on the slippery road. I was tightening the cinch by the time Joel came out with Mr. Clapp.

"You be careful," Clapp warned us as Joel led a horse from the stall and started saddling him. "There's a picket line about a half mile down the road."

"That's all right," Wheeler said. He paused, one foot in the stirrup. "Any pickets been out this far?"

"Early this morning," Clapp replied. "Not since. The bulk of Lincoln's troops are still in their billets in Hadley."

Wheeler chuckled. "Good place for them."

Just as he started to swing up into the saddle, his horse shied and his hands slipped. He twisted his body as he fell, kicking himself free, and landed hard on one knee. He was up before I could get to help him and Clapp grabbed the horse's bridle, talking softly to him to steady him down.

"You all right?" I asked anxiously.

Wheeler rubbed his knee. "All right, I guess. Damn bones of mine are getting old." He mounted from the offside. "Ready, Joel?"

"Ready," Joel returned.

"Good luck, boys!" Clapp called.

And we were on our way again.

As Mr. Clapp had told us, there was a picket line across the road near the Amherst Meeting House. A squad of Horse, their mounts tied up at the hitching rail, were lolling on the steps, resting, presumably just in from a patrol. That was a good sign, too, for if they had discovered anything suspicious, they would certainly be on their way back to Hadley to report.

We were stopped and examined, Wheeler talking for us. Lincoln's soldiers weren't particularly unfriendly, but I can't say they were friendly, either. They were more like workmen, interested only in doing a necessary job. The young lieutenant wanted to disarm us, but, the pistols being valuable, we compromised by firing them and giving up our spare ammunition. Four men were assigned to escort us to General Lincoln.

All along the road, people stopped and stared at us with curiosity. Some were friendly. Some were hostile. Just as we came into Hadley we met a detachment of militia marching up to relieve the pickets in Amherst. A riot almost ensued when we refused to remove the pine tuft badges from our hats. The sergeant of the cavalry nervously asked us to at least hide the badges.

"We're Regulators," Wheeler replied grimly. Then, he added with a smile, "Besides, we don't want to be shot as spies."

General Lincoln had set up his headquarters at the home of one of the wealthier citizens of the town. Two uniformed soldiers stood guard at the gates and, when the sergeant knocked on the door, a smiling colored servant came in answer. The sergeant stated his business and the servant wagged his head and smiled.

"The Gin'l is in the study, sars. Wait here, please."

There was a chair next to the side table in the entry hall and Wheeler sank into it, rubbing his knee.

"How is it?" Joel asked.

"Not so good." Wheeler grunted. "I nicked a piece out of it during the war—the other war," he added with a grin. "It never did heal properly."

The servant came out of the study and bowed. "The Gin'l will see you now, sars."

We filed into the warm, book-lined study. There was a thick turkish carpet on the floor and massive leather-bottomed chairs were set in a semi-circle before the low mahogany desk. General Lincoln looked small and bulky in the big chair and his blue eyes held a twinkle as we came to attention before him.

"Gentlemen, you're wasting time," he said dryly. "That is, unless you've come to surrender. Have you?"

"No, sir," Wheeler said firmly.

"Very well. It won't do you any good, but I'll look at your petit—" He caught sight of me, stared a moment. "Well, it's Mr. Hascott. Or is it General Hascott? I understand commissions are cheap in your army, military brains being so scarce."

I flushed. "You've been misinformed, General—as you will learn if you choose to fight us."

"Indeed? Interesting. Frightening, too." General Lincoln rubbed his smooth forehead. "The petition, please."

Captain Wheeler handed it over and looked around. "May I sit down, General? I bunged my knee on the way over."

530

Lincoln waved. "Go ahead, you may all sit."

We did. Benjamin Lincoln leaned back, a bored smile on his round face as he opened the petition and read it.

"You seem to have run out of imagination, gentlemen," he commented when he had finished. "This is virtually the same as the one you presented the other day." He dropped the paper on the desk, leaned forward, clasping his hands. "Why don't you men be sensible? Lay down your arms and take the oath of allegiance. You know I can't entertain petitions of this sort. They're an affront to the dignity of the Commonwealth."

I coughed. "Is the dignity of the Commonwealth more important than justice, sir?"

"Let's not go into that, Mr. Hascott. I'm a soldier, not a politician."

"We hear," Joel drawled, "that you expect to run for lieutenant-governor with Bowdoin, General."

"That has nothing to do with the present situation, my man. This is a military matter. I've been ordered by His Excellency to do a job and I intend to do it."

"You won't lift a finger to save the peace?" I asked.

Lincoln showed slight irritation. "I've made my offer, Mr. Hascott. You can accept it or not, as you choose."

"You've offered nothing, sir, not even to the privates. You ask them to sign a pledge of allegiance without the assurance that they will be purged of their wrong."

"Oh, you admit you're in the wrong," Lincoln said.

"I admit nothing, sir. Amend the statement to be: what the state considers wrong. Offer us honorable terms and we'll lay down our arms in a moment. You can't expect us to do otherwise."

"And what do you consider honorable terms?"

"Order demobilization of your army. Give us a pledge—privates and officers—that no one will be prosecuted for having participated in this affair until after the election, after the people have shown their will at the polls."

Lincoln snorted. "You think I'm a fool, young man? What would prevent you from mobilizing again as soon as my troops had been sent home?"

"What's to prevent you from remobilizing?" I countered. "The Legislature is now in session, isn't it? You'd then have proper authority for your actions."

Lincoln stood up abruptly. "That's enough, young man. You're being insolent."

I flushed and started to answer but Wheeler silenced me with a glance. He said, "Maybe we'd surrender if you disposed of our cases. But if we lay down our arms, General, how can we be sure we won't be deprived of our citizenship and our property? How can we be sure the people won't have punishments laid on them? How can we be sure we who took the lead won't be hounded and jailed and maybe hanged? Assure us that the Government will not take a vindictive attitude toward us and you can have my surrender right now."

"I repeat, gentlemen," Lincoln said coldly, "the time for discussion is over. I have my orders and I shall carry them out. That I can promise you. Good day, gentlemen."

Wheeler hopped up, favoring his hurt leg. "All right, you win, General. We're still anxious to prevent a civil war—so anxious we'll even consider surrender." He smiled and spread his horny hands. "'Course, we couldn't say it while we had a chance of getting decent terms. I see your mind is set. Will you give us time to discuss surrender? Some of the boys might be a little hard to swing over."

Lincoln's lips tightened and he stared at Wheeler for a long moment. "I promise nothing. Unless you lay down your arms immediately, you will take the consequences. Good day, gentlemen."

"That's good enough for us, General. And thank you, sir." Wheeler hobbled to the door, paused. "Will you give us a pass back to our lines, sir?"

General Lincoln scowled at us, then raised his voice. "Sergeant!" The cavalryman poked his head in. "See that these gentlemen are escorted back to their lines."

Wheeler gurgled deep in his throat, barely managing to stifle his curse. That was exactly what we did not want, for our mission was ruined unless we could stay in Hadley. Perhaps not completely ruined. Lincoln had shown himself as not overanxious to open hostilities. He may have been led to believe we actually would consider surrender and do nothing about the rumors. Yet, Lincoln was not a stupid man. We could only hope that his desire for our surrender would blind him to realities.

Joel tried to whisper something to Adam Wheeler, but

Wheeler motioned him to keep quiet. The sergeant was right behind us. As we came out of the house, Wheeler's limp miraculously grew very bad. He was barely dragging himself along by the time we reached our horses. He stumbled and I grabbed him. The greyish pallor on his face denied that he was wholly acting.

"You'd better get me to a doctor, Warren," he said heavily. "Joel, ride back to camp quick. There's no time to lose."

The sergeant looked dubious. "This is irregular, sir. If you stay behind, you'll have to stay as a prisoner."

I feigned impatience. "For heaven's sake, this is no time for technicalities. Escort Lt. Billings back to our lines. I'll take care of Captain Wheeler. Where's the nearest doctor?"

"Down there—Dr. Greenwood. But I'll have to. . . ."

"Young man," Wheeler broke in sharply, "don't you understand? There's. . . ." He winced as he tried to put his weight on his foot. "There's no time for delay. General Lincoln's waiting a little longer to get our surrender. If Billings doesn't get back to Pelham in a hurry, Lincoln will think we rejected his offer and order an attack. Would you like to be responsible for the outbreak of war, young man? Joel, get moving."

Joel leaped to the saddle, the gleam in his eye showing he understood perfectly. The sergeant looked up and down in confusion a moment, then called one of the other men in the escort.

"Take these gentlemen to the doctor, Peters. Don't let them out of your sight. I'll be back in a half hour to escort them to the lines if this gentleman can travel. Wait for me." He scowled at Wheeler. "If you can't go you'll be a prisoner."

"All right, all right, just as long as somebody gets back to Pelham with the news." Wheeler motioned impatiently. "Hurry along, Joel. I'll come later."

Joel, with three of the four cavalrymen, started away at a rapid clip. Wheeler gruffly ordered the guard who remained to bring our horses along and we started down the road. I couldn't see how this solved anything, but Wheeler evidently had a plan. He sent a quick glance over his shoulder, then leaned closer to me.

"Make for Sam Barlow's—two houses up from the tavern. You can stay there. He's one of us."

533

"But you. . . ." I began, and shut up as Wheeler waved.

Wheeler's knee was really in bad shape, for every step he took was agony. I could feel him trembling with pain as he leaned against me for support. Luckily, Dr. Greenwood's modest residence was not far, barely a hundred yards down from Lincoln's temporary headquarters. Wheeler sighed heavily as the cavalryman tied up the horses.

"Thanks, Warren. You can get along now. You can catch them if you hurry. They're not out of sight yet."

"You can't do that," our guard protested. "I have orders. . . ."

"You heard the sergeant, didn't you?" Wheeler demanded. "He's coming back for me. Lt. Hascott can go ahead. You'll catch up to them easily, Warren. And don't forget to tell Captain Shays I recommend surrender. I'll be along as soon as I can."

The cavalryman looked very dubious, but Billings and the others were still in sight, so he made no attempt to stop me when I mounted. Wheeler called out "Good luck!" as I spurred my horse. I saluted ostentatiously, turning my head quickly. I had snatched the pine tuft from my hat. I was now a spy.

Not until I passed the tavern did I dare look back. Captain Wheeler and his guard had disappeared into the house. Joel and his cavalry escort were gone beyond a bend in the road. There were a number of soldiers on the street mostly heading for the tavern. No one paid any attention to me as I turned into the yard of the house I believed was that of Sam Barlow. I rode around to the back door and dismounted.

A thin, grey haired woman came to the kitchen door in response to my knock. "Is Mr. Barlow in, m'am?"

"I am," came a nasal voice from inside. The woman opened the door a little wider and I walked in. Mr. Barlow was sitting by the fire, whittling a new axe handle. "What kin I do fer ye, son?"

"A friend—Adam Wheeler—sent me here."

Barlow picked his nose thoughtfully. "Do tell. So, Adam's in town, eh? Well, if that don't beat all." He stood up, looked around, as if expecting to find an enemy hidden in his kitchen. "I reckon you be one of them Regulators, eh?"

"Yes. Captain Wheeler said you'd give me shelter."

He picked his nose again, glanced down the short hall to

his front door. "I got a Cunnel Boyd stoppin' by us . . . not by invite, yew understand. But what kin a body do? Yew jest want shelter, son, or kin I do somethin' else for yew?"

Mrs. Barlow stirred. "Sam, do you think it's wise. . . .?"

"Shore, Ma, nawthin' to worry 'bout. The cunnel only comes to sleep. Stays at the tavern all day, soppin' up rum. Shore I can't do nawthin' else for yew, young feller?"

"No, just let me stay here for a while. You can put my horse in the barn, if you don't mind. I won't be here so very long—just until nightfall. Or until Lincoln mobilizes."

I was again compelled to submit to the exquisite torture of waiting. The longer I waited, I knew, the better for the safety of our army. But the thought was slim compensation for the endless, wearying watching from the window. Nothing happened with uncanny regularity.

Around noontime, I became more nervous and jumpy. Sam had warned me to rush down into the cellar if the colonel took a notion to come here for dinner. Colonel Boyd didn't often have his midday meal at the house, which proved to me that he could not have been a very intelligent officer, for Mrs. Barlow was an exquisite cook. The main dish was pork, as usual, but she had cooked it into a pie, cut in small pieces and mixed in with carrots, turnips and herbs of various kinds that gave it a wonderful flavor. Her dried apple pie was almost as good as my mother's, and her cheese, home made, was a trifle better. I would have enjoyed that meal a lot better, however, if I hadn't expected at any moment to be forced to make a dive for the cellar.

During the afternoon, Sam Barlow went out to scout around for me. The news he brought back was meagre to the extreme, which was all to the good as far as I was concerned. Sam hadn't dared call on Dr. Greenwood, who he said was a secret sympathizer, but he had learned that Adam Wheeler was gone. Since no trouble had been reported down at the doctor's, I could assume Wheeler had managed to explain away my absence when the sergeant returned.

Dusk slowly crept over the town of Hadley, blurring the faces of the passersby, softening the gauntness of the leafless trees lining Main Street, blotting out the stark, unpainted houses across the smooth snow covered fields. I was almost sorry it had turned out this way, for I was thinking it might have been better if the two armies had clashed and come to decisive grips. This way, the rebellion would go on and on, to the detriment of trade. Business in Springfield, I had heard, was virtually at a standstill, as was business in Boston, itself. Thinking about Springfield reminded me I ought to take a trip there and see how much money I could pry out of Salderman's agents there. I certainly didn't want to call on Salderman himself and have to explain what had happened. I supposed our poor showing was the reason why that man Jaeger hadn't been around to see me.

Around six o'clock I gave up my vigil and returned to the warmth of the kitchen. The monotony of watching wouldn't have been so bad if the parlor hearth had been lit. Sam Barlow was on our side, all right, but that was no reason in his eyes for wasting fuel on a parlor fire. Sam wasn't niggardly, don't get that idea. When he heard I had been forced to hand over my ammunition when coming through the lines he gave me half his supply, which was certainly more precious to him than his firewood.

With supper time coming on, I felt my nervousness returning. "Maybe I'd best go along, Mr. Barlow. You'll get in trouble if I'm caught here."

"Bah, the cunnel won't never know y're around. He'll flop into bed when he gets home. Don't you worry none about us, young feller. Worst they kin do is send me to jail."

"Sam," Mrs. Barlow said softly. "I hear drums."

I listened intently, but for long moments I could hear nothing. Then faintly, far in the distance, I heard the throbbing of drums. Despite her years, her hearing was much more acute than mine. Finally Sam caught the sound, too, and frowned.

"That's crazy," he growled. "It's night."

"Do you think he'll march now?" I asked incredulously.

I didn't wait for an answer, but half turned to run into the parlor to see if the troops were mobilizing. A sharp rapping on the back door stopped me in my tracks. I whirled, drawing my pistols. The door rattled, but the bolt was on. Barlow waved me into the parlor, waited until I had partly closed the door, then went to admit the impatient visitor. I gripped my pistol hard as I heard the back door creak open.

"Well, for—Joel! Goshamighty, son, I'm danged glad to see yew. Come in, come in."

I poked my head out cautiously. A weight dropped from my shoulders as I was assured it was really Joel Billings.

"Is Warren Hasc—" He spied me. "Warren! I thought I'd find you here." He turned to Barlow. "Listen, Sam, I need a horse. Mine just cast a shoe."

"Shore thing, Joel, yes, siree. Looks like yew got some riding to do tonight, eh?"

"Looks like," Joel conceded without enthusiasm. He shivered slightly, pulled off his mittens and warmed his fingers. "It's getting colder, a lot colder."

"Is Lincoln marching?" I asked impatiently.

Joel nodded. "He sure is. Listen to that."

The beat of the drums was getting louder and coming this way. Horsemen were galloping up and down the street and men were shouting hoarsely to one another.

"Lincoln's mad as hell," Joel went on with a grin. "He just heard how we tricked him. I stopped by the tavern for a drink before coming here."

"That wasn't so smart," I commented. "You're well known in these parts. How did you know I was here?"

"Adam told me. He stopped by at Clapp's on his way back. Clapp hired him a sleigh to take him home. His knee's really in bad shape. I tried to get back here several times, but every time I got chased by Lincoln's pickets."

"What do we do now?" I asked.

Joel shrugged. "Let's wait and see. One of us will have to go on to Petersham to warn Dan, but there's no big hurry. I can't really believe he's going to march. Certainly he won't go all the way to Petersham. That's crazy."

I chuckled without mirth. "That's what Sam Barlow said when he heard the drums."

"Well, it is crazy," Joel insisted. "But I suppose maybe he's crazy enough to march as far as Shutesbury, anyway."

Sam took his lantern. Joel and I went to the barn to get the horses. The barn seemed horribly dark. The horses stomped restlessly and a mouse rustled through the harness room. I could hear Joel breathing hard as he watched the house through a small crack in the door. My pulses were pounding in rhythm to those crisp, authoritative drums.

The night was suddenly livid with the sound of marching feet, the hiss of sleigh runners, the clacking of hooves on the frozen road, the voices barking orders. We did not have to see those men to know they were better disciplined than ours. Yet, Lincoln's army was essentially the same as ours, the same mixture of veterans and raw recruits. I wondered if his soldiers could fight any better than ours. I could only hope they'd never be put to the test.

We said a hasty goodby to Sam and eased our mounts out into the bitter night. We were careful not to show undue haste when we got on the road. No one challenged us. Some distance from the house, we stopped and watched Lincoln's troops, still swarming down toward the common.

"Think he meant it?" Joel asked suddenly. "About not resting 'til he smashes us?"

I lifted my shoulders. "Who knows?"

"I think he did," Joel said slowly. "Warren, know what I think? I think we're finally going to have a showdown."

My jaw hardened. "We'll be ready for him."

Joel scowled. "I hope so."

Chapter 41

A T CLAPP'S TAVERN, we stabled our horses and had our dinner while waiting to see what Lincoln would do. He was certain to pass by the tavern, but where he'd head or how long he'd march was uncertain. It seemed highly unlikely that he'd make an all night march to Petersham. Such a course could gain him a smashing victory—if he managed to surprise our army. But if he didn't and found our troops drawn up in battle array, woe to Lincoln. It would be fresh men against sleepy, weary soldiers. And Lincoln would find that storming Petersham was every bit as difficult as storming Pelham.

Lincoln had two possible routes, depending on his intentions. The longer way would be to go straight to Pelham, thence along the road north on the inner side of East Hill. He would take that route if he intended to break the march into two parts, stopping at Pelham overnight and going on at dawn to reach Petersham about three o'clock the next afternoon. The shorter route was by way of the north road which branched off the east-west highway out of Amherst on this side of West Hill. That north branch would take him up to Shutesbury, thence northeast to Petersham. If he marched all night, he'd arrive at Petersham possibly about four in the morning, a disastrous time for our army if caught napping.

I was inclined to think Lincoln would take the short route. Joel still insisted that was a crazy idea and believed that Lincoln would stop over at Pelham. Accordingly, we decided to back our own choices. Joel would station himself on West Hill. If Lincoln came that way, Joel would ride on ahead of him into Pelham, make sure he stopped there, then ride on to

539

Petersham, I would station myself some distance up the north road to Shutesbury. If Lincoln went to Pelham, I would ride straight to Petersham, arriving before Joel and giving the news. If, however, he came my way, I would ride on ahead, making sure Lincoln did not stop at Shutesbury or New Salem. Joel, meantime, would be taking the longer road direct to Petersham. Either way, Shays would get ample warning of Lincoln's coming.

Clapp posted a man up the road to keep watch for the army, so we'd be able to get out in time. And it was nine o'clock before Lincoln's army finally came. Joel and I had a last drink. We postponed paying Clapp for that drink, for Joel jubilantly bet that Lincoln was only going to Pelham. I should have asked odds. Taking the short route now appeared insane, for the hour was so late that Lincoln could hardly hope to reach Petersham before dawn. Our pickets would certainly discover him long before he got within striking distance of the town, for there was a wide, flat plain before the hill on which Petersham was set.

Clapp warned us both to take along a flask of rum and, as soon as we were out on the road, we were not sorry we took his advice. The night was bitter cold and a sharp, stinging wind was sweeping in from the south. Joel and I kept our beasts to a trot, watching over our shoulders for a sign of Lincoln's army. The night was too black to see very far, even though the whiteness of the snow gave some illumination. There were no stars, only unfriendly, glowering clouds. At the crossroads, we reined our horses and listened carefully, trying to keep our mounts quiet.

"There—hear it?" Joel whispered sharply.

Far up the road, artillery—blessed noisy artillery—was rumbling and crackling over the frozen road. I could hear, too, the shuffling of a thousand and more marching feet.

"Too bad they don't use drums," I commented wryly. "Well, Godspeed, Joel. I hope they come your way."

"So do I." Joel's grin was barely visible in the dimness. "And not because I want you to pay for that drink."

We gave each other a last wave and separated. I rode slowly up the road, keeping a sharp eye back on a squat pine tree at the junction of the highways in an effort to establish my range of vision. Naturally I wasn't going to stand in the middle road and wait to learn if Lincoln came this way. Nor could I conceal myself in the brush and watch until the column had passed by. I had to keep ahead of the army. The pine tree blurred at four hundred feet and at five hundred it dissolved into darkness. Such a distance hardly gave me enough margin of safety. I had to move further up the road.

I prodded my mount to a trot, searching for a suitable place to stop. Behind me the thumping of artillery wheels in the ruts was growing louder. The road was hilly, but not hilly enough, winding, but not winding enough. Finally, I came to a sharp curve which seemed suitable. I rounded it, dismounted and tied the bridle to a bush at the side of the road, then made my way back. I found a convenient boulder, crouched behind it and took my watch. If everything went well, I felt sure I could get around the curve to my horse and be away before Lincoln's troops got anywhere within sight or sound of me. . . .

I blinked rapidly, half rose, an artery in my throat suddenly throbbing. I was sure I had seen something human moving about up there on the hill. Yes, it was a man. Four dim figures rose at his back. They were soldiers. My doubts were over. Lincoln was taking the short route direct to Petersham.

All through the night, the sound of Lincoln's army traveled with me. Sometimes, the sound receded far into the background, only the rumbling of the artillery wheels distinct. Sometimes, the column drew so close that I could hear the brittle clank of iron shod hooves on the hard ground and the softer shuffling of an indeterminate number of boots. At all times, I managed to keep far enough in advance to be safe.

The night was cold—Lord how cold. The chill crept through my woolen gloves and numbed my fingers, my shins ached, the icy wind clawed down my shoulderblades like raking fingers. Yet, Lincoln's army pushed on and on. At Shutesbury, I was certain Lincoln would stop and billet his men. The wind was inhuman and his men could only be frozen flesh and blood. No, he did not stop.

New Salem was the next—and last—town on the route. It was too small a town to accommodate his army. There could thus be only one more doubt in my mind. From which direction would he attack? Would he take the North fork of the road and attack the town from the rear? Or would he make a frontal attack on Petersham? I spurred my horse up the eastern fork and dismounted.

I almost collapsed, my feet were so numb. Pain seemed to burn paths from my feet to every part of my body. I waited, and waited, and waited, stomping and swinging my arms to get some semblance of comfort back into my aching body. Then, it started to snow. How hard it was snowing I was too pain wracked to notice—until something black wavered on the road a scant ten yards away. Then, as I whirled, I made a frightening discovery. My horse had wandered away. She was lost somewhere behind that swirling white curtain. And I was in the midst of Lincoln's army.

I hesitated only a few seconds, though it seemed like hours. I decided to mingle with the soldiers and try to slip on ahead. That didn't seem as if it would be so hard, for the wind was whipping the snow about with such violence that only a fool pulled his head out of his coat collar unless it was absolutely necessary.

Gradually, by quickening my pace a little, I pulled farther and farther up the line. I came abreast of a field piece dragged along by four men. The officer, marching in front of the gun, gave me a sharp look. My heart leaped as he edged over to me.

"Who are you?" he yelled over the howls of the storm.

I mumbled something in a rising cadence. ". . . of the Brookfield Volunteers," I shouted. "I guess I've lost my company."

"I guess you have," he screamed back. "This is Colonel Haskill's Artillery Company." Then, he added, as if uncertain of his position, "We headed the line of march up to New Salem. How did you get here? Did your company pass us?"

"I don't think so. I stopped for . . . for relief and I must have wandered into the field and taken a short cut."

He grunted. "All right. Stick with us."

The gripping in my chest eased away as he faded back to his regular place in line. I shuddered to think of what would have happened if this had been the Brookfield Volunteers.

Hour after hour, we plodded on and on. There was no rest. There could be no question of rest. Of all the places in the state to be caught on such a night, this stretch of road was probably the worst. The land was diabolically flat. No forests gave us momentary respite from that brutal, driving wind. No hills broke the ceaseless pounding on our bodies and nerves. This was infinitely worse than the experience suffered with the Berkshire men in their return from Worcester last December. These men were better clothed and none lacked shoes. But these men did not dare pause, not even for a brief moment.

I assure you this steady, ceaseless pushing ahead soon became a serious problem. I had used as an excuse my need for relief, but I hadn't understood what that meant. When the torture became unbearable, I decided to chance the icy wind. That proved one of the most harrowing of all my experiences, for the cold drove deep into my viscera and never left me. Many of the men preferred to soil themselves rather than brave the agony.

As I was making my way back to the column—battering my way against the wind would be more accurate—I tripped over what I thought was a log. But when I stepped down and felt something soft and squashy underfoot, I realized it was a man. He was curled up, his eyes closed as if he was asleep. I prodded him with my toe, but he would not stir. I dragged him into a sitting position, slapped his face sharply. He whimpered and raised his arms to ward off the blows. I dragged him to his feet.

"Lemme be, sir . . . please, sir . . . please. So . . . so tired . . . I wanna . . . can't . . . can't."

"Oh, yes you can," I said impatiently.

I shouted for help. Several soldiers glanced at me indifferently, if at all, and plodded on and on. I became a bit angry and I half dragged, half carried my burden over to the line.

"You, there!" I shouted authoritatively. "Take care of this man. Run him up and down and. . . ."

A slight fellow stepped from line. "My God, it's Rufe! Eli! Eli! It's Rufe!"

Another man came from the ranks and grabbed the stricken man. "Thank ye, sir. We'll take care of him."

I fetched out my almost empty flask. "Here. Give him some of this. Don't drink it all yourself, understand?"

They thanked me profusely and called the others of their comrades over to help revive Rufe and I left the half frozen man in their charge. I felt a bit uneasy about helping the men who would soon be fighting against my friends. Then I shrugged. If these men could defeat us in the condition they'd be in when they reached Petersham, our army would deserve to lose.

I was tired, Lord, how tired. Many times I almost yielded to the warm drowsiness that tempted me to seek a bed in a comfortable snowdrift. Once I staggered off the road and had to be dragged back by an apologetic private. Another time I performed the same service for another man who broke from line. My fight to keep awake was more strenuous than any fight I had engaged in with swinging cutlass and flaming powder belching into my face.

During the whole of that raging snowstorm, the night was oppressively dark yet never wholly black, a phenomenon entirely without interest to me until at length I became aware of a weird greyness creeping into the gloom. Many moments slipped by while I tried to adjust myself to the novelty of real men, instead of vague shapes. Actually, they looked more like stiff, frozen snowmen than human beings. It somehow disconcerted me to discover that I could see more than twenty feet ahead of me. Then as if awakening from a nightmare, I knew morning had come. The wind had lost its fury. The storm was passing away.

Soon, I regretted the end of the storm, for life was coming back to my deadened limbs. The sensation was not pleasant. Needlelike pains drove into my feet and ankles and tearing agony settled in my thighs. A patch of dull ache formed in the small of my back. My mind was clearing and my senses thawed. My fears returned. I was only too aware now that I was in the midst of Government troops, only too conscious that I could be seized and hanged as a spy. But I was much too tired to even think of making a move which might bring down suspicion and disaster upon me.

There was no escape. Even had I been able to muster the strength to run, there was no place to go. The land was comparatively level in this vicinity and huge drifts had piled up, in weird, writhing shapes, some as high as a horse. The impossibility of running on ahead was all too evident. I was close to the head of the column and I could see the soldiers struggling valiantly to break through the endless succession of small and large snowbanks.

"There she is!" someone yelled. "Petersham!"

Instantly, the shout rippled down the line. Immediately, the order to hush was passed along, for the enemy must not be warned. Enemy! Curious word in my ears. I peered ahead at the low ridge of hills in the distance. Petersham was nestled in there, elevated from the flat ground over which we were coming. I could see one spume of smoke rising from among the jagged hilltops. I wondered if our troops were up and about, if Joel had managed to get through. Again I considered trying to sprint on ahead. Again, I abandoned the idea as hopeless. I'd be shot like a rabbit as I floundered over those snow barriers set across the road.

The progress of the army was no greater than before, but the spirit of the men was definitely higher. As tired as they were, many could laugh and chatter and even indulge in some horseplay. The confidence of that crew was amazing. To them, their task was nearly over. All they'd have to do, according to them, would be to drive into the town, swoop down on the centers of resistance, round up the prisoners and go home. I wasn't willing to admit it would be as easy as that. Yet, one grim fact made me afraid. The smooth blanket of snow, marred only by infrequent mounds and furrows, undulated endlessly from horizon to horizon. Not a square inch of that vast expanse of whiteness had been broken by human foot and it was now close to nine o'clock.

Now we were almost within shouting distance of the town. And still no sign of the pickets. Then, just off the road at the crest of the hill, I spotted the back of a rude lean-to, almost completely covered with snow. That's where the pickets were, sitting and basking their toes before the fire whose smoke spume was now rising straight up. I nearly groaned aloud. Those fools! Looking back, I could see that Colonel Haskill's Artillery Company, with which I was travelling, was a good half mile ahead of the main body of troops. The rest of the column stretched out like a gigantic black snake, visible for miles against the dazzling whiteness covering the silent countryside. Yet we seemed to be approaching without being detected.

Then, only one barrier remained—a long hill. The company slowed almost to a halt and I thought for a moment that Colonel Haskill was going to wait for the main force to come up.

But no, it was the snowdrift at the bottom of the hill that had forced us to slow down. The front ranks were battering themselves against that wall of snow, clearing the way for the rest. There was not yet a single picket in sight.

An officer at the head of the line turned, cupping his hands and looking directly at me.

"Fix bayonets!" he called in a subdued voice.

Since he had mistaken me for an officer, I could do no more than accept the situation. I turned and called in a loud voice, loud enough, I hoped, to carry over the hill:

"Fix bayonets!"

The clink of metal against metal rippled down the line and faded into nothingness. We were halfway up the hill when the sunlight broke through the clouds and startling flashes flickered from the bared steel. Everyone was tense, but no one tenser than I. Incongruously, many of the soldiers were grumbling, not about the cold or their weariness, but about their hunger. That was a sure sign that the troops had regained their morale.

And still no sign of our pickets.

Progress was becoming slower and harder and some of the men virtually disappeared under the snow that blocked our way. I seized upon my opportunity, thankful for my long legs which would carry me on a bit faster than the rest. I pushed through to the very head of the line. No one challenged me. Everyone was too intent upon knocking down the wall of snow and clearing the way for the artillery. I fought my way ahead, pretending to urge the men on faster, but frantically trying to get over the top first. From what hidden well I managed to summon the energy for such strenuous exertions, I'll never know.

A head popped up, less than twenty feet in front of me, then a second, then a third. As if hypnotized, the three men walked out to the very brink of the hill, their mouths open, eyes bulging. I shouted to them, but they did not seem to hear. Even when I came right up to them, they did not move. They stood like stone statues, paralyzed with astonishment.

"Government troops!" I bellowed. "God dammit, get going! Spread the word!"

I jostled past them, sprinted with all my might, shouting at the top of my lungs. Behind me, an officer roared with rage and ordered his men to fire. Two muskets clicked futilely. A third cracked viciously and the ball sped over my head. Oddly, the road here had been swept almost bare by the wind. Even so, I could not run very fast. The pickets rushed by me, waving their arms and shrieking in shrill terror:

"Lincoln! Lincoln! Lincoln!"

I was yelling like a fool myself.

Heads popped from every window and door and, as soon as the men caught the meaning of the shouting, they, too, started yelling. Then, they came out and dashed about aimlessly. My shouts turned to curses of consternation. They were panic stricken!

Men tumbled out of every house and barn along the way, some half dressed, some throwing away their muskets and greatcoats as they ran. Senseless fist fights broke out in the middle of the street. Many tripped over discarded equipment and sprawled on their faces, scrambling up again to run they knew not where. Behind me, Lincoln's men were pouring over the hilltop, bayonets leveled, spreading out like the black spew of a roaring volcano. And our men were running, running, running, like stampeding sheep.

I tripped and fell on my face and crawled a good ways before I could regain my feet. I was actually crying tears, tears of rage and frustration and remembrance. The officers were out among our men, flaying them with their swords, begging them to stand and fight, picking up muskets and shoving them into unwilling hands. No use, no use, no use. The refrain was pounding in my head as I ran blindly down the street searching for the tavern.

Then, I saw Dan Shays. He, too, was snarling and flailing and cursing his men, vainly trying to rally them. No use. They were streaming out of town at the other end of the street, never looking back, never stopping, anxious only to escape from Lincoln's descending horde.

"Warren!" Shays yelled suddenly. "Warren, how in God's name. . . . No, no time for explanations. Get busy. Stop these madmen."

He flung himself into the path of a baying horde of fear-crazed men. They bowled him over and almost trampled him to death before I could hammer my way through to him. He was pale and shaken and screaming incoherently.

I shook him. "Dan! Dan! Don't be a fool! You can't stop them. No one can stop them. Escape! Escape or hang!"

Shays stared stupidly at me for a long moment. He turned his back to the oncoming Government troops and stared at his army, the bulk of which was clambering through the snow drifts on the road to Athol. The vanguard of Lincoln's men was now within fifty feet of us. I grabbed Dan's arm and started dragging him along. He shook me off angrily, turned deliberately toward the Government troops and raised his sword. Then, his arm dropped. He spat contemptuously and cursed his troops.

"I'll reform my ranks!" he shouted defiantly. "By God, I will! And I'll meet you again if it's the last thing I do."

He elbowed me out of the way and started running. He no longer knew me. His eyes were blinded by rage and despair.

Just in time, I regained my senses and started running again. Every step was agony. Then I saw a group of men standing by a big oak tree at the last house in town. Their leader, a big, barrel-chested man, was deploying them for an attempt to stop the Government advance. That man was Luke Day. He was not going to lose his head. He was not going to run. By the Lord Harry, he and his men would fight like men. It was a brave band, but too pitifully few to hope to stop the Government advance.

His square, heavy features brightened. "Hascott! Damn my soul, I'm glad to see you! Has. . . . Fall on your face! Fall on your face!" Instinctively, I did, just as he roared: "Fire!"

Twenty muskets cracked and the Government troops scattered for cover. Luke Day laughed wildly. He shoved a musket into my hands.

"We'll fight those bastards! We'll fight. . . ." His voice cracked and he brushed his hand over his eyes. "God help us, it's too late. Cowards! Come back there and fight! Stop, you! Come here, you!"

The last of our men were struggling to get out of town. They gave Luke Day no heed. Luke Day cursed them up and down. Lincoln's men were rounding up stragglers, more intent upon taking prisoners than fighting. A hundred men could have stopped them in their tracks and possibly knocked them back out of town. But Luke Day didn't have a hundred. He had only twenty. He knew he was licked.

"I told you this army was brittle," he said bitterly. "You and your goddam moderation! Look what it's done to us." He shook his fist at the tremendous wave of troops rolling toward us. "We're not through. This is only the beginning. We'll gather the best of the men in the hills and come back. I'll smear the countryside with their lousy carcasses." He grunted and nodded to his men. "Come on, let's get out of here. We've got guts, but we're not idiots like the rest of our lousy army."

Luke Day, too, hastened up the road to Athol.

The stop had done me no good. The stiffness was gathering in my limbs and I could hardly put one foot in front of the other. A musket butt smashed against the back of my skull and I dropped into a horrible dark pit.

I groaned and stirred and felt hard boards under my back. I could hear a fire roaring in the distance. The smell of ale and rum and cider was strong in my nostrils. Then, as I opened my eyes, I gazed up at the round, lumpy face of General Lincoln.

"The Government has been upheld, Mr. Hascott," he said softly. "Your rebellion is over."

As I slipped back into the depths of oblivion, the echo came up with hollow despair:

"Your rebellion is over."

Chapter 42

ЮЮ

I AWAKENED briefly several times, just long enough to assure myself I was in a comfortable bed with comfortable blankets over me, then quickly yielding to the almost forgotten luxury of untroubled sleep. True, I was acutely aware that my left ear was frostbitten, swollen to twice its normal size and burning like mad. I knew I was a prisoner of war. But I could see no profit in worrying about anything until later . . . much later.

The last time I came swirling up from my warm dreams, I just lay still, hoping I could return to the wondrous bliss of oblivion. But I had slept myself out. I was reluctant to return to the ugly realities of living. The vivid pictures of that bestial stampede passed before my eyes like a distorted nightmare. "The rebellion is over," someone had told me. I strove to disbelieve it. In my heart, I knew it was true.

The army of the Regulators was shattered beyond repair. The men had thrown away their weapons, fled from their billets without even taking along their food which they'd been cooking in the ovens. The provision sleighs must have fallen intact into Lincoln's hands. Shays might be able to rally some of the men. But most of them, the men of property and substance who had given our cause dignity and backbone, those men would now be on their way home. Never again could Shays raise a formidable army. Never again would the people support a discredited army that had broken not once, but twice.

I couldn't stay in bed forever. Tentatively, I opened my eyes and looked around. I was in a barely furnished chamber, the usual sort found in a wayside tavern. Two men shared the bed with me, the one next to me snoring lustily. The other man was in misery, groaning and grinding his teeth and mumbling as if he was out of his head. That man needed medical attention.

I almost died trying to get out of bed. Not an inch of my frame was without a kink or twinge or an excruciating pain. My head felt like a cannonball and I expected any moment it would drop from my shoulders and crash through the floor. I walked to and fro gingerly, hoping my legs wouldn't snap off. They didn't. Slowly, the dizziness passed away and some of the pain left me. Having been through this before after long sieges of violent activity and no sleep, I expected to be as spry as ever in a few moments. My recuperative powers were not what they had once been. Sadly, as I staggered to the door, I had to admit I was growing old.

A tiny wisp of a man bumped into me as I opened the door. He stepped back, blinked and smiled.

"My, my, you've recovered quickly, my man. Let me introduce myself, sir. Dr. Dwight Mallory, at your service." He pulled up the tail of his coat and drew forth a flask. "Here, take a little of this. It will do you good."

I mumbled my thanks and accepted the flask and took a generous pull. I coughed and sputtered and spewed the liquid out over the wall. Poor innocent me. I had thought he was offering me rum. The bitterness of that devilish brew was nauseating.

"Tsk, tsk, young man, it's good for you."

"Indeed!" I said coldly. "If it's so damn good, take it yourself."

He pouted and seemed ready to burst into tears. I laughed and apologized for hurting his feelings. I strode away before he could give me any more of his infernal treatments.

"But your ear!" he protested. "I really should. . . ."

"Your patient is inside," I called back.

I wanted nothing more to do with his kind of doctor.

Not until I came downstairs was I fully aware that it was dark outside. All the candles were lit in the taproom and the tables were well filled. The landlord looked awfully sleepy. I had assumed I had slept through the day and it was now early evening. But the patrons seemed to be eating breakfast. Then, I spied someone I knew.

"Joel!" I called in delight.

Joel lifted his hand, but did not smile. He glanced pointedly at the man sitting at the table near which he was standing. It was General Lincoln. He was nibbling on his breakfast and watching the man bending over and signing a paper. He glanced up and saw me and a broad smile broke on his round face.

"Good morning, Mr. Hascott!" He beckoned to Joel. "You're next, Mr. Billings. Sign directly below the last name."

The long, lean man who laid down the pen and was straightening up was Tom Packard. He winked at me and grinned. Joel picked up the pen, fidgeted a moment.

"I'm an officer," he said finally.

"I know that, Mr. Billings," Lincoln replied. "Just sign and we'll let the General Court worry about your part in the affair. . . . Well, Mr. Hascott, I fancy you're next." He gave me an amused look. "If your men had the spirit of the officers, this wouldn't have been so easy."

"We're not through yet," I said grimly. "Shays will reform the army and lick you yet."

Lincoln waved. "Bosh! Shays is through and you know it. I'm almost disappointed I had no more opposition. Sign this, Mr. Hascott, and you may go."

"What is it?" I asked suspiciously.

He handed me the paper. "The oath of allegiance. Perhaps you would like to read it first?"

I would and I did. Since the document has a bearing on the attitude of the state towards us, permit me to insert the text:

"I do truly and sincerely acknowledge, profess, testify, and declare that the Commonwealth of Massachusetts is, and of right ought to be, a free, sovereign and independent state. And I do swear that I will bear true faith to the said Commonwealth, and that I will defend the same against all traitorous conspiracies and hostile attempts whatsoever. And I do renounce and abjure all allegiance, subjection and obedience to the king or government of Great Britain, and every other foreign power whatsoever. And that no foreign prince, person, prelate, state or potentate hath or ought to have any jurisdiction, superiority, preeminence, authority, dispensing any other power in any matter, civil, ecclesiastical or spiritual, within this Commonwealth—except the authority and power which is or may be invested by their constituents in the Congress of the United States. And I do further testify and declare that no man, or body of men, hath or can have any right to absolve me from the obligation of this oath, declaration or affirmation, and that I do make this acknowledgement, testimony, declaration, denial, renunciation and abjuration heartily and truly, according to the common meaning and acceptance of the foregoing words, without any equivocation, mental evasions or secret reservations whatsoever, So help me God. . . ."

"This must have been drawn up by a lawyer," I commented.

Tom guffawed and the other rebels gathered around the table joined him. Even General Lincoln chuckled.

"America is the land of the lawyer," he said dryly. "You gentlemen should remember that and thank God for it. As long as we have lawyers and laws for them to evade, we have freedom. Will you sign below Mr. Billings' name, Mr. Hascott?"

"If I refuse? If I prefer to remain a prisoner of war?"

Lincoln shook his head. "I took no 'prisoners of war', young man. This is—was—a rebellion. Rebels have no belligerent rights. Persist in defying the Government and you hang as a Rebel. Sign and possibly you'll get off with a lighter punishment."

I shrugged and signed. "At least, I'm not being asked to acknowledge any wrong."

Lincoln's brows went up and he turned the paper, scanning it quickly. "A lawyer's interpretation, Mr. Hascott. However, that's not my business. If you remain loyal to our Constitution in the future, according to your oath, I shall be satisfied."

"I trust Governor Bowdoin and his administration takes such a liberal view of the matter, General."

"I trust so, too. I assure you I shall work to that end. I believe our country's interests will be better served if justice is tempered with common sense instead of vindictiveness." General Lincoln extended his hand. "Our wounds will heal more quickly if we harbor no resentments."

553

I shook hands and assured him I held nothing personal against him or his men, some of whom were my neighbors. But, as I stepped away from the table, I had a momentary doubt. A group of Government soldiers were standing by the door. Among them was my cousin Jesse. Our eyes met with coolness, wavered, and I half turned away. Then, I decided Lincoln was right. Perhaps I didn't and never would agree with the Government position, but it would profit no one to nurse the grudge forever. The issue had been decided too decisively to deny the defeat of my viewpoint.

Jesse kept his eyes averted as I walked over to him.

"Howdy, Jesse," I greeted, a bit stiffly.

A smile pulled at his lips. "I—I heard you'd been hurt. I thought I'd come over and. . . ." He gulped. "How's Anzel?"

"Pretty low the last time I saw him . . . about a week ago, that was. We'd have heard if . . . if anything happened."

He shifted uneasily, avoiding my eyes. "I hope he gets better quick. Tell him that when you see him, will you?" He looked embarrassed. "You'd better get that ear of yours fixed."

I instinctively touched it and winced. "I'd almost forgotten it, I've got so many other pains." I cleared my throat. "I'm going home today."

"That's fine. Tell Pa and Ma I'm all right, will you? I'll be home in two or three weeks." He gave me a strained smile. "Well, I gotta go. I'm glad you're all right. 'By."

Jesse didn't see me put out my hand, he turned away so quickly. I was satisfied that the meeting hadn't lasted any longer. Jesse and I wouldn't hate each other, but I knew it would be a long time before we could again discuss politics. However, I felt greatly encouraged that neither Jesse nor any of the other Government soldiers showed elation over their victory. Actually, they had not won a victory. Then, it occurred to me that perhaps, after all, the war had ended, in fact if not in appearance, in the manner in which Dr. Hynds had hoped it would end.

Joel and Tom were at breakfast. I now learned that the time was four in the morning, instead of early evening, and that I had slept eighteen solid hours. I felt it. Before sitting down with them, I hunted up Dr. Mallory and had him fix up my ear. He tried to inflict some medicine on me, without success, but I allowed him to smear some salve on my ear. The stuff

554

smelled strongly of sulphur and skunk. The bandage he applied was virtually a sultan's headdress. Dr. Mallory pish tushed my protests, saying he had plenty of bandage. The good women of Petersham had contributed liberally of their petticoats for that purpose. My bandages were of fine cambric, donated by the parson's pretty eighteen year old daughter, no less. My head ached just as much, however.

While he worked, he gave me the results of our disastrous rout. Only a hundred and fifty of the nearly two thousand in our army had been captured. Most of them had already signed the oath and gone home. None of our men had been killed. None had even been wounded, beyond minor cuts and bruises. The Government troops had suffered far worse, almost every man having had a frostbite of some kind. Except for a handful of cases, however, most were as minor as mine. Dr. Mallory's cheerful opinion was that only a few would require amputations of legs or arms. In all seriousness, that is a remarkable record considering the cruelty of the experience.

Having been tended to, I thanked Dr. Mallory and offered him payment, which he indignantly refused. Then, I returned to the taproom and sat down with Tom and Joel and had breakfast. I might have been dopey from my long sleep and full of aches from my march, but the inner man was still sound. I was wolf hungry. I consumed enough to make up for all the meals I had missed.

While I packed away nourishment, Tom and Joel told me how they happened to be captured. Tom said that he had rushed out in his shirtsleeves when he heard the noise. By the time he gave up trying to rally the men, he found he had been swept too far away from the house where he had been billeted and couldn't return for his clothes. So, he joined the retreat. He knew, of course, he'd either have to get a coat or freeze on the road. So, he stopped in at the nearest farmhouse, and, while the farmer was hunting up his old greatcoat, Government troops surrounded the place. Tom ducked into the cellar and hid there all day. Unfortunately, troops were billeted there and the farmer was caught taking food down to him. Tom was brought back to town and kept here at the tavern until Lincoln came down just now.

Joel's tale was equally distressing. "After I left Pelham, I rode as fast as I could and figured to get here around half past three or four o'clock. I was just about halfway when a big chunk of snow fell off some branches and plopped on the road right in front of me. The horse shied and threw me and ran away. I cut across country and got to Shutesbury and got a horse from John Powers' father. Lincoln's troops were in Shutesbury then. I had to ride around the whole damn army, which took a lot of extra time. When I was about five miles from here I ran right into some Government pickets."

Tom lifted his shoulders. "Here we all are. Maybe it's all for the best. I hear nobody got hurt on either side—from fighting, I mean. Maybe Dan can still keep to the plan."

"Let's not fool ourselves," I said. "The rebellion is over. Dan will be lucky if a hundred men stick to him."

"There'll be more than that," Tom surmised. "Some of Parsons' men will rally 'round. So will some of Luke Day's men. I'd say Dan can salvage about five hundred."

Joel slumped in his chair. "Just think, if it weren't for me, this wouldn't have happened."

"And me," I added.

Tom shook his head. "No, I don't think either of you were to blame. I don't even blame those pickets who should have warned us in time. It was the whole army's fault."

"Luke Day once told me it was brittle," I put in.

"Yes, that's it, exactly," Tom agreed. "The men were divided and confused. If we had vilified the Government the way the Tories vilified us, the men wouldn't have doubted. That's what you need for a fighting army—no doubts. We should have used a good rousing slogan like: 'Down with the dirty rich!' We should have let Luke Day's crowd pump junk like 'Bowdoin wants to be a tyrant!' into the men."

"Well, he may try now to set up a new tyranny," Joel pointed out mournfully. "Who's to stop him?"

"The people," I answered. "If Bowdoin or the autocratic elements in his administration try to turn our Government into a dictatorship of any kind, our cause will revive overnight. Bowdoin can't be completely stupid. He must know he'll inflame public opinion and start a new revolt if he hangs us and denies us our civil liberties. Deny civil liberties to one group and you deny them to all. The people won't stand for that. Anyway, let's worry about it when it happens."

"I'm gonna hire me a good lawyer," Joel commented. "I

want enough postponements to keep my neck in one piece until we know." He pushed himself away from the table. "If you're done, Warren, let's go. We've hired a sleigh to take us home."

About three in the afternoon, we reached the junction of the Pelham-Amherst highway. Joel wanted to get out and walk the rest of the way home, but Tom and I insisted on taking him into Amherst. Joel allowed us to take him as far as Clapp's Tavern. He wanted us to come in with him and have a drink, but Tom and I refused, for we knew we'd be kept there for hours performing the autopsy on our movement.

"See you in jail, Joel," Tom said cheerfully as our friend stepped out of the sleigh.

Joel laughed. "Bring your own blankets." He held out his hand to me. "I suppose I'll be seeing you, too, Warren."

"Maybe not, Joel. I've been thinking of going to Boston. My other trips did no good, but maybe I can talk my friends into working for leniency for us."

Joel looked dubious. "You might be put in jail."

I smiled. "What's the difference? Here or in Boston."

"Yah, that's right." He gripped my hand hard. "Give my regards to Job Shattuck. And I hope this isn't goodby."

"I hope not, Joel."

Joel Billings stepped back and waved and Mr. Enders, our driver, whipped up the horse. Turning back, Tom and I saw people swarming out of Clapp's and clamoring for news.

"I'm glad we escaped that," Tom said, settling again. "What's this about going to Boston? I thought you were going to marry Beulah."

"I'll take her along," I replied uncomfortably.

I was sorry he had brought that up. There was no way of escaping her, of course, even if I wanted to—which I didn't particularly. But I wasn't eager to face her, not after what had happened. She might very well blame me for not being able to warn the army in time. Yet, even if I were mistaken in this, I doubted that I'd ever be wholly happy with her. I didn't love her.

557

Tom didn't break the silence until we were over West Hill and passing Bruce's Tavern. Then:

"Warren, why don't you take her to her grandfather's in Attleboro. Let Dave Corbett know. He'll go to her and take her off your hands."

I shook my head. "That wouldn't be fair to her. It would be the same as deserting her. I don't think she loves him."

Tom snorted. "Beulah never loved any man—including you." He was silent a moment. "I don't know exactly why I say that, but I feel it's true."

I burrowed deeper under the blanket. "It's too late to worry about that now."

"I suppose it is," Tom agreed.

As we passed my house, I saw my father crossing to the barn in a path he had dug. He was visible only from the chest up. I didn't stop, since I wanted to see Beulah first and settle things there. . . .

The sleigh stopped in front of Beulah's and I got out. Tom gave me his hand. "Good luck, Warren, whatever happens." He smiled slowly. "Maybe I'll see you on the scaffold. Anyway, it's been nice having you around long enough to get you into trouble."

I grinned. "I'll be back if any more causes turn up. Just holler 'Dictator' or 'Freedom' and I'll come running."

Tom gave me a mock salute. "Down with the dirty rich!" He waved and the sleigh went on into the waning afternoon.

I knocked on the kitchen door and walked in. Beulah was standing on a stool, taking a powder horn down from its hook over the mantel. She glanced over her shoulder, teetered a moment on the stool, then jumped down, her eyes widening. "Warren!" She rushed over to me. "Warren, are you all right? Your head."

I touched the bandage lightly. "I'd almost forgotten about that. A frostbitten ear, that's all. Nothing serious."

"Wh—what happened?" she asked breathlessly. "Why—what brings you home so soon?"

"The war is over—finished." Then I noticed someone sitting in the rocker by the fire. "Joe! I thought you'd be gone by now."

"I changed my mind," Joe said brusquely.

Beulah shook my coat sleeve. "What happened?"

I told her as briefly as possible. Joab hadn't given me any greeting when I entered, but he turned now from his work-bench and listened closely to my account of Lincoln's march to Petersham and the rout of the Regulators. Though it was not yet dark, the candles had been lighted to brighten his gloomy corner and the yellow light glistened on his full, flat face. His eyes and mouth hardened as I spoke and, when I was finished, he turned back to his work. I distinctly saw a tear fall on the bench.

Beulah didn't say anything. She nodded absently, went back to the mantel and took down a silver butterboat that had belonged to her grandmother. Then I noticed an open traveling trunk on a chair by the door to Joab's downstairs bedroom. It looked very much as if Beulah was packing.

Someone behind me cleared his throat gruffly and, for the first time, I noticed Dave Corbett. He had risen from his seat and his massive fists were clenched as he glared at me. I looked from him to Beulah in bewilderment. Beulah's fingers were trembling a little as she wrapped the butterboat carefully into that cambric dress I liked so well. She set it into the trunk and went back to the mantel for the powder horn. She avoided my eyes.

"Beulah," Dave rumbled finally, "Ain't you gonna tell him?"

Beulah nodded without turning. "Warren, I—I'm going away t—tonight—now." She bit her lower lip. "I'm going away with David. We're going to be . . . to be married tomorrow."

I gasped, as if she had hit me on the breastbone. Automatically, I said, "That's nice."

"Please, Warren, don't . . . don't take it that way. I. . . ." She looked to Dave. "I want to talk to him . . . alone. It's the last time."

"I forbid. . . ." Dave began in a throaty voice.

Beulah ignored him. "Come in here, Warren, please." And she walked into Joab's bedroom.

I was rooted to the floor. I glanced at Dave. His anger was fading and a tight, uncertain smile was fixed on his lips. Joe grinned and winked and went back to his perennial whittling. I found my legs and strode into the bedroom.

"Close the door, please, Warren." Beulah waited until I obeyed, then turned away and stared out the window, still avoiding my eyes. "David turned his farm over to his younger brother, He and I . . . we . . . we're going west in the Spring."

Almost without willing it, I walked over to her. "I'm afraid I don't understand this at all."

She smiled and touched my cheek lightly. "Does it hurt? I mean, to learn you don't really understand what's inside a woman's heart?" Her eyes clouded and dropped. "I thought it all over while you were away. I decided this would be the best. I had hoped to be gone before you got back."

"But why?" I asked desperately.

I suppose I was more piqued by the shock than from any desire to argue her into changing her mind again. Curiously, I felt no joy over this sudden release. The old magic was working once more, the smell of her clean brown hair, the softness of her skin, the loveliness of her heaving bosom. I had an almost uncontrollable desire to take her into my arms. But her cool grey eyes held me off.

"Remember when we quarreled, I told you we were . . . different? I really didn't know it at the time, but it's true. We are different. You're going to live in Boston. I'd never fit in there. I'd feel stifled living in town, hemmed in by bricks and narrow streets. I despise the kind of people you like . . . those shallow women and grasping men. Oh, I know you don't think they're shallow and grasping. But I do. I want a man who won't be a parasite. I want to stand by his side on the edge of a new world. I want my man to build. He'll never have fame or money or fine manners, but he'll have—well— something finer. You see, don't you, Warren?" her eyes misted as she timidly rubbed my lapel. "You do see, don't you? We . . . my kind. . . . Someday, we might have to fight your kind, fight to keep what we build and get back what you steal from us in the name of civilization."

I only half heard her. Her moist, warm lips were too close, much too close. I kissed her.

"God help me," Beulah breathed huskily. "Don't make me weaken, Warren . . . Don't. . . ."

Her arm slipped over my shoulder and tightened about my neck. Her touch rekindled my passions and her ardent lips swept away everything, everything but my burning urge to have her for my own, forever. She swayed closer and my eager fingers pressed deeper into her yielding waist.

Her lips drew away but she did not. "This is goodby,

Warren. Go to Judith. She's your kind. She . . . she knew it all along. I hated her once for her calm acceptance of the fact. But not any more." She put her cheek against my chest. "Oh, Warren, it's too late now, but why . . . just once, even if you didn't mean it . . . why didn't you tell me you loved me?"

I opened my mouth to reply, then closed it again. It was the truth. It had never occurred to me before.

Beulah smiled. "Maybe it's better that way. I'll always remember that, Warren. You never lied to me."

She kissed me hard, fiercely, then tore loose.

"You'd better go now, Warren . . . please."

"Yes." I cleared the huskiness from my throat. "All right. Goodby, Beulah." At the door, I paused. "Oh, Beulah, just one thing more. That nonsense . . . about town people being different from country people. It is nonsense, Underneath the superficial manners and such, we've got a lot in common. If ever we fight against each other, both of us will lose our freedom."

Beulah laughed lightly and shook her head. "Warren, you're incorrigible. I guess that's one reason I lo . . . like you so much. I hope you never change." She touched her fingertips to her lips and threw me a last kiss.

I closed the door softly behind me.

Dave Corbett was glaring sullenly at me. I walked over to him, my hand outstretched.

"I won't say you've won, Dave. Let's just say we've all come to our senses. Goodby . . . and take care of her. She deserves happiness and I know a good man like you can give it to her."

Dave Corbett's lips twitched, then he allowed a friendly smile to break his stern features. He almost crushed my hand.

"The past is past, Warren. Goodby."

Joe walked me to the door. "Going to Boston?"

"Yes."

"The schooner's at Griffin's Warf. I'll be there by Saturday, I think. I have to go over to Northampton tomorrow with Beulah and Dave."

"I'll see you Saturday, then." I glanced over to Joab. "Goodby, Joab. I'll drop in again next time I'm home."

"I'll be here." His voice was infinitely bitter. Then, his

561

mouth softened. "I—I'm glad it turned out this way, Warren. It's better for everybody. Goodby, Warren."

The cold air was refreshing as I trudged up the long slippery path. Dusk was closing down rapidly. I was whistling softly to myself. Yes, I was glad I had been released from an unwanted obligation, glad I was free to walk a path of my own choosing. Not exactly of my choosing. This day had taught me the folly of believing man moved by free will in matters of the heart. But I could not now quarrel with woman or fate.

At the top of the hill, I stopped and turned back and waited. Soon, Dave Corbett, a tremendous man even at this distance, came out of the house and stowed the traveling trunk in the sleigh. Then Joe and Beulah came out. She looked tiny alongside her brother, tinier alongside the man who was to be her husband. Joab came out, too, dragging himself along with that curious, painful gait. And lastly came Mrs. Crane, the drab, lifeless woman who had died with her husband at Saratoga.

The farewells were brief. Dave handed Beulah into the sleigh and took his own place. She kissed her mother and said something to Joab. But Joab was not listening. He was staring over the horizon, the western horizon, where virgin land was so desperately in need of strong, fearless men.

The sleigh started off and Beulah waved back. She saw me and lifted her hand high. I lifted mine in farewell. She took with her a part of my affections that would be hers forever.

Chapter 43

A CRESCENT moon hung on the dusky blueness over the
jagged edges of East Hill. As I turned in from the
road and plodded up the path to our kitchen door, my
mother opened the door.

"Warren!" she said. "Are you all right?"

I grinned and touched the bandage. "Sure. Just a mite of
frostbite in my ear, that's all. It's all over, Ma. There isn't going to be any war."

"Thank God." She wiped her eyes with the hem of her
apron. "I couldn't help worrying about you." She sniffed. "Oh,
gracious! My sauce!" And she scurried back to her cooking.

Pa drew his feet in. "The war's over, you say?"

"All over. The army's broken . . . routed . . . scattered. Dan
may still be running, for all I know. So, the rebellion's over
. . . finished. No one was killed, either, as far as I know."

"You didn't desert Dan, did you?" Pa asked.

"No, no. I was caught. I'm home on parole. I had to sign
the oath of allegiance and Lincoln let us go."

"You mean you may be arrested later?"

"Well, no," I lied, not wanting to worry my mother. "Lincoln says he'll get us pardons. How about something to eat,
Ma? I haven't had a decent meal since . . ."

I heard the door opening and my voice faded off. My
brother stared at me, flushed with embarrassment. He closed
the door and hung up his hat and coat, avoiding my eyes.

"I thought you joined Lincoln's army, Increase."

"Changed my mind," Increase replied shortly. He gave me a
morose look. "Gosh, Warren, how could I fight against my
own friends . . . and my own brother?"

My brows went up. "How about Hope?"

He shrugged. "What could she say? It wasn't her idea, anyway, it was her father's. I'm not marrying him."

"Wasn't she angry?"

"Well, yes, a little," Increase admitted seriously. "But goshamighty, if I let her rule me now, how will it be after we're married? I told her it was her Paw or me, and she finally decided she loved me more."

I laughed. "Bravo, Increase!" I put my arm around his shoulders. "Anyway, I'm glad you weren't against us."

"I'm neutral. Politics don't interest me much. Later, maybe I'll make up my mind one way or the other. But I'm not going to be ruled by a petticoat, I can tell you that."

Pa chuckled. "That's what you think."

"I'm not going to be ruled by a woman," Increase insisted. "How about you, Warren?"

"Down with petticoat rule, eh, Ma?" I winked and she giggled. "Oh, and that reminds me. It's all off—about me marrying Beulah."

My mother gasped. "Warren, you can't do that to her."

"She decided, not me. She's going away with Dave Corbett. They're getting married at the registrar's office in Northampton tomorrow. They're going west in the Spring and I'm going to Boston."

"When do you figure on leaving, Warren?" Increase asked.

"Tomorrow morning," I replied. "If all goes well, Ma, I expect to live in Boston."

My mother smiled gently. "I know. I never did have much hope we could keep you with us, even when you were little. You were always my ugly duckling, Warren." She hesitated, then timidly, "I suppose you'll be marrying . . . maybe Judith?"

I lifted my shoulders and mother nodded slowly. "I don't know her as well as I know Beulah, but I do believe she's a good and very sensible girl. And she'll be a big help to you, I'm sure. She'll fit in better with the kind of a life you want."

"I'll bet she can't cook like Beulah," Increase said.

Ma patted my hand. "Warren can bring her here and I'll teach her—if she ever has to cook." She gave me a shy, sidelong glance. "I'd like to be at the wedding, Warren."

"Assuming there is one," I said with a grin, "I'll try to have it here or with her folks in Amherst."

Pa raised his cider cup. "Well, here's luck, Warren. Whatever you do, we're with you."

I rose early the next morning, for I wanted to make the nine o'clock stage which passed through Amherst. Our farewells were brief, almost casual, for my mother and father had long since recognized the inevitable. I was going away as I had come home such a short time ago, less than an intimate of the family, yet more than a stranger. My mother and father would always be a part of me. My home in Pelham would always be my anchor to windward.

Mother made me promise I wouldn't be like Joe Crane, but write often and come home once in a while. Increase, true brother of mine, reminded me of that little matter of a wedding present and his pay for the trip to Fenwick. I told him I'd try to be home in time for his wedding to Hope, but, in any case, he would get his due and more. I didn't mention I might be delayed by a slight matter of a date with the hangman.

Pa walked down to the road with me and, for the first time, I realized how bent and grey he was getting. But his lean, angular face seemed the same as always.

"I'll send that money home if I can't come myself, Pa. And I'll send a list of those I owe. You take care of it, will you?" I clapped him on the shoulder. "Keep out of jail, Pa."

He grunted. "Keep out of jail yourself, son. Seems I remember you were in jail seven years and me only seven months."

I laughed. "If you ever need money, Pa, come to me before you borrow. If I have it, it's yours."

"I'll always have a living, son." He swept his arm to his snow-covered fields. "God never fails a man willing to work his land." Then, he chuckled and poked me in the ribs. "Only, if you Boston aristocrats start taking away honest men's land again, you can expect some more rebellions."

"I hope to God we all remember that." I shook hands with my father. "I'll be back in the Spring, Pa."

"I'll be here, son. As long as there's a field to plow, I'll be here in the Spring."

My mother waved to me from the kitchen door and I waved back and started down the road. The echo of my father's final words were still with me. Yes, those words were true. Not jail, not exile, not even the grave itself could keep father and mother from the land in the Spring.

Lest I give the impression that everyone believed that the rebellion was over, let me hasten to stress that the contrary was true. My traveling companions were two gentlemen from Albany and one from Great Barrington. To them, the rebellion was very much alive and the Regulators still a burning subject of discussion. Burning is hardly the word. The Regulators were verbally seared and flayed and dismembered quite thoroughly. I maintained a discreet silence on the subject, for, while I am perennially willing to debate, I scorn to fling vituperation around the countryside—that is, unless aroused. These gentlemen were too ignorant and narrow minded to be worthy of my mettle.

I was cheered to learn that Shays had managed to salvage three hundred men from the wreck. But I couldn't agree that the others would flock back to him. Yet, with that view prevalent, you can see the rebellion was by no means completely over. The movement could revive quickly if circumstances warranted it.

In my turn, I asked for news of the work done by the General Court. The answer was exasperatingly familiar. To date, the Legislature had done nothing. It hadn't even acted on our petition sent from Pelham on the 30th of January. Nor had the esteemed General Court gotten around to acting on Lincoln's urgent request that a state of rebellion be proclaimed.

At dusk on the 7th of February, I arrived in the town of Boston. My predilection, naturally, was to go directly to the Burdicks' and Judith. But I wasn't so sure my parole, granted so casually by General Lincoln, would be recognized here in Boston. If I were to be arrested, I preferred that the Burdicks be kept in ignorance. I anticipated enough trouble winning over Mrs. Burdick without having a second jailing sour her completely. Of course, if Judith wanted me, her mother wouldn't be able to stand in our way. But I figured there was no sense in starting married life with mother-in-law trouble if it could possibly be avoided.

Accordingly, I stayed with the coach until its final stop at Pease's Tavern on Common Street. There, I engaged a room and had a manservant take my baggage up. Then, I settled to dinner and tried to decide what my first move should be.

Joe wasn't in town yet, so I couldn't very well put my things aboard the schooner. I hesitated about seeing Mr. Blair at the Salvation Inn, for the patrons there knew me by sight. They would clamor for news of the rebellion and might thereby attract a constable. I had no feeling of being a fugitive, but I didn't think it necessary to go out of my way to find trouble. For a time, I played with the idea of going straight to State House and finding out once and for all whether Lincoln's parole was any good. I decided instead to go to Fitch's. Even if Fitch had gone over to government, I felt sure he wouldn't turn me in. Thus, after settling my bill, I turned my steps down to the waterfront.

Mr. Fitch's store was still open and still cluttered with idlers standing around the Franklin stove. There was an elegantly clad young woman standing by the counter, ordering groceries, her fur muff lying on the head of a nearby sugar barrel.

As I entered, she turned and squealed with delight and flung herself into my arms. I backed against the door, feeling that she had mistaken me for someone else. She had not. That beautiful blond young woman was Amy.

"Mr. Hascott!" She threw her arms around my neck and planted a kiss on my chin, which was as high as she could reach. "Mr. Hascott, I'll never forgive you."

"Forgive me? For what? Excuse me if I seem a bit confused, Amy."

"For not being at my wedding, silly."

"No! You're married? When did it happen?"

My jaw must have fallen halfway to my knees, for she laughed and clapped her hands.

"Last week. It's true. I'm really married. We wrote you," she added chidingly, "and you didn't even answer."

"I'm sorry, Amy, truly sorry. I've been away from home. As a matter of fact, the letter didn't reach home. It must have gone astray. Post deliveries are pretty uncertain the way things are out there."

Mr. Fitch, who had been standing by and chuckling like a contented hen, suddenly blinked. "Yes, yes, of course. How . . . how are things out there?"

"I'm out of it, at any rate. Technically, I'm General Lincoln's prisoner. I was captured at Petersham and released on parole." I went on hurriedly to avoid further questioning. "But this news is amazing, Amy. However did it happen?"

Before she could reply, the door bumped me in the back as someone opened it from outside. Amy giggled and took my hand, turning me around.

"Look, Ethan! It's Mr. Hascott."

Ethan seized my other hand and wrung it dry. "I'm delighted to see you, sir, delighted. I suppose you heard?"

"I'm still breathless." My brows lifted. "And I do believe I've forgotten something. Congratulations, Ethan, and you, too, Amy. Now, do I get to kiss the bride?"

She pecked my lips. "Tell him what happened, Ethan."

"Well, my father finally relented," Ethan said.

"I gathered that much, Ethan. But how and why?"

Ethan grinned. "Well, you helped some to change his mind. Mostly, though, it was Beulah. Remember the night of the Burdicks' party? Well, he thought over what happened and decided Amy was as good as any of those girls there, so he withdrew his objections. Now, he thinks Amy's a lot better than any of them. We had him over to our home one evening and she cooked him a meal—and, I mean, a meal! Father said it was almost as good as mother could do."

"You're a lucky man, Ethan, getting a pretty girl who can cook. One of these days, she'll be a charming hostess."

"Soon, Mr. Hascott, soon. Mr. Gorham tells me I'm to be taken into the firm in the Spring. I'll be a junior partner."

"And how is Beulah?" Amy asked.

"Oh, fine," I replied, flushing a little. "She's married."

Amy pouted. "But not to you? I thought . . ."

I laughed. "No, she decided to marry a childhood suitor. He got there first. They're going west in the Spring."

"Oh, that reminds me," Ethan broke in. Then grinned. "My father has some . . . something of yours."

"Uh huh. Where can I find him, do you know? I hesitated to go up to the inn. I'm not sure my parole holds here in Boston."

Ethan frowned. "Father's still working. The reb—the troubles have kept him very busy lately. The General Court sits in the evenings sometimes these days. I'll be glad to do anything I can for you, Mr. Hascott. I'll fetch him right now and have him meet you any place you suggest. At our house, if you like."

I thought it over, wondering if I dared take the chance of going to State House. My eye fell on Mr. Fitch.

"How are things in Boston these days, Mr. Fitch?"

"Quiet, very quiet. There's a good deal of sentiment favoring your side, Mr. Hascott, a good deal."

"Suppose the rebellion ended without bloodshed and the Government decided to hang the rebels, what do you suppose would happen here? I mean, would public opinion favor such hangings?"

"Certainly not." Fitch fingered his spectacles. "That is, most people would be only too happy if the affair blew over without serious fighting. No, not many would want to see the Rebels hanged." He leaned closer, his voice dropping. "I've heard talk. Mind, this is confidential: I heard that, if the Government dares condemn Job Shattuck, the mechanics would tear down the jail and release him. I'm sure there would be rioting if Shattuck was condemned to hang."

I rubbed the edge of my jawbone. "Is the Government aware of this feeling in town?"

Mr. Fitch lifted his shoulders. "How can I tell? I suppose so. You can't very well escape it if you visit any of the taverns, not unless you're deaf." He peered at me anxiously. "Is there hope of avoiding bloodshed? We hear Daniel Shays has seventeen thousand men, with Ethan Allen ready to come over from Vermont to support him with ten thousand more troops."

"The strength of Shays' army has been greatly exaggerated, Mr. Fitch. As for that Ethan Allen story, this is the first I've heard of it." I came to my decision. "I'm going to State House. If I must be arrested, it may as well be now as later. I don't enjoy slinking down alleys to avoid constables."

"I had hoped you'd dine with us tonight," Amy said. "Ethan and I have a place on Pudding Lane. It's not very elegant, but it's nice—and Ethan will vouch for my cooking."

"Not tonight, Amy, thanks just the same. I've already had my supper."

"You'll come soon?" Amy asked.

"Just as soon as I can. That's a promise, Amy. I've sampled your cooking once. I'd like to sample it again and again."

I shook hands with Ethan. "You know you and Amy have my best wishes for your happiness, Ethan. I'm sorry I couldn't be at the wedding, but I'll make up for it some other way."

"Just come and visit us often, Mr. Hascott," Ethan said earnestly. "That's all we ask. We owe you a lot, sir."

"Nonsense." I waved to Mr. Fitch. "Goodnight, sir."

"Come back soon, will you Mr. Hascott?" Fitch fiddled with his glasses and scowled. "I'm neutral, you understand, but I'd sure like to hear what's been going on out there. Seems we're getting a lot of false reports around here."

"I'll be back," I promised. "Goodnight, everybody."

With some trepidation, I started toward State House, the lair of my enemies.

Chapter 44

M Y COURAGE was practically gone by the time I came
out on State Street. The memory of my previous stay
in the Boston jail made me extremely reluctant to
tempt my enemies to put me back in there. Of course, the
Northampton and Springfield jails were as bad, if not worse.
But, while my family could provide for me if I were jailed
out there, here I felt I had the opportunity of getting better
legal talent. Too, I could count on my friends to help me get
bail, friends who had influence with the Government. Yes, I
would be much better off, if I must be jailed, to face the unpleasantness here in Boston.

Having thus decided, I boldly approached the door to State
House. The place was going full blast, except for the legislative chambers. Those rooms were darkened, but the upstairs
offices were ablaze with light. Then, as my hand fell on the
door latch, I hesitated. Perhaps I ought to think this over a
bit more carefully. After all. . . .

The door flung out and nearly knocked me from the steps.
A pot-bellied gentleman, his eyes distressed, seized my arm
and prevented me from falling.

"I'm extremely sorry, sir." He held the door open for me.
"You were just going in, I gather?"

I couldn't very well say I was just coming out, so I nodded
and walked in. As I passed down the corridor toward the
circular stairway, the clerks looked up momentarily from their
work. None of them hissed: "Rebel!" Upstairs, a number of
gentlemen were lingering in the rotunda. They didn't even
glance at me.

Mr. Blair was bent over his papers, the candlelight shining

on the part of his bald pate visible beyond his wig, which was askew as usual. He heard me come in, glanced up and nodded absently. He started to lower his eyes, then jerked upright.

"Warren!" he breathed. "Warren, what are you doing here?"

I smiled and sank into the chair by his desk. "I came to see you, of course."

"B—but they'll arrest you." He glanced nervously at the door. "His Excellency is here . . . over in that office across the way. If he sees you. . . ."

"Technically," I interrupted, "I'm a prisoner. General Lincoln released me on parole. If I'm arrested, I'm arrested. I'm just as liable to be put in jail at home."

Blair's thin lips tightened. "As bad as the Northampton jail is reputed to be, you should know the Boston jail is a lot worse." He threw down his quill. "Well, you're here and that's that. What's the news?"

"The rebellion's over," I answered. "Shays was routed at Petersham. I was taken prisoner there. It's finished."

"We had a dispatch from Lincoln," Blair said. "But we didn't get that impression. Lincoln tells us that Shays had managed to gather some of his army together again and is retreating toward the New Hampshire border. He ought to be over the line by tomorrow'."

"That's good. If I know Dan, he'll swing around and re-enter Massachusetts in Berkshire County and hold out, if he can, until Lincoln's army starts breaking up."

"I thought you said the rebellion is over."

"It is, actually, but I doubt that Shays realizes it yet. Not if he has a substantial number of men with him. But he's not going to attack Lincoln, you can bet on it. He'll try to hold out until election day. If Bowdoin is out of office then, he'll surrender. He doesn't want to hang. You can't blame him for that. I don't want to hang, either."

"You pick a fine way of showing it," Blair said dryly. "Was that the reason the army moved from Pelham? We were wondering. People who know that section of the country told us the terrain was very favorable to Shays. We couldn't understand his moving."

"Well, that was it, we didn't want to precipitate a clash. There may be clashes now. Luke Day and Eli Parsons will have more influence than Shays with what's left of the army. But you can take my word for it, the rebellion's over."

Blair clucked his tongue. "And only today, the General Court got around to voting on that petition you sent from Pelham. The House voted to reject it. The Senate votes on it tomorrow."

"On what grounds did they turn down our petition?"

"Oh, a lot of reasons, none of them very sensible. You avow yourselves to be under arms. The petition doesn't say which or how many officers know about it. You acknowledge an 'error' but only consider it as a 'failing.' You're presumptuous in considering yourselves as good as the Legislature. You seem to threaten bloodshed unless a 'reconciliation' is effected. You'll imply you'll continue in arms if you don't get a pardon. And lastly, the Government can't be sure you'll keep your promises."

"No offer of pardon or leniency?"

"None."

"No offer of a redress of grievances?"

"Certainly not. Who do you think you are, anyway?—citizens with rights in the Government?"

I slumped in my seat. "Maybe I was wrong. Maybe the rebellion isn't over, after all. Dan still has some men. If the Government insists on continuing to be stupid, maybe a lot will flock back to him. No hope of leniency?"

"Well, I don't know. It's really too early to tell. If, as you say, Shays is finished, Bowdoin will hesitate to take full vengeance. He knows public sentiment here in Boston. In fact, he doesn't even dare put Job on trial. Prescott wrote in and asked bail for Oliver Parker and Ben Page. They've been released."

"Prescott's the man who originally asked the Governor to arrest them, isn't he?"

"The same. Prescott says people up around Groton will be angry if corporal punishment is inflicted on any of the prisoners. He seems to think—Oh, my gosh." He jumped up, bowing and straightening his wig. "Good evening, Your Excellency."

I winced, got up slowly, turned around, hoping against hope it wasn't true. It was. James Bowdoin was standing in the doorway, glaring at me.

573

"In all my life," he rumbled, "I have never seen such colossal insolence. You dared come here." He glanced over his shoulder. "You were right, Sam. It's that Rebel. Call a constable."

My stomach suddenly sagged as if filled with stones. I almost fell ill. Sam Adams spoke to someone hidden by the side of the door, then came into the office.

"You were very foolish, young man."

I worked the kink out of my throat. Then, "I'm a prisoner, sir. I was taken by General Lincoln at Petersham. I gave my word not to leave the state."

The Governor glowered at me. "I didn't know Lincoln would be that soft. His orders were to release only privates and sympathizers, not officers or instigators of this insurrection."

"I signed the oath of allegiance, Your Excellency."

"Oh, you did, did you? And what brings you here to State House? More petitions?"

"No, sir. I hoped . . ." I gulped the lump out of my throat. "I hoped I could persuade someone to speak to you, sir . . . about adopting a lenient policy toward the Rebels. The rebellion's virtually over, Your Excellency. If you show the people you will be lenient, the state will be quiet in thirty days."

"That's a threat!" the Governor roared.

I tried to hold my annoyance in check. "It wasn't intended as a threat, sir. It's common sense. We know Shays' army is broken. We're willing to take the oath of allegiance. But our friends and neighbours—and I've spoken to many, sir—don't believe the state would be served by having us hanged. Every second person out in my country has friends and relatives who have been in on this. They're worried. Show leniency, Your Excellency, and peace will be inevitable. Surely, a vindictive policy cannot strengthen the Government and heal the wounds this affair has opened."

"They whine when cornered, don't they," Bowdoin said coldly. "Young man, you and your ilk have committed crimes against the state. It would be a sorry Government that encouraged more crime by allowing treason to go unpunished."

I spread my hands. "All right, take that attitude, Your Excellency, and you're sure to have more trouble—and a lot of explaining to do to the voters before election day. That isn't a threat, sir, that's a prediction."

Bowdoin caught his breath angrily, but he was interrupted by the appearance of a man in the doorway. He handed a paper to Sam Adams and retired. Sam Adams went over it carefully. I recognized it as the paper I had signed at Petersham.

"Yes, here it is—Warren Hascott. He's signed the oath, Jim. You can revoke his parole if you like, but . . ."

Bowdoin stared at Sam Adams a moment, then shrugged. "All right, dismiss the constable." With his lips pressed together, he strode from the room.

Sam Adams paused at the door. "You're sure the rebellion is over, Mr. Hascott?"

"Quite sure, sir—unless the Government unleashes a reign of terror against us. I can truthfully say that the people generally deplore our resort to arms, but they sympathize with us and our aims. They won't stand idly by and see us murdered."

Adams waved deprecatingly. "You're biased."

"I wouldn't take a chance on that, sir, if I had any voice in forming Government policy toward the Regulators."

Sam Adams smiled and nodded and left.

Mr. Blair and I virtually collapsed into our chairs. I hadn't realized how truly scared I'd been during the interview. And small beads of sweat were glistening on Mr. Blair's wrinkled brow.

"I almost talked myself into jail, didn't I?" I asked breathlessly. "Do you suppose I did any good?"

Blair's chuckle was shaky. "I think so. Bowdoin's not a very good politician, but he has to consider political realities. Though, you can't tell. Feeling around here is hardening against the Regulators. I thought for a minute I'd be discharged when he saw you talking to me."

"I'm sorry. I shouldn't have jeopardized your position this way."

"Nonsense. I've decided to quit, anyway. I have some money and property. I'm wasting my time here."

"You mean, you're going into business?"

"Yes, I do." Blair shook a skinny finger at me. "It took this insurrection to open my eyes. If we get peace, this country is going to grow. We're going to develop our own resources. I signed that declaration to encourage home manufactures. But I'm going to do more. I have an opportunity to invest some money and my services in a new cotton mill. Why must we import finished goods from England? I think we can make cloth here more cheaply. And I have another proposition in view. I've agreed, with a number of other gentlemen, to put money into a silk farm."

"I heard about attempts to grow silk here. I saw a young lady wearing a ribbon made of silk grown in this state. It was a handsome ribbon, too."

"There you are, Warren. There are limitless opportunities here in America for men with some courage and a little capital. I've been a clerk long enough. I can do better than that. I'm only sixty four—which isn't very old."

I smiled. "Age is a stage of mind, Mr. Blair. A man is only old when he settles back and complains there're no more opportunities for a man of his age."

"Exactly." He beamed and rubbed his thin shanks. Then, he snapped his fingers. "I almost forgot. I have your money. You can have it any time you want it."

"Fine. And thank you, I'll take it tomorrow, or in a few days, whenever I go home. You'll hold it until then? What did Burdick say when you got the money from him?"

"Nothing much. He asked me if I was going over into the Rebel camp. I said no, but I knew a Rebel I could trust to deliver the money to you. He understood you couldn't leave the money in his hands under the circumstances."

I reached for my hat. "I'm going over there now and let them know I'm back in the fold."

Blair winked slyly. "And see Judith?"

"And see Judith," I admitted. "This seems to be the marrying season. Maybe I can get in on it myself. You know, I saw Ethan and Amy a while ago. There's a fine couple."

Blair pursed his lips, nodded slowly. "Yes, I'll have to concede that now. She's an excellent cook, excellent. You were right about her. I can see that now."

"But I can't see now why you didn't approve of Amy right along."

Blair squirmed. "All right, I'll admit it. I did believe Ethan's career could be furthered if he married into a family with 'connections.' It's true and probably always will be that a man who has 'connections' can get ahead faster. But a man can get along without such an advantage. All an American needs is ability—and honest sweat."

He hopped up from his chair. "Enough of lecturing. I know you have more important business on your mind. You'll be in town for awhile?"

"Yes, I have an invitation to dine at Amy's. Maybe I can wrangle you an invitation, too."

Mr. Blair laughed. "Do, do. Drop in here tomorrow, if you can. I'll make the arrangements. Goodnight, my boy—and good luck!"

He gave me a broad wink.

I walked right by the Burdicks'. The parlor drapes were drawn, but from the side I had seen that the dining room was all alight. I felt sure they must have company. I swore softly. Must those people always be entertaining when I called? Of course, I knew their position demanded that they entertain almost constantly, and generally I was eager to meet the interesting people their table attracted. But this time, I wanted neither amusement nor information. I wanted to talk to Judith —alone.

My hat had been badly battered since that day in June when I first came to this house and my serges were showing the effects of hard wear. But my eagerness to see Judith—just to see her, if nothing else—overcame my consciousness of my shabbiness. I rapped boldly on the shiny brass knocker.

Polly opened the door. "Why, Mr. Hascott. It's been a long ti . . ." She suddenly became frigid. "Whom did you wish to see, sir?"

I pinched her cheek. "You first, then Judith."

She giggled and widened the door. "I don't know about Miss Judith. I'll ask, though. Come in, sir."

The dinner party would be a big one, judging from the sounds of male voices in the dining room and female chatter and rattling of coffee cups in the parlor. Polly was in there a long time and I grew warmer and warmer, acutely aware that

577

I had not chosen an appropriate moment for the mission I had in mind.

Finally, before I got cold feet, Judith came sweeping out of the living room. As usual, she was gorgeously dressed, this time in an off shoulder gown of white satin trimmed with blue lace. But my heart sank as she came over to me, extending her hand. She seemed cold. She had no smile for me.

"Warren, you shouldn't have come. The rebellion. . . ."

I breathed easier. "It's all over. I'm a prisoner, on parole. I won't be arrested—not yet, at any rate. I've just seen the Governor at State House."

"Oh." She seized my hand and pulled me to her father's den. "Then, I'm glad you came. I've been dying to talk to someone about this. I haven't dared—not even to father."

She went to the bookshelves. Along the bottom shelf was a row of paper novels and plays, evidently hers. She selected one, took a letter from among the pages and thrust it into my hands.

"Read it, Warren, Tell me what I should do."

I glanced at the signature, saw that it was from a woman, a friend of Judith's in New York. The contents of the letter made my eyes widen, bit by bit, until they nearly popped out. This was the passage that struck me so hard:

". . . . You will be positively shocked when I tell you what I overheard this afternoon. Papa and Mr. Salderman dined at the King's Arms Tavern with Baron Von Steuben and several other gentlemen. When they came home, Papa and Mr. Salderman had a very violent quarrel, which nearly ended in blows. You can never, never guess the subject of their quarrel. Papa accused Mr. Salderman of supplying money to the rebels. And Mr. Salderman admitted it! I nearly swooned—actually. Papa and Mr. Salderman had spoken to Baron Von Steuben, who is interested in the rebellion, about turning it to their advantage. Mr. Salderman claims to have influence with the rebels and, when they win, he says he will be in a position to seize the power— by killing Shays, if necessary. They intend to put a KING on the throne of Massachusetts! The Baron has suggested Prince Henry of Bavaria and is even now negotiating with him to come to America to rally the monarchists, of which there are many here in New York, I know. Mr. Salderman expects the rebellion to spread to other states—Rhode Island first, where the rabble has made a shambles of business with their horrible paper money. New York will be next. They said Connecticut will be a hard nut to crack, but if the surrounding states proclaim for Prince Henry, Connecticut will be brought into line—by force, if necessary. Papa has washed his hands of the matter. He says he did not know he was contributing toward this kind of a monarchist plot. . . ."

I folded the paper carefully. "Interesting, if true. Is Salderman here?" She nodded and I considered her a moment. "Judith, do you love that man?"

She stiffened slightly. "I told you I was going to marry him."

"I didn't ask you that," I said quietly. "You see, I'm going to destroy him. That's my duty and I'm afraid nothing you could say would make me swerve from that duty. But if you love him, I'll do it some other time, as unobtrusively as possible."

Judith smiled and slid her hand under my arm. "That's the nicest thing you've ever said to me. If you must do your duty, there's no time like the present."

I was too determined to feel self-conscious about my clothes as I came into the dining room. The assemblage was unusually distinguished. Most of the guests I already knew, General Ward, Salderman, my Tory friend, Graham; the liberal lawyer, Lang; the elderly merchant, Mr. Trowbridge. In addition General Putnam, our own "Old Put," was present and, lastly, Mr. Elbridge Gerry, the distinguished merchant and statesman.

Mr. Burdick at the head of the table saw me first. He was startled to say the least. But he quickly rose to the occasion. He put down his pipe and came over to me smiling genially, as if my presence was perfectly natural.

"Warren, it's a pleasure to see you again." He took my other arm. "You know everyone here." He frowned at his daughter. "I'll take care of him, Judith."

"I'll stay for a few moments, if you don't mind, Papa. Our rebel has an interesting bomb to throw."

General Ward jerked his head up, coughed. "I wouldn't

579

doubt it, Miss Judith. Don't tell me that damned rebel is still a friend of yours, Moses. Why, I saw him at practically every one of those court-stopping outrages last Fall."

"A rebel? A real live rebel?" Mr. Gerry was smiling. "You do have such interesting friends, Moses."

"Mr. Gerry, Mr. Hascott," Burdick introduced hastily.

He was a little red in the face, which wasn't anything to compare with Mr. Graham. His face was like a boiled lobster, hot enough to spout steam. Salderman's long face was thoughtful. He seemed to sense what was in my mind.

I walked over to his place. "I really came to see Mr. Salderman. You gentlemen didn't know, I suppose, that he has been a generous backer of the Regulators."

A stunned silence ensued. Ward sputtered on his brandy.

"Jothan? Backing the rebels? Absurd."

Salderman snickered. "Mr. Hascott has an odd sense of humor, to say the very least."

"If Mr. Salderman's only crime were supplying money to the rebels, naturally, I wouldn't be here. Whether you agree with our position or not, you can understand we would be grateful for any donations we received. But I don't think you understand what the Regulators stand for. Let me assure you, our object has always been to maintain and defend the democratic principle, the principle for which so many of us fought during the late war. We despise dictatorship in any form. We particularly despise monarchy. Thus, you can understand our anger when we learned that Mr. Salderman was in reality trying to foist such a government upon us. Mr. Salderman, and certain other gentlemen, are right now negotiating to bring Prince Henry of Bavaria to America to occupy the throne of Massachusetts."

The room was in an uproar when I finished, everyone demanding that I prove my assertions. Gradually, the clamor died and all looked to Jothan Salderman for a denial.

"Mr. Hascott is having hallucinations," Salderman said fliply. "Or bad dreams. Imagine anyone trying to set a king over us, a people who fought to do away with kings."

"I can imagine it," Mr. Gerry replied promptly. "In fact, I have spoken to men who told me frankly that it might be better to have a king to keep order. The rebellion has made those people bolder, Mr. Salderman."

"Surely, Mr. Gerry . . . General Ward . . . all of you . . . you won't take the word of a rebel against my word?" Salderman's eyes narrowed shrewdly. "I may add, gentlemen, that Mr. Hascott has a personal grudge against me."

General Putnam stared at Salderman a moment, then looked up at me. "Can you prove your statements, young man? You've made serious charges, you know."

I hesitated a moment. "Perhaps I've been a little hasty. I have knowledge of the plot to enthrone Prince Henry from a confidential source. I should have waited until I had full evidence. However, I'll get the proof. As for the other charge, that Mr. Salderman has been supplying the Regulators with funds, I can vouch for the truth of that. He gave money to me. He gave money to Daniel Shays. Give me a few days and I can get a deposition from Captain Shays to that effect. I believe I can produce other testimony, too, in proof of that contention."

The table was quiet for a long time.

General Ward cleared his throat. "Is it true? The second charge—that of supplying the rebels with funds?"

"Why, yes," Salderman said blandly, "in the beginning I believed they were only seeking justice—and you must admit there was some justice on their side. Had I known their object was to overthrow the Government, I certainly would not have given them a farthing."

I smiled without mirth. "I deny our object was to overthrow the Government. But, assuming that it was, would you say, General Putnam, that this object was known in December—at the time the court was stopped in Worcester?"

"Yes, I would," Putnam replied briskly. "I was there and I talked to Daniel Shays. I'm convinced—not exactly that Shays himself sought revolution—but that his fellows did."

"You remember, sir, that Mr. Salderman was in Worcester at the time?"

"Why, yes, I believe I saw him at the Sun Tavern."

"At that time, Mr. Salderman was on his way to New York. He saw Shays in Worcester while he was there, General. He gave Dan Shays five hundred pounds for the cause."

Putnam's mouth hardened. "If that's true, there can be no doubt that he has been supporting the rebellion."

General Ward leaned over. "You would be willing to file charges against this man, Mr. Hascott?"

"I would."

Ward folded his thick fingers. "The monarchist charge may or may not be true, Mr. Salderman. But the other charge, aiding and abetting the rebellion, seems to have some basis in fact. It looks, my dear fellow, as if you'll have to submit to arrest. You'll be granted bail, of course, but you'll have to refute Mr. Hascott's testimony in court. You know what that means, naturally?"

Trowbridge grunted. "Financial ruin, at the very least—if the charges are proven in court."

The room became hushed. Mr. Salderman was unruffled as he glanced from face to face. The eyes were hostile, the mouths were hardening. He wiped his lips daintily, set the napkin on the table and rose, calmly pulling down his waistcoat.

"I'm sure you gentlemen will excuse me?" he asked blandly. "I have a business appointment I'd quite forgotten." He bowed to Burdick and tried to kiss Judith's hand. She drew away sharply and he lifted his shoulders. His lips were smiling, but his eyes held cold hate as he gazed at me. "It was a nice game while it lasted. Too bad the rebellion wasn't a complete success. Goodnight, gentlemen."

"Salderman!" Goulding called. Salderman paused and looked back. "There's a ship of mine leaving tomorrow morning for Halifax."

"Indeed?" Salderman nodded slowly. "I've been thinking of making a trip there. But tomorrow morning is much too soon. It will take a week, at least, to wind up my affairs. I have a ship of my own I can use. Good night, gentlemen."

No one looked at him. No one stirred for long minutes. The chattering of the women in the parlor was very loud in the utter hush. Then, the front door closed with a soft thump.

"Well!" General Ward explained. "He admitted his guilt!" He pointed a stubby finger at me. "And you, young man, how dared you come here?"

"The rebellion's over, gentlemen," I replied simply.

Graham went white. "Over? We heard . . . that is . . . Shays was routed at Petersham, but that doesn't mean . . ."

"I'm afraid it does, Mr. Graham."

I was enjoying this moment. I knew that he, like Salderman,

had not sent his agent to see me, preferring to wait until he saw how the tide would turn. The glaze in his eyes, the horror on his handsome, rugged face told me he had gambled and lost. I considered denouncing him, too, but I was aware I didn't have a shred of evidence against him. However, if he was losing money by being stuck with his muskets, that was ample punishment for him. I was only wondering how much he'd lose. And Ward got me the answer.

"Well, Graham, looks as if you won't be able to sell Lincoln those muskets you're bringing from New York."

Graham shrugged and managed a weak smile. "Oh, well, I shan't lose much. I'll sell them to the Ohio Company."

"You'll take a big loss, I'll wager," Mr. Gerry put in with a chuckle. He turned to me. "You have no definite evidence of that monarchist plot, Mr. Hascott? Unfortunate, in a way. But I shall investigate. I've heard rumors myself. I doubt, though, if we'll ever be able to track them down. Plotters against our Government usually take great care to cover themselves."

"I'll do all I can to clear up the matter," I promised.

"Sit down, Mr. Hascott," Lang invited. "We'd all be interested in hearing your experiences. I daresay, you're the first to reach Boston with a first hand account of the events."

"If you'll excuse me for a while, gentlemen, I . . ." A blush heightened on my cheeks. "I have something of importance to . . . ah . . . impart to our hostess."

Judith's brows arched and she smiled. "I'm sure the gentlemen will excuse us."

As we crossed the big entry hall, I caught a glimpse of Mrs. Burdick in the parlor. She gasped as she recognized me and her lips tightened with disapproval. I bowed politely in greeting and hurried on to Mr. Burdick's den. I closed the door carefully. Judith turned and faced me, her brown eyes wide and shining, her smile a bit mocking.

"You have business with me, Warren?"

"Important business," I acknowledged. "Will you sit?"

"Lest I faint?" she asked mischievously.

I laughed, feeling strangely at ease. "I've changed my mind. Don't sit. I may want to kiss you."

Her head cocked quickly. "The mouse is lionish."

I cleared my throat, struggled for a beginning. "Judith . . . Judith . . . I mean, Judith."

"Well, we're over the first hurdle," she said, amused.

"Oh, bother, you know what I want to say. I suppose I should have waited for a romantic moment, but I can't. Now that I've eliminated my rival, I guess I can speak out. I'm in love with you, Judith. I want you for my wife."

"Yes, I know," she replied softly. "What about Beulah?"

"She's gone—out of my life forever. She married Dave Corbett. They're going west. You know I never loved her."

"Yes, I knew." She turned away slowly, picked on the chair upholstery. "I . . . I really expected you to speak out that night at your house, Warren."

"I couldn't. It wasn't as simple as that. I'd been seeing so much of her, everyone assumed . . . well, you know how it is in a small town . . . the gossip . . . the pressure."

"I lived in Amherst twenty years," she reminded me gently. "I know . . . I knew then . . . I just . . . well, I suppose my pride was hurt a little. I didn't believe you'd be happy with her . . . knowing you'd virtually been forced to marry her. You can be glad you escaped . . . and so can she."

"No, I won't be glad unless. . . ." I took her shoulders and turned her to me. "Judith, I love you. Will you marry me?"

"This is sudden, Warren." Her eyes were shining and her moist lips inviting. "I really should have time to think."

My spirits drooped. "Well, I guess I should give you time. Lord knows, I must have time myself—to prove my worth. I have no right to speak now. I'm virtually a pauper. But give me six months. . . ."

"No." She drew closer to me. "No, Warren, I won't wait. Six months would be six years. I'm old enough as it is." Her arm slid around my neck. "I've had time enough to think, Warren. I knew the very first day you came here this would happen. I didn't decide it. You didn't. It just had to be. We were fated to belong to each other." Then, she added, wryly, "Barring accident, of course." The mirth faded from her eyes. "I won't wait, Warren. I've already waited six months. I don't need six months more to know I'd marry you, with money or without."

I kissed her then. I had never really kissed before.

Our lips parted reluctantly and she brushed her soft fingers over my temples.

"We'll be happy, Warren, I can feel it, I know it. Perhaps you think I'm fragile, but I'm not. I promise you, Warren, if ever—God forbid—we must, I can cook and clean and wear gingham instead of satin. I'll be a good wife to you—and a good mother, God willing, to your children."

"I know, I know." My lips brushed her fragrant brown curls. "But we must be practical, too, darling. We can't live without money. I have next to nothing. I'll have enough soon. I have a deal in mind. . . ."

"Silly. You don't have to worry about money. Father is just waiting to take you into the business."

I stiffened slightly. "No, I'm sorry. I wouldn't marry you on that basis. I have to make my own way."

She drew back a little, frowning. "Now, Warren, you're not going to be foolish about this. There's no sense quarreling about something that's settled. You must . . ."

"I must not. There's no quarrel and no discussion of the matter. I'm not going into your father's firm until I can buy my way in. Please, Judith, see it my way. I've got a little money. And I have plans. With Joe's schooner and my capital, I think we can build a real business in no time. Joe is a fine young man, but I flatter myself I have a trifle more business talent. You'll see, Judith. In six months, or maybe a bit longer. . . ."

She studied me for a long time.

"Warren, I have confidence in your plans. I have confidence in you. Do you have as much confidence in yourself? I mean, would you expand your plans now—on borrowed money?

I hesitated, but only for an instant. "With a little more capital, and you behind me, I could lick the problem in three months."

Her nose crinkled and she kissed me. "We've had our first disagreement and our first compromise. You can borrow the money from Papa—at regular interest rates, of course."

I considered it with a frown. After all, I had borrowed money from him before. Indeed, if I hadn't, I wouldn't have a farthing of my own right now. And, at regular rates of interest, the transaction would be purely a business one, not a family affair at all. Yes, I had that much confidence in myself.

"Our first compromise," I said finally, and kissed her.

She was breathless when I released her.

"You can let me go now," she whispered. "You'll have plenty of time to hold me later on, I promise."

"Well, as long as it's a promise."

She laughed and took my hand and opened the door. The gentlemen had at last broken away from their pipes and brandy and had joined the ladies. I was a little uneasy about going in there, but I had no choice. Judith held tight to my hand and literally dragged me into the parlor. She took me directly over to the long couch where her mother was sitting with Mrs. Ward and Mrs. Lang. Mrs. Burdick froze up as we approached.

"Mother," Judith said, with more calmness than I could have mustered, "Warren has asked me to marry him. I've promised to be his wife."

Mrs. Burdick's mechanical smile did not waver, but her eyes seemed stunned. Slowly, her features thawed and she pursed her lips.

"Permit me to use some of my daughter's frankness for once, Warren. There have been times when I believed my daughter to be headstrong and unwise. I think I was mistaken. I wish you both all happiness and prosperity. Yes, I sincerely do."

"Eh? Eh? What's this?" Burdick came through the group that was already gathering about us. "What's this I hear?"

Mrs. Burdick was bland. "You're to have a son at last, Moses —and I'm sure he'll be a good son."

Moses Burdick pumped my arm. "I can't say this is unexpected, Warren. But I do say you both make me very happy."

Chapter 45

I t would be pleasant to report that all of my problems were automatically solved with the winning of my lady. Ruefully, I must admit life had some unpleasant surprises in store for me. Indeed, in many respects, my troubles were just beginning.

My first disconcerting discovery was that business was virtually at a standstill, not only in Boston, but throughout the Commonwealth. The merchants of Boston were paralyzed with fear, expecting momentarily that the Regulators would storm the town and seize the Government. I tried to tell everyone that the rebellion was over, as did travellers from the country districts, but no one would listen. Indeed, the Legislature didn't get around to proclaiming a state of rebellion until the 8th of February. On the 9th, Bowdoin issued a proclamation, setting a price of a hundred and fifty pounds on the head of Daniel Shays, and a hundred pounds on the heads of several other of the more prominent leaders, including Luke Day, Eli Parsons and Adam Wheeler.

My next shock came when I found I was less than a genius as a trader. On reports that the building industry was reviving in New York, I sent Joe there with a load of bricks. I nearly lost my shirt, but I did learn that the New York kilns could supply the city at a much lower price than I could. However, I had great confidence in the general idea. I was sure it was only a matter of time before that section of the city which had been burned out by the British during the Revolution would be rebuilt. Other towns and cities were in a run down condition and ripe for a building boom.

Accordingly, I decided to deal exclusively in hardware,

587

imported and domestic, but especially the latter. I traveled extensively along the coast and into Worcester County, contracting to take the entire output of several iron foundries. I also made deals with a number of individual farmers and smiths who made small items as a sideline. I was capitalizing on the wave of enthusiasm sweeping the state for domestic products. Thus, I managed to keep my head above water and, when trade finally did revive, I found that I had the jump on my competitors.

During the time I was struggling to establish myself, I kept a close watch on developments in Berkshire County. The reports of the whereabouts of Dan Shays were bafflingly unreliable. He was reputed to be in Pittsburg, Montreal, New York, Philadelphia, Halifax and somewhere in Massachusetts. He was reported have ten thousand men with him. He was supposed to be raising new levies in Vermont with the help of Ethan Allen. Even the years have not clarified, with any real certainty, Dan's movements after he made that hasty departure from Petersham.

As nearly as I can piece together the story, this is what happened: From Petersham, Shays fled to Athol. There he reformed the remnants of his army. He had some four hundred out of the nearly two thousand. He told the men frankly that, since the baggage train had been captured, every man would have to take care of himself. Half the men promptly departed for home, only two hundred staying with Shays. Hearing that Lincoln was sending troops to capture him, Shays retreated toward the Vermont border. He struck northwest and was known to have passed through Bennington. There, he dropped out of sight. It seems likely, however, that he turned south and reentered Massachusetts somewhere near the western border of Berkshire County.

Meanwhile, Royal Tyler and a company of soldiers, whom Lincoln had dispatched to capture Shays, passed across the border into Vermont hot in pursuit. Whether Royal Tyler had permission of the Vermont authorities, I've never been able to learn. It seems doubtful. He went as far as Bennington, where he lost Shays' trail. Lincoln, himself, hearing of a concentration of Rebels at the town of Washington in Berkshire County, moved on to Pittsfield. By the time he reached there, the Rebel force had dissolved, so Lincoln stopped and set up headquarters.

Coincident with Lincoln's movement, the bill outlawing the Rebels had been promulgated. All Rebels were forbidden to dispose of their property or leave the state until purged of treason. A mass movement of Rebels towards the adjourning states thereupon began. Most of them took all of their portable belongings and headed west. Hundreds of cattle and sheep became a part of this exodus. The Tories were thoroughly alarmed at this turn of events.

Governor Bowdoin sent urgent messages to the governors of Rhode Island, Connecticut, New Hampshire, New York and Vermont, asking them to apprehend the Rebels and turn them back. New Hampshire and Connecticut agreed. Governor Clinton called a special session of the New York legislature to enact a law to that effect. Rhode Island, under control of radicals who sympathized with our cause, flatly refused and welcomed the Rebels. Royal Tyler called upon the Governor of Vermont—which was virtually a sovereign nation at this time—and asked him for help in rounding up Rebels. The Governor was evasive, saying he would do what he could. For one thing, the people of Vermont were in sympathy with our cause. For another, that territory was sparsely settled and thus looked with favor on immigration. Bowdoin finally prevailed on the Governor to issue a proclamation, calling upon the people of Vermont to aid in the apprehension of the Rebels. The request was ineffectual, but to us remaining in Massachusetts, Bowdoin's action was ominous. Our worst fears seemed to be coming true. Bowdoin seemed determined to pursue a vindictive policy.

Out in Berkshire County, Luke Day and Eli Parsons—and possibly Dan Shays—were trying desperately to pull the army together again. The task was impossible. The prestige of the Regulators was gone. The people would no longer contribute food and supplies to our soldiers. The homeless among the Rebels were splitting into small groups which wandered all over the county. They soon became marauding bands.

Those men were, I must admit sadly, the dregs of our once respectable army, the thieves and rowdies and general scum. They burned and pillaged and terrorized wherever they went. The natural result was a wave of revulsion against the Regulators. The Tories gleefully seized upon every criminal incident and screamed that these proved what they had been saying all along, that the Rebels were knaves and abandoned scoundrels. The Rebels and their friends had to keep their mouths shut, for the treason trials were coming up soon. And thus you can see how the Tory view and Tory libels on our character entered the pages of history without challenge.

Blood was shed, too, out in Berkshire County. On the 26th of February, a party of a hundred and fifty Rebels under the command of Lt. Perez Hamlin came over the line from New York and plundered Stockbridge. Since the government had announced its intention of persecuting all Rebels, Hamlin seized a number of Tories and held them as hostages, vowing to hang them if any Rebels were hanged. The Berkshire militia leaped up in arms and made after Lt. Hamlin. After rushing hither and yon in confusion, the militia stumbled on Hamlin's company near Springfield. The two forces clashed. Hamlin was driven from the field. The Rebels lost two dead and thirty wounded. The militia lost two dead, one wounded, and two additional militiamen died of exhaustion and exposure. Hamlin himself escaped.

Here again, the Insurgents had had an opportunity to smash a decisive blow at the Government, but had let it slip by. If Hamlin had struck farther north at Pittsfield instead of at Stockbridge, he would have captured General Lincoln, and thus revived the army of the Regulators. As we had anticipated, Lincoln's army began to disintegrate during February, since his men had enlisted only for thirty days. The General Court had authorized a new levy of fifteen hundred men, enlisted for four months, but it took considerable time to raise the men, equip them and send them from the coast out to Berkshire. On the 21st of February, Lincoln's army at Pittsfield had been reduced to thirty men.

Besides Hamlin's foray into the state, there were a number of more minor clashes between Rebels and militia. None were important. Most were raids for food and clothing, though many people suffered outrageous indignities at the hands of Rebels who still called themselves Regulators. The Tories made political capital of the many tales of murder and rape coming out of Berkshire. Unfortunately, some of those tales were true.

Thus, with dread and trepidation, we awaited the treason trials.

Late in March, I had to go home to answer my own case. I did the same as all sensible Rebels who had the money. I hired a good lawyer and asked for a postponement. Although the people no longer supported the Regulators, there was still much sympathy left for our cause. Public opinion was hardening against harsh and vindictive measures. Bowdoin, with an election coming up in May, couldn't ignore this feeling. So, on the 12th of March, he announced to his council that the rebellion had been quelled and recommended bail for some of the Insurgents. One of the first to be let out on bail was Job Shattuck. The selectmen of Groton had attested that Shattuck was no longer a menace to the state. Which was true. That wound in his knee had left him a permanent cripple.

The General Court, too, sensed the trend of public opinion and passed an act of indemnity. Insurgents were to be freed on these conditions: After laying down their arms and taking the oath of allegiance, they must keep the peace for three years. They would be ineligible to vote or to hold any town or state office, and were barred from becoming schoolmasters, inkeepers or retailers of spiritous liquors. However, the legislature could, after the first of May, discharge the Rebels from these disqualifications if they showed evidence of an unequivocal attachment to the Government. Exempted from these conditions were: non-citizens, the members of any convention or Rebel committee, those who had acted as advisors, councilers, or commissioned officers and members of the General Court. Our own Tom Johnson came under that last exemption.

This being the situation, you can imagine our surprise and shock when the first to be convicted was, of all people, Hank McCullock of Pelham. Poor Hank. He had been loud mouthed, but so obscure in the movement that no one outside of our town had ever heard of him. Hank was the only man in Hampshire County to be condemned to hang. The reaction of the people to this sentence might have had something to do with it. The day Hank was sentenced, a petition started circulating. Everyone of importance in Pelham signed it. Many staunch upholders of Government in surrounding towns signed. It was even signed by such a respectable man as Judge Eleazer Porter of Hadley, our avowed enemy.

In Worcester County, Henry Gale and Johnny Wheeler were condemned to the gallows. In Middlesex County, Job Shattuck was tried and sentenced to hang. Immediately the people were in an angry uproar. The Governor did not dare let those men die. On the 21st of April, Bowdoin asked the council to delay the execution of these convicted "criminals." He said that many petitions had been received in their favor, but complained that the Rebels themselves should plead for mercy. He also hinted that the judges should forward recommendations for a commutation of sentence. The judges quickly complied.

Then, in the middle of April, John Hancock announced that he had recovered sufficiently from the illness which had forced him into retirement. He was standing for election against Bowdoin.

The trials went on and many Rebels were convicted of seditions. No one was hanged. Bowdoin was again hesitating. Hancock wasn't saying much, but his supporters were promising the release of all the Rebels if Hancock were elected. The Tories heaped mud on Hancock, but Bowdoin was getting plenty of abuse heaped on his head, too. Hancock wasn't getting himself up as an Insurgent sympathizer, mind, but he referred to them as misguided men, rather than terrible criminals.

On the first Monday in May, the people went to the polls. I was back in Boston by that time and you can imagine how avidly I watched the voting in Fanueil Hall. Hancock was not beloved of the Insurgents, but we all knew that a vote for Hancock was a vote for leniency. I got a sick feeling when the Boston vote was finally announced: Bowdoin 765, Hancock, 13.

It was almost a month before all the votes were in and counted. It was a month of agony, rising hopes and sinking hearts. Bowdoin was sweeping the eastern seaboard with majorities of four and five to one. But soon, the tide turned. The results from the western counties were going resoundingly for Hancock. And there were more people out there. The final tally was: Bowdoin, 6,129; Hancock, 18,459!

You can well imagine the joy and cheering among the Insurgents. We had lost the battles. But we had won the war!

Hancock's first act as Governor was to reprieve all the Rebels who were under sentence to hang. On June first, the new General Court passed a general pardon to all the Insurgents, discharging us of all penalties, pains, disabilities and disqualifications. All our citizenship rights were restored and the weapons which Lincoln had confiscated were ordered returned to their owners. There were several exceptions to this pardon, the most notable being Daniel Shays, Luke Day, Adam Wheeler, Eli Parsons and Perez Hamlin. All were safely out of the state.

Now, at long last, I could claim my bride.

My brother, Increase, and Hope Pennington had been married in April while I had been in Hampshire to attend the trials. By the time I got home in June, he had his fields all planted and his barn had been raised. The boys told me that Increase's barn-raising bee had been quite a celebration. Among those missing was our fat lawyer friend, Toby Plummer.

My own wedding was set for the 18th of June. Mrs. Burdick wanted to have it in Boston, with pomp and lavish display. I left it up to Judith. She passed the problem on to her father. Mr. Burdick decided for Amherst . . . which is where both Judith and I wanted it.

Since Burdick no longer maintained a home in Amherst, we held the wedding at his brother's farm. Aspath Burdick was a man much like my Uncle Enoch, the same kind of a careful, conscientious farmer. His place was on the west side of town. His house was about the same size as my uncle's and as well kept, though his parlor was better furnished, for his brother had sent him imported furniture at wholesale prices.

Mrs. Burdick showed pique all the way from Boston. But once she was in Amherst and among old friends, most of whom were disgustingly deferential, she thawed very nicely. My mother and Mrs. Burdick had known each other slightly in the old days, but I worried a bit about how they'd get along. Not too well, I found, but well enough for the occasion. Pa and Burdick got on famously. Like so many who had fled the farm and gone to town, Burdick was always planning to return to the soil—as soon as he had money enough to retire. Pa and Burdick, with Uncle Enoch and my new Uncle Aspath, did nothing but talk scientific farming the whole time they were together. Ah, yes, they enjoyed themselves.

You will pardon me, I am sure, if I become a bit sentimental when I recall my wedding day. I can't remember if the sun was shining or if the birds were twittering in the trees, but I do know that it was a beautiful day. All my family and all of my friends were on hand to see me joined to the girl who had waited. Tom Packard, uncomfortable in his black serge Sunday suit, stood up as my best man. Anzel was there, still weak and wan from his wound, but able to hobble around with a cane. Jesse had come. I had made a special trip to his place to insist that he be on hand. I had the pleasure of seeing Jesse and Anzel shake hands that day. Joe Crane had come, with Reuben and his mother, but I hadn't been able to persuade Joab to attend. Reuben told me that Joab seemed to be wasting away, as if he no longer wanted to live.

I must confess that the details of the greatest moment of my life are vague and muddled. Tom seemed to think that I should be well fortified for that moment, and he had proceeded to petrify me. But the memory of Judith coming into the parlor in her simple white satin gown will ever remain with me. She was gorgeous. I could not be frightened when, at long last, I stood at her side before the Rev. Parsons.

For one brief moment, the years faded away and Judith was sixteen again. Her full red lips were half parted and her eyes were shining with the same trust, the same happiness. Her voice was a bare whisper as she said she would be mine. I bent my head to kiss her and I could feel her trembling.

"Will you wait?" I breathed.

"Forever . . . forever," she replied breathlessly. Then she smiled and crinkled her nose impudently. "Anyway, until you've sobered up."

There was laughter in Amherst that day, and feasting and drinking, and music and dancing. Ah, yes, and in the evening when I carried my bride away, there was love.

When we returned to Boston, the Burdicks held a reception for us at their home. That, too, was a gay occasion. Since the rebellion was over and the Legislature had pardoned the Regulators, I was once more respectable. And, with elections and politics no longer of urgent concern, Governor Hancock found himself quite well enough to attend and enjoy himself.

General Ward was on hand, as were Mr. Trowbridge, Lang,

and other gentlemen whom I had met. Naturally, Mr. Blair was on hand—his wig on straight for once. He winked slyly and told me his barber had set it on his scalp with glue. Amy and Ethan were there, too. Amy wasn't too warmly received by the younger crowd. She was too strikingly beautiful in a gorgeous white satin gown. But she was so modest and demure that the elders took her to their hearts. Mr. Blair had to admit he had been wrong about her. Amy was proving to be Ethan's most valuable social asset.

Even Mr. and Mrs. Ormund Graham were among those present. Mr. Burdick had scratched Graham's name from the invitation list, but I had it put back on. As a businessman, I might have dealings with that man sometime. Now that I was married to a Burdick, the Grahams decided I was acceptable. It was amusing to see how polite they were to me that night. All in all, our party was a huge success.

I might add here that I did finally settle my score with that man Graham. Late in the fall, Joe came back from Baltimore with the news that the migrations toward the western frontier were gathering momentum, despite the trouble with the Indians. Muskets were getting premium prices down there. So, I sent Joe to buy those muskets from Graham. I don't remember the exact price Joe paid, but Graham lost slightly on his original purchase price. I wish you could have seen his face when I told him I had turned a neat profit of nearly a thousand pounds on those muskets.

Of the rebellion itself, there is little more to say. Bands of Rebels were still operating in Berkshire County as late as July of 1787. Lincoln stayed on the field all summer and didn't disband his army until September. On the 12th of September, Gov. Hancock disposed of the last of the Insurgent prisoners. He granted pardons to Job Shattuck, Henry Gale and Hank McCullock.

The triumph of our cause didn't begin to take shape until the following year. While leniency was being shown the rebels, the jails still overflowed with those for whom we had fought, the debtors. The public clamor for their release grew more and more insistent.

At long last, in November of 1787, the General Court acted to lance the festering boil. On the 19th, it passed an act "For the Relief of Poor Debtors." The bill provided that the debtor must take a Pauper's Oath, swearing he had no property, no assets, no means of satisfying the debt or of sustaining himself in jail. The creditor was to be given the opportunity to show cause why the debtor should not be released. The judgment, however, remained in force and could be executed against any property the debtor might acquire in the future, with this notable exception: his clothing, household goods and the tools necessary for his trade or occupation could never, at any time, be seized for a debt.

This was a tremendous victory. A wave of exultation swept over the Commonwealth as the jails opened and hundreds of men held for trifling sums were turned loose. But this was not merely a victory for those individuals. It was a victory for the nation, a victory for democracy. Here was an expression of the forces gathering to bring forth a truly United States, a nation in which Government must bow to the needs and will of the people, a nation in which property rights must bow to human rights.

The final echoes of the insurrection didn't die out until the following year. On the 3rd of April, 1788, Governor Hancock issued a proclamation, repealing the law which called for the apprehension of the leaders. They were given full and complete pardons. They were no longer wanted.

Adam Wheeler returned from Vermont and spent the rest of his days in peace on his farm. Luke Day, having been disowned by his family, remained in New York where he finally died in poverty. I never did learn what happened to Eli Parsons and Perez Hamlin. They never came back. Dan Shays hesitated a long time before he ventured from his hideout in upper New York. His fears of being an outcast were unfounded. When he did return to Pelham, he was received with respect and elected a town warden.

On a visit home, shortly after Dan had returned, I dropped over to Conkey's to see him. He had changed. Even before I came into that familiar taproom, I could hear him declaiming in a loud voice, reminiscent of Luke Day. He was sitting by the dead hearth, his audience very quiet, watching him with serious expressions. His breeches were of dark blue homespun, but he still clung to his old uniform coat, which was now patched in many places. His once rosy complexion was sallow and his cheeks were shrunken. His eyes were red-rimmed and harassed.

When he spied me, he leaped from his chair and rushed over to me. He seized my hand and held it tightly.

"Warren! Warren Hascott! It's good to see you again. Here . . . sit down, sir, sit down." He pounded the table. "Conkey! Conkey! Refreshments for my friend, Mr. Hascott."

Conkey was scowling when he came over. "Howdy, Warren." He eyed me up and down. "You're prospering."

"Tolerably," I admitted.

I grinned and waved to the boys. Tom Packard winked solemnly and folded his lank frame into the chair next to mine. But he said nothing. The rest of the boys gave me a half smile in greeting, which struck me as odd. I thought their coldness might be due to my clothes. I must admit they were finely tailored. Then, I noticed they were not watching me as much as they were eying Dan Shays—with distaste, it seemed.

I pulled aside my tails and sat down. Then, with a shock, I realized Dan had a skin full. He didn't show it much, except by his hard breathing and his vague eyes. But it was certain that he was drunk.

"And what is the news from Boston, Mr. Hascott?" he demanded in a loud voice. His diction was perfect. "Has the Governor called a special session, yet?"

I was puzzled. "Not that I heard. Why should he?"

"Are you joking?" Dan asked incredulously. "To redress grievances, of course." He pounded the table. "How long must we wait for a redress of grievances?"

I smiled. "I've often wondered myself, Dan."

Dan waved his finger under my nose. "Mr. Hascott, the people are getting sick of inaction. Must we fight again to compel those bastards to disgorge our liberties?"

I blinked, assuring myself that this was Dan Shays and not Luke Day. "That's all in the past, Dan."

Dan Shays glared at me, than took a deep draught of his liquor. "Warren, our war was a rehearsal. We made mistakes last time—bad mistakes. Those stinking aristocrats don't understand any other language but force. All right, if it's war they want, it's war they'll get."

I glanced wide-eyed at Tom Packard. His features were set in a cynical smile and he lifted his hands.

"Dan doesn't come here so often any more," Tom drawled. "He thinks we're kinda . . . ah . . . blind."

"And stupid!" Dan added fiercely. He glared about him. "It's happening right under your very noses. They throw a bone to you and you think you have your liberties. But the countryside will rise again, mark me."

"Oh, come now, Dan," I protested, "it's all over. We're getting what we wanted gradually."

"Warren," Dan said in a low, confidential voice, "I misjudged the temper of the people last time. I won't make that mistake again. I shall strike when the moment is right. Why, if I should gather a hundred men right now and march in any direction, multitudes would flock to my standard . . . multitudes."

"Perhaps they would, Dan," I agreed. I finished my drink and got up. "You'll have to excuse me now. I have some visits to make while I'm here."

Tom Packard got up, too. "I'll walk a ways with you, Warren." He paused and looked down at his friend. "Perhaps we'll see each other again, Captain Shays."

Dan Shays leaned back in his chair and looked up with cold haughtiness. "*General* Shays, if you please."